RITA MAE BROWN

& SNEAKY PIE BROWN

THE *THIRD* THREE MRS. MURPHY MYSTERIES

Cat on the Scent

Pawing Through the Past

Claws and Effect

Other Mrs. Murphy omnibuses from
Random House Value Publishing:

Three Mrs. Murphy Mysteries in One Volume:
Wish You Were Here
Rest In Pieces
Murder at Monticello

Three More Mrs. Murphy Mysteries in One Volume:
Pay Dirt
Murder, She Meowed
Murder on the Prowl

RITA MAE BROWN

& SNEAKY PIE BROWN

Illustrations by Itoko Maeno

THE *THIRD* THREE MRS. MURPHY MYSTERIES IN ONE VOLUME

Cat on the Scent

Pawing Through the Past

Claws and Effect

Wing Books • New York

Originally published in three volumes by Bantam Books under the titles:

Cat on the Scent, copyright © 1999 by American Artists, Inc.
Illustrations copyright © 1999 by Itoko Maeno

Pawing Through the Past, copyright © 2000 by American Artists, Inc.
Illustrations copyright © 2000 by Itoko Maeno

Claws and Effect, copyright © 2001 by American Artists, Inc.

This edition contains the complete and unabridged texts of the original editions.

This 2007 edition is published by Wings Books ®, an imprint of Random House Value Publishing, by arrangement with the Bantam Doubleday Dell Publishing Group, Inc., divisions of Random House, Inc., New York

Wings Books® and colophon are trademarks of Random House, Inc.

Random House
New York • Toronto • London • Sydney • Auckland
www.valuebooks.com

Printed and bound in the United States.

A catalog record for this title is available from the Library of Congress.

ISBN: 978-0-517-22966-8

10 9 8 7 6 5 4 3 2 1

CONTENTS

Cat on the Scent

To a cat queen,
Elizabeth Putnam Sinsel

Cast of Characters

Mary Minor Haristeen (Harry), the young postmistress of Crozet

Mrs. Murphy, Harry's gray tiger cat

Tee Tucker, Harry's Welsh corgi, Mrs. Murphy's friend and confidante

Pewter, Market's shamelessly fat gray cat, who now lives with Harry and family

Pharamond Haristeen (Fair), veterinarian, formerly married to Harry

Mrs. George Hogendobber (Miranda), a widow who works with Harry in the post office

Market Shiflett, owner of Shiflett's Market, next to the post office

Susan Tucker, Harry's best friend

Big Marilyn Sanburne (Mim), the undisputed queen of Crozet society

Tally Urquhart, older than dirt, she says what she thinks when she thinks it, even to her niece, Mim the Magnificent

Rick Shaw, sheriff

Cynthia Cooper, police officer

Herbert C. Jones, pastor of Crozet Lutheran Church

Blair Bainbridge, a handsome model who lives on the farm next to Harry's

Sir H. Vane-Tempest, a modern Midas who proves there is nothing like the greed of the rich

Sarah Vane-Tempest, the much younger, fabulously beautiful wife of the imperious H. Vane

Archie Ingram, as a county commissioner he has been a strong advocate of controlling development and preserving the environment. Too bad he couldn't preserve his marriage

Tommy Van Allen, tall, dark, and handsome, he's been wild as a rat ever since childhood

Ridley Kent, an easygoing man who has inherited enough money to sap all initiative. He means well

1

The intoxicating fragrance of lilacs floated across the meadow grass. Mrs. Murphy was night hunting in and around the abandoned dependencies on old Tally Urquhart's farm, Rose Hill. Once a great estate, the farm's main part continued to be kept in pristine condition. A combination of old age plus spiraling taxes, and wages forced Thalia "Tally" Urquhart, as well as others like her, to let outlying buildings go.

A huge stone hay barn with a center aisle big enough to house four hay wagons side by side sat in the middle of small one-and-a-half-story stone houses with slate roofs. The buildings, although pockmarked by broken windows, were so well constructed they would endure despite the birds nesting in their chimneys.

The hay barn, whose supporting beams were constructed

from entire tree trunks, would outlast this century and the next one as well.

The paint peeled off the stone buildings, exposing the soft gray underneath with an occasional flash of rose-gray.

The tiger cat sniffed the air; low clouds and fog were moving in fast from the west, sliding down the Blue Ridge Mountains like fudge on a sundae.

Normally Mrs. Murphy would hunt close to her own farm. Often she was accompanied by Pewter, who despite her bulk was a ferocious mouser. This evening she wanted to hunt alone. It cleared her mind. She liked to wait motionless for mice to scurry in the rotting burlap feed bags, for their tiny claws to tap against the beams in the hayloft.

Since no one paid attention to the Urquhart barns, the mousing was superb. Kernels of grain and dried corn drew the little marauders in, as did the barn itself, a splendid place in which to raise young mice.

A moldy horse collar, left over from the late 1930s, its brass knobs green, hung on the tack-room wall, forgotten by all, the mules who wore it long gone to the Great Mule Sky.

Mrs. Murphy left off her mousing to explore the barn, constructed in the early nineteenth century. How lovely the farm must have once been. Mrs. Murphy prided herself on her knowledge of human history, something the two-legged species often overlooked in its rush to be current. Of course, she reflected, whatever is current today is out of fashion tomorrow.

The tiger cat, like most felines, took the long view.

Her particular human, Mary Minor Haristeen, or Harry, the young, pretty postmistress of Crozet, Virginia, evinced interest in history as well as in animal behavior. She read voraciously and expanded her understanding of animals by visiting Virginia Tech in Blacksburg and the Marion DuPont Scott Equine Research Center in Leesburg, Virginia. Harry even studied the labels on crunchy-food bags to make certain kitty nutrition was adequate.

She cared for her two cats, one dog, and three horses with love and knowledge.

The flowers continued to push up around the buildings. The lilac bushes, enormous, burst forth each spring. The sadness of the decaying old place was modified by the health of the plant life.

The cat emerged from the barn and glanced at the deepening night clouds, deciding to hurry back home before the fog got thicker. Two creeks and a medium-sized ridge were the biggest obstacles. She could traverse the four miles in an hour at a trot, faster if she ran. Mrs. Murphy could run four miles with ease. A sound foxhound could run forty miles in a day. Much as she liked running, she was glad she wasn't a foxhound, or any hound, for that matter. Mrs. Murphy liked dogs but considered them a lower species, for the most part, except for the corgi she lived with, Tucker, who was nearly the equal of a cat. Not that she'd tell Tucker that. . . . Never.

She trotted away from the magical spot and loped over the long, flat pasture, once an airstrip for Tally Urquhart in her heyday, when she had shocked the residents of central Virginia by flying airplanes. Her disregard for the formalities of marriage did the rest.

Tally Urquhart was Mim Sanburne's aunt. Mim had ascended to the rank of undisputed social leader of Crozet once her aunt had relinquished the position twenty years ago. Mrs. Murphy would giggle and say to Mim's face, *"Ah, welcome to the Queen of Quite a Lot."* Since Mim didn't understand cat, the grande dame wasn't insulted.

On the other side of the airfield a rolling expanse of oats just breaking through the earth's surface undulated down to the first creek.

At the creek the cat stopped. The clouds lowered; the moisture was palpable. She thought she heard a rumble. Senses razor sharp, she looked in each direction, including overhead. Owls were deadly in conditions like this.

The rumble grew closer. She climbed a tree—just in case. Out of the clouds overhead two wheels appeared. Mrs. Murphy watched as a single-engine plane touched down, bumped, then rolled toward the barn. It stopped right in front of the massive doors, a quarter of a mile away from Mrs. Murphy.

A lean figure hopped out of the plane to open the barn doors. The pilot stayed at the controls, and as the doors opened, the plane puttered into the barn. The motor was cut off. Mrs. Murphy saw two figures now, one much taller than the other. She couldn't make out their features; the collars of their trench coats were turned up and they were half turned away, dueling gusts of wind. As each human braced behind a door and rolled it shut, the heavens opened in a deluge.

A great fat *splat* of rain plopped right on Mrs. Murphy's head. She hated getting wet, but she waited long enough to see the two humans run down the road past the stone houses. In the far distance she thought she heard a motor turn over.

Irritated that she hadn't gone down the farm road and therefore might have missed something, she climbed down and ran flat out the entire way home. She could have stayed overnight in the Urquhart barn, but Harry would panic if she woke up and realized Mrs. Murphy wasn't asleep on the bed.

By the time she reached her own back porch forty-five minutes later, she was soaked. She pushed through the animal door and shook herself twice in the kitchen, spattering the cabinets, before walking into the bedroom.

Tucker snored on the floor at the foot of the bed. Pewter snuggled next to Harry. The portly gray cat opened one brilliant green eye as Mrs. Murphy leapt onto the bed.

"Don't sleep next to me. You're all wet."

"It was worth it."

Both eyes opened. *"What'd you get?"*

"Two field mice and one shrew."

"Liar."

"Why would I make it up?"

Pewter closed both eyes and flicked her tail over her nose. *"Because you have to be the best at everything."*

The tiger ignored her, crept to the head of the bed, lifted the comforter, and slid under while staying on top of the blanket. If she'd picked up all the covers and gotten on the sheets, Harry might have rolled over and felt the wet sheets and the wet cat. Mrs. Murphy was better off in the middle; and she would dry faster that way, too.

Pewter said nothing but she heard a muffled *"Hee-hee,"* before falling asleep again.

2

The slanting rays of the afternoon sun spilled across the meadows of Harry's farm. The hayloft door, wide open, framed a sleeping Mrs. Murphy, flopped on her back, her creamy beige stomach soaking up the sun's warmth. The cat's tail gently rocked from side to side as though floating in a pool of sunlight.

Simon the possum, curled in a gray ball, slept at the mouth of his nest made from old hay bales. A worn curb chain glittered from the recess of his den. Simon liked to carry off shiny objects, ribbons, gloves, even old pieces of newspaper.

Below, in the barn's center aisle, Tucker snoozed. Each time she exhaled, a tiny knot of no-see-ums swirled up, then settled down again on her shoulders.

May, usually the best month in central Virginia, along with colorful Octobers, remained unusually cool this year, the temperature staying in the fifties and low sixties. One week earlier, the last of April, a snowstorm had roared down the Blue Ridge Mountains, covering the swelling buds and freezing the daffodils and tulips. All that was forgotten as redbuds bloomed and dogwoods began to open, lush white or pink. The grass turned green.

This afternoon the animals couldn't keep their eyes open. Sometimes an abrupt change of season could do that, wreaking havoc with everyone's rhythm. Even Harry, that engine of productivity, dozed in the tack room. She had every intention of stripping and dipping her tack, a monotonous task reserved for the change of seasons. Harry had gotten up that morning in an organizing mood but she had fallen asleep before she had even broken down the bridle.

Alone—if one counts being divorced but having your ex much in evidence as "alone"—Harry ran the small farm bequeathed to her by her deceased parents. Farming, difficult these days because of government regulation, made enough money to cover the taxes on the place. She relied on her job at the Crozet Post Office to feed and clothe herself.

In her thirties, Harry was oblivious to her charms. Her one concession to the rigors of feminine display was a good haircut. She lived in jeans, T-shirts, and cowboy boots. She even wore her cowboy boots to work. Since the Crozet Post Office was such a small, out-of-the-way place, she need not dress for success.

In fact, Harry measured success by laughter, not by money. She was extremely successful. If she wasn't laughing with other humans she was laughing with Mrs. Murphy, wit personified, Tucker, or Pewter, the cat who came to dinner.

Pewter, curled in Harry's lap, dreamed of crème brûlée. Other cats dreamed of mice, moles, birds, the occasional spider. Pewter conjured up images of beef Wellington, mashed potatoes, fresh buttered bread, and her favorite food on earth, crème brûlée. She liked the crust thin and crunchy.

In the distance a low purr caused Mrs. Murphy to flick her ear in that direction. The marvelous sound came nearer. She opened one eye, casting her gaze down the long dirt road dotted with puddles of water from last night's rain. She stretched but didn't rise.

The throaty roar sounded like a big cat staking out territory. She heard the distinctive crushing sound of tires on Number 5 gravel. Curious, she half raised her head, then pushed herself up, stretching fore and aft, blinking in the sunlight.

Pewter lifted her head as well.

Tucker remained dead to the world.

Mrs. Murphy squinted to catch sight of a gleaming black car rounding the far turn.

"Company's coming."

No one below paid attention. She leaned forward, sticking her head out the second-story space as Harry's nearest neighbor, Blair Bainbridge, cruised into the driveway behind the wheel of a black wide-body Porsche 911 Turbo.

Tucker barked. Mrs. Murphy laughed to herself—*"Dogs!"*— as she sauntered over to the ladder. She excelled at climbing ladders and at descending them. The latter took longer to learn. The trick was not to look down.

She scampered across the dusty center aisle and out to Blair. Harry woke up with Pewter licking her face. Tucker, sniffling about interrupted sleep, emerged into the sunlight.

"Hello, Mrs. Murphy." Blair grinned.

"Hello." She rubbed against his leg.

"Anybody home?" Blair called out.

"Be there in a minute," a foggy Harry replied.

The tiger cat walked around the low-bodied, sleek machine. *"A cat designed this."*

"Why?" Tucker viewed the car without much enthusiasm, but Tucker never had much enthusiasm when awakened.

"Because it's beautiful and powerful."

"*You don't like yourself much, do you?*"

Harry walked out, then stopped abruptly. "Beautiful!"

"Just delivered." Blair leaned against the sloping front fender. "Makes all the crap I do worthwhile."

"Modeling can't be that bad."

"Can't be that good. It's not..."—he paused—"connected. It's superficial." He waved his hand dismissively. "And sooner or later I'll be considered over-the-hill. It's ruthless that way."

"I don't know. You're too hard on yourself. Anyway, it got you this. I don't think I've ever seen anything so beautiful. Not even the Aston Martin Volante."

"You like Aston Martins?" His dark eyebrows rose.

"Love 'em. Not as much as horses, but I love them. The Volante is a sleek car, but you need the mechanic to go with it. This is more reliable."

"German."

"There is that." She smiled.

"Would you like a ride?"

"I thought you'd never ask." She spoke to the two cats and dog. "Hold down the fort."

"*Yeah, yeah,*" Mrs. Murphy grumbled. "*I think we should all go for a ride.*"

"*No room,*" Tucker sensibly noted.

"*I don't take up much room—unlike you.*"

"*What's that supposed to mean?*"

"*Nothing.*" Mrs. Murphy raised her tail straight up, sashaying toward the house as Blair backed out. Mrs. Murphy thought the baritone perfect, not too deep, yet velvety.

"Only one hundred Turbos made for the U.S. market each year," Blair said as he straightened out the wheel.

Pewter waddled toward the house. She gave the $110,000 internal-combustion machine barely a look. "*Don't go so fast,*" she chided her cohort.

To torment her, the tiger cat bounded gracefully onto the screened-in porch, pawing open the unlatched screen door.

"I hate her," Pewter muttered.

"Me, too." Tucker walked alongside the gray cat. *"The biggest show-off since P.T. Barnum."*

"I heard that."

"We don't care," Tucker replied.

"You're bored." Mrs. Murphy ducked through the doggie door in the kitchen.

"Did she say I was boring?"

"No, Pewter, she said we were bored."

"Nothing ever happens in May."

Mrs. Murphy stuck her head out the magnetic-flap door. *"Blair Bainbridge bought a Porsche Turbo. I count that as an important event."*

Pewter and Tucker, walking more briskly, reached the screen door. The corgi sat while the cat opened it.

"That doesn't count." Pewter flung open the door.

Mrs. Murphy ducked back into the kitchen. Pewter dashed through the animal door first.

"What would you like to happen?" Mrs. Murphy inquired.

"A meat truck turns over in front of the post office." Tucker wagged her nonexistent tail.

"Remember the Halloween when the human head turned up in a pumpkin?" Pewter's pupils widened.

"Yech!" Mrs. Murphy recalled the grisly event that happened a few years back.

"Yech? I found it. You didn't."

"I don't like to think about it." Mrs. Murphy fastidiously licked the sides of her front paws, then swept them over her face.

She noticed the side of the barn facing north, the broad, flat side where the paint was peeling. A painted ad for Coca-Cola, black background underneath, peeled out in parts.

"Funny."

"*What?*" Pewter leaned over to groom her friend, whom she loved even though Mrs. Murphy often irritated her.

"*How the past is bursting through—all around us. That old Coke sign—bet it was painted on the barn in the 1920s or '30s. The past bursts through the present.*"

"*Dead and gone,*" Tucker laconically said.

"*The past is never dead.*"

"*Well, maybe not for you. You have nine lives.*"

"*Ha-ha.*" Mrs. Murphy turned her nose up.

"*I bet the past wasn't as boring as today,*" Pewter moaned.

"*Things will pick up,*" Tucker advised.

Truer words were never spoken.

3

Blair glided down Route 250 toward Greenwood at 60 miles an hour. He was only in second gear and the tachometer wasn't even close to the red zone.

Harry couldn't believe the surge of power or the handling. They hit 0 to 60 mph in 4.4 seconds. The balance of the car astounded her. The old farm Misfit blurred by, then Mirador (Misfit's big sister), then Blair downshifted, turned right, and headed back toward the Greenwood school, the road snaking and the car sweeping around each sharp curve without a shudder, a roll, or a skid.

"Don't you love it?" Blair laughed out loud.

She sighed. "Deep love."

A short stretch of flat land beckoned. He smoothly shifted.

The speedometer glided past 100, then Blair expertly down-shifted as a curve rolled off to the right.

Unfortunately, Sheriff Rick Shaw was rolling, too, right out of Sir H. Vane-Tempest's driveway. He hit the siren and snapped on the whirling lights.

"Damn," Blair whispered.

"What's he doing out here in the boonies? He ought to be on Route 29." Harry glanced in the rearview mirror.

"Is it Rick or Cynthia?" Blair squinted at the distant object, which was fast approaching.

"Rick. Cynthia doesn't wear her hat in the squad car."

"That makes sense. Turn your head and the brim hits the window."

"Rick's balding, remember."

"There is that." Blair half smiled as he pulled over. The Porsche stopped as smooth as silk. He lowered the window and reached in the side pocket of the door for the relevant papers as Rick lumbered up.

"As I live and breathe, Blair Bainbridge." Rick bent over. "And our esteemed postmistress. License, please," he sang out.

"Oh." Blair fished around in his hip pocket, pulled out his crocodile wallet, and handed the license to Rick.

"Blair, do you have any idea how fast you were moving?"

"Uh—yes, I do."

"Uh-huh. You know, of course, that the speed limit in the great state of Virginia is fifty-five miles per hour. Now I don't think that's the smartest law on the books, but I have to en-force it."

"Yes, sir."

"When did you get this vehicle?"

"This morning."

"Uh-huh. Why don't you get out of the car a minute."

In a show of sympathy, Harry unfastened her seat belt and got out, too.

"Lemme see the engine."

Rick popped up the back, revealing a giant turbo covering the engine.

"That's a pain in the ass," the sheriff grumbled.

"It's the turbo, chief, it forces air back in here,"—Blair pointed to the inlet side—"which boosts the horsepower to four hundred. Here's the delivery side."

"Four hundred horsepower?" Rick whispered reverently.

Blair smiled, knowing the sheriff was hooked. "The intake, or flow, is split toward the left and right exhaust turbochargers. The air gets reunited, flows past the throttle, and goes into the cylinder heads in virtually direct sequence." He paused, realizing he was getting too technical. "The pollution level falls below government requirements, which is a good thing. Drive a turbo and be environmentally responsible."

"Uh-huh." Rick ran his hand over the rear fender, which slightly resembled a horse's hindquarters, then ducked his head inside the driver's side. "Not much room in the back."

"Big enough for Mrs. Murphy, Tucker, and Pewter." Harry finally said something.

"I'm surprised they aren't with you." Rick pushed his hat back on his head. "Now in order to be fair here, I need to know a little more about this car. Can we all fit in?"

"Sure," Blair said.

"Tell you what, guys, I'll stay with the squad car. You two roll on," Harry said.

Rick furtively looked around. "Well—"

"No one will know a thing. If anyone stops, I'll say you're investigating a rustling call and I came along for the ride. You're out in the pasture."

"Well—all right," Rick agreed. "If H. Vane-Tempest happens to come by, don't say a word."

"Got his nose out of joint again?" Harry casually asked.

Rick grunted. "He's a little different."

"Different!" Harry giggled. "He's got more money than God and he acts like he *is* God."

"He and Archie Ingram pester me with more calls than anyone else in the county, and this is a county full of nutcases."

Archie Ingram, one of the county commissioners, a handsome man, courtly to women, was so violently opposed to most development schemes that he had attracted radical detractors and equally radical supporters.

"H. Vane is a big noise in the environmental group. I guess he and Archie have to work closely together."

"Ideas are one thing. Temperament's another." Rick hooked his thumb in his gun belt. "I predict those two can't stay on the same team for long."

"Sheriff, would you like to drive?" Blair asked.

"Well—"

"Go on."

Rick slipped behind the wheel.

Blair winked at Harry, then folded his six-foot-four-inch frame into the passenger side. "That button will push the seat back or forward. There you go. And you can raise or lower the seat, too."

"Isn't that something?" Rick's seduction would be complete once he touched the accelerator. He reached to the right for the key.

"On the left."

"That's weird."

"A leftover from the great racing days when drivers had to sprint to their cars. If the ignition was on the left it gave them a split-second advantage. The driver could start the car and shift into gear simultaneously."

"I'll be damned." Rick turned the key. The pistons awakened like Sleeping Beauty.

Rick stalled out.

"Takes a while to get used to the clutch. Everything is much more sensitive than you or I are accustomed to—it's not so much about technology, it's about feel."

"Yeah." Rick engaged the clutch and touched the gas, then shot down the road.

Harry folded her arms across her chest, watching the car lurch into second. It would take Rick a few more tries.

She walked back to the squad car, sat down, and clicked on the two-way radio.

Milden Hall, the estate of Sir H. Vane-Tempest, was immediately behind her. The overlarge sign, emblazoned with a gold griffin on a bloodred field, swung slightly in the breeze.

Harry turned off the radio, swung her legs out, and closed the door. The day was too pleasant for sitting in the car. She walked back toward the sign. A car cruised around the corner, having turned off 250.

Harry waved and Susan Tucker pulled her Audi to the side of the road.

"What are you doing out here?"

Harry walked over to her best friend. "Joyriding. Blair bought a Porsche Turbo and as luck would have it, Rick Shaw came out of H. Vane's driveway just as we slowed down to eighty-something."

"Where's Blair now? In jail?"

"No. He's letting Rick drive the Turbo."

Susan laughed. "That's a good one."

"What are you doing out here?"

"On my way to drop off books for Chris Middleton. I want to persuade him to give a talk at the high school for career day."

Chris was a small-animals veterinarian, one of the best.

"Good idea."

"And then I have to meet Mim, Her Royal Pain in the Ass, at the club. She's fussed up about this board meeting over the water supply. The county's been fighting about the reservoir so long I don't know why she still lets it get to her."

"We've got to do something with the development in the northwest corner of the county. They need water."

"Exactly, but the reservoir plan is already outdated and it hasn't been built yet." Susan pouted for a minute. "Archie Ingram, as usual, wants to turn the clock back to 1890."

"Make it 1840. Then he could own slaves." Harry approved of conservation but Archie Ingram took it too far.

"Good one, Harry." Susan smiled. "Oh, that reminds me, the battle reenactment at Oak Ridge—you have to be there."

"No I don't."

"Yes you do, because Ned needs camp followers."

Ned was Susan's husband, a lawyer by trade and a reenactor in Civil War battles on weekends. The latter was becoming a passion.

"Susan, I hate that war stuff."

"Living history."

"I'll think about it."

"Harry..." Susan lowered her voice.

"Susan..."

"You do it."

"Takes two women to keep your husband happy these days."

"That's right, girlfriend. And I even have your costume."

"Susan, you're both nuts."

"You'll look fetching in a bonnet."

"I'm not wearing period clothes—period!"

Harry heard the distant, distinctive sound of the Porsche. "Push on, because Rick will be embarrassed if he gets back and finds you here. We don't want Blair to get a ticket."

"Tell Blair that Ned expects him in the First Virginia." That was the name of Ned's unit. The reenactors were fanatical about detail, down to the last button.

"I will." Harry kissed her on the cheek. Susan kissed air in return, then drove away.

By the time the Porsche drove into view, Harry was back

leaning against the squad car. A beaming Rick Shaw stayed behind the wheel.

"You deserve a car like that, Sheriff."

"I never drove anything like that in my life," Rick said, his
voice full of wonder. He wouldn't get out of the car. He was like
a child at Christmas, sitting under the tree, fondling his favorite
present.

"I just had to have it." Blair smiled. "Boys with toys, as Harry
would say."

"Hate to leave this baby." Rick finally slid out from under the
wheel. He walked alongside the front of the car, running his top
finger over the curving, graceful lines. "Kind of like an egg on its
side."

"Yes."

Rick opened the creaking door of the squad car. "Blair, stay
inside the speed limit."

"Yes, sir."

"Harry, mum's the word."

"Okay." She smiled at Rick, whom she liked even though he
chided her about being an amateur detective. His word was
busybody.

He flicked on the radio.

"Car 1. Car 1."

"Car 1," Rick answered.

"Where you been, boss?" Deputy Cynthia Cooper's voice
crackled.

"Sir H. Vane-Tempest's. His wife says Archie Ingram threatened her husband with bodily harm. H. pooh-poohs it. Said
they simply had a disagreement over sensitive environmental
issues."

"Oh la!" Coop sang out.

"See you in ten. Over and out." Rick started the motor and
Harry backed away from his window. Rick winked at her, then
pulled out, made a U-turn, and cruised back to 250.

Blair folded his arms across his muscled chest. "Man fell in love before my very eyes."

"Doesn't everyone?" Harry enjoyed her double entendre, for Blair was stunning to the point of leaving women breathless—and a few men, too, for that matter.

"How about you, then?" He held open the driver's-side door, ushering her into the cockpit.

Harry sat still, inhaling the rich leather smell as she reached for the key on her left. Blair closed the passenger door behind him.

"Ready, Eddy?" She turned over the key.

"Shoot the goose, Bruce."

"I never heard that."

"Maybe it's shoot the juice." Blair laughed.

She did and they roared into Greenwood, around the little town, and back to Crozet by every back mountain road she could remember.

When they finally pulled into her driveway, Tee Tucker burst through the animal door of the house, then pushed open the screen door, happy to see her mother.

Mrs. Murphy turned to Pewter, both of them reposing on the kitchen table, forbidden to them and therefore more appealing. *"That dog will never learn."*

Pewter tapped her skull with one extended claw. *"Dog brains."*

Mrs. Murphy jumped over to the window over the kitchen sink. *"They're coming inside. Off the table."*

Pewter waited until she heard the screen door slam before leaving the table.

"Hi, kids," Harry greeted her cats, who ignored her.

"Make her suffer for leaving us here." Mrs. Murphy stalked into the living room.

Pewter, knowing some manner of food would be placed on the table, decided to be mildly friendly.

Harry spied the cat hair on the table and wiped it off with a wet dishrag. "You were on the table."

"Was not," Mrs. Murphy called from the living room.

"Was too," Tucker tattled.

"Shut up, you little brownnose," Mrs. Murphy yelled at the dog.

"Blair, thank you again for letting me drive a dream." She opened the refrigerator door, removing corn bread and butter. Not that she had made the corn bread; Miranda had given her a big pan of it Friday after they left work.

"Any time."

"Oh, I forgot to tell you. Susan drove by while I was waiting for you and the sheriff. She said Ned expects you in the First Virginia for reenactment at Oak Ridge."

"I'll call him."

"I didn't know you were into that battle stuff."

"I'm not. They're short of bodies."

"Isn't it expensive to get the gear?"

"Yeah, but I can't complain if I've just bought a Turbo, can I?" He laughed. "Some of these guys are a little extreme, but I'm looking forward to it."

"Extreme?" Mrs. Murphy sardonically replied as she walked back to the kitchen, pointedly not paying attention to Harry. *"They're a quart low."*

"I think it's fascinating." Tucker sat down on Blair's foot.

"You think anything's fascinating that has dead bodies in it."

"Well, dogs eat carrion. That's what they're for, I guess." Pewter pressed against the refrigerator door. *"Nature's garbage collectors."*

"People hang out deer for a few days," Tucker rejoined.

"Better gut them the minute you kill them or you'll have some terrible-tasting deer." Mrs. Murphy wasn't fond of venison, but she could eat it if prepared in buttermilk.

Pewter moved back to the table. *"There aren't going to be any dead bodies at the reenactment, just people pretending to be dead."*

"The way things have been going, the commission meeting coming up might have a few dead bodies." Tucker giggled.

Pewter turned her full attention on Harry, who had set out some thinly sliced roast beef.

"Stay on the floor." Harry read her mind, not difficult under the circumstances.

"One teensy piece," Pewter begged.

"Me, too." Tucker had been transformed into Miss Adorable.

"No," Harry said, but without much oomph.

"She'll weaken if you sit by the chair." Pewter hurried to get on Harry's right side.

"You say that every time." The tiger cat laughed but she hurried to Blair's side, figuring he'd weaken before Harry.

"I had no idea that Sir H. Vane-Tempest pestered Sheriff Shaw so often."

"Tempest in a teapot is what Miranda calls him." Harry stuck her knife into a pot of creamy homemade mustard. "But Archie's picking fights with everyone. Even though he and H. Vane seem to be in a phase of political agreement. He's even fighting Mim."

"Not a smart move."

"Getting on the wrong side of Sir H. isn't smart either. His net worth is more than the gross national product of Chile."

"Mrs. Murphy, what do you know about H. Vane?" Tucker never took her eyes off Harry's hands.

"He doesn't have cats or dogs, which bespeaks an empty life."

Blair dropped her a sliver of roast beef, which she daintily ate.

"Are you going to the commission meeting?" Harry asked her guest.

"You bet. It's going to be the best show this spring."

4

Archie Ingram, a handsome man in his early forties, smiled at the assemblage. The only hint that he was nervous was the tension in his cheek muscles. The classroom at Crozet High School spilled over with people, many standing in the hall. A topographical map of the county was on a bulletin board behind the front table.

"I told you we should have used the auditorium," Archie complained to Jim Sanburne, the mayor of Crozet, as well as Mim's husband. As mayor he chaired the county meeting in his town.

"Archie, these meetings usually number three people, each of whom wants a zoning variance for a trailer, a business, or a nursing home. The only reason all these people are here is that you've stirred up a hornet's nest."

"Bullshit," he growled at the large, genial man.

Jim ignored him, waving a greeting to the Reverend Herbert Jones.

"Jim, I brought my dowser." Herb held up the wooden divining rod, which worked well despite naysayers.

"Spare me," Archie muttered under his breath, his eyes scanning the room, resting a second on the beautiful Sarah Vane-Tempest before darting away.

"What?" Jim asked.

"Where's Tommy Van Allen?" Archie demanded. "I'm not delaying this meeting one more time for him."

"I don't know. I called and he wasn't at work."

"Typical." Archie tapped his pencil on the tabletop. "The only reason he ever wanted this thankless job was to find out when and where we'd be making road improvements and granting commercial zoning permits. Gives him more time to put together a good bid."

"Come on, Arch, you don't believe that."

"The hell I don't." Archie snapped his mouth shut like a turtle.

Harry, Mrs. Murphy, Tucker, and Pewter sat in the middle next to Harry's colleague in the post office, Miranda Hogendobber. Also there were Susan and Ned Tucker; Harry's ex-husband, Fair Haristeen; and BoomBoom Craycroft. The widow Craycroft was not Harry's favorite person.

Blair accompanied Mim's daughter, Marilyn.

Little Mim, as she was known, stood up in front with her mother, who was already poring over the large map of the county.

Sir Henry Vane-Tempest—called H. or H. Vane by everyone—sat off to the side, his horn-rimmed spectacles sliding down his long nose. He had taken the precaution of bugging each county commissioner's office. Once a week the transcript was discreetly brought to him at his farm by Tareq Said, head of

Said and Trumbo Investigations. Vane-Tempest made certain that his wife knew nothing of this. No one knew and H. would keep it that way. Next to him was Ridley Kent, a rich ne'er-do-well whose primary occupation was staring at women's bodices. He happened to be sitting beside a good one. Sarah Vane-Tempest was H. Vane's trophy wife, an elegant blonde whose cool beauty owed little to the expensive clothes she wore.

"The gang's all here," Susan said to Harry.

"Frightening, isn't it?" Harry sarcastically replied.

"Holding negative feelings will eat you up and destroy your good health," BoomBoom crooned.

"Shut up, Boom."

"That's exactly what I'm talking about." BoomBoom cast her violet eyes at Harry.

Archie noticed Mrs. Murphy sauntering up to the map. "Get that cat out of here."

"I beg your pardon." Mrs. Murphy stared at him.

"Mary Minor Haristeen, those animals have no place here." Archie pointed to Pewter, on her lap, and Tucker, seated at Fair's cowboy-booted feet.

"Hey, Murphy, jump on the table and blow a tuna fart right in his face," Pewter called out.

"How rude." Mrs. Murphy giggled but she did jump on the desk to stare Archie directly in the eye.

"Murphy—" Harry called to her.

"You are a sorry excuse for a mammal." Mrs. Murphy insulted Archie, who blinked as she spoke.

"She's saying that she's a resident of Albemarle County, too, and the water supply affects her." Mim's upper-class voice hushed the room.

"That's right, honeybun," Jim, not upper-class, said.

Everyone laughed.

"Then at least keep this feline with you," Archie told Harry.

Mrs. Murphy, the full attention of the room on her, flopped on her side, cocking her head at the audience.

"Isn't she adorable. She knows we're talking about her," one of the older ladies said.

"*Gag me,*" Pewter sniped.

"Mrs. Murphy, come back here," Harry said firmly. She was put out at Mrs. Murphy's showing off, but secretly she was also enjoying Archie Ingram's discomfiture. He could be so pompous.

Naturally, Mrs. Murphy flopped on the other side, again gazing at her fans. She emitted a honey-coated meow.

"Precious," another voice cooed.

Even Tucker looked queasy.

Harry handed Pewter to Fair, stood up, and stepped along a row of desks to the center aisle. "Madam, you get off that desk."

"*One for the money, two for the show, three to get ready and four to go,*" the tiger cat sang out, sat up, grabbed Archie's pencil in her teeth, and leapt off the front table.

"Hey!" Archie boomed as everyone in the classroom laughed at him. "Hey, I want that back."

Mrs. Murphy pranced over to Sarah Vane-Tempest, dropping the pencil at her expensively shod feet.

"*I can't believe you did that,*" Pewter hollered at her.

"*Watch me.*" She skidded out to the hallway, dodging legs, and finally sat down under the water fountain. By the time Harry caught up with her, she was intently grooming the tip of her tail.

"Monster."

"*Broccoli eater.*"

"If you even move your eyebrows I'm taking you out to the truck."

"*Take me to Blair's Porsche. I don't want to sit in the truck.*"

"Don't you mouth off at me," Harry warned her.

"*Who else am I going to mouth off to?*"

Harry paused, wondering whether to take her back into the meeting or go directly to the truck. Well aware of Murphy's lethal temper, she thought the cat would be safer in sight than out of sight. She scooped up the silky-coated creature, holding her bottom while Murphy leaned on her shoulder, winking at passersby.

By the time Harry reached the classroom door her seat had been taken. Pewter stood on Fair's lap, paws on his shoulders, looking for her buddy. Upon seeing Mrs. Murphy, she jumped down and walked to the back of the room.

Meanwhile Archie was explaining to the assembled why the reservoir plan was outdated. He couldn't resist reminding them that he had always been an opponent of unchecked growth. However, the population had grown, the water supply had not, and as a public servant he had to find a solution. Before he could finish his presentation, the county commissioner next to him dropped his tablet. It hit the floor with a loud clatter.

Archie glared as Donald Jackson bent over to pick it up, tipped off balance, and fell over, still in the chair.

Jim Sanburne quickly hopped out of his seat to assist Don, which made Archie look like a jerk, since he was standing above the fallen man.

Irritated, Archie continued reading off his figures.

"Archie, we know all that." Don tried to divert him.

"Everyone in this room knows the cost of building a new reservoir?" He slapped his hand on the table, the papers in his other hand shaking.

"Yes. It's on the handout sheet. You don't need to read that. In case anyone missed a handout sheet, a new reservoir in the northwest quadrant will cost us thirty-two million dollars."

"What's wrong with rehabilitating Sugar Hollow?" a voice from the middle piped up.

Sugar Hollow was the site of an old reservoir.

"After what Hurricane Fran did?" Archie imperiously dismissed the question.

"Not so fast, Archie." Ned Tucker spoke up. "Given the importance of the issue, a feasibility study on reviving Sugar Hollow isn't a frivolous suggestion."

"Maybe we need them both," Sir H. Vane-Tempest suggested in his soothing voice.

"And where would the money come from?" Little Mim asked a sensible question yet received a frown from her mother.

Big Mim preferred to speak before her offspring did, at which time she expected Little Mim to rubber-stamp whatever she had said. Aunt Tally, leaning on her silver-handled cane, cast a sharp eye at her family. The handle itself was carved in the shape of a hound's head. It had become Tally's signature accessory.

"From my pocketbook," Miranda good-naturedly called out.

A few people laughed. Others nodded.

"The county's population has tipped over 112,000." Jim, deep voice rumbling, folded his hands. "The original plan for the reservoir between Free Union and Earlysville was drawn up in 1962, when the population was half of what it is today and projections were not even close to our current rate of growth."

"That's the problem. Unrestrained growth," Archie again said.

"We can't throw people out." Jim sighed, tacitly acknowledging the problem.

"No, but we can certainly put the lid on development."

"You've done a good job of that all by yourself," Sir H. Vane-Tempest jocularly interjected.

"With little support from my colleagues." Archie's eyebrows twitched upward as he stared at the Englishman. "You've been opposed to growth, H. Vane, and I appreciate your vision."

"Un*planned* growth. A master plan for this county would go a long way to solving these woes." Sir H. Vane-Tempest appeared to shift politically ever so slightly.

"We don't have a master plan!" Archie's eyes narrowed. What was Vane-Tempest up to?

"This reservoir plan is not worth the paper it's printed on." Don Jackson shook his head. "Earlier commissions did not foresee this population boom nor the encroachment of Richmond and even Washington, on weekends, anyway. Our infrastructure is woefully inadequate and that includes our water supply."

"Wouldn't it make sense to identify all of our water resources?" Fair Haristeen stood up. "We have the runoff from the Blue Ridge Mountains, which I believe figured into the original reservoir plan. We have the remains of the reservoir at Sugar Hollow. We have the Rivanna, Mechum, and James rivers, which may yet prove useful."

"He's right." BoomBoom smiled, which made the men smile back.

"Yuk," Harry whispered to Mrs. Murphy and Pewter.

"And if we try to dam up the rivers, do we know what the state will do to us? Ha!" Archie threw up his hands. "To say nothing of the catastrophic environmental damage."

"We can't be the only county trying to absorb new people." Sir H. Vane-Tempest now stood up. In his early seventies, exuding vitality, he was well turned out, although the ascot seemed pretentious for the occasion. "The concept of a major reservoir serving ourselves and even the lower counties, such as Buckingham, isn't a frivolous idea."

"Well, what about the water table?" Dr. Larry Johnson joined in. "Whatever we do, we have to examine the underground effect. This isn't just about building a reservoir."

Archie sat down, folding his arms across his chest.

Don leaned forward. "Precisely the reason for these local meetings. Our commission has to present your ideas to the state. There's no way Albemarle County can fund a reservoir. Even if you double taxes, we can't pay for it."

"So we have to go to Richmond no matter what?" Jim Sanburne half asked, half informed the audience.

"Too much government! Richmond will only make it worse. Look at the bypass." Aunt Tally referred to a bottled-up traffic mess that the state couldn't resolve, each plan being worse than the former.

People nodded their heads in agreement.

"There's got to be enough water under the ground. Got to be." Ridley Kent shook his head.

"Ridley, if you had a brain you'd be dangerous." Vane-Tempest guffawed at his own joke.

Ridley, not one to take offense, laughed back. "I mean it. There're underground rivers as well as overground rivers."

"Exactly. Identify the water sources." Fair spoke again.

"I agree, but aren't these feasibility studies also expensive?" Blair finally spoke. As a relative newcomer to Crozet he had learned to wait his turn. Of course, you couldn't wait your turn until you knew your place on the totem pole, which he was finally figuring out. Given his income and his stunning good looks, he hovered in the middle, much higher than had he been shorn of his attributes. Not being southern, there were moments when the elaborate, unspoken rules overwhelmed him. Harry usually translated for him.

"Hideously expensive." Archie leaned forward again.

"We know there's plenty of water, plenty." Herb Jones's gravelly voice filled the room. "But no matter how much we have, no matter where it is, we can't dam it up or pull it up without goring somebody's sacred cow."

"I resent that!" Archie jumped up.

"Sit down, Arch," Jim calmly commanded.

Archie didn't listen. "You're implying that because my farm is in the path of the reservoir I stand to gain. I think I stand to lose!"

"Oh, hell, Archie, I implied nothing, but you proved my

point." The room erupted in laughter, then quieted as the elderly minister, beloved of all, continued. "There's no way a project like this can go forward without enriching some and harming others. Once the state comes in and appraises your land or exercises eminent domain and claims land for the so-called greater good, whatever they do is going to be a real shell game."

"You got that right." Susan's husband, Ned, chimed in.

"And what about the bids for the jobs? Who would build the reservoir? You don't think that's political?" Vane-Tempest stood up again.

"Well, H. Vane, I'm not in the construction business." Archie glared at his former colleague, since he mistakenly assumed the criticism was directed at him.

"No, but Tommy Van Allen is." Vane-Tempest appeared triumphant.

"He's hardly my best friend." Archie cleared his throat. "What are you implying?"

"Gentlemen, Van Allen's books are open. I have known him all my life." Jim Sanburne wanted to get this meeting over with.

"Means you've known Archie all his life, too. You have my sympathy," Vane-Tempest catcalled, tired of Archie's oversensitivity. A few people laughed. Sarah elbowed her husband to stop.

"You know, if I weren't an elected official, I'd smash your face in." Archie clenched his fists, surprising people. He had a temper but he was taking offense where only leavening humor was intended.

"That's quite enough." Mim rose, facing the gathering. "We need more information. If we ask the state for another study it will be at their convenience and our expense. We are perfectly capable of identifying water sources ourselves. Once we have done that we can formulate our own plan and then present that plan to the state—a preemptive strike, if you will. Archie and Donald, you take the Keswick-Cismont area."

"Wait a minute. We have to vote on this." Archie's face changed from red to pale white.

"Call to question," Miranda said.

"There's no motion on the floor," Jim said.

"I move that the county commissioners identify all possible water sources in Albemarle County before our next meeting." BoomBoom succinctly put forth the motion.

"I second the motion," Vane-Tempest said.

"Call to question," Miranda repeated.

"All those in favor say aye." Jim cast his gaze over the room.

"Aye," came the resounding reply.

"Opposed."

"Me," Archie said. "I've got enough work to do."

"If you want to be reelected to the county commission you'd better change your attitude," Mim warned. Coming from her it was no idle threat.

As the meeting broke up, BoomBoom pushed her way to the back. "Harry, don't forget you're going to Lifeline with me Thursday night."

"I know." Harry showed no enthusiasm.

"Eight at the church."

"Eight."

"Ha-ha," Mrs. Murphy giggled. *"BoomBoom's got her."*

"She promised. Poor Mom. She got caught on that one." Tucker thought it was funny, too, for Lifeline was a group that looked inward, a spiritual awakening larded with lots of psychobabble. Harry was going to hate every minute, but she'd been hornswoggled into it in front of her friends last fall and now that a new cycle of Lifeline was starting, she had to make good on her promise.

Miranda bustled out, surrounded by her church friends. They sang in the choir at the Church of the Holy Light. "See you tomorrow, Harry."

"Bright and early." Harry smiled.

Fair caught up to her and leaned down. "Do you think some-one has paid Archie off to be so obstructionist? It doesn't make sense. He's so touchy."

"He's opposed to anything that will allow more people to move into the area. A reservoir would do that. At least, I think that's what's going on. He's saying one thing but doing another."

Fair smiled at his ex-wife's shrewd observation, but wondered what had happened to Archie Ingram, never the most likeable man but always a principled one.

BoomBoom, her back to Harry, was talking to Blair about his Porsche.

Sir H. Vane-Tempest and Sarah hurried by, glancing over their shoulders. Archie was in slow pursuit. They escaped out the front door as Ridley Kent bagged Archie, demanding to know when the next meeting would be.

"I don't know." Archie shoved him aside.

Don Jackson, together with Jim Sanburne, caught up with Archie. "Jesus, Arch, what's the matter with you?"

"Nothing. These studies will take forever. I'll be an old man before we come to any conclusion, and the state will do whatever they want, which would be the rape of Albemarle County, her natural resources, her extraordinary beauty, and her historical value."

"Can't be that bad." Jim frowned, worried for Arch, who had a promising political future if he could learn to control his temper.

"It will take forever. Christ, some of us will be pushing up daisies." Then he stormed out the door.

"*He's scared,*" Mrs. Murphy said to her friends. They could smell the fear, too.

5

Harry shot mail into the brass mailboxes as Mrs. Murphy sat on the ledge underneath the top section of boxes. The bottom section contained the big boxes, big enough for Murphy to sit in. Harry hummed to herself as Miranda played with the computer at the right side of the open counter.

As much as Miranda hated computers, the tiny post office had finally received one and Miranda had applied herself to the instructions that came with it. Being a bright woman, she had figured the machine out but she didn't like it. The green letters on the screen, a touch fuzzy, hurt her eyes.

Also, every time the power fritzed out, which happened often in the country, down went the computer. She could figure much faster with her trusty scale. No matter what the computer said she still double-checked with the scale.

Both women, early risers, came to work at seven. Usually, by the time residents opened the front door of the post office much of the mail was sorted—except during holidays. In late spring a few love letters filtered in, a few postcards from those taking early vacations, and the bills never stopped. Harry's secret ambition was to burn everyone's bills, announce she'd done it, and see what happened. The night of April 15, when lines curled across the railroad tracks as people hastened to dump their IRS forms in the mail, her ambition flamed beyond disposing of bills—she wanted to tear down every IRS building in America. She figured every other postal worker felt the same.

Low clouds and a light drizzle didn't dampen her mood. The warmth of spring brought out the best in Harry.

A squawk from the computer elicited "I know I did it right, why is it talking to me?" from Miranda.

"Zero out and try it again."

"I don't feel like it." Miranda, chin up, strode away from the offending machine.

A knock on the back door awakened Tee Tucker. Before she could bark, Susan Tucker, her breeder, jumped inside. She held her umbrella out the door, shook it vigorously, then closed the door, propping the umbrella to the right of it.

"Gloomy day, girls."

"Good for my irises," Mrs. Hogendobber, a passionate gardener, replied.

"Miranda, did you make orange buns again?" Susan sniffed the beguiling scent.

"Indeed, I did, you help yourself."

Susan gobbled one before Miranda finished her sentence.

"Pig." Harry laughed at her best friend.

"It's true." Susan sighed as she licked her lips. "I might as well live up to my billing." She ate another one.

"She'll ask for a rowing machine next Christmas," Mrs. Murphy remarked.

"*Won't use it. No one ever uses those things,*" Tucker said.

"*BoomBoom uses hers.*" Pewter opened one eye. She'd been snoozing on the chair at the small table in the rear.

"*She would.*" Mrs. Murphy stuck her paw in an open mailbox. "*Don't you love the way the clear window on bills crinkles when you touch it?*"

"*Bite it.*" Pewter egged her on.

"*Better not. Mom's still mad at you for your shameless display at the meeting last night.*" Tucker, ever obedient, chided her.

"*Hee-hee.*" Mrs. Murphy's whiskers twitched forward.

Susan walked over to scratch her ear. "You were the best part of the water-commission meeting."

"Say, wasn't Archie a pip?" Mrs. Hogendobber, beyond sixty, although she'd never admit her exact age, used slang from her generation's youth.

"Pip? He was a flaming asshole." Harry laughed.

"Don't be vulgar, Harry. That's the trouble with you young people. Cursing betrays a paucity of imagination."

"You're right." Harry smiled. "How about my saying that Archie was fraught with froth."

"A firth of froth or a froth of firth?" Susan kissed Murphy's head.

"*I like that,*" Murphy purred.

"What's a firth?" Mrs. Hogendobber asked.

"I don't know. It sounded right." Susan laughed at herself.

"To the dictionary, girls." Miranda pointed to the old Webster's, its blue-cloth case rubbed shiny, the cardboard sticking out at the corners.

"Is there really such a word?" Harry wondered.

Miranda silently pointed to the Webster's again.

Susan sat down at the table, thumbing through. The orange buns screamed under her nose. She snatched another. "*Firth,* old Scandinavian word meaning an 'arm of the sea.'"

"The English language is a lifelong study," Miranda pronounced.

The Reverend Herbert Jones strode up to the big counter, the ladies on the other side. "I smell orange."

"Come on in," Harry lifted the divider.

He helped himself to an orange bun. Pewter ate one when no one was looking. It made the cat so full she couldn't move. The humans were surprised that Pewter wasn't begging until Miranda counted the orange buns.

"Susan, did you eat four?"

"Three."

"Uh-huh." Miranda sternly reproached the cat with a look.

It had no effect whatsoever.

"This whole water business worries me." Herb licked his fingers, then found a napkin. "I don't know why Archie is behaving the way he is. He's known about the old study for years." His voice shot upward. "The various conservation groups in the county are on top of this one. Anyway, there are more-pressing political issues."

"Like what?"

"Like a new grade school in Greenwood."

"Yeah, that is pretty important," Harry agreed.

"That fop Sir H. Vane-Tempest—and if he's a knight or a lord or whatever, I'm John the Baptist—" Herb arched an eyebrow, "called me up and chewed me out for having too much brass on my foraging cap."

"What?" The three women stared at him.

"Like a fool I agreed to be in this reenactment. Now look, girls,"—he always called them girls, and there was no point in mentioning that might not be desirable—"I'm no fanatic. I agreed to fill out the ranks. He wants me to be one hundred percent accurate, though. He says that no real soldier would have all that brass on his cap because it's just one more thing to keep clean."

"Exactly what is on your cap?" Miranda asked.

"VA 1st—and then he said I had to wear something called a havelock—it's a piece of white canvas that buttons over the cap. He said it might be hot and a real soldier would want to keep the sun off. I told him I'd spent enough money and if I wasn't one hundred percent accurate that was too bad. He huffed and puffed. Finally I told him he wasn't an American, and far more important, he wasn't a Virginian and he shouldn't tell one born and bred how to dress. My great-granddaddy was *in* the war. His was living high on the hog in England. He sputtered some more and said nationality had nothing to do with it. This was living history." He shook his head. "Obviously, the man has nothing better to do with his life."

"What about Ned?" Harry turned to Susan. "Is he getting obsessive?"

"He started out like the Rev." She smiled at Herb when she said that. "Now he's really into it. Why do you think I'm getting involved?"

"*That settles it. I'm going.*" Mrs. Murphy spoke from the depths of the mail cart.

"*Fat chance,*" Tucker replied.

"*I am too going and I'll tell you why, midget fatso.*"

"*I'm not fat.*"

"*You're so low to the ground, how can I tell?*" The tiger cackled. "*I'm going because there were Confederate cats. They were vital to the war effort. We kept mice out of the grain supplies.*"

"*What about Union cats?*" Pewter, a glorious Confederate gray, said.

"*We don't mention them.*"

"What are you all talking about?" Susan, sensitive to animals, asked them.

"*The reenactment,*" came the reply.

"You know Blair Bainbridge bought everything authentic,

not reproductions but real stuff. Must have cost him a fortune," Herb mused.

"I'd kill for his Porsche." Harry's eyes clouded over.

"You'd have to." Susan poked at her. "You can't even afford a new truck."

"Ain't it awful?" Harry hung her head in mock despair.

"Your ex is going as a cavalry officer. No one can find a jacket large enough for him, so he's wearing a period muslin shirt and gray pants."

"I hope he's considered the small fact that most of our horses aren't accustomed to continuous gunfire and cannon fire."

"He mentioned that." Herb folded his arms across his chest so he wouldn't reach out and grab another orange bun. He was on yet another diet and he'd cheated already.

"I have mixed emotions about Civil War reenactments. I think we're glorifying violence," Harry said. "I can't help it, I think there's a nasty reactionary undertow to all this."

"Never thought about it." Susan wrinkled her brow. "I figured it was what they said, living history. Besides, Ned gets dragged to so many things with me, I have to go along with this."

"Well, if it's living history, then why aren't we reliving inventing the reaper or the cotton gin? Why are we instead reliving the most horrible thing that's ever happened to this country? Sixty percent of the War Between the States was fought on Virginia soil. You'd think we, of all the people, would have the sense not to glorify it."

"Maybe it's not over." Herb stared at the ceiling.

"He hit the nail on the head." Mrs. Murphy played with her tail.

6

Later that afternoon the clouds grew darker still.

Deputy Cooper walked through the back door. "Hey."

"Hey," Harry answered.

"Where's Miranda?"

"Ran home for a minute." Harry pointed to a chair. "Sit down."

"Have you seen Tommy Van Allen?"

"No."

The two cats, dozing in the canvas mail cart, woke up, sticking their heads over the top.

"He's been missing for two days—two days that we know of—and his plane is missing, too."

Mrs. Murphy put her paws on the edge of the cart, with rapt attention.

"Cynthia, how could his plane be missing for two days and the airport not realize it?"

"They thought the plane was in Hangar C, the last hangar for repairs. Apparently Tommy had scheduled a maintenance check for Monday morning."

"How could the plane take off and not return without anyone noticing?"

"I wondered about that myself. The airport closes at midnight. He could have gone off then, and he *is* in the habit of staying a night or two at his destination. Still, it's odd."

"*I know where the plane is!*" Mrs. Murphy shouted.

"Quiet." Harry shook her finger.

The cat jumped out of the cart and bounded into Cynthia's lap. "*I don't know where Tommy is but I know where the plane is.*"

"She's affectionate." Cynthia scratched her ears.

"*Don't waste your breath,*" Pewter advised Mrs. Murphy.

"*Do you really know where the plane is?*" Tucker asked.

"*Tally Urquhart's old barn. I'll take you there.*"

Rain rattled on the windowpane.

Pewter settled back down in the mail cart. "*Wait for a sunny day.*"

Mrs. Murphy jumped off Cynthia's lap back into the mail cart, where she rolled over Pewter. "*You don't believe me.*"

"*I don't care.*"

"*Sunday night when I came to bed wet—that's when I saw the plane.*" She swatted the inattentive Pewter.

"Temper tantrum." Harry rose and separated them.

"Has anyone picked up Tommy's mail?" Cooper asked.

"His secretary." Harry held Mrs. Murphy on her shoulder.

Miranda came through the back door. Cynthia asked her about Tommy.

"He'll show up. It's hard to hide a six-foot-five-inch man," Miranda advised. "He's done this before."

"He stopped drinking," Harry reminded her.

"Maybe he slipped off the wagon." Miranda frowned.

"I know where the plane is!" the cat bellowed.

"God, Murphy, you'll split my eardrum." Harry placed her on the floor.

7

The longer days helped Harry finish her chores when she returned home from work. She pulled Johnny Pop, her 1958 John Deere tractor—as good as the day it was built—into the shed.

When she cut the choke the exhaust always popped—one loud crack—which made her laugh. She cleaned stalls, throwing the muck into the manure spreader. Since it was raining she'd have to wait until the ground dried before spreading anything on it.

Harry always put her equipment back in the shed. Her dad had told her that was the only way to do it. Stuff would last for decades if well built and well cared for.

She missed her father and mother. They were lively, hardworking people. As she grew up she realized what good people they really were. They'd had a German shepherd, King, when she was in her teens. King lived to an advanced age and when her mother died, King followed. Harry told herself that one day she'd get another German shepherd but she hadn't gotten around to it, maybe because a shepherd would remind her of her mother and make the loss even more apparent.

Tucker had been given to her as a six-week-old puppy by Susan, one of the best corgi breeders in Virginia. Harry didn't like small dogs but she learned to love the bouncing, tough corgi. Then she decided if she brought in a shepherd puppy it would upset Tucker—another reason to procrastinate.

Actually, the shepherd would upset the cats more. Tucker, outnumbered, might have been happy for another canine on the place.

She dashed back to the barn, rain sliding down the collar of her ancient Barbour. "I've got to rewax this thing." Water was seeping through the back of the coat.

The phone rang in the tack room. "Hello."

"Harry, Ridley Kent here. I've agreed to help Archie canvass landowners. I'm looking at a topo map and a flat map. You've got a creek in your western boundary."

"Yep."

"Strong creek?"

"In spring, but even in summer it never dries out completely. The water comes down from Little Yellow Mountain."

"What about springs?"

"There's one at the eastern corner."

"North or south?"

"Northeastern."

"Have you ever had your well run dry in a drought?"

"No. Neither did Mom and Dad, and they moved to this farm in the forties."

"Thanks."

"Sure." She hung up the phone.

"Mother, there's an underground spring in the depression in the cornfield," Tucker told her. *"I can hear it."*

Harry rubbed the dog's soft fur. "I don't have any treaties on me."

The horses, munching hay in their stalls, lifted their heads when Mrs. Murphy jumped on the stall divider from the hayloft. Pewter, on the tack trunk, her favorite spot, watched her nimble friend. She could jump like that if she wanted to but she never wanted to; it jarred her bones.

"Simon's found a quarter," Murphy announced.

"Don't tell," a tiny voice complained.

"I don't want your quarter," Tucker called up as the possum's beady little eyes peered over the hayloft ledge.

Harry looked up at him. "Evening, Simon."

He blinked, then scurried back to his nest. Simon wouldn't show himself at first but over time he'd learned to trust Harry. That didn't mean he was going to talk to her. You had to be careful about humans.

The rain pounded down.

Harry checked the barometer in the tack room. The needle swung over to stormy. She walked up and down the aisle. She'd filled each water bucket, put out hay, put new salt cubes in the bottoms of their feed buckets. But Harry liked to double-check everything. Then she unplugged the coffeemaker in the tack room, folding up the cord and slipping it in the top drawer of the tall, narrow chest of drawers. She kept bits in those drawers as well as hoof-picks, small flat things. She'd learned her lesson when the mice ruined her first coffeepot by chewing through the cord. They had electrocuted themselves but they could have started a fire in the barn. Since then she ran light cords through a narrow PVC tube that she attached to the wall. This was the only exposed cord.

Harry also kept fire extinguishers at both ends of the barn

plus one in the hayloft. Right now she was in less danger of fire than of being blown off the surface of the earth.

She paused at the open doorway. "You know, I'd better close the barn doors." She walked to the other end and pulled the doors closed. Then she returned to the end of the barn facing the house. "Kids, you with me?"

Three little heads looked up at her. *"Yep."*

She pulled the barn doors at that end closed, with a sliver of room for her to squeeze out. Then she ran like mad for the screened porch door. The two cats and the dog jetted ahead of her.

"I hate to get wet," Pewter yowled.

"Slowpoke." Mrs. Murphy pulled open the door.

"You guys are smart." Harry admired her brood.

The animals shook on the screened porch. Harry removed her coat and shook it, too. "I swear—when it dries I will re-wax it."

She lifted a thick-piled towel off a peg, kneeling down to dry off the animals.

Apart from the rain drumming on the tin roof it was a quiet night. She made herself a fried-egg-and-pickle sandwich, fed the animals, then sat down to read *The Life of Cézanne* but couldn't keep her eyes open. Low-pressure systems made her sleepy.

Mrs. Murphy listened to the rain. *"As soon as it dries we're going over to the old barn."*

8

An open one-pound can of gunpowder sat on the butcher-block kitchen table. Paper cartridges, laid out in rows like tiny trapezoidal tents, covered one edge of the table. Ridley Kent bent his handsome head over the litter. Determined to outauthenticate everyone, he was rolling his own cartridges. It wasn't as easy to roll sixty grains of 2F black powder as he had anticipated.

Rolling with both hands, he then fumbled with the tie-off. Outside the rain beat down the kitchen window. It was a filthy night.

"Damn it to hell!" he exploded when the paper opened, spilling gunpowder over the table. Now he'd have to count out grains again.

It occurred to him to line up sixty grains behind every piece of paper. That served the purpose, too, of calming him down so he wouldn't botch his next tie-off job.

Archie Ingram came through the door, sending the carefully cut paper sailing around the room.

"I could kill you, Archie."

Archie hung his raincoat on the doorknob to drip. He surveyed the white papers, then knelt down, picking them up. "Get a grip."

"Do you know how long I've been sitting here with these cursed things?"

"Half the day?"

"Two hours. It took one hour just to cut the paper."

"Right weight. You've done your homework. After all, you could have cheated and bought ready-mades."

"Not me. Plenty of others do."

"Here, let me show you how to do this." Archie sat down, took a flat knife, and scraped the sixty grains into the paper, rolling it so a tiny piece, the longest piece, stuck over the final edge. He tied off the end. "Where'd you get the dowel?"

"Made it." Ridley referred to the wooden dowel, about half an inch with a head cut like a bullet head or minnie ball. Rolling the paper on this wooden dowel made the task more congenial but Ridley's fingers, none too steady at any time of day, still couldn't tie off the cartridge.

"And I suppose you'll go as an officer?"

"Since I'm one of the few who can afford the gear, yes," came Ridley's testy reply.

"Don't even think about giving an order. You give enough in real life."

"What did officers do?" Ridley questioned, half laughing.

"Die by the truckload."

"I've no intention of doing that. Anyway, the Union men fire over our heads and we fire over theirs. Aren't the rules never to point a firearm directly at your opponent, and not to ram a real ball down your rifle?"

"Yes. But don't give orders. You're new to this and even though you're a—"

"Colonel."

"How perfect," Archie slyly said. "You don't give orders. You walk by the side of your men, on the front corner."

"I'll ride."

"Ridley, you can't ride a hair of a horse. Walk or be an artillery officer."

"All I have to do is walk along. I think I can manage that."

"Listen, bonehead, Fair Haristeen's worried about riding and he can *ride*. None of the horses are accustomed to gunfire. You'll walk."

"But I've got yellow trim on my uniform and a golden sash for my sword," Ridley protested.

"Light blue. Infantry. Don't make an ass of yourself. Take this back to Mrs. Woo and have her sew on blue facings. Her shop is that little building behind Rio Road Shopping Center. Just do what I tell you. I know what I'm talking about and I don't want to see you make a fool of yourself."

Ridley wanted to say, "You're making a fool out of your own self. Why worry about me?"

Archie droned on. "We're going to shut up H. Vane. The man thinks he can run the world. Pompous limey! He's upset because we're filling the rank with men who aren't true reenactors. I said we had to do it. The public will be in attendance and we need this battle to warm up for the Wilderness reenactment."

"Still bodies in that Wilderness." Ridley shuddered.

"There's so many bodies in the ground in Virginia, you can't plow without hitting one, especially around Richmond."

"Maybe that's why our crops grow so well."

Archie narrowed his greenish eyes. "You're not taking this seriously."

"Seriously enough to spend good money."

"Hell, Ridley, if you aren't throwing your money away on women..."

"You've got room to talk?" A thick auburn eyebrow jutted upward.

Crimson washed over Archie's face. He blushed easily. "A gentleman doesn't discuss those matters."

"Who said we were gentlemen?" Ridley laughed.

"We were raised gentlemen even if we can't always be gentlemen." A guilty conscience haunted the county commissioner.

"Archie, one of these days you're going to get caught, and if your wife doesn't kill you somebody else will." A half-smile gave Ridley a rakish air. "You're a Casanova in disguise."

"What's the disguise?" Archie liked the description more than he cared to admit.

"Pug ugly." Ridley laughed.

Archie breathed in, thought a second, then laughed himself. He rolled another cartridge. "Charles Bronson wasn't classically handsome."

"Charles Bronson's ass would make your Sunday face," Ridley teased, for Arch was good-looking.

"Ridley, you really know how to hurt a guy." Archie's gloom lifted a bit.

Ridley could make anyone laugh. His infectious spirit, too often fueled by booze, made him a boon companion. Women adored him. The compliment was returned.

Ridley got up, returning with a three-banded Enfield rifle. Four hundred and eighty dollars. Was I robbed?"

"No, that's the going price."

He polished the brass on the musket.

"If you're behind a line of infantry, you hold your rifle so that the first and second bands of your weapon are over the ear of one of your men." He pointed to the part of the barrel. "That way no one will get a singed ear."

They worked quietly, then Ridley, voice low, said, "Arch, if you don't mend some fences you're going to lose your commission seat. Mim's in a rage."

Archie flared his nostrils. "She is?"

"What did you expect? You acted like a jerk at the commission meeting." He smiled to soften his words. "You didn't seem like yourself."

Archie shrugged. "I'm sick of being the bad guy in the county-commission meetings."

"You're only the bad guy to the developers. Plenty of people think you're doing a fine job. No one understands why you're so emotional about the reservoir, though. I'm on your side, Arch, that's why I'm telling you what others won't tell you. You need to mend fences," he repeated.

"H. Vane is behind this."

"He may be behind it but I'm telling you Mim's in front of it." Ridley put his cartridges in stacks of ten. "And why did you deny Vane-Tempest's request for a zoning variance last winter? Establishing a quarry on the north side of his land is a good idea. No one will see it and it will create jobs."

"He needed better plans."

"Come on, Arch, his plan included a responsible solution to reclaim the pits. It was environmentally progressive." Ridley lowered his voice. "Are you on the take?" Archie's jaw fell slack. Ridley pressed. "That's what some people are saying. I'll never tell but I'd sure like to know because you're acting like you're a nickel short of a dime these days. People think hard-line environmental groups are slipping you money. Crazy. But they're talking like that."

Archie got up, heading for the door. Ridley ran after him. "Arch! Come on, Arch. I'm trying to help."

"Help? You accuse me of betraying the public's confidence!"

"I don't want you to lose what you've worked so hard to get. Come on, sit down."

Archie rejoined him. "I am not on the take."

"Okay." Ridley paused. "Hey, did you hear that Tommy Van Allen is missing?"

"He's not missing. He's probably in Santa Fe or Buenos Aires, for God's sake. That is the most self-indulgent man I've ever met."

"Rick Shaw called me. They're treating it as a missing-persons case. His plane is missing, too."

"I'm glad we never pitched in and bought that twin engine. I don't know how I could have fallen for that."

"It was fun...our flying club, but I don't get the power charge from flying that you guys do."

"At least you could afford it." Archie absentmindedly polished the brass bands on the rifle.

"Tommy and I already knew how to fly, of course, courtesy of the U.S. Air Force. And H. Vane learned in the RAF. Maybe being up in the air again reminded me too much of my service days or maybe I really am up in the air. It was too close for comfort."

"Blair sure learned quickly. I thought a pretty guy like that would chicken out. I'd rather he had dropped out instead of you."

"I can't warm to that guy." Ridley offered Archie a beer. He passed. "He's not cold-blooded but he's not hot-blooded either. Like last fall, when he had that affairette with Sarah Vane-Tempest—"

Arch interrupted, "He did not."

"The hell he didn't. They were discreet about it, that's all."

"I can't believe she'd go to bed with Blair Bainbridge," Archie said with disgust.

"Didn't last long. Maybe he got bored with her or she got bored with him. Then, too, I wouldn't want H. Vane breathing down my neck."

"What's H. Vane expect, marrying a woman half his age?"

Ridley walked to the fridge. "Drink a beer, buddy, you look peaked."

"Huh? Okay." Archie took the cold beer, peeling back the pop-top. "I know I've been irritable. Too much work, Ridley. Just too much. My wife complains that she never sees me and since she only complains when she does see me, I don't want to go home." He drank a long, slow swallow. "Being a county commissioner can sometimes, well, let me put it this way—if there's a buffoon, an asshole, or a certifiable psycho, not only will I meet them campaigning they'll show up in my office. And this reservoir stuff brings them all out of the woodwork."

"Forget about it for a night. I'll make popcorn. We can tell lies about the women we've conquered."

"Sounds good to me." Archie drained the beer can, got up, and fetched another.

9

The rain stopped Wednesday morning. That evening after supper, Mrs. Murphy gathered Pewter and Tucker on the screened-in porch.

"*Four miles is too far in the muck. Let's wait a few more days,*" Pewter whined.

"*For all we know, the plane will be gone by then.*" Mrs. Murphy sniffed the wind, a light breeze out of the west. "*I'm heading out.*"

"*I'll go with you.*" Tucker's big ears moved forward.

"*I'm staying home.*" Pewter sat down.

"*Chicken,*" the dog teased her.

"*I'm not chicken. I don't feel like getting dirty, especially since I've just given myself a bath.*"

"*Well, let's go.*" Murphy opened the screen door, Tucker immediately behind her. The door flapped twice. Pewter watched them bound over the meadow by the barn. She felt a pang of missing out but not enough to follow. She walked back inside, deciding to curl up on the 1930s chair with the mohair throw. She liked to snuggle in the mohair but wished Harry were wealthy enough to afford cashmere. Pewter craved luxury.

Reaching the first creek dividing Harry's property from Blair Bainbridge's, the cat and dog were stopped by high water.

"Ugly." Tucker paced the bank.

"Let's go up to the beaver dam."

"If it's standing."

"Hasn't been that much water. Come on."

"I hate those beavers." Tucker did, too.

"We'll be across before they know it."

A quarter of a mile upstream the log-and-sapling lodge dominated the creek along with the sturdy dam the beavers had constructed.

Carefully, Mrs. Murphy put one paw on the dam. She tested its sturdiness, then sped across, small splashes of water in her wake.

Tucker whined but followed. Her progress wasn't as graceful but she made it. They were halfway across Blair's easternmost meadow before the beavers emerged from their lodge to inspect their dam.

Lights at Blair's place caught their attention. A white Land Rover was parked in the driveway.

"Wonder what Archie's doing at Blair's?"

Mrs. Murphy kept moving. *"Trying to borrow the Porsche."*

They laughed until they reached the ridge, about seven hundred feet above sea level. They paused at the top, which bristled with rock outcroppings. Although only four miles across, the terrain was rugged in parts.

After catching her breath, Mrs. Murphy nudged Tucker. *"Ready?"*

"Yeah."

They swept down the ridge, skirting the thorn creepers and the underbrush, where they startled rabbits and one lurking fox. Mrs. Murphy hoped the bobcat was hunting somewhere else tonight.

The last creek had an upturned tree fallen over it. Mrs. Murphy danced across it. Tucker chose to swim the creek.

The abandoned buildings of the Urquhart farm shone silver in the moonlight, the slate roofs sparkling as though obsidian.

The doors to the barn were shut.

The two animals circled the barn, searching for burrows, preferably uninhabited. Mrs. Murphy looked up.

The Dutch door of a stall was partially open, flapping in the gentle breeze.

"I'll try it." Mrs. Murphy squatted down, paused a second, then sprang upward, reaching the slight opening before the top door banged back again. She dropped to the old hay on the stall floor.

Walking over to the big doors, she pulled with her paw just enough to create a crack. Tucker wedged her nose in and both cat and dog pushed. The big door creaked back on its overhead track just enough for the powerful dog to push herself inside.

Tucker stopped. Tommy Van Allen's plane was still parked in the middle of the vast center aisle. *"I'll be."*

"You sniff around the plane," Mrs. Murphy ordered. *"I'll get in the cockpit."*

The tiger unleashed her claws, vaulting at a stall post. She shimmied up, reaching a massive cross beam, and walked along the top of it until the white plane was directly underneath, ten feet below.

"That's a big drop, Murphy."

"I know." Murphy stared down at the wing, backed up a bit,

then jumped off the beam. She hit the wing with a thud, sliding a little in the process, leaving red clay marks to disturb the pristine whiteness.

"You okay?" the dog called.

"Yes, but it's slick." The cat tiptoed to the edge of the cockpit. She easily opened the door, as the handle was large and turned down, and the door was slightly ajar. Then she hopped inside, leaving the door hanging wide open. The odor of old leather filled her nostrils.

"See anything?" Tucker called up.

"Lots of dials and a throttle."

"Blood?"

"No, squeaky-clean."

Tucker, somewhat disappointed, returned to the task of sniffing around the plane. The odor of gas killed other scents.

Mrs. Murphy poked at knobs, put one eye close to the throttle to see if anything had fallen into the slidpath. She hopped around, unwittingly leaving muddy paw prints as a signature.

Finding nothing, she readied to jump back down on the wing. Then, on the pilot's-side door, she noticed a leather pocket like a map pocket on an old car door. She reached over but couldn't quite get to it. She reached again and caught the very inside of the pocket, slowly moving the door toward her. She didn't want to shut the door since the inside handle might not open easily.

With one paw, claws out, she pulled open the pocket while with the other paw she held the door from closing. She fished in the pocket, pulling out the only thing in there, a folded-over map, used so many times, the creases were worn to nothingness. She grabbed it between her teeth, hopping onto the wing. She skidded on the flap side of the wing and launched herself to the soft center-aisle turf below.

The two friends walked to the door, squeezed through, and opened the map in the moonlight. Mrs. Murphy carefully sat on the edge of the map so it wouldn't blow away; she loved the smooth feel of paper under her bottom.

"What is it?" Tucker strained to make sense of the colors and lines.

"Your face is too close. Step back."

"Oh." She did as instructed. *"It's the U.S. Geological Survey map for the county. Pretty colors."*

"Can you carry this back home? I'll hide it in Simon's house."

"Why not leave it here?"

"Because I think someone will come back for it."

"Tommy?"

"No. Tommy's dead."

"How do you know that?"

"I don't. Cat intuition. I saw two people leave this plane. One had to be Tommy, a very tall person, but it was raining, fog was swirling down, and I couldn't get a good look. Plus I was already at the creek and had climbed up in the oak tree. The other person was short."

"Anyone would be short compared to Tommy Van Allen."

"Tucker, put your paw on both corners. If I can look down at this map maybe I can see better." The cat drew herself to her full height, glancing down. *"Hmm. Pieces are outlined."*

"Maybe an old flight path."

"These are more like squares and a big outline outside that."

"Was there a flight plan up there?"

"No."

"Why would two people take off, not tell anyone, and land here? And one of them is now missing."

"I haven't a single idea. But they planned to put the plane in the barn. I really think they did."

"You don't think the fog and bad weather drove them down?"

"There are better place to land than Tally's old airstrip. There are lots of airstrips in Albemarle County. To come down here you have to shoot between Little Yellow Mountain and that ridge we crossed. It's

not threading a needle but you have to be pretty darned good, especially with the downdraft and winds that swirl around mountains. Whoever landed here in the fog was a hell of a pilot."

"Tommy was good."

"But it wasn't Tommy. I saw him hop out and open the doors. At least, I think that was Tommy."

"How will we ever get Harry over here?" Tucker wondered.

"Only if she visits Tally or if she rides over. She hardly ever comes this way, because the second creek crossing changes every time there's a storm. Who knows how long it will take the humans to find this plane?"

"If Rick Shaw is logical he'll eventually search each private airstrip."

"That's true. I wonder when he'll get to that?" The cat noticed Mars, pulsating red in the sky. *"I do believe whoever flew that plane will be back for this map."*

"There have to be thousands of survey maps of the county. This one isn't valuable."

"If it has fingerprints on it, it is." Mrs. Murphy studied the map again, paying attention to the hand-drawn lines. *"That's it."*

"What?"

"The big outline—it's the watershed. I remember from the map posted on the bulletin board at the commission meeting. I was up on the desk. I could see it clearly."

10

"Do I have to do this?" Harry leaned against the truck door.

"Yes." Miranda offered no hope of escape. "I'll take Mrs. Murphy, Pewter, and Tucker home with me. No one will miss supper. If you take them home, you'll be late."

"All right." Harry climbed up into the old Superman-blue 1978 Ford half-ton.

"Good luck, Mom," Mrs. Murphy saucily called out.

She needed more than luck. She needed the patience of Job. Lifeline, held in the basement of the Lutheran church, provided support and direction for many seekers.

Harry thought she had direction enough, and as for support, she was raised not to broadcast her troubles.

The adherents of this self-discovery process really surprised her, though. Ridley Kent; Cynthia Cooper—of all people; Dr.

Hayden McIntire, Larry Johnson's much-younger partner; and several other people she'd known for years were among the crowd that filled the church basement.

BoomBoom stuck next to her.

The leader of the group, Bill Oster, worked at the University of Virginia library. It had taken years of training for him to become a group leader.

"Each of us carries negative programming, negative information. The purpose of Lifeline is to clear that away so you can more fully experience the people around you and so you can more fully experience yourself. It's strange, isn't it? We are raised to practice good manners, we're taught how to treat other people, but we're not taught how to treat ourselves. The first task, therefore, is to establish a proper relationship with yourself."

BoomBoom beamed with each word, casting significant glances at Harry. By the end of the evening Harry couldn't say she'd heard anything silly but she couldn't say the program was for her either. By nature a self-contained person, she found the idea of exploring emotions or even cleansing herself of negativity in front of others to be anathema. Still, she had to admit the ideas were worth considering.

"I hope you'll return," Bill Oster warmly said.

"You are a motivating leader." Harry, manners to the fore, complimented him.

"And that means you won't return." He believed in constant honesty, which at times had a touch of ruthlessness to it.

"No." Harry hated to be direct in this fashion. It violated everything she'd been taught all her life. "It's not for me but I think it's a good process."

He clasped both her hands in his. "If you change your mind you know where to find us. We start new groups every six weeks."

BoomBoom, disappointed in Harry, said, "Would you go if I

weren't part of the group? I'm training to lead a group but I can put it off for another six weeks."

"It has nothing to do with you, Boom."

"Eventually you overcome your discomfort level."

"You have to want to and I don't. Whatever my deepest inner flaws are, I've learned to live with them."

"That's not the point." BoomBoom felt rejected because Lifeline was rejected.

Cynthia joined them. "Boom, Harry is the stubbornest woman I've ever met. Neither of us can talk her into anything. Besides, she kept her promise."

"That's true." BoomBoom offered her hand to Harry, who graciously shook it.

"Thanks, Boom."

"Will we ever be friends?"

"I—I don't know, but our relationship has improved." Harry was truthful. Ever since BoomBoom's fling with Fair, the very sight of her set Harry's teeth on edge, but she was able to have a civil conversation with her now.

A somewhat mollified BoomBoom Craycroft bid them good-night.

"You're the last person I'd think to find in a group like this," Harry confided to Coop. "Well, Ridley Kent is a big surprise, too."

"I was getting jaded," Cynthia softly replied. "I see liars, drunks, irresponsible shits day in and day out. The drug dealers are a real treat, too. I was losing my faith in the goodness of people."

"Guess you would."

"I thought, this can't hurt me and I might even learn something."

"Good for you. No wonder I haven't seen you around much lately."

"Actually, this is my first night. I've been on overload because the spring flu is moving through the force. In the last month we've had two or three people out each week. I'm pulling a lot of overtime, anyway."

"When things even out, come on over. We'll have a Chinese-and-video night."

"Great. I'll bring the Chinese."

Harry walked Coop to her car, then hopped into her truck.

As she walked through Miranda's door she smelled freshly fried liver, not her favorite.

Miranda sat at the table, the animals eating from places set for them. Sheepishly Harry's hostess said, "They're the only creatures I can get to eat fried liver with me."

"I'll eat fried liver."

"You don't really like it."

"I wouldn't buy it in a restaurant but everything you make tastes good."

"I happen to have a piece left, smothered in my special sauce with caramelized onions. And I know you love brussels sprouts, a hint of molasses and lemon with them, but only a hint."

As Harry ate this unexpected feast, Miranda peppered her with questions to satisfy herself that Lifeline wasn't leading people away from the Scriptures.

"Didn't mention the Bible. It's about personal growth, not religion."

"The two are connected."

"Now, Miranda, I am not capable of a theological discussion. You take that up with Herbie. After all, the meetings are held in his church."

"People need the Good Book."

"Lifeline and Christianity are not mutually exclusive." A brussels sprout melted in her mouth.

"The essence of Christianity is forgiveness."

"I think in Lifeline they teach you to forgive yourself."

This thought hit Miranda like a Ping-Pong ball: It bounced off but left a small impression. She would have to ponder it. "Seems you got more out of Lifeline than you realize."

11

Pewter, wild-eyed and puffed up, charged through the animal flap at the back of the post office. *"Come quick!"*

Without arguing, Mrs. Murphy rushed outside, closely followed by Tucker. Pewter's short, furry tail disappeared around the corner to the front of Market Shiflett's grocery store. She leapt onto the fruit display outside the front door.

Mrs. Murphy followed, finding herself amid the banana display. *"Ever see a banana spider?"* she hissed.

She soon forgot about the furry spiders hiding among the yellow bunches because inside, Sir H. Vane-Tempest and Archie Ingram were shouting at the top of their lungs. A small crowd was gathered, including Market Shiflett, who stood beside the screened front door of his store. It was still too cool for air-conditioning.

"You've forgotten—" Vane-Tempest sputtered.

"I've forgotten nothing."

"You've forgotten who your friends are." Vane-Tempest stepped closer to Archie, who suddenly hit him on the left cheek. He lashed out so quickly that Archie surprised both himself and the Englishman.

Reeling backward, Vane-Tempest lifted a soft hand to cover the red mark.

Still in a fury, Archie taunted the old man. "You're the one who forgets, Vane-Tempest, and it will catch up with you!"

Before the Englishman could lunge forward, a rattled Archie had backed out of the store, parting the gaggle of people.

Harry stuck her head out of the post office, since the shouts had penetrated even there. She stuck it back in. The altercation was none of her business. Besides, people were soon pouring into the post office, all telling their versions of the tale.

Mrs. Murphy moved over to sit on the apples. *"Friendship is like a love affair. When it sours, pfff-t!"*

"Ours won't." Pewter rubbed her cheek against the slender tiger.

"We're cats. We're smarter than people," Murphy purred. She liked attention and she especially liked being groomed.

"Don't you wonder what's happened?"

"It's the rock quarry," Pewter said.

"That was ages ago," Mrs. Murphy remembered.

"Some people are on slow fuses," Pewter remarked.

Tucker stepped away from the fruit stand to better see the cats. *"Bet there's a woman involved."*

"Maybe," Mrs. Murphy noted.

"Who would go out with H. Vane-Tempest apart from his very expensive wife? A puff adder, that man!" Pewter likened people to animals.

"Who said it was H. Vane?" Tucker winked.

"Gross," came the tiger's tart comment.

They walked over to the post office, going in by the front door as yet another resident opened it. Sir H. Vane-Tempest was loudly explaining his side of the story.

"He's become irrational. He thinks everyone is against him. Even Aileen has noticed it. I spoke to her last week about Archie's personality disintegration."

Aileen was Archie's wife.

"It's difficult being on the county commission when opinion in the county is so divided," Miranda offered.

"He asked for the job," Big Mim tartly observed.

"Won't have it for long," Little Mim said, which made her mother smile slightly.

"Ever since the storms this winter when Sugar Hollow washed—the terrible flooding—he's not been the same," Vane-Tempest said.

"It can't be that," Miranda shrewdly noticed. "You don't think so either."

Vane-Tempest eyed her. "Well—well, whatever has come over him has been intensifying since that time. I was the man's friend...when no one else wanted to hear about preserving the environment."

Tucker interrupted. *"He's sure tooting his own horn."*

"Quiet," Harry reprimanded her.

Vane-Tempest continued. "He's argued with everyone. Aileen says he hardly speaks to her when he comes home at night. He goes into his den and pores over papers and maps. And yes, I am angry that he lobbied the commission to deny permission for me to establish a rock quarry. But I'll get over it."

"Will *he*?" Mim sharply said.

"I didn't act that badly," Vane-Tempest defended himself. "He did."

"He certainly did today." Little Mim played with the soft leather weave of her Bottega Veneta bag.

"You should have offered him a share of the business when his term expired." Mim surprised everyone with her comment, then added, "Really, people, how do you think anything gets done here?"

"That's a bribe," Miranda said firmly.

"No. You don't ask him to vote your way, you simply offer him a job when his term expires. It's done in Washington on an hourly basis and the pity of it is, it isn't done well. We'd have better government if it were."

"Cynic." Vane-Tempest smiled.

"Realist." Mim tapped her foot on the polished wooden floors, polished with use. "People in government can't make money while they're in government. So you must use your position to develop contacts for when your term expires."

No one said a word for a minute. Mim had a way of boring straight to the heart of a problem. The truth was that Archie, a small printer by trade, didn't make much money. The county-commission post carried no stipend and the time it sucked up diverted his attention from a business that could have been more lucrative.

"He'd never give up his business." Vane-Tempest betrayed his own thoughts, which was exactly what Mim had hoped to achieve by being forthright. Being an Englishman, he couldn't have known she was baiting him. The Virginians knew exactly what she was doing, which was why they fell silent after she spoke.

"Aileen could run it." Little Mim worked well with her mother despite her irritation with her overbearing parent. "She runs it anyway."

"Archie lacks the common touch and a good printer has to be able to deal with people who have little idea of how long it takes to print anything or what it costs. You're right. He ought to turn the whole business over to Aileen. As for why he wanted to be a county commissioner, well, he has his pet concerns, but truthfully, he wanted the power." Vane-Tempest cracked a knuckle, revealing his rare nervousness.

"*Human meetings waste time,*" Pewter blandly noted. "*Everyone has to express an opinion. Then everyone else has to rebut it or add to it. I say shut up and get the job done.*"

"*They can't,*" Mrs. Murphy shrewdly observed. "*Most cats are roughly equal, if you think about it. I mean, we can all jump about the same height, run about the same speed. They're very different from one another. Their talents are wildly different. The only way they can survive is to talk to one another and reach a consensus. All herd animals are like that. We're not herd animals.*"

"*Neither am I,*" Tucker protested.

"*You're a pack animal. Same difference.*"

"*I am an individual.*"

"*I never said you weren't an individual, Tucker. But dogs tend to run in packs and kill in packs.*"

"*I herd cows, sheep, anything. I'm not a hunting dog.*"

"*You're an argumentative one.*" Mrs. Murphy flicked her tail.

"*Tucker is the exception that proves the rule.*" Pewter didn't feel like a fight. Hearing Archie and H. Vane was enough for her.

Vane-Tempest threw back his shoulders. "I can't talk to Arch, obviously, but I do think some of you can. Maybe you can cast oil upon the waters."

" 'Yet man is born into trouble, as the sparks fly upward.' " Miranda quoted Job, Chapter 5, Verse 7.

"What's that supposed to mean?" the Englishman mildly inquired.

"I don't know. Just popped into my head." Mrs. H. laughed at herself.

Just then the Reverend Herbert Jones pushed open the door. Everyone stopped to stare at him.

"What do you think?" Herb asked.

He stood there, shoulders back, head erect, wearing his

Confederate sergeant major's uniform with the red facings of the artillery.

Then everyone started talking at once.

"Odd," Tucker said.

"Why?" the cats asked.

"Like the dead coming to life, isn't it?"

12

The Reverend Herbert Jones, accustomed as he was to the confessions of his flock, still managed to be surprised by them.

He ushered Archie Ingram into his cozy library, where Herb's two magnificent cats, Lucy Fur and Elocution, snoozed on a bearskin rug before the fire. Herb had shot the bear as a boy. Lost in the woods, he had riled the normally passive animal although he didn't know how he had done it. All he knew was that a black bear was charging him. Luckily he had his .22 rifle, but it was too light to bring down the animal. He stood his ground, waited, and then fired, hitting the beast in the eye and killing it instantly. And then he started to shake all over. His daddy, thanks to the gunfire, found him.

Archie Ingram took a seat near the fire.

"I'll be brief, Herb. I'm having an affair. My wife suspects.

Sooner or later this will blow up in my face. Even though we've drifted apart, I know I have a good wife but...I can't seem to help myself. And the strange thing is, I don't feel guilty."

Herb poured a small glass of port, Dow's 1972, for Archie and for himself. Port and a fine cigar were the perfect finish to an evening. He'd sworn off cigars, missing them terribly, but he still enjoyed his evening glass of port. Stashed away in his small wine cellar he had a bottle of Cockburn's from 1937. He was saving it for a special occasion but he could never figure out what would be that special.

He held the glass in his hand, admiring the ruby color, which came to life as the firelight flickered through it. "Archie, we've known each other a long time."

"Yes, we have."

"How old are you now?"

"Forty-three."

Herb sipped, leaned back in his chair, and thought awhile. "Ever think how wine is made?"

"Peasants step on grapes."

Herb laughed. "I guess we could say the grapes are bruised and tortured, but out of this suffering, combined with time, comes a liquid of refinement and comfort. I enjoy port, you know. I've got bottles ranging from the recent—say ten years ago—all the way back to 1937. Port improves with age. Men do, too. You're being bruised now."

"Except I'm the one committing the sin."

"You hurt yourself more by sinning than you hurt anyone else. Some people never realize that. You're at a vulnerable age."

"Yeah, youth is checking out..."

"And leaving no forwarding address." Herb laughed. "It's a hard time for both men and women. Takes us differently, though. So many marriages break up."

"I don't want to lose my wife."

"Then you'd better lose the other woman."

Sweat poured down Archie's face. "I know that. Each time I see her I tell myself, this is it . . . break it off and then . . ."

"Younger?"

"A little," Archie admitted.

A rueful smile covered the minister's expansive face. "You've heard that feminist joke, 'When God made man she was practicing.' I don't think of myself as a feminist but I agree with that one." He paused. "Arch, there's not a man alive who hasn't been torn between two women at one time in his life. And I expect there isn't a woman alive who hasn't been torn between two men at one time in her life. Pray for guidance. Consider what has drawn you to the other woman and what has drawn her to you. There may be answers there that surprise you."

"Should I tell Aileen?"

"I can't answer that." He shook his head. "I don't know."

Archie drained his glass. "Crazy time."

"You've ruffled a lot of feathers lately. I always say it's easy to be an angel if no one ruffles your feathers."

Archie carefully placed his glass on the coaster. "Everybody wants something, don't they?"

"Most times, yes. Quid pro quo makes sense in the business world but it has no meaning in the spiritual world. God's love is unconditional."

Archie smiled weakly. He wanted to believe that but he didn't. No matter, talking to Herb had helped him. He now felt he could sort this out somehow, over time.

As Herb opened the door for Archie and waved good-bye he noticed how cool it was. May could be tricky.

13

Mrs. Murphy loped along fields swallowed in darkness, skirting the creek dividing Harry's land from Blair Bainbridge's picturesque farm. She wanted to visit the 911 Turbo. The humans hadn't given her enough time to thoroughly inspect the car.

A movement out of the corner of her eye caught her attention, about fifty yards away, a swaying in the bushes along the upper creek.

She stopped. In a split second she whirled around, blasting for home as fast as she could run. She heard the quick swish of the spring grasses behind her. Longer strides than hers were gaining on her.

With a surge of her own turbo, Mrs. Murphy ran flat out, her belly skimming the earth, her tail horizontal, her whiskers and ears swept back.

She charged into the paddock on the west side of the barn where Poptart, Gin Fizz, and Tomahawk were munching.

"Help me!" She streaked past Harry's horses.

The three horses spread out as the forty-pound bobcat tore over the earth. They pawed, snorted, and ran around, forcing the big cat to weave. It gave Mrs. Murphy just enough time to dodge into the barn and climb into the hayloft. She ran to the open hayloft door.

"Tucker, help me!"

The horses continued to chase the bobcat, who easily evaded them.

The powerful animal slid out of the paddock to sit outside in front of the hayloft, where she eyed her quarry above.

The owl, on a trip back to her nest with a mouse, swooped low over the bobcat but the animal wasn't afraid.

Simon, in the feed room, gobbling up sweet feed that had fallen on the floor, froze stiff. He was all ready to flop over and play dead if necessary.

Gin Fizz, old and wise, ordered the others, *"Make a lot of noise. We've got to wake Harry."*

Pewter, asleep on the kitchen table, woke up at the din of neighing and dashed to the window. Seeing in an instant what was going on, she hurried into the bedroom, leaping on Harry with all her weight.

"Uh." Harry opened one eye.

"Tucker, wake up!" Pewter shouted at the dog, sleeping on her side. *"Bobcat!"*

"Huh?"

"The bobcat's sitting under the hayloft and she'll get Murphy."

"Where's Murphy?"

"In the hayloft, stupid!"

Tucker shook her head. Why did cats hunt at night? Nonetheless the corgi scrambled to her feet and barreled through the animal door in the kitchen door.

"Wake up! Wake up!" Pewter jumped up and down on Harry.

The neighing and snorting finally filtered into Harry's ears.

"Dammit!" She shot out of bed, switched on a light, and grabbed her shotgun from the closet. She slipped four shells into the pocket of her robe, which was half on, half off, as she ran in her bare feet for the kitchen door.

Tucker squared off against the bobcat, who was spoiling for a fight.

"Don't risk it." Mrs. Murphy leaned so far over the hayloft opening, she nearly fell out.

The bobcat coolly waited until Harry switched on the outside lights. Then she turned, calling over her shoulder, *"Beware, little cousin, the hunter can become the hunted."*

With one mighty bound the bobcat cleared the paddock fence and ran out the northern side, Gin Fizz giving chase.

By the time Harry reached the fence line she saw the bobcat cruising along, maybe one hundred yards out. She put down the shotgun to climb over the fence.

"You guys all right?" In the moonlight she carefully checked the horses for scratches or injuries. Dawn was a half hour away. Then she hurried back to the barn, looking up at her friend. "Are you all right? Come down here so I can see you."

She walked into the barn and clicked on the lights. As Mrs. Murphy was backing down the ladder, Harry ducked her head in the feed room to see if any mice were in evidence.

"Simon."

Simon was playing possum. He'd been so traumatized by the bobcat that when he heard Harry's voice he couldn't move forward or backward, so he dropped over.

One eye opened when Harry cut off the light.

Mrs. Murphy landed on the tack trunk. "Let me look at you. If I have to make a screaming run over to Chris Middleton's at this hour I won't stay friends with our vet for long. You'd better be okay."

"I am." Mrs. Murphy's fur was still puffed.

Tucker, who'd run around the other side of the barn in case the bobcat pulled a fast one, trotted down the center aisle from the back.

"Brave dog." Harry patted the broad head.

"I'm a corgi." Tucker shrugged.

"Thanks, Tucker. I owe you one." Mrs. Murphy jumped down to rub along Tucker's side.

The three walked back to the house, Harry stepping lively since her bare feet were cold.

Pewter greeted them at the door. *"I told you not to hunt far from the barn!"*

"You stayed inside, chicken."

"I'd have come out and fought if I had to," she growled.

And in truth, Pewter could be a lion when needs be.

Mrs. Murphy laughed now that the danger was over. *"Close call."*

Harry, wide awake, made a pot of coffee as she fed the animals. She'd grown up in the country. She understood the ways of predators. She knew that life could change in the blink of an eye. One false step and you were a bigger animal's breakfast—or a smaller animal's, if it was smart and strong enough.

14

Oak Ridge rises out of the land south of Lovingston, Virginia. Built in 1802 by a Revolutionary War veteran, one of the Rives family of Albemarle, the estate was buffeted from the scalding rises and freezing plunges of unregulated capitalism. The originator of Oak Ridge rode the economy like the tides. His progeny fared less well and over the nineteenth century the place changed hands, sometimes for the better, sometimes for the worse.

Finally Thomas Fortune Ryan, a local boy born in 1851, made good in the New York stock market and bought the place he remembered from his impoverished childhood. By that time, 1904, Ryan was the third-richest man in America—true riches, for there was no Internal Revenue Service.

He set about creating a great country estate, not on the scale of Blenheim but on a Virginia scale, which meant he kept a sense of proportion. The mansion was twenty-three thousand square feet, and eighty other smaller houses, barns, and water towers completed the plan. A hothouse, built as a smaller version of London's famed Crystal Palace, sat below the mansion.

The place bore the mark of a single, overriding, rapacious mind. An alley of oak trees guided the visitor to the main house from the road—the northern, back side of the house. The grander entrance was on the other, southern side facing the railroad tracks because that was how Mr. Ryan rode to his country estate from New York, in his sumptuous private car. The buggies, phaetons, gigs, and the occasional coach-and-four drove up the back way.

Given that the glory days of rail travel were over, the approach now was from Route 653, the paved highway to Shipman, the back road.

The reenactors camped on the miles of front lawn and former golf course, their Sibley tents resembling teepees, common tents and larger officers' tents dotting the verdant expanse like overlarge tissues.

The reenactors would have to tramp a half mile to the oak tree, reckoned to be 380 years old. The Yankees would rise up out of the eastern woods surrounding Trinity Episcopal Church, while the Southerners would be marching due north from the edge of Mrs. Wright's hayfields.

The view was better for the public from the oak tree and it reduced the possibility of a raid on the main house.

Having that many people on her front lawn caused the petite and pretty Rhonda Holland some inconvenience, but she bore it with good grace. John, her dynamic husband, delighted in strolling along the neatly laid out avenues of tents to chat with the fellows cleaning rifles, fiddling, and singing. A convivial man wearing a floppy straw hat, he had plans for Oak Ridge as magnificent as Thomas Fortune Ryan's.

John worked more slowly than Ryan, thanks to the proliferation of government agencies choking him with regulations, but he never gave up.

The entire Holland family was on hand to view the reenactment, as were thirty thousand other people, a far larger crowd than anyone had anticipated.

Add in the five thousand reenactors, including camp followers, and there were a mess of people.

Harry sat on a camp stool. Tucker sat next to her, and Mrs. Murphy and Pewter lounged on a camp table spread with maps. The cats weren't supposed to come but they'd hidden under the seat of the truck, then raced to freedom when the door was opened.

Pewter nibbled on a square of hardtack. *"How could they eat this stuff?"*

"With difficulty," the tiger said, watching Fair Haristeen struggle with his gold sword sash.

"Here." Harry wound it around his middle, the two tasseled ends of the sash tempting Mrs. Murphy, but not enough to leave her perch, just enough for her to swat at the tassels when he walked by.

Fair, a twinkle in his eye, said, "I love it when you fuss over me."

"Stand still." Harry commanded but she smiled when she said it.

"You know I never looked so good as when you bought my clothes."

"Fair, stand still. You're a vet. Coveralls aren't that glamorous. You look the same now as when we were married."

"Meant my Sunday clothes." He playfully pinched her buttock. "I liked it best when you undressed me."

"Pulease." Harry drew out the word. Pretending to ignore the banter, she secretly enjoyed it. "There. A proper Confederate officer."

"I'd rather be improper."

"What's with you? Maybe the prospect of battle is an aphrodisiac." She laughed.

"No, *you're* the aphrodisiac. I'm only doing this for Ned
Tucker." He kissed her on the cheek.

A shout outside the tent sent them onto the grass avenue.

Archie Ingram and Sir H. Vane-Tempest fought in Sir H.'s
tent, next to Fair and Ned's tent. Archie, lean and quicker than
the Englishman, cracked him hard on the jaw.

The larger man, about forty pounds overweight, sagged for
an instant against the corner tent pole. The tent wobbled dangerously. Then Vane-Tempest collected himself, lunging for
Archie, grabbing him by the waist and bulling him out onto the
grassy avenue.

Sarah, in a pale melon gown complete with hoop skirt,
rushed out. Smart enough not to get between them, she hissed,
"Stop it!"

The men paid no mind.

Vane-Tempest clumsily ducked Archie's blows but enough
landed that red marks swelled on his cheeks. Archie danced
around him. One solid blow from Vane-Tempest would have
picked the smaller man off his feet, then sent him crashing to the
ground.

Fair watched for a moment, then grabbed Archie's upraised
hand. Archie whirled around and caught Fair on the side of his
head.

Ned Tucker, running from the other end of the avenue, seized
the Englishman before he could land a telling blow on Archie.
Although thirty years older than Archie, Sir H. wanted to fight.

Vane-Tempest shook Ned off more easily than Ned thought
he could. The two antagonists pounded each other again.

Herb Jones, dressed in his artillery sergeant major's outfit,
hurried out from the headquarters tent. Larry Johnson, Hayden
McIntire, and a host of other Crozet men followed.

Two men from Rappahannock County dashed over, canteens banging against their hips.

The four of them finally separated Vane-Tempest, who was sputtering "bloody this" and "bloody that," from Archie, who grimly said nothing.

Sarah rushed to her husband's aid. He needed ice held to his cheek. He grandly pushed her aside with one arm and advanced on Archie once more. Fair and Bobby Forester, from Rappahannock, lunged for him again.

"Leave me alone!" the florid peer of the realm commanded.

Herb Jones strode into the middle of everyone. "Gentlemen, save it for the Yankees."

This made everyone laugh except for Archie and his opponent. Even Vane-Tempest evinced a small smile.

Tucker, Mrs. Murphy, and Pewter sat quietly at their campsite, watching the exchange.

"They can't abide each other." Tucker scratched her ear.

"H. Vane gave beaucoup money to Archie's campaign last year." Mrs. Murphy swatted at a fly. *"You'd have thought they were two peas in a pod then."*

"Guess Archie didn't keep his promises."

"I'll settle with you later." Archie's jaw jutted out, his facial muscles tense.

"You'll settle with me? That's a laugh." Vane-Tempest smoothed his hair with his right hand. "And you had no business invading my tent in the first place!"

"Archie, come with me." Herb put his hand under Archie's elbow. "Fair, you keep an eye on H. Vane until we draw up in formation."

"Yes, sir." Fair saluted.

The gray line parted as Herb propelled the county commissioner toward the HQ tent.

Men listened to Herb. He'd attended VMI and then fought in Korea, where he experienced a revelation about his calling on earth. When he returned home he entered the seminary, which provoked no end of amusement among his contemporaries. They'd known him as a hell-raiser at military school.

"Now, Arch, what is the matter with you? You're becoming..."

"A liability," Archie snapped, his knuckles bleeding.

"I was going to say 'an embarrassment.'" Herb didn't mince words. "You're an elected official."

"We're in Nelson County now, not Albemarle." Archie hung his head, half mumbling.

"You know this will get into the papers."

Archie glumly said nothing as Herb continued to guide him toward the large HQ tent.

As the crowd dispersed, Sarah allowed herself a flash of temperament. "H., you're a perfect ass."

"And you're a perfect bitch," he evenly replied.

"That does it. You can play soldier by yourself. I always thought this was silly to begin with, grown men dressing up and waving swords about. At least your father was a real soldier."

"That's below the belt, Sarah." His mouth clamped shut like a vice. "But then that's your favorite geography, isn't it? You forget I served in the RAF. I just didn't have the good fortune of being born in time for the big war."

Fair, face reddening because he didn't want to hear this exchange, stepped away from the sparring couple. "You won't run after Arch?"

"No." Vane-Tempest turned on his booted heel and disappeared into his tent.

Mrs. Murphy and Pewter ran over and peeped under the tent flaps. Sarah, cooling down, walked inside after her husband.

"Why do you let him get under your skin?"

Vane-Tempest sagged heavily on a big trunk. "A man who's been bought ought to stay bought."

"Oh, Henry,"—she called him by his Christian name—"you didn't contribute that much."

"Five thousand dollars at the county-commissioner level seems rather large to me. We aren't talking about the Senate, my dear, and I didn't leave the money in a brown paper bag either. I'm not that crude." He motioned for her to stop speaking as Ned Tucker entered the tent.

"Think you can go out today?"

"Why not?" Vane-Tempest answered the soft-spoken lawyer, Susan's husband.

"You took a couple of good pops to the face."

"He can't hit that hard."

Not exactly true, since Archie had rocked him with the blow to the jaw, but his punches were light otherwise.

"Can you put this aside? I mean, you two are marching in the same company."

Vane-Tempest shrugged, the shrug of superiority. "He won't bother me. I apologize for losing my temper in the first place. I don't like his attentions to my wife."

"Henry!"

He laughed. "He does look at you all the time."

"That's not why you were fighting. Leave me out of this."

"It's none of my business." Ned took a step back to leave. "But please keep a lid on it out there."

The two kitties ducked their heads, scampering back to Fair and Harry.

"What'd you make of that?" Mrs. Murphy felt something was unexpressed, something beyond anger.

"Unevolved." Pewter scooted in under the tent bottom, nearly emerging between Harry's feet. *"Humans are unevolved."*

"Where have you two been?" Harry pointed a finger.

"Eavesdropping."

"I'm taking you to the truck. I'll leave the windows cracked, but you all aren't going to get into that crowd. I can't believe you snuck under the seat of the truck to begin with, little devils."

That fast and without consulting each other, the cats tore out of there.

"Mrs. Murphy! Pewter!" Harry ran after them and Fair started after her but the bugle called him to formation.

"Should we stay just in view or dump her?" Pewter asked.

"Let's just stay in sight and run her to exhaustion." Mrs. Murphy laughed, turning to see Harry, mad as a wet hen, tearing after them, Tucker right at the human's heels.

15

Sarah Vane-Tempest rustled with each step, her long pastel skirts swaying. H. Vane and company had departed to join their regiment, already marching toward the old racetrack on the west side of the oak tree. From there they would wheel out of sight, marching southeast until the land flattened out. They'd be at the edge of beautiful hayfields.

Her parasol provided some relief from the warming sun. She twirled it in irritation.

Mrs. Murphy and Pewter raced by her. She barely noticed them but she did notice Blair Bainbridge, long legs eating up territory as he hurried to fall in with his regiment. He waved as he dashed by.

Harry, panting, slowed down by Sarah. The cats slowed, too, walking the rest of the way but keeping well ahead of Harry.

Miranda Hogendobber joined Harry and Sarah. She'd been in the hunter barn, which was on the way to the oak tree from the main house. She'd brought Fair some hotcakes, a recipe from her grandmother, who remembered the time of Virginia's sorrows. Since Mrs. Hogendobber's great-grandfather had ridden with the cavalry, she gravitated toward the barn.

"The more I think about those two the madder I get." Sarah's parasol whirled savagely.

"Making me dizzy," Mrs. Hogendobber remarked. She meant the twirling parasol.

"What I should have done is crown them with it." Sarah stopped twirling. "They're like two little boys fighting over a fire truck."

"Exactly which fire truck?" Harry got to the point.

"The zoning variance." Sarah closed her parasol. "H. Vane is still livid over Archie squashing his request for a variance to open the quarry. His revenge is to push for the reservoir."

"But Archie appears to support the reservoir, although, God knows, he has obstructed everything. I told Fair after that commission meeting that Archie is saying one thing but doing another. Who knows what he's really going to do about the reservoir when the chips are down?" Harry hated politics, especially in her own backyard.

" 'Appears' is the operative word. Behind the scenes he's doing everything he can to retard progress. My husband knows all of this, of course." She sighed. "Henry adores political intrigue."

"So what side *is* Sir H. on?" Harry bluntly asked.

"His own." Sarah laughed, spirits a bit restored.

"Well—" Miranda fanned herself with a program advertising whalebone corsets and hoop skirts as well as bayonets and haversacks. "I hope they mend their fences."

"Ego! Neither one will make a peace offering." Sarah tapped her foot with the closed parasol. "How did women wear these things?" She pushed her crinolines forward, and the entire bell of the skirt flowed with them. "The heat doesn't help." A warm front had moved in and the weather was sticky.

"If you were dropped out of a plane you'd be safe." Tucker snickered.

Sarah glanced down at the dog, a frown on her pretty mouth; it was as if she knew what the corgi was saying to her. "Damn! I forgot H.'s extra canteen. He'll be furious."

"What's in the canteen?"

"Glenlivet." She raised an eyebrow. "He's cheating. I really do think this authenticity thing has gone too far. Do you know they even have rules about how to die?"

"You're kidding!" Harry laughed.

"If you're shot you have to fall down with your head to the side so you can breathe, with your firearm in your hand a bit away from your body. There are other rules but that's the only one I remember. And they decide who will be injured, who will die, and who will survive. That's if it's a general reenactment. If it's a *true* battle reenactment, like Sharpsburg, the men take on the identities of real soldiers. They have to fall in the exact spots where the real soldiers were hit."

"Strange," Miranda muttered.

"Rules for dying?" Harry stooped over to pick up Pewter, who had slowed.

"The obsession with violence. The obsession with *that* war, especially. No good ever came of it." Miranda shook her head.

Harry disagreed with her. "The slaves were freed."

"Yes," Miranda said, "free to starve. The Yankees were hypocrites. Still are."

Sarah, raised in Connecticut, smiled tightly. "I'm going back to get my lord and master's canteen. I'll see you at the battle." She turned and ran as fast as pantaloons, a hoop skirt, and yards of material would allow. Her bonnet, tied under her neck, flapped behind her.

Harry and Miranda reached the beautiful oak tree. Fair had

given them tickets for seats on a small reviewing stand. They took their places.

"Follow me!" Mrs. Murphy joyfully commanded as she scampered to the base of the tree, sank her razor-sharp claws in the yielding bark, and climbed high.

Pewter, a good climber, was on her tail.

Tucker, irritated, watched the two giggling felines. She couldn't see anything because everywhere she turned there were humans.

Harry shaded her eyes, glancing up at the cats, who sat on a high, wide branch, their tails swishing to and fro in excitement. She nudged Miranda.

"Best seats in the house." Miranda laughed.

Tucker returned to Harry, sitting in front of her. *"I can't see a thing,"* the peeved dog complained.

"Hush, honey." Harry patted Tucker's silky head.

A low drumroll hushed everyone. A line of Union cannons ran parallel to Route 653. The Confederate cannons, fourteen-pounders, sat at a right angle to the Union artillery. The backs of the artillerymen were visible to the crowd. As both sides began firing, a wealth of smoke belched from the mouths of the guns.

In the far distance Harry heard another drum. Goose bumps covered her arms.

Miranda, too, became silent.

"Do you think if Jefferson Davis had challenged Abe Lincoln to hand-to-hand combat they could have avoided this?" Pewter wondered.

"No."

Pewter didn't pursue her line of questioning; she was too focused on all she could see from her high perch. The tight squares of opposing regiments fast-stepped into place. On the left the officer in charge of his square raised his saber.

Ahead of the squares both sides sent out skirmishers. For this particular reenactment, the organizers had choreographed hand-

to-hand combat among the skirmishers. As they grappled, fought, and threw one another on the ground the cannons fired now with more precision, the harmless shot soaring high over everyone's heads.

Harry coughed. "Stuff scratches."

Miranda, hanky to her nose, nodded.

As the drumbeats grew louder the crowd strained forward.

They could hear officers calling out orders. The Union regiment at the forefront stopped as the Confederates, still at a distance, moved forward.

"Load," called out the captain.

The soldiers placed their muskets, barrels out, between their feet. As the officer called out further loading orders, they poured gunpowder down the barrels and rammed the charges home.

"Ha!" Pewter was watching Fair, struggling with his frightened horse.

Mrs. Murphy, knowing Fair was a fine rider, didn't find it quite as funny as Pewter did. *"I don't think anyone knows how to get the horses used to this noise and the sulphur smell."*

Fair's big bay shied, dancing sideways. At the next volley of cannon fire the horse reared up, came down on his two forelegs, and bucked straight out with his hind legs, a jolting, snapping, hell of a buck. Fair sat the first one but the succeeding ones, spiced up with a side-to-side twisting action, sent him into the sweet grass with a thud. The horse, no fool, spun around, flying back toward the hunter stables. Fair, disgusted, picked himself up, then looked around, realized he was in a battle, and ran over to join his unit.

Sir H. Vane-Tempest, on the front corner of the first regiment, grimly stared into the billowing smoke. Archie Ingram was farther back in the square, as was Blair Bainbridge. Ridley Kent marched in the second unit behind them.

Mrs. Murphy strained to see through the smoke, which would clear, then close up again with new fire. Reverend Herb

Jones, red sash wrapped around his tunic, sat on an upturned wagon to the rear of the battle. The heat had exhausted him.

Dr. Larry Johnson and Ned Tucker were in the third line of the regiment, faces flushed. Everywhere the two cats looked they saw familiar faces in unfamiliar clothes. The smoke thinning over the men's faces like a soft silver veil made them look even more eerie.

The first volley of rifle fire from the Yankees rolled over the turf with a crackle: Small slits of flame leapt from muzzles. Mrs. Murphy hoped they would be smart enough to keep their hands away from the barrel nozzles when ramming home the next charge. A man could lose fingers or part of a hand that way if a spark smoldered deep down in the gun.

By now all but one of the mounted officers had bought some real estate. The only animal moving forward was a huge Belgian draft horse, the horse calm as if on parade.

A few "corpses" dotted the field. Then a shroud of smoke enveloped the field as all guns fired at once. *Pop, pop, pop,* rifles and handguns reported between the rhythmic firing of the elegant cannons.

"Poor suckers died blind." Mrs. Murphy's whiskers twitched.

"Ugh." Pewter shuddered. *"Only a human would die for an idea."*

"That's the truth." The tiger blinked when a bit of smoke floated over the branches. *"You know, they can't accept reality. Reality is that everything is happening at once to everybody. There's no special sense to it. So humans invent systems. If one human's system collides with another human's system, they fight."*

"The only reality is nature." Pewter, not a philosophical cat like Mrs. Murphy, was nonetheless a smart one.

"True enough." The cat squinted as the smoke cleared. She saw Sir H. Vane-Tempest break from the ranks, never to be outdone, and sprint toward the enemy.

A loud *crack*, another volley of cannon fire and he went down, a hero to the cause.

The battle grew more intense. Tucker, since she couldn't see, lay on the reviewing stand between Harry's feet. She hated the noise, and the sulphur fumes offended her delicate nose.

After fifteen more minutes of the hardest-fought section of the reenactment, the Yankees broke and ran. That, too, was choreographed. It would never do for the Union troops to wallop Southerners on Southern turf unless it was a precise reenactment of an actual battle won by the Yankees. Not only was this a sop to Southern vanity, but it was also pretty accurate. The North hadn't begun to routinely chalk up victories until the latter part of the war, when victories in the west ensured victories in the east, and tens of thousands died.

The drummers kept drumming as the last smoke wafted over the flat expanse of hayfield, formerly an old airfield. The routed Yankees ran toward Route 653, collected themselves, and turned left, heading for the racetrack.

The wounded, in the name of authenticity, were being carried off on stretchers. A few of the dead had gel packs, which squashed when they fell. The fake blood gave them a realistic appearance.

As the last of the wounded were carried to the hospital tent the dead began to stir. The cats sat in the tree and laughed. Tucker watched with curiosity. She'd moved to the front of the reviewing stand.

One corpse didn't move.

A Confederate, resurrected, walked by without paying attention.

Archie Ingram, formerly deceased, also walked by. He stopped, nudging the body with his boot. Nothing happened.

Many people in the crowd were walking back to the main house, unaware of the unfolding drama.

That fast the two cats backed down the tree, streaking across the field.

"Tucker!" Mrs. Murphy hollered.

The dog left Harry, just now noticing the curious sight, to join the cats.

Archie, down on his hands and knees, turned over the body. It was Sir H. Vane-Tempest.

Mrs. Murphy reached Vane-Tempest before Pewter or Tucker.

As the breathless gray cat caught up, the tiger sniffed the body. *"Powder,"* was all she said.

The corgi, famous for her scenting abilities, gawked for an instant. *"He looks like a piece of swiss cheese."*

16

People slowly began to return to the field. At first the sight of Archie kneeling over Vane-Tempest looked like acting. Distraught, he loosened the older man's collar.

Harry, a sprinter, had been the first person out from the sidelines. She grasped Vane-Tempest's wrist to take his pulse. Irregular. His breathing was shallow.

Miranda, slower but hurrying, motioned for Dr. Larry Johnson to join her. The gray-haired Confederate dumped his weapon and ran. Reverend Jones solicited a four-wheel drive to take him to the victim.

Vane-Tempest, in shock, stared upward with glassy eyes. His lips moved.

Larry tore open his tunic. The bullet holes, neat, could have been drawn on his chest except that blood oozed out of them.

Susan Tucker jumped into a farm truck parked on the side out of view of the battle. She pressed hard on the horn, making her way through the crowd, looking for Sarah. Sarah, returning with her husband's canteen, was slowed by the distance, the heat, and now the retreating crowd. Susan caught sight of her at the hunter barn, standing at the open door, shielding her eyes against the sun.

Finally reaching Sarah, she shouted, "Get in."

"Oh, God, he's really mad at me, isn't he? I had to catch my breath for a minute. It's sweltering in this dress."

Susan didn't answer Sarah. She was trying to return to the battlefield as fast as she could, given the crowd, which slowly got out of her way as she laid on the horn.

She pulled up close to where Larry was working on Vane-Tempest. Sarah, at first, didn't realize it was her husband lying on the ground, the focus of grim activity. Susan nudged her out of the farm truck.

Sarah stood by the truck door for a second, then ran for the prostrate figure. She tore away her hoop skirt to run faster.

"Harry, keep people away," Larry ordered, then barked at Miranda, "See to Sarah."

Sarah, mute, fought Miranda. BoomBoom ran up to help the older woman. Together they pulled Sarah a short distance from her husband so Larry could work unmolested.

"Hold his head still. You might have to clear his mouth out." Larry spoke low, and calmly.

Harry, on her knees, placed a hand on either side of Vane-Tempest's florid face as Larry crossed one hand over the other and pumped on the wounded man's chest with all his weight.

The two cats watched, as did Tucker. She put her nose to the ground but knew it was hopeless; too many feet had trod the earth, too many guns had been fired.

"Shot in the back for sure," Mrs. Murphy softly said.

"What a terrible accident." Tucker hung her head.

"*No accident,*" Mrs. Murphy crisply remarked. "*Three bullets in the back is no accident.*"

Pewter stared at the tiger.

Archie knelt on the other side of the gasping man. "I'm sorry. I'm so sorry."

Vane-Tempest blinked. His eyes cleared for a moment and he seemed to recognize everyone. But his left lung was filling with blood.

In the distance an ambulance squealed.

Harry watched Larry work. She'd known him all her life as a family doctor but this was the first time she had seen him dealing with an emergency. She admired his cool proficiency and his physical strength. In his middle seventies, Larry acted like a man in his fifties.

The ambulance rolled out onto the field. Within seconds the crew, headed by Diana Robb, had Vane-Tempest on a stretcher and inside the vehicle. Larry hopped in behind, and the door slammed.

"Waynesboro," Diana called to Harry and Miranda. "It's the closest hospital."

Miranda and BoomBoom guided Sarah back to the farm truck. They squeezed in, heading to Waynesboro, a good twenty-five miles away and up over treacherous Afton Gap.

As the humans continued to mill around in disbelief, Mrs. Murphy suggested, "*Fan five feet apart, and move toward the tree.*"

"*What are we looking for?*" Tucker inquired.

"*Spent bullets. The holes in his chest were made by clean exits.*"

Archie, shaking, walked toward the main house, a vacant look on his face. Harry caught up to him.

She called over her shoulder, "Come on, kids."

"*In a minute,*" Tucker barked.

"*Hurry. It won't take long for one of these fools to grind the bullets into the earth,*" the tiger urged.

"Found one." Pewter stopped.

The other two ran over. Sure enough it was a lead bullet, fattish, with three concentric rings on the bottom and a squashed nose lying in the grass.

"Can't call her back." The tiger thought out loud. *"Tucker, carry it in your mouth."*

The corgi happily pinched the bullet between her teeth.

"Don't swallow," Pewter teased.

They trotted after Harry, who eased Archie toward the hunter barn.

"I need to get back to my tent."

"Arch, there will be questions. You're better off here."

"I didn't shoot him." Archie was beginning to comprehend the full impact of this dolorous event.

"Of course you didn't. However, why subject yourself to strangers or even friends asking questions you may not be emotionally prepared to answer? Come on in here. I'll find Cynthia Cooper. I know she's around."

"This is Sheriff Hill's territory," Archie vaguely protested.

"I know that but it can't hurt to have an Albemarle deputy with you. Archie, trust me."

His emotions crystallized into anger. "Trust you! For Christ's sake, you're the goddamned postmistress. You don't know what you're doing."

He pushed right by her, plunging into the crowd.

Harry said nothing. She walked into the barn. Fair was brushing down his horse. He looked up.

"Hi."

"H. Vane's been shot."

"What?" Fair stopped, brush held midair.

"Shot through the back."

"Really shot?" It was sinking in.

"Really shot."

"Some fool was back there actually firing bullets? Of all the stupid—"

"Maybe it wasn't stupid."

"Don't let your imagination run away with you, Harry. Who would shoot H. Vane on purpose? He's not worth the lead." That popped out of his mouth before he realized it.

"A lot of men marched behind him, including Archie Ingram. You know how people think."

"It's absurd." He paused. "Is he going to make it?"

"I don't know. Larry Johnson worked on him. He's on his way to Waynesboro Hospital."

"Well, they've dealt with gunshot wounds before."

Tucker walked up to Harry and opened her mouth, dropping the bullet smack onto Harry's foot.

"Good job." Pewter praised the dog.

Mrs. Murphy studied her human's face. Harry bent over to pick up the fired bullet.

"Good Lord," she said, then stared at Tucker, who smiled back.

17

Miranda's house, centrally located behind the post office, provided a gathering place for old friends. Her cooking drew them in as well. Few things delighted Miranda Hogendobber as much as feeding those she loved and even those she didn't love. Holy Scripture bade her to love all mankind but many times she found the theory easier than the practice.

Harry helped serve apple cider and Tom Collinses. Boom-Boom had remained at the hospital, but then BoomBoom flourished amid tragedy, especially if the tragedy was visited upon someone other than herself. However, since she and Sarah were friends, her staying on might serve some good purpose.

Cynthia Cooper sat next to Fair. They were both such light blonds they could have been twins, although they were not related, not even distantly, which is always a disappointment to a true Virginian.

"I can understand someone taking a shot at Archie but not Sir H. Vane-Tempest." Cynthia sipped the most delicious apple cider she had ever tasted. In conjunction with Miranda's piping hot scones it was perfection.

"You don't know that it was on purpose." Harry passed around the silver tray filled with jellies, preserves, and unsalted butter. She thought the shots were intentional but she wanted to see what others would say.

"Actually, I should be the one to say that." Cynthia dumped mounds of persimmon jelly on her scone.

"You're off duty." Harry smiled at her.

"Tell me again about the bullet." Cynthia split open the scone, releasing a thin waft of moist, fragrant air.

"Tucker dropped it at my feet and I gave it to Sheriff Hill."

The dog, greedily gobbling the raw hamburger mixed with raw egg that Miranda had made for her, didn't even glance up when her name was spoken. Nor did Mrs. Murphy or Pewter, faces deep in cooked, diced chicken.

"I wonder why she picked it up?" Miranda thought out loud.

"Maybe it had blood on it," Harry replied, then noticed that everyone stopped eating for a moment. "Sorry."

A light rap on the back door followed by a "Yoo-hoo" diverted them from the unpleasant thought.

"Come in," Miranda called from the kitchen.

Herb Jones eased through the door, a blade of cooling night air following him. "Any word?"

"No."

He sat down. Harry offered the minister his choice of beverage. He requested coffee since Miranda always had a pot on the stove. Miranda bustled in with a tray of fresh scones. She set them on the tea trolley.

"Sit down, Miranda, you work too hard," Herb told her.

"I will in a minute." She walked back to the kitchen, returning in moments with a cup of hot coffee.

"People are already saying that Archie shot him." Herb dabbed his lips with a cocktail napkin. "That's all they're talking about. Even Mim, who's usually circumspect, says it bears all the marks of Archie's scheming."

"Scheming? In front of everyone?" Harry said.

The taciturn Fair spoke up. "That's her point. No one will ever be able to prove that Archie fired at H. People can talk all they want. They can't prove it. Archie's devious by nature."

"Fair, I'm surprised to hear you say that." Miranda's voice shot upward.

"He's played both ends against the middle all his life. That doesn't mean he's bad, just devious."

"Can't they test weapons?" Miranda directed the question to Cynthia.

"Yes." She swallowed, then continued, "And I'm sure Sheriff Hill will do just that. But everyone was loading and firing so all the barrels will be filled with powder. And no one was supposed to have real bullets. This could prove very interesting."

"You know, H. Vane has spent a lifetime abusing his body. I wonder if he can pull through this." Harry watched Mrs. Murphy and Pewter change dishes. "Why do they each think the other one got something better?"

"We don't." Mrs. Murphy brushed a bit of chicken off her chin.

"It's our food dance," said Pewter, nose in the bowl.

"It is not." Tucker giggled.

"It is too," Murphy called to the tailless dog. *"I can smell what she has in her dish and she can smell what I have in mine. We like to do it, that's all. You stick your face in your food and inhale it. We cats have more delicacy of manner."*

"And more taste buds," Pewter said.

"You do not."

"Yes we do. We even have better taste buds than they do." Pewter indicated the humans.

"That's not saying much." The dog sat down. She was too full to stand.

"You all are getting awfully chatty over there," Harry reprimanded her pets as the decibel level of their conversation increased.

Three pairs of eyes glared at her but the animals did pipe down.

"Where's Susan?" Herb asked.

"I don't know, but before Archie left the campground he asked Ned to represent him."

"Harry, why didn't you say something?" Cynthia was surprised.

"It doesn't mean he did it. The only reason I know is I passed Susan on my way out of the hunter barn." She paused. "I can't stand Archie Ingram. I really don't give a damn what happens to him and I might even lower myself to enjoy his discomfort."

Everyone stared at her, including the animals.

"Harry, your mother didn't raise you to be like that," Miranda chided her.

"No, but my mother didn't have to deal with Archie after he became a county commissioner either. He got the big head. Anyway, I can't always be a proper Virginia lady. I'm too young to be that proper." A raffish grin crossed her face.

"Lifeline." Cynthia half smiled.

"I'd sooner bleed from the throat. How do you stand it?"

Since no one there had realized that Cynthia attended the self-help group, they smiled nervously, waiting for her rejoinder.

Cynthia smiled reflexively. "I've seen people bleed from the throat."

"I'm sorry," Harry apologized, genuinely upset with herself.

"Does it work?" Fair innocently asked.

"I've only been once but I think it will teach me techniques to handle situations better. It's not really therapy or anything, more of a learning session."

Miranda was dying to ask more questions but decided she'd do it in private.

The phone rang.

"Hello." Miranda didn't cover the mouthpiece. "Mim." She listened. "He's what!" She listened some more. "Thanks." Miranda hung up the phone and ran over to the television.

She clicked on Channel 29's news. An interview with Archie Ingram was in progress. Archie, dressed in a three-piece suit and a turquoise tie, was answering a reporter's questions. He stood outside the county offices.

"—unfortunate incident. I realize many will point the finger at me because of my recent strained relationship with Sir H. Vane-Tempest but our friendship is deeper than this recent disagreement."

"What is the nature of the disagreement, Mr. Ingram?"

"We have different visions of how best to serve Albemarle County—political differences."

The reporter interrupted before Archie could cite his record. "It's about water, isn't it?"

"I'm sick of talking about the damn reservoir!" Archie's face purpled. "Yes, we disagree but I wouldn't shoot him over it."

"But at the meeting at Crozet High School last week—"

"The hell with you, lady." Archie walked off camera.

The cameraman swung around and followed him. Archie loomed into the lens of the camera, and the camera bobbled. The sound of it hitting the sidewalk could be heard, then the picture went black for a second. The image switched back to the studio.

"Is he stone stupid or what?" Harry blurted out.

"You know, the funny thing is, it would make sense if someone had shot Archie. Doesn't make sense that H. got it." Herb shook his head.

"Maybe Archie was the target and H. Vane got in the way," Harry said. "There's a lot of H. Vane and not much of Archie."

"Archie's protesting too much," Mrs. Murphy announced to no one in particular and everyone in general. *"He's covering something up."*

"Yeah, he's covering up that he shot H. Vane in broad daylight before thirty thousand people." Tucker stood up again, felt the effort too great, and sat back down.

"Something else." The tiger blinked, then swayed in that way that cats do, a light forward and backward motion.

18

Sarah Vane-Tempest slept at the hospital for two nights. When her husband was moved out of intensive care and onto the critical list, she allowed Miranda to take her home.

Exhausted, raccoon-eyed, Sarah invited Miranda in for tea.

"Honey, I brought some quiche. I'll warm it up for you while you take a shower. By the time you're finished the food will be ready."

"If the hospital calls, come get me even if I'm in the shower."

"I will, and don't worry. You've worried enough for three women." Miranda smiled. "Anyway, Blair Bainbridge is taking a turn with your husband. I had no idea they'd gotten that close."

"Outsiders. They both feel like outsiders since their families aren't from Virginia. Oh, well, it is like the Cotswolds, so H.

mostly loves it here." Vane-Tempest had been born in a particularly lovely part of England.

"Go on now." Miranda pushed her in the direction of her bedroom.

She warmed the oven and unwrapped her homemade breads, the dishcloths slightly damp to prevent them from drying out. She hummed a hymn as she set the table.

Miranda held that the way a woman organizes her kitchen tells you everything you need to know about her—that and her shoes.

Sarah's kitchen, the latest in high-tech gadgetry, boasted an enormous brass espresso maker from Italy. It rested on the marble countertop.

Velvet-lined drawers contained Tiffany silver for everyday use. The evening silver was locked in the pantry. Miranda couldn't imagine using Tiffany silver for breakfast and lunch.

The refrigerator, dishwasher, microwave, and double oven had black, shiny surfaces. At the top of the wall, six inches from the ceiling, a green neon line acted as molding. It was all very playful and hideously expensive, but at least it was extremely well organized.

While the quiche warmed, Miranda opened the closet. Two Confederate uniforms hung there, each of them clean. Both sported the blue facings of the infantry.

Sarah walked back into the kitchen, her slippers scuffling.

Miranda turned around. "Two uniforms?"

"You know how H. gets when he suffers these—deliriums."

"Mmm." Miranda did know.

Like many wealthy people, H. Vane-Tempest rarely glided into an activity. He jumped in with both feet, spent oo-scoobs of money for equipment, only to abandon the passion a year or two later. Since he had nothing to work for anymore, he needed constant new challenges to occupy his mind. He had bought every possible book on the War Between the States, going so far as to pester the government of England to let him see any correspondence Queen Victoria might have penned on the matter.

Sarah sat down, eyes half closed as the moist aroma of fresh bread curled into her nostrils. "Rye?"

"And cornbread." Miranda opened the oven, removing the warming breads. Hotpads at the ready, she pulled out the quiche.

They ate in silence, Sarah haggard from the crisis. Anyone who knew Miranda Hogendobber longer than a half hour would figure out that the good woman made a lot of room for both your personality and your situation.

"Herb says port is fortifying. Might it pick you up?"

"Put me down. I'm so worn-out I don't trust my system," Sarah replied. "Do you think he'll be all right, Miranda?"

"I don't know. He's in God's hands."

"God's hands are full."

Miranda smiled. " 'Beloved, do not be surprised at the fiery ordeal which comes upon you to prove you, as though something strange were happening to you. But rejoice insofar as you share Christ's sufferings, that you may also rejoice and be glad when his glory is revealed.' " She drew a breath. "First Peter. I forget the chapter."

"How do you remember all that?"

Miranda shrugged. "Just do. When I was a little girl my sister and I would have memorizing contests. You've never met my sister, have you?"

Sarah shook her head.

"Lives in Greenville, South Carolina. Loves it." She cut another piece of quiche for Sarah.

"I'm full."

"Just a nibble. You need your strength."

Sarah poked at the bacon-and-cheese quiche. "You draw such comfort from the Bible."

"Were you raised in the church?"

"Yes. Episcopalian. *Very* high church."

"I see." Miranda sipped sparkling water. "You might enjoy a more, mmm . . . personal church."

"Perhaps," came the noncommittal reply.

Miranda marveled at how beautiful Sarah was, even exhausted. Impeccably groomed, hair the perfect shade of blond, eyes startlingly blue, strong chin, full and sensuous lips—Miranda noted these visual enticements. She herself felt no pull toward female beauty. It was rather like watching a sleek cat. She felt men paid dearly for such wives.

"A cup of coffee?"

"No. I've imbibed enough caffeine in the last two days to qualify me for a Valium prescription."

"Well then, I'll just clean up and be on my way. Would you like me to call someone to stay with you tonight? I'd hate for you to wake up and be frightened."

"BoomBoom will come over, after one of her interminable Lifeline meetings. I don't know why. She keeps meeting the same men over and over again."

"Yes." Miranda wanted to say that was probably the point. "Will you be all right until then?"

"Of course I will. You were a dear to tend to me."

"I wasn't tending to you. I was enjoying your company."

19

"*Bite her leg,*" Mrs. Murphy ordered Tucker.

"*I will not. That will get me in trouble. You get away with every-thing.*"

"*No, I don't.*"

"*You bite her, then.*"

"*Cats scratch. Dogs bite.*"

"*Bull.*"

Pewter piped up. "*Nothing's going to work. Forget it.*"

They looked out the truck window forlornly as Harry passed Rose Hill, Tally Urquhart's place.

"*Bite her!*"

"*We'll go off the road.*" Tucker bared her fangs at Mrs. Murphy.

"*My, what big teeth you have, Grandma.*" Mrs. Murphy burst out laughing, joined by Pewter.

"I hate you." Tucker laid her ears against her pretty face.

"What's going on here?" Harry, eyes on the road, grumbled. "If you all can't behave I'm not taking you out again."

"She told me to bite you." Tucker indicated Mrs. Murphy by inclining her head.

A lightning-fast paw struck the dog on the nose. A bead of blood appeared.

"Oo-oo-oo," the little dog cried.

"Dammit, Murphy." Harry pulled off the road onto the old farm service road of Rose Hill. She stopped, checked the dog, opened the glove compartment for a tissue and held it to the long nose. "You play too rough."

"Tough." The tiger thought the rhyme funny. Pewter had to laugh, too.

"Bunch of mean cats," Tucker whined.

"Play it for all it's worth, bubblebutt." Mrs. Murphy stepped on Tucker's back, then stepped on Harry's lap.

The driver's-side window, halfway open, was her goal. She soared through it off Harry's lap.

"Mrs. Murphy!" Harry shouted.

The cat sat outside by the driver's door, her lustrous green eyes cast up at her mother's livid visage. *"I've got something to show you."*

"Good idea." Pewter stepped on the dog, then on Harry's lap, and then she, too, jumped out of the truck, although not as gracefully as Mrs. Murphy.

"You don't know where I'm going."

"Yes I do." Pewter loped down the grassy lane.

"Don't go without me. Oh, don't you dare go without me," the dog howled.

"Jesus." Harry opened the door, struggling out with the dog in her arms. The corgi was heavy.

Before Harry's feet hit the ground Tucker wiggled free,

landed, and rolled. She hopped to her feet, shook her head, and tore after the cats.

"Tucker, you come back here!" Harry called. "I don't believe them."

She ran after them. Little good that did, as all three barreled on, out of reach but clearly in sight. The cats didn't deviate or dash off the lane as usual. Harry watched, cursed, then hopped into her truck and followed them at fifteen miles an hour.

In ten minutes Tally Urquhart's stone cottages and the huge stone hay barn came into view.

Harry pulled into the middle of the buildings, cut the motor, and got out just as the cats pushed open the barn door a crack and flattened themselves to get inside. She beheld two paws— one tiger, one gray—sticking through the slight gap in the door. It was as though they were waving at her to follow.

Tucker put her sore nose in the door and pushed. She, too, squeezed inside.

"They're trying to drive me crazy," Harry said out loud. "Really, this is an orchestrated plan to send me round the bend."

She walked to the door, rolled it back with a heave, and blinked.

"Holy shit."

"You got that right," Mrs. Murphy catcalled.

20

Warm spring light flooded the barn, illuminating Rick Shaw's face as he stood under the wing of the Cessna. Behind him a young woman dusted for fingerprints.

Not a drop of blood marred the shiny surface of the airplane or the cockpit, although there were muddy paw prints on the wings and the cockpit. No dings, dents, or smears of oil hinted at foul play.

The wheels of the small plane were blocked. In fact, everything was in order. The gas tank was almost full. They could have crawled up into the Cessna to cruise through creamy clouds on this, a gorgeous day.

Cynthia spoke to Tally Urquhart. Miss Tally's sight remained keen, her hearing sharp, but her powers of locomotion had diminished. After fervid wrangling sprinkled with the utterance of unladylike epithets, she had agreed to stop driving. No longer able to ride astride, she allowed herself the pleasures of driving a matched pair of hackney ponies, to the terror of the neighbors. Her majordomo, Kyle Washburn, had the honor of transporting her to her many clubs and good deeds. It was also his duty to hang on when she took the reins. There were many in Albemarle County who thought no amount of money was too much to pay Kyle.

"I told you that," Tally snapped.

"I know it's irritating, ma'am, but my job is to check and double-check."

She tossed her white curls, hair still luxuriously thick. "Tommy Van Allen put his plane in my big hay barn and walked away, never to return. And I heard nothing."

"At no time did you hear a plane buzz the house?" Cynthia braced herself for the blast.

"Are you deaf? No."

Kyle stepped in. "Miss Tally is in town a lot, Deputy. Anyone who knows her and her busy schedule would have no trouble landing here when she was out of the house."

"You hear anything?" Cynthia smiled at him.

"No."

"Mr. Washburn." She leaned toward his weathered, freckled face. "How could this plane sit here and you not know it?"

"Winter hay barn," Tally snapped as though that simple description would be enough for any intelligent person.

"Miss Tally fills this barn up with hay in the fall. Usually I open it wide in May. Air it out. I'm behind this year—a little."

"So you two think whoever parked the plane here—do you park a plane?—well, whoever did this knows Miss Tally's schedule?"

"Yes," Kyle answered while Tally glared. This was damned inconvenient and she knew the situation would bring her bossy niece over to once again interfere.

Using her cane with vigor, hand clutched over the silver hound's head, Tally stalked Harry.

"I don't know any more than you do." Harry shrugged.

"You know a good deal less." Tally pointed her cane at Harry. "You say you chased these varmints here?"

"I'm no varmint," Tucker yipped.

"They led me right to the barn."

Tally studied the animals at Harry's feet.

"Sometimes animals know things. Your mother had a marvelous sense of animals. She could talk to them and I swear they talked back," Tally said, her smile momentarily tinged with melancholy. Then, steeling herself, she again eyed Harry. "You get used to it. By the time you're my age everyone's dead. Dead. Dead. Dead. No use crying over spilt milk." She took a little breath. "And if you ask me, Tommy Van Allen is dead, too."

Rick, respectfully silent until now, asked, "Why do you say that, ma'am?"

"Tommy Van Allen is wild as a rat. He'd be here if he were alive."

"Some people think he was selling drugs, made a big haul and disappeared," Rick suggested.

"Piffle."

"Ma'am?"

"He might use them. He wouldn't sell them. That boy was a lot of things but stupid wasn't one of them. He wouldn't sell drugs." She pointed her cane at Rick's chest. "Every time something happens around here everyone yells 'Drugs.' Too much TV." She turned to Harry. "You're a nosy kid. Always were. In the blood. Your great-grandfather was nosy."

"Which one?"

"Biddy Minor. Handsomest man I ever saw. Had to know everything, though. Killed him, of course."

Rick, a student of local crime, said gently, since it wouldn't do to correct her, "It was never proven."

She raised an eyebrow, barely deigning to refute his prattle. "Proving and knowing are two different things, Sheriff. Just like I know Tommy Van Allen is dead. I know it. You have to prove it, I suppose."

"Ma'am, we can't convict anyone without proof."

"Convict them?" Her thin voice rose. "Convict them—they're out on the streets in six months."

Rick blushed. "Miss Tally, I feel exactly the same way but I have a job to do. I'm elected to this position."

She softened. "And so you are. Well—what else do you want to know?"

"Can you think of any reason why someone would want to kill Tommy Van Allen?"

She paused thoughtfully. "No more than anyone else. By that I mean he had his share of angry ex-girlfriends, his share of people who plain didn't like him."

"Can you think of any reason why someone would shoot Sir H. Vane-Tempest?"

"Pompous, silly ass." She shrugged her bony shoulders. "You're going to canvass my neighbors, aren't you? Surely one of them heard this airplane."

"We'll speak to everyone," Rick assured her.

A crunch of tires on gravel turned all heads in the direction of the Bentley Turbo R pulling into the open barn.

Tucker barked as the motor was cut off and one elegant leg swung out the driver's side. *"Mim!"* The little dog rushed forward to greet the haughty Mim, who nonetheless loved dogs. She bent over to pat Tucker's head, and the dog happily tagged at her heels.

"Don't you start telling me what to do." Tally's lower lip jutted out.

"I'm not. I'm here to help." Mim stopped to study the plane. "Extraordinary," she said quietly.

"If you all don't need me any longer I'll go." Harry began to move toward the open door.

"Go on." Sheriff Shaw nodded.

Cynthia called out, "I'll catch you later."

Miss Tally placed her left hand on Harry's arm. Her thin ring gleamed. "Mary Minor, you never believed the story about my brother shooting your great-granddaddy because Biddy walked up on his still, did you?"

"No."

She nodded, satisfied. "Good girl."

Harry herded Mrs. Murphy, Pewter, and Tucker into the truck, hearing Mim say, "Now, Aunt Tally, why would anyone put a plane in your barn?"

"To give me excitement in my declining years."

21

That evening Harry walked out to the creek dividing her land from Blair Bainbridge's. A soft *squish* accompanied each step. Pewter picked her paws up, periodically shaking them.

"It was much worse the other night," Mrs. Murphy nonchalantly remarked.

"I'll have to spend half the night washing my feet."

"Stick 'em under the faucet," the dog joked.

"Never." Pewter shook her paws again.

Harry stopped at the creek. The sun was setting, crowning the mountains in pink clouds suffused with gold.

Tucker sat down.

"I'm not sitting down in this," Pewter complained.

"You're cranky. Bet you've got a tapeworm."

"I do not!" The cat slapped at the dog, who laughed.

"You should talk." Mrs. Murphy hated those monthly worm pills but they worked. She knew Tucker sometimes cheated and spit hers out. Then she'd feel bad, Harry would discover evidence of roundworms, and Tucker would really get a dose of medicine.

Harry drank in the sunset and the sound of peepers. She studied her animals; uncanny, as though they knew where the plane was stashed.

It occurred to Harry that whoever deposited Tommy Van Allen's airplane would not be happy to know that she had discovered it. But someone would have eventually done so. She didn't think she'd be in the line of fire.

But Sir H. Vane-Tempest was.

"Just doesn't compute," she said out loud.

"It's not our problem." Pewter felt that suppertime started with sunset. She turned to face the distant house, hoping Harry would take the hint.

Instead Harry climbed the massive walnut tree. Mrs. Murphy joined her, as did Pewter.

"What am I supposed to do?" the dog whined at the base of the tree.

"Guard us, Tucker," Mrs. Murphy said.

"I might have to," the dog grumbled, *"and lest you forget, egotist of all time, I ran and chased the bobcat."*

"You did. I really am grateful."

"How often do humans climb trees?" Pewter watched Harry swing her legs as she sat on the low, wide branch.

"Not very often. As they get older they don't do it at all, I think," Mrs. Murphy answered. *"You see so much more from up here. You'd think they'd want to keep doing it."*

"No claws. Must be hard for them." Pewter kept her claws dangerously sharp.

"Everything's hard for them. That's why all their religions are full of fear. You know, hellfire and damnation, that sort of thing."

"And being plunged into darkness." Tucker agreed with the tiger cat.

"If they could see in the dark as well as we do, their gods would be dark gods." Mrs. Murphy pitied humans their wide variety of fears.

"If they were bats their gods would be sounds." Tucker suffered no religious anxiety. She knew perfectly well that a corgi presided over the universe and she ignored the cats' blasphemous references to a celestial feline.

"How long do you think Harry will live?" Pewter rubbed against the cobbled trunk of the tree.

Walnuts, beautiful trees, possessed the exact right type of bark for cats to sharpen their claws on—and it was good to rub against, too.

"She's strong. Into her eighties, I should say, maybe as long as Tally Urquhart," Murphy replied.

"Then why are humans scared, really? They live much longer than we do."

"Nah. Just seems longer." Tucker giggled.

The cats laughed.

Mrs. Murphy watched Harry hum to herself, swinging her legs as she enjoyed the slow shift of colors from pink to salmon to bloodred shot through with fingers of gray. She truly loved this human and wished Harry could be more like a cat. It would improve her life.

Harry suddenly noticed the animals all observing her.

She burst out laughing. "Hey."

"Hey back at you," they replied.

"Isn't it beautiful?"

"Yes," came the chorus.

"It's time for supper."

"Pewter," Mrs. Murphy corrected her.

Pewter fell silent. If she complained she'd probably be stuck out in the walnut tree longer. With luck, Harry's bucolic rapture would pass soon.

"Do you ever worry about who will take care of Mom when we're dead?" Tucker soberly asked Murphy.

"She'll bring in a puppy and a kitten by the time we're old. We'll train them."

"I'm not training any kitten," Pewter huffed.

"That's because you have nothing to teach the next generation."

"Aren't we clever?" Pewter boxed Murphy's ears.

Murphy boxed right back, the two felines moving forward and backward on the heavy branch as Harry laughed at them. Pewter whacked Murphy hard and the tiger slipped. She grabbed at the branch with her front paws but her hind legs dangled over the edge.

"Here." Harry reached over and grabbed her by the scruff of the neck, pulling her up. She put the tiger cat in her lap.

Pewter advanced on Murphy.

"Don't you dare or I'll fall off." Harry shook her finger at Pewter, who grabbed her finger. She sheathed her claws but her pupils were big so she appeared ferocious.

"Who will open the cans if Harry gets hurt?" Murphy spit in Pewter's face.

"Now that's enough!" Harry tapped the tiger's head with her index finger.

It didn't hurt but it was irritating.

A sweet purr attracted everyone's attention. A pair of head-lights, a mile off, swung into view. Blair pulled into his driveway. He got out of his car, then opened the door for Little Mim.

"Can she see?" Pewter asked Murphy.

"It's clear enough. She can see that far. Interested, too."

"Who wouldn't be interested in the Porsche," Tucker said.

"She's curious about him."

"Oh." Tucker watched a twig by the creek. *"What was that about Biddy Minor? Miss Tally said curiosity killed him?"*

"I don't know. Long before my time. That's way back in our great-grandmothers' time, I guess."

"You'd think they'd talk about it." Pewter backed down the tree. If the others weren't going home, she was. There might be some dried crunchies left in the bowl on the countertop.

"Maybe they did and we didn't hear it. But I don't think Harry's talked about it." Mrs. Murphy hopped out of Harry's lap and backed down the walnut also. She talked as she felt for her footing, the slight piercing sound of her claws sinking in bark audible even to the human. *"Maybe she made a passing reference. It would have happened in the twenties, I think."*

"That long ago?"

Murphy reached the bottom as Tucker walked over to her. *"Well, if Biddy was Harry's great-grandfather, you figure he was born in the 1880s, not much later than 1900 for sure."*

"Let's look it up in the family Bible," Tucker suggested, *"when she's asleep."*

"Okay." Pewter would have agreed to anything just to get to the house.

Harry "skinned the cat," turning upside down from the branch and dropping to the ground below.

"Very good," Murphy praised her.

As they walked back together Harry asked them, "Did you all know about Tommy Van Allen's plane?"

"Yes," Mrs. Murphy and Tucker replied.

Pewter said nothing because she hadn't seen it before, even though Mrs. Murphy had told her everything.

Harry smiled at them, oblivious to their answers.

"Smart kids."

"Sometimes," Tucker, more modest than the cats, responded.

"What I don't like about this is it's too close to home." Murphy emphasized *home*. *"Tally Urquhart's only four miles away."*

"It doesn't concern Mom no matter how far away or how close it is." Pewter had taken to calling Harry Mom even though she had

been raised by Market Shiflett and she occasionally helped out in the store.

"This is a small town. Everything concerns everybody and we led Mom to what may become damaging evidence for someone else. We were stupid." Murphy realized her mistake.

"I never thought of that." Tucker pressed closer to Harry.

"Me neither. I wish I had."

"Don't worry until they find a body," Pewter said.

"Whoever landed that plane had guts. The fog that night was thick as Mrs. Hogendobber's gravy. Bold ones like that do things other people don't dream of, they take wild chances. Whoever was with Tommy probably killed him, which means I saw the killer. I couldn't tell you one thing about him, though, except that he was shorter than Van Allen. But whoever killed Tommy can't be but so far away."

"You don't know that." Pewter played devil's advocate.

"But I do." Mrs. Murphy dashed ahead a few paces. *"What would someone far away have to gain by removing Tommy Van Allen—"*

"And removing H. Vane-Tempest," Tucker interrupted.

"He's still hanging on." Pewter wasn't convinced.

Mrs. Murphy continued her thoughts. *"If Van Allen has some distant relatives who might inherit his construction business, well, it might be someone far away, but I doubt that's the case."*

"Everyone will know when his will is read." Pewter shrugged.

"Since no one knows that he's dead yet the will won't be read. His property will stay intact," Murphy said, her tail straight out horizontally.

"Someone has to run the business." Tucker began to feel uneasy.

"Whoever is vice president of his corporation will. But think about it, it doesn't matter who runs the business. What matters is where the profits go. And they won't go into anyone's pocket until he is legally declared dead."

"Mrs. Murphy, if the killer stands to profit from Tommy's death

then the body must be revealed." Pewter was hungry and frustrated. This didn't make a bit of sense to her.

"Exactly."

"I don't get it," Tucker forthrightly said, her voice high.

"Be patient." Mrs. Murphy smiled at them as they caught up to walk beside her. *"Whoever killed Tommy is in no hurry. I don't know what Virginia laws say about when you're legally declared dead, but I guarantee you our killer knows. Someone has a great deal to gain by this."*

"Could be love gone sour." Pewter searched for a different tack.

"Could be." Murphy inhaled the sharp fragrance of the shed bursting with wood shavings.

Pewter was happy they were home.

Tucker was growing more concerned by the minute. *"You're making me nervous."*

"Maybe we're looking at this from the wrong angle." Mrs. Murphy bounced through the screen door when Harry opened it. She liked to let Harry open it. It wouldn't do for Harry to know all her tricks. *"Maybe the question is, what do Tommy Van Allen and H. Vane have in common?"*

"Nothing," Pewter said.

Tucker demurred. *"Plenty."*

The two animals looked at each other as Harry wiped off the kitchen counter and pulled out cans of food.

"They don't have anything in common." Pewter defended her position. *"Tommy is young and handsome. H. Vane has got to be in his seventies. The face-lift makes him look a little younger."*

"He had a face-lift?" Tucker asked.

"I can always tell. The eyes. The faces lose some of their expressiveness—even with the good jobs," Pewter authoritatively declared. *"But those two don't have anything in common. Tommy is divorced. H. Vane is happily married, or appears to be. Tommy is wild and boisterous, H. Vane has a stick up his ass."*

"My turn. If you're finished."

Pewter waited by her food bowl, which said LOYAL FRIEND. *"I'm finished, I think."*

"Okay, they're both well-off. H. Vane is beyond well-off. He's Midas. But they can do whatever they want. They belong to the same clubs. They go to the same parties. They both like to fly. And Tommy was going to do the reenactment."

"Every man in Crozet was going to do that. That's not enough." Pewter purred when Harry scooped out tuna.

"Maybe Tommy had an affair with Sarah." Tucker buried her face in her food.

They tabled the discussion until after they ate.

Harry whistled, tired of her own whistle, and turned on the radio. She liked the classical station and country and western. She tuned to the classical station out of Lynchburg. She heated the griddle, pulled out two slices of bread and two fat slices of American cheese. She loved cheese sandwiches, dressing them up with mayonnaise and hamburger pickles. Sometimes she'd squirt on ketchup, too.

Tucker finished first, as always. *"Hurry up."*

"You don't savor your food." Pewter did, of course.

"It tastes good to me. I don't know why you hover over yours."

"Tucker, you're such a dog," Pewter haughtily replied.

Mrs. Murphy, a slow eater, paused. *"If Tommy slept with Sarah, the question is, did H. Vane know? He certainly seemed friendly enough to Tommy."*

Pewter pitched in her two cents. *"H. Vane would hardly kill Tommy, then get it in the back himself. This is screwy."*

"No, it isn't. We haven't found the key yet, that's all." Murphy was resolute.

"And now that we've somewhat compromised Mom we'd better figure this out." Tucker had lived with Mrs. Murphy a long time. She knew how the cat thought.

"Yes."

Pewter, food bits clinging to her whiskers, jerked her head up from the bowl. *"She'd stick her nose in it even if we hadn't taken her to the airplane. Even Miss Tally said it was in the blood."*

"You got that right." Mrs. Murphy thought Pewter looked silly. *"Remember what she said about Biddy Minor?"*

"Curiosity killed him," Tucker whispered.

"I thought curiosity killed the cat." Pewter swallowed some carefully chewed tuna.

"Shut up." Murphy hated that expression. *"I prefer 'Cats have nine lives,' myself."*

"Well, I only have one. I intend to take good care of it." Tucker snapped her jaws shut with a click.

22

The shadows etched an outline of the budding trees onto the impeccably manicured back lawn of the Lutheran church. The Reverend Herbert C. Jones, in clerical garb, fiddled with his fly rod as he stood on the moss-covered brick walkway to the beige clapboard office, window shutters painted Charleston green.

He'd finished his sermon for Sunday and since this was Tuesday he felt on top of the world. True, his desk contained four mountains of neatly ordered paperwork but a man couldn't work around the clock. Even the Good Lord rested on the seventh day. And the afternoon, balmy and warm, enticed him from the grind of paperwork. He got his fishing rod and went outside.

Usually Herb parked the church's 1987 white Chevy truck on the corner to let people know he was at church. Since he received many calls to pick up this and drop off that for a parishioner in need, it was also useful for the truck to sit ready, keys in the ignition. However, at the moment the Chevy had a flat left-front tire, which irritated him no end because he'd endured a flat just last year on the right front and had replaced both front tires. He had parked the Chevy in the brick garage behind the office until he could fix it. Lovely winding brick paths meandered from the church to the garage, formerly the stable, and to his graceful residence, a subdued classic in flemish bond.

The tail of the Chevy poked out from the garage. His Buick Roadmaster was parked next to the old truck.

"I'll stand here and cast at the taillight," he told himself.

Lucy Fur watched her human with detached amusement. Mrs. Murphy and Pewter were visiting from the post office. The animal door that Harry had installed there was a godsend because the animals didn't have to lurk by the front door waiting for a person to open it. All too often the human would close the door fast or step on them, because humans lacked a sharp sense of how much space they took up or how much other creatures needed. They were always bumping into things, stepping on tails, or tripping over their own feet. With the animal door at the rear of the old frame building the creatures could come and go at will. The cats especially enjoyed prowling the neighborhood to visit other cats.

Lucy Fur, a gorgeous young Maine coon cat, had walked into Herb's life one stormy night. He kept her because Elocution was getting on in years and he thought a younger companion would do her good. At first Elocution had hissed and spit. That lasted two weeks. Then she tried the deep freeze. Every time the kitten would walk by she'd turn her back. After a month she accepted Lucy Fur, teaching her the duties of a preacher's cat. The first, for any cat, is to catch mice. However, there were communion wafers to count, vestments to inspect, sermons to read, parishioners to comfort, and a variety of functions to attend.

Both cats excelled as fund-raisers, mingling with the crowd and encouraging generosity with both checkbooks and food.

The three cats sat abreast in the deep window ledge of the house. Sunlight like golden butter drenched their shiny fur. They watched Herb wryly.

Herb put his right foot back as he lifted his right arm. He wiggled a minute, then cast toward a taillight. He'd done better.

"Damn," he muttered under his breath, reeling his line, a tiny lead weight dangling on the end, his hand-tied fly, white and speckled black, slightly above it.

"Is this some Christian ritual?" Pewter asked.

"Not the way he does it." Lucy Fur giggled.

Again, the gentle reverend cocked his wrist, placed his feet in the correct position, and softly flicked his line out. This cast was worse than the first one.

"Hell's bells." His voice rose.

"Might prayer help?" Mrs. Murphy dryly noted.

"As far as I know there is no prayer specific to fishing." Lucy Fur's opinion was an informed one. She studied her texts.

"What about Jesus talking to the men casting their nets?" Mrs. Murphy suggested.

"Luke 5, Verses 1 through 11. It's the story where the men fished all night, came up empty, and Jesus told them to go out and throw their nets. They caught so many fish their ships began to sink. And that's when Simon Peter joined Jesus. He was one of the fishermen."

Impressed, Murphy gasped, *"You should talk to Mrs. Hogendobber. She'd have a fit and fall in it!"*

"Oh," Lucy Fur airily replied, *"she wouldn't listen. You know she believes in this charismatic stuff. She ought to submit to the rigor of the Lutheran catechism. I don't believe you sit around waiting until the spirit moves you."*

"She hardly sits," Pewter noted, herself a sharp critic of human mystical leanings. But in the case of Miranda, the good woman practiced what she preached.

"Uh-oh. I don't think biblical references are going to help now." Murphy stared upward.

Herb cast into a tree.

"Christ on a crutch!" he bellowed, then glanced over his shoulder to see if anyone was within earshot.

"Cats to the rescue." Murphy leapt off the window ledge, quickly followed by Pewter and Lucy Fur.

Elocution, watching from inside the house, laughed so hard she had to lie down.

The tiger was halfway up the tree before Lucy Fur even reached the trunk. Pewter, not a girl to rush about, sashayed with dignity toward the puce-faced clergyman.

"Now how am I going to get my hook out of the tree? That's one of my best flies." He threw his lad's cap on the grass.

"Thank you." Pewter immediately sat on the herringbone cap.

Herb stepped to the right, giving the line a tug. No release. He walked to the left. Pewter watched.

"What pretty feathers." Murphy inspected the tied fly.

"He sits up for hours tying these things. He won't let Elocution or me help. He sputters if we even touch one of these precious feathers. I personally can't understand why fish would grab a feather if a bird isn't attached."

"Life's too short to try and understand cold-blooded creatures." Mrs. Murphy unleashed one white claw, wedging it underneath the hook. *"Stop pulling,"* she ordered Herb.

He stopped. "That's my best fly. Don't you eat it!"

"Get a grip." Murphy laughed.

"Let me help." Lucy Fur put her weight on the line so that if Herb did jerk it there'd be a little slack so Murphy could pry up the hook.

"Here it comes." Murphy popped it straight up.

Herb stared up at the cats. He glanced around again. "His wonders never cease." Then he laughed. The cats joined in.

Slowly he reeled in his line, picking up his favorite fly to inspect the damage. None.

He spoke to Pewter, who was all rapt attention. "Best fly in the world for rockfish bass."

"*Good eating,*" Pewter replied; she liked freshwater fish, especially if fried, but more than any other seafood she liked crabmeat.

"You're on my cap."

"*You threw it on the ground, you big baby.*" Nonetheless, Pewter removed herself from the cap, which he promptly slapped back on his head.

"*Why is he wearing that now? Herringbone is for fall.*" Mrs. Murphy paid attention to fashions.

"*He has to get in the mood. You should see him rehearse his sermons. Once when he used* cowboy *as a metaphor he put on cowboy boots and a big hat.*"

"*He's funny.*" Murphy shimmied back down.

"*They all are.*" Lucy Fur backed down.

"*Watch out!*" Pewter warned. "*He's going to cast again.*"

"*Jesus, preserve us,*" Lucy Fur blurted out.

He popped out the line. It sailed over the cats' upturned heads and nicked the bed of the truck, just above the taillight.

Ding.

"Pretty good, if I do say so myself." He grinned ear to ear. "Amen." He smiled outright, following his line in to the truck.

The cats scampered along. The shiny sinker tumbled into the truck bed.

Mrs. Murphy leapt into the bed with Pewter and Lucy Fur on her heels.

"Practice makes perfect," he sang out to himself, reaching into the bed and lifting out his sinker and fly as if they were gold-plated.

"*Well done,*" Lucy Fur congratulated him.

He patted her on her magnificent head.

Pewter noticed that the door was slightly ajar to the passenger side of the truck. *"That broke, too?"*

"Hey." Mrs. Murphy peered into the cab.

Lucy Fur got on her hind legs and looked inside. Pewter stood next to her.

"What?" Pewter said.

"That bomber jacket." Lucy Fur's tail flipped left, then right.

"Herb doesn't own a bomber jacket." Murphy jumped out of the bed. She tried to pry open the heavy truck door, but, although ajar, it was too much for her.

"Whoever used the truck last forgot their jacket." Pewter shrugged.

"Open the door!" Murphy hollered at the top of her not-inconsiderable lungs.

"You could wake the dead." Herb leaned his rod against the truck, walking over to the howling cat. "Oh." He noticed the door and opened it wider to shut it firmly. As he did, the cat hopped into the seat. "Now Mrs. Murphy—" He opened the door. "What's this?"

23

With no corpse, no motive, and no witnesses, Rick Shaw was in an unenviable position regarding the disappearance of Tommy Van Allen. By contrast he had 30,000 witnesses to the shooting of Sir H. Vane-Tempest—30,003 if he counted Mrs. Murphy, Pewter, and Tee Tucker.

He looked into Mrs. Murphy's green eyes, which stared right back into his own. "Sure of yourself, aren't you?" he whispered to the cat. Then he turned to Herb. "She shows up in the damnedest places. They both do." He stroked Pewter.

Herb was holding Lucy Fur, more to comfort himself than anything.

"Now, Herb, who used this truck last?"

"I did."

"When?"

"A week ago." He sheepishly continued. "I've been meaning to fix the flat but it's always one thing or another."

Cynthia Cooper pulled up to join them. Rick held out the bomber jacket. He wore gloves. "T.V.A." Coop read aloud the initials embroidered on the inside map pocket.

"So the truck has been in the garage for one week," Rick went on. He turned back to Herb. "Have you checked it? You know, come on out to get something from the glove compartment? Anything?"

"No."

"How many people—" Rick stopped himself. Everyone knew where the garage was. In fact, everyone knew everything— almost.

"Do you have any idea why this jacket is in your truck?"

"Sheriff, that's the sixty-four-thousand-dollar question." Herb betrayed his age when he used that phrase.

"Maybe Tommy put it in there himself." Lucy Fur posited her idea.

"No." Mrs. Murphy concentrated fiercely on the jacket.

"You know, when H. Vane was hauled away in the ambulance, I established the range for muzzle-loaders. About one hundred yards. That meant anyone in either of the two companies could have fired on him. I met the doctor the second she walked out of surgery. I did everything by the book. Three bullet wounds can't be an accident but I have no complaint filed by the victim. Isn't that odd?"

"Yes." Herb crossed his arms over his chest.

"And I have a missing person I am treating as, shall we say, an unfriendly disappearance. We find the airplane. Nothing, except it's covered with pussycat paw prints." He cast an eye at Mrs. Murphy, even though he didn't realize those were her prints. "I've combed through Tommy's house and his office with his housekeeper. Nothing has been taken. The only things missing are what he was wearing—the clothes on his back, a signet ring, and his forty-five-thousand-dollar Schauffenhausen watch."

Herb whistled at the price.

"We've alerted pawnshops across the country. We've sent out photographs to every law-enforcement agency. Not a trace. What I'm driving at is—things are just too damned curious." Rick slapped his thigh in disgust. "I'll check this for prints, fibers, you name it." He sighed audibly. "But I can't put it together."

"Nobody can, boss." Coop brightened. "At least we've got another clue."

"There is that." He smiled.

"Do you think the killer is trying to implicate me?" Herb reached for his rod as though the touch of it would make everything all right.

"No, I don't." Rick smiled. "And I have a suspicious mind. There are so many places to dispose of a jacket. . . . *Whoever* put it here is in effect giving us the finger—begging your pardon, Reverend."

"Van Allen was probably wearing this jacket when he disappeared," Cynthia said. "Herb, if you don't mind, leave the truck here for a day. We need to check it for prints."

"We've got a portable compressor. I'll fill your tire. Once we're finished tomorrow you can take it down to the garage."

"Thanks, that would be a big help."

Lucy Fur rubbed his leg. *"Don't worry, Poppy. Everything will be all right."*

"Tommy Van Allen was wearing a trench coat, collar turned up, when I saw him at Tally Urquhart's."

"You saw him?" Lucy Fur stopped midrub.

"I couldn't see his face but how many six-foot-five men are there? I was far away, it was getting foggy with a hard rain. But he wasn't wearing that bomber jacket."

"*Maybe he left it in his car and grabbed the trench coat because it was raining?*" Pewter said.

"*It doesn't matter whether he was wearing it, left it in a car, or whether this jacket was in someone else's car or someone else's house. That's really irrelevant at this point.*" Murphy's words were clipped.

Pewter disagreed. "*I think it's relevant. The killer or accomplice wanted to get rid of evidence. Maybe he forgot this jacket was in his car or trunk or something?*"

"*No way.*" The tiger stood up. "*He's putting down bad scent.*"

"*Deliberately misleading us?*" Lucy Fur sat on Herb's sturdy walking shoe.

"*You'd better believe it—and enjoying himself in the bargain.*" Mrs. Murphy felt the whole complexion of the events had changed, like a lighting-change during a play. The mood shifts with the light. It can suddenly become treacherous.

24

Tubes invaded H. Vane-Tempest's body. Alert but in pain, he lay in the hospital bed counting the minutes until the next shot would bring him relief. What hurt most was his reset shoulder blade.

"Honey, drink a little water. You'll get dehydrated." Sarah held a plastic water cup with a big plastic bent straw in it.

Dutifully he drank. "Where's that goddamn nurse?"

"She'll be here in a minute." Sarah checked her watch.

The heavyset nurse appeared, right on time. "How are you feeling?"

"I've felt better."

She checked his chart and took his pulse.

"He's very uncomfortable. Can't you increase his dosage?"

"No. Only the doctor can do that." The nurse gently removed her fingers from his wrist. "This will help for now. I know it wears off sooner than you'd like, but Dr. Svarski is a firm believer in getting people up and out of here as soon as possible. If you become dependent on painkillers it's that much harder."

H. Vane glared at her as she stuck the needle into his left arm.

"What about his sleep? If you give him a higher dosage at night he'll at least be able to sleep right through. As it is now, he wakes up."

"Mrs. Tempest—"

"Lady Vane-Tempest." Sarah was testy.

"Ma'am, you'll have to discuss this with Dr. Svarski. I cannot increase your husband's dosage." She abruptly left the room.

"I hate nurses." Sarah closed the door, then sat next to him. "Would you like me to read to you?"

He smiled at her. "Thank you, but I can't seem to stay focused on anything. My mind wanders. I couldn't even answer Shaw's questions."

"He understands." She lowered her voice. "Henry, it's just us. No repercussions. I understand you don't want to make accusations you can't support. You're exceedingly fair that way. But between us, who would want to shoot you? Is there something I don't know?"

He looked into his wife's imploring eyes. "Sarah, the only person I can think of is Archie."

"Yes, of course." She put her hand on his.

"Lately I'd have gladly shot him." He laughed but it hurt so badly he stopped.

She shook her head. "He's snapped, I suppose. The sheriff

can't arrest him until they have more proof.... How are you holding up, honey, you look done in."

"Tired."

"Sleep. You need lots of sleep."

"Yes, but it's so boring." He squeezed her hand and promptly fell asleep.

25

News of the bomber jacket appeared in the *Daily Progress*. A storm of speculation followed and a plethora of leads—all dead ends.

This Saturday, Harry was determined to wax her Barbour coat. If she didn't do it now she'd regret it in about two days, when more rain was predicted.

She warmed the wax as she brushed the coat, inspected the seams, emptied the pockets. An old movie ticket fell out.

"I can't even remember the last time I went to the movies."

"You need to get out more often," Tucker advised.

Mrs. Murphy, grooming her tail, listened to the blue jay squawking outside the barn door. Birds excited her senses. Blue jays were saucy, fearless, and expert dive-bombers.

"Shut up," Pewter called out.

"Shut up yourself, fatso!"

"I have half a mind to go out there and teach him a lesson," Pewter grumbled.

Murphy admired her tail. Having this appendage gave her better balance than Harry but the maintenance could be tiresome. If she forgot to hoist it, she picked up mud or dust. If she was caught in pouring rain, her tail looked like a very long rat-tail, which offended her exalted vanity. If she brushed by a lily she would smear her tail with sticky rust-colored pollen. In fall she picked up "hitchhikers." Biting them out of her tail was a time-consuming process. Still, she'd rather have a tail than not.

She thought Harry would be much improved with a tail. Tucker could certainly use one.

A flurry of squawks, screeches, and whistles drew her from her grooming. She dropped her tail, which she had picked up in her paw.

"That jay family is pushing it too far." Pewter shook herself and strolled to the barn door.

"Death to cats!" The jay swooped down on Pewter, flew through the barn, and zoomed out the other end.

"I'll break your neck!" the humiliated cat hollered.

"I'll help you." Mrs. Murphy trotted over to Pewter.

Tucker joined them, too.

Again the jay swirled around the hayloft, then dove at a forty-five-degree angle.

Murphy leapt straight up, the swish of tail feathers by her ear. She clapped both paws together but missed.

"Ha!" the jay called out.

"Let's lure him into the hayloft. We'll cut down his air space," Pewter sagely advised.

Mrs. Murphy blinked. *"Forget him, I've got an idea. Follow me."*

The two animals trailed after Murphy as she loped across the field.

"Where are we going?" Pewter asked.

"To Tally Urquhart's."

"Why?" The day was pretty enough that Pewter felt she could endure exercise.

"The blue jay made me think of it."

"What?" Tucker's soft brown eyes scanned the fields.

"I should have thought of this before. We need to work in circles around the barn. A human can't see the nose on his face."

The animals arrived at the abandoned barn a half hour later. Since the weather was good they had made excellent time.

"The sheriff has scoured the barn and the outbuildings. My plan is that we each work fifty yards apart in a circle. Pewter, take the closest circle. I'll take the second circle. Tucker, you take the farthest circle. If anyone finds something, yell. If we don't find anything let's work three more circles."

"When you saw the two humans, where did they walk?" Tucker lifted her head to the wind.

"Down the dirt road."

"If Tommy was killed out here he could be buried anywhere," Pewter said.

"Yes, but the other human was little. He wouldn't be able to drag that heavy carcass far."

"Let's go to work." Tucker trotted out 150 yards from the barn and shouted back, *"We'll use the road as our rendezvous point, but remember, I'm on the farthest circle, so it will take me longer to get back here."*

"Okay." The two cats fanned out.

Murphy worked quietly. She found old smoothed-over bits of glass from long-ago bottles for poultices, worm remedies, even liquor. Here and there she turned up a rusted horseshoe or a rabbit's nest. She throttled her instincts to hunt.

They worked in silence for an hour. Murphy, on the second circle, came back about ten minutes after Pewter.

"What'd you get?"

Pewter shrugged. *"Ratholes and high-topped shoes."*

"Come on."

"A piece of an upper, I think, anyway. Humans sure put their bodies into some pinchy clothes and shoes."

"Whee-ooo."

The sound, to their right, sent them scrambling. Tucker sat on the edge of an old dump. Pieces of tractor stuck out through the brambles, which seemed to grow overnight.

"What have you got?" Pewter thought the graveyard of machines eerie.

"Nothing, but wouldn't this be a great place to dump a body?" Tucker said.

"Yes, but we would have smelled it when we led Harry to the barn." Mrs. Murphy marveled at how quickly brambles grow in the spring. They were already twirling through an old discarded hay elevator.

"Yeah." Tucker, disappointed, bulled through the thorns into the pile, her thick coat protecting her. *"I'll just nose around."*

"No hunting, Tucker. We've resisted."

"Pewter, I wouldn't dream of it."

The cats stuck around just in case. The strong, low-built dog pushed straight into the dump. She would nose through some of the debris, a delightful prospect.

Being next to mountains, the area had shifted over the years with small tremors. A rusted truck, an ancient Chevy from the 1930s, had been turned on its side by quake tremors. Vines and rusting were slowly pulling it apart.

A faint but tantalizing odor curled in Tucker's nostrils. She sniffed around the truck, then started digging underneath it.

As she ripped into the soft earth, the corner of a sturdy, small suitcase appeared. It might once have sat on the seat of the truck but had probably slid out once the glass broke. Over the decades the truck had settled on top of it, and it was covered with fallen leaves and vines depositing layers of humus.

"Found an old suitcase."

"So what?" Pewter catcalled.

"It's heavy leather, got steel corners. It has an alluring odor— faded, very faded."

"What's she babbling about?" Murphy grumbled.

"Let's go see."

Tucker gave a hearty tug on the suitcase, then another.

The latch gave just a bit. She tugged some more.

"Will you get back to work?" Murphy circled around the worst of the brambles, crawling low to avoid the others. She walked over an old Massey-Ferguson tractor, then dropped onto the side of the Chevy.

"I'm not going in there!" Pewter shouted.

"Who asked you?" Then Tucker yelled again. *"Golly!"*

The cat stepped up as the dog sniffed the musty odor of old death.

The two friends blinked.

"It's a tiny skeleton." A bit of lace still hung over the skull. *"A tiny human skeleton!"* Mrs. Murphy gasped.

"What will we do?" Tucker's voice was almost a whisper.

"Will you come out of there?" Pewter paced, irritated to the point of putting up her tail.

"We've found a skeleton," Murphy called out.

"You're just saying that to get me in there."

"NO, we're not," they answered in unison.

Pewter paced, sat, paced, cursed, then finally crawled in. *"You're lying. I know you're lying."*

"Look." Mrs. Murphy leaned back.

"Liar." Nonetheless Pewter did look. *"Oh, no."* She sat down.

"Nobody buries their baby in a suitcase." Tucker was indignant.

"You're exactly right." Murphy licked the dog's ear.

"Are you thinking what I'm thinking?" Pewter asked.

"Someone killed this little thing." Mrs. Murphy sighed. *"Tucker, do you think we can pull the suitcase out of this rubble?"*

"No."

"The rats will get at it, or raccoons." Pewter felt quite sad. *"Can you cover it again?"*

"Yes. It wasn't very deep. If you two help it won't take long."

Tucker pushed the suitcase back, then turned around, throwing dirt on their discovery with her hind legs.

The cats threw dirt on it as well.

Once it was covered they took a breather, then crawled back out.

"Let's go home," a subdued Pewter requested. *"We won't find Tommy Van Allen."*

26

At the eastern end of Crozet, on Route 240, the large food plant, which had been through successive corporate owners, dominated the skyline. On the south side of the white buildings ran the railroad tracks, a convenience should they need carloads of grain shunted off onto sidings. These days huge trailers pulled in and out of the parking lot, a sea of macadam. Each time a driver shifted gears a squelch of diesel smoke would shoot straight upward, a smoke signal from the internal-combustion engine.

The giant refrigerator trucks hauled the frozen foods to refrigerated warehouses from whence the product made it directly to the freezer sections of supermarkets.

Loading the behemoths in the docking area plunged men from cavernous freezers into the baking temperature outside and then into the long, cold trailers. This was not the most desirable job in the United States and many a Crozet High School graduate working on that platform rued the day he had decided not to try for college.

While a lot of the town's residents worked in the food factory, just as many did not. It was odd, really, how little social impact the big corporation had on the town except for creating traffic in the morning and then again at quitting time.

For a manager on the way up, Crozet was a good stop. Most deplored the small town, calling it Podunk or some other put-down. For those who weren't southern, the jolt of Virginia life came like unexpected turbulence at twenty thousand feet. Charlottesville, offering some cultural delights, was disdained because it wasn't Chicago, a fact that Charlottesvillians were keen to perpetuate.

Wilson C. McGaughey, thirty-two, ambitious, organized, and a student of time-management schemes, daily outraged those people working in his unit. Bad enough that he mocked their speech, called them slow and inefficient; now he'd taken to putting up flow charts for the workers' edification. Next to the flow chart and the weekly productivity quota McGaughey had what his underlings dubbed the Weenie List—workers who had excelled. Two were chosen each week. Next to that was the Shit List, the names of those who did the poorest work. If your name made the Shit List three times in one year Wilson fired you. Simple as that.

The huge refrigerated units were part of Wilson Mc-Gaughey's responsibility. The freezers housed the raw foods that would be processed into turkey dinners or roast beef or linguini. Occasionally a bottle of shine or store-bought alcohol would be secreted in a back corner far from Wilson's eyes.

Dabney Shiflett, cousin to Market, didn't have a drinking problem as much as he had a specific thirst. A good worker, he nimbly sidestepped Wilson. Chewing Fisherman's Friend lozenges helped.

Dabney slipped away from the loading dock, telling his buddy he was heading to the bathroom. Instead he made straight for the meat locker in the back. He walked in and turned on the lights, revealing sides of beef hanging overhead. The back corner had a joist, slightly separated, providing the perfect place to wedge a slender flask of shine. He needed only a nip to feel wondrous warmth, a general flow of well-being. He hurried to the back, unscrewed the cap, and knocked back a healthy swallow. He opened his eyes, midpull. His mouth fell open, grain alcohol spilling onto his shirt. He dropped the flask, running flat out for the door.

27

"You won't mention the company? We aren't responsible." Wilson McGaughey pressured Rick Shaw. "Nobody could blame us."

"Facts are facts, Mr. McGaughey. The body was found in a Good Foods refrigerator."

Wilson, revulsion turning to anger, wheeled on Dabney. "Do you have something to do with this? It's bad enough you were drinking on company time—"

Rick interrupted, motioning for Dabney to follow him. "If you don't mind, Mr. McGaughey, I'd like to question Mr. Shiflett alone."

Wilson did mind but he held his tongue.

Rick took Dabney away from the corner where the corpse of Tommy Van Allen hung, by handcuffs dangling from a meathook. He'd been shot once in the temple, a neat job, very little mess. His Schauffenhausen watch remained on his wrist, his signet ring was on his finger, and $523, cash, was in his pants pocket along with his keys.

His glazed eyes were staring; his mouth hung open. But he was perfectly preserved, being frozen stiff.

"Now Dabney, pay that Yankee son of a bitch no mind."

"He's gonna fire me."

"He can try. Man can't be fired for finding a corpse."

At the mention of the word *corpse*, Dabney paled and began shaking. "I feel bad, Sheriff."

"It's a terrible shock."

"I didn't kill him."

"Didn't think you did." He clapped Dabney on the back. "How often is this meat locker checked?"

"Daily." He lowered his voice. "In theory. Maybe someone sticks their head in once a day. But, you know, probably no one has walked all the way back here since Tommy's been missing."

"Unless they're in on it."

"Hadn't thought of that." Dabney was feeling better, as long as he didn't look at the body.

"Do you know anyone who might bear a grudge, who—"

"No. He didn't have anything to do with the company, Sheriff, other than building the new office wing, and that was eleven years back."

"I know you came back for a swig, Dabney. Why hadn't you come in here before?"

Dabney looked away from Rick. "Used up the rest of my stash. This was my last bottle until I refilled the others and started all over again." He lifted his head, his smile weak.

"And Wilson knew nothing?"

Dabney shook his head. "No."

"How long ago did you put your flask back here?"

"Uh . . . three weeks, I reckon. I dunno."

Rick wrinkled his forehead. "Go on, Dabney. I'm sorry you had to go through this. I might want to talk to you later."

Wilson McGaughey sidled up. "You have influence with the press—"

"McGaughey, you haven't lived here long enough to feel anything for that slab of human beef hanging back there, but let me tell you, as men go, he was a good man, not a perfect man, not always an even-tempered man, but a decent man." He stopped for breath. "I can't keep this out of the news. If you obstruct justice in any way, I'll have your ass. Am I clear?"

"Yes."

"You sounded like a New Yorker for a minute." Cynthia had been standing behind her boss.

He turned around. "Is that a compliment or an insult?"

"Depends."

"Mr. McGaughey, did you know the victim?"

"Only in passing." He clipped his words.

"Did you like him?" Rick felt his nose get colder by the minute.

"What little I knew of him, yes. He was a pleasant fellow."

"All right. You can go." Rick paused. "One last thing. Don't fire Dabney Shiflett."

"Man's got a problem." Wilson was furious that the redneck had put one over on him.

"He performs his duties."

"Drinking during work hours is against company regulations."

"Then get the man into a program. Don't fire him. He has three mouths to feed and he's a hard worker. I've known him all my life. If you want to get along in Crozet, work with people. Do you understand?"

Wilson understood that the sheriff was mad at him. But he didn't understand exactly what was being asked of him.

Cynthia spoke up. "The sheriff is saying that you will lower

your productivity and maybe even harm your career if you don't
learn that showing a little concern for your workers might boost
morale. If Dabney was slacking off on the job, okay, then be a
hard-ass. But help him. You might need help yourself someday."

"I'll take it under consideration." He walked off, nearly as
stiff as Tommy Van Allen.

"Jesus, what a bonehead. And I'll bet he has his M.B.A.,"
Shaw said.

"Boss, this was in Van Allen's trench-coat pocket." Cynthia
held a condom wrapper in her gloved hand.

"Any sign of the condom?"

"No."

"Coop, how do you think he got on that meathook?"

She shrugged. "He could have been hoisted up the same way
they hoist the beef. Come on, I'll show you."

They walked outside and Cynthia pointed out a squarish machine used to move pallets loaded with heavy cartons; modified,
the machine could also lift up sides of beef.

"Possible." He walked over. "How much does one of these
things cost?"

"About sixteen thousand dollars retail."

"How do you know that?"

"Asked Wilson."

"Ah, yes, he'd know." He heard the gurney rolling down the
outside walkway. "Coroner's good. Body may be frozen blue but
I bet he can establish the time of death. What he can't establish
is, was he killed here or brought here? And why here? Why not
just dump him up in the waste unit like dead meat?" His voice
rasped. "I have never seen anything like this in my years of law
enforcement."

"Me neither."

He shot her a sharp glance. "You, you're still wet behind the
ears."

"I've seen enough murders to know most of them are committed in a white-hot rage. This was not."

"The bomber jacket in Herb's truck was a neat trick, too. A little flag to let us all know we aren't on top of this case."

The gurney rolled past them, Tommy tucked into two body bags, since his arms were frozen straight up. Diana Robb, the paramedic, couldn't get him into one bag without breaking his arms, and that would compromise evidence.

She stopped as her coworkers continued to push the body to the ambulance. "Weighed a ton. Like moving a boulder."

"Better than shaking off the maggots that crawl up your leg. Those suckers bite." Rick hated that stench.

"You've got a point there. Never would have thought Tommy would end this way. I could have pictured a jealous husband shooting him maybe, but nothing like this."

"Nasty, isn't it?" Coop said.

"Yep." Diana grimaced, then rejoined her crew.

Rick half closed his eyes to hide his frustration.

28

Mrs. Murphy watched a bejeweled hand reach into the post-office box. Playfully she swatted.

Big Mim withdrew her hand. "Murphy, stop it."

"Hee-hee."

"Harry, your cat is interfering with federal property again." Mim reached in once more.

"Murphy, behave." Harry walked over to the postboxes. She peered through the brass box as Mim peered in from the other side. "Peekaboo."

"Back at you!" Mim was in a good mood.

Aunt Tally, however, was not. "A sixty-two-year-old woman acting like a silly schoolgirl."

"I am not sixty-two."

"And I'm not ninety-three. Or is it ninety-one?" She sighed.

"I've lied about my age for so many years, I can't remember how old I really am. But I remember exactly how old you are, Mimsy." A light hint of malice floated through her voice. "My sister said you kicked in the womb so hard you gave her a hernia."

The turned-up collar of Mim's expensive English-tailored shirt seemed to stiffen. "Harry and Miranda aren't interested in that."

"Oh yes we are," came the chorus, the animals included.

Tally leaned across the divider. "Urquharts conceive with no difficulty at all, of course." She called over her shoulder to Mim, sorting her mail, "And Little Mim gave you a couple of whacks." Mim ignored her, so she continued. "I never had children myself but I've spent a lifetime observing them—from birth to death sometimes. I've outlived everyone except my imperious niece and her daughter."

"I'm not imperious, Aunt Tally. That honor belongs to you."

"Oh la!" Tally's eyebrows rose, as did her voice.

Pewter, sound asleep on the table, was missing the exchange but Murphy and Tucker drank in every word.

"I never knew your mother," Miranda Hogendobber told Tally, "but everyone says she was beautiful."

"She was. Jamie got her looks and I got Daddy's brains. We'd have all been better off if that genetic package had been reversed." Jamie Urquhart was Tally's deceased brother. "Maybe not these days, but certainly in mine."

"You're fishing for compliments." Mim joined her at the wooden divider. "You looked good then and you look good now."

"Ha. Every plastic surgeon in America could work on me and I'd still look two years older than God." Her bright eyes darted to Miranda. "Sorry."

"That's quite all right."

"You're still a religious nut, I take it." Tally's smile was crooked and funny.

Miranda opened her mouth but nothing came out.

"This is getting good." Tucker giggled. *"Think we should wake up Pewter?"*

"No, let her suffer. We can tell her every syllable and she'll scream that we made it up." Mrs. Murphy ducked her head and rubbed it under Tucker's ruff. The cat had jumped off the eight-inch wooden divider behind the mailboxes to sit with the dog.

"Tally!" Mim admonished her.

"She is. She quotes the Scriptures more often and more accurately than those jackleg TV preachers. Ought to get *your* own TV show, Miranda. Make a bloody fortune." She threw back her head and laughed. " 'This moment of Jesus brought to you by General Motors. If the Good Lord were with us today he'd drive a Chevy. Trade in your sandals on a V-8.' "

All eyes fixed upon Tally, her red beret tilted at a rakish angle. Her eyes were merry, her lipstick disappearing into the crevices above her still-full lips.

"Think Mrs. H. will pitch a hissy?" Tucker took a step backward.

"No. She'll chalk it up to advanced age, then go pray for her." Murphy leapt onto the counter. *"Mim's face is crimson, though. Whoo-ee."*

"We'd better be going now." Mim put her hand under Tally's bony elbow.

"I'm not going anywhere until I hear what Miranda has to say. You were the cutest little girl in Crozet."

Harry looked at Miranda with new eyes. It had never occurred to her that her friend might have once been cute, although she wasn't unattractive now—just plump.

Miranda cleared her throat. "I attend the Church of the Holy Light, from which I draw great comfort, Tally, but I don't think I'm a religious nut."

"You weren't like this while George lived. It's a substitute."

"Aunt Tally, that really is going too far." Mim stamped her Gucci-shod foot.

"I can say what I want, when I want. That's a benefit of advanced age. Not that you'll listen. Like Sir H. Vane getting shot. If you ask me, it's a wonder nobody shot that warthog earlier. All this drivel about being knighted. He hasn't done a damn thing. Probably made his money selling drugs to British rock stars."

"He was knighted. Susan and I got on the Internet to the library of the British Museum in London and searched through peers of the realm. Then we went to the London *Times* and pulled up a bio."

"You didn't tell me." Miranda was more upset by this omission than Tally's assault.

"Slipped my mind. Anyway, we did it over lunch hour."

"Well, what did you find out?" Mim demanded.

"He built airports throughout Africa in the countries formerly part of the British commonwealth. He built other things, too, but he made the millions building these airports. He is the genuine article."

"Oh, hell. I liked believing he was a fake." Tally pouted.

Susan screeched up in her Audi station wagon and hopped out, forgetting to close the door. She was in her spandex workout clothes. She threw open the door to the post office.

"They found Tommy Van Allen!"

"Pewter, wake up!" Murphy jumped on the table to pat Pewter's face.

Grumbling, the fat kitty opened her eyes.

Tucker hopped up and down, trying to get closer to the humans. Harry opened the divider door for her to go out front as she and Miranda walked out to Susan.

"He was hanging in the big freezer room at Good Foods."

"What? Why hasn't Rick Shaw informed me?" Mim believed

herself to be the first citizen of Crozet. And her husband was the mayor to boot.

"Mim, even Jim doesn't know," Susan breathlessly said.

"Then how do you come by this unsettling knowledge?" Tally asked.

"I dropped by Ned's office just as the phone rang. Dabney Shiflett was fired by his boss for drinking on the job. It was Dabney who found Tommy. He'd snuck into a meat locker for a quick nip and he found Tommy Van Allen hanging from a meathook by a pair of handcuffs. Frozen. Just totally frozen."

"My God." Mim couldn't believe it.

"Did Dabney tell Ned how he was killed?" Harry kept a cool head, as always.

"Yes. Shot straight through the temple. 'Neat as a pin,' Dabney said, 'neat as a pin.' Can you imagine?"

"People've been shot around here since gunpowder. Before that the Indians used bows and arrows, clubs and knives. Killing is one of our favorite pastimes," Tally flatly stated.

"*She's got a point there.*" Pewter, riveted by the news, agreed with the old lady.

"*Yeah, but this is—*" Tucker was interrupted by Susan continuing.

"The only good thing is, he wasn't pinned on the meathook. At least he was hanging by handcuffs."

"*It's the handcuffs that worry me.*" Murphy paced the counter.

"*Why?*" Tucker's pink tongue contrasted with her white fangs.

"*This was thought out. I wonder how long Tommy was alive wearing those handcuffs before he was killed?*"

Pewter flattened her ears, then swept them forward again. "*Torture?*"

"*Physical or psychological... or even sexual. Those handcuffs bother me.*"

29

The other news of the day, not quite as shocking as the discovery of Tommy Van Allen, concerned Archie Ingram. When Deputy Cooper met him at the county offices to question him further about the shooting at Oak Ridge he asked her about the Van Allen murder.

He said he had heard about it on his C-band radio.

Cooper, suspicious as to how quickly information like that would get on the C-band, drilled him on this. He lost his temper and slugged her.

The county commissioner was sitting in the county jail for assaulting an officer. Bail wouldn't be set until the next morning.

Cynthia, glad to put Archie in his place, nonetheless called around to check Archie's story. Dabney Shiflett had put the news on C-band along with a most unflattering portrait of the man who had just fired him.

Since Wilson McGaughey drove a car, not a truck, and had no two-way radio, Dabney rightly figured it would be days before McGaughey learned what had been said about him. This small revenge gave Dabney some comfort.

30

Harry and Mrs. Hogendobber drove over to Tommy Van Allen's the evening of the body's discovery. His housekeeper, Helen Dodds, now in her late fifties, thanked them for their offer of help but was afraid to make any decisions until Tommy's estranged wife, Jessica, showed up. She was due in from Aiken, South Carolina, in the morning. Aileen Ingram, Archie's wife, joined them in the living room.

Mrs. Dodds said everyone had come by to help—the Tuckers, Reverend Jones, Sarah Vane-Tempest, Mim and Little Mim, just everyone, no matter what was happening in their lives. She was grateful, she went on, and was only sorry Tommy hadn't known he had so many friends. Then she burst into tears.

Aileen, petite and curly-haired, put her arm around Helen's

shoulders. "There, there, Helen. I'm so sorry for all this." She glanced up at Miranda. "Helen feels this is her fault."

Helen sobbed anew. "I always tried to keep track of Tommy's schedule but lately I've fallen behind and"—she dropped her voice—"he's been secretive."

Helen had been a dear friend of Aileen's now-deceased mother, and Aileen had remained close to the older woman. As soon as she heard the news of the body's discovery, she hurried to Helen's side.

"Helen, this isn't your fault. It may not even be Tommy's fault. Terrible things happen."

Before Miranda could guide Helen toward heavenly support, Helen startled everyone by shouting. "Well, I hope they get him. I hope whoever killed Tommy fries in the electric chair!"

Harry cut off any attempt by Miranda to describe the Lord's justice. "Helen, I'm sure Sheriff Shaw will get to the bottom of this. We all need to keep our eyes and ears open. The smallest thing may have significance."

Mrs. Murphy climbed out of the truck. Tucker was stuck in the cab, complaining bitterly. Pewter had stayed back at Market Shiflett's store to be picked up on the way home.

Tommy's fiery red Porsche 911 Targa was parked in the garage. Tommy, Vane-Tempest, and Blair Bainbridge had indulged in competitive consumption. Murphy sniffed the driver's-side door, the tires, the front and back of the machine. Not that she expected to find anything—just force of habit.

On her hind paws, she stretched her full height to look in the driver's window. The keys were in the ignition.

"Mrs. Murphy," Harry called.

The cat scampered back to the truck. Miranda was already in the passenger side, Tucker wedged between her and Harry. The cat soared onto Harry's lap, then snuggled next to Tucker.

Harry backed out, heading toward town. "It was good of Aileen Ingram to come by, considering her troubles."

"Archie needs to turn to the Lord. How much plainer must his message be?"

"Miranda, these days when people are in trouble they think of turning to a therapist if they think of anything at all."

"Won't work."

"I wouldn't know." They passed BoomBoom and waved. "My point proven."

"Mmm." Miranda let pass the opportunity to reprimand Harry for her snideness toward BoomBoom. "I suppose Aileen was on her way to bail out Archie."

"If she had any sense she'd leave him in there."

"'Whoever exalts himself will be humbled, and whoever humbles himself will be exalted.'" Mrs. Hogendobber quoted Matthew 23, Verse 12.

"Did that just pop into your head or is there a point to it?"

"Harry, don't be ugly."

"I'm sorry. You're right." She sighed heavily. "I'm upset. Seeing poor Mrs. Dodds break down like that—and what's going to happen to her? Who knows what's in Tommy's will or if he even had one."

"He had one. You don't run a big construction company without something like that. Probably had a fat insurance policy, too. I suppose Jessica will get all of it, even if they have separated."

"He could have changed his will."

"Yes, but they aren't legally divorced yet."

"What made you think of the Bible verse about pride?"

"Oh." Mrs. Hogendobber had forgotten to answer Harry's query. "Tommy, H. Vane, Blair, and even Archie. Ridley was part of it for a little while. It's a rich-boys' club. Expensive sports cars, airplanes..."

"Archie doesn't have that much money," Harry interrupted.

"Enough for a Land whatever-you-call-it."

"Land Rover." Harry paused. "I never thought about that. I mean, it seemed discreet enough. White."

Cynthia Cooper's squad car was parked in front of the bank although it was after banking hours. Harry turned into the parking lot, pulling in front of the old brick freestanding bank building.

"Hey."

"Hey there." Cooper rolled down her window.

"We just came from Tommy Van Allen's. Poor Mrs. Dodds."

"And Aileen Ingram was there to help out." Miranda spoke over the animals' heads.

"She can't spring Archie until tomorrow."

"What?" both women said.

"The judge won't set bail until then."

"He can do that?" Harry wondered.

"He can do whatever he wants. He's the judge." Coop smiled.

"You've had a hard day," Miranda said sympathetically.

"I've had better ones." Cooper smiled weakly.

All heads turned as Sarah Vane-Tempest drove by with H. Vane-Tempest in the passenger seat.

"He's made a remarkable recovery," Miranda noted.

"For how long?" Mrs. Murphy cryptically said.

31

Sir H. Vane-Tempest had recovered sufficiently to fight with his wife, who started it.

"Why are you protecting him?" Sarah tossed her shoulder-length blond hair.

"I'm not protecting him."

"The man tried to kill you. I insist you press charges."

"Sarah, my love, he was behind me. Hundreds of men were behind me. Anyone could have fired that shot."

"Archie had it in for you. The other hundreds did not. Why are you protecting him?"

"I am not protecting him."

"Then what are you protecting?" She sat across from him as he reclined on the sofa, more tired from this exchange than from his physical trauma.

"Nothing. Why don't you fix me a real cuppa? That tepid slop at the hospital was torture."

Angry but composing herself, Sarah walked into the kitchen. It was six-thirty, and the maid and cook had left for the day. However, she could brew an invigorating cup of tea without help. She measured out the loose Irish blend, placing it in the ceramic leaf tray of the Brown Betty teapot. She shook her head as if to return to the moment and brought out two fragile china cups delicately edged in rose gold. These had belonged to H. Vane's mother. She hoped the sight of them would improve his mood.

He beamed indulgently when she returned pushing the tea caddy. Scones, jams, white butter, and small watercress sandwiches swirled around the plate, a pinwheel of edibles. The cook made up scones and tea sandwiches fresh each day. The Vane-Tempests practiced the civilized tradition of high tea at four.

He eagerly accepted the cup filled with the intoxicating brew.

He put raw sugar, one teaspoonful exactly, into the cup.

"Ah." He closed his eyes in pleasure as he drank. "My dear, you are unsurpassed."

"Thank you." She sipped her cup of tea.

"My mother loved this china. It was given to her as a wedding present from her aunt Davida. Aunt Davida, you know, served as a missionary in China before World War I. I always thought she was a little cracked, myself, but her china wasn't." He lifted his eyebrows, waiting for the appreciative titter.

Sarah smiled dutifully. "H., you're awful."

Pleased, he replied, "You wouldn't have me any other way."

Sarah wanted to say that she'd be happy to have him forty pounds lighter, with a full head of hair, and perhaps twenty years younger. Some wishes were best left unsaid. "Darling, you're right. I knew from the first moment I saw you that I couldn't live without you."

He nibbled on a scone. "Americans do some things supremely

well. Airplanes, for instance. They build good airplanes. However, they can't make a decent scone and they haven't a clue as to how to produce thick Devonshire cream. Odd."

"That's why you brought over a Scottish cook, yes?"

"Indeed." He reached for another scone. "They want their country back, you know. I read the papers front-to-back in the hospital. Just because I was slightly indisposed didn't mean I should alter my regimen. Why England would even want to *keep* Scotland or Wales is beyond me. And Ireland? Pfft." He made a dismissive motion with his hand.

"That's why we live here."

"Yes. Except here we have to listen to the bleatings of the underclass, interwoven as it is with color. Silly."

"Not to them," Sarah said a mite too tartly.

"Reading the speeches of Martin Luther King, my pet?"

She recovered. "No. What I'm saying is, there is no perfect place, but some are closer than others. And this is very close to heaven."

"Americans are too rude to develop proper tea culture. It takes a great civilization to do that: China, Japan, England. Do you know even the Germans are starting to get it?"

"With ruthless efficiency, I'm sure." She smoothed her dress skirt.

He held out his cup for a refill. "They aren't that efficient. That's a myth, my dear. I've done business with them for years."

"I never appreciated how good a businessman you were until you were nearly taken away from me."

"Oh?" He reveled in the compliment.

"You never discuss business with me."

"Dull, my darling. With you I savor the finer things in life: music, dance, novels. I adore it when we read together and I love it when you read to me. You have such a seductive voice, my sweet."

"Thank you. But I must confess, H., I rather like business. I read *The Wall Street Journal* when you're finished with it and I puzzle my way through *Süddeutsche Zeitung* sometimes. I wish I had gone further in school."

"Beauty is its own school."

"The more I know, the more I admire your acumen."

He placed the cup on the tray. "Sarah, building airports is not a suitable venue for a woman."

"But darling, you don't do that anymore. Now you invest in the stock exchange, here and in London. And you have other irons in the fire. It's fascinating. You're fascinating." She stood up and pressed her hands together, standing quite still. "If you had died, if that fool had killed you, I would have been totally unprepared to administer your empire."

He guffawed. "That's what I pay lawyers for and—"

"But who will watch them? You may trust them. Why should I?"

"Really, my dear, they would serve you as faithfully as they have served me."

"Henry, my experience of life is that each time money changes hands it sticks to somebody's fingers. That army you pay is loyal to you—not to me. And there is the small matter of your ex-wife and your two daughters residing in palatial splendor in England. Well, I forgot, Abigail is in Australia now, in outback splendor."

"My ex and my daughters are provided for. They can't break my will and they'd be fools to try because the astronomical costs would jeopardize their resources. I pay the best minds on two continents. Rest yours."

"No. I want to be included."

"Sarah, you have twenty thousand dollars a month in play money. You can do whatever you like."

"That's not what I'm asking and I am not impugning your generosity to me. What I want is to understand your business holdings."

"I—" Flummoxed, Vane-Tempest began to stutter.

Still standing with her hands pressed together, Sarah half whispered, "Because I did not know whether you would live or die, I sat at your desk and I read your papers. I opened the safe and I read the papers in there. You are an amazing man, Henry, and I don't even know the half of it. I only know what you're doing here in Albemarle County. I haven't a single idea of what you may be doing in Zimbabwe or New Zealand or Germany. I do know you avoid the French like the plague."

His mouth twitched. "I see."

"You formed a corporation with Tommy Van Allen, Archie Ingram, and Blair Bainbridge, I learned. Teotan Incorporated. To date Teotan has purchased over two million dollars' worth of land. I had no idea Archie Ingram had resources at that level. The others, of course, aren't paupers, although no one is in your league."

His eyes narrowed. "Archie put up sweat equity."

"Archie is your conduit to and from Richmond. I'm not in your league either, H., but my brain does function. Archie is a county commissioner. He could point toward those areas that the state will develop or claim for highways and bypasses. Am I correct?"

"Yes."

"And now he has cold feet."

"Yes."

"If the full extent of his participation is discovered, he will certainly lose his seat and may even be raked over the coals, politically and legally, for peddling influence. I believe that's the term for it."

"Precisely."

"Is that what he's been fighting about?"

Sir H. Vane-Tempest sat for a moment. His beautiful wife, that trophy of all trophies, surprised him. He'd been married to the woman for seven years and he'd had no idea her mind was this good. She shocked him. He was also shocked at his own blindness. He had discounted her. Oh, he loved her, he lusted after her, but he had discounted her.

He drew a deep breath. "In part, Sarah, that is what we have been fighting about. Archie is a coward. He wanted the money and he has been handsomely paid by the three of us in terms of his share of the corporate profits. He has a ten-percent share. On top of that we pay him an annual stipend through a complicated trust that I set up, one that leaves no trail to him. I'm too tired to go into the details."

"Some other time, my love?"

His eyes brightened under his ginger brows. "Some other time. Yes."

"But Archie had to have known what he was doing."

"He did. As the county hearings and various other meetings heated up he realized that if his involvement with Teotan ever saw the light of day these grillings would be as little minnows to the whale of discontent, to paraphrase Boswell on Johnson."

"Is there more?"

He shrugged. "He's having problems in his marriage. Tupping some damsel, I should think. That's usually what happens. I don't know who the unfortunate might be. Archie has little to offer, although I suppose he's handsome to women."

"There's no accounting for taste. Some country girl might be thrilled to be sleeping with a county commissioner." She burst out laughing, the silver, tinkling, infectious sound filling the room.

This made Vane-Tempest laugh, too.

Sarah, still smiling, said, "Darling, I want to be part of Teotan."

"Everything comes to you when I die."

"I want to work with you. I want to learn. I don't want to wait until you die. And I want to know why you men have been buying these properties."

"I'm tired." He was, too.

"You can't avoid this. Henry, I want to learn. I've watched you. You can turn a shilling into a pound and a pound into a fortune. I do know that before you built those airports in Africa you bought the land on which they were built."

"Ah." He smiled. "You've been doing your homework."

"Yes."

"Have you studied a map of this county?"

"I have, which is why I want to know why you have bought the particular lands you have bought. There seems to be no rhyme or reason to it."

"Have you spoken to Blair or Archie or Tommy about any of this?"

"Of course not. And I'll never speak to Tommy again. He was found hanging in a refrigerated vault at Good Foods today."

"What!" Vane-Tempest's eyes seemed to bug out of his head.

"Gruesome, isn't it?"

"Why didn't you tell me before?"

"I thought you could hear about it tomorrow. I wanted tonight just for our business. But it occurs to me, darling, that Tommy's death *is* our business."

"In what way?"

"He was a partner in Teotan. He's been murdered and someone tried to kill you. Which is why you must prosecute Archie. You must. He'll strike again. Don't you see? If he kills each of you he's safe. Not only will he cover his tracks, he'll reap the profits of whatever you all have created—you saved him with that trust, that untraceable trust."

"I don't believe it," Vane-Tempest blurted. "Archie Ingram isn't smart enough to do that."

"Weren't you worried when Tommy disappeared?"

"No. Off on a toot, I thought. Slumming." He grimaced. "And then I had other things to think about. I haven't given Tommy much thought. Hanging? Did he hang himself?"

"Sheriff Shaw isn't forthcoming with the details but it's all over town, mostly because the manager of the plant fired the man who found him. Said he was remiss in his duties. And that man, Dabney Shiflett, has been babbling nonstop. I really don't know the details. But Tommy didn't hang himself. Now will you pick up the phone and call the sheriff?"

"No, but I will pick up the phone and call Ingram."

She stepped toward him, stooping down to meet his eyes. "Henry, if that man makes one move to harm you, I will kill him."

Secretly excited by her ardor, he replied, "That won't be necessary. Archie Ingram has neither the intelligence nor the guts to pull off a scheme such as you imagine. As for Tommy's death, I wouldn't rush to conclusions. His demise and my—well—accident are unrelated."

"Will you include me in Teotan?"

"Yes. But I must discuss this with Blair Bainbridge—"

She pressed her hands together again. "Unless someone kills him, too!"

"Calm down, Sarah. I must have the approval of the other partners, and that includes Archie. As for Tommy, the corporation is set up so that if one principal dies, his share is parceled out equally among the survivors."

"You can't ask for the vote of a man who tried to kill you!" Her eyes were wild.

"I can and I must. Now if you would bring me the handy, I will arrange a meeting."

She gave him the cell phone. He dialed and got Archie's answering machine. "Hello, H. Vane-Tempest here for Archie Ingram. Call tomorrow after nine. Good-bye." He folded the phone, putting it on the tea trolley. "Now I can't very well call Sheriff Shaw, can I?" He paused, a dark shift clouding his features. "I liked Tommy Van Allen. Did you?"

"Yes."

"Terrible thing."

She settled on the chintz sofa, squeezing in next to him. "Henry, you must be careful. You must. I don't want to lose you."

"Promise." He leaned forward and kissed her.

32

Lilacs surrounded the brick patio behind Archie's house in Ivy Farms. Once, open meadows had surrounded the strong-running Ivy Creek, before the property was developed in the early seventies. Now dotted with upper-middle-class homes and manicured grounds, the area had lost all vestiges of its farming heritage.

Aileen Ingram, director of the Jefferson Environmental Council, made a decent salary. She poured what extra money she had into their home and garden. Archie was appreciative of her domestic gifts and he appreciated her. Her fine qualities only exacerbated his guilt.

Sitting on the Brown Jordan lawn chair, smelling the profusion of lilacs, he was startled when she appeared at his side.

"I must have been half-asleep."

"Arch, bail was twenty-five hundred dollars. Blair Bainbridge lent me the money and I don't even know why he offered to help. Your lawyer's bills will be double that. I don't know what's wrong. You won't talk to me. I don't think you talk to anyone. You're unraveling. Resign as county commissioner before it's too late."

"Too late for what?"

"Your political career is over. Get out with as much good grace as you can."

"No."

"You're mad."

"No, I'm not. The worst I've done is lose my temper."

"Smashing Cynthia Cooper in the face was stupid."

He crossed his right foot over his left knee, holding his ankle. "I have one year left of my term. I won't run again. It would cost the county too much money to run an election in an off year."

"The mayor would appoint an interim commissioner."

"You've been scheming behind my back!"

"No. I've been trying to save what I can of your reputation." She twisted her wedding ring, thin gold, around her finger. "But I don't think I can save our marriage. That takes two."

"What's that supposed to mean?"

"I'm not an idiot. I know there's another woman—or women. You don't hang around Tommy Van Allen or Blair Bainbridge without partaking of their castoffs."

"I resent that!" He blushed.

"Because I nailed you or because I insulted you by indicating you're playing with their discards instead of seducing a woman on your own merits?" Steel was in her voice. "Your vanity is touching, under the circumstances."

"I admit I have feet of clay. I don't like myself much but"—he warmed to his subject—"I am trying to salt away money for us. A lot of money. I need one more year. Then I'm off the commission. I won't waste my life in these dull meetings with people picking at everything I say or do. I can apply myself to other pursuits, like making you happy again."

"Better to have money than not but I am not waiting a year for you to get your act together. You've lied to me."

"I have not."

"Omission is a kind of lie."

"What man is going to come home and announce to his wife that he's having an affair? I said I wasn't proud of myself." He dropped his eyes, then raised them. "Did you hire a detective?"

"No. Any detective I could hire around here would know the sheriff. If someone tailed you Rick Shaw would find out in a heartbeat. He's on the county payroll. You're a commissioner. I swallowed my pride and my curiosity."

"I'm sorry, Aileen."

"So am I."

"I can't resign. I can explain it later, but not now. I have to stay on and I have to keep my lines to Richmond open."

"You're a political liability now."

"I'm under a dark cloud, but it's passing. And at the next open meeting at the end of the month I am unveiling a workfare plan that will employ people and create new housing. It's a good plan and won't cost the county much at all. One-cent surcharge on luxury purchases inside the county."

She wondered if he was a blockhead or purposefully opaque. "Intriguing. Archie, I want you out of the house. If you can resolve this affair, clear up your garbage, then we can talk."

"You can't throw me out of my own house."

"I can and I will. Your clothes are packed. Your computer is in the black-and-white box along with your disks. Everything is neatly stacked in the rented U-Haul in the garage, which is attached to your Land Rover. If you aren't out of here by noon I'm calling the sheriff. I figure it will take you that long to pack whatever else you might want."

"And what's the sheriff going to do?" Archie was belligerent.

"Throw you out, because I'm going to accuse you of wife beating. That will be the end of your career. Totally."

He hurried to the garage. She wasn't kidding. There was a loaded U-Haul. He dashed into the kitchen. Aileen was unloading the dishwasher.

"Where am I going to live?"

"Blair Bainbridge said he'd put you up in his extra bedroom. Failing that, there's an apartment for rent on Second Street off High. Seven hundred and fifty dollars a month. The number is on a Post-it on your steering wheel." She closed the dishwasher door. "And I informed your mother."

"Why don't *you* run the world?"

"I could."

33

The *Daily Progress* spread over the table carried the Tommy Van Allen story on the front page. Pewter sat on the paper. The big news was that cocaine was found in his blood.

The post office buzzed. People were in shock but everyone had a theory. No one was quite prepared for the sight of Tommy's widow, Jessica, cruising down Main Street behind the wheel of Tommy's blazing-red Porsche.

Harry and Mrs. Murphy noticed her first. "She could have waited until he was cold in the ground." Realizing what she'd said, she quickly added, "Sorry."

The group crowding into the post office all talked at once. The Reverend Jones was still upset that Tommy's bomber jacket was discovered on his truck seat. Big Mim declared that no one had manners anymore so they shouldn't be shocked at the behavior of Mrs. Van Allen—formerly of Crozet and now hailing from Aiken. It was rumored she had a polo-player lover who had discreetly stayed back in South Carolina. Tally Urquhart sorted her mail. Sarah Vane-Tempest suggested the whole world had gone nuts. Susan Tucker warned people about jumping to conclusions.

When Blair walked in, Big Mim buttonholed him at once.

"What do you think?"

"It's macabre," he replied.

"Not that. What do you think of—" She stopped mid-sentence because she had spotted Archie Ingram driving by, pulling a U-Haul trailer behind his Land Rover. "What in the world?"

Blair swallowed. "Damn. Pardon me, Mrs. Sanburne. I've got to go."

"Blair, your mail," Harry called out.

He shut the door, not hearing her.

"Isn't that the most peculiar thing?" Miranda Hogendobber walked out to the door.

Cynthia Cooper pulled up, as did Ridley Kent, dapper even in an old tweed jacket. He bowed and opened the door for her as Miranda stepped back. Cooper wished Ridley's courtesies presaged genuine interest but she knew they did not.

Everyone said their hellos.

"I knew I'd find the gang here," Cynthia muttered, walking over to her mailbox.

Tucker sat outside the front door. She figured the cats could tell her who said what to whom. She wanted to watch the cars and pick up tidbits of conversation in the parking lot.

"Herb, when's the service?" Mim asked.

"Thursday at ten."

Mrs. Murphy sat next to Pewter on the divider counter, both cats careful to avoid the burgundy stamp pad.

"Why haven't you arrested Archie Ingram?" Sarah pursued Cynthia.

"We did yesterday. He's out on bail today."

The silence was complete.

"For murder?" Mrs. Murphy asked.

All eyes swiveled to the cat, who meowed, then back to Cooper, her left cheek covered with a reddish bruise soon to turn other colors. Cynthia walked over and petted Murphy and Pewter.

"I don't mean for hitting you—I mean for shooting my husband." Sarah's pleasant voice turned shrill.

"Mrs. Vane-Tempest, we don't know that," Cynthia said simply.

Ridley Kent spoke up, his rich baritone filling the room. "We're all worried. How could we not be?" He glanced around the group for affirmation. "We're all here now. Why don't we put our heads together?"

Mim, usually the group organizer, coolly appraised the usurper. "Good idea."

Ridley, appreciating his mistake, deferred to the Queen of Crozet. "With your permission, Mim. You're better at this kind of thing than any of us."

She smiled and stepped forward. "The circumstances of Tommy's death are still unknown, are they not?"

Cynthia nodded. "We know he was shot in the head, just as the paper tells you. It will take a while to establish the time of death because he was perfectly preserved, you see. But he did have coke in his blood."

"I don't care about Tommy. He's gone to his reward. I care about Henry. What if the killer comes back for him?" Sarah's eyes filled.

"Is it possible it was an accident?" Herb suggested, not believing that it was.

"Three shots? No." Ridley folded his arms across his chest.

"Is there a connection between Sir H. Vane-Tempest and Van Allen? Something that one of us might have overlooked?" Harry interjected.

"On the surface, no, but we're digging," Cynthia replied. "These things take time, and I understand your frustration. Be patient."

"Wouldn't it make sense to question the people who sold the guns and uniforms?" Harry thought out loud. "Maybe there's something peculiar. You've tested Archie's Enfield rifle, and other people's rifles,"—she nodded to the assembled—"but what about other suppliers? Whoever shot H. Vane had to come up with the stuff. He had to have contact with these people."

"Along with every other reenactor. But yes, we are chasing them down one by one. I had no idea that Civil War reenactments were this precise."

"Obsessive," Sarah said curtly.

"Do you know of any connection between Tommy Van Allen and your husband, other than social?" Herb asked Sarah.

"No," she lied.

"Doesn't Mrs. Woo make period uniforms?" Harry remembered the seamstress with a small shop behind Rio Road Shopping Center.

"She does everything." Mim nodded. "She can whip up a dress from the 1830s that would fool a museum curator. She made a lot of the uniforms."

"She's on our list. We haven't gotten there yet. Initially we concentrated on the firearms people, hoping we could trace the rifle since we have two bullets, one intact and one flattened, the one that lodged against Sir Vane-Tempest's shoulder blade. The third one is missing."

"Arrest Archie Ingram." Sarah pounded the table, making the cats jump.

"Mrs. Vane-Tempest, you can't imagine the pleasure that would give me, but I can't arrest him without evidence."

"He was behind my husband."

"So was I," Ridley said. "So were Blair, Herb, and half of Crozet."

"You don't care what happens to Henry. You don't like him!" Sarah shouted.

"Ma'am, I abide by the laws of the land and I can't arrest Archie Ingram. Not without compelling evidence."

Herb raised his impressive voice. "What's important is we've got to communicate with one another. If we see anything untoward, call the sheriff or the deputy. Call one another."

"Do you think we're all in danger?" Mim neatened her mail stack. She wasn't frightened as much as she was curious.

"No," Cynthia replied.

"Lucky you." Sarah, furious, stalked out of the post office.

This set everyone off again. Ridley Kent hurried after her.

Tucker listened intently, then came in by the back animal door. *"She's hot."*

The cats jumped down to join her. *"Can't blame her."*

"What did you make of Blair running out like that when he saw Archie?" Pewter asked the dog.

"He folded himself into that car and flew down the road in the direction of home. Makes me wonder."

"Let's go over there tonight after work," Murphy suggested.

"Yes, let's," Pewter chimed in.

One by one the townspeople left. Cynthia, Tally, and Mim lingered.

Miranda made Tally a bracing cup of tea, as she was flagging a bit.

"Not every question has an answer." The old lady sipped her tea, straight.

"I think they do. But we don't always want to hear it." Mim contradicted her aunt.

"Speak for yourself."

"No one wanted to know the answer when Jamie shot Biddy

Minor." Big Mim hated being contradicted, even by Tally—or especially by Tally. "Every place has unsolved crimes because people don't want to know."

"What good would it do to know? Everyone is dead. How they arrived at that state is irrelevant!" Tally snapped.

The cats knew better than to leap on the table with Tally present. They hung out in the canvas mail cart instead, heads peeping over the top. Tucker sat under the table.

"Moonshine," Harry called over her shoulder as she emptied the wastebasket into a plastic garbage bag. "I know that's not the reason but that was the excuse given."

"My brother didn't make any more moonshine than anyone else in Albemarle County in those days," Tally said. "Bad blood."

"Had to be awfully bad if Jamie shot him," Miranda said. "Both such handsome men. I've seen their pictures."

"Never see their like again." Tally stared off in the distance.

"Didn't Jamie have a gambling problem?" Big Mim asked her aunt.

"Mim, my brother had many problems. You name it—gambling, horses, women, wine. Prudence was not his watchword."

"Wasn't Tommy Van Allen's either." Harry, finished with her chore, leaned on the sink behind them.

"Somewhat similar personalities. You'd have thought it would have been Jamie who got shot, not Biddy. Biddy was a sensible man most ways." Tally allowed Miranda to refill her cup.

"Guess we'll never know." Harry walked to the divider and folded up the newspaper. The back section fell on the floor. She picked it up without reading it.

"People do terrible things. They just do," Tally said. "We're animals with a gloss of manners."

"I resent that." Murphy's tail twitched.

Harry opened a jar of Haute Feline, giving each cat a fishy.
"Hey."

She handed Tucker a Milk-Bone.

"You remind me of your great-grandfather, Mary Minor. You have his eyes and you have his curiosity."

"Did you like my great-grandfather?"

"I adored him. Had a schoolgirl crush. Biddy was the handsomest man. Curly black hair and those snapping black eyes. And the biggest smile! He could light a room with that smile. He bet on horses and cards, chickens . . . everyone did. He and Jamie bred fighting cocks together. Often wondered if that wasn't it. But it wasn't moonshine, I'm sure of that."

"Where'd they fight chickens?" Miranda said. "Didn't you have a pit out on the farm? Oh, I barely remember. My momma wouldn't allow me anywhere near."

"A beautiful pit out by the back barn." She pointed to Harry. "Out where you found the airplane. Nothing left of it anymore. It's full of rusted trucks and tractors. All illegal now." She shrugged.

After Mim and Tally and Cynthia left, Harry picked up the paper to throw it into the garbage bag. She glanced at the back page. "Miranda, did you read this?"

"What?"

They bent over the story. A big photo of a golden retriever behind the wheel of a Dodge Ram made them giggle.

Harry read aloud. " 'Maxwell, a golden retriever owned by Stuart Robinson of Springfield, Massachusetts, received a ticket today for driving without a license. Robinson said the dog was in the cab of the truck when he got out at the gas station, leaving the motor running. He doesn't know how but Maxwell drove the truck down the street, finally running into a mailbox.' "

Miranda laughed. "Art Bushey will kidnap that dog and put him behind the wheel of a Ford."

They laughed harder.

Pewter said, *"I could drive a truck if I had to."*

"You could not," Tucker said. *"You don't have the strength to hold the steering wheel."*

"I do so."

"She could." Mrs. Murphy took Pewter's part.

"I'll believe it when I see it."

After work the cats crawled into the parked truck and practiced.

"This is harder than I thought," Pewter confessed.

"Yeah, and we aren't even moving." Murphy laughed until she rolled over.

"Come on, let's go over to Blair's."

34

The cats reached the deep creek separating Harry's land from Blair's before Tucker caught up with them.

Running flat out, she skidded to a stop, her hind end whirling around, leaving a semicircle in the grass. *"Cheaters!"*

"You were asleep."

"I was not. I was resting my eyes."

"Sure." Pewter viewed the steep bank with zero enthusiasm, but vaulted over.

Archie Ingram's U-Haul was parked next to the divine Porsche.

The animals inspected it thoroughly, then Murphy bounded onto the Porsche, leaving delicate paw prints on the hood and roof.

"Babe magnet." She leaned over from the roof and stared inside at the luscious leather.

"He hardly needs that." Tucker sniffed the tires. *"He's been over to Little Mim's. That ridiculous Brittany spaniel of hers has marked it."*

"You can't stand him because he's perfectly groomed."

"Murphy, that's silly." Tucker turned her back on the cat and walked to the house.

"You can't go in there without us." Pewter fell in next to the dog.

"Don't go in," Murphy commanded as she carefully slid off the car.

"Why not?"

"We'll interrupt them."

"They won't pay any attention to us. Blair will open the door, feed us something, and then go back to whatever he was doing." Pewter pulled open his back porch door, which was easy since it was warped.

"The truth comes out." Murphy whapped her paw from the door. *"Listen to me. Don't you find it odd that Archie Ingram has pulled into Blair's driveway with a U-Haul? You and I should climb up in the tree. We can see everything—the windows are open."*

"You climb in the tree. I'm sitting on the kitchen windowsill." Pewter walked to the window and jumped up on the sill.

If there hadn't been a screen in the window she would have vaulted into the kitchen.

"What about me?"

"Tucker, I'll open the door for you a crack. Lie down with your nose in the door. You can see and hear everything that way. If they notice you, act glad to see them and go right in. I'm staying in the tree."

Pewter watched as Blair brewed coffee. His top-of-the-line machine cost more than the industrial Bunn at Market's store. A

pint of cream sat on the counter next to it. Archie was slumped in a chair at the table, his head resting in one hand.

"Come on, Arch, this will start your motor again."

Archie sighed, toying with his cup. "Yeah."

"Will you snap out of it? She didn't shoot you. She isn't running around town telling tales." He handed him the cream. "You're being given a vacation to sort things out."

"Yeah." He drank some coffee.

"Good?"

"Yeah."

"Dazzle me, Arch. Vary your vocabulary. How about 'Yes'?"

The corner of Archie's mouth curved up. "Yes." He drank more coffee.

"If this doesn't enliven you we'll have to look for cocaine," Blair joked.

"People are saying that's why Tommy was killed. That you and Van Allen bring in cocaine in the hubcaps of your Porsches."

"People will say anything."

Archie shrugged. "You use it?"

"I have in the past. I don't now."

"Get you in trouble?"

"No." Blair sat across from him. "I saw it get a lot of other people in trouble and figured I'd quit while I was ahead."

"Aileen wants me to resign my seat on the county commission."

"Not a good idea." Blair drained his cup, rose to pour another.

"H. would shoot me." Archie laughed a dry laugh. "That damned Sarah is screaming all over the county that I shot H. Christ, I wouldn't shoot him. Strangle him, maybe, but not shoot him."

"What went down between you two? One minute you were—"

Archie slapped the table with his open palm, startling Blair and the watching animals. "I got sick of taking his shit. Who was taking all the risks? Me! Whatever I did wasn't enough. He wanted to know more and he wanted it yesterday. Damn, how many times can I run up and down the road to Richmond?"

"Our peer of the realm likes to give orders." Blair checked the time on the old railroad clock on the wall, a duplicate of the one in the post office. It was six-thirty.

"If my involvement comes out, I'm down the tubes."

"Don't be so dramatic," Blair admonished him. "The law is murky in this area. Someone would have to prove that you abused your office for personal gain. Furthermore, the information you passed on to us concerning road development is public knowledge."

"The timetable is not public knowledge."

"Yes, it is."

"The *real* timetable," Archie shot back, in no mood for Blair's rebuke.

"So? It would have to be proved. Archie, for chrissake, you knew what you were getting into. Information is bought and sold every day in every profession. If you're smart enough to get on the inside track, you win." Blair, leaning against his refrigerator, shoved his hands into his back pockets. "We're almost finished with our buying. All that's left is the Catlett property. But even without it, we're in good shape. After that, Arch, it's all over but the shouting."

"It's the shouting I'm worried about."

"Toughen up. Are you hungry?"

"I've lost my appetite."

"I haven't," Pewter called from the windowsill.

"You ditz!" Murphy would have boxed her ears if she could. Pewter had no restraint.

The cat's meow startled the two men.

Blair laughed. "Pewter, you shameless eavesdropper."

Tucker pushed open the door, waltzing in. *"Hi."*

"Wonder if Harry's around?" Archie rose, walking outside to check. He came back in. "No, but I hear her on the tractor."

"That thing is a museum piece." Blair put out cream for Pewter and gave Tucker stale bread he'd been saving for the birds.

Furious, Mrs. Murphy backed down the tree, practically vaulting into the kitchen.

"Idiots!"

"Party pooper." Pewter licked her lips; a drop of cream dribbled from her chin.

The aroma of rich cream overcame Murphy's scruples. She hopped up next to Pewter.

"Full house." Blair scratched the base of Mrs. Murphy's tail.

"Damn cat." Archie, eyes squinting, glared at Murphy.

"She had a big time at the meeting." Blair laughed.

Archie held on to his coffee cup with both hands as though it might fly away. "Do you think Sarah cheats on H.?"

Blair raised an eyebrow. "I wouldn't know."

"Ridley said she was going at it with Tommy." Archie, cunning, did not divulge that Ridley also told him Sarah had slept with Blair.

"Was Ridley drunk or sober?"

"Sober."

"I don't know." He did know, of course, because Tommy had told him about the affair, but Blair had given his word not to repeat it. "Sex gets us all into trouble."

The phone rang. Blair picked it up. "Hello." Then he covered the mouthpiece. "H. Vane."

Archie got up and put his ear to the receiver. Murphy joined them. Archie pushed her away but she was persistent.

"Blair, I'd like to have a meeting with you and Archie tomorrow at three. Can you make it?"

"Yes."

"What about Arch? I know he's with you. He drove past the

post office and people saw you run out. You know how small this town is."

"He'll be there."

Archie grabbed the phone. "I'll be there."

"Did you shoot me?"

"No."

"I didn't think so."

"Where's Sarah? I can't believe she'd let you call me after the stuff she's saying."

"She drove down to the market. The way she drives, that will take two minutes. I figured I'd call while I could."

"How will you get away for a meeting? And where do you want to have it?" Blair asked.

"Your place. I can drive."

"Goody," Murphy told the others. *"H. Vane will be here tomorrow at three for a meeting."*

"We'll be at work." Tucker was disappointed.

"Leave that to me." Murphy strained to hear more.

"If Sarah knows you're going to meet with me she'll bring out the cannon," Archie said.

"She'll do what I tell her. I pay the bills, remember?"

"I remember," Archie replied, a splash of acid in his tone.

35

"Where is that cat?" Harry opened closet doors to make certain she hadn't shut the nosy Mrs. Murphy in one.

The phone rang. Harry figured the caller was Miranda or Susan, early risers like herself. Sometimes Fair called after returning home from an all-night emergency.

It was six o'clock. She'd been up for half an hour.

"Good morning, camper, zip, zip, zip. We sing a song to start the day."

Before Harry could launch into the second obnoxious lyric, Mrs. Hogendobber tersely said, "More violence."

"What?"

"Mrs. Woo's shop burned down. They think it's arson."

"I don't believe it."

"On the news. If you'd ever turn on your television, you'd . . .

Just turn it on. It's the lead story on Channel 29. Her shop burned to a crisp."

"Roger. See you at work." Harry hung up, stretched over the counter, and clicked on the small TV, which she hated with all her heart. Since Fair had given it to her for her birthday this year she couldn't toss it out.

"...high today expected to be seventy-two degrees Fahrenheit, a light breeze from the south, clouds moving in tonight, and a fifty-percent chance of rainfall after midnight. Back to you, Trish." Robert Van Winkle, the weatherman, smiled.

Soberly facing the camera, the young woman said, "Our top story this morning, Expert Tailoring Shop behind Rio Road Shopping Center was burned to the ground last night. Nothing is left except the charred remains. Chief Johnson says..."

The fire chief faced the camera in the tape from the night before. "We are fully investigating this incident. If anyone saw or heard anything out of the ordinary in the area around two o'clock in the morning, please call the fire department." He rattled off the number, which was shown on the screen.

"Do you think it was arson?"

Pure frustration on his face, Ted Johnson spoke directly into the camera. "We are investigating all possibilities." He repeated himself. "If you have any information concerning these events, please call our hotline. It's manned twenty-four hours a day." The number ran again several times at the bottom of the screen.

"Then you have no leads?"

"I have nothing further to say at this point." He turned his back on the camera.

"What in holy hell is going on?" Harry exclaimed. "Mrs. Woo is the sweetest person in the whole county."

Murphy popped out from behind the sofa where she was hiding.

"Mrs. Woo had her shop torched," Pewter yelled out.

"I know. I heard the TV."

"Where have you been?" Harry glared at Mrs. Murphy.

"Hiding. I need to stay on the farm today." She was determined to attend the 3:00 P.M. meeting at Blair Bainbridge's.

"Here." Harry opened another can of cat food.

Pewter sidled over next to Murphy. *"Mariner's Pride."*

"Butt out," Murphy growled.

Harry scooped a big spoonful into Pewter's oatmeal-colored crockery dish.

UPHOLSTERY DESTROYER was painted on Mrs. Murphy's dish, while Tucker's read SUPER DOG.

"This goes back to the reenactment at Oak Ridge." Tucker stated. She sat down while the cats ate and Harry dialed Susan Tucker to discuss the latest news.

"The new guys had to have uniforms made or altered in a hurry. Everybody went to Mrs. Woo. She knew who was in that reenactment," Pewter said.

"Yes, but so do Herb Jones, H. Vane-Tempest, Rick Shaw—each company commander has a list of men. That's what's sticking in my craw. We know!" Mrs. Murphy pushed her food bowl away.

"Mrs. Woo had to know something."

"It could be unrelated, Tucker." Pewter pounced on Murphy's rejected food.

"Don't talk with your mouth full. Humans do that. Vile." Murphy sniffed.

"Miss Manners." Pewter swished her tail once.

"Listen to me. Tucker, you go with Mother. Stick with her no matter what. We've got to stay here today."

"Only one of you needs to go to the meeting."

"Both Pewter and I need to read the map. Really study it." Mrs. Murphy sat still like the famous Egyptian statue of the cat with earrings in its ears.

"Why are you so worried?" Tucker cocked her head.

"Because Harry found the airplane—my fault. And because Harry suggested checking out all the suppliers for Civil War reenac-

tors. Remember? She mentioned gun sales, uniforms. She's eventually going to go one step too far."

"She'd better carry her gun," Pewter sagely advised.

"Let's mention that to her." Mrs. Murphy rubbed against Harry's arm while she was speaking to Susan. "Carry your side arm."

"She's—" Pewter's attention was diverted by the bold blue jay swooping by the kitchen window.

Seeing Pewter, he sailed straight for the window, then turned, feetfirst, wings flapping while he threatened at the window.

"I hate that bird!" Pewter spit.

"Not my fave either. Come on," Murphy said.

He returned for another pass, the bird version of giving the finger. Pewter leapt at the window and smacked it.

"Come on, Pewter." Murphy kicked her with her hind leg.

Pewter slid down off the counter. Leaping wasn't her first recourse. If she could put her front paws on cabinets and reach way down, sliding, then she'd hit the floor with less of a thump. Hitting with all that lard made a big *baboom*.

The three hurried into the bedroom. The bedroom door, usually closed, was open, since Harry was still in her robe.

The .357 was in a hard plastic carrying case.

"Ugh. This thing is heavy." Murphy tried to push it out.

"Let's all three try." Tucker wedged in next to Murphy on the left, pushing over sneakers and old cowboy boots.

Pewter was already on Murphy's right side.

"On three," Murphy called out. "One, two, three."

"Uh." They all grunted but succeeded in moving the gun case halfway out of the closet. She'd trip over it if she wasn't looking and she had to go to the closet for her boots.

"Think she'll get it?" Pewter scratched behind her ear.

"Fleas?"

"No," she angrily replied. "An itch."

"Gray animals have more trouble with fleas." Mrs. Murphy pronounced this as solemnly as a judge.

"You're so full of it."

Pewter swatted Murphy, and the two girls mixed it up. Tucker, no fool, stepped away just as Harry stepped into her bedroom.

"Hey!"

Two angry faces greeted hers.

"She started it."

"I did not," Mrs. Murphy defended herself.

"Don't you dare fight in my bedroom. The last time, you knocked over Mom's crystal stag's head. Luckily it fell on the carpeted part of the floor. I love that stag's head."

She bent over to fetch her boots.

"Take your gun," Pewter said.

Harry pushed the gray box back in, then stopped. She pulled it out and opened it up. The polished chrome barrel shone. She liked revolvers. They felt better in her hand than other types of handguns. Being a country girl, Harry had grown up with guns and rifles. She knew how to use them safely. Guns made no sense in the city, but they made a great deal of sense in the country, especially during rabies season. In theory rabies occurred all year long, but Harry usually noticed an upswing in the spring. It was a horrible disease, a dreadful way for an animal to die, and dangerous for everyone else.

"Take the gun." Tucker panted from nervousness.

Harry plucked out a clear hard plastic packet of bullets. She laid the bullets and gun on the bed, then pulled on her socks, stepped into her jeans, threw on her windowpane shirt, finally yanked on the old boots, and slipped the packet into her shirt pocket. Although the gun was unloaded she checked again just to be sure. Then she carried the gun to the truck and placed it in the glove compartment.

She walked back into the house for her purse and the animals, calling, "Rodeo!"

Tucker bounded through the screen door. The cats followed but then flew into the barn.

"Murphy, come on!" Harry put one hand on the chrome handhold she had installed outside both doors so she could swing up.

"Forget it." Tucker sat on the seat.

Harry dropped back down. She trudged into the barn. The horses walked up to the gate to watch. Harry turned them out first thing each morning.

"Blown her stack," Tomahawk said to Gin Fizz.

"Uh-huh."

Poptart joined them. Human explosions amused them so long as they didn't take place on their backs.

"Let's go!" Harry stomped down the center aisle, not a cat in sight, not even a paw print.

Both cats hid behind a hay bale in the loft. A telltale stalk of hay floated down, whirling in the early sunlight.

"A-ha!" Harry climbed the ladder so fast she could have been a cat.

"Skedaddle." Murphy shot out from her hay bale, streaking toward the back of the loft where the bales were stacked higher.

Pewter flattened as Harry tromped by, not even noticing her. Then the gray cat silently circled, dropping behind an old tack trunk put in the loft with odds and ends of bits, bridles, and old tools.

Harry craned to see around the tall bales. A pair of gleaming eyes stared right back at her.

"Go to work."

"Come on out of there."

"No."

She checked her watch, her father's old Bulova. "Damn."

"Go on."

"I know you're saying ugly things about me."

"No, I'm not." Murphy didn't like Harry's misinterpretation of her meow. *"Just go on."*

Harry checked her watch again. "You'd better be in that house when I come home."

"I will be."

"Me, too," Pewter called out.

Harry put her hands outside the ladder and her feet, too, to slide down.

As she walked toward the truck a fat raindrop splattered on her cheek.

"The weatherman said it wouldn't rain until after midnight."

Tucker, sitting in the driver's seat, said, *"He lied."*

36

The two cats walked over to Simon's nest. He opened an eye, then closed it.

"I know you're awake." Murphy tickled the possum's nose with her tail.

"I'm tired. I was out foraging all night," he grumbled.

"In the feed room." Pewter laughed.

"Go back to sleep. I'm borrowing this map that I stashed here. I'll bring it back."

"Fine." He closed his eyes again.

They carried the map to the opened hayloft door, unfolded it, and studied it.

"It's the watershed, like you said." Pewter sat on the corner.

"Wish I knew what the separate squares meant. Any ideas?"

"No. They're in or adjacent to the watershed."

"Well, let's put this back. There may be a good time to show the humans."

The blue jay streaked past the hayloft, spied the cats, and shrieked, *"Tuna breath!"*

Pewter lunged for the bird but Murphy caught her. *"Don't let him bug you like that. Do you want to fall out of the hayloft?"*

"I will kill that bird if it's the last thing I do."

"Self-control."

Complaining, Pewter put the map in Simon's nest along with his ever-expanding treasures. The latest find was a broken fan belt.

"Mrs. Murphy, let's do nothing today. Nothing at all."

"Good idea."

37

The massive green Range Rover, outfitted for its owner with a hamper basket from Harrods, rolled down Blair Bainbridge's driveway at precisely 2:55 P.M. Mrs. Murphy and Pewter, halfway across Blair's hay field, observed Sir H. at the wheel. He wore a bush hat, which offset his safari jacket nicely.

Sir H. Vane-Tempest never believed in buying a bargain when he could pay full price. He'd bought his attire at Hunting World in Paris. The French soaked him good.

The brief morning rain had subsided, leaving a sparkling sky with impressive cumulus clouds tipping over the mountains.

Pewter loathed mud. She hated the sensation when it curled up between her toes. She'd have to wait until it dried, then pick it out with her teeth. Mrs. Murphy, while not lax in her personal grooming, wasn't as fastidious as Pewter. But then Pewter was a lustrous gunmetal-gray, which showed any soiling, whereas Mrs. Murphy was a brown tiger with black stripes, her mottled coat hiding any imperfections.

Pewter felt that she was a rare color, a more desirable color than the tabby. After all, tabbies were a dime a dozen.

The cats reached the porch door as Sir H. Vane-Tempest stepped out of his Rover. He'd lost weight since the shooting and actually looked better than he had before he'd been drilled with three holes.

He knocked on the screened-porch door.

"Come in, H." Blair walked out to greet him. "Arch is in the living room."

Mrs. Murphy shot through Blair's tall legs. Pewter slid through, too. "You stinkers!" He laughed.

As Blair served drinks, Murphy and Pewter edged to the living-room door. Vane-Tempest noticed them when he entered the house, but he paid little attention. To him cats were dumb animals.

"Arch—" Vane-Tempest nodded.

"H.," Arch replied coolly. "How did you leave Sarah?"

"I told you she'd do as I asked." A wrinkle creased his brow. "Actually, BoomBoom came over to give her some soothing herbs. Don't look at me like that—it's what she called them, soothing herbs."

"She still selling that herb stuff? What's she call it, aroma-therapy?"

"Yes. The girls are going on a shopping spree. BoomBoom will share her latest catharsis. I'll come home. Sarah will forget to be out of sorts but she'll suggest that we both try Lifeline. That's BoomBoom's latest salvation—she's quite predictable." He laughed.

Archie didn't laugh. "I don't think any woman is predictable. Mine threw me out."

"Won't last. Make amends. Buy her a new car or something."

"I don't have that kind of money." Archie sourly turned and noticed Mrs. Murphy seated under the coffee table.

"You will."

"Blair," Archie called out, impatiently.

"I'm coming." He returned with a silver tray bearing two Irish-crystal decanters and three matching glasses. "Sherry, if you're so inclined, or Glenlivet."

Vane-Tempest longingly stared at the scotch, then sighed. "A cup of coffee or even tea. Early for tea, but I'll brave it. Cutting back." He indicated the booze.

"Tea it is. Arch?"

"I'm fine. What is that cat doing here again? Harry's cat." He didn't see Pewter. She had ducked behind a wing chair.

"*I beg your pardon.*" Murphy brazenly strolled into the middle of the room.

"Two days in a row. I guess I rate." Blair loved Harry's cats.

"Get Murphy out of here," Archie grumbled.

"Are you allergic?" Vane-Tempest politely inquired.

"To that damned cat, I am. She made a fool of me at that meeting."

"Hardly needed the cat for that," Vane-Tempest dryly noted.

"I don't trust her. Something uncanny about her." Archie pouted.

Blair scooped up Murphy. "Come on, sweetie. I'll give you a treat, but outside."

Murphy wrinkled her nose. "*You're an asshole, Archie Ingram.*" Then she called to Pewter, "*Hide under the sofa. I'll meet you outside later.*"

Blair put Mrs. Murphy over his shoulder while Pewter squeezed under the large sofa. He intended to poach salmon for supper, so he sliced off a bit, then diced it while the teakettle boiled. He placed a small bowl of the fresh salmon outside for the tiger.

Murphy prowled around the cars. The windows were open. She might as well investigate the interiors.

Once the tea was served, Vane-Tempest got down to business. Since he had called this meeting no one else could start it.

"I'll get straight to the point: Sarah wants to be a partner in Teotan Incorporated."

"Does she know what we're doing?"

"No, Arch, she does not." Vane-Tempest shot him a baleful glance. "But she knows we're purchasing land."

"Did you tell her?" Archie's right eye twitched nervously.

"No. She went through my papers when I was in hospital. Under the circumstances that was normal. I told her the lawyers would handle everything, but that didn't satisfy her. She was terribly worried. Also, she doesn't trust my lawyers."

"Do you?"

"Of course I do. Some of these men have served me for over twenty-five years. Sarah's feeling is that should the worst befall me, they won't work with her, they won't reveal to her the full extent of my holdings."

"She's worried about them stealing from her?" His tone revealed curiosity as well as irritation.

"No. I don't think that's it. She wants to be in charge. The only way she can make intelligent decisions is to have accurate information. I never thought about it until she raised the issue, but I can see her point of view."

"Why can't you teach her about your investments without bringing her into Teotan?" Blair asked sensibly.

"Oh, I can." Vane-Tempest held up his hands. "But she read some of the real-estate transactions. She understands property, of course, so she wants to be part of this. She doesn't know the full significance of our purchases."

"I see." Blair poured himself a glass of sherry. He enjoyed the nutlike flavor.

"I tried to dissuade her."

"What if we refuse her?" Archie crossed his arms over his chest and leaned back in the chair.

"I don't know." He shrugged. "But I do rather think—what's the expression . . . it's distasteful but, ah yes—I think she's better inside the tent pissing out than outside the tent pissing in."

Blair and Archie remained silent for a moment.

"I sense this is unwelcome."

Blair cleared his throat. "A surprise. My concern is not her response to the purpose of our corporation. Sarah can appreciate profit as well as the next man—woman." He stroked his chin. "My concern is, what would be her function? Whatever resources she puts into the corporation would, in effect, be your resources."

"Quite true. She hasn't a penny that doesn't come from me."

"And she'd have a vote. You'd control Teotan." Archie neatly summed up the situation.

"It does rather appear so, but I would never assume that Sarah would always agree with me. If you two present something sensible she might be swayed. I don't know. I mean, there's little potential for disagreement. Our business plan is clear but I understand your concern. It would throw Teotan out of balance."

Archie rose, put his hands behind his back, and paced. "She's bright. She's beautiful. Once Teotan goes public she'd make a hell of a spokesperson. People tend to trust women more than they trust men."

Blair raised an eyebrow. "Exactly what do you mean by 'going public'?"

"Not public-issue stock, obviously. No, I meant when Teotan presents its plan to the county commission. Who better to present it than Sarah? She's perfect."

"I never thought of that." Vane-Tempest smiled.

Blair poured him another cup of tea. "Do *you* want her in the corporation?"

"Quite frankly, at first, I did not. I was offended when she suggested it and put out that she'd read my papers. She had access only to the papers at home, but still. However, once she explained her fears, I considered what I would do in her circumstances: the same thing."

"Having Sarah in Teotan at this late date..." Blair paused. "You would control the corporation after I've pumped in seven hundred and fifty thousand dollars. That's—"

"I understand." And Vane-Tempest did. He was a businessman, after all. "You, Tommy, and I put in equal shares and Archie put in sweat equity. We have—I forget the exact term— right of survivorship, in essence, to Tommy's share. We don't need another partner. And she'll be hell to live with." He wiped his brow. "On the other hand, apart from being a spokesperson, she does have a way about her. Sarah could—how did Ridley put it one day? Could talk a dog off a meat wagon." He smiled. "You people have such colorful expressions."

"You could put her in my place," Archie soberly suggested. "She could cover my tracks."

"Your tracks are well covered, Archie." Vane-Tempest spoke forcefully. "An investigator would have to go through two dummy corporations in Bermuda and there are no papers with your name on them. You're paid in cash."

"Aileen told me my career was over."

"Aileen doesn't have the facts," Vane-Tempest flatly stated.

"What I've done is immoral." A flush covered Archie's angular face.

"Balls!" the Englishman exploded. "Spare me Aileen's refined morality. You've made a sound business decision. You supply us with pertinent information, connect us with the proper people in Richmond, and serve your county. Our plan will save Albemarle millions of dollars." He gestured expansively. "And why shouldn't we be amply rewarded for our foresight?"

"Buck up, Archie." Blair agreed with Vane-Tempest, although he recognized Archie's moral predicament. Still, Archie had known what he was getting into.

Archie mulled this over. Their plan *would* save the county money. "It is a good plan, isn't it?"

"We have Tommy to thank for the first glimmer." Blair missed the fun-loving Tommy. "If he hadn't pushed me into flying lessons I'd have never studied the watershed from the air."

"Nor would we have applied ourselves to underground streams and rivers." Vane-Tempest perked up; the tea was giving him a lift. "If one studies the land mass one can pick out those depressions, those possible water sources. The fact that no one had considered this is evidence of precisely how stupid elected officials are. Present company excluded, of course." He nodded to Arch.

"Some are dumb, others are on the gravy train." Archie's eyes glittered with anger. "No one can tell me that fortunes won't be made with a reservoir, and those fortunes won't necessarily be made here. Outsiders will bid on the job and, oh, how interesting that state process can get. I've watched this bullshit mumbo jumbo for years. All they do is waste money, siphon off a nice piece into their own pockets, and let the taxpayer pay through the nose."

"Right. Which is why our plan of wells to service the northwest corner of the county is brilliant." Blair sat up straight. "The wells we have already dug are moving at eighty-eight gallons of water a minute. That's extraordinary. With the underground water we're tapping we can service Free Union, Boonesville, Earlysville, that whole northwestern corner all the way to the county line. The only expense will be for constructing cisterns or water towers, and that's a hell of a lot cheaper than building a reservoir. The county buys the water from us at an attractive rate. If this works, which I know it will, we can do the same thing for the other sections of the county."

"But we'll have more competition. Other people will copy us and start buying up the land." Archie sat down again. "There's talk about these wells being dug but so far as I know no one has figured out the purpose. But people will buy up land. Just wait."

"I'll attend to that. There's no reason we can't absorb some of these entrepreneurs into an umbrella corporation or create limited partnerships for, say, the southeastern corner of the county. We can worry about that later." On a roll, Vane-Tempest continued. "Your job, Arch, apart from keeping us informed of what's cooking at the statehouse, is to introduce the idea of floating a bond to set up those water towers and cisterns."

"I can't do that until you present your idea to the public."

"Which is where Sarah comes in." Vane-Tempest smiled without warmth.

"Let me think about this. I'm not saying no, I just want to think. Give me a week."

"Fair enough." Vane-Tempest opened his palms, a gesture of appeasement. "Now, another matter. Which one of us killed Tommy Van Allen? We all had something to gain."

Stunned, Archie reacted first. "That's a sick joke!"

As the men wrangled, Mrs. Murphy emerged from the Range Rover. She'd already investigated the 911, loath to leave it because it smelled so good. Being small, the Porsche took no time at all. The Range Rover, however, sucked up almost forty-five minutes of precise sniffing and opening compartments.

Next on the list was the U-Haul.

The U-Haul had an open back like a stall with a Dutch door. It hadn't been unpacked. Looked like Archie couldn't make up his mind what to do.

Once inside, Mrs. Murphy picked her way over the suitcases, one small desk, and a chair. Her eyes were adjusting to the light. She noticed a cardboard box with a picture of handcuffs on the outside, haphazardly tossed into a carton. She pushed the box, and something rattled inside. She tried to open it but it was shut tight.

Claws out, Murphy smashed into the cardboard full-force. With her claws embedded all the way through the cardboard, she easily lifted the lid. A pair of shiny handcuffs, key in the lock, gleamed up at her.

The slapping shut of the porch door alerted her to the approach of a human.

The tiger scrambled over the desk and chair, managing to propel herself out the back. She dropped onto the ground as H. Vane-Tempest reached his car.

Archie cursed on seeing her. "If that damn cat peed on my stuff I'll kill her!"

Pewter scurried out of the house, racing for the old graveyard. *"Vamoose!"*

Mrs. Murphy flew down the farm road to catch her, Archie's curses still ringing in her ears.

38

The old gravestones, worn thin by time, stood out bleakly on the meadow's horizon. The buried were members of Herb Jones's family who had once farmed the land now owned by Blair Bainbridge. As is the custom in Virginia, when land passes hands, family members nonetheless continue to care for the graves of their ancestors.

Once a year Herb righted tombstones, planted flowers, and trimmed the magnificent English boxwood hedge bordering the southwest side. Over time Herb's bad back hurt him more and more. Blair had begun to help tend the graveyard and to learn the history of its inhabitants.

Blair mowed the lawn, pruned trees, and trimmed around the edges of the stones. He performed this service out of respect for Herb, who had a large flock and not much help. The good reverend's natural generosity meant he had but little time for himself and even less money.

Pewter caught her breath on a flat gravestone set on graceful piers. *"You won't believe what I heard!"*

"Well, I found handcuffs."

"You did?"

"In the U-Haul."

"So it is Archie Ingram." Pewter scanned the fresh green shoots in the field.

"How many people carry handcuffs?"

"Cops and cop wanna-bes. Now listen to what those guys were talking about. The map makes sense. The marked-off squares are lands they've bought through a corporation called Teotan. They've tapped underground rivers and streams. They're sinking wells on these properties and the flow is so strong they can sell water to the county. The county will need to put up water towers or build cisterns—which are a lot better-looking. This plan will save the county a mess of money and provide a good water supply for all of the newcomers. So far no other humans have put two and two together although the well drillers know a mess of wells are being dug."

"Hmm, where's the hole?"

"There isn't one. I mean, except for Tommy Van Allen winding up as a frozen TV dinner. He was one of the four partners and, the most extraordinary thing, Sir H. Vane-Tempest said, 'Which one of us killed Tommy Van Allen?' Archie screamed so loud I thought my eardrums would burst. He said H. was sick to even say such a thing. Blair wasn't overfond of H.'s crack either. Sir H. Vane said Sarah wanted to come into the deal in place of Tommy. At first Archie was opposed, then he thought it over and said she might be a good spokesperson for when they go public."

"Blair?"

"He's not sure yet. He's afraid it will give the Vane-Tempests control over Teotan. He's right, too."

Mrs. Murphy, hearing geese, squinted into the sun. She spied the telltale V formation, flying low. The rustling of the birds' wings was growing louder and just as quickly growing faint as the formation passed.

"I wouldn't want to be in Teotan right now."

"Me neither," Pewter agreed. *"One partner hung on a meathook and the other got blasted."*

"The brilliance of their business plan is the money is steady. Millions will come in over the years. If they sold the land or the water outright to the county they'd lose an enormous chunk of their profit to taxes." She shook herself, then squeezed through the iron fence around the graveyard. *"Blair's smarter than I gave him credit for."*

"Smart? He'll be dead soon enough. Archie will control everything."

They walked across the soft earth, crossing over the creek into Harry's hay field. Tomahawk, Poptart, and Gin Fizz, mouths full of clover and timothy, raised their heads, spotted their feline friends, then returned to grazing.

Mrs. Murphy finally spoke. *"Blair isn't our human. He isn't our responsibility, but I like him."*

"I'm not risking my neck for anyone but Harry."

"No one is asking you to, but we need to be alert. I'm inclined to help him up to a point. He's our next-door neighbor."

"That's what worries me: He's next door."

39

When Harry returned from work that evening, Mrs. Murphy was asleep on the sofa and Pewter was dozing by her food bowl.

Tucker burst through the door to share the day's gossip. The cats, at first grumpy, woke up fully and told the corgi of their adventure.

As they were filling Tucker in, Deputy Cooper drove up. She emerged from her squad car, carrying Chinese food.

Harry selected some morsels of chicken for the cats. Cynthia had thoughtfully brought a knuckle bone from Market Shiflett's grocery for Tucker.

"Hear about Little Mim's party?"

Harry shook her head since her mouth was full of chicken-fried rice, so Cynthia continued.

"She's planning an apple-blossom party. Impromptu."

"Ha," Harry replied, knowing that Little Mim's version of *impromptu* meant a small army of workers at the last minute instead of a small army planning months in advance. *Spontaneity* wasn't a word associated with either Mim senior or Mim junior.

"She's renting small tables, setting them out in the apple orchard. She's hired a band. Her mother is lending her the outdoor dance floor. That takes an entire day to put together. Anyway, she's in a state."

"Where'd you hear this?"

"From the horse's mouth. I met her this morning to ask if she took clothing to Mrs. Woo. Turns out she doesn't since Gretchen, Big Mim's utility infielder, also does the mending. That's when she waxed eloquent about the party."

"Bet she doesn't invite me."

"She has to invite you." Cynthia grabbed pork lo mein with her chopsticks.

"No she doesn't."

"Yes she does, because if she doesn't everyone will notice. She cares about appearances as much as her mother."

"Maybe I'll go and maybe I won't."

"You'll go. Since when have you missed a party?"

"When I first separated from Fair."

"Forget about that. Hey, where's he been?"

"Foaling season. From January through May he's delivering the Thoroughbred foals. When we were married I'd sometimes go days without seeing him."

"There are other vets. He could have passed on some of the work."

"No, he really couldn't. People have a lot of money tied up in a mare. First there's the purchase price of the mare herself. If she's a Thoroughbred with good bloodlines and of a good age that could be, in these parts, anywhere from five thousand to thirty thousand dollars. Then there's the stud fee. Again, the price varies widely. So when that baby hits the ground some of the breeders already have fifty thousand dollars invested in it. For the hunter people it's a little different. But still, it's not just money, it's emotion, too. Fair's the best, so everyone wants him."

"There's a lot I don't know about the horse business."

"Incredible business, because it's not just money and it's not just the study of bloodlines, there's a certain something, a sixth sense. That's the hook. Otherwise, everyone could do it. Harder and harder to make money at it, though."

"Everything's that way. Do you think we'll live to see a revolution?" Cynthia offered the rest of the lo mein to Harry, who refused, so she dumped it all on her plate.

"Yeah, but I don't know what kind of revolution. I do know you can't punish people for productivity and expect a society to last long. Right now an American's answer is to work harder but the harder he or she works the more the government takes. Think of all the money we've already put into Social Security from our wages. By the time the whole system collapses will we be too old to fight?"

"Look at you and me. Single women in our thirties."

"Never too old to fight." Cynthia smiled. "Think you'll stay single?"

"Yes."

"I don't. You'll get married in the next few years."

"Nope." Harry shook her head for emphasis. "I have nothing to gain from another husband. I'm not saying I won't have an affair but, really, what can I get from marriage except double the laundry?"

"Cynic."

"Yep."

"If Little Mim doesn't snag Blair Bainbridge, I think she'll have a nervous breakdown." Cynthia opened a brown paper bag filled with brownies. "Dessert."

Harry inhaled over the bag. "Miranda! She didn't tell me she was making brownies."

"I stopped by after work. She happened to be making some for tomorrow. Hot out of the pan."

"God, these are good." Harry bit into one. "This business about Little Mim and Blair is delicate. Blair and I are buddies. Nothing more to it than that, but it drives her bats."

"Yeah, well, his reticence about the situation doesn't help matters."

"He likes you." Mrs. Murphy swallowed the last of her cashew chicken.

"More?" Harry dropped another chicken bit on her plate.

"Hey!"

She dropped one for Pewter, too. Tucker, engrossed in her bone, paid no attention to the Chinese food or the conversation. A joint bone required intense concentration.

"Blair's changed." Harry chose her words carefully since she knew Cynthia, like many women, had a crush on him. "He's distant."

"You know, I thought it was just me—he didn't want to be bothered with me."

"Cynthia, he likes you. It's not you. He's worried about his age. After all, his work is his face. He's getting crow's-feet around his eyes and a few gray hairs around the temples."

"Makes him look even better, I think."

"Me, too, but models have a short shelf life. As he ages he'll wind up in catalogs for tie companies. That's not the same as a spread in *GQ*."

"Never thought of that. It's bad enough when women worry about their looks. It seems somehow"—she groped for the right word—"frivolous when a man does it."

"Yeah. Then again," Harry continued, "I guess the money dries up."

"He's invested wisely, I bet."

"I don't know. He never talks about money. I just see how he spends it." Harry sighed. "I can't imagine buying whatever I want when I want it."

"Me neither," Cynthia agreed. "Course, if he married Little Mim, he'd never have to work another day in his life."

Harry paused. "I don't think he could do that."

"Too moral?"

"Well—he likes beautiful women. Little Mim is nice-looking but she's not a *Vogue* model. Know what I mean?"

"Yep."

"And when the woman has the bucks, the man dances to her tune unless she's a flat-out fool, and Little Mim is not. Whoever has the gold makes the rules."

"Guess he'll never go out with me." Cynthia smiled wanly.

"Cynthia, Blair's nice enough but you need a good old country boy. A man who isn't afraid to get his hands dirty."

"Oh, I don't know."

"Think you'll ever get married?" Harry asked.

"I hope so."

A horn beeping down the driveway broke the moment.

"Whoo-ee," Susan Tucker called.

"Whoo-ee back at you." Harry didn't get up as Susan stuck her head through the kitchen doorway. "Grab a plate. Cynthia's demolished all the pork lo mein, but there's lots of everything else."

Needing no prompting, Susan did just that. "Since you guys are on dessert I'll assume everything else is mine." She smiled.

"Pig out, Suz."

As she shoveled food into her mouth, Susan's bright eyes danced. "You won't believe what happened to me. Mmm, can't talk with my mouth full."

"We'll talk to you. When you've slowed down you can tell us everything."

Susan held up her hand, indicating that was a good idea, and kept eating.

Mrs. Murphy jumped onto the kitchen counter. The sun was setting; a shaft of scarlet spiraled into the sky. Very unusual, just that one vertical column of color. She dropped down on top of the closed plastic garbage can, then to the floor, and walked out the door. Pewter and Tucker ignored her.

Susan recovered enough to talk. "I was on the fifteenth hole at Keswick. I like to play once a week there and once a week at Farmington. Actually, I'd play every day if I could, but that's neither here nor there. Anyway, there I was moving along at a pretty good clip when who should roll by me in her personalized golf cart but Sarah Vane-Tempest. She was by herself, so I asked if she wanted to join me. She said no, she was on her way home. She'd lost track of the time. She wanted to be there when H. Vane got home. Said she was furious with him because he was driving his car and she didn't think he should be doing that. Then she zoomed on by."

"She's overprotective." Harry reached for another brownie.

"Treats us like dirt." Cynthia shrugged. "But then, a lot of people do."

"What have we here?" Susan noticed Mrs. Murphy carrying what looked like folded paper in her mouth.

Pewter stopped eating. *"Won't help."*

Murphy dropped the map at Cynthia Cooper's feet.

She bent over to pick it up, carefully opening it. The name in small block print on the right-hand corner read TOMMY VAN ALLEN.

Her expression motivated both Harry and Susan to rise out of their chairs and lean over her shoulder.

"Good Lord!" Susan exclaimed.

Harry picked up her cat and kissed her cheek. "Where'd you find this, pusskin?"

"In the airplane."

Cynthia traced the outlined blocks with her forefinger. She

quickly folded the map back up and headed for the door. "Not a word of this to anyone. I mean it. Not even Miranda."

Harry followed her out to the car as Susan cleared the table.

Cynthia slid behind the wheel, buckled up, reached over onto the passenger seat, and gave Harry a folder. "I came over so we could read this together, but I don't think it matters too much if you keep it for tonight. I'll pick it up from you at work tomorrow." She started the motor. "Do you have any idea where Mrs. Murphy could have gotten this map?"

"Not one."

Cynthia handed her the file, labeled BARBER C. MINOR, and drove off.

40

"Umph." Pewter bit at her hind claws, trying to pull out the mud caked there.

"Why don't you relax? The stuff will fall out tomorrow," Mrs. Murphy advised.

"I'm not going to bed with mud in my claws."

"Least you're not complaining about how you came by it."

"Wish I'd been with you guys." Tucker lay down with her head between her paws, her expressive eyes turned upward to the cats, each of which sat on an arm of the old wing chair. Harry was intently reading the file on her great-grandfather.

"You're good at what you do," Murphy complimented Tucker.

"Anything big happen in the P.O.?" Pewter yanked out another tiny pellet of mud.

"Reverend Jones said Elocution is on special foods to control her

weight. Harry wrote down the information." Tucker gleefully directed this at Pewter. *"Then BoomBoom and Sarah waltzed in. Major shopping spree but Sarah said that even though she'd spent a lot of H. Vane's money she was still mad at him for driving himself around. She thinks he should go slow and after all, they can afford a chauffeur. Then Big Mim arrived for her mail, told Sarah to shut up and let her husband do whatever he wants, the worst thing she can do is make him feel like an invalid. So Sarah got mad and huffed out to the car. Said she had to play golf. BoomBoom fussed at Mim, said Sarah'd suffered a hideous shock. Mim told Boom to get a life and stop feeding off other people's tragedies. Then Boom huffed out and Harry and Big Mim laughed themselves silly. That was my day."*

"We told you ours."

"What's she so absorbed in?" Tucker rolled over to reveal a sparkling white stomach, a tiny paunch growing ever more noticeable.

Murphy moved to the back of the wing chair and read over Harry's shoulder. *"File. Barber Clark Minor, aka Biddy. Born April 2, 1890. Shot dead, May 30, 1927. Born in Albemarle County. Duke University, B.A. 1911. Law school, University of Virginia. Left before receiving degree. Enlisted in the Army. Saw action in France. Achieved rank of captain. Wounded three times. (Awarded Bronze Star.) Returned to Crozet. Finished law school. Entered practice with firm of Roscoe, Commons. Later Roscoe, Commons, and Minor.*

"'Married Elizabeth Carhart, 1919. Three children. Howard, born 1920. Anne, born 1921. Barber Clark Jr., 1923.

"'No criminal record.

"'Killed by James Urquhart. Mr. Minor's widow did not press charges.'"

Tucker broke into the cat's oration, saying, *"You'd think Mrs. Minor would have brought charges. What else does it say?"*

"'Testimony of witnesses. Sheriff Hogendobber'—must be

George's father or uncle or something." She referred to Mrs. Hogendobber's deceased husband, George. *"Anyway the sheriff questioned three eyewitnesses, the first being Isabelle Urquhart, Mim's mother. She saw Biddy drive up to the Urquhart farm the morning of May 30. She was being driven by her father to market. They had passed the Urquhart driveway and Biddy waved."*

Harry turned the page, absentimindedly reaching up to tickle Mrs. Murphy under her chin.

"Go on," Tucker urged as Pewter also moved to the back of the chair to read over Harry's shoulder.

" 'The second witness was James Urquhart himself, aged nineteen. The boy stated, "Mr. Minor called on me at ten in the morning unexpectedly. One thing led to another. I lost my temper and struck him in the face. He hit me back. I usually carry a side arm. Copperheads. All over this spring. I pulled it out and shot him in the chest. He kept coming at me and I shot him again. He fell down on his knees and then fell over backward. When I reached him he was dead."

" 'The third witness was Thalia Urquhart, aged twenty. "Mr. Minor called on my brother," she stated. "They had words. Jamie went into a rage and shot him. He should have never shot Biddy Minor. He was such a nice man." ' "

Three brown photographs of the body were neatly pasted on the last page—Biddy's stiff, prone body, blood spreading over his white shirt, his eyes open, gazing to heaven. But even in death Biddy Minor was a fabulously handsome man.

"That's it?" Tucker asked.

"Except for the three old photographs." Pewter added, *"You've seen a lot worse."*

Harry closed the folder, crossing her legs under her. "Not much of an investigation for a murder. You'd think Sheriff Hogendobber would have shown more curiosity and you'd think Biddy's wife would have thrown the book at him," she thought out loud as the three animals hung on each word. "Course, the Urquharts were rich. The Minors were not."

"*He admitted to the shooting,*" Pewter mentioned. "*She had an open-and-shut case.*"

"Know what I think?" Harry leaned against the backrest. "A gentleman's agreement. And gentlewoman's. Bet Tally knows the truth."

"*Maybe.*" Mrs. Murphy listened. The owl hooted in the barn. "*What's she blabbing about?*"

"*Who?*"

"*The owl.*" Murphy crawled into Harry's lap before Pewter had the chance to think of it.

"*Calling for a boyfriend.*" Tucker giggled.

"*That's all we need. More owls,*" Murphy grumbled.

"*I'd rather have owls than blue jays.*"

"*Pewter, you're obsessed with that blue jay.*" Harry rubbed Murphy's ears so she purred the last part of the sentence.

"*Apart from the insults, blue jays steal. Anything shiny. They're so greedy.*"

41

Rick Shaw's ashtray overflowed with butts. As he absentmindedly put a live cigarette into the deep tray, the whole mess caught
on fire, a miniature volcano of stale nicotine and discarded ideas.

Coop, laughing, trotted to the water cooler, filled a cup, and
dumped the contents onto the smoldering ashtray. She had prudently carried a paper towel with her to clean up the mess.

"Goddammit!" He stood up, knocking his chair over backward.

"*You* set the place on fire, not me, grouch."

"I didn't mean you. I meant me."

"Boss, you take these cases too personal."

"I liked Tommy. I like Mary Woo. Hell, I can't even find out
who burned her shop down, and she's too upset to remember

anything to do with her records. Or maybe too scared. Yes, I take this *personal*." He parodied Cynthia's incorrect English.

"Come on, let's go home." She pointed to the wall clock.

It was two-thirty in the morning.

"No. Not yet."

"Your wife probably forgets what you look like."

"Right now that's good. I look like a vampire reject. One more time." He pointed to the map on the table. "What do these properties have in common?"

"Nothing that I can tell. They aren't connected. They aren't on major roadways or potential road expansions. They aren't in the path of the beltway that the state threatens to build but never does. Just looks like speculation."

"Land speculation ruined Lighthorse Harry Lee."

"And plenty more." Like Rick, Cynthia knew her history— but most Virginians did.

Before schools became "relevant," teachers led you to the facts. If you didn't study them willingly they simply pounded them into you. One way or the other a Virginian would learn history, multiplication tables, the Queen's English, and manners. Then a child would go home for more drilling by the family about the family, things like: "Aunt Minnie believes that God is a giant orange. Other than that she's harmless, so be respectful."

"God, I'm tired." Rick sighed. His mind was wandering. He sank back in his chair.

"Roger." Cynthia rubbed her eyes.

"Let me review this again. Mrs. Murphy brought you the map. Dropped it right at your feet."

"Yes."

"Harry had never seen the map?"

"No. Boss, I told you exactly how it happened. Mrs. Murphy walked outside and returned with the map. She was quite deliberate about it. She didn't give it to Harry. She gave it to me."

"If we ever go to court, what do we say? A cat gave us evidence?"

"Sure looks that way." Cynthia smiled. She genuinely liked her boss.

"Let's keep this out of the papers. I can't bring myself to drag the pussycat into the glare of publicity. Where did she find it!"

"We've gone over this. Behind the post office? Near the house? In the bomber jacket? The map could have been dropped anywhere. But wherever it was, Mrs. Murphy found it."

"Why would she bother to pick it up?" He threw his hands in the air.

"Because cats love paper."

"Next you'll tell me she reads."

"That one, I wouldn't be surprised." She pulled the coroner's report over to her one more time and thumbed through it. "Guess you have to release this."

"Yes. It confirms he was killed on the night he disappeared. And I guess I'll have to release the fact that he was loaded with cocaine. They'll have a field day with that one."

"You need some sleep before facing reporters again."

"I need a lead. A clear lead." Rick pounded the table.

"We can start visiting these land parcels."

"Yep." He rose, sighed, and clicked off the bright, small desk lamp. "You're right. We both need sleep."

They waved to the graveyard-shift dispatcher.

The cool night air, bearing a hint of moisture, smelled like fresh earth.

"Night, Rick."

"Coop?"

"Yeah?"

"Think H. Vane is in on the drug trade?"

"We don't know if Tommy was dealing. We only know he was full of the stuff."

"That's not what I'm asking."

"H. Vane loves a profit." She turned up her collar.

"H., Tommy, Blair, and Archie took flying lessons. I questioned Ridley, too, but he wasn't in the club for long. Makes sense." He sighed. "Well, let's both get some sleep. Then we can drive over the land marked on the map."

42

Earlier that same night Sarah, in a rage, had slapped her husband in the face. He slapped her back.

"You forget your station, madam." He coldly turned his back on her.

"You can't go out alone. You hire a bodyguard or I will!"

"Don't tell me what I can do. And don't worry that I'll be killed. Whoever tried was a damned poor shot."

"You can be insufferably smug."

"And you can be a bloody nag."

With some effort, she composed herself. "What happened at the meeting today?"

"Surprisingly, Archie thought your joining us was a good idea, once he had time to adjust to it."

"And?"

"Blair wants to consult his lawyer. It would give you and me overwhelming control of the corporation and there is the small matter that you haven't invested your share of capital."

"Ass."

"He's a better businessman than I assumed he would be. I thought he was just a pretty face and an empty head."

"What does he care what I put in or what percent of the stock we own? He'll still make a boatload of money."

"Give him time."

"You'll persuade him?"

"Actually, I think you will."

The telephone rang.

Sarah picked it up. "Hello. What are you doing calling here?"

Archie replied on the other end, "I'd like to speak to your husband."

She handed the phone to H. "Archie."

"Hello, Arch. Forgive Sarah. She still believes you shot me." He listened a bit, chewed his lip, nodding in agreement with Archie's ideas. Finally, he turned to Sarah, who had flopped down on the sofa and pointedly picked up a magazine. "He'd like to speak to you."

"No."

He put his hand over the receiver. "Sarah, I insist. You must get over this absurd notion that Arch tried to kill me."

Furiously, she stood; her magazine slithered to the floor. She took the offered phone. "Yes."

"I'm sure H. filled you in on our meeting today."

"Yes."

"I think it would be beneficial to all parties if we sat down and talked."

"I have nothing to say to you." She glared at H., who made appeasing gestures.

"Well, I have a great deal to say to you." He hurried his words before she could cut him off. "We need to talk, especially if we're going to be in business together."

"That's up to Blair Bainbridge."

"Sarah . . ."

"Hold on." She covered the mouthpiece. "He wants to talk to me privately. Do I have to do this?"

"I think it would be best for all concerned."

She removed her hand from the mouthpiece. "All right."

"How about my office tomorrow afternoon?"

"Make it Friday. I have a dentist's appointment tomorrow."

"Fine. Friday. My office."

She hung up the phone. "Friday. His office. Are you happy now?"

"Yes, the sooner we get this behind us, the better." His jaw tightened, his eyes narrowed, then just as quickly as the tension showed on his face, he erased it.

"It would be helpful if we knew who killed Tommy Van Allen and why." She flopped back down on the sofa, bending over to retrieve her magazine. "You don't think it was Archie?"

Vane-Tempest lowered his bulk next to her. "Much as I trust my instincts in business, I have learned not to jump to conclusions. We both know Archie Ingram doesn't have the guts to kill anyone in cold blood. You're using these events to express other, repressed emotions such as anger at the fact that I have kept you from my business. I've shut you out of a large part of my life. I've treated you like a child."

"Yes, you have." She lowered her eyes, then looked into his eyes again.

"I'm turning over a new leaf. If Blair obstructs your inclusion in Teotan, I'll start another corporation and you can be president." He put his arm around her. "But, I think he'll see the light of reason just as you will when Archie speaks to you. We were all such good friends once. Let's go back to the way things were."

She put her head on his shoulder. "I'd like that."

43

Tommy Van Allen's memorial service on Thursday, intended to be a subdued affair, scandalized Crozet because his widow chose not to attend. It wasn't because she was too shocked to fulfill this last duty to her husband. She just didn't care. She'd already returned to Aiken and she had given Rick Shaw carte blanche to ransack Tommy's records. She also allowed him to impound the Porsche for a week. He promised to send it on to Aiken after it had been searched.

Big Mim hosted a small luncheon after the memorial for Van Allen. Her prize-winning peonies picked that moment to open.

Miranda Hogendobber strolled through Mim's magnificent gardens, which undulated down to the lake. The catamaran, *Mim's Vim*, gently bobbed in the water. The reverend escorted her.

"Young people today have no discipline." Mrs. Hogendobber's hazel eyes were troubled. "Jessica Van Allen should have come to the funeral. God knows she'll inherit all his money."

"Miranda, if people no longer dress as they should it's an outward sign that they've lost all sense of propriety. Dress isn't superficial."

"I quite agree."

"Even Harry, who does have manners, falls down in the dress department."

"Poor dear. She has to be dragged kicking and screaming to shop. Susan and I are considering putting silver duct tape over her mouth on our upcoming foray."

"Not like my dear departed. Her motto was, Shop until you drop." Herb Jones chuckled.

They sat on the wrought-iron bench, two old friends together. "What's become of the world, Herbert?"

"I don't know. Maybe every old person asks that question. But it's a cruder and more vulgar world than the one I knew as a boy. And it's more violent."

"We thought the violence would end with World War II."

"Now we turn it back on ourselves." He drank in the refreshing sight before him. "If nothing else, the gardens are flourishing." He patted Miranda on her gloved hand. "Your tulips this year could have won national awards."

"Do you really think so?"

"You outdid yourself."

A sharp voice interrupted their enjoyment. "You two spooning?"

"I haven't heard that word since grade school." Herb burst out laughing.

Tally Urquhart, moving slowly, but moving, descended upon them. "Just what are you doing down here, off by yourselves? You don't appear to be grieving."

"Are you?" Miranda, usually not at all saucy, had been emboldened by Herb's praise.

"No. I've grieved enough in my life. After a while you learn to say good-bye and be done with it. When your number's up it's up. I should have been dead years ago, but here I am."

"You'll outlive us all." Herb stood up, offering her his seat.

Tally balanced on her silver hound-headed cane, lowering herself next to Miranda. "The sheriff is taking Tommy's and Blair's cars apart."

"Yes, we heard that, too." Miranda shifted her position to face the vinegary lady.

"Won't do a bit of good."

"Why is that?" Herb mildly inquired.

"Because science, machines, fingerprints, oh, it's all very impressive. The *how* fills page upon page. But it's the *why* that matters."

"Ah, yes," Mrs. Hogendobber mused while watching two children paddle a dark green canoe at the far side of the lake.

"Such as, why doesn't Blair Bainbridge call on Marilyn? He doesn't appear to be in love with anyone else. She's certainly the most eligible young lady in the entire county."

"I think Harry is the most eligible young lady." Miranda surprised herself by contradicting Tally.

"She hasn't a sou," Tally grumbled, then half smiled. "But she's a far more interesting soul than my great-niece. Don't tell Mimsy, though." She laughed in earnest.

"We ought to get Harry out of that post office. She's too intelligent for that job."

"Thank you, Herbert," Mrs. Hogendobber said with unaccustomed sarcasm.

"Miranda, your husband was the postmaster. It's something else entirely."

"Oh?"

"She graduated from Smith College in art history." Herb

hoped this would explain his point of view without further insulting the memory of Miranda's husband.

"I graduated from Mary Baldwin," Tally said, "and I never worked a day in my life. Of course, we weren't expected to then."

"You did work," Miranda said.

"Of course I worked. I worked harder than a stevedore but you know what I mean. For money. I think it's better now."

"You do?" Herb pressed.

"Yes. People ought to be able to pursue their talents."

"My point." Herb beamed. "Harry is not pursuing her talents."

"But perhaps she is," Tally said. "She enjoys life. She appreciates the clouds and the peonies and us. She has before her every day at the post office the peerless entertainment of the human comedy."

"I never thought of that."

"Of course not, Herbie, you're thinking of your next sermon." Tally flicked her cane out at him. "Now, what are we going to do about Little Mim and this Bainbridge fellow? She'll perish if she doesn't land him. I tell her she's better off alone but I don't think a young woman like Marilyn believes that."

"Nor do I." Herb folded his hands behind his back.

"Naturally. Men need women. Women don't need men." Tally sounded triumphant.

"Fiddlesticks." He restrained himself from saying *bullshit*.

Harry headed down to join them. "Why is everyone suddenly shutting up?"

"Because we were talking about you," Tally replied.

"Only good things." Miranda smiled.

"That's a relief."

Mim trooped down to the lake a few moments after Harry's arrival. "What are you all doing down here? I need you in the garden. You all are the social spark plugs of Crozet."

The small gathering looked at one another with resignation,

then Miranda piped up. "And what are you doing here, Mim, dear?"

"Came here to get away from all of them."

They laughed together, which lightened the unexpressed tension and worry.

44

The day started quietly enough. It had dawned crimson, then gold. Harry knocked out her chores quickly, then decided to walk to work, given the exceptional beauty of the morning.

Pewter complained long and loud about Harry's decision. Pewter hated being stranded without wheels.

Harry hadn't gone a half mile down the road before a low rumble captured her attention. Blair Bainbridge snaked around the corner, saw her, and braked. He opened the door from the inside.

"Hop in."

"I've got the critters."

"We'll squeeze in."

"I've been dying to ride in this car." Murphy sat in Harry's lap, forcing Tucker and Pewter onto the small backseat.

Blair turned toward the farm.

"I've got to go to work."

"You need the truck. Didn't you listen to the radio this morning?"

"No."

"Big storms are moving up from the south. Fast. You need the truck."

"When they come from the south they're wet. How long before they arrive?"

"The weatherman isn't sure, of course. They always cover their butt. There's a high off the coast that might hold it up for a bit."

"Oh, goody," Murphy sarcastically said.

"Not fair that you're in the front." Tucker stuck her nose between the seats.

"Get over it."

"Selfish." Pewter leaned on Tucker as they turned down the long dirt driveway.

"Are you coming or going?" Harry asked.

"Ever hear the one about the duke who died in the prostitute's arms? The bobby asked what happened and she said, 'He was coming and going.'" Blair scratched his head. "Did I get that right?"

"I don't know, but you're certainly in a good mood."

"I have four hundred horsepower at 5,750 rpm. Of course I'm in a good mood." He pulled up next to Harry's truck. "I'll see you later."

"Come on, gang."

Pewter stubbornly waited to be lifted into the truck. *"I told you to take the truck. Nobody listens to me."*

"Pewter, stop bellyaching." Tucker found an old rawhide chew wedged in the seat just under the unused middle seat belt. Harry turned the key; that old familiar cough-then-shake was followed by the motor turning over.

"See that?" Pewter put her paws on the windshield.

"What?"

"The blue jay is sitting on the lamppost by the back door. Because he sees us pulling out."

"Could be because Mom throws out birdseed there for Simon and the birds."

Miranda was carrying a big tray into Market Shiflett's just as Harry pulled into her parking space in back of the post office.

"Let me help."

"There's a second one on the kitchen table. You fetch that one."

Harry brought the light, flaky biscuits to Market's.

He wiped down the counter, said hello to his former cat, Pewter, and threw scraps to the animals. "H. Vane-Tempest called to tell me there's a reenactors' meeting at his house tomorrow to discuss *safety* measures. I like that." He shook his head cynically.

"Are you going?" Harry asked.

"Well, I bought all that stuff for the Oak Ridge affair, I suppose I ought to get my money's worth."

"You could sell it," Pewter, ever the realist, suggested.

He fed her another small beef scrap. "She's a good mouser."

"Can't catch a bird, though, to save her life." Murphy stood on her hind paws to catch a tossed morsel.

Tucker, too, grabbed a piece of meat from the air. She was very quick.

"Did he ask Archie to the meeting?" Harry inquired.

"I don't know."

The post-office crew hurried over to the frame building as Rob Collier tossed in the canvas sacks from the main office on Seminole Trail, also called Route 29.

"Time to work." Harry started sorting.

The phone rang and Harry picked it up.

Cynthia Cooper was on the line. "Harry, can you come with me this lunch hour?"

"Sure. What are we doing?"

"Tell you when I see you."

She hung up. "Miranda, will you mind Mrs. Murphy, Pewter, and Tucker for lunch? Cynthia asked me to go with her but she won't say why. Official business, I guess."

At twelve Cynthia picked up Harry in the squad car. Harry asked Miranda to cover for her for two hours.

Within fifteen minutes they were at the airport, at the private hangar.

"Are you afraid of small planes?" Cynthia asked.

"No."

"Glad to hear it." Cynthia bent over to fit through the small door, then reached out to pull Harry in. "This is Bob Green. He's a pilot for FedEx. In his off time he still loves to fly."

"Hi." The square-jawed pilot nodded a greeting.

They taxied down the runway, lifted off, and were airborne in minutes. Harry, on the passenger side, looked down on the patchwork quilts of green, beige, and forest. Creeks and rivers glittered. The tops of the buildings at Fashion Square Mall were flat.

"Boy, hope we never get five feet of snow. Bet those roofs wouldn't take the stress load."

"Bet they can." Bob smiled. "Or there will be lawsuits up the wazoo."

Cynthia, hand on the back of Harry's seat, leaned forward between Bob and Harry to hand her Tommy Van Allen's map. "You grew up here. We're flying you over these parcels. Tell me what you know."

Bob flew over the first parcel, a high meadow adjacent to Sugar Hollow.

"Well, that used to belong to Francie Haynes, an old lady who raised Herefords, the horned kind."

"Haynes. The black Haynes?"

"Yeah."

"Anything special about the land?"

"Not that I know of."

As they flew over each parcel, Harry recounted the history as she knew it.

"Bob, can we go up just a little bit, another thousand feet or so, and make a big circle?" Harry requested.

"No problem."

"Coop, look down. Can you see how the land folds together? Can you see the old reservoir at Sugar Hollow?"

"Yes."

"Okay, we're flying over the watershed. See how everything drains, essentially, in one direction? That's where the state and some in the county want to put the new reservoir, between Free Union and Earlysville."

"I can see it."

"Let's go lower over Sugar Hollow."

Bob pushed in the steering wheel and they gently descended.

"Really obvious here." Cynthia strained to look over Harry's head, out the passenger window. "And I can see Francie Haynes's land."

"Now, wouldn't it make more sense to use Sugar Hollow?" Harry said.

"From up here, yes."

"Hey, you two, it's just us and the birds up here," said Bob. "The landowners are bigger and richer at the other place. This is poor people. Used to be poor people, I mean. Other folks are moving in now."

"And let's not forget the contractors." Cynthia shielded her eyes as they turned toward the sun. "You know when the state writes the specs for these massive projects they write them so only a few firms can truly compete. What a crock of shit it all is. Sorry, Bob, I don't know you well enough to swear."

"Fine by me."

"So, there's nothing special about these parcels of land?"

"Some are in the watershed and some aren't. But no, there's nothing that I know of that marks these off. Why?" Harry asked.

"Can't tell you that part."

"Since we're up here, can we fly over Tally Urquhart's?"

"Good idea." Cynthia raised her voice because the propeller noise drowned out normal conversation. "The back side of Little Yellow Mountain. I guess Mint Springs is a better coordinate."

"Okay."

Within a few moments they were cruising over the verdant acres, the miles of crisp white fencing that constituted the Urquhart place. The old hay barn and stone buildings came into view.

"Bob, see that barn down there? How hard would it be to land there? I'm not asking you to land," she hastened to add as he descended, "but how hard would it be?" Cynthia asked.

"Not much of a strip. A little like threading the needle between the two hills. Take a good pilot."

"How about in rain and fog?" Harry asked.

"Take a pilot with brass balls and a sure touch."

45

The map lay open on Rick's desk. A pile of financial statements, account books, and manila legal-sized folders were stacked on the floor next to his chair.

"The watershed . . ." He rubbed his chin.

"It's easy to see from the air," Cynthia said, then added, "I checked the weather the night Tommy Van Allen died, or we think he died."

"You doubt the word of our coroner?"

"When someone's frozen like a fish stick, yes."

He slapped her on the back. "That's what I like—an independent thinker."

"A storm came in quickly and hung on a long time that night. And then today, we just got up in time. As we landed the clouds rolled down like a dirty gray rug."

"Was there any similarity of the properties from the air?"

"Not really."

"Hmm, Harry pepper you with questions?"

"No, she was pretty good."

He sat in his chair. "Close the door." He paused until she returned.

"I've read every comma, semicolon, period, and smudge on Van Allen's account books. He's clean." He swiveled around. "What you're telling me is that Tommy was a damn good pilot."

"Yes. After seeing the small landing strip, he was better than good," Cynthia affirmed.

"H. Vane and Tommy already knew how to fly," Rick said out loud, even though he was really talking to himself. He had found no double set of account books. He wondered if perhaps the other fellows kept accounts. He was pursuing the drug angle. "And they were all part of the Oak Ridge reenactment. At least, Tommy would have been." She nodded and he continued, "Coop, we're in the ballpark, at least, but we still aren't on base."

"Could it be that these land parcels represent just what they appear to: investments against future growth? I guess I should say, for future growth?"

"With the exception of two here bordering Sugar Hollow they're generally in this quadrant." He took out a color copy he'd made of the map and put a ruler on the copy. With a red pencil he drew lines, and a pattern began to form. "See." He slapped his thigh. "I'd like to think this map represents drug customers, but when we checked the farms—before they were purchased—no. There's no way old Ephraim Chiles would buy drugs. I want to make this fit and I can't. And I'm not sure why some of these parcels have new wells on them and others don't."

"I see that there are two roughly parallel lines."

"I see it and I don't know what it means. Think about what you saw in the air. Was there anything to suggest this type of alignment, something obvious like a low hill chain or a creek?"

"No. Besides, if there were a creek it would be on the map. We'd have noticed it before."

He dropped his forehead onto his hand. "When's the next commission meeting?"

"Next Tuesday."

"Okay. We'll tack this on the wall without saying anything. Has to be on the wall before anyone gets to the meeting. We might at least flush out Arch." He smiled. "I think we're getting a little closer to our killer."

"Good idea," she said with little enthusiasm.

He fired his pencil at her end-over-end. "What?"

"Nothing."

"Out with it."

"I've inherited your gut feelings. This doesn't feel right. Maybe half-right. Not complete."

"Yeah, I feel that way, but the look on your face..."

"He's going to strike again. I just know it."

"Something off-the-wall like Mrs. Woo's store. I think that was definitely part of this. The fire destroyed her files—all those reenactor files."

"Well, she does bring us back to the reenactors. You're right."

"In a funny way serial sex killers are easier to figure than this one," Rick mused.

"But there may have been sex. Don't forget the empty rubber packet in Tommy Van Allen's trench coat."

"Nah. I don't buy it."

Coop sat on the edge of the desk. "I hope I'm wrong, but this is far from over. H. Vane better hire a bodyguard." As she said that a loud clap of thunder startled them both and the heavens opened.

46

When the natural light struck Sarah Vane-Tempest's hair, the blond highlights glimmered like beaten gold. Her fingernails, perfectly manicured, complemented long, graceful hands. Not only was she a beautiful woman, she had perfected young those wiles so useful in reducing men to putty.

Since most men are taller than most women, the first trick she mastered—by fourth grade—was the disarming habit of lowering her eyes, then raising them as though only the object of her glance could call forth such a promising response. She modulated her voice so it was never loud, never strident, a bit soft so that he would have to strain to listen.

The more sophisticated snares, such as inflecting each sentence subtly so that it seemed a question only he with his superior wisdom could answer, she acquired by eighteen.

Lowering her shoulder a tad in his direction also sparked fire in the male of the species. The fact that these were calculated postures, as studied as an actress's blocking on the stage, never occurred to men. Even a man as highly intelligent as Sir H. Vane-Tempest devolved into a quivering hormonal puddle in Sarah's presence.

Her demeanor changed completely in the company of women. Her voice, straightforward, was not harsh but certainly not music to female ears. She looked her friends straight in the eye. She said what was on her mind. She never once dropped a shoulder or slightly turned her body to make a woman appear larger.

Her women friends giggled when she'd switch gears the second a man entered the room. Her profound falsity, although a subject of amusement to most and disgust to a few, did not make women mistrust her. Each woman, even Harry, knew why women performed as Sarah performed. It was an unequal world.

Beauty, short-lived, was a weapon to secure food, clothing, shelter, and status. Few women could stand alone and live well. They had to be attached to a breadwinner.

Although bright, Sarah was essentially afraid of the world, afraid she couldn't move in it on her own at the level she desired. She wasn't wrong. Few women have as much power or money as Sir H. Vane-Tempest.

She'd hit the jackpot. It was simple, really. She studied where the rich played. Since it was easier to get to Florida from Connecticut than to some other places like Aspen, she showed up, fresh out of school, then carefully edged closer and closer to the good parties.

She had also been careful not to do something stupid, like sleep with the wrong man or take a job in a clothing shop. That would diminish her mystery. She'd attend polo matches at Royal Palm Polo Club in Boca Raton. She'd watch, alone, hoping to catch a man's eye or that of an older woman needing an extra for a party. Usually men were needed as extras, but occasionally a young woman was needed to pep up an older visiting gentleman.

One Sunday at Wellington, west of Palm Beach, she happened to be standing near a string of ponies. The groom, called away by another groom needing help to catch a runaway, left a pile of polo mallets on the ground. They were organized by length and whippiness of shaft.

Sir H. Vane-Tempest thundered up. "Manuel, 51 green."

Sarah reached into the pile of 51's, having the presence of mind to grab the one with green tape carefully placed where the shaft meets the head. H. Vane noticed immediately that Manuel had been changed by the good fairy into one of the most beautiful young women he had ever beheld.

The rest, as they say, was history. An expensive divorce from Wife Number One—who was, after all, showing wear and tear—soon followed.

That was seven years ago. Soon, very soon, actually, Sarah would be showing wear and tear herself.

Had someone whispered in her ear, as she walked down the aisle, that the price of marriage would be high, she would never have believed it. Lured by surface glamor, she didn't recognize the price was herself. She had lost herself. Once she realized it, she panicked. Such women seek solace in religion, booze, drugs, charitable work, children, and of course, other men.

When she walked through Archie Ingram's office door on Friday she closed the door behind her. She had made a point of never going to his office or calling him at the office.

"Did you shoot H.?"

"No."

"Why not?"

"I'd never do such a thing. You know that."

"Wish you would," she said in jest, throwing her purse on the desk.

He seized her by the waist, drawing her to him.

She didn't resist. She kissed him, starting with the cleft in his chin. "I haven't seen you for two long weeks."

Once the frantic mingling of body fluids was over, they had time to review their predicament. A black cloud seemed to follow Archie wherever he moved. As for her, glad though she was that Archie was out of his house, Sarah would never leave her husband. That was what she told Archie. Poor Archie cried.

"It's not that bad." She ran her fingers through his hair.

"It's not that good."

"H. is a vindictive, combative man. He'd stop at nothing to ruin you. Discretion is the better part of valor." She sighed. "He's old. He's not as vigilant as he once was where I'm concerned, probably because his testosterone level has dropped. All will be well."

Blinking back the tears, Archie moaned, "I hate that bastard. I hate him because he's smarter than I am and I hate him because he has you."

"He has me in body only, not in soul," she quietly said.

"Maybe." He frowned, for as much as he loved her, he was learning to distrust her. "But he knew I'd fall for the Teotan plan. The money is good. More money than I could dream of in my job. It wasn't until that meeting in Crozet, the one where Harry's cat jumped on the table, that I realized I had the most to lose. H., Blair, and Tommy risk far less than I do but their profit is higher!"

She smoothed her hair. "Arch, you'll clear a good two million and possibly more. I can't see what you have to lose."

"My reputation. My political career. I'll never be governor."

"Ah." She hadn't realized his ambition reached that high. "Other men have overcome scandal."

"This is Virginia," he snapped.

"Well, yes, there is that. Do you really think you could vault from the county commission to Richmond?"

"Yes. I know I could get elected to the state House of Representatives, for starters. One step at a time. But I blew it." He wiped his brow.

"Maybe you can buy your way in."

"Doesn't work quite that way. Money helps, but—" He smiled sadly. "You haven't lived here long enough, Sarah. Disgrace stains through generations. The reverse of that is all those silly, empty snobs living off the grand deeds of their ancestors. No one forgets anything here."

"That's absurd." She didn't believe it.

"Sarah, you're married to a powerful man. People would like you even if you weren't, but don't let surface acceptance fool you."

"I can ride, garden, and shoot with the best of Virginia's country squires," she boasted.

"So you can." He gave up trying to teach her the real rules of the road. Archie was on the verge of giving up everything, he felt so profoundly miserable.

"Sure you didn't try to kill him? It was a brilliant plan." She changed the subject, a jocular tone to her voice.

"No. I didn't." He pulled himself together, retied his silk rep tie, brushed off his pants. "Sarah, you could have any man you want to play with. Why me?"

"You have imagination. Most men don't."

He nuzzled her neck. "What kind of imagination? Did Tommy Van Allen have imagination?"

She drew back. "About what?"

"About you."

"Arch, don't be absurd."

"I know you had an affair with him."

She waited, sighed, lowered her eyes, then raised them. "I haven't always used the best judgment. He made me—reckless. Of course, I had no idea he was snorting coke. I was as shocked as the next person when the *Daily Progress* reprinted the autopsy results. I never saw any sign of it, but then I'm not sure I know the signs." She sounded convincing.

"Is that why you went up in the airplane with him late at night with a storm coming? To be reckless?" Archie played his wild card, for he didn't really know if she'd been with Tommy or not. He thought maybe he could trip her up.

"No."

"What'd you do, give H. sleeping pills?"

"I never flew with Tommy. Are you suggesting I killed him?"

"Maybe he got in the way."

"Of what?" She pulled back, viewing him with dispassion.

"Your well-ordered life. Maybe he threatened to tell your husband. He might have thought H. would throw you out. He'd have you all to himself."

"Tommy was reckless but he wasn't in love with me. We occupied each other's thoughts for a while—that's all."

"You occupied more than thoughts. Tell me, were you sleeping with him when you were sleeping with me?"

"No," she lied.

"Well—that's something, at least."

"Arch, sometimes if you let things alone they work out better. My husband is an old man."

"And strong as an ox. He'll live to be as old as Tally Urquhart. I wish I did have the guts to kill him, but I need him."

"For what?"

"Teotan. In for a penny, in for a pound. I can't back out now no matter what I'm sacrificing."

"Blair's smart enough to run the corporation. Don't underestimate him. And thank you for speaking up for me at the meeting." She kissed him on each cheek and then the mouth. "I was only kidding about killing H. I could understand if you had shot him. But I'm glad you didn't."

"You certainly ran your mouth about it all over town."

"Arch, what better way to cover *our tracks*?"

"Your tracks." He coolly appraised her but couldn't protect himself from her beauty.

"My tracks?"

"Sarah, you could have shot H. You weren't at the reenactment."

"I ran back for H.'s canteen."

"Prove it." He smiled softly.

"You're as bad as Rick Shaw." She laughed it off. "I found witnesses who saw me running back to the tent."

"You could easily have ducked behind the hunter barn or into the woods or even into your Range Rover if you ran fast enough and managed to creep out of the woods. You could have fallen in at the back of the marching line."

"In that gown and hoop? Are you insane?"

"No. You'd change, of course."

He breathed in sharply. "I did not shoot H. Vane. Tommy was already dead. If he had a motive it died with him. You are the only other person with a motive."

"What about Blair? If H. were out of the way, you and he could run Teotan. Two people would control the new water supply."

"It's an interesting theory. But if Blair and I were in cahoots I'd know about it and—" He held up his hands in question.

Unperturbed, she said, "You could have killed Tommy. And tried to kill H. And intend to kill Blair. All threads would be in your hands."

"Thank you for giving me credit for being that intelligent. But I didn't do it. I wouldn't do it and the rock-bottom reality is, I'm not smart enough to pull off a crime like that and not get caught. You, on the other hand, are."

"I didn't kill Tommy Van Allen."

"Not even to cover your tracks, as you say?"

"Well, then you'd be next on my list, wouldn't you?"

"I think I would. Am I?"

"No, darling. I adore you. Can't you tell? Can't you tell when you hold me?"

He sighed. "Sarah, I don't know what I know anymore."

"You're angry at me because I won't leave H. right now. I can't, Archie. We'd have a year of passion if we were lucky, but sooner or later the outside world would tear us apart. My way takes longer but the result is more solid. H. is an *old* man."

"Old and healthy. Old and frighteningly intelligent."

"But still old." She put her forefinger to his lips to silence him, then kissed her forefinger and his lips simultaneously.

"Arch, let me keep saying dreadful things about you. It's the only hope we've got. It's the only cover we've got. You know the truth and you know every chance I get, I'll come to you." She ran her finger across his lips, then along the side of his jaw.

He kissed her hard. "That fool doesn't know what he has in you."

"As long as you know."

"It's funny. I would have thought you'd have the affair with Blair, not me. He's a lot better-looking than I am." He still didn't know whether to believe what Ridley Kent had told him.

"Chemistry." She brushed her hair with a few practiced flips of her wrist. "Besides, Little Mim would die. We've got to leave her something."

"Ridley told me you had a brief fling with Blair." Archie couldn't stand it any longer. He had to hear her response.

Coolly, too coolly, Sarah said, "Ridley's put out that I refused his advances. Why listen to him? I can't believe you listen to him."

"I don't know." His voice wavered.

"Well, I do." She kissed him again and then left for home.

47

The underside of a Porsche is sealed. It's as though the bottom is covered by a series of interconnecting skid plates. The mechanic, in white overalls, removed one gray underbody rectangle. Rick peered up as the mechanic shone a light.

"Couldn't hardly hide a tin of snuff up there," the mechanic said.

"Would you like us to remove each panel?" Mike Gage, the owner of Pegasus Motor Cars, politely asked the sheriff.

"No, bring her down. Body panels make more sense."

"Of course."

Blair Bainbridge watched. "You aren't going to cut the upholstery, are you?" He had cooperated with the search, not demanding a warrant, but he wasn't sure what he'd do if it went that far.

"I don't know." Rick ducked his head in the car once it re-turned to earth. "There's no place to hide anything in those backseats. Hardly big enough for a cat."

"Somebody could remove the padding in the front seats and replace it with cocaine. I think you'd be able to feel it, though." Mike pressed down on the seat.

"Harvey, bring up the new Targa. Let him feel those seats so he has a point of comparison."

Within minutes a lush polar-silver Targa gutturally an-nounced its arrival. Rick opened the door. The smell of a new car made him giddy with possibilities. Dutifully, he pressed on the seats, then pressed again on the seats of Blair's Turbo.

Blair, clasping and unclasping his hands, murmured, "Look, I don't know why you're doing this. You know I'm not involved in drugs."

"Your buddy Tommy Van Allen sure was. Cocaine packed be-hind his hubcaps—come on, it must have given you a charge to fake out everybody."

"No," Blair flatly replied.

"Fast money. Fast cars."

"I don't sell drugs."

Mike Gage interrupted the increasingly tense exchange. "Let me show you something, Rick. See these air inlets on the front end?"

"Yes." Rick pressed at the small sloops in the metal.

"Could stash small amounts of coke in them but it would lead to undesirable consequences later." Mike had briefed Rick earlier on the basics of an air-cooled engine.

Blair spoke up. "If I was going to deal drugs I'd find a better place than that."

Rick ignored him as Mike continued to point out small areas where drugs could be secreted.

Blair shifted his weight from foot to foot. "You know I'm in-nocent."

"You knew about Tommy." Rick pushed him.

"Tommy didn't run drugs. It's crazy. A Porsche attracts attention. It'd be crazy to carry drugs in a Porsche."

"If you don't calm down I'll haul you out of here," Rick threatened.

"Listen, I'm allowing you to search my car out of courtesy. You don't have a warrant. I have nothing to hide, so give me some credit."

Mike looked away as Rick scowled.

Rick hesitated a moment, then spoke to Mike. "Don't rip up the leather. Keep searching, though. Mr. Bainbridge and I will be right over there in the squad car if you need me."

"Okay." Mike nodded.

Blair slid into the squad car passenger seat, slamming the door.

Rick wedged himself behind the wheel. "Would you like to tell me the purpose of Teotan? I have Tommy's maps. I know you've sunk wells. Let's have it."

Blair waited a moment, then cleared his throat. "Teotan's purpose is to supply potable water to the northwest quadrant of the county while saving the taxpayers considerable expense. We were intending to present our plan at the next water commission meeting—next week, in fact."

"No new reservoir?"

Blair shrugged. "My hope would be no. Teotan could save this county a fortune in construction costs. There's enough water running underground to fill the need. Millions of gallons."

Rick dropped his head a moment, then raised it. "Sir H. Vane-Tempest said the same thing."

"It *is* a good plan."

"Have you approached Archie Ingram? He opposes any idea of Vane-Tempest's." Rick didn't know of Archie's involvement, for Vane-Tempest, true to his word, had said nothing.

"Archie's a weathervane." Blair sounded noncommittal. "He's not the same man since his wife kicked him out."

"Wasn't impressed with the original." Rick sighed a long sigh. "I'm a paid public servant. I'm not supposed to harbor political opinions."

Blair shrugged. "Won't go past me."

"Changing the subject, what are you going to do if the county rejects your concept? I suppose you have supporting figures?" Rick asked.

"We do. Much of the seven hundred and fifty thousand dollars apiece we each put up to create Teotan went for a feasibility study. We used a firm out of Atlanta. Washington, New York, and Richmond were too close in the respect that too many people from Albemarle work in those cities or have strong ties there. What we are about to offer this county is economical and sound."

"What if they reject it?"

"If we can get it on the ballot as a referendum, I think we'll prevail despite the vested interests in a reservoir and dam. But, should we fail, we'll sell the water as bottled water."

"You'll have to tap-dance again on that one. Environmental studies and water purity." He shook his head. "We're so over-regulated. It's lunacy. Generations of Virginians drank water right out of the ground. They had more common sense. They didn't build on drained marshland or put their homes where runoff would leak into the well. People sit in front of computers and know nothing of the real world."

"We're prepared for the bottled-water battle. We've retained Fernley, Stubbs, and Marshall in Richmond."

"Then you are prepared." He tapped on the steering wheel. "One member of your company is dead. No suspects. One member was shot. Many suspects, including Mr. Ingram. Is there something about Teotan I ought to know?"

"No."

Rick warned Blair, "If I were you, I'd look over my shoulder. I don't think it's coincidence but I still couldn't say why, exactly."

"Unfortunately, I don't know why either. If our plan works it means a steady flow of profits for as long as we live. If one partner dies, his share is equally divided among the survivors. On the surface of it that would be motivation for murder."

"Blair, have you seen this ticket before?" Rick reached into his breast pocket and pulled out a white locker ticket, Number 349.

Blair examined the Greyhound locker ticket. "No."

"We found this in Tommy's car."

"I assume you went to the locker?"

"Yes. We found accounting books for cocaine deals."

"That's too easy. I know Tommy Van Allen wouldn't sell drugs. No way!"

Rick paused. "Actually, Blair, I think you're right but I have nothing else to go on."

"I don't sell drugs. Tommy didn't sell drugs. I don't know what this is all about or why, but it's not true."

"Is there something about Teotan I don't know? That might have a bearing on this case? Blair, for God's sake, a man has been killed and another wounded. *Tell* me."

Blair inhaled sharply. "Archie is a hidden partner."

"Arch doesn't have that kind of money. You other boys put up big bucks."

"He put in work." Blair left it at that.

Rick whistled. "He's using public office for private gain. And H. Vane-Tempest risks nothing. Archie risks everything."

"H. Vane risks the start-up money."

"That's nothing to him and you know it." Rick turned to face Blair. "This changes everything."

"I don't know. I mean, yes, it compromises Archie politically but people's attention span is two minutes. Look at all the crap politicians get away with, Rick."

"I'd say Archie Ingram has more motivation to kill than any of you. He'd be sitting atop a fountain of profits."

"It doesn't seem possible."

"A lot of things don't seem possible but they happen anyway. Blair, I'd be careful if I were you."

48

Mrs. Murphy slept on the divider counter, her tail hanging down. Pewter, on her back on the small table, meowed in her sleep. Tucker snored under the big canvas mail cart.

Harry felt like sleeping herself. A low-pressure system was moving in.

The front door swung open as her head nodded. She blinked. Dr. Larry Johnson waved.

"I'm ready for a nap, too, Harry. Where's Miranda?"

"Next door. She's planning a menu for Market. He wants to sell complete meals. It's a good idea."

"And Miranda will cook them?"

"Part of them. She works hard enough as it is, and the garden comes first."

Larry eyed Murphy's tail. "Tempting."

Harry stood on her tiptoes, leaning over the counter. "She's proud of that tail."

Mrs. Hogendobber entered through the back door. "Hello," she sang out.

Mrs. Murphy opened one eye. *"Keep your voices down."*

Sarah and Sir H. Vane-Tempest came in with Herb right behind them.

"Glad I ran into you," Larry said. He walked back outside and returned, handing Vane-Tempest his Confederate tunic top. "Is this genuine homespun?"

Vane-Tempest examined the material in his hands.

Miranda flipped up the countertop and walked out to the front. "I can tell you."

"I wish everyone would shut up." Mrs. Murphy opened both eyes.

Tucker lifted her head. *"They complain when I bark."*

Miranda held the material in her hands, rubbing it between forefinger and thumb. "Machine."

"How can you tell?" Vane-Tempest held the other sleeve.

"If this were spun on a home loom there'd be more slubs and the color dye wouldn't be as even. Also, the boys in gray were often called butternut. Dyes weren't colorfast, you see, and dyeing could be an expensive process. A foot soldier would wear homespun for so long that the color would go from a sort of light brown to a gray-white over time."

Harry joined them. "Bet that stuff itches to high heaven."

"Your shirt would be spun from cotton. Probably better cotton than what you buy today," Miranda noted. "So you wouldn't feel your tunic so much."

Harry took the jacket from Vane-Tempest, slipping it on.

Herb laughed. "You'll drown in that."

Mrs. Murphy sat bolt upright. She soared from the counter into the mail bin. *"Wake up."*

"Dammit!" Pewter, surprised and therefore scared, spit at Murphy.

Tally and Big Mim dropped by to pick up their mail.

"You know what I don't understand?" Tally put one hand on her hip. "If a man dresses as a woman, everybody laughs. They'll pay money to see him. If a woman dresses as a man, stone silence."

By now Pewter had hopped onto the divider counter and Murphy roused Tucker, who padded out front to the people.

"Want to try?" Harry handed the tunic to Big Mim.

"I'll leave that to the boys."

"That's it!" Murphy crowed.

Pewter blinked, thought, then she got it. So did Tucker.

That same afternoon, as Sarah fed the domestic ducks on her pond, private investigator Tareq Said discreetly delivered county-commission tapes to her husband, as he did once a week. He'd bugged Archie's office along with the others. Vane-Tempest did not fully trust Arch and wanted to make certain he was getting his money's worth. Also, this way he could keep tabs on the other commissioners. Surprisingly, Arch had not disappointed him. He really was working for Teotan's acceptance. He was all business.

However, this week's tape proved substantially different. Tareq handed over the legal-sized folder, then swiftly left.

49

The brass buttons rolled around in the palm of her hand with a dull *clank*. Harry pushed them with her forefinger.

"First Virginia." Blair leaned against his 110 HP John Deere tractor—new, of course, like everything on his farm. "They're genuine. Cost five hundred and fifty dollars."

"Wonder who wore them and if he survived the war?"

Blair shrugged. "I don't know."

The warm sun skidded over Mrs. Murphy's coat; she glistened as she lounged on the hood of the 911 Turbo. Neither human had yet noticed her chosen place to display her glories.

Pewter prowled around Blair's equipment shed with Tucker. She was on a blue-jay kick. Determined to find and bait the raucous bird wherever she could, she had sharpened her claws on the side of the shed. Pewter could perform surgery with those claws.

"Looks like you're throwing yourself whole hog into reenacting," Harry said.

"I kind of thought it was silly at first. But I felt something at Oak Ridge, and, Harry, that wasn't even a true reenactment. We weren't on sacred ground, if you will. I want to go to the Seven Days, Sharpsburg." He looked sober at the word; Sharpsburg was the scene of the worst carnage in that bloodiest of wars. "I can't explain what I felt, just—just that I have to do this."

"Have you ever noticed that all the reenactors are white?"

"The combatants were mostly white."

"I'll feel a little better about this when someone resurrects the 54th Massachusetts." Harry cited the all-black regiment renowned for its courage.

"Harry, I'm sure someone is already doing that. Really, I don't think this is a racist program." His warm hazel eyes flickered.

"Maybe you're right." She sighed. "Maybe it's me. Maybe I don't like being reminded of a war of supreme foolishness, a foolishness that soaked this state in blood. So many battles have been fought here in Virginia since the Revolutionary War. All that blood has soaked into our soil. Makes me sick, kinda. I think I fail to see the romance of it."

"Maybe it's a guy thing." He smiled.

"Guess so." She paused, then swung up into the cab of the elegant, expensive, coveted John Deere. "Blair, I've been thinking. A guy thing?" she said, louder than she intended. "What if Sarah was in uniform? What if she shot H. Vane?"

"*What?*"

The animals stopped in the shed. Mrs. Murphy, on the Porsche, pricked her ears.

"I know it sounds crazy but today in the post office when I tried on the jacket, it occurred to me—she could have worn the trousers under her hoop skirt, stepped out of it.... Of course, she'd have to run back like mad, get out of the uniform, stash it, and get back into her dress—but it's not impossible. Heavy smoke covered everything. You couldn't see the hand in front of your face sometimes. And it was pandemonium. Who would notice one person sneaking off? And besides, nobody noticed H. had been shot for quite a while. She'd have had time."

He blinked. "I don't know. Never thought of it."

"Mrs. Woo made lots of the uniforms—too many to remember. But she probably kept receipts, if not records. So what happens? Her store gets burned down."

Blair wondered if Sarah was capable of murder. "Harry, that's pretty extreme."

"But why? Everyone just jumped to the conclusion that it was Archie Ingram."

Slowly, his deep baritone low, Blair said, "Well, I don't know. It's possible. But why kill him? She'll eventually inherit his estate anyway, most of it."

"He's a tough bird and a demanding one. She's in the prime of life. Servicing H. Vane, you'll forgive the expression, may be losing some of its luster."

His face reddened. Mrs. Murphy carefully slid off the Porsche hood. She walked over to the tractor as Pewter and Tucker joined her. Harry stepped down from the cockpit.

"Nice, huh?"

"Beautiful. If I had to pick between your Porsche and your John Deere it would be one of the hardest decisions of my life." She laughed, leaning against the giant rear wheel. "I think I'd better talk to Coop."

"Don't do that," he said too rapidly.

"Why not?"

"Because you can't ruin someone's name like that."

"She's not ruining her name," Mrs. Murphy said. *"She's only conveying an idea. Coop has tact."*

"Hadn't thought of that."

"Mother, you're not ruining her name. And you're right!" Pewter meowed.

Harry picked up the cat, putting her on her shoulder. "Hush."

"Put me down." She wiggled.

"Pewter, stay put. You'll get her mind distracted. Humans can't focus for very long. That's why they can't catch mice."

Pewter glared at Mrs. Murphy but settled down on Harry's shoulder.

Tucker lifted her nose in the air. *"Blair's body temperature is rising. He's upset."*

"The other flaw in your theory is that if Sarah shot at H. Vane, then who killed Tommy Van Allen?" Blair said.

"There's no proof that the two murders are connected. We've all been assuming. They could be unrelated."

"They're related. We just don't know how." Tucker was resolute on this point.

Blair blushed. "Yeah."

"What's the matter?"

"Took her a while," Pewter dryly commented.

"Oh." He clasped his hands behind his back. "Nothing. Say, would you like to borrow my tractor? You could disc your fields in one-third the time." He pointed to a disc, its round metal spheres tilted slightly inward toward a center line.

Murphy noted, *"That's a quick change of subject."*

Harry eyed the huge implement, which would make short work of her chores. Good farmer that she was, she disced first before plowing. She disced the fields for hay, too. They didn't need plowing but she was a great believer in working the soil thoroughly before planting. If the hay was already established she'd merely thatch and aerate every few years. She loved farming, desperately wishing she could make a good living from it. But she just squeaked by.

"This is brand-new."

"Hell, you know how to use this equipment better than I do."

"Tell you what." Harry would feel better if she could make a trade. "I'll show you how to prepare that cornfield you want to put in down on your bottomland. Then I'll borrow this baby." She patted the field-green side of the square, powerful tractor.

"Deal." He stuck out his hand then withdrew it. "Sorry. Forgot my manners."

"Oh, Blair, I don't care. I think that stuff's outmoded." She referred to the fact that a man wasn't supposed to extend his hand to a lady, but wait for her to extend hers first.

"Big Mim would kill me." He grinned.

Harry noticed Archie's U-Haul. "Is he ever leaving?"

"Today, in fact."

"Bet you're relieved."

"Archie is curiously stubborn."

"What a nice way to put it." Harry smiled as she headed for her truck. "Where's he going?"

"Tally Urquhart's."

"What?"

"She'll let him live in one of her outbuildings if he'll restore it. He said he needs a positive project."

"I'm nervous." The tiger walked over to Harry's truck. *"We've got to get her to call Coop."*

It was too late for that.

50

Sir H. Vane-Tempest noticed the peculiar waxiness of the magnolias—grandifloras—he'd planted along his southern drive. The long shadows of late afternoon heightened the colors and the sense of melancholy at the day's passing.

A troop of gardeners worked behind the house.

Usually the garden delighted him. Vane-Tempest was not a man to delight in people, since he viewed all relationships as a power struggle, a struggle he must win in order to feel important. He saw people in terms of a vertical scale. Perhaps the Windsor family ranked above him, certain Rothschilds and Von Thyssens, but he believed he sat very near the pinnacle. Usually that fact thrilled him.

Since reading Tareq's transcription he'd been unthrilled, indeed, deeply miserable.

"The days are drained into time's cup and I've drunk it dry," he whispered to himself, turning on his heel to go inside.

He stopped, turned around, and looked again at the gardens. He noticed Sarah walking among the workers. Her beauty soared beyond explanation, like the beauty of creamy peonies. It just was.

He turned once more and walked into the house. He strolled down the long parquet-floor hallway, barely noticing the Monet. He strode into Sarah's room, opened her closet, clicked on the lights, and closed the door behind him.

Row upon row of cashmere sweaters in plastic see-through boxes attested to her acquisitiveness as well as to her insight into the fact that she was valuable only as long as she was beautiful.

He headed for the long rows of canvas garment bags. He unzipped them one by one. Sumptuous evening gowns of emerald, sapphire, ruby, silver, white, and gold spilled over the sides of the opened bags. He could picture his wife in each of these extravagantly expensive confections.

He reached into the bottom of each garment bag, swished around with his hand, then moved to the next one. The last bag tucked in the cedar-lined closet swayed slightly.

He opened it. The zipper clicked as the tab moved down. Her shimmering peach gown fluttered. He reached down. Nothing.

The door opened. "H., what are you doing?"

"Where is it?"

"What?" She noticed the shine on his brow, the gleam in his eye.

"Your uniform."

"What uniform?"

"Don't play games with me. You dressed up and shot me. Archie doesn't have the guts."

"I did no such thing."

"Liar!" He lunged toward her but the closet was huge.

She slammed the door, locked it, and cut off the lights. She took her unregistered snub-nosed .38 out of the nightstand by her bed and threw it into her purse. Then she ran like hell for her car.

51

Harry was just turning into her driveway when Sarah flew past her without waving, her car a blur.

She stopped at her mailbox, watching as Sarah turned into Blair's driveway a quarter of a mile down the road.

"I wonder—" she said out loud, then shook her head. "Nah."

Sarah roared up to the house, parked her car next to the Porsche, and ran to the door.

"Archie! Archie!"

Archie, who'd just come back from dragging the U-Haul to Tally's, was surprised to see Sarah burst through the doorway, even more surprised when she flung herself into his arms.

"I think I'll go to my office." Blair, who'd been helping Archie, put his papers in a box, then walked upstairs.

Sarah waited until she heard the door close. "He's going to kill me."

"H.?"

"Archie, I've got to get out of here. Help me!"

"Why does he want to kill you?"

"Because I tried to kill him."

"What!"

"It *was* me at Oak Ridge. You were right. I dressed as a soldier, just as you said. Those damned old rifles—it's a wonder anybody hit the broad side of a barn during that war."

Archie held her at arm's length. "Sarah, you really shot H. Vane?"

"I'm only sorry I missed killing him."

"He knows?" Archie was amazed.

"He thinks he knows. I caught him in my closet going through my garment bags—looking for the uniform, damn his eyes. Well, he won't find it. I'm not stupid. I burned the thing."

"So he has no proof?"

"No, but what does that matter? He's in a rage. He'll kill me if he finds me and he's so rich he'll get off. People like him always do."

"Why did you want to kill him?" Archie coolly asked.

"Because I couldn't stand his fat body one more minute. Because I hate him. I hate the sight of him. You've never been a servant, Archie, you wouldn't understand."

"You were a very well-paid one."

Sensing his withdrawal, she said, "I couldn't tell you. You would have tried to stop me. As long as he's alive I can't be with you. And why should I go to the poorhouse? I've worked for that money. If he caught us together my divorce would be an open-and-shut case. Shut the door. Bang."

"I see."

"Archie, help me!" She threw her arms around him.

"Where is he now?"

"Locked in my closet. He'll eventually break the door down. His shoulder still hurts but he's strong. You've got to hide me until I can figure something out."

"Jesus, Sarah, didn't your mother tell you, Look before you leap?"

"If I'd done that I'd never have fallen in love with you."

"I wish I believed that." He sighed. Beautiful women acquired men like dogs acquire fleas. All they had to do was walk through a room.

"Did you shoot Tommy? Tell me the truth this time."

"No. I loved Tommy once." She looked him square in the eye. "He had magic. It didn't last long but I was so miserable with H. Archie, can't you understand?"

"I—"

"He'll kill me!"

"All right. All right." He stroked her hair.

Try as he might, he couldn't stop loving her. He kissed her. "Everything will be all right." He walked to the foot of the stairs. "Blair."

The door opened. "Yes."

"I'm taking Sarah to the airport."

Blair clomped halfway down the stairs. "Everything okay?"

"No," Sarah tearfully confessed. "Blair, I can explain everything later. I just have to get out of here."

Archie hustled her into his Land Rover. Blair watched them start down the driveway. If he'd watched longer he would have seen that Archie turned right out of his driveway, not left toward the airport.

52

Pewter wedged herself underneath the camellia bush. She felt certain the blue jay would perch there and since she'd squeezed herself in and was still, he wouldn't notice.

Hunting was best in the morning or late afternoon. No animal likes to go to bed on an empty stomach. She knew she could grab the blue jay. She'd even gone to the trouble of scattering about bread crusts, which she fished out of the garbage when Harry's back was turned.

Pewter dreamed of ways to dispatch the bird, her favorite being a straight vertical leap, grasping the offender between her mighty paws, pulling him to the ground, and staring him in the eye before breaking his neck.

"She who laughs last laughs best!" she told herself, revving her motor.

She was ready!

Pop.

Mrs. Murphy, sitting on the haywagon next to the barn, out of Pewter's way, heard it, too. She looked out toward Harry, who'd been inspired by the vision of that new John Deere to get up on Johnny Pop and overseed the front acres. Harry rolled along, the small seeder attached to the back of the tractor.

"Pewter."

Pewter wouldn't answer.

Tucker, half-asleep under the haywagon, did. *"What?"*

"Hear that?"

"Yes."

"That wasn't Johnny Pop." Mrs. Murphy was worried.

The old tractor would *pop, pop, pop* along but this *pop* was crisp.

Pop!

"Pewter, get out from under there. We've got to get to Blair's."

Pewter backed farther underneath the camellia bush. *She'll do anything to spoil this. She* doesn't *think I can kill the blue jay. She thinks she's the Great Striped Hunter. I'll show her,* she thought to herself.

Mrs. Murphy peeled off the haywagon, covering eight feet in the launch without even pushing hard. Tucker scrambled out.

Pewter noticed the two racing across the fields toward Blair's house. Torn, she grumbled, then slowly extricated herself from her perfect hiding place.

"Fatso!" The blue jay, who'd been perched on the weathervane on top of the barn, screamed as he swooped over Pewter's head.

She leapt up, twisting in the air, but missed. *"You're toast,"* she threatened but hurried after Mrs. Murphy and Tucker. The jay dive-bombed her part of the way, shrieking with delight.

Mrs. Murphy didn't turn to look for Pewter or wait.

Pewter switched on the afterburners, her ears swept back, her whiskers flat against her face, her tail level to the ground. She veered right toward the creek, then dropped down onto the bank, ran alongside, found a shallow place, and ran through the water. No time to fool around and find another path. She reached Mrs. Murphy and Tucker as they crossed over by the old graveyard on the hill. The three animals flew down to Blair's house.

"*Too late,*" Mrs. Murphy said.

Blair sat in his car, the door open. Blood ran down his forehead, marring the leather seat. He was slumped over to the right, his long torso behind the gearshift, his head on the passenger seat. The motor was running. He appeared to have been shot.

Tucker licked his hand but Blair didn't move.

Sarah Vane-Tempest's car was parked in front of the barn. Archie Ingram's car was gone.

Mrs. Murphy jumped into his lap. Pewter followed by gingerly stepping onto the floor on the driver's side. The car was in neutral. Blair's left foot was on the clutch, his right had turned up sideways.

"*Where's he hit?*" Tucker stood on her hind legs.

"*I don't know.*"

"*His legs are okay.*" Pewter sniffed for blood. "*What about his head?*"

Mrs. Murphy put her nose to Blair's nose. She sniffed his lips, put a paw on his lower lip, and pulled it down. "*Gums are white.*"

"*But is he hit in the head?*"

"*There's a lot of blood, but I can only see the left side of his face.*"

"*Put your nose to the seat. See if you smell blood or powder,*" Tucker advised.

Murphy carefully laid the side of her face on the seat, her eye level with Blair's closed one. "*Blood's oozing on the seat. Must be the right side of his head,*" she said, cool in a crisis. "*Pewter, sit in his lap and lean on the horn. I'll keep licking him.*"

Pewter, both paws on the horn, put her weight into it. The horn sounded.

"Who's going to hear it?" Tucker sat down. *"Archie's not here. Mom's on her tractor."*

"He's in a bad way." Murphy kept licking Blair's face. *"We've got to do something fast."*

"Let's think." Pewter, over with Murphy now, put her paw on Blair's wrist. His pulse was erratic.

"We could run back to Harry," Pewter said.

"She's on the tractor. Can't hear us. She might not notice us. We've got to convince her to come over here." Murphy checked the gearshift on the floor. *"Tucker, are you thinking what I'm thinking?"*

"It's his only chance," the dog solemnly said.

"I wish somebody would tell me!" an upset gray kitty exploded.

"We're going to drive this sucker," Murphy resolutely stated.

"You're out of your mind!"

"Pewter, go home then," Murphy sharply told her. *"Tucker, give him a shove."*

Tucker nudged Blair with her front paws and her head. He slowly slumped over just a bit more.

"Pewter, are you in or out of this car?"

"I'm in. What do you want me to do?"

"We've got to get the car in first gear."

"His foot is on the clutch," Pewter said.

"Okay, Tucker, can you fit in down there?"

"Yes."

"Sit on his foot while Pewter and I push the gearshift into first. Then slowly move his foot off the clutch and we'll steer."

"Won't work. We'll stall out," Tucker panted. *"The trick is, I have to get his foot off the clutch and mine on the gas pedal. Luckily his foot isn't on the gas pedal."*

"We have to get this right on the first try." Murphy crawled over

into Blair's lap while Pewter sat in the passenger seat, patting his face with her paw.

The idea was for Murphy to push the shift stick from the top while Pewter pulled from the bottom.

"Ready?" Murphy tersely asked.

"Yes," the other two replied.

The cats moved the gearshift into first. That part was easy. The next part was hard because if they stalled out they'd have to turn the key and feed gas at the same time. They didn't think they could do that.

"Tucker, it's better if we shoot ahead than stall out," Murphy advised.

Pewter had joined her in the driver's seat. She stood on her hind legs, staring out the window. Murphy sat in Blair's lap, her paws on the bottom of the steering wheel.

"God, I hope this car is as responsive as all those ads say it is." Murphy sent up a little prayer to the Great Cat in the sky for Blair. *"Let's go."*

Tucker pushed off Blair's foot as she pushed down on the gas pedal with her right paw. The car lurched forward and sputtered.

"More gas."

Tucker, both feet free now, pressed on the accelerator.

The car smoothly accelerated at amazing speed.

"Keep on the road! Not so much gas!"

"Help me," Murphy called out.

Pewter, claws unleashed, sank them into the leather steering wheel. She struggled to keep the car on the gravel driveway. Even a small motion turned the wheels. *"Tucker, let up a little,"* Pewter screamed.

"I'm trying." Tucker took her full weight off the flat pedal. *"We've got it now. We got it."*

"What are we going to do when we get to the paved road?" Pewter shivered with fear.

"Pray that no car is coming our way because if we stop we won't get started again."

Pewter, eyes huge, chin quivering, steered for all she was worth. By God, she might be afraid but she wasn't a coward.

They reached the end of Blair's long driveway. A truck was past them on the right. With all their might the two cats turned the wheel to the left. The car door still hung wide open.

"Not too much! Not too much!" Pewter directed.

"More?" Tucker couldn't see a thing. This was truly an act of blind faith.

"No, keep it right like it is, Tucker. You're doing great. Okay, okay, here's our driveway. Another left. Not too much, it's curvy." Murphy kept her voice calm.

"Slow, slow. Oh no—there's another car!" Pewter's fur stood on end.

"He sees us. He's not going to hit us without messing himself up."

The car swerved around them, horn honking.

"Asshole!" Murphy spat. *"Yeah, okay, now keep your eyes on the road, Pewts. We'll make it."* The car dropped down a bit on the dirt road; the stones had moved to the sides, as they always do. It's a waste of money putting stone on a driveway, but who can afford macadam?

"I see Mom!" Pewter almost wept with relief.

"Tucker, keep it steady. We have to roll past her line of vision. Okay, okay, she sees us. Pewter, hit the horn."

Pewter laid on that horn for all she was worth.

"Off?"

"Yeah."

Tucker lifted her weight off the gas pedal. The car shuddered to a stop. Harry stopped the tractor and hit the ground running. She tore over her newly seeded field.

"Oh my God," was all she could say when she reached the stalled-out Turbo. She put it in neutral, started it, then picked up the activated car phone and dialed 911.

"Crozet Emergency—" Diana Robb didn't get to finish her sentence.

"Diana. Harry. Blair's in my driveway. He's been shot. There's blood everywhere. For God's sake, hurry!"

She dropped the phone. She was shaking so hard that Tucker, now on the ground, licked her hands. Then she remembered to turn off the motor. She no longer needed the power for the telephone. Harry felt Blair's pulse, which was surprisingly strong. Fearful of moving him, she ran around to the passenger side of the car and opened the door. The two cats got out of the car and looked up at her blankly.

Within minutes they heard the siren. The rescue squad halted behind the Porsche. Diana reached Blair first.

"Call the E.R. Let's get him out of here."

"Is he going to make it?"

"I don't know." Diana held his head. "Help me lift him upright from the passenger side. We'll slide him out on the driver's side." She turned to Harry. "How did he ever make it over here?"

"If I told you, you wouldn't believe me."

The animals watched, tears in their eyes, their ears drooping.

As Harry and Diana lifted out the injured man, Joe Farham, Diana's assistant, rolled out the gurney from the back of the ambulance.

The three humans gently placed Blair on the gurney.

Joe took Blair's pulse as Diana, still stabilizing his head, examined the wound.

"I can't find an entry point." She stared at the bloody right side of Blair's head.

Blair moaned.

"Dear God, what can I do to help him!" Harry, in tears, cried.

"Take a couple of deep breaths. We'll get him to the E.R. as fast as we can. You wait for Rick to get here. I'll call for him on my way to the hospital. Oh, Harry, don't touch the car. Okay?"

"Okay." Harry wiped her eyes.

Joe had shut the ambulance doors and hopped into the driver's seat as Diana jumped in next to Blair, closing the doors behind her. They hit the siren and flew down the gravel road as Harry tried to collect herself.

"Please let Blair live," Tucker whimpered.

"I don't believe what I saw." Harry cried anew, reaching down to stroke her animals. "You guys are heroes."

"We couldn't let him die. He has a fighting chance," Murphy solemnly said.

Harry sat down on the grass to wait for Sheriff Shaw.

53

A crowd of people kept vigil in the hospital hallway: Harry, Miranda, Big Mim, Little Mim, Herb Jones, BoomBoom, Susan and Ned, Market Shiflett, Jim Sanburne, and Dr. Larry Johnson. Finally, Larry's young partner, Hayden McIntire, emerged from the operating room.

Everyone stood up.

"He'll live."

A collective sigh of relief passed through the group and tears withheld from fear suddenly flowed in gratitude.

"Dr. Chan's closing him up now, but he'll definitely make it."

Larry rushed down immediately once he heard the news. Hayden took him to look at the X rays.

"There's swelling in the area of damage. The brain is fine. Luckily the bullet didn't shatter his skull. It made a deep crease."

Hayden pointed to the X ray. "Right here is where the bullet grazed. Like a crease in a piece of paper that tears just a bit."

"Thank God." Larry closed his eyes for a second.

"It's very hard to say what his prognosis is until the swelling goes down. He should be fine. He's young, strong, healthy, but this is the last place you want swelling. Time and rehab will tell."

Later Larry walked with Hayden to see Blair in post-op.

"Any ideas about what happened?" he asked.

"Yes. Given the position of the wound, I think he'd turned away from his attacker."

"He didn't anticipate being shot?" Larry rubbed his forehead with the palm of his hand.

"No. He turned his back."

"Any other signs of struggle on the body?" Larry gazed at the tall man, seemingly asleep except for all the tubes running into him.

"No. Not a mark."

54

When Blair regained consciousness Rick and Cynthia were there waiting for him.

Hayden gave them five minutes only, because Blair's condition was still critical.

"Did you see who shot you?" Rick quietly leaned over Blair's bed.

Blair didn't answer because he could barely focus. He had the world's worst headache.

"Archie?" Rick whispered to the wounded man.

"No." Blair whispered, then lost consciousness again.

55

The high sun shone over central Virginia. Each leaf, a bride in spring green, smiled at the radiant afternoon light. The trumpet vines opened their orange flowers. Bumblebees appeared in squadrons. Honeybees, decimated by a fatal mite, buzzed but in reduced numbers.

Harry, dazed that her friend had been shot, worked hard but her mind kept returning to yesterday's sight of the cats driving the car with Tucker down in the well. She knew that any animal recognizes injury and pain in any other animal. What was remarkable was that they brought the bleeding man to her. They drove him right in front of her.

Each time she envisioned Murphy and Pewter, both with their paws on the steering wheel, she'd get the shakes.

Living close to nature, Harry was better connected to reality

than many people. Now she had to face the depth of her ignorance. She had credited her animal friends with human traits.
She'd insulted them. By masking their true natures with human
characteristics, she missed what was unique about each species. It
was entirely possible that Mrs. Murphy and Pewter, along with
Tucker, operated at another level of intelligence than she did. It
was also possible that theirs was higher but not measurable by
human standards.

Harry was being humbled by life in its myriad forms.

56

In the west an inferno illuminated the sky, the spring sun setting in a scarlet blaze. The sky, as though put to the torch, exploded in scarlet and gold.

Cynthia noticed the drama of it as she checked her service revolver. Rick, his mouth a straight line, carefully coasted down the road toward Tally Urquhart's haybarn, where Tommy Van Allen's plane was stowed.

He'd stopped at Miss Tally's to inquire if she'd seen Archie. She said he was renting a room in her house while he fixed up an old farmworker's stone house down the farm road.

When Cynthia inquired as to how they'd get along, Tally curtly replied, "I need somebody to fight with."

Rick ordered her to stay in her house. She said she had seen Archie's white Land Rover go back there a while ago. She'd heard another car not ten minutes ago but she didn't get to the window in time to see it. However, she was sure it was another car going in, not one coming out.

Rick was no sooner out her front door than Tally phoned Mim.

"Boss, should we wait for backup?"

"No time. God, I hate these kinds of things." Like all police officers, Rick knew domestic violence to be the most irrational of situations. Armed robbery was easy compared to this.

After speeding down the old farm road toward the haybarn, Rick cut the motor at a curve out of sight from the barn door. Both cops got out, drew their guns, and slowly walked toward the old barn, which they could not yet see. Before they rounded the curve they heard a curse, two shots, and a scream. They ran but with practiced caution.

As the two officers approached the barn doors they saw Sir H. Vane-Tempest bent over Archie Ingram. Sarah was clinging to her husband.

"Freeze!" Rick commanded.

Vane-Tempest spun around, a .357 in his right hand.

"Drop your weapon," Rick ordered, and Vane-Tempest threw the gun on the ground.

Rick kept his gun on the Englishman while Cynthia ran over to Archie. She pressed her index finger into his neck.

"Gone."

"He tried to kill me after abducting my wife," Vane-Tempest said calmly.

Sarah, sobbing, stood between her husband and her lover.

"Have you anything to say?" Cynthia stood up, facing Sarah.

"Sarah, you have the legal right to remain silent," Vane-Tempest forcefully said. "This has been a dreadful situation. You take a deep breath. You're safe now."

"Am I?" She put her face in her hands.

"Put your hands behind your back, sir."

"Rick, I killed him in self-defense. You're making a mistake."

"That may be true, but for right now, the handcuffs go on." Rick snapped the steel bracelets on quickly.

"Don't handcuff him. He had no choice." Sarah wiped her eyes. "Archie abducted me from our home after locking H. in my closet."

"Why would he do that?" Rick put his gun in its holster.

"Because I was having an affair with him. He wanted us to ride off into the sunset together." She didn't realize the irony of her words as the gorgeous sunset deepened.

"You knew about this?" Cynthia directed this to the hand-cuffed Sir H. Vane-Tempest.

"I did. Yes."

"Oh, H., I'm sorry. I'm so sorry. I never thought he'd try to kill you." She walked over to her husband and threw her arms around his neck.

"I'm an old man. You're a young and beautiful woman. Maybe one of the most beautiful women on the face of the earth," he whispered.

Another squad car pulled up along with the Crozet Rescue Squad. Diana Robb had had a busy day.

Rick motioned to his officers to go slow, then he put his hand under Vane-Tempest's elbow. "Let's go down to HQ."

"May I phone my lawyer?"

"When we get there."

"Do I have to wear these?"

"Until we get to the station, you do. Come on, before the goddamned television crews get out here." That made the old man pick up his feet.

Sarah slid into the backseat next to her husband. She never looked backward at Archie, sprawled on the ground, her snub-nosed .38 in his right hand.

57

Mim watched with her aunt as the last of the police cars drove out.

"Shall we go down there?" Mim asked.

"Not in the dark. Let's go in the morning." Tally watched the flickering red-and-blue lights. "Mimsy, stay here tonight, please."

"Of course."

58

News of Archie's death spread like a prairie fire.

Susan Tucker burst through the kitchen door to tell Harry, who'd already heard it via telephone from Mrs. Hogendobber, who'd heard it from Mim, who'd heard it from Rick Shaw.

"I can't believe Archie would kidnap Sarah." Harry lay at one end of the sofa while Susan stretched out on the other end. The cats joined them, stretched across the back. Tucker curled up on the wing chair nearby.

"Well, he did," Susan matter-of-factly stated.

"Bull," Pewter said.

"Sex does short-circuit people's brains," Tucker agreed with Susan. *"But why would Archie shoot Blair?"*

"Her car was parked at Blair's when we found him," Mrs. Murphy said.

"Well, why would she go to Blair's?" Pewter stretched her hind leg straight out for grooming.

"Pewter, do that later. I hate that licking sound when I'm having a conversation," Harry ordered.

"Priss," Pewter complained, but nonetheless tucked her hind leg under her.

"All the girls go to Blair's," Tucker said.

"Archie was at Blair's, too. He didn't kidnap Sarah," Murphy said.

"Blair must know that. When his mind is clear and he feels better." Pewter tried to think who else might know.

"Archie was moving out," Mrs. Murphy continued. *"She went there for him. Archie didn't kidnap her."*

"He's not here to defend himself," Tucker sagely noted.

Murphy lay down. *"A wasted life, Archie's."*

"H. is out on bail." Susan put her hands behind her head. "Big surprise."

"Was Sarah harmed?"

"No. She says Archie kidnapped her. He wanted to live with her. He wanted her to run away. He didn't mean to harm her."

"What do you think?" Harry asked.

"I don't know what to think. I'm glad it's over."

"Is it? We still don't know who killed Tommy Van Allen."

"Sarah confessed to Rick Shaw that Archie confessed to her that he killed Tommy over a drug deal gone sour."

"I don't believe it," Harry said.

"He did not," Murphy protested.

"Hush. You've had enough to eat."

"Sarah shot H. Vane. I don't know who killed Tommy Van Allen but she shot H." Murphy stuck to her guns.

"She gets a notion..." Harry commented on Murphy's conversation.

"And they're usually on the money," Tucker said.

"*Thank you.*" Murphy rested her head on her paws. "*We'd better get over to Tally's place tomorrow. First light.*"

"*Why so early?*" Pewter moaned.

"*Before people start crawling over it. The ghouls will show up whether Tally wants them or not.*"

"*Weird. Humans fear death but they can't stay away from it,*" Pewter remarked.

59

A line of gray illuminated the eastern horizon. Mrs. Murphy, Pewter, and Tucker were already on the ridge above Rose Hill.

As they dropped down into the fertile plain the golden rim of the sun pushed over the horizon and shafts of gold, like spokes on a wheel, radiated into the lightened sky.

By the time they reached the barn and stone buildings they were surprised to find Big Mim and Tally already there.

A pool of blood, dark brown, stained the dirt road where Archie had fallen. Big Mim and Tally stood in silence in the circle of buildings. When Mim finally spoke, she said nothing of the evidence of murder. The women knew each other too well for Tally to be surprised.

"Why don't you let me restore these?"

"I've got no use for them," Tally replied.

"You could rent them out. Make a little money. After all, you were going to rent one to Archie." Mim smiled suddenly as Mrs. Murphy and Pewter came up to her. "Why, look who's here." Tucker lingered at the blood until Murphy sharply reprimanded her.

"You characters certainly cover the miles." Mim petted the cats' heads.

"I say let the whole damn place fall down." Tally thumped the ground with her cane.

"That's foolish."

"Who are you to tell me what's foolish? I knew you in diapers."

"The day may come when you want to sell Rose Hill. You need to keep up the place. I can repair all this. I have a good crew."

"I don't know." She paused, looking skyward as the colors changed from gold to pink to red to gold again and the sun flooded the world with light. "Crazy."

"Hmm?"

She pointed with her cane to the pool of blood.

"Yes. It's all over now."

"It certainly is for Archie. Damn fool. This is the South. You don't steal another man's wife without expecting retribution."

"That's why the rest of the country thinks we're uncivilized. We erupt. Underneath the veneer of manners we're animals."

"Are you an animal, my dear?" Tally raised a silver eyebrow.

"Yes. If pushed hard enough I am. Why kid myself?"

"The question is, what pushes people? Love? Money? Prestige? Property? I don't know. What people kill and die for seems thin gruel to me."

"You're old. You forget."

Tally whirled on Mim, her cane over her head. "Damn you."

"Passion, Aunt Tally. You see, you still have it."

Tally brought her cane down, then laughed. "You are clever. Sometimes I forget how clever you are."

"Back to business." Mim deflected the compliment.

"Oh, what!" came the irritated response.

"First order of business, let me get my men in here and clean this barn. I'll bring this place back to the way it was when I was a child. How I loved to play back here. And the barn dances! Mother would wear gingham dresses and Daddy would laugh and laugh. What days those were before—well, before everything changed so."

"Change is part of life. Sometimes it's good and sometimes it's not. Most times it's both. A change can be bad for me but good for the man down the road."

"Maybe I can get them to look at the suitcase." Tucker wagged her tailless bottom as Mim winked at her.

"You can try." Pewter shrugged.

Tucker bounded into the thicket, barking like a maniac.

"What's she got in there?" Mim wondered.

"Tractor graveyard. Rats or mice."

The two women returned to arguing about the stone houses but Tucker continued to bark.

"I'll go see. Maybe she's hurt." Mim pushed through the budding bushes, which included nasty thorns. She heard the little dog under the Chevy.

Raised in the country, Mim was hesitant to squat down and find herself face-to-face with a snarling fox or other burrowing creature. But Tucker's entreaties overcame her natural caution. She knelt down, noticing dirt fly up as Tucker dug furiously in the loam.

"Look!" Tucker tugged at a corner of the suitcase.

Mim reached in and grabbed the corner sticking out. She edged it toward her, grasping the handle. As soon as Mim had the suitcase Tucker shut up.

"This is what you want?" Mim stared into the beautiful round eyes.

"Open it."

Mim clicked open the top. "Oh, God," she gasped, stepping back.

"What are you doing in there?!"

"Tucker dug out an old suitcase with a tiny skeleton in it and what's left of a lace headcap and dress." She closed the suitcase, fighting her way back through the foliage, Tucker at her heels.

"I don't want to see it." A ghastly pallor covered Tally's face. "Put it back, Marilyn."

"I can't do that. I have to turn this skeleton over to Rick Shaw. The child was murdered. Why else would she or he be stuffed in a suitcase?" Mim noticed Tally clutch at her chest and falter. "Aunt Tally." She dropped the suitcase, the skeleton tumbling out, and grabbed her aunt.

"Oh, no." Tally saw the child's bones.

Mrs. Murphy and Pewter silently watched. Tucker sat by the skeleton.

"Put it back," Tally sobbed.

Mim sank to her knees with the old lady. No fool, she said, "What do you know about this child?"

"It's mine!" Tally sobbed so hard Mrs. Murphy thought her old heart would break.

"Is this why Uncle Jamie shot Biddy Minor?"

"Yes. I wanted to die. I loved Biddy Minor. I loved him like no other man on earth and he loved me."

Mim put her arms around her aunt and softly asked, "Did you kill your baby?"

"No, no, I could never do that."

"Did Biddy?"

"No."

"Who, then?"

"Daddy. He took the baby from my arms and he smothered her."

Mim shivered. "I'm so sorry."

"I didn't show much. I got away with being pregnant. Momma suspected but I lied through my teeth."

"What did Biddy do?"

"Daddy said if Biddy set foot on his property he'd kill him—a married man trifling with a young thing, that's what he called me, a young thing. But, oh, I loved Biddy Minor and I found a way to get a message to him. Veenie—do you remember our maid? She was born in slavery she was so old—Veenie told him I delivered the baby and Daddy killed her. I wanted that baby. She was all I would ever have of Biddy. He couldn't divorce, you see. Nobody could then."

"Yes, I remember."

"And Daddy wanted me to marry well. If anyone knew I'd had an illegitimate child he couldn't have married me off to the milkman."

"I see." Mim stood up and brushed off her knees. She helped Tally up.

Tally, once on her feet, walked over to the skeleton with hesitant steps. She knelt down. Tucker whimpered.

Tally looked at Tucker. "She was the most beautiful little girl, with red curls, red curls just like mine when I was little." She touched the hand. "And I'll never forget when she wrapped her tiny fingers around my finger. She was my living memory of Biddy." Tally put her head in her hands and sobbed, racking sobs.

Mim, eyes wet, too, knelt down and gathered up the bones, putting them back into the suitcase.

"I thought Daddy buried her but one night he got drunk and said he put her in a suitcase and threw her in with the junk. I thought about looking for her but I couldn't, you know, Mimsy, I couldn't."

"You were a girl and had no control over your life. How is it that Jamie shot Biddy?"

"When Biddy heard what Daddy did to the baby, he came up here to kill him. I told Jamie I trusted him, and he loved me, I thought. Wild as he was, you could trust Jamie. But as soon as Biddy put one foot on our land Jamie killed him because he knew Biddy would kill Daddy for what he'd done. And I think in Jamie's heart he thought he was protecting me. He knew I'd run after Biddy again and ruin all our lives. I never hated Jamie for what he did but I hated Daddy. I hated Daddy for the rest of his life and I hate him still." She touched a piece of pink ribbon on the bonnet and pleaded, "Don't give her to the sheriff."

"I won't. We'll bury her on the hill with the rest of the family. She's one of us. You can tell or not tell." Mim closed the suitcase as though it carried the most precious items in the world, then she helped up Tally and they both walked slowly back to Mim's Bentley.

Tucker walked over to the girls. *"Poor Tally."*

"It's like a tom killing kittens," Pewter said.

"Bet old man Urquhart went to his grave believing he did the right thing." Tucker watched as Mim opened the door for her aunt, setting the suitcase on her lap.

"Humans can justify anything. Kill one. Kill millions. They'll come up with a reason why it's all right." Pewter had the last word.

60

On a glorious afternoon the following week, Sarah Vane-Tempest was directing her gardeners. H. Vane-Tempest, in a cashmere-and-linen turtleneck, worked in his secondary office, used only in good weather, a twenty-by-twenty glassed-in porch with French doors across the entire breadth. He could open all the doors on an especially good day.

He had little sense of the ordinary work week. He did whatever he wanted whenever he wanted and expected his help to be there. For this demanding schedule he paid quite well.

Seated across from him, Howard Fenton organized blue-covered legal packets, twelve of them. His assistant, a young man fresh out of Yale Law, carefully double-checked each document.

Vane-Tempest, using a fountain pen, the only appropriate writing utensil, signed the last one. Behind him stood his two secretaries, whose function today was to witness the documents and affix their signatures to the bottoms.

Howard viewed the two men—Vane-Tempest would employ only male secretaries, multilingual at that. "Does the subject appear to be in full possession of his mental faculties?"

"Yes," they answered in chorus.

"Does he appear to sign this document freely and without coercion?"

"Yes."

Vane-Tempest raised an eyebrow. "Would you like my blood type?"

Howard, humorless, replied, "Not necessary, sir."

"Next." Vane-Tempest held out his hand, his ultrathin watch half hidden by his cuff.

The Yale Law graduate handed him another legal-sized document. This one had beige covers to distinguish it from the others.

"Mmm." Vane-Tempest read quickly. He understood the law quite well for a civilian. Then, too, those many decades of business, real estate, and one jarring divorce had taught him the basics: Screw them before they screw you.

In this instance he wasn't interested in besting someone. He was acting with largesse.

"I think you'll find it is just as you dictated, sir. . . ."

"I know, Howard, but it's a damn fool who signs a contract without reading it, even if he did dictate it. If you're bored,"—his voice dripped acid and well it should, since he kept this law firm on a million-dollar retainer—"walk with my beautiful wife in her beautiful garden."

"I'm not bored."

"I'm so glad to hear it." He read on and ten minutes later signed the beige-covered documents, again twelve copies.

The black ink, specially purchased from Italy for its richness of hue, glistened on the last page of the last document. Vane-Tempest blew on the page.

The young assistant surreptitiously sneaked a glance at Sarah, the lush light outlining her breathtaking features. *This is what money buys,* he thought to himself.

"Shall I hand deliver the Teotan papers to Mr. Bainbridge?"

"Yes. Mr. Bainbridge, as you know, is in hospital. Don't tire him."

"Despite his injuries I do believe this will revive his spirits."

"Hope so, Howard. Nasty business. The police will never find the criminal. They never do, you know. You Americans display a curious disregard for punishment and deterrence."

"Sir?" Howard stood as his client got to his feet.

"If you catch them you let them off on parole. If they're in jail they work out with weights or watch TV. Devil's Island, by God, send them to Devil's Island. You'll see your crime statistics plunge."

"I agree." And he did.

"Off with you, then." Vane-Tempest smiled genially as Secretary Number One showed the two lawyers the front door.

He clasped his hands behind his back. Butterflies covered his Italian lilacs, late bloomers, but everything was late this year.

He strode outside feeling better than he had in a while. Putting his arm around Sarah's shoulders, he guided her to the expanse of manicured lawn, the croquet pitch, facing the north. The direct western view, the best mountain views, he wisely left unmolested, the lawn merging with the edge of a hayfield.

"Spring. Finally. Unequivocally."

"Yes."

"I have resigned my interest and by extension your interest in Teotan," Vane-Tempest informed his wife.

"What?" Dismay read over her face.

He held up his hand. "Patience. Hear me out. I have turned over the corporation to Blair, to which he has agreed. He has only to sign the documents I have prepared and Teotan is his with my investment. I apologized for taking out my jealousy on him and speaking harshly to him. He apologized for an 'immoral escapade.' Exact words."

"What about me?"

"I thought we could go into business together. The two of us. What would you like?"

Turning to view her garden she replied, with a hint of determination and excitement, "A nursery. A wholesale business to supply the landscape architects."

"How interesting. I thought you might pick a dress shop or a theater."

"A nursery. It's healthier." She beamed at him.

"So it is."

"H., why are you relinquishing Teotan? There are other ways to buy off Blair Bainbridge."

"The fellow doesn't have to be bought off. He doesn't remember much about that afternoon. Not uncommon with head injuries, I'm told. So let's just call it insurance...in case he does remember on some distant day. Besides, I think it imprudent for us to be in business with your former lover. I thought I was very clever in keeping Blair and Tommy close to me. They never suspected, I know, and I had ample time to study them. Archie, however, was a complete and dismal surprise." He didn't admit that he figured out about Blair from hearing her answer Archie's accusation during their tryst in Archie's office. He knew from the tone of her voice.

Not missing a beat, she said, "I hated you, H. You dismissed me."

"How did you keep all those balls in the air, forgive the pun." He heard what she said but changed the subject.

"I've always been good at scheduling." She stifled a laugh.

"Did you love any of them?"

"No. Blair is a sweet fellow but too languid, ultimately. And that *was* the briefest of affairs, H. Two weeks."

"Tommy Van Allen?"

"A flameout. It was fading before he died." She bit her lower lip, turning to face her husband. "I hated you and I wanted to hurt you. Don't change the subject. I wanted to hurt you, Henry. You hurt me."

H. Vane-Tempest could withstand news, no matter how bad, as long as he was the center of it. "You succeeded."

"I'm desperately sorry."

"No, you're not. But you will behave and we will create a successful nursery. And I suggest you give Mrs. Woo a great deal of business, for all the trouble you've caused her." As Sarah remained silent he continued. "The reason you'll behave, Sarah, is that I changed my will just now. If my death is in any way suspicious you inherit nothing. Nothing. You do understand?"

"I understand that you will live a long and healthy life." She kissed him on the cheek.

"You had pluck trying to kill me. I underestimated you, undervalued you. That won't happen again."

"You killed Tommy Van Allen, didn't you?"

He shrugged. "I doubt Rick Shaw will solve that crime."

"Henry, I know you . . ."

"Tommy Van Allen was an impulsive fool. He had enough cocaine in his bloodstream to kill three people. The rest was window dressing." He neglected to mention that he had shot the cocaine into Tommy's veins. Cocaine was ridiculously easy to get in this wealthy county. She stuck her thumb in the waistband of her wraparound skirt. "Teotan is, I should think, generous recompense to Blair." She paused. "Do you think the county will buy the well water?"

"I do. I think Blair will become a wealthy man, not serious money, but some money."

Sarah laughed, because in her husband's world, less than ten million dollars qualified as some money.

He kissed her lightly on the mouth. "I'm going to lose forty pounds. I've let myself go." He kept to himself the daily shots of testosterone he would be taking. Some things were best left unsaid.

As for putting Tommy's bomber jacket in Herb Jones's truck, and the handcuffs in Archie's van—no one had even found those, more's the pity—he did that for the sheer devilment of it. It was exciting to watch everyone come unglued.

The presence of Sarah's black Jaguar at Blair Bainbridge's still bothered the police. But Vane-Tempest had crawled to the top of the heap by understanding people in a cynical fashion. If the police had a solution that the public accepted, then what was one odd piece that didn't fit into the puzzle? They could prove nothing against Sarah or him.

He knew Sarah had been in the plane with Tommy. He had gotten up in the middle of the night, called Tommy to meet him at the food plant under the pretext of a Teotan emergency, shot him, and loaded him with cocaine. It took all of fifteen minutes. He was home in bed by three o'clock, with no one the wiser. Planting cocaine and a locker storage ticket in Tommy's car was child's play. Faking a set of accounting books was easy, too. He'd run numbers off his computer, then put them into a leather binder.

As for himself, he didn't fear Sarah. This episode, as he chose to consider it, only whetted his appetite for her. He saw her now for what she was, a tiger. And so was he.

61

Harry and Miranda sat on two chairs next to Blair's bed. Each woman had visited him two and three times a day since his shooting.

"Is any memory coming back at all?" Miranda politely inquired.

"No," he truthfully replied. "But the doctor said bits and pieces may come back to me. Then again, I may never remember. The last thing I remember—and it's so stupid—is I heard a car come up the driveway. I opened the back screened door and I tripped. Just took a mistep. That's all I can remember."

"You must be tired of everyone asking you." Harry smiled. "You look good."

"I feel pretty good. The swelling is down. Doc wants me to wait a few more days to be certain. I'll tell you what's driving me crazy." He pointed to the bandages on his head. "My scalp itches like poison ivy. I can't scratch it."

"Means it's healing." Miranda patted his hand. "You'll be back to good health in no time. Thank you, Jesus." She closed her eyes in fervent prayer.

"Yes. I have been very lucky." Blair's eyes misted. "Thank God for you, Harry."

"You've thanked me enough already." Harry warmly smiled.

"And Mrs. Murphy, Pewter, and Tucker." Blair smiled broadly.

"Yes." Harry hadn't told him or anyone the full extent of their efforts. She knew no one would believe her.

"Maybe it's better not to remember. You and Archie had been friends." Miranda assumed Blair's attacker had been Archie.

"I just don't know, Miranda. I don't know if it's better to know or not to know and there's not much I can do about it. I'm just so grateful to be alive." He stopped as his eyes filled with tears, and Harry's and Miranda's eyes filled also.

62

Miranda's hand flew to her face. "I hate to hear about drug deals. I so liked Tommy."

Cynthia, in regulation sunglasses, continued her story. "He must have brought the stuff in by private plane after picking it up in Florida or from local airports closer by. You know those training runs that Tommy used to do? They weren't training runs."

"Good job," Miranda congratulated her.

"We've got the records. That's the real break. We found cocaine and a locker ticket from the bus station in Tommy's Porsche. So we went over to the bus station, of course, opened the locker, and that's where the accounting books were."

"How about that?" Tucker watched people drive by the post

office. Spring worked its magic on everyone. People were smiling.

It galled Cynthia that Blair could not remember whoever shot him. The bullet had never been found—the sign of a careful killer. She knew the other shoe hadn't dropped and she suspected H. Vane-Tempest. Whatever her suspicions might be, suspicions weren't facts, and Blair's doctors confirmed he could have "lost" the hours leading up to his being shot. She sighed. "How is Blair today?"

"His color is better." Mrs. Hogendobber offered a biscuit to Cynthia after shooing Pewter off the table.

Too late, though, for Pewter had yet another fresh biscuit firmly clamped in her jaws. She chewed some of it, then tore the remainder with her claws. *"That's what I'm going to do to that blue jay."*

"Dream on." Murphy listened, unmoved, to the details.

"Doubting Thomas," cooed Pewter, who at that moment felt glorious, since she had successfully stolen a biscuit.

"We're lucky." Murphy hopped off the counter and rubbed against the corgi's snow-white chest. She dearly loved that dog, although she wouldn't say it out loud.

"We saved Blair." Tucker licked Murphy's ear.

"Yes." She rubbed her cheek against Tucker's cheek.

Big Mim, Little Mim, Herb, and Tally came in. Cynthia didn't tell them the news about finding the drug records because Big Mim already knew. If Rick Shaw didn't call her the second he knew something, she'd make his life miserable. It helped that she made major contributions to various law-enforcement events and charities.

"We're all feeling better, thanks to you." Mim shook Cynthia's hand.

"I don't deserve any credit, really."

"You're too modest. All those hours of questioning people, in-

vestigating sites, poring over evidence—no one sees how much work there is." Mim smiled.

Tally spoke up abruptly. "This Saturday at three at my place, the old cemetery, you are invited to a funeral."

"Oh, no! Who has—" Miranda rushed to console Tally, who held up her hand for silence.

"I'll explain at the funeral. Reverend Herb will conduct the service and afterward I will serve refreshments with the help of my niece and tell you who died and why. I won't live much longer myself. I need to tell you—" She paused, reaching for the counter to steady herself. "I need to tell you how things stay with you. The past, I mean. The past lives right through us. Even if no one ever reads another history book, even if whole nations resign themselves to ignorance, the past pulls like the moon on tides. Please come."

"Of course we'll come." Miranda's voice, filled with warm sympathy, almost made Tally cry.

"I'll be there. Thank you for inviting me," Harry said.

"How about that?" Pewter was amazed.

After the group left, including Cynthia, Harry and Miranda sorted, then swept the floors.

"I wonder why Tally invited me to this funeral?" Harry asked.

"I believe it has something to do with you."

"Me?"

"Your blood. There was talk about Tally and your great-grandfather. I was too young to pay attention. But there was talk. This was before my time. Mother remembered, though."

"I guess we'll find out on Saturday."

"You know that you were ransomed from the futile ways inherited from your fathers, not with perishable things such as silver or gold, but with the precious blood of Christ, like that of a lamb without blemish or spot." She put the broom back into the broom closet. "Redemption. I should think that whatever she tells us, Saturday is about redemption."

"What chapter and verse?"

"First Peter, Chapter 1, Verses 18 and 19."

"You amaze me."

"In my day we learned by rote. Stays with you."

Harry scooped up Murphy and kissed her head. She was thinking about the animals driving the Porsche and knowing she couldn't tell anyone.

"Miranda, do you really believe that people can be redeemed? A murderer can be redeemed?"

"Certainly I do, if he but accepts Christ as his savior."

"What about Murphy and Tucker, and Pewter, even though she's a little thief?" She smiled.

"A thief is the only person guaranteed a place in paradise. Remember, it was a thief crucified with Christ who accepted him as the Son of God, and Jesus promised him everlasting life."

"Hope for Pewter."

Miranda, years ago, would have been offended at this discussion, at the idea that animals have immortal souls and spiritual lives . . . but working with them and watching them, she had changed her mind. Not loudly. Not even so much that others might notice by observation. "There's redemption for Pewter. God loves all his creatures and I believe we will be reunited in heaven." She stopped, and this, for her, was a revelation. "Harry, sometimes I think that animals are closer to God than we are."

"Not blue jays," Pewter announced, being uninterested in theological discussions.

"I do, too." Harry looked around. "It's a wrap, partner."

Miranda put her hand on Harry's shoulder. "I've known you since you were born, Mary Minor. And I know you have doubts. Your faith gets shaken. But it's there. Your mother and father gave you rock-solid beliefs. When you need it, it's there."

"I hope so."

"In time of trouble—" Then Miranda stopped herself. "Let's hope few troubles come your way. I think of them as tests, God's tests. Blair is being tested. He needs us. He's hurt physically and harmed morally."

"Little Mim will be at his side."

"We must all be there." She glanced at the old railroad wall clock. "Oh, dear, I'd better hustle my bustle."

Harry laughed as Miranda scooted out of the post office. Her old-fashioned phrases delighted Harry. She dropped the paper shades and double-checked the lock on the sliding door that closed off the office part of the post office, then walked to the back, dropped the hard plastic sheet in metal slots through the animal door, and secured it with a steel pin. Lastly she opened the back door. "Come on, gang."

Three furry behinds scampered into the late afternoon as Harry locked the back door to the post office.

She opened the door to the blue Ford truck, lifting Tucker in. Pewter and Mrs. Murphy had already jumped up onto the bench seat.

Harry turned the key. The starter clicked, then the motor turned over. She let it idle for a few minutes. No point in pushing the old girl.

Once the motor hummed, she pushed down on the clutch, reaching for the long black stick shift on the floor.

Mrs. Murphy moved over to sit in her lap.

"Want to drive?" Harry asked her as Pewter laughed.

"I only drive Porsches." Mrs. Murphy giggled.

Pawing Through
the Past

Dedicated to Cindy Chandler

In a dog-eat-dog world,
she hands us our napkins

Cast of Characters

Mary Minor Haristeen (Harry), the young postmistress of Crozet. She won double senior superlatives in high school: Most Likely to Succeed and Most Athletic.

Mrs. Murphy, Harry's gray tiger cat, calm in a crisis and sassy, too.

Tee Tucker, Harry's Welsh corgi, Mrs. Murphy's friend and confidante, is a solid, courageous creature.

Pewter, Market Shiflett's shamelessly fat gray cat, who now lives with Harry and family. Her high intelligence is usually in the service of her self-indulgence.

Pharamond Haristeen (Fair), an equine veterinarian, formerly married to Harry. He wants to get back together again with Harry.

Susan Tucker, Harry's best friend. She tells it like it is. She won the Best All-Round senior superlative in high school.

Olivia Craycroft (BoomBoom), a buxom dilettante who constantly irritates Harry. Her senior superlative was Best Looking.

Cynthia Cooper, a young deputy in the sheriff's department, who is willing to use unorthodox methods to capture criminals.

Sheriff Rick Shaw, a dedicated, reliable public servant. He may not be the most imaginative sheriff but he is the most persistent.

Tracy Raz, the former All-State football player, who comes home for his fiftieth high-school reunion and rekindles his romance with Miranda.

Chris Sharpton, a newcomer to Crozet, she jumps right into activities hoping to make friends.

Bitsy Valenzuela, a socially active woman who includes Chris in her circle.

Marcy Wiggins, an unhappily married woman, who looks forward to her outings with Bitsy and Chris. She needs the diversion.

Big Marilyn Sanburne (Mim), the undisputed queen of Crozet, who can be an awful snob at times. She knows the way the world works.

Little Marilyn Sanburne (Little Mim), a chip off the old block yet quite resentful of it.

Charlie Ashcraft, a notoriously successful seducer of women. Voted Best Looking by his high-school class.

Leo Burkey, was voted Wittiest.

Bonnie Baltier, was voted Wittiest.

Hank Bittner, was voted Most Talented.

Bob Shoaf, was voted Most Athletic later playing cornerback for the New York Giants.

Dennis Rablan, voted Best All-Round and now a photographer. He squandered his inheritance and is regarded as a failure.

Miranda Hogendobber, last but not least on the list: A woman of solid virtue, common sense, she works with Harry at the post office.

1

The huge ceiling fan lazily swirled overhead, vainly attempting to move the soggy August air. Mary Minor Haristeen, Harry to her friends—and everyone was a friend—scribbled ideas on a yellow legal pad. Seated around the kitchen table, high-school yearbooks open, were Susan Tucker, her best friend, Mrs. Miranda Hogendobber, her coworker and good friend, and Chris Sharpton, an attractive woman new to the area.

"We could have had this meeting at the post office," Susan remarked as she wiped the sweat from her forehead.

"Government property," Miranda said.

"Right, government property paid for with my taxes," Susan laughed.

Harry, the postmistress in tiny Crozet, Virginia, said, "Okay, it is air-conditioned but think how many hours Miranda and I spend in that place. I have no desire to hang out there in my free time."

"You've got air-conditioning at your house." Miranda stared at Susan.

"I know but the kids are having a pool party and—"

"You left the house with a party in progress? There won't be a drop of liquor left," Harry interrupted.

"My kids know when to stop."

"Congratulations," Harry taunted her. "That doesn't mean anyone else's kids know when to stop. I hope you locked the bar."

"Ned is there." Susan returned to the opened yearbook, the conversation clearly over. Her husband could handle any crisis.

"You could have said that in the first place." Harry opened her yearbook to the same page.

"Why? It's more fun to listen to you tell me what to do."

"Oh." Harry sheepishly bent over the yearbook photo of one of her senior superlatives, Most Likely to Succeed. "I can't believe I looked like that."

"You look exactly the same. Exactly." Miranda pulled Harry's yearbook to her.

"Don't compliment her, it will go to her head." Susan turned to Chris. "Are you sorry you volunteered to help us?"

"No, but I don't see as I'm doing much good." The newcomer smiled, her hand on her own high-school yearbook.

"All right. Down to business." Harry straightened her shoulders. "I'm in charge of special categories for our twentieth high-school reunion. BoomBoom Craycroft, our fearless leader"—Harry said this with a tinge of sarcasm about the head of the reunion—"is going to reshoot photographs of our senior superlatives with us as we are today. My job is to come up with other things to do with people who weren't senior superlatives."

"That's only fair. I mean, there are only twelve senior superlatives, one male, one female. That's twenty people out of one hundred and thirty-two, give or take a few, since some of us were voted more than one superlative." Harry paused for a breath. "How many were in your class, Miranda?"

"Fifty-six. Forty-two are still alive, although some of us might be on respirators. My task for my reunion is easier." Miranda giggled, her hand resting on the worn cover of her 1950 yearbook.

"You all were so lucky to go to small high schools. Mine was a consolidated. Huge," Chris remarked, and indeed her yearbook bore witness to the fact, being three times fatter than that of Harry and Susan or Mrs. Hogendobber.

Susan agreed. "I guess we were lucky but we didn't know it at the time."

"Does anyone?" Harry tapped her yellow wooden pencil against the back of her left wrist.

"Probably not. Not when you're young. What fun we had." Miranda, a widow, nodded her head, jammed with happy memories.

"Okay, here's what I've got. Ready?" They nodded in assent so Harry began reading, "These are categories to try and include others: Most Distance Traveled. Most Children. Most Wives—"

"You're not going to do that." Miranda chuckled.

"Why not? That one is followed by Most Husbands. Too bad we can't have one for Most Affairs." Harry lifted her eyebrows.

"Malicious," Susan said dryly.

"Rhymes with delicious." Harry's eyes brightened. "Okay, what else have I got here? Most Changed. Obviously that has to be in some good way. Can't pick out someone who has porked on an extra hundred pounds. And—uh—I couldn't think of anything else."

"Harry, you're usually so imaginative." Miranda seemed surprised.

"She's not at all imaginative but she is ruthlessly logical. I'll give her that."

Harry ignored Susan's assessment of her, speaking to Chris, "When you're new to a place it takes a long time to ferret out people's relationships to one another. Suffice it to say that Susan, my best friend since birth, feels compelled to point out my shortcomings."

"Harry, being logical isn't a shortcoming. It's a virtue," Susan protested. "But we are light on categories here."

Chris opened her dark green yearbook to a club photo. "My twentieth reunion was last year. One of the things we did was go

through the club photos to see if we could find anyone who
became a professional at something they were known for in high
school. You know, like did anyone in Latin club become a Latin
teacher. It's kind of hokey but you do get desperate after a time."

Harry pulled the book toward her, the youthful faces of the
Pep Club staring back at her. "Which one are you?"

Chris pointed to a tall girl in the back row. "I wasn't blonde
then."

"I can see that." Harry read the names below the photo, finding Chris Sharpton. She slid the book back to the owner.

"What we also did which took a bit of quick thinking on the
spot was, we had cards made up with classmates' names written
on them in italics. They were pretty. Anyway, if the individual had-
n't fit into some earlier category we did things like Tom Cruise
Double—anything to make them feel special."

"That's clever," Miranda complimented her.

"The other thing we did was make calls. As you know, people
disperse after high school. Each of us on the committee called
everyone we were still in contact with from our class. We asked
who they were in contact with and what they knew about the
people. This way we gathered information for things like Most
Community Service. After a time it's a stretch but it's important
that everyone be included in some way. At the last minute we
even wrote a card up, Still the Same."

"Chris, these are good ideas." Harry was grateful. "You're
wonderful to come help us. I mean, this isn't even your reunion."

"I'm not as generous as you think," Chris laughed. "Susan bet
me she'd beat me by three strokes on the Keswick golf course. The
bet was I'd help you all if I lost."

"What would you have gotten if you'd won?"

"Two English boxwoods planted by my front walkway."

Since moving to Crozet four months ago, Chris had thrown
herself into decorating and landscaping her house in the Deep
Valley subdivision, a magnet for under-forty newcomers to Albemarle County.

An outgoing person, Chris had made friends with her neighbors but most especially Marcy Wiggins and Bitsy Valenzuela, two women married to men who were classmates of Harry's.

"Good bet," Harry whistled.

"I told you my golf game was improving." Susan gloated. "But Miranda, I don't think we've done one thing to help you."

She smiled a slow smile. "Our expectations are different than yours. At your fiftieth high-school reunion you're thrilled that all your parts are moving. We'll be happy to eat good food, share stories, sit around. I suppose we'll pitch horseshoes and dance. That sort of thing."

"Are you in charge of the whole thing?" Chris was incredulous.

"Pretty much. I'll need to round up a few people to help me decorate. I'm keeping it simple because I'm simple."

Before anyone could protest that Miranda was not simple, Mrs. Murphy, Harry's beautiful tiger cat, burst through the animal door.

"What have you got?" Harry rose from the table expecting the worst.

Pewter, the plump gray cat, immediately followed through the animal door and Tee Tucker, Harry's corgi, burst through behind her, bumping the cat in the rear end, which brought forth a snarl.

Susan focused on the animals. "I don't know what she's got but everyone wants it."

Mrs. Murphy blew through the kitchen into the living room, where she crouched behind the sofa as Pewter leapt onto the large stuffed curving arm.

"Selfish!"

The tiger cat did not answer her gray accuser because if she did, the mole she had carefully stalked would have popped out of her mouth and escaped.

Harry knelt down. "Say, Murphy, good job. That's a huge mole. Why, that mole could dig to China."

"*She didn't catch it by herself,*" Pewter complained loudly. "I blocked off the other exit. *I deserve half of that mole.*"

"*I helped.*" The corgi drooled.

"*Ha!*" Pewter disagreed.

"Thank you for bringing me this prize." Harry carefully reached behind the sofa, petted Murphy, then grabbed the limp mole by the scruff of its neck.

The tiger cat opened her jaws. "*Moles are dangerous, you know. William of Orange, King of England, was killed when his horse stepped in a mole hole. He broke his collarbone and then took a fever.*"

"*Show-off.*" Pewter's pupils narrowed to slits.

Mrs. Murphy sashayed into the kitchen, ignoring her detractors.

"Excuse me, ladies." Harry walked outside, depositing the mole at the back of the woodpile. The minute it was on the ground it scurried under the logs. "That's Murphy for you. She didn't even break your neck, little guy. She was bringing me a present. Guess she expected me to dispatch you."

When Harry returned, Chris said, nose wrinkled, "I don't know how you could pick up that mole. I could never do that. I'm too squeamish."

"Oh, when you grow up in the country you don't think about stuff. You just do it." She pointed to Chris's yearbook. "Lake Shore, Illinois, must be a far cry from the country."

"That it is." Chris laughed.

Susan, flipping through her yearbook, bubbled. "I'm getting excited about this reunion. October will be here before we know it. Time flies."

"Don't say that. I'm nervous enough about getting organized for the damn thing," Harry grumbled.

"Maybe you're nervous about seeing all those people," Chris said.

"I'm as nervous about them seeing me as me seeing them. What will they think? Do I look like a . . ." Susan paused.

"Well, do I look older? Will they be disappointed when they see me?"

"You look great," Harry said with conviction. "Besides, half of our class still lives within shouting distance. Everyone knows what you look like."

"Harry, we hardly even see the people who moved to Richmond—like Leo Burkey. Shouting distance doesn't matter."

Harry cupped her chin in her hand. "Leo Burkey will be just like always, handsome and B-A-D."

"Hey, I'd like to meet this guy." The single Chris smiled.

"Is he between wives?" Harry asked Susan.

"BoomBoom will know."

"Of course she will." Harry laughed. "Miranda, we really aren't doing a thing for you but I'm glad our reunions are at the same time. We can use a skateboard to go up and down the halls to visit."

"I'll bet you think I can't even use a skateboard," Miranda challenged her.

"I never said that!"

"You didn't have to." Miranda winked. But just you wait, Miranda thought to herself, smiling.

"*It's not fair that Murphy gets all the attention,*" Pewter wailed as she jumped on the kitchen counter.

"*I don't get all the attention but I did bring in a fresh mole. Jealous.*"

"*I am unloved,*" Pewter warbled at a high-decibel range.

Harry got up, opened the cupboard, and removed a round plastic bowl of fresh catnip. She rolled it between her fingers, releasing the heavenly aroma. Then she placed the bits on the floor where Pewter dove in, quickly followed by Murphy. Harry handed Tucker a Milk-Bone, which satisfied her.

A little coo from Pewter directed all human eyes to her. Blitzed on catnip, she lay on her back on the heart pine floor, her tail slowly swishing. Mrs. Murphy was on her side, her paws covering her eyes.

"Bliss." Miranda laughed.

"*I love the whole world and everyone in it*," Pewter meowed.

Murphy removed one paw—"*Me, too*"—then she covered her eyes up again.

"That ought to hold them." Harry sat back down after pouring everyone iced tea. Mrs. Hogendobber had brought homemade icebox cookies, cucumber sandwiches, and fresh vegetables.

"Do you know that some schools now regard senior superlatives as politically incorrect?" Susan reached for a sandwich.

"Why?" Miranda wondered.

Susan pointed to the senior superlative section, one full page for each superlative. "Elitist. Hurts people's feelings."

"Life is unfair." Harry's voice rose slightly. "You might as well learn that in high school if you haven't already."

"You've got a point there." Chris shook her sleek blonde pageboy. "I can remember crying hot tears over stuff that now seems trivial but I learned that disappointments are going to come and I've got to handle them. And all that surging emotion going through you for the first time. How confusing."

"Still is." Harry sipped her tea. "For me anyway."

"Is everyone in your class still alive?" Chris asked Susan and Harry.

"We've lost two," Susan answered. "Aurora Hughes." She turned the page to Most Talented and there a willowy girl in a full-length dress was in the arms of a young man, Hank Bittner, wearing a top hat and tails. "She died of leukemia the year after graduation. We were all in college and you know, I still feel guilty about not being there. Aurora was such a good kid. And she really was talented."

"Who was the other one?" Chris asked.

"Ronnie Brindell." Harry spoke since Susan had just stuffed a cookie in her mouth. "They say he jumped off the Golden Gate Bridge in San Francisco. He left a note. I still can't believe he did it. I liked Ron. I can't imagine he'd—well—what can you say about suicide?"

"Here." Susan flipped to the senior superlative for Most Popular. A slender, slightly effeminate young man sat on a merry-go-round with Meredith McLaughlin, her eyes sparkling with merriment.

"He doesn't look depressed." Chris studied the picture.

"People said he was gay and couldn't handle it." Harry also studied the picture. "He was a nice boy. But the bruiser boys used to pick on him something terrible. I bet it was rough being a gay kid in high school but back then no one said anything like that. The gay kids must have gotten roughed up daily but it was all hidden, you know."

"I do, actually. We had the same thing at Lake Shore. I guess every school did. It's sad really. And to think he jumped off the bridge." Chris shuddered.

"May the Lord be a tower of strength for the oppressed." Mrs. Hogendobber cited a verse from Psalm Nine and that closed the subject.

"Who knows what secrets will pop up like a jack-in-the-box?" Susan ruminated. "Old wounds might be opened."

"Susan, it's a high-school reunion for Pete's sake. Not therapy."

"Okay, maybe not therapy but it sure is a stage where past and present collide for all to see."

"Susan, I don't feel that way. We know these people."

"Harry, when was the last time you saw Bob Shoaf?" Susan mentioned the star athlete of their class, who became a professional football player.

"On television."

"You don't think he'll have the big head? Those guys snap their fingers for girls, cars, goodies . . . and presto, they get what they want. He won't be the same old Bob."

"He sounds fascinating, too." Chris's eyes widened.

"He thinks so. He was always conceited but he is good-looking and I guess he's rich. Those people pull down unreal salaries." Harry sighed, wishing a bit of money would fall her way.

"Maybe he blew it all. Maybe he's suffering from depression. Maybe he's impotent." A devilish grin filled Susan's face. "Secrets!"

"She's right, though. At our twentieth people who had crushes on one another in high school snuck off, marriages hit the rocks, old rivalries were renewed. It was wild, really. I had a good time, though." Chris shyly grinned.

Susan wheeled on Harry. "Charlie Ashcraft!"

"Not if he were the last man on earth!"

"You slept with Charlie. That's your secret."

"Is not," Harry protested.

"Girls." Mrs. Hogendobber feigned shock. She'd spent enough time around this generation to know they said things directly that her generation did not. She still couldn't decide if that was wise or unwise.

"You know, Harry, it will all come out at the reunion if what Chris says holds true for us."

"You're one brick shy of a load." Harry considered flicking a cucumber at her face. "Anyway, a woman has to have some secrets. People are boring without secrets."

Mrs. Murphy raised her head, her mind clearing somewhat from the delightful effects of the homegrown catnip. *That depends on the secrets.*

2

Canada sent down a ridge of cool dry air which swept over central Virginia, bringing relief from the moist, suffocating August heat.

That evening Harry, on her knees weeding her garden, rocked back on her heels to inhale the light, cool fragrance. With the mercury dipping to sixty-five degrees Fahrenheit, she had put on a torn navy blue sweatshirt.

Mrs. Murphy stalked a maple moth who easily saw her coming; those compound eyes could see everything. The yellow and pinkish creature fluttered upwards, fixing on the top of the boxwoods. From this lordly perch it observed the sleek cat, who, intelligent as she was, couldn't climb a boxwood.

The pile of weeds grew to a mound.

"Better toss this before it gets too heavy." Harry lifted the pitchfork, wedged it under, and in one neat motion picked up the debris. She walked past to the compost pile some distance from the manure spreader.

"*Dump it on the manure spreader,*" Murphy suggested.

"You don't have to come along," Harry replied to her cat, who she thought was complaining. She walked to the edge of the woods where she chucked the weeds. Murphy caught up with her.

"*If you'd put it in the manure spreader, Harry, it would have been a lot easier.*"

Harry leaned on her pitchfork and looked out over the hay field. The bees were heading back to the hives as twilight deepened. Even the nasty brilliant yellow digger bees headed to their labyrinthine underground nests. The bats stirred overhead, consuming insects.

"Farmer's friend," Harry said. "Did you know, Mrs. Murphy, that bats, black snakes, praying mantis, and owls are some of the best partners you can have among the wild animals?"

"*I did. I forgot to tell you that the black snake that winters in the loft is now close to four and a half feet long and she's on the south side of the garden. Her hunting territory is a giant circle and she moves counterclockwise. The sight of her is a fright. 'Course, the sight of Flatface, the barn owl, is a fright, too. She's grown twice as tall as last year. Thinks she's better than the rest of us.*"

Harry reached down, picked up her little friend, and kissed the top of her head. "You are the most wonderful cat in the world. Have I told you that lately?"

"*Thank you,*" Murphy purred, then wiggled to get down. The night creatures emerging were too tempting. She wanted to stalk a few.

Harry grabbed the pitchfork which she'd propped against a hickory: "Come on, time for supper."

The sweet smell of redbud clover filled their nostrils as the thin line of ground fog turned from seashell pink to mauve to pearl gray. A bobwhite called behind them. The magnificent owl of whom Mrs. Murphy had just spoken, flew out from the barn cupola on her first foraging mission of the evening.

Part of the rhythm of this place and these animals, Harry placed the pitchfork on the wall of the small storage shed. The night air cooled the temperature considerably. She put her hands in her jeans pockets as she hurried into the house.

"*What took you so long?*" Pewter complained. "*I thought you two were weeding the garden.*"

"*We did but we had things to talk about.*" Mrs. Murphy brushed past her, then quickly turned as she heard the can opener. "*Hope it's tuna tonight. I'm in the mood for tuna.*"

A bark outside and then a whap on the doggie door announced Tucker's presence.

"*Where were you?*" Mrs. Murphy asked from the counter as Harry spooned out the tuna into the two cat dishes, one marked Her Highness and the other, Upholstery Destroyer.

"*Blair Bainbridge's.*" The dog mentioned Harry's nearest neighbor to the west. "*Bought starter cattle and I had to help him herd them. He doesn't know beans and he's still moving a little slow after his injuries from last year. Wait until you see the calves. Weedy, spindly legs and thin chests, not good specimens at all but at least they've been wormed and had their shots. Wait until Mom sees them. It will be interesting to see how she manages to praise him without telling him these are the worst heifers she's ever seen.*"

"*She'll find a way.*"

"*Tucker. You've been busy. You're getting lamb bits in gravy.*" Pewter sniffed the distinctive mutton aroma.

"*Yeah!*"

As the three ate, Harry popped a pasta dish in the microwave. She wasn't very hungry but she ate it anyway since she had a tendency to lose weight in the summers.

Afterward they all sat on the sofa while Harry tried to read the newspaper but she kept rattling it, then putting it down. Finally, she got up, threw on her jacket, and walked outside.

"*What's she up to?*" Pewter, quite comfortable, wondered.

"*I'll go.*" Tucker roused herself and followed.

"*Me, too.*" Murphy shook herself.

"*Damn,*" Pewter grumbled. She flicked her tail over her gray nose, finally got up to stretch, and tagged along.

Harry walked to the paddocks behind the barn where she leaned against the black three-board fence to watch her horses, Gin Fizz, Tomahawk, and Poptart, enjoying the refreshing air.

They looked up, said hello, and returned to grazing.

Overhead the evening star appeared unreal, it was so big and clear. The Big Dipper rolled toward the horizon and Yellow Mountain was outlined in a thin band of blue, lighter than the deep skies.

"Kids, I couldn't live anywhere else. I know I work fourteen to sixteen hours a day between the post office and the farm, but I couldn't work in an office. I don't know . . ." Her voice trailed off. Pewter climbed up one fence post, Mrs. Murphy climbed up on another one while Tucker patiently sat on Harry's foot. "I kind of dread this reunion. I went to the fifteenth—still married then. It's a lot easier when you're married—socially, I mean. The ones from far away will look at me, then look at BoomBoom. I guess it's pretty easy to see why Fair hopped on her in a hurry. Wonder if he'll come? He was in the class ahead. But of course he will, he knows everybody. He's a good man, guys. He went through a bad patch, that's all, but I couldn't endure it. I just couldn't do it."

"*He's over that now,*" Tucker stoutly replied. The corgi loved Fair Haristeen, DVM, with all her heart and soul. "*He's admitted he was wrong. He still loves you.*"

"*But she doesn't love him.*" Pewter licked her paw and rapidly passed it over her whiskers.

"*She does love him,*" Mrs. Murphy countered, "*but she doesn't know how much or in what way. Like she wouldn't want to marry him again but she loves him as a person.*"

"*It's awfully confusing.*" Tucker's pretty ears drooped.

"*Humans make such a mess,*" Pewter airily announced.

"*They think too much and feel too little,*" Murphy noted. "*Even Mom and I love her, we all love her. It's the curse of the species. Then again I sometimes reverse that and believe they feel too much and don't think enough. Now I'm confused.*" She laughed at herself.

"You all have so much to say tonight." Harry smiled at her family, then continued her musings. "I watch television some-times. You know, the sitcoms. Apart from being the same age, I have nothing in common with those people. They live in beautiful apartments in big cities. They have great clothes and no one worries about money. They're witty and cool. A drought means nothing to them. Overseeding is a foreign word. They drive sexy cars while I drive a 1978 Ford half-ton truck. My generation is all those things that I am not." She frowned. "Not too many of us live in the country anymore. The old ways are being lost and I suppose I'll be lost with them but—I can't live any other way." She kicked the dewy grass. "Damn, why did I get so involved in this reunion? I am such a sucker!" She turned on her heel to go back to the house.

Mrs. Murphy gracefully leapt off the post while Pewter turned around to back down. No need to jar her bones if it wasn't absolutely necessary. Tucker stayed at her mother's left heel.

As they passed the front of the barn, Simon, the possum who lived in the hayloft, peered out the open loft door.

The animals greeted him, causing Harry to glance up, too. "Evening, Simon."

Simon blinked. He didn't hurry back to his nest, and that was as close as he got to greeting them.

"You want marshmallows, I know." Harry walked to her screened-in porch and opened the old zinc-lined milk box that her mother had used when Monticello Dairy used to deliver milk bottles. She kept marshmallows and a small bag of sunflower seeds for the finches there. She walked back with four marshmallows and threw them through the hayloft door. "Enjoy yourself, Simon."

He grabbed one, his glittering black eyes merry. "I will."

Harry looked up at Simon, then down at her three friends. "Well, I bet no one else in my class feeds marshmallows to their possum." Spirits somewhat restored, she trotted back into the house to warm up.

After sorting everyone else's mail, Harry finally sorted her own. If the morning proved unusually hectic she'd slide her mail into her metal box, hoping she'd remember it before going home.

Sometimes two or three days would pass before she read her own mail.

This morning had been busy. Mrs. Hogendobber, a tower of strength in or out of the post office, ran back and forth to her house because the hot-water heater had stopped working. She finally gave up restarting it, calling a plumber. When he arrived she went home.

Fair stopped by early. He kissed his ex-wife on the cheek and apologized for delivering four hundred and fifty postcards to mail out. Each containing his e-mail address. He had, however, arranged them by zip code.

Susan stopped by, grabbed her mail, and opened it on the counter.

"Bills. Bills. Bills."

"*I can take care of that!*" Mrs. Murphy swished her tail, crouched and leapt onto the counter. She attacked the offending bills.

"Murphy." Harry reached for the cat, who easily eluded her.

"Murphy, you have the right idea." Susan smiled, then gently pushed the cat off her mail.

Mrs. Hogendobber came through the back door. "Four hundred and twenty dollars plus fifty dollars for a house call. I have to buy a new hot-water heater."

"That's terrible," Susan commiserated.

"I just ordered one and it will be here after lunch. I can't believe what things cost and Roy even gave me a ten-percent discount." She mentioned the appliance-store owner, an old friend.

"Hey." Susan opened a letter.

"*What?*" both Harry and Mrs. Murphy asked.

"Look at this." She held open a letter edged in Crozet High's colors, blue and gold.

It read, "You'll never get old."

"Let me see that." Harry took the letter and envelope from her. "Postmarked from the Barracks Road post office."

"But there's no name on it," Susan remarked.

"Wonder if I got one?" Harry reached into her mailbox from behind the counter. "Yep."

"Check other boxes," Susan ordered.

"I can check but I can't open the envelopes."

"I know that, Harry. I'm not an idiot."

Miranda, ignoring Susan's testiness, reached into Market Shiflett's mailbox, a member of Harry and Susan's class. "Another."

Harry checked the others, finding the same envelope. "Well, if someone was going to go to all that trouble to compliment us, he ought to sign his name."

"*Maybe it's not a compliment,*" Mrs. Murphy remarked.

Pewter, asleep, opened one eye but didn't move from the small table in the back of the post office. "*What?*"

"*Tell you later,*" Mrs. Murphy said, noticing that Tucker, on her side under the table, was dreaming.

"Oh, whoever mailed this will 'fess up or show up with a face-lift." Susan shrugged.

"We aren't old enough for face-lifts." Harry shuddered at the thought.

"People are doing stuff like that in their early thirties." Susan read too many popular magazines.

"And they look silly. I can always tell." Miranda, still upset about her hot-water heater bill, waved her hand dismissively.

"*How?*" both women and Mrs. Murphy asked.

Miranda ran her forefinger from the corner of her cheekbone to the corner of her mouth. "This muscle or ligament, whatever you call it, is always too tight, even in the very, very good ones."

"Like Mim's?" Susan mentioned Crozet's leading citizen.

"She won't admit to it." Harry liked Mim but never underestimated the woman's vanity.

"*Cats are beautiful no matter how old we are,*" Mrs. Murphy smugly noted.

Harry, as if understanding her friend, leaned down. "If I had a furry face I wouldn't care."

Susan tossed the mailing in the trash. "You'll never get old. Ha!"

Ha, indeed.

4

"Now what?" Harry, hands on hips, sourly inspected her truck.

"*Battery,*" Tucker matter-of-factly said.

Harry opened the hood, checked her cables and various wires, kept the hood open, then got back in the driver's seat and turned the ignition. A click, click, click rewarded her efforts.

"Damn! The battery."

"*That's what I said.*" The corgi calmly sat, gazing at the hood of the old blue truck.

The truck, parked in the alleyway behind the post office, nose to the railroad tie used as a curb bumper, presented problems. Many problems. With over two hundred thousand miles on the 1978 V-8 engine, this machine had earned its keep and now had earned its rest. Harry had investigated rebuilding the engine. She might squeeze another thirty thousand miles out of the truck with that. She'd gone through eight sets of tires, three batteries, two clutches, but only one set of brakes. The upholstery, worn full of holes, was covered by a plaid Baker horse blanket Harry had Mrs. Martin, the town seamstress, convert into a bench seat cover. The blue paint on the truck was so old that patches glowed an iridescent purple. The rubber covers on the accelerator and clutch were worn thin, too.

Mrs. Hogendobber, having changed into her gardening clothes, including a wonderful goatskin apron, walked across the alley from her backyard to the post office. Apart from singing in the choir and baking, gardening was her passion. Even now—being the end of a hot summer—her lilies, of all varieties, flourished. She misted them each morning and each evening.

"Miranda, do you have jumper cables?" Harry called to her.

"Dead again?" Miranda shook her head, commiserating. "And this such a beautiful afternoon. I bet you want to get home."

Just then Market Shiflett stuck his head out of the back door of the store. "Harry, Pewter—half a chicken!"

"Uh-oh. I'll pay for it, Market. I'm sorry." Secretly, Harry laughed. The fresh chickens reposed in an old white case with shaved ice and parsley. Pewter must have hooked one when Market opened the case. She was clever and she knew Market's ways, having spent her earlier years as his cat. "Did you see Mrs. Murphy?"

"Oh, yes." Market nodded. "Aiding and abetting a criminal! I often wonder what your human children will turn out to be should you have them."

"From the sound of it—chicken thieves." Out of the corner of her eye she saw Pewter valiantly struggling to haul the half-chicken to the truck. Mrs. Murphy tugged on the other side of the carcass.

"*Let me help.*" Tucker gleefully leapt toward them.

"*No, you don't,*" Mrs. Murphy spat, then saw Market. "*Pewter, quick, into the crepe myrtle!*"

The two cats dragged the chicken under the pinkish-purple crepe myrtle.

"Here." Harry dug into her pocket, handing Market a ten-dollar bill.

"It's not a gold-plated chicken." He fished in his pocket for change.

"Forget it, Market. You do plenty for me and I'm sorry Pewter behaved so badly."

"Breathed her last?" He turned his attention to the truck.

"No, just the battery."

"You've got cables, don't you?" Miranda smiled at Market, who was getting a little thick around the middle.

"I do."

"Well, if you don't mind, I'll let you two recharge Old Paint here. I am determined to dust for Japanese beetles. And I'm enduring a grub attack, too. Maybe I should get some chickens. That would take care of that." Then she saw the two cats crouched under the crepe myrtle, passionately guarding the plucked corpse. "Then again, I think not."

Harry laughed. "Go on, Miranda. Market and I will fix this."

As Miranda walked back to her lawn, Market hopped in his Subaru, next to a large new dumpster, backed out, maneuvering his car so that its nose was at a right angle to the blue truck. This saved Harry from attempting to coast backwards.

"The cables will reach." He clipped the tiny copper jaws onto the battery nodes. "Off?"

"Yep."

He switched on his ignition. "Just give it two minutes. Did you check for a loose connection?"

"I did."

Market slid out from behind the wheel and came over to lean on the truck. "Harry, it's time to bite the bullet. You'll never get through another winter with this baby."

"I know," Harry mournfully agreed.

"Call Art."

"I can't afford a new truck."

"Who said you had to buy a new one? Buy a used one."

"Market, the bank won't give me a loan on a used truck."

"They will if it's a recent one, like two or three years old."

"Yeah, but then the price will be way up. It's damned if I do and damned if I don't."

Market, hearing the distress level in Harry's voice, put his arm around her shoulder. "Chill out, honey. Art is one of our buddies.

He'll help. He makes enough money off everyone else. Go talk to the man."

"Well . . ." Her voice weakened. "I don't want to be disappointed."

"There are worse disappointments than that and we've both had them," Market genially encouraged her.

He was right, too. They'd both had a few hard knocks along the way—his divorce being more acrimonious than hers, but no divorce is happy. He had one beloved daughter, now in college. Poor Market had married the day he graduated from high school. His senior superlative was Friendliest and that friendliness meant his daughter was born seven months after the wedding.

"You know, time forges bonds of steel, doesn't it?" Harry said.

"What do you mean?"

"You, me, Miranda, Herbie, the gang. We know everything about one another—almost." She smiled.

"Yep. I can't believe we're having our twentieth. I'm"—he hummed a minute, a habit—"half-excited and half-apprehensive. How about you?"

"Same."

"Well, let's see if this baby is fired up." He walked back and cut his motor. "Crank her up."

Harry hopped in. The engine turned over, then rumbled. "I think I'd better let her run for a few more minutes."

"Good idea. How are you coming along with ideas for the reunion?"

"Okay. We had our first meeting yesterday. I've gotten everything written out for the calendars of local newspapers for all the major towns in the state. And I've written up ads to run the week before the reunion—ads with photos. I'll have to fight BoomBoom for the money. The publicity part I can do with no problem. It's coming up with some special moniker for everyone that's driving me crazy."

"Speak of the devil," he said under his breath as BoomBoom, in a new 7-series BMW—to replace one wrecked during a theft attempt—rolled down the alleyway. She pulled over. The electrical windows purred as she lowered them.

"Hi." BoomBoom's voice purred like her windows.

Marcy Wiggins, Chris Sharpton, and Bitsy Valenzuela said "Hi" along with her.

Harry returned the hellos of the trio, all neighbors in the Deep Valley subdivision. Bitsy had married E.R. Valenzuela, a classmate who'd worked in Silicon Valley and moved back home last year to establish a cellular phone business. Since E.R. worked all the time no one ever saw much of him, including his wife. Marcy, a somewhat withdrawn woman, had married Bill Wiggins, who'd gone to medical school in upstate New York, returning to the University of Virginia Hospital for his residency in oncology. No one saw much of Bill either, but he was congenial when they did.

"How'd you do?" Market asked the ladies, who all wore golf clothes.

"Not bad. We played in the Cancer Society tournament, captain's choice, and we each won a sleeve of balls. We came in seventh out of a field of twenty teams," BoomBoom bragged.

Chris leaned out the back window. "I've never played at Waynesboro Country Club. It's fun. I don't think I'll ever win boxwoods from Susan, though."

"Keep trying. Anyone roped into working on our reunion deserves boxwoods," Harry replied. "Do you all need mail?"

"No, everyone's husbands did their duty."

"Except for me," Chris laughed.

"Stay single, girl, believe me. Marriage is work," Marcy grumbled.

"Need your mail?" Harry inquired of Chris.

"No, I'll get it tomorrow. We're on our way to the big sale at Fashion Square," Chris answered. "Next time you see any of us—complete makeover." She crinkled her freckled nose.

The ladies waved and drove off.

"Cute, that Chris." Market winked.

"Yes. She reminds me of someone but I can't place it."

"Meg Ryan in a pageboy."

"You have made a study, haven't you?" Harry poked him.

"Hey, she's living in one of those new houses. She isn't going to look at a guy who owns a convenience store. I'm realistic. She's a stockbroker. Stockbrokers don't date grocers."

"The right man is the right man. Doesn't matter what he does."

"Bull. Especially from you."

"You trying to say I'm not romantic?"

"You're as realistic as I am and you always were. The Minors are solid people." He referred to Harry's paternal ancestors. She'd kept her married name, Haristeen.

"I wish someone in our family had had a head for business. Solid is good but a little money would have been wonderful."

"Mim Sanburne's got enough brains and money for the whole town, I guess." He folded his arms across his chest. "This morning a lady came in as Mim was picking up a big rack of lamb, beautiful piece of meat. She's having another one of her 'dos.' Anyway, these two ladies come in, tourists. They'd crawled over Monticello and Ash Lawn and they'd driven up to Orange to see Montpelier. They were on their way to Staunton to see Woodrow Wilson's birthplace and they needed gas. Anyway, they wound up right here in the middle of Crozet. The tall one says, 'This is kind of a dumpy town, isn't it?' The short one, maps under her arm, replies, 'Yes.' Then she looks at me and says, 'Is there anything of interest here?' Before I could open my mouth, Mim says, 'Me.' Gives them the freeze stare"—he rubbed his hands when he said that—"then opens the door, gets into her Bentley Turbo R, which these two ladies had no appreciation for, and drove off. 'Well, who does she think she is?' says the short one. 'The Queen of Crozet,' says I." He chuckled. "Guess they complained all the way to Fisherville. By that time they were probably consulting their maps again."

Harry laughed. "Crozet isn't exactly picturesque, but I think the painting the kids did on the railroad underpass is pretty nice." She leaned next to Market, shoulder to shoulder. "I guess we aren't much to look at but the land is beautiful. That's what counts. Buildings fall down and so do we. Can't be but so bad." She changed the subject abruptly, a habit of hers. "How do you get a name like Bitsy?"

"Probably the same way you get a name like Harry. You do something when you're little and it sticks. You picked up more injured animals than anyone I know. You were and remain dappled with an interesting assortment of animal sheddings."

"Which reminds me—give me a plastic bag so I can take that chicken home and boil it for them."

He fetched a beige plastic bag from the store. They both approached the two cats and Tucker, squatting before them, making them crazy.

"All right, girls, hand it over."

"Death to anyone who dares touch this chicken!" Pewter growled.

"Don't be melodramatic." The dog salivated.

Pewter lashed out, catching one of the corgi's long ears. Tucker yelped.

"Pewter, hateful thing." Harry knelt down. "Market, want your cat back?"

"Hell, no. She ate me out of my profit." He knelt down beside Harry. "Pewter, you're a bad cat."

"Put one over on you."

"Don't brag, Pewter, let's see if we can make a bargain." Mrs. Murphy swept her ears forward. *"Harry, if you don't throw the chicken away, we'll come out."*

"I'm going to cook the chicken."

"She understood!" Tucker was ecstatic.

The cats, equally amazed, released the chicken from their fangs and claws. Harry scooped it into the plastic bag.

"Come on."

They slunk out from under the bush just in case Market was going to take a swat at them.

Harry put the chicken on the seat, which meant three animals gladly scrambled into the truck. "Market, ask that Chris out. She'll say yes or she'll say no. And you've heard both before."

"I don't know."

"Hey, before I leave I forgot to ask you. Did you get a letter saying 'You'll never grow old'?"

"Yeah. In Crozet colors."

"I checked the envelopes. Each of our classmates living here got the same envelope, but that doesn't guarantee the same content. Thought I'd ask."

"No name." He stepped back from the driver's window. "I thought it was a joke because it's our twentieth reunion. Thirty-seven or thirty-eight, most of us, you know. I figured someone was panicking about turning forty."

"I didn't think of that. Susan thought it was a compliment. We look good. I guess." Harry smiled her beguiling smile.

"I'll take it." Market smacked the door of the truck like a horse's hindquarter and Harry drove off.

5

"Call to question." BoomBoom, sitting behind a long table, raised her voice.

"What are you talking about?" Harry, failing at hiding her irritation, snapped.

"Robert's Rules of Order. Otherwise we'll descend into chaos."

"BoomBoom, you're full of shit," Harry blurted out. "It's just us. Susan, Market, and Dennis."

Dennis Rablan, voted Best All-Round, volunteered to be in charge of the physical plant. That meant cleaning the gymnasium at Crozet High School, setting up the sound system for taped music, and working with the decorating committee. He'd gotten only one volunteer, Mike Zalaznik, to help him. Dennis was lazy as sin so Mike would wind up doing most of the work.

Dennis had learned to ignore the whisperings behind his back about how he had squandered away the large nest egg his father had left him. He owned a photography studio in downtown Crozet. Weddings, anniversaries, high-school graduation, red-haired Dennis was always on hand toting two or three cameras. He was the one classmate who saw the other local classmates during the turning points of their lives.

The small group sat in a history classroom at Crozet High, the windows wide open to catch the cool breeze since that wondrous Canadian high still hung around.

"Harry, don't lose your temper," Susan admonished her best friend. "BoomBoom"—she turned to the chair sitting opposite them—"you don't need to be so formal about this meeting. I don't like it any more than Harry does. Let's discuss ideas without the hoopla."

"What do you think, Dennis?" BoomBoom smiled at Dennis, her big eyes imploring him.

"Well, I never learned Robert's Rules of Order, I doubt I could contribute much, but then I might not be able to contribute much anyway." He brushed a bright forelock back.

"Aren't you going to ask me?" Market folded his arms across his chest.

"You'll vote with Harry. You always do."

"Because she has good sense." Market laughed. "Look, you want to reshoot our senior superlative pictures and have them blown up life-size to place around the auditorium. I'm not opposed to the idea but how are you going to get the superlatives from out of town to duplicate the photograph?"

"Easy." BoomBoom loved showing up Harry, although she told all who would listen that she bore Harry no ill will. After all, she had cavorted with Harry's husband after they separated but were not yet divorced, so, morally Harry was in the right. BoomBoom thought that by recognizing this she'd be absolved of her misdeeds. But small-town memories were long.

"Well?" Susan leaned forward in her seat.

"We shoot the original locations, ask the away people to duplicate their pose in a studio, and we superimpose it on the location photograph. Dennis knows how to do it. Right, Dennis?"

"Right."

"For how much?" Harry asked.

"Seven hundred dollars." BoomBoom smiled broadly, as though she'd scored a coup.

"Mostly that's for gas, chemicals, paper. There's not much in there for me," Dennis quickly added.

"You'd better not take it out of my publicity budget," Harry warned.

"You don't have a publicity budget." BoomBoom dismissed the idea.

"Oh, *yes*, I do. I worked it out over the weekend and I've made copies for everyone. If you want a bang-up reunion then you've got to cast wide your net." She handed out budget copies as Mrs. Murphy walked into the room, sitting down under the blackboard. "And don't forget, the day after Labor Day weekend I have to send a mailing with details to each class member. That's in the budget, too."

The school, built in 1920 out of fine red brick with a pretty white four-columned main entrance, exuded a coziness that Mrs. Murphy liked. Pewter and Tucker peeped around the doorjamb.

"*Are they finished yet?*" Pewter had found nothing in the hallway to entice her.

"*No,*" Murphy replied. The other animals came in and sat next to her, watching the humans as humans watch animals in a zoo.

"Harry, we can go over your budget later. We need to nail down this superlative idea first." BoomBoom barely glanced at the paper. BoomBoom herself had been voted Best Looking.

"I think it's a good idea. And I assume you will blow up the original senior superlative photograph and put it next to the new one." Susan nodded.

"Exactly! Won't it be wonderful?"

"Not if you're going bald," Market moaned.

BoomBoom pounced on him. "If you'd take the herbs I drop

off for you it would help, and if that doesn't give you results fast enough, then get those hair transplants. They really work."

"You'd look adorable," Dennis teased, "with those plugs in your scalp. Just like cornrows."

"I'll get you for that, Dennis. You know why God made hair? Because not everyone could have a perfect head."

"Three points for Market." Harry chalked up the air.

"Are you going to agree with my plan or not?" BoomBoom folded her hands, staring at Harry.

"Yes. There, bet that surprised you, didn't it?"

"Kinda." BoomBoom sighed with relief. "Dennis, when can you start?"

"The sooner the better. How about this week?"

"Fine," everyone said in unison. They wanted to go home. The weather was good and everyone had things to do.

"*Let's go.*" Pewter shook herself.

"*Not yet,*" Tucker sighed as BoomBoom plucked another paper off her pile.

"We still don't have a ball chairman. So many of us live in the central Virginia area—you'd think someone would volunteer."

"People are overcommitted," said Susan, a shining example.

"If I can't buttonhole someone soon, we'll have to do it," BoomBoom announced.

"No, we won't." Harry put her foot down.

"*BoomBoom plucks Mom's last nerve. Beyond that, what is it about people sitting in a meeting? Everything takes three times as long. Big fat waste of time,*" Murphy commented.

"*Passing opinions is like passing gas. They can't help it,*" Pewter giggled.

"Harry, are you still our liaison person with Mrs. Hogendobber so we don't have any conflicts with their reunion?" BoomBoom ignored Harry's small rebellion.

"Liaison person? I see her five or six days out of the week."

"Thought I'd ask."

"BoomBoom, what's your idea for the decorating committee?" Susan had visions of a bare auditorium save for the senior superlative photographs.

"Marcy Wiggins and Bitsy Valenzuela have volunteered to help us if we help organize the Cancer Ball fund-raiser in December. I think Charlie Ashcraft will head the committee."

"You can't be serious," Harry blurted out. "Charlie is such a womanizer."

"He's all we've got. Plus"—BoomBoom lowered her voice conspiratorially—"he's already putting the moves on Marcy."

"I hope you've warned her." Susan frowned.

"She's a big girl." BoomBoom tidied the few papers on her desk.

"Boom, he's one of the handsomest men God ever put on earth and utterly irresponsible. His idea of going slow is to ask a woman to bed after being introduced to her instead of before. Come on." Harry leaned forward.

"She's married." Market waved off the subject, feeling Marcy's wedding ring offered protection—sort of like garlic against a vampire.

"Unhappily," BoomBoom demurred.

Dennis finally spoke. "Remember Raylene Ramsey and Meredith McLaughlin getting into a fight over Charlie at our fifteenth reunion?"

"I thought they'd kill one another." Market checked his watch.

"I'd rather hoped they'd kill Charlie," Harry laughed.

"I never could see what you girls saw in him." Dennis laughed, too.

"Don't look at me. I think he's an asshole." Harry held up her hands.

BoomBoom, having seduced Charlie in their youth, or vice versa, kept silent on this.

Susan jumped in. "I don't mind that he had sex with both of

them at our fifteenth. I do mind, however, that he saw fit to do it in the pool at the Holiday Inn. Just because it was three in the morning didn't mean we weren't awake." Susan shook her head in disgust.

"Back to the subject. Charlie as head of decorating?" BoomBoom tapped the desk with her pencil. "And Marcy Wiggins and Bitsy Valenzuela," she added.

"But they didn't go to high school with us," Market protested.

"Who cares, Market? We need workers. Chris was a big help at our meeting at my house." Harry punched him lightly. "Anyway, they married into our class. That counts for something."

"Chris says maybe she'll meet some men. It's hard for new people to fit in. We were born here. We never think about breaking into a new place," BoomBoom replied.

"Did she really say she wanted to meet men?" Market whispered.

"Yes," Harry whispered back.

"She's not half bad," Dennis whispered as he overheard them. This earned him a stern glare from Market.

"Are we okay on Charlie then?" BoomBoom pressed on.

The others looked at one another, then reluctantly raised their hands in agreement since no one could think of a substitute.

"One last item of business before we adjourn." BoomBoom couldn't help but notice how fidgety her classmates had become. "I received a bordered letter, run off at Kinko's or KopyKat, I think. Anyway, it said, 'You'll never get old.' Harry, did you send that out?"

"Why me?" Harry was surprised.

"You're the postmistress. I thought you might be playing a practical joke on us."

"No. It wasn't me."

BoomBoom looked from one to the other as each one shook his or her head. "Well, I think it's in bad taste."

"Boom, what are you talking about?" Susan asked.

"Yeah," Market and Dennis said.

"'You'll never get old.' I should think it would be obvious. We'll never get old if we're dead. Here I am trying to create the best reunion ever and someone is sending out a sick joke."

"I didn't take it that way." Susan frowned since she didn't like BoomBoom's interpretation.

On that note the meeting broke up.

"It *is odd*," Mrs. Murphy mused to no one in particular.

6

"Are you really going to buy a truck?" Fair Haristeen asked his
ex-wife as he picked up his mail the next morning.

"Gonna try."

"She's taking a two-hour lunch to visit Art Bushey." Miranda
helpfully supplied him with information.

"Serious." He rubbed his chin.

*"She cruises the lot at night, looking at trucks, but this is the first time she's
going over in the day,"* Mrs. Murphy told Fair, who pulled a metal foil
wrapper out of his pocket and gave it to her.

"Here, Houdini, open this." His deep voice rumbled.

Mrs. Murphy surreptitiously looked around. Pewter, asleep in
the mail cart, remained unaware of the gift which Murphy
inspected and then tore open. The aroma of moist fish tidbits
caused one chartreuse eye to open down in the mail cart.

"Don't you have anything for me?" Tucker implored.

Fair reached into his other pocket, bringing forth a foil
packet with a plum-colored edging marked Mouth-Watering Dog
Divine Treats. He pulled open the pouch, spilling the contents on
the floor.

"Thank you!" Tucker gobbled up the round meat treats.

Pewter, on her back, rolled over. She crawled out of the cart to join Mrs. Murphy, who wasn't wildly happy about it but she wasn't selfish either.

"Are you going to add a small-animal practice to your equine practice?" Mrs. Hogendobber laughed.

"No. I get freebies from feed companies. Which reminds me, I've got a bag of rich alfalfa cubes. I'm wondering if you'd help me, Harry? If I give you a feed schedule, three cubes per day along with your standard timothy, will you keep weight charts for me?"

"Sure," Harry happily agreed.

"You don't put your horses on a scale, do you?" Mrs. Hogendobber, not a horse person, inquired. "That would be awfully difficult, wouldn't it?"

"Miranda, the easiest way to keep track of gain is a tape measure. Just the kind you'd buy from the five-and-dime."

"Except there are no more five-and-dimes." Miranda wrinkled her forehead. "When I think of the times I ran into Woolworth's with a quarter as a child and thought I was rich . . ."

"You were." Fair smiled, which only made him more handsome. He strongly resembled the young Gary Cooper.

At six feet four inches, with blond hair, a strong jaw, kind eyes, and broad shoulders, Fair was a man women noticed. And they usually smiled when they noticed.

"Those were the days." The older woman rolled up the blue nylon belts used to hold large quantities of mail. "Do you know, Fair Haristeen, that this year is my fiftieth high-school reunion. I have to pinch myself to realize it."

"You don't look a day over thirty-nine and no one in Crozet can hold a candle to your gardening powers."

She smiled broadly. "Better not say that in front of Mim."

"If I had three gardeners I'd be on the garden tour, too." He tossed catalogues in the garbage can. "You do it by yourself."

"Thank you." She was mightily pleased.

"Almost lunch hour." Harry flicked two letters into Susan Tucker's mailbox.

Fair glanced at the clock. "Want me to go with you to Art's?"

"Why, you think I can't make a deal?"

"No. I think you'll cry if you part with that heap out back."

"I will not." Color came to her cheeks.

"Okay." He winked at Miranda when Harry couldn't see him, walked to the door, then turned. "I'll drop the alfalfa cubes off tonight."

"I don't know if I want to talk to you. I can't believe you think I'd cry over a truck."

"Uh-huh." He pushed open the door and walked into the breezy air. It felt more like late September than the tail end of August.

"He gets my goat," Harry mumbled as she rolled up lingerie catalogues and slid them in Little Mim's mailbox. "Why does she get all these underwear wishing books?"

"Because she's wishing," Miranda answered.

Little Mim, divorced a few years back, was lonesome, lonesome and carrying a torch for Harry's neighbor, Blair Bainbridge.

"Oh." Harry blinked. She never thought of stuff like that.

"It's noon. Are you going to the Ford dealer, or not?"

"I'm going. I said I was going. I know none of you think I can count beans much less make a deal."

"I never said that."

"You didn't have to."

"Harry, calm yourself. I think you have a good head for figures. I admire your frugality. After all, I'm still driving my husband's Falcon and how many years has my poor George been called to heaven? Really now, I'm on your side."

Harry regretted her crabby moment. "I know you are, Miranda. I don't know what made me cross."

"Your ex."

She shrugged. "I think I can do better without the three musketeers. Mind letting them work through lunch hour?"

"*Take me?*" Tucker wagged her nonexistent tail.

"I'm *staying right here*." Pewter put one paw on the collapsed foil packet.

"I'll *stay, too. Good luck, Mom.*"

Twenty minutes later Harry rolled down Pantops Mountain, for she'd driven down on I-64, turning left on Route 250 at the Shadwell exit. The Ford dealership, spanking blue and white, covered the north side of the road just before the river. In the old days there had been a covered bridge over the Rivanna River, called Free Bridge, since there was no toll to use it. A big storm would find horse and buggies lined up in the bridge waiting for the worst to blow over. Today such chance encounters and sensible acceptance of Nature's agenda had been pushed aside. People thought they could drive through anything. The covered bridge gave way to a two-lane buttressed bridge, which in turn gave way to a four-lane soulless piece of engineering. People zoomed across the river with never a thought for stopping and looking down or having a juicy chat with a friend while the thunder boomed overhead.

Harry pulled in front of the plate-glass windows at the older part of the Ford building.

Art Bushey walked out to see her. "Hi, beautiful. Did I ever tell you, I have a thing for postmistresses. I like that word 'mistress.' Just gives me chills."

"Pervert." Harry punched him, then hugged him.

"Knew you were coming. Half of Crozet called me, including your ex-husband. Still loves you, Harry. But hey, men fall all over you."

"You are so full of it."

"Love hearing it, though, don't you? You're a good-looking woman. I want good-looking women driving Ford trucks." He ducked his head into the 1978 truck to look at the speedometer. "How many times has this thing turned over?"

"Over two hundred thousand."

"We build 'em good, don't we?" He patted the nose of the blue truck. "Come on, let me show you what I've got and Harry, don't panic about the money just yet. Let me show you what's here. You drive them. I'll work something out. I want your money, now, don't misunderstand me. I love money. But Busheys, Minors, and Hepworths"—he mentioned her mother's maiden name—"go back a long way. I remember when your father bought this truck."

"I do, too. His first new truck. You still had your mustache." Harry recalled the flush on her father's lean face when he told his wife and daughter he'd bought a brand-new truck.

"Come on." He opened the door to a red half-ton 4 x 4. "Thinking about growing my mustache back."

"I guess you were expecting me—got the plates on and everything." She smiled. "About the mustache: do it. Makes you look dangerous."

Art liked that. "They're all ready for you and I've got two used ones for you to look at as well."

She hopped in the cab, turned the motor over as he clicked on his seat belt in the passenger seat.

"Now this truck is maxed out. AC over here, tape deck and CD, speakers everywhere, captain's chairs—nice on the back—plush interior, which your cats will enjoy. Cats are fussy."

"Yeah, I'd hate to disappoint them." Harry hit the accelerator, they backed out, and in a minute they were heading toward Keswick. "Jeez, this thing drives like a car."

They roared down the road and as she touched the brakes, the machine glided to a smooth stop.

By the time they returned to the dealership she was amazed at how the truck felt. One by one they got into the different trucks, different trim packages.

After an hour of driving new and two very nice used trucks they repaired to Art's office. "What do you think?"

"I'm scared of the cost," she forthrightly replied.

He punched in a mess of numbers. "Look." He yanked out the computer printout. "I can get you an F250 HD 4 by 4 for twenty thousand, four hundred and seventy-eight dollars. That's stripped and doesn't figure in your trade-in, which I will know in a minute because while we were out cruising, one of my guys was going over your truck."

"It's in good shape."

"I know that. You take care of everything including yourself." He pointed to figures on the right-hand column. "Add in your tags, title transfer, documentation service—and I don't know whether you want the extended service plan or not but figure another five hundred. Hold that number in your head. Round numbers are easier to remember. If you buy this now, I can give you a six-hundred-dollar rebate. That expires September fifteenth. Don't ask me why. Ford makes those decisions and the dealer has nothing to say about it. Good for you, though. But here"—he punched in some more numbers—"I can get you the XLT package for another fifteen hundred. If you buy things piecemeal like the tape deck and AC it doesn't make sense. I know this sounds crazy but if you spend money you can save money on the payments. I'm figuring you'll finance for five years. Look, I can get you the bells and whistles—" He pointed to a figure on the bottom of a new page he pulled out of the computer.

Her eyes grew large. "But that's almost four thousand more dollars."

"It is. But if we spread it over the five years it means about another thirty in your payment schedule. And Harry, this isn't the final figure. Aren't you going to badger me about the price?"

"Uh . . ."

The phone rang. "Yeah," Art said. "Great." He punched the button. "One thousand five hundred dollars on your 1978. And here's what I'll sell you the F250 HD 4 by 4 for." He scrawled numbers.

"That's almost twenty percent less." She scooted to the edge of her seat.

"That's right. You're paying what I pay plus the paperwork. What color do you want?"

"Red."

"What interior?"

"Beige."

He pointed to a red truck sitting on the lot. "You got it. Now Harry, I know you don't make a lot of money. I also know you'll drive this truck for twenty years. Why don't you take the truck home? If you don't like it, bring it back but don't go telling everyone what the cost is or everyone will want the same deal and then I'd go broke."

"Art?"

"Hey." He threw up his hands. "Like I said, I've got a thing for postmistresses. Go on, get out of here before Miranda calls and says she's overloaded."

Harry drove the new machine along I-64 feeling certain that everyone on the highway was admiring the beautiful truck. She'd done her sums at home and knew she could carry, with care, about four hundred and fourteen dollars a month.

When she drove to the front of the post office instead of the back, Miranda, Mrs. Murphy, Pewter, Tucker, and Market—in picking up his mail—ran out.

"Wow!" Market whistled.

"*Open the door!*" Mrs. Murphy excitedly demanded, and as the door swung open for everyone to see the plush interior, the cat jumped up on the floor and then on the seat.

"O-o-o." She dug her claws in the upholstery just a tiny bit.

Within seconds, Pewter sat next to her. "*Snuggly.*" She patted at the divider between the two seats, a console with trays, cup holders, all manner of niceties to make the truck a little office. "*Even a place to store catnip.*"

"*I want to see!*" The dog whined as the humans opened the door on the other side.

"Here." Harry picked up Tucker, a heavy child, putting her on the seat after wiping off her paws.

"*Neat.*" The dog smiled.

"*Not bad.*" Pewter squeezed next to Tucker.

"Did you buy it?" Miranda eagerly asked.

"I think I did. I have to call my banker. I didn't give Art a firm yes."

"You can put the fifth wheel in the back—haul your horses. The old half-ton was straining," Market counseled.

"What saved me was I only hauled one at a time." Harry laughed because it did make life that much harder not being able to take two horses in her two-horse trailer.

Chris Sharpton drove up and parked. "This is new."

Harry smiled. "I haven't bought it yet."

"BoomBoom called me"—Chris pulled her mailbox key out of her purse—"asking me to come up with more ideas for the 'welcoming committee.' That's what she's calling you guys now. I told her I wouldn't mind but I hoped you wouldn't mind. After all, it's your reunion and your committee."

" 'Course, I don't mind."

Chris smiled. "The Boom is getting desperate—not so much about the work for this thing but because she wants to make certain that *she* is *perfect* by homecoming—head to toe."

"Big surprise," Harry giggled.

"Can we meet tomorrow night?" Chris walked into the post office as Harry nodded yes.

Later that night, Harry turned off the lights in the barn, walked across to the house, and burst into tears. She'd lived with her old truck for so many years she couldn't imagine living without it.

No sooner had she walked into the house then Tucker barked, "Intruder!"

Harry walked back outside.

Fair was driving her old 1978 blue truck, followed by Art Bushey in a new silver Jeep.

"Hi," she said as they both got out of their vehicles.

"Here's your truck." Fair handed her the keys.

"Huh?" She was confused.

"Fair put up the down payment on the F250 so you don't

have to trade in your dad's truck." Art crossed his arms over his chest and leaned against the silver Jeep. "I told him he's nuts. You still aren't going to take him back but he did it anyway."

"Art, you're awful." She burst out laughing as the cats hopped into the bed of the old blue truck. The vantage point was better.

"Fair, I can't take your money."

"A late divorce settlement." He shrugged. "Now do you want the F250 or the F350 dually?"

"I'd better stick to the F250 HD."

"Doing it my way it's twelve hundred more for the dually. So you have everything you've ever wanted—your half-ton and a dually," Art said. "Big F350 in red with a beige interior just like the 250 here. And those extra wheels in the back are what you need when you're hauling weight."

"Deal!" She shook his hand.

"Red." Fair slapped his baseball cap against his thigh. "I bet Art a hundred bucks you'd buy another blue truck."

"Gotcha." Art smiled.

"Hey, wait." Harry ran into the barn, returning with a paper. "Here's the figures on the horses. I measured them tonight."

"Damn, I knew I forgot something. I'll drop off the alfalfa cubes tomorrow."

"Fair."

"Huh?"

"You're a good man." She put her hand behind his neck, drew him down, and kissed him.

"What about me?"

"How could I forget?" She kissed Art, too.

"All right, buddy, drive this back." Art shepherded Fair to the Jeep. Art would drive back in the F250. "You can pick up your dually tomorrow unless you want me to send it to Cavalier Camper for the fifth wheel."

"That's a good idea," Harry agreed.

As they drove off, Pewter asked Mrs. Murphy, *"How'd he know she'd never part with her father's truck?"*

Tucker called from the ground, "*He's very sensitive.*"

"But it's metal," Pewter protested, finding the emotion around the 1978 truck silly.

"*Metal but it has so many memories.*"

"*A cruise down Memory Lane.*" Tucker walked back toward the house.

"*If she got this worked up over a truck, what's she going to be like at her high-school reunion?*" Pewter gingerly stepped onto the back bumper and thence to the ground.

7

"A big smile. There. Cover of *People* magazine." Dennis Rablan clicked away, his black Nikon camera covering his face. "Boom, get your face closer to the steer. You, too, Charlie, get in there."

"Yuk." Charlie grimaced. "I didn't like this the first time we did it, twenty years ago."

"Least it's not a horse's ass," Harry quipped. She had been conned by Susan to help with the first superlative shoot.

"No, I've got Boom for that."

"You know, Charlie," she hissed through clenched teeth, "you won Best Looking but you sure didn't win Best Personality and you never will."

"Like I care." He beamed to the camera.

Susan stood to the side holding up a reflector, which the steer distrusted. Crouched beside the large animal were Fair Haristeen on one side and Blair Bainbridge, equally tall, on the other.

Although Blair was a professional model, Charlie Ashcraft held his own. He was a strikingly handsome man, with curly, glossy black hair, bright blue eyes, and a creamy tan. At six foot one with a good body, he bowled women over. He knew it. He used it. He abused it. He left a trail of broken hearts, broken marriages, and broken promises behind him. Despite that, women still fell for him even when they knew his history. His arrogance added fuel to the fire. He was loathed by those not under his spell, which was to say most men.

Her shoulders ached, her deltoids especially, as Harry held the silver reflector behind Denny Rablan. She thought, *How like BoomBoom to take her own photo first. No matter what, her visage will be plastered all over the gym.* Instead she said, "Denny, I'm putting this down for a minute." The heat was giving her a headache, or was it the reunion itself? She wasn't sure she had improved with the passage of time.

Click. He said without looking at her, "Okay. All right, take a break, especially Hercules here."

Fair stepped up and put a small grain bucket in front of Hercules, whose mood improved considerably.

Marcy Wiggins in her candy-apple red Taurus GL drove down the farm lane followed by Chris Sharpton and Bitsy Valenzuela in Bitsy's Jaguar XJR, top down.

"Oh no, are we late?" Chris wailed, opening the car door.

"No, we're taking a break. Harry's arms are tired," BoomBoom answered.

"I'll hold the reflector," Chris eagerly volunteered.

"Great. You've got a job." Harry handed her the floppy silver square.

"Boom, you look fabulous—professional makeup job, I bet," Bitsy cooed.

"Oh . . ." BoomBoom Craycroft had no intention of answering that question.

Charlie glided over. "I don't believe I've had the pleasure."

"You have, too." Bitsy laughed. "I met you at the Foxfield Races. My husband is E. R. Valenzuela, the president of 360° Communications here in town. You let me know if you need a cell phone in your car, you hear now?"

"Foxfield, well, that is a distracting environment." He

smoothed his hair, which sprang back into curls. "I had no idea E.R. had such good taste in women."

Then brazenly, Charlie swept his eyes from the top of Chris's head to her toes. "A model's body. Tall and angular. Have I ever told you how much I like that?"

"Yes." She laughed. "Every time you see me."

He beamed at each lady in turn. Marcy turned beet red. "I'll call you the three Amuses. Good, huh?"

"Brilliant." Chris's eyelids dropped a bit, then flickered upward.

"God, Charlie, I hope you don't say that to my husband." Marcy swallowed hard.

"Do you know what I say to any woman's husband? 'If you don't treat her right, some other man will. Just because you're married doesn't mean you can relax. A woman's got to be won over each and every day.' " He smiled from ear to ear.

"Good Lord," Marcy whispered.

"I think I'll help Boom," Bitsy brightly said as she skipped past her friend.

Bitsy wiped the shine from BoomBoom's nose, adding a dab of lipstick to her mouth.

Denny clapped his hands, which disturbed Hercules, who let out a bellow. "Let's go."

Harry, arms crossed, watched Charlie stoop down, Hercules on one side and BoomBoom on the other.

"Harry, why don't you take away this bucket?" BoomBoom pointed at the bucket.

"You crippled?" Harry turned on her heel, striding to her old Ford truck. "*Adios.*"

"You're not going to kiss me good-bye?" Charlie called out. He puckered his lips.

"I wouldn't kiss you if you were the last man on earth," Harry said, as Susan's jaw nearly dropped to her chest.

"Hey, I love you, too."

"Charlie, is this a command performance?" Marcy asked, voice wavering.

He winked at her, then called after Harry, "I understand you called me a body part at the reunion meeting."

"I should have called you an arrogant, empty-headed, vainglorious idiot. 'Asshole' showed a lack of imagination." She smiled a big fake smile, her head throbbing.

"You've been divorced too-o-o long," he said in a singsong voice.

She stopped in her tracks. Fair's face froze. Susan covered her eyes, peeking out through her fingers. BoomBoom squared her shoulders, ready for the worst.

"You know what, Charlie? My claim to fame is that I'm one of seven women in Albemarle County who hasn't gone to bed with you."

"There's still time." He laughed as Marcy Wiggins' face registered dismay.

"You'll die before I do." Harry turned, heading back to the truck.

This icy pronouncement caught everyone off guard. Charlie laughed nervously. Dennis took over, rearranging the principals except for Hercules, who was firmly planted close to the grain.

Then Charlie yelled after her, "I knew you sent that letter about me not growing old."

"Dream on." Harry kept walking. "I wouldn't waste the postage."

"Susan, you aren't going, too?" BoomBoom's voice, drenched in irritation, cut through Hercules' bellow as he cried for his grain bucket. Susan left with Harry.

Susan leaned over to Harry as they walked away. "You got a wild hair or what?" she said, *sotto voce*.

"I don't really know. Just know I can't take any more." Harry rubbed her temples. "Susan, I don't know what's happening to me. I have no patience anymore. None. And I'm sick and tired of beating around the bush. Hell with it."

"M-m-m."

"I don't want to be rude but I'm fresh out of tolerance for the fools of this life."

"Your poor mother will be spinning in her grave. All the years of cotillion, the Sunday teas."

Harry put her hand on the chrome door handle of the 1978 truck. "Here's what I don't get: where is the line between good manners and supporting people in their bullshit? I'm not putting up with Charlie for one more minute." She opened the door but didn't climb inside. "I've turned a corner. I'm not wearing that social face anymore. Too much time. Too much suppressed anger. If people are going to like me they can like me as I am. Treat me right and I'll treat you right."

"Within reason."

"Well . . . yes." Harry reluctantly conceded.

Susan breathed in the moist air. The heat had finally returned and with it the flies. "I know exactly how you feel. I'm not brave enough to act on it yet."

"Of course you are."

"No. I have a husband with a good career and two teenagers. When the last one graduates from college—five more years—" She sighed, "Then I expect I'll be ready."

"*Tempus fugit.*" Harry hopped in the truck. "Charlie Ashcraft has not one redeeming virtue. How is it that someone like him lives and someone good dies? Aurora Hughes was a wonderful person."

"Pity. He is the most divine-looking animal." Susan shrugged.

"Handsome is as handsome does."

"Tell that to my hormones," Susan countered.

They both laughed and Harry drove home feeling as if the weight of the world had been lifted off her shoulders. She wasn't sure why. Was it because she had erupted at BoomBoom? At Charlie? Or because she had gotten tired and left, instead of standing there feeling like a resentful martyr? She decided she wasn't going to help with any other senior superlative photographs and she wasn't even sure she'd go through with her own. Then she thought better of it. After all, it would be really mean-spirited not to cooperate. They were all in this together. Still, the thought of BoomBoom hovering around . . . Of course, knowing Boom she'd put off Harry's shot until last and then photograph her in the worst light. Harry thought she'd better call Denny at the studio tomorrow.

After the chores, she played with Mrs. Murphy, Pewter, and Tucker. They loved to play hide 'n' seek.

The phone rang at nine P.M.

"Har?"

"Susan, don't tell me you just got home."

"No. I just heard this instant—Charlie Ashcraft was shot dead in the men's locker room at the Farmington Country Club."

"What?"

"Right between the eyes with a .38."

"Who did it?"

"Nobody knows."

"I can think of a dozen who'd fight for the chance."

"Me, too. Queer, though. After just seeing him."

"Bet BoomBoom's glad she got the photograph first," Harry shot from the hip.

"You're awful."

"No, I'm your best friend. I'm supposed to say anything in the world to you, 'member?"

"Then let me say this to you. Don't be too jolly. Think about what you said this afternoon. We have no idea of who he's slept with recently. That's for starters. He was gifted at hiding his amours for a time, anyway. I'm all for your cleansing inside but a little repression will go a long way right now."

"You're right."

After she hung up the phone she told Mrs. Murphy, Pewter, and Tucker, who listened with interest.

"*A jilted husband finally did what everyone else has wanted to do,*" Tucker said.

"Tucker, you have the sweetest eyes." Harry stroked the soft head.

"*Weren't there any witnesses?*" Mrs. Murphy asked.

"*Right between the eyes.*" Pewter shook her head.

Farmington Country Club glowed with the patina of years. The handmade bricks lent a soft paprika glow to the Georgian buildings in the long summer twilight. As the oldest country club in Albemarle County, Farmington counted among its members the movers and shakers of the region as well as the totally worthless whose only distinguishing feature was that they had inherited enough money to stay current on their dues. The median age of members was sixty-two, which didn't bode well for Farmington's future. However, Farmington rested secure in its old golf course with long, classic fairways. The modern golf courses employed far too many sharp doglegs and par 3's because land was so expensive.

Charlie Ashcraft, a good golfer, had divided his skills between Farmington and its challengers, Keswick and Glenmore. At a seven handicap he was much in demand as a partner, carrying pounds of silver from tournaments. He also carried away Belinda Harrier when he was only seventeen and she was thirty and had won the ladies' championship. That was the first clue that Charlie possessed unusual powers of persuasion. Charlie's parents fetched him from the Richmond motel to which they had fled and Belinda's husband promptly divorced her. Her golf game went to pot as did Belinda.

Rick Shaw, sheriff of Albemarle County, and his deputy, the young and very attractive Cynthia Cooper, knew all this. They had done their homework. Cynthia was about twenty years younger than Rick. The age difference enhanced their teamwork.

The men's locker room had been cordoned off with shiny plastic yellow tape. The employees of the club, all of whom had seen enough wild stuff to write a novel, had to admit this was the weirdest of the weird.

The locker room, recently remodeled, had a general sitting room with the lockers and showers beyond that. The exterior door faced out to the parking lot. An interior door was about thirty feet from the golf shop with a stairway in between which first rose to a landing and continued into the men's grill, forbidden to women. If a man walked through the grill he would wind up in the 19th Hole, the typical sort of restaurant most clubs provide at the golf course.

Getting in and out of the men's locker room would have been easy for Charlie's killer. As the golfers had come and gone, the only people around would have been those who'd been dressing for dinner in the main dining room or down in the tavern way at the other end of the huge structure. There would be little traffic in and out of the locker room. The housekeeping staff cleaned at about eleven at night, checking again at eight in the morning since the locker rooms never closed.

Charlie Ashcraft had been found by a local attorney, Mark DiBlasi. The body remained as Mark had found him, sitting upright, slumped against locker 13. Blood was smeared on the locker. Charlie's head hadn't slumped to the side; blood trickled out of his ears but none came from his eyes or his mouth. It was a clean shot at very close range; a circle of powder burn at the entry point signified that. The bullet exited the back of his head, tore into the locker door, and lodged in the opposite wall.

Mark DiBlasi had been dining with his mother and wife when he left the main dining room to fetch his wallet from his locker. He'd played golf, finished at six-thirty, showered, and closed his locker, but forgot his wallet, which was still in his golf shorts. The moment he saw Charlie he called the sheriff. He then called the club manager. After that he sat down and shook like a leaf.

"Mark, forgive me. I know this is trying." Cooper sat next to him on a bench. "You think you came back here at eight?"

"Yes." Mark struggled for composure.

"You noticed no one."

"Nobody."

She flipped through her notebook. "I think I've gotten everything. If I have other questions I'll call you at the office. I'm sorry your dinner was disturbed." She called to Rick, "Any questions?"

Rick wheeled around. "Mark, who was Charlie's latest conquest?"

Mark blushed and stammered a moment. "Uh—anyone new and pretty?"

Rick nodded. "Go on. I know where to find you. If you think of anything, call me."

"Will do." Mark straightened his tie as he hurried out.

"He'll have nightmares," Cynthia remarked.

"H-m-m." Rick changed the subject. "Charlie's four ex-wives. We'll start there."

"They all moved away, didn't they?"

"Yeah." He whistled as he walked through the men's locker room to fix the layout in his mind.

A knock on the door revealed Diana Robb, head of the Crozet Rescue Squad. "Ready?"

"I didn't hear the siren," Cynthia said.

"Didn't hit it. I was coming back from the hospital when you called, not more than a mile away." She looked at Charlie as she walked back into the lockers. "Neat as a pin. Even his tie is straight."

"Mark DiBlasi found him."

Diana called over her shoulder, "Hey guys, bring in the gurney and the body bag." Her two assistants scurried back out for the equipment.

"Mark said he was warm when he found him," Rick informed her.

"Fresh kill."

"We've already dusted. He's ready to go." Cynthia watched as the gurney was rolled in; the quarters were a bit tight.

"Put on your gloves and let's lift him up, carry him out to the sitting room," Diana directed. "Sucker's going to be heavy."

"Any ideas?" Cynthia asked Diana.

"Too many."

"Yeah, that seems to be the problem." Rick smiled.

"I do know this." Diana wiggled her fingers in the thin rubber gloves over which she pulled on a pair of heavier gloves. "Charlie always was a snob. If you didn't have money you had to have great bloodlines. There were no poor people involved."

9

The post office buzzed the next morning. As it was the central meeting point in town, each person arrived hopeful that someone would have more news than they had. Everyone had an opinion, that much was certain.

"Can't go sleeping with other men's wives without expecting trouble," Jim Sanburne, mayor of Crozet and husband of Mim, announced.

As Jim, in his youth, had indulged in affairs, the elegant Mim eyed him coldly. "Well said."

"*This is getting good.*" Mrs. Murphy, whiskers vibrating, perched on the counter between the mailroom and the public room.

Pewter, next to her, licked her paw, then absentmindedly forgot to wash herself. Tucker, mingling out with the people, believed she could smell guilt and anger.

"Will even one person lament his death?" Mim asked.

Jim Sanburne rubbed his chin. "Whoever he was carrying on with at the time, I reckon."

The Reverend Herb Jones growled, "He was a rascal, no doubt. But, then again, he was a young man in his prime—never forget redemption."

Miranda nodded her head in agreement with the Reverend.

"Something wrong with that boy." The massive Jim leaned over the counter so close that Pewter decided to rub against his arm to make him feel loved.

"Male version of nymphomania," Big Mim said as her daughter, Little Mim, blinked, surprised at her mother's boldness.

Fair, who'd walked in the door, picked up the word "nymphomania." "I came just in time."

Marcy Wiggins and Chris Sharpton also pushed open the door. Fair stepped aside. The small space was getting crowded.

Chris shyly blinked. "It's so shocking. I mean, we were all watching the superlative shoot and then this."

"Chris, don't waste your time feeling sorry for that s.o.b.," Susan Tucker told her. "You didn't know him well enough to be one of his victims—yet. He would have tried."

"Charlie should have been shot years ago," Fair laconically said, then turned solemn. "But still you never think something like this would happen to someone you know."

Noticing the look on Marcy's face, Harry added, "We're not as cold as you might think, Marcy. But ask E.R. about Charlie's past. He upset too many applecarts without giving a thought to what he was doing to people's lives. He remained unacquainted with responsibility for his entire life."

"Oh," Marcy replied, looking not at all comforted.

" 'The way of a fool is right in his own eyes, but a wise man listens to advice.' Proverbs. Twelfth chapter, fifteenth verse," Mrs. Hogendobber quoted. "Charlie Ashcraft was told many times in many ways by many people that he had to change his habits. He didn't. Someone changed them for him; not that that's right. No one has the right to take a life. That power belongs only to God."

"*Tucker, smell anything?*" Murphy called down.

"*No, although Jim Sanburne has dog pee on his shoe. Bet Mim's dog got him and he doesn't even know it,"* the corgi gleefully reported. *"Of course, I haven't sniffed everyone yet. There's too much coming and going."*

BoomBoom flounced through the door, breathlessly put her tiny hand to her heart. "Can you believe it? Right after our superlative shoot."

"Aren't you glad you shot yours first?" Harry dryly commented. "As it is we'll have two people missing in our shoots. This way you would have had three."

"Harry, I can't believe you said that." BoomBoom folded her arms across her chest. "Do you really think I would be more concerned about our senior superlative photographs than a man's life?"

"In a word, yes." Harry also folded her arms across her chest.

"This is getting good," Pewter purred with excitement.

"Our classmate is dead," BoomBoom nearly shrieked. "After that damned letter you sent."

"I didn't send that stupid letter!" Harry lowered her voice instead of raising it.

"Harry would never do anything like that," Fair curtly said.

"She likes to stir the pot."

"Look who's talking." Harry squared off at BoomBoom.

"Pipe down," Big Mim commanded. "You aren't solving anything. This is about Charlie's murder, not your history with one another." She turned to her ex-husband. "If every man in Crozet were shot for infidelity, who would be left?"

"Now, honey, let sleeping dogs lie." His *basso profundo* voice rumbled.

"It's not sleeping dogs we're talking about," Mim snapped.

Little Marilyn tugged at the ends of her white linen jacket and suppressed a smile.

"We're all upset." Herb smoothed the waters. "After all, everyone of us here, with the exception of the two lovely young additions to our community"—he nodded toward Chris and Marcy—"have known Charlie since childhood. Yes, he was flawed, but is there anyone standing here who is perfect?"

A subdued quiet fell over the room.

"*I'm perfect,*" Pewter warbled as the humans looked at her.

"*Oh la!*" Mrs. Murphy laughed.

"*Girls, this is serious.*" The corgi frowned. "*You know sooner or later the murderer will pop up and what if he pops up here?!*"

"*You've got a point,*" Mrs. Murphy, stretching fore and aft, agreed.

"*Doesn't change the fact that I am perfect.*"

"Harry, what do you feed them?" Chris lightheartedly said, which broke the tension in the room.

The chatter again filled the room but the acrimony level died down.

Herb leaned over to Harry. "What's this letter business?"

"I'll show you." She walked back to the small table where she'd left three days' worth of mail. She returned, handing it over the counter.

He read it. "Could mean a lot of things."

"Exactly," Harry agreed.

"But it is creepy," BoomBoom intruded.

"Now it is, but we're viewing it through the lens of Charlie's death," Herb sensibly replied.

Fair put one elbow on the counter divider. "I wouldn't make too much of this unless something else happens—something, uh, dark."

Chris joined in as Marcy was tongue-tied and uncomfortable. "I agree, but reunions are such loaded situations. All those memories."

"My memories are pretty wonderful." Fair winked at Harry, who blushed.

"You were the class ahead. Our memories might be different." BoomBoom sighed.

"I thought you had a great time—a great senior year," Harry said.

"I did."

"Well, then, Boom, what are you talking about?"

Mrs. H., fearing another spat, left the Sanburnes and Marcy

Wiggins to go back behind the divider. "Let me tell you about memory. It plays tricks on you. The further I get from my youth the better it looks and then some sharp memory will startle me, like stepping on a nail. It might be a fragrance or a ring around the moon at midnight, but then I remember the swirling emotions—the confusion—and you know, I'm quite glad to be old."

"You're not old," Fair gallantly said.

Jim, overhearing, agreed. "We're holding up pretty good, Miranda, and of course, my bride"—he smiled broadly—"is as beautiful as the day I married her."

As the friends and neighbors applauded, Marcy slipped outside.

"*Odd.*" Tucker noticed as did Chris, who also walked outside.

"*Marcy?*" Mrs. Murphy knew her friend's mind.

"*Yes . . . such a little person with such a heavy burden.*" The dog put her paws on the windowsill.

Jim checked his gold watch. "Meeting at town hall." He kissed Mim on the cheek. "Home for dinner."

One by one the old friends left the post office.

"When's the next shoot?" Harry asked BoomBoom as she slipped the key into her mailbox. She was beginning to regret her anger at the high-school shoot and she really regretted saying she'd outlive Charlie even though she loathed him.

"Saturday."

"Who is it?"

"Bonnie Baltier and Leo Burkey. She's driving down from Warrenton and he's coming over from Richmond. I promised them dinner as a reward."

"Better do the shoot soon. I mean, you never know who else will die." Harry rolled the full mail cart over to the counter.

"That's ghoulish," BoomBoom indignantly replied.

"You're right." Harry sighed. "But I couldn't resist. I mean I could keel over right here. We're all so . . . fragile."

"Prophesy." Fair raised an eyebrow and Harry whitened.

"Don't say that. That's worse." BoomBoom, an emotional type, crossed herself.

"I didn't say it was a prophecy. I said *prophesy*."

"I'm a little jangled." Boom's beautiful face clouded over.

"Your affair with Charlie was in high school," Harry snapped. "That's too far back to be jangled."

"That is uncalled for, Harry, and you're better than that," Miranda chided.

"Don't know that I am." Harry stuck her jaw out.

"Charlie Ashcraft was a big mistake. That was obvious even in high school. But I had to make the mistake first." Boom's face was pink. "I know you think little of me, Harry Haristeen, and not without just cause. I've apologized to you before. I can't spend my life apologizing. I am not promiscuous. I do not go around seducing every man I see and furthermore when my husband died my judgment was flawed. I did a lot of things I wouldn't do today. When are you ever going to let it go?"

Harry, amazed, blurted out, "It's easy to be gracious now—I even believe you. But it wasn't your marriage that hit the rocks."

"That was my fault." Fair finally spoke up. He'd been too stunned to speak.

"Why don't you three go out back and settle this?" Miranda saw more people pulling into the parking lot. "I know this is federal property and you have a right to be here but really, go out back."

"All right." Harry stomped out, slamming the back door behind her.

"I think *we're* on duty." Mrs. Murphy jumped down, then scooted across the back room.

Pewter followed. Tucker walked out the front door when Fair held the door for BoomBoom. She tagged at their heels as they walked between Market Shiflett's store and the post office to the parking area in the rear.

In the parking lot by the alleyway they stood mutely staring at one another for a moment.

"*Come on, Mom, get it out. Get it over with,*" Mrs. Murphy advised.

"I'm being a bitch. I know it." Harry finally broke the silence.

Fair said, "Some wounds take a long time to heal. And I am sorry, truly sorry. Harry, I was scared to death that I was missing something." He paused. "But if I hadn't made such a major mistake I wouldn't have known what a fool I was. Maybe other people can learn without as much chaos, but I don't think I could have grown if I hadn't gone through that time. The sorrow of it is, I dragged you through it, too."

Harry leaned against the clapboard side of the post office, the wood warm on her back. All three animals turned their faces up to her. She looked down at them, opened her mouth, but nothing came out.

"*Go on,*" Mrs. Murphy encouraged her.

Harry picked up the tiger cat, stroking her. "I don't guess there is another way to learn. I don't know if it's worse being the one who goes or the one who stays. Does that make sense?"

"It does, sort of," BoomBoom replied. "We're so different, Harry, that if this hadn't happened we still wouldn't be best friends. I'm driven by my emotions and you, well, you're much more logical."

"I apologize for my rude remarks. And I accept your apology."

"*Mom is growing up at last.*" Tucker felt quite proud of her human.

Before more could be said, Mrs. Hogendobber opened the back door. "Cynthia Cooper here to see all three of you."

They trooped back in, feeling a bit sheepish.

Cynthia noticed their demeanor and after a few pleasantries

she asked them about the shoot, if they noticed anything unusual about Charlie, if they had any specific ideas.

Each person confirmed what the other said. Nothing was different. Charlie was Charlie.

Cooper stuck her notepad in her back hip pocket. "Harry, I
need to see you alone." She shepherded Harry out to the squad
car. Mrs. Murphy and Pewter watched through the window. They
could clearly see from their perch on the divider.

"*What's going on?*" Tucker, intently staring out the window,
asked.

"*Mother is frowning, talking, and using her hands a lot.*"

"*I can see that. I mean what is really going on?*" the dog snipped.

"H-m-m." Pewter blinked, not pleased with the turn of events.

The air-conditioning hummed in the squad car. Empty potato chip bags lay on the seat. Harry removed them to the floor.

"Whatever possessed you to tell Charlie Ashcraft he'd die
before you'd sleep with him?"

"Coop, I don't know. I was mad as hell."

"Well, it doesn't look good. Because of that outburst I have to
consider you a suspect. It was a dumb thing to say."

"Yeah . . ." Harry bent over, picked up the potato chip bags,
and folded them lengthwise. "I hated that guy. But you know perfectly well I didn't kill him."

"Can you account for your whereabouts from six-thirty to
eight last night?"

"Sure. I was on the farm."

"Can anyone corroborate this?" Cooper wrote in her steno
pad.

"Murphy, Pewter, and Tucker."

"That's not funny, Harry. You really are a suspect."

"Oh come on, Cynthia."

"You are a member of the country club. It wouldn't have been
difficult for you."

"No, I'm not," Harry quickly spoke. "Mom and Dad were but

after they died I couldn't afford the dues. I'm allowed to go to the club once a month, which I usually do with Susan if she needs a tennis partner."

"But your presence at the club wouldn't seem unusual. Everyone knows you."

"Coop, let me tell you: there are old biddies, male and female, who have nothing better to do than cast the searching eye. If I had been there, you can be sure someone would have reported me because I've already played with Susan this month. I've used up my allotted time."

Cynthia flipped her book closed. "Do you think you could kill?"

"Sure, I could. In self-defense."

"In anger?"

"Probably," she replied honestly.

"He sexually baited you."

"He'd been doing that since high school."

"You snapped."

"Nope." Harry folded her arms across her chest.

Cynthia exhaled through her nostrils. "Rick will insist on keeping you an active suspect until better shows up. You know how he is. So don't leave the state. If an emergency should arise and you need to leave Virginia, call me."

"I'm not leaving. Now I'm insulted. If you don't find the killer, I will."

"What I'd advise you to do, Harry, is watch your mouth. That's why we're sitting in my squad car on a hot August day."

"I suppose BoomBoom couldn't wait to tell how I lost my temper."

"Let's just say she performed her civic duty."

"That bitch."

"Yes, well, if that bitch winds up dead you are in trouble."

"Coop, I didn't kill Charlie Ashcraft."

Relenting, dropping her professional demeanor, Cynthia replied, "I know—but shut up. Really."

Harry smoothed the folded potato chip bags on her thigh. "I will. I don't know what's come over me. It's like I just don't give a damn anymore." She stared out the window. "You think it's this reunion? I'm getting stirred up?"

"I don't know. Your high-school class seems, well, volatile." She paused. "One more question."

"Sure."

"Do *you* think this murder has anything to do with your high-school reunion?"

"Nah. How could it?"

10

"*Have you ever seen anything like it?*" Tucker inquired of Mrs. Murphy and Pewter as the animals watched Harry fall in love with her new truck.

"*She's read the manual twice, she's crawled under the truck, and now she's identifying and playing with every single part she can reach in the engine. Humans are extremely peculiar. All this attention to a hunk of metal,*" Pewter said.

A little breeze kicked up a wind devil in front of the barn door where the animals crouched in the shade. Harry worked in the fading sunlight.

"*It's a perfect red.*" Mrs. Murphy felt more people would notice her riding in a red truck than in any other color. "*Look who's rolling down the road.*"

They heard the tire crunch a half mile away, saw the dust and soon Blair Bainbridge's 911 wide-body black turbo Porsche glided into view, a vastly different machine than the dually but each suited for its purpose.

Harry put down the grease gun she'd been using and wiped her hands on an old towel as Blair stopped. "Hey, had to see the new truck. I didn't believe it when Little Mim told me, but when

Big Mim said you truly had a new truck, one that could haul your trailer, I had to see it."

"Big Mim is interested in my truck?" Harry smiled.

"The only topic of conversation hotter than your red truck is the end of Charlie Ashcraft. Everyone has a suspect and no one cares. Amazing." He stretched his long legs, unfolding himself from the cockpit of the Porsche. "It seems like everyone knew Charlie but no one *really* knew him."

"You could say that about a lot of people."

"Yes, I guess you could," he agreed.

She lingered over the big V-8 engine, admiring the cleanliness of it, touching the fuel injection ports, which meant she had to stand on an old wooden Coca-Cola box to lean down into the compact engine. "Blair, men talk. What are they saying?"

"Oh," he waved his hand, "I'm not in the inner circle." He took a breath.

"You know I value your judgment. You were born and bred here and, uh . . ." He stopped for a moment. "I find myself in a delicate situation."

"Too many women, too little time." Harry laughed.

He laughed, too. Harry relaxed him. "Not exactly, but close. Over the years we've become friends and I think I would have committed more blunders without you. I'm afraid I'm heading for a real cock-up, as the Brits say."

"Little Mim."

"Yes." He glanced up at the sky. "See, it's like this: women accuse men of being superficial over looks. Trust me. Women are equally as superficial."

"You would know." She smiled at the unbelievably handsome model.

Blair flew all over the world for photo shoots. The biggest names in men's fashions wanted him.

"You're not going to put up a fight? You're not going to tell me men are worse than women?"

"Nope." Harry jammed her hands in her back pockets. "Now tell me what's going on."

"Little Mim has a crush on me. Okay, I've dealt with crushes before and I like her. Don't get me wrong. But over the weekend I was at a fund-raiser and, of course, the Sanburnes were there. Big Mim pulled me away from the crowd, took me down to the rathskeller, and closed the door."

"This is getting serious," Harry remarked. The rathskeller was a small stone room in the basement of the Farmington Country Club.

"She offered me cash if I would stay away from Marilyn. She said modeling was not a suitable profession for her son-in-law."

"No!" Harry blurted out.

"I make a lot of money, but let's just say my business is time-sensitive. I'd be a liar if I said I'm immune to a big bribe. And I've had enough scrapes and breaks to my body to wake me up to that fact. My Teotan Partnership Investment is doing very well, though. But really, I was shocked that the old girl would try to buy me off."

Through various twists and turns Blair wound up sole director of a corporation originally set up to sell water to Albemarle County. However, he'd begun bottling it and selling the mountain water—purified, of course—in specialty stores. This proved lucrative.

"You don't need her money." Harry thought to herself that it must be nice.

"No. But the Sanburnes control Crozet. If I spurn Little Mim, I'm cooked. If I ignore Big Mim's wishes, I'm cooked."

"M-m-m." Harry removed her hands from her pockets and rubbed them together absentmindedly. "Do you like Marilyn?" She called Little Mim by her Christian name.

"Yes."

"Love?"

"No. Not yet, if ever. That takes time for me." He pursed his lips.

"Well, squire Little Mim around to local functions, spend some time with her and her family. Sometimes when you really get to know someone things look different. You look different, too."

He paused and rephrased his thoughts. "If I'm up-front about getting to know her daughter, the family, Mim will take it better if I choose to spend my life with her daughter?" he questioned, then quietly added, "If the relationship should progress, I mean."

"He is a Yankee." Mrs. Murphy laughed because Blair missed the subtlety of Harry's suggestion.

"Because he's only thinking of his feelings about Little Mim." Pewter had gotten a spot of grease on her paw, licked it, and spit.

"Go drink water," Tucker told her.

The gray cat scampered into the barn, standing on her hind legs to drink out of the water bucket in the wash stall.

"He's missing the point, that this gives Little Mim and Big Mim plenty of time to assess him." Tucker stood up and shook. "Mom's betting on Little Mim getting the stars out of her eyes."

"No. I think Mom is giving everyone a chance to draw closer or gracefully decline. If he walks away from Mim's offer she'll be furious. And if he took it he'd be held in contempt by her forever."

"He's in a fix. You don't think Little Marilyn knows?"

"Tucker, it would kill her."

"Yeah."

Pewter mumbled back, "Let's drag that grease gun into the woods."

"You'll have even more grease on you."

Pewter eyed the dog. "I hate it when you're smarter than I am."

All three animals laughed.

". . . no hurry," Harry continued. "If you go slow and be honest, things will turn out for the best."

"I knew you'd know the right thing to do."

"And pay court to Big Mim even if she's cold to you. She loves the attention."

"Right." He folded himself back into his car. "Glad you finally got a new truck."

"Me, too."

He drove back down the driveway without fully realizing that now he really wanted Little Mim precisely because her mother refused him. Suddenly Little Mim was a challenge. She was desirable. People are funny that way.

As soon as he was out of sight, Harry raced for the phone in the tackroom.

"Susan."

"What?"

"I was just thinking about how people say one thing and do another—sometimes on purpose and sometimes because they don't know what they're doing."

"Yes . . ." Susan drew out the yes.

"Well, I was just talking to Blair about another matter but it made me think about people concealing their true intentions. Like Charlie's behavior toward Marcy Wiggins at the shoot."

"He didn't pay much attention to her at the shoot." Susan thought back.

"Exactly," Harry said.

"H-m-m." Susan thought it over.

"Let's raise the flag and see who salutes." Harry's voice filled with excitement.

"What do you mean?" Susan wondered.

"Leave it to me." Harry almost smacked her lips.

"She's incorrigible." The tiger cat sighed.

11

By eight-thirty the next morning, they had all the mail sorted and popped in the mailboxes.

Harry and Mrs. Hogendobber felt wonderful. Their job was easier in the summer. The catalogue glut diminished—only to return like a bad penny in the fall. A rise in summer postcards couldn't compete with the tidal wave of mail from Thanksgiving to Christmas.

Harry enjoyed reading postcards before sliding them in the boxes. Maine, an excellent place to be in mid-August, claimed four Crozetians. Nova Scotia, that exquisite appendage of Canada, had one. The rest of the postcards were from beach places, with the occasional glossy photo of a Notre Dame gargoyle from a student on vacation dutifully writing home to Mom and Dad.

Miranda had baked her specialty, orange-glazed cinnamon buns. The two women nibbled as they worked. Miranda swept the floor while Harry dusted down the backs of the metal mailboxes.

"*Why do humans have flat faces?*" Pewter lazily inquired, made tired by this ceaseless productivity.

"*Ran into a cosmic door.*" Mrs. Murphy cackled.

"*If they had long faces it would throw them out of balance,*" Tucker said.

"*What do you mean?*" Mrs. Murphy didn't follow the canine line of reasoning.

"*They'd be falling forward to keep up with their faces. Flat faces help them since they walk on two legs. Can't have too much weight in front.*"

"*You know, Tucker, you amaze me,*" Mrs. Murphy admiringly purred as she strolled over from the back door.

Harry had put an animal door in the back door so the kids could come and go. Each time an animal entered or left a little flap was heard. Mrs. Murphy was considering a stroll in Miranda's garden. Insect patrol. She changed her mind to sit next to Tucker.

The front door opened. Susan came in carrying a tin of English tea. "Hey, girls, let's try this."

"Darjeeling?" Harry examined the lavender tin.

"Miranda, tea or coffee?"

"This is a tea day. I can't drink but so much coffee when it's hot unless it's iced. Don't know why." She bent over to attack the dust pile with a black dustpan.

"Let me hold that, it's easier." Susan bent down with the pan as Miranda swept up.

"Have you made your morning calls?" Harry asked. Susan liked to get all her calls and chores done early.

"No, but Boom called bright and early, a switch for her. She wants to shoot the Best All-Round photo after Wittiest and I told her no. I need a month to lose seven pounds."

"Susan, you look fine."

"Easy for you to say." Susan felt that Harry would never know the battle of the bulge, as both her parents were lean and food just wasn't very important to her.

"She have a fit?"

"No, she asked again if I would help with Wittiest."

"Will you help?"

"Yes." Susan sighed. "What about you?"

"No!" Harry said this so loudly the animals flinched.

"One hour of your time," Susan cajoled.

"BoomBoom wanted to be the chair of our reunion, let her do it. I'm doing my part."

"Okay . . ." Susan's voice trailed off, which meant she was merely tabling her agenda until a better time.

The front door opened, and a well-built man of average height stood there, the light behind him. He had thick, steel-gray hair, a square chin, broad shoulders. He opened wide his arms as he walked toward the counter.

"Cuddles!"

Miranda squinted, looking hard at the man, thrust aside the broom, and raced to flip up the divider. She embraced him. "Tracy Raz!"

"Gee, it's good to see you." He hugged her, then held her away for a moment, then hugged her again. "You look like the girl I left in high school."

"What a fibber." She beamed.

Mrs. Murphy looked at Pewter and Tucker as the tiger cat whispered, *"Cuddles?"*

12

"How many of us are left?" Tracy reached over for another orange-glazed bun.

Harry, upon learning that Tracy Raz was a "lost" member of Mrs. Hogendobber's high-school class, forced her to take the day off. Miranda huffed and puffed but finally succumbed. She took Tracy home, setting out a sumptuous breakfast—homemade buns and doughnuts, cereal with thick cream, and the best coffee in the state of Virginia.

"Forty-two out of fifty-six." Miranda munched on a doughnut. "Korea accounted for two of us, Vietnam one—"

"Who was in Vietnam?"

"Xavier France. Career officer. Made full colonel, too. His helicopter was shot down near the Cambodia border."

"Xavier France, he was the last kid I would have picked for a service career. What about the others?"

"The usual: car accidents, cancer—far too much of that, I'm afraid—heart attacks. Poor Asther Dandridge died young of diabetes. Still, Tracy, if you think about it, our class is in good shape."

"You certainly are."

"You haven't changed a bit."

"Gray hair and twenty more pounds."

"Muscle." And it was. "How did you hear about the reunion? We'd given up on ever finding you."

"It was a funny thing." His movements carried an athlete's grace as he put the cup back on the saucer. "Naturally, I knew this was our fiftieth year. I hadn't much interest in attending the other reunions and I'll come to that later. I remembered that Kevin McKenna worked for Twentieth Century-Fox. I'd see his name in the papers. He's director of marketing. Got to be worth a bundle. I called and got the usual runaround but I left a message with my phone number and damned if he didn't call me back. He sent me a copy of the invitation. I was footloose and fancy-free so I came early. Thought you might need an old fullback to help you."

"Where do you live?"

"Hawaii. The island of Kauai. After high school I enlisted, which you knew. Well, in our day, Miranda, you enlisted or you were drafted. I figured if I enlisted I'd get a better deal than if I let myself get drafted. Army. Got good training. I wound up in intelligence, of all the strange things, and once my tour was up I re-enlisted but I made them promise to put me through Ranger school. Now it's Green Berets but then it was Rangers. They did. I stayed in for ten years. Left after being recruited by the CIA—"

"A spy?" Her kind eyes widened.

He waved his hand to dismiss the notion. "That's TV stuff. I had a wonderful job. I was sent all over the world to see events firsthand. For instance, during the oil crisis in the seventies I was in Riyadh. Worst posting I ever had was Nigeria. But basically I was a troubleshooter. I'd be the first one in, scope the situation and report back. They could make of my data what they wished— everyone in Washington has his own agenda. My God, Miranda, bureaucracy will ruin this country. That's my story. Retired and here I am."

"Did you ever marry?"

He nodded. "A beautiful Japanese girl I met in Kobe in 1958. That's when I bought a little land in Kauai. Li could get back to her family and I could get to the States."

"I hope you'll bring her to the reunion."

He folded his hands. "She died two years ago. Lymphatic cancer. She fought hard." He stopped to swallow. "Now I rattle around in our house like a dried pea in a big shell. The kids are grown. My daughter, Mandy, works for Rubicon Advertising in New York, John runs the Kubota dealership in Kauai, and Carl is a lawyer in Honolulu. They speak fluent Japanese. I can carry on a conversation but the kids are fluent, which makes them valuable these days. They're all married with kids of their own." He smiled. "I'm kind of lost really." He slapped his thigh. "Here I am talking about myself. Tell me what happened to you."

"I married George Hogendobber, he became the postmaster here, and we lived a quiet but joyful life. He died of a heart attack, nearly ten years ago. Sometimes it seems like yesterday."

"I don't remember George."

"He moved here from Winchester."

"Kids?"

"No. That blessing passed me by, although I feel as though Mary Minor Haristeen is a daughter. She's the young woman you just met."

"Miranda, you were the spark plug of our class. I've thought of you more than you'll ever know, but I never sat down to write a letter. I'm a terrible letter writer. You'll always be my high-school sweetheart. Those were good times."

"Yes, they were," she said simply.

"I wanted to see the world and I did. But here I am. Back home."

"I feel as though I saw the world, too, Tracy. I suppose my world was within. I've drawn great strength from the Bible since George died. Harry calls me a religious nut."

"Harry?"

"The girl in the post office."

"Yes, of course. Minor. The people out on Yellow Mountain Road. He married a Hepworth."

"Good memory. She's their daughter. They're gone now."

"Whatever happened to Mim Conrad? Did she marry Larry Johnson?"

"No." Miranda's voice dropped as though Mim were in the next room. "Larry was four years older than we were. Remember, he was finishing college as she was finishing high school? Well, he did go to medical school. They dated and then the next thing I knew they weren't dating anymore. He married someone else and she married Jim Sanburne."

"That oaf?"

"The same."

"Mim marrying Jim Sanburne. I can't believe it."

"He was big and handsome. He runs to fat now. But he's a genial man once you get to know him."

"I never tried. Larry still alive?"

"Yes, he practiced medicine here for decades. Still does, although he sold his practice to a young man, Hayden McIntire, with the provision that Larry'd work just one more year, get Hayden settled with the patients. That was several years ago. Still working, though. Hayden doesn't seem to mind. Larry's wife died years ago. He and Mim are friendly."

"They were such a hot item."

"You never know how the cookie will crumble." She giggled a little.

"Guess not. Here I am. Miranda, it's as though I never left. Oh, a few things are different, like that old-age home by the rail-road underpass."

"Careful. No one calls it that anymore, not since we're getting so close ourselves. It's assisted-care living."

"Bull."

"Well—yes." She smiled. "The town is much the same. There are subdivisions. One on Route 240 called Deep Valley and one on the way to Miller School. There's a brand-new grade school which cost the county a pretty penny. But pretty much Crozet is Crozet. Not beautiful. Not quaint. Just home."

"Do you need help with the reunion?"

"What a delightful question." She folded her hands together gleefully.

"That's a yes, I take it." He smiled. "Say, how does Mim look?"

"Fabulous. You know it's her fiftieth reunion this year, too, at Madeira. She endured her second face-lift. She goes to the best and truthfully she does look fabulous. Slender as ever."

"H-m-m." He dusted his fingertips to rub off the sticky icing. "Jim Sanburne . . . I still can't believe that. Is he good to her?"

"Now. For a long time he wasn't and the further apart they drifted the haughtier she got. She was an embittered woman and then a miracle happened. I don't know if you believe in miracles but I do. She was diagnosed with breast cancer. Larry broke the news. She had a mastectomy and reconstructive surgery. Jim stopped running after women."

"Stop drinking, too?"

"He did."

"He'd put it away in high school, I remember that. Class of '49. Good football player. I was glad I had a year after he graduated. Selfish. I wanted the attention."

"You were All-State."

"We had a good team for as small a school as we were." He paused. "I closed up the house in Kauai. I'm looking to rent a house here, or rooms. Would you know of anything?"

"I don't wish to pry but what would you be willing to pay?"

"A thousand a month for the right place."

She thought long and hard. "For how long?"

"Well, until December first at least. Our reunion is Homecoming so I might as well stay a month after that."

She smiled broadly. "I have an idea. Let me check it out first. Where are you staying now?"

"Farmington Country Club—pretty funny, isn't it? The way I used to rail about that place being full of stupid snobs. Now I'm one of them—on a temporary basis, of course. And I heard a young fellow was murdered there—what? Two days ago?"

"Unlamented, I'm afraid. People are lining up to lay claim to the deed." She stopped. "Not very charitable of me, but the truth is no one is very upset about the demise of Charlie Ashcraft. How about if I call you tonight, or tomorrow at the latest? I may have just the place."

"Whose animals were those in the post office?"

"Oh, those are Harry's. If they aren't the smartest and cutest helpers."

"I don't remember you being that fond of animals."

She blushed. "They converted me."

He laughed. "Then they do have special powers."

13

"Use this italics pen." Chris handed Harry the fountain pen with the slanted nib.

"Let me practice first." Harry gingerly scratched the pen over scrap paper. "Kinda neat."

"I've divided up those cream-colored cards, the two-by-threes. See? Print the person's name like this." She held up a card. "*Carl Ackerman*, with the name at the top, leaving room for the title below. Got it?"

"I'll never think of stuff."

"You will, but if all the name tags are done now it will make life easier at the reunion. You'll be surprised at the ideas that will pop into your head between now and then. I bet by the time of your reunion—when is it, again?"

"End of October. Homecoming weekend."

"Right." Chris picked a card off her stack, her deep maroon nail polish making her fingers seem even longer and more tapered than they were. "That's lots of time. How about if I take the first half of the alphabet and you take the second."

"All those M's and S's," Harry laughed. "Thanks for having me over. The cats and dog thank you, too."

"*Thanks.*" Mrs. Murphy sat on the floor, her eyes half-closed, swaying.

"*The air-conditioning is perfect.*" Tucker wedged next to Harry, who sat on the floor, using the coffee table as a desk.

"*Right-o,*" Pewter agreed. She rested on the silk sofa.

Harry eyed the gray kitty. "Get off that sofa."

"Oh, I don't care."

"Silk is very expensive." Harry leaned over. "I told you to get off."

"*You touch me and I'll sink a claw into this gorgeous silk.*" For emphasis Pewter brandished one razor-sharp claw.

"Hussy." Harry backed off.

"She's fine. I rather like having animals about. When I bought this house I liked the fact that it's on an acre. I thought someday I might get a cat or dog."

"*Cat,*" Pewter encouraged.

"*Dog,*" Tucker countered.

"*Both,*" Mrs. Murphy compromised.

"They're funny." Chris laughed.

"That they are. Why did you come here? After the big city it must seem like the back of the beyond."

"Chicago was all I knew. I came through here two years ago on a vacation—a history tour. I just fell in love with the place. Being a stockbroker makes me pretty mobile and when an opening popped up at Harold and Marshall Securities I said, 'Why not.' I'd saved a good deal of money, which I think will tide me over as I build a new client base."

"People are cheap here. What I mean to say is, it won't be as easy to sell as it was in Chicago."

"I already know that," Chris said matter-of-factly as she inscribed names, "but I needed a shake-up. I broke up with my boyfriend. My walls were closing in on me."

A car rolled into the driveway.

"*Who goes there!?!*" Tucker sprang to the door.

"Tucker, this isn't your house."

"*Oh—yeah.*" Tucker returned to Harry as Chris opened the door, letting Bitsy Valenzuela into the cooler air.

"Hi."

"Hi, Bitsy." Harry didn't rise.

"A drink?" Chris asked.

"A Tom Collins would be heaven. I'll mix it myself." Bitsy knew the way to the bar in Chris's house, a rounded steel bar with squares cut into the polished steel harboring lights: red, green, yellow, and blue. "Harry, you drinking?"

"Coke."

"Such virtue," Chris teased her.

"That's me." Harry hated inscribing the names.

Bitsy joined them at the coffee table. She sat next to Pewter, who stared up at her and then looked away. "I'm not up to snuff," Bitsy observed.

"*She can be snotty,*" Murphy commented.

"*Flies on your tuna,*" Pewter grumbled, then shut her eyes.

"Where's E.R.?" Chris inquired.

"Home for a change. He's vacuuming the swimming pool. I told him I'd be back in a half hour. It's his turn to cook. He's a good cook, too. Say, if you're hungry I'll pick up two more steaks."

"No, thanks," Harry declined. "I am determined to knock out my half. I've got forty left."

Bitsy picked up a card. "Bonnie Baltier. Great name."

"Wittiest," Chris said.

"How do you know that?" Harry asked.

"Senior superlatives," Chris said. "I've studied your yearbook so much I think I know them almost as well as you do."

"This goes above and beyond losing to Susan Tucker at golf," Harry said.

"Well, I'm enjoying it. And to be honest, I'm hoping to meet some unmarried men through this. You never know." She shyly smiled.

"Take E.R.," Bitsy laughed. She loved him but she liked to complain of his foibles, one of which was the irritating habit of reading magazines backwards to forwards. "I could use a rest."

"Any husband that cooks, I'd keep," Chris told her.

"Amen," Harry said.

"Anyone seen Marcy today?" Chris asked. "I thought she might drop by this afternoon."

"I passed her on the road and waved." Bitsy swallowed half her drink. "She looked miserable. I wish she'd come out with it and say her marriage is crumbling—we all know. I think all this stress is making her sick. Her face is drawn."

"I'm sorry to hear that." Harry's eyebrows moved up in surprise.

"Another Deep Valley divorce." Bitsy drained the glass. "They barely speak to one another."

"People go through phases," Chris blandly said.

Mrs. Murphy opened her eyes. *That's a nice way to put it.*

"That's true." Bitsy got up to make herself another Tom Collins. "Chris, I owe you a bottle of Tanqueray. But how do you know what's a phase and what's a permanent part of character?" She returned to the original subject.

"You don't for a long time. By the time I figured out my boyfriend was a self-centered jerk, I'd put three years into the relationship," Chris complained.

The ice cubes tumbled into the tall frosted glass as Bitsy listened.

"What's the story on Blair Bainbridge?" Chris asked. "I can't quite get a fix on him."

"He's a model," Harry said. "Makes a ton of money. He dates Little Mim Sanburne as well as women from other places. He's kind of"—she thought for a minute—"languid."

Bitsy flopped on the couch, again disturbing Pewter, who grumbled. "He can be as languid as he wants as long as he stays that gorgeous."

"Amen, sister." Chris held up her glass, as if toasting Bitsy.

Bitsy asked Harry, "We all thought you and Fair might be getting back together."

"Did Mrs. Hogendobber tell you that?"

"No," Chris answered, "but it just seemed, uh, in the cards and Fair is very handsome."

"Fair Haristeen is the best equine vet in central Virginia. He's a good man. He was a so-so husband. If he interests you, tell him. You won't upset me."

"Harry, I wouldn't do that." Chris blushed.

"I don't care."

"*You do, too,*" Tucker disagreed.

Bitsy took a long swallow. "Harry, no woman is that diffident about her ex-husband."

"Uh." Harry changed the subject. "Market Shiflett is single. He's a nice guy."

"Doesn't look like Blair Bainbridge," Bitsy frankly stated.

"If you marry a drop-dead gorgeous man you have to accept that other women will chase him and sooner or later he'll be unfaithful. A man like Market is responsible, loyal, and true. Personally, I find those qualities very sexy. I didn't at twenty-two but I do now," Harry said.

"You've got a point there," Chris agreed.

14

There were three reasons that people attended Charlie Ashcraft's funeral. The first was to support his mother, Linda, who had never made an enemy in her life. Married young, dumped at twenty-one with a six-month-old baby, she had struggled to make ends meet. Like many an abandoned woman she spoiled her son—the only man who truly loved her—and she had bailed her offspring out of innumerable crises. Poor Linda could never see that she was part of the problem. She fervently believed she was the solution.

The second reason people came to the funeral was to see who else was there—namely, were there any teary-eyed women? Surprisingly, there were not.

The third reason people came was to make sure he was really dead.

A lone reporter from *The Daily Progress* covered the event but Channel 29 sent no cameras to mar the occasion. Then, too, the station manager had had his own brush with Charlie and enjoyed denying the egotist coverage of his last social event.

As people filed out of the simple Baptist church, Harry leaned over to Susan and whispered, "Did you notice there were hardly any flowers?"

"I did. Maybe people will give to charity."

"More than likely they'll give to an abortion clinic. That's where most of his girlfriends wound up."

Susan gasped, choking on a mint, and Harry patted her on the back. "Sorry."

Thanks to her beautiful voice, Miranda Hogendobber, a stalwart of the choir of The Church of the Holy Light, was invited to sing solo at the funeral. Linda Ashcraft asked her to sing "Faith of Our Fathers," which she did. Walking out of the back of the church, her choir robe over her arm, she caught sight of Harry and Susan.

"Unusual," Mrs. Hogendobber said under her breath.

"Uh-huh," the two friends agreed.

They walked up the hill, the church cemetery unfolding in the deep green grass before them. Ahead walked BoomBoom, Bitsy, and Chris.

"Maybe they knew Charlie better than we thought." Susan kept her voice low.

"BoomBoom's tugboats. They're missing Marcy Wiggins, though. H-m-m." Harry thought a minute. "Boom probably called in tears saying she needed support since he was her first high-school boyfriend. Amazes me how she manages to be the center of drama." She stopped as they neared the gravesite.

Linda, already at the grave, was being supported by her brother-in-law. The poor woman was totally distraught. As they gathered around the opened earth, Harry, in the back, scanned the band of mourners—if one could call them that. Apart from Linda, the mood was respectful but not grief-stricken. Meredith McLaughlin, Market Shiflett, and Bonnie Baltier were there, all from their high-school class.

Big Mim Sanburne attended, Little Mim was absent. Who was there and who was not was interesting, and Sheriff Rick Shaw and Deputy Cynthia Cooper had attended just to study the gathering.

Although they were too discreet to make notes at such a time.

"Why don't we slip away before Linda comes back through the crowd?" Rick put his hand under Cynthia's elbow, propelling the tall woman toward the church.

Harry, noticing, left Susan and Miranda to catch up to Cynthia and Rick. She said, "Sad. Not because he's dead but because nobody cares other than Linda. Can you imagine living a life where nobody truly loves you and it's your own damn fault?"

"A waste." Cynthia summed it up.

The three stopped before a recent grave festooned with flowers. The granite headstone bore the inscription Timothy Martin, June 1, 1958 to January 29, 1997. A racing car carved at the base of the tombstone roared from left to right. At the corners of the grave two checkered flags marked Tim's final finish line.

"I didn't know they'd done that." Rick remembered picking up what was left of Tim after he spun out on a nasty curve coming down Afton Mountain. He turned too fast on Route 6 and literally flew over the mountainside. He raced stock cars on weekends, was a good driver, but never saw the black ice that ended his life.

The flags fluttered. "It's nice that his family remembered him as he lived. He'd love this."

"They keep him covered in flowers," Cynthia remarked. "I hope someone loves me that much."

"Someone will—be patient." Rick smiled as he flicked open his small notebook with his thumb. "What do you think, Harry?"

"I'd question whoever isn't here and should have been."

He smiled again. "Smart cookie."

The crowd was dispersing from the gravesite.

"Let's forgo the reception. This is hard enough for Linda Ashcraft without two cops at the table." Cynthia headed toward her own car. They hadn't taken a squad car, and since the body was carried directly from the church to the cemetery there was no need for a police escort. Rick and Cynthia were uncommonly sensitive people.

Moving at a slow pace, Miranda, choir robe folded over her arm, and Susan came over the rise. They waved to Harry, who waited at the back church door.

Miranda exhaled, focusing on Harry. "I'd like a word with you." The two walked under the trees as Miranda encouraged Harry to take in a boarder, namely Tracy.

15

Like many doctors, Bill Wiggins, an oncologist, was accustomed to getting his way. "Stat" was his favorite word, a word meaning "immediately" in hospital lingo.

Sitting on his back deck surveying his green lawn, not one dandelion in sight, he also surveyed his wife.

"Marcy, you've lost a lot of weight."

"Summer. I can't eat in the heat." She watered the ornamental cherry trees at the edge of the lawn.

"You need to get a thorough checkup. I'll call Dinky Barlow."

Dinky Barlow was an internist at the hospital. He was unbelievably thorough.

"Honey, I'm fine."

"I'm the doctor." He tried to sound humorous.

"Probably need a B-12 shot." She smiled weakly. It would never do to tell Bill what was off was their relationship. They rarely communicated other than simple facts—like bring home milk and butter. Bill, like most doctors, worked long hours under great stress. He never quite adjusted to his patients dying, feeling in some way that it was a blot on his skills.

Marcy needed more. Bill had nothing left to give her.

Then again, he didn't look inward. As long as supper was on

the table, his home kept in order and clean, he had nothing to complain about.

His silence, which Bitsy and Chris interpreted as hostility in their friend's marriage, was really exhaustion. He had little time for chatting up his wife and none for her girlfriends, whom he thought boring and superficial.

Bill flipped open his mobile phone, dialed, made an appointment for his wife, then flipped the phone so it shut off. "Next Tuesday. Eight-thirty A.M. Dinky's office."

"Thank you, honey." She hated it when he managed her like that but she said nothing, instead changing the subject. "You didn't want to go to Charlie Ashcraft's funeral?"

He swirled his chair to speak directly to her. "Marcy, the last place I ever want to go is a funeral," he ruefully said. "Besides, he was an empty person. I've no time for people like that."

"But doesn't it upset you just a little bit that someone in your class was killed? Murdered?"

"If it were anyone but him, maybe it would." He sat up straight. "You know what gets me? Death is part of life. Americans can't accept that."

"But Charlie was so young."

"The body has its own timetable. In his case it wasn't his body, it was his mind. He brought about his own end. Why be a hypocrite and pretend I'm upset? As I said, my dear, death is a part of life."

"But you get upset when a patient dies."

"You're damned right I do. I fight for my patients. I see how much they fight. Charlie squandered his life. I wish I could give my patients those hours and years that he tossed aside." He glared at Marcy. "Why are we having this argument?"

"I didn't think it was an argument."

"Oh." Confused, he slumped back in his chair.

She continued watering, moving to the boxwoods, which were far enough away to retard conversation.

16

The 1958 John Deere tractor, affectionately known as Johnny Pop, *pop-popped* over the western hay fields.

Bushhogging was one of Harry's favorite chores. She would mow the edge of the road, all around the barn and then clear around the edges of her pastures and hay fields.

The hay needed to be cut next week. She'd arranged to rent a spider wheel tedder to fold the freshly cut hay into windrows. Then she'd go back over the flattened, sweet-smelling hay with an old twine square baler.

Hard work in the boiling sun, but Harry, born to it, thrived.

Today she chugged along in a middle gear, careful not to get too close to the strong-running creek.

The horses stayed in the barn during the day in the summers, a fan tilted into each stall to cool them and blow the flies off.

Mrs. Murphy and Pewter were hanging out at the spring house. The cool water running over the stones produced a delightful scent. The mice liked it, too.

Tucker, sprawled in the center aisle of the barn, breathed in and out—little no-see-ums rising and falling with each breath— like an insect parasol opening and closing.

Harry loved this patch of Virginia. She had great pride in her state, which boasted two ancient mountain ranges, a rich coast-line fed by three great rivers, and a lushness unimaginable to a Westerner. But, then, the Westerner was freed from the myriad gossamer expectations and blood ties inherited by each Virginian. So much was expected of a Virginian that ofttimes one had to escape for a few days, weeks, or years to rejuvenate.

A poplar tree downed in an early-summer storm loomed ahead. Harry sighed. She had to cut up the big tree, then drag the sections and branches to those places in her fence line that needed repair. Poplar didn't last as long as locust, but still, it was for free, not counting her labor.

She cut off Johnny Pop and dismounted. The spotted tree bark remained home to black ants and other crawlies. Although flat on its side, roots exposed, the crown of the poplar was covered in healthy green leaves.

"Life doesn't give up easily," she said aloud, admiring the tenacity of the desperately injured tree.

She bent over the creek, cupped her hands and washed her face. Then she let the tumbling cool water run over her hands.

It suddenly occurred to her that her feelings about Charlie Ashcraft as an individual were irrelevant. The swiftness of his end sobered her. Security was a myth. Knowing that intellectually and knowing it emotionally were two different things.

She shook her hands, enjoying the tingling sensation. The sensation of death's randomness was far less pleasant.

"Given the chance, I'll fight to the end. I'll fight just like you." She patted the thick tree trunk before climbing back onto the tractor.

17

"*Smells okay.*" Tucker twitched her nose.

"*You rely on your nose too much. You have to use your other senses.*" Pewter sat impassively on the sofa, watching Tracy Raz carry a duffel bag over his shoulder.

"*Think this will work?*" Tucker, also on the sofa, asked.

"*Yep.*" Mrs. Murphy, alertly poised on the big curving sofa arm announced, "*Tracy Raz will be a godsend.*"

" *'Cause of the money? Mom's new truck payments don't leave much at the end of the month.*" Tucker, conservative about money, fretted over every penny because she saw Harry fret. A rent check of five hundred dollars a month would help Harry considerably. Tucker was grateful to Mrs. Hogendobber for sitting down both Harry and Tracy Raz to work out a fair arrangement.

"*That, too, but I think it's going to be great for Mom to have someone around. She's lived alone too long now and she's getting set in her ways. Another year and it'd be—concrete.*"

Pewter and Tucker laughed.

Harry led the athletically built man upstairs. She walked down a hall, the heart pine floor covered with an old Persian runner, deep russet and navy blue. At the end of the hall she opened the last door on the right to a huge bedroom with a full

bath and sitting room. "I hope it suits. I turned on the air conditioner. It's an old window unit and hums a lot but the nights
are so cool you won't need it. There's always a breeze."

Tracy noticed the big four-poster rice bed. "That's a beauty."

"Grandmother gave it to Mom as a wedding present.
Grandma Hepworth was raised in Charleston, South Carolina."

"Prettiest city in the country." He walked across the room,
turned off the air conditioner, and threw open the window. "The
reason people are sick all the time is because of air-conditioning.
The body never properly adjusts to the season."

"Dad used to say that." Harry smiled. "Oh, here are the keys
although I never lock the house. Let's see, I'm usually up by five-
thirty so I can knock off the barn chores. If you like to ride you
can help me work the horses. It's a lot of fun."

"Rode Western. Never got the hang of an English saddle." He
smiled.

"I can't promise meals . . ."

"Don't expect any. Anyway, Miranda told me you eat like a
bird."

"Oh, if you don't shut your door at night the animals will
come in. They won't be able to resist. Any magazines or papers
you leave on the floor will be filed away—usually under the bed.
If you take your watch off at night or a necklace of any sort put
it in your bureau drawer because Mrs. Murphy can't resist jewelry. She drags anything that glitters to the sofa, where she drops
it behind a cushion."

Mrs. Murphy, curiosity aroused, followed them upstairs. "I
resent that. You leave stuff all over the house. With my system everything is in one
place."

"Where we can all sit on it," Pewter, also brimming with curiosity,
said.

"Those two culprits?" Tracy nodded at the two cats now pos-
ing in the doorway.

"Murphy's the tiger cat and the gray cannonball is Pewter. She
used to belong to Market Shiflett but she spent so much time at

the post office with my animals that he told me to just take her home. She also flicked meat out of the display case, which didn't go down well with the customers."

"They're beautiful cats."

"*I knew I'd like this guy.*" Pewter beamed.

"*He's handsome for his age.*" Mrs. Murphy purred, deciding to bestow a rub on Tracy's leg. She padded over, slid across his leg, then sat down. He stroked her head.

Pewter followed suit.

"I'll leave you to get settled. You can use the kitchen, the living room. I figure if something upsets you you'll tell me and vice versa. I'm going out to finish my barn chores."

"I'll go along. There's not that much in the bag to worry about. I thought I'd do a little shopping this week."

"You don't have to help me."

"Like to be useful." He beamed.

And he was. He could toss a fifty-pound bale of hay over his shoulder as though it weighed one-tenth of that. Although not a horseman, he had enough sense to not make loud noises around them.

Tracy whistled as he worked. Harry liked hearing him. It suddenly hit her how stupid it was to retire people unless they decided to retire. The terms "twilight years" and "golden years" ought to be stricken from the language. We shove people out of work at the time when they have the most wisdom. It must be horrible to sit on the sidelines with nothing vital to do.

Simon, belly flat to the hayloft floor, peered over the side. A new human! One was bad enough.

Harry noticed him. "Patience, Simon."

Tracy glanced up. "Simon?"

"Possum in the hayloft. He's very shy. There's also a huge owl up in the cupola and a blacksnake. She comes back to hibernate each fall. Right now she's on the south side of the property. I've tracked her hunting circle. Pretty interesting."

"That was the one thing I hated about my work. Kept me in

cities most of the time. I worked out in gyms but nothing keeps you as healthy as farmwork. My father farmed. You wouldn't remember him, he worked the old Black Twig apple orchard west of Crozet. Lived to be a hundred and one. The worst thing we ever did was talk Pop into selling the orchard and moving to Florida. I'll never forgive myself for that."

"He's forgiven you."

Tracy stopped a moment to wipe the sweat from his face. The temperature hovered in the low eighties even though it was seven at night. "Thanks for that."

"Possums are interesting, too." Harry tactfully returned to the subject of Simon. "They'll eat about anything. There's a bug that infects birds and if the possums eat a bird with the bug they'll shed it in their poop. If horses eat the poop they come down with EPM, an awful kind of sickness that gets them uncoordinated and weak. If you catch it in time it still takes a long time to heal. Anyway, I love my Simon. Can't kill him but I don't want my kids here to, by chance, munch some hay that Simon has—befouled. So each night I put out sweet feed and the occasional marshmallow. He's so full he doesn't roam very far and there's no room for birds."

"I can see you're the kind of person who loves animals."

"My best friends." She slid the pitchfork between the two nails on the wall. "Mr. Raz—"

"Please call me Tracy."

"Thank you. And call me Harry. I hope you don't think I'm prying but I've just got to ask you. How did Mrs. Hogendobber come by the nickname 'Cuddles'?"

As they watched the ground fog slither over the western meadow and the meadowlarks scurry to their nests, the bob-whites started to call to one another and the bats emerged from under the eaves of Harry's house. Tracy recalled his high-school days with Miranda.

"*Love bats.*" Mrs. Murphy fluffed her fur as a slight chill rolled up with the ground fog.

"*Never catch one.*" Pewter liked the way bats zigged and zagged. Got her blood up.

"*My mother caught one once,*" Murphy remembered. "*It was on its way out, though. Still, she did catch it. You know they're mice with wings, that's how I think of them.*"

"*Maybe we'd better catch the mice in the barn first.*"

Mrs. Murphy moved over to Pewter, leaning against her in the chill. "*I heard them singing in the tackroom this morning. I expect them to be saucy in the feedroom. But the tackroom. It was humiliating. Fortunately, Harry can't hear them.*"

"*An original song?*"

The tiger cat laughed. "*In those high-pitched voices everything sounds original but it was 'Dixie.'*"

"*Well, at least they're Southern mice.*"

"*Pewter, that's a great comfort.*" Mrs. Murphy laughed so loudly she interrupted the humans.

"Getting a little nippy, Miss Puss?" Harry scooped her up in one arm while lifting Pewter with the other. "Pewts, light and lively for you."

A cat on each shoulder, Harry walked back to the house as Tucker trailed at Tracy's heels.

Tracy picked up where he'd left off when Murphy let out what sounded to him like a yowl. "—one of the prettiest girls in the class. Natural. Fresh."

"Was she plump?"

"Uh . . . full-figured. You girls are too skinny these days. Miranda sparkled. Anyway, we'd go on hay rides and trips to other high schools for football games. I played on the team. Afterwards we'd all ride back to school in our old jalopies. Fun. I think I was too young to know how much fun I was having. And World War Two ended five years before our graduation so everyone felt safe and wonderful. It was an incredible time." He chuckled as he opened the porch door for Harry. "Every chance I had I got close to Miranda and I nicknamed her 'Cuddles.' "

The kitchen door, open to catch the breeze, was shut behind

them as the night air, drenched in moisture and coolness, was drawing through the house.

Harry put the cats on the kitchen counter. "Must be a cold front coming through. The wind is picking up. This has been an unusual summer. Usually it's brutally hot, like the last few days have been."

"Nothing like a Virginia summer unless it's a Delta summer. One year in the service I was stationed in Louisiana and thought I would melt. Heat and hookworm, the history of the South."

"Cured the latter. Did I interrupt you? If I did I apologize. You were telling me about Miranda."

"In my day we were all friends. It wasn't quite as much sex stuff. I had a crush on Miranda and we did a lot of things together but as a group. I took her to the senior prom. You know, I loved her but I didn't know that either. It wasn't until years later that I figured it all out but by then I was halfway around the world, fighting in Korea. I wish you could have known Miranda as a youngster."

"I'm glad to know her now."

"More subdued now. She said you thought she was a religious nut."

"I give her a hard time. She needs someone to give her hell," Harry half-giggled. "She's more religious than I am but I don't know as she's a nut. You know, Tracy, I've known Miranda from the time I was a child but what do children know? She was bright and chirpy. George died and she took a nosedive. That's when she turned more to religion, although she was a strong churchgoer before. But I've noticed this last year she's happier. It's taken her a long time."

"Does. Lost my wife two years ago and I'm just pulling out of it."

"I'm sorry."

"Me, too. You live with a woman for half of your life and she's the air you breathe. You don't think about it. You simply breathe."

"*Poor fellow.*" Tucker whimpered softly.

"*He's on the mend and he's sure good with chores so I hope he hangs around.*"

Mrs. Murphy, ever practical, batted water drops as they slowly collected under the water tap.

The phone rang. Harry picked it up. Tracy noticed Mrs. Murphy and walked over to the faucet. He unscrewed the tap with his fingers, so strong was his grasp. The washer was shot. He put it back and grabbed a notepad by the phone and made a note to himself which he stuck in his pocket.

"All right. Susan, all right."

Susan, on the other end of the line, said, "Now the hysteria is, should BoomBoom use the picture with Charlie or not?"

"She should look at the proofs first."

"One of them is bound to turn out."

"Susan, what does she intend to do with the superlatives that Aurora and Ron are in? They're dead, too."

"She can't make up her mind whether to use their old photographs either."

"I'll make it up for her. Tell her we all suffered in the heat for that photograph of her and Charlie, so use it."

"You know, Harry, that's a good idea. Hang up and call her before she emotes anymore. It is tiresome." Susan paused. "Go on, Harry. You call her."

Harry, grumbling, did just that and BoomBoom blurted out three or four sentences of inner thoughts before Harry cut her off and told her to just use the new photo. The whole idea was to see the passage of time!

Harry finally got off the phone. "This reunion is becoming a full-time job."

"Ours is going to be real simple," Tracy said. "We'll gather in the cafeteria, swap tales, eat and dance. I don't even know if there will be decorations."

"With Miranda as the chair? She can't have changed that much in fifty years, I promise you." Harry smiled.

"That's something about one of your classmates getting shot." Tracy noticed the weather stripping on the door was ragged. "Everyone seems calm about it."

"Because everyone thinks they know the reason why. They just have to find out which husband pulled the trigger. What has upset people, though, is the mailing that went out to our classmates before Charlie was killed. 'You'll never get old!' it said."

"*Ever hear the expression, 'Expect a trap where the ground is smoothest'?*" Mrs. Murphy commented as she wiped her whiskers.

"*What made you think of that?*" Tucker, now rolled over on her back, inquired.

"*People have jumped to a conclusion. Charlie Ashcraft could have been killed for another reason. What if he was involved in fraud or theft or selling fake bonds?*"

"That's true." Pewter, now on the table, agreed. "*No one much cares because they think it doesn't have anything to do with them.*"

"*Like I said, 'Expect a trap where the ground is smoothest.'*"

18

The dually's motor rumbled as Harry leaned over to drop Tracy's rent check and her deposit slip in the outdoor deposit box on the side of the bank.

The truck gobbled gas, which she could ill afford, but the thrill of driving her new truck to town on her lunch hour superseded prudence.

Susan had given her expensive sheepskin seat covers, which pleased the animals as much as it pleased Harry. They lounged on the luxurious surface, the cats "kneading bread."

Harry flew through the morning's chores, then drove over to Fair's clinic at lunch.

"Hi, Ruth." She smiled at the receptionist.

"He's in the back." Ruth nodded toward the back.

Harry and the animals found him studying X-rays.

"Look." He pointed to a splint, a bone sliver detaching from a horse's cannon bone, a bone roughly equivalent to the human forearm.

"Doesn't look bad enough to operate." She'd seen lots of X-rays during their marriage.

"Hope not. It should reattach. Splints are more common than not." He switched off the light box. "Hello, kids."

The animals greeted him eagerly.

"Here, you're a peach." Harry smiled on the word *peach*. She handed him a check.

"What's this?"

"Partial payment on my old truck. Five hundred dollars a month for four months. I called Art for the real price. He told me to take anything you'd give me but I can't—really. It's not right."

"I don't want the money. That was a gift." He frowned.

"It's too big a gift. I can't take it, as much as I appreciate it."

"No strings. I owe it to you."

"No you don't." She shoved back the check that he held out to her.

"Harry, you can be a real pain in the ass."

"Who's talking?" Her voice raised.

"*I'm leaving.*" Mrs. Murphy headed for the door, only to jump sideways as Ruth rushed in.

"Doc, Sheriff Shaw has Bill Wiggins in the squad car."

"Huh?"

Ruth, almost overwhelmed by the mass of curly gray hair atop her head, breathlessly said, "Margaret Anstein called from the station house. She's the new receptionist at the sheriff's office—or station house, that's what she calls it. She just called me to say Rick was bringing in Bill Wiggins for questioning about Charlie's murder."

"You can't get away with anything in this town." Fair carefully slid the X-rays in a big heavy white envelope.

"That Marcy is a pretty girl. Just Charlie's type." Ruth smacked her lips.

"They were all Charlie's type," Harry said.

"She wasn't at the funeral," Ruth said.

"Why should she be? She's new," Fair replied, irritated that Ruth and most of Crozet had jumped to conclusions.

"The other new people were there. A funeral is a good place to meet people," Ruth blathered.

"*Unless they're dead.*" Pewter twitched her whiskers and followed Murphy to the door.

19

Harry no sooner walked through the back door to the post office than Miranda rushed over to her.

"There's been another one."

"Another what?"

"Mailing. Open your mail. You're always late in opening your mail."

Harry picked up her pile on the little table in the back.

"This one." Miranda pointed out a folded-over, stapled sheet.

"Who else . . . ?"

"Susan, BoomBoom, Bill, and—"

Harry exclaimed, "What a jerk!"

Mrs. Murphy and Pewter stuck their heads over the paper that Harry held in her hands.

"What is it?" Tucker asked.

"Typed. 'Sorry, Charlie. Who's next?' and a drop of red ink like a drop of blood," the tiger answered.

Harry flipped over the page, which allowed Tucker to see it. "22905. The Barracks Road post office again. It's funny no one said anything this morning."

"Because none of your classmates came in before lunch. BoomBoom was at her therapist's and Susan spent the morning in Richmond. The only reason I know that Bill got one was that Marcy called once she got home. Guess she opens his mail. Not right to do that." Miranda believed mail was sacrosanct, the last intimate form of communication.

Harry dialed Vonda, the postmistress at Barracks Road. "Hi, Vonda, Harry. How you doin'?"

Vonda, a pretty woman but not one to babble on, said, "Fine, how are you?"

"Okay, except my classmates and I have gotten another one of these mailings from your post office. Folded over, stapled. Looks to be run off from a color Xerox."

"Bulk?"

"No. They're too smart for a bulk rate. A regular stamp and yesterday's postmark. Did anyone come to the counter with a handful?" Harry knew Vonda would remember, if she'd been behind the counter.

"No. Let me ask the others." Vonda put down the phone. She returned in a minute. "They were pushed through the mail slot. Mary says they were in the bin when she started sorting at elevenish. Second full bin of the day."

"Keep your eyes open. This is getting kind of creepy."

"I will. But it's very easy to walk in and out of here without attracting notice."

"Yeah, I know. Thanks, Vonda." Harry hung up the phone.

"Barracks Road gets more traffic in a day than we get in a week," Pewter remarked.

"Second busiest post office in the county." Mrs. Murphy knew enough to be a postmistress herself. "Even busier than the university station." The main post office on Seminole Trail was the busiest, of course.

"Does Rick know?" Harry asked.

"Yes. Susan called him the minute she picked up her mail." Mrs. Hogendobber paused. "Did you hear that Rick hauled in Bill Wiggins for questioning?"

"Ruth told me. I stopped by Fair's clinic."

"Doesn't look good, does it?" Miranda pursed her lipstick-covered lips.

"For Bill?"

"No, in general."

"I want to know why Bill?"

"Perhaps he was Charlie's doctor. It's entirely possible that Charlie had cancer. He'd never tell."

"I never thought of that." Harry looked down at Tucker, who was looking up. "That doesn't mean Bill will reveal anything. Aren't doctor-patient relationships privileged?"

"I think they are. Doesn't mean Rick won't try."

Mrs. Murphy batted at the paper. Harry dropped it on the table. "What a sick thing to do. Send out . . ." She didn't finish her sentence.

Mrs. Murphy and Pewter both stared at the 8½" x 11" white page.

"*Looks like a warning to me,*" Pewter said.

"*What happened back then? Back when Harry graduated,*" Tucker sensibly asked.

"*I don't know. And more to the point, she doesn't know.*" Mrs. Murphy looked up at Harry. "*If something dreadful had happened and she knew about it, she'd tell the sheriff.*" Mrs. Murphy sat on the paper.

"*Yes. She would.*" Pewter shuddered.

20

Rick Shaw made drawings, flow sheets, time charts, which he color-coded, sticking them on the long cork bulletin board he installed at the station. Being a visual thinker he needed charts.

Every employee of the Farmington Country Club was questioned. Every member at the club that evening had been questioned also, which put a few noses out of joint.

He paced up and down the aisle in front of the bulletin board, eighteen feet. Although pacing was a habit he declared it burned calories. When he slid into middle age he noticed the pounds stuck to him like yellow jackets. You'd brush them off only to have them return. He'd lost fifteen pounds and was feeling better but he had another fifteen to go.

"You're wearing me out." Cynthia tapped her pencil on the side of her desk.

"Get up and walk with me." He smiled at her, his hands clasped behind his back. "This is such a straightforward murder, Coop, that we ought to be able to close the case and yet we haven't a firm suspect. Bill Wiggins is our most logical candidate but the guy has an airtight alibi. He was with a patient at Martha Jefferson Hospital."

She plopped her pencil in a Ball jar she kept on her desk for that purpose and joined him. "The fact that Charlie was shot at such a close range implies he knew who killed him."

"No, it doesn't. There's not a lot of room in the men's locker room. A stranger could have come in as though going to a locker. Charlie wouldn't have paid much attention."

"Yeah." Coop knew he was right, and it frustrated her.

"All we have is Hunter Hughes' testimony that he thought he saw a slender man come down from the landing. He heard the footsteps because he had left the counter in the golf shop and had walked outside for a smoke. He worked until nine that evening. He assumed the man was leaving the men's grill, heard the footsteps and as he turned to go back into the golf shop he saw the back of an average-sized male wearing a white linen-like jacket. This was close to the time of the murder. That's all we've got."

They both stopped in front of the detailed drawing of the country club golf shop, grill, and the men's locker room, along with a sketch of the buildings on that side of the club.

"But when we questioned the manager of the grill, he doesn't remember anyone at the bar about that time."

"Could have been a member passing through from the 19th Hole to the back stairway on the second floor, since it would be a faster route to the men's locker room."

"What if our killer came out of the pool side?" She pointed to the pool, which was behind the long brick structure containing the locker room and golf shop.

"Easy. It would have been easy to park behind the caretaker's house. The car would have been in the dark. Walking up here behind the huge boxwoods would have made it easy to escape detection." He pointed to the sketch. "For that matter the killer could have sat in his car. Who would notice back here? Whoever he is, he knows the routine and layout of the club. He knew no big party was planned that night. Then again, the schedule is published monthly, so it's easily accessible. It goes to each member plus it's posted at the front desk."

"A member." She nodded. "Knowing the layout points in that direction."

"Yeah, or an employee"—Rick folded his arms across his chest—"possible but unlikely."

"A jealous husband could have paid a professional."

"Could have."

She turned to face her boss. "But it smacks of a deeper connection. 'Up close and personal,' like they used to say during the Olympics coverage."

"Sure does. Our killer wanted to get right in Charlie's face."

21

"Not so fast!" Denny Rablan called from behind the camera. He was beginning to wonder why he was doing this, even if it was for his class reunion.

Bonnie, black curls shaking with laughter, sped on her bicycle toward a short but handsome Leo Burkey, also pedaling to pick up momentum. Bonnie and Leo screamed at one another as they approached. Chris Sharpton buried her face in her hands since she thought they'd crash.

BoomBoom, standing behind Denny, appeared immobile while Harry giggled. She knew Bonnie and Leo were thoroughly enjoying discomfiting BoomBoom, who was determined to follow through on her before-and-after idea.

The two pedaled more furiously, heading straight for one another, at the last minute averting the crash.

"That's not funny!" BoomBoom bellowed.

"Olivia, you have no sense of humor. You never did." Bonnie called BoomBoom by her given name.

Her maiden name had been Olivia Ulrich but she'd been called BoomBoom ever since puberty. Only Boom's mother called her Olivia, a name she loathed although it was beautiful. Once she married Kelly Craycroft she happily dumped all references to Ulrich, since the Craycrofts carried more social cachet than the Ulrichs.

Eyes narrowed, BoomBoom advanced on Bonnie, who merrily pedaled away from her. "Get serious, Baltier! This is costing us. Time is money."

"God, what a rocket scientist." Leo smiled, revealing huge white teeth.

"You're a big, fat help." BoomBoom pointed a finger at him.

"I thought dear Denny was giving us his services for free." He innocently held up his hands, riding without them.

"I am. Almost," Dennis growled. "A greatly reduced rate."

"Well, Denny, my man, if you hadn't pissed away a fortune, you could do this for free, couldn't you?"

"Leo, shut up. It's over and done. I live with my mistakes and I don't throw your screwups in your face."

Leo rode in circles around the tall, thin, attractive photographer. "Maybe you're right."

"I could name your screwups. They all have feminine names."

Leo stopped the bike. He put his feet on the ground and walked the few steps to face Dennis. "So many women. So little time. Not that I'm in Charlie's league."

"Guess not. Charlie's dead."

"Did you get that asinine letter?"

"I figured you did it." Dennis smirked.

"Sure. I drove all the way from Richmond to Charlottesville to send a mailing with fake blood drops. Get real."

"I wouldn't put anything past you."

"No?" Leo's light hazel eyes widened. "Remember this: I'm not stupid. You were stupid. Sex, drugs, and rock and roll. Jesus, Denny, by the time you got off the merry-go-round you were broken. How could you do that?"

"Too loaded to care, man." Dennis's mouth clamped like a vise.

"I think you broke bad in high school."

"Leo, I don't give a damn what you think." Dennis turned his back on the shorter but more powerfully built man.

The others glanced over at the two men, then glanced away. Dennis and Leo were oil and water. Always had been.

"Shiny nose," Bitsy Valenzuela, in charge of makeup, called out.

Bonnie, ignoring BoomBoom—something she had perfected throughout high school—glided over to Bitsy.

Chris Sharpton picked up the orange cone she'd dropped when she thought the two were going to crash at high speed. Stationed at the entrance to the high-school parking lot, she put the cone upright. If anyone drove in they'd see the blaze-orange cone, see her and stop. She could direct them toward the rear. She stood there forlorn since no one drove through this early September afternoon. Many of the kids were behind the school at football practice.

"Listen, you two, we haven't got all day. Just get in position. Put the bikes down."

Finally obeying, both Bonnie and Leo approached one another and screeched to a halt.

"Put that bike down carefully, Leo, it's an antique," BoomBoom again commanded.

"No one is going to know if this bike is twenty years old or not. You're getting carried away with this," Leo said, but he did restrain himself from saying other, less pleasant things.

Bonnie laid her bike down, turning the wheel up just as it was in the original photograph. Leo's bike took more work. It stood on its front wheel in the original photograph as though the wreck had just happened. Harry, Susan Tucker, and a very subdued Marcy Wiggins set two blocks on either side of the front wheel. Since Leo would be sprawled on the ground his body would cover the blocks. They then braced the back side of the bicycle with a thin iron pole. As this was a balancing act, the two principals lay on the ground. The first time the shot had been taken, in 1979, the bike kept falling on Leo. The next day he was covered with bruises. Harry, Susan, and Marcy hoped they had secured the bicycle better than that but they also held their breath, hoping Nature would do likewise.

"Hurry up, Denny, this asphalt is hot!" Leo barked.

"Stay still, idiot." Denny said "idiot" under his breath. He shot the whole roll in record time.

Bonnie, thinking ahead, had taped bits of moleskin and padding on her one elbow and knee. She was on them as though she'd just hit the ground on her side. Still, the heat came through the padding.

Leo got up. "That's enough."

"We just started!" BoomBoom exploded.

The propped bicycle wobbled, falling with a metallic crash, spinning spokes throwing off sunlight.

Harry ran over, picked it up. Luckily there were no scratches.

"If that bike is broken, I'll kill you," BoomBoom, often the butt of Leo's high-school pranks, hissed.

"Don't get your ovaries in an uproar, Boom. If the damned bicycle is scratched I'll fix it. You know, here it is twenty years later and you still haven't learned how to lighten up."

"Here it is twenty years later and you still haven't grown up," she fired back.

Chris left her cone. This was too good to miss.

Bonnie, ever the pragmatist, walked over to Denny. "Think you got it?"

"Yeah, that asphalt really is too hot to shoot this picture. The first time we did this it was later in the fall, remember?"

"October." Harry rolled the bike over to the two of them. "We voted on senior superlatives mid-October."

"What a good memory." Denny couldn't remember what he'd eaten for supper the night before but then, given his past, a bad memory was a blessing.

"Remember when Leo made a crack to Ron Brindell in the cafeteria the day after the results were announced? Remember?

Ron won Most Popular and Leo said they should shoot his picture in the locker room." Harry continued to wipe down the bike.

Leo had joined them. "Yeah."

Chris innocently asked, "Why'd you say that?"

"Ron was such a limp-wristed wimp. I said they should shoot him in the showers bent over with the naked guys behind him. He took a swing at me, that skinny little twit. I decked him and got a month of detention."

"Was he gay?" Chris wondered.

"He moved to San Francisco." Leo laughed as though that proved his point.

"That doesn't mean he was gay," Harry piped up. "I liked him."

"Yeah, you aren't a guy." Leo smoothed back his light brown hair.

"Speak no ill of the dead," Susan Tucker admonished as she picked up Bonnie's bike.

"Three of the superlatives are dead." Leo slipped his hands in his back pants pockets. "Maybe it's a bad omen." Then he imitated the *Twilight Zone* music.

"Ron and Aurora died long before now," BoomBoom, tired of Leo, said. Her alto voice carried over the parking lot. "As for Charlie, bad karma."

"He should have gone into pornographic films. Charlie Ashcraft, porn star. He would have been happier than as a stockbroker," Leo laughed.

"Funny thing is, he was a good stockbroker." Bonnie peeled off the moleskin.

"He was?" Leo was surprised.

"Prudent. He made a lot of money for people." Susan added, "Odd, how a person can be so reckless in one aspect of his life and so shrewd in another."

Marcy and Bitsy had joined them, Marcy adding to the conversation, "My husband says that men can compartmentalize better than women. There's a compartment for work, for family, for sex. It's easy for them." She'd taken to talking more fondly of Bill lately, perhaps to ward off gossip about her alleged relationship with Charlie. She was too late, of course.

Denny shrugged. "I don't know. Charlie must have had some thick walls between those compartments."

Harry took one of the bicycles, rolling it over to her red truck. She'd placed blankets on the floor of the truck bed so neither the bicycle nor the truck would get scratched. She wanted to buy a bedliner for the truck but hadn't had time to get one installed. She lifted the bike onto the dropped tailgate.

Chris came over. "Let me help."

"Okay, I'll hop in here and if you hop in on the other side we can lift it to the back. I've got ties to keep it from slipping."

"Who's taking the other bike?" Chris asked.

"Susan. It's her son's. Good thing. I'd hate to stack the bikes on one another. I think the first scratch to this truck will be a blow to my heart." She smiled. "Silly."

"Human." Chris wrapped yellow rope under the bike frame.

Bonnie and Susan walked over. "Are you going to dinner?"

"No," Harry responded.

"What about you, Chris?"

She turned to Susan. "BoomBoom told me she'd promised dinner to Bonnie and Leo since they had to drive a bit to get here. I don't want to intrude."

Susan said, "We've decided on Dutch treat. Come on. It will be fun. If for no other reason than to watch Leo torment Boom. Sure you don't want to come, Harry?"

"No, thanks. I've got chores to do." She tried to tolerate BoomBoom better these days but she'd not volunteer to spend time with her.

As she opened the door to the truck, Chris asked, "Denny asked me to dinner this Saturday. I don't know much about him. Is he an okay guy?"

Susan replied, "He's made a lot of bad decisions but, yeah, he's okay. At least he has learned from his messes."

Chris looked to Harry, who shrugged. "Go."

"He's divorced?"

"Years ago. I don't know why he married in the first place. They had nothing in common," Susan said.

"Date a lot of men, it helps refine your standards." Harry laughed. "Advice I should have taken myself."

"Thanks." Chris smiled, then walked back to Dennis, who was putting away his equipment. He smiled as she approached him.

When Harry arrived home she found that the washer in the kitchen faucet had been replaced, the weather stripping on the door was replaced, a blackboard hung next to the kitchen door, a box of colored chalk was suspended by a chain attached to the blackboard. Written in green on the blackboard was the message, "Taking Cuddles to the movies. See you in the morning. Pewter has something to show you."

"Pewts," Harry called.

A little voice answered from the living room. Harry walked in to find Pewter proudly guarding a skink that she'd dispatched. Mrs. Murphy and Tucker flanked the gray cat.

"I caught him all by myself," Pewter crowed.

"Sort of," Mrs. Murphy added.

"Pewter, what a good kitty." Harry petted her. She went outside to check the horses, finished up her chores with fading light, and went to bed, glad she wasn't forced to relive old times at dinner.

22

The phone rang at the post office at seven-thirty A.M. just as Rob Collier, the delivery man from the main post office on Seminole Trail, dropped off two bags of mail.

"Sorry I'm late. Fender bender at Hydraulic Road and Route 29." He tipped his hat as he jogged back to the truck.

Mrs. Hogendobber answered the phone as the cats dashed to the mailbags. "Crozet Post Office. Mrs. Hogendobber speaking."

"I think movies were better in our day," Tracy replied on the other end. "That movie last night was all special effects. Was there a story?"

"Not that I could decipher."

"The best part of the movie was sitting next to you."

"You flatterer." She blushed and winked at Harry.

"I'll stop by on my way to Staunton. Harry left me a note this morning thanking me for the washer and leaving me five dollars for fixing it. You tell that girl she's got to learn to let people do things for her."

"Yes, Tracy, I'll try, but a new voice might get through. See you later."

"He's still got a crush on you," Harry teased Miranda, as she untied the first mailbag to the delight of Mrs. Murphy, who wriggled through the opening.

"*Isn't paper the best?*" The cat slid around in the bag, which was about three-quarters full.

"*Tissue paper is better but this isn't bad.*" Pewter squeezed into the second mailbag.

"*Paper? I don't get it.*" The dog shook her head, retiring to the small table in the back upon which Mrs. Hogendobber had placed a fresh round loaf of black bread, a damp dish towel over the top of it. The aroma filled the post office. Freshly churned butter in a large covered glass dish sat next to it.

"Come on, Miss Puss, out of there." Harry reached in and grabbed Mrs. Murphy's tail. Not hard.

"*Make me.*" Mrs. Murphy batted away her hand, claws sheathed.

"You're a saucy wench this morning." Harry opened the bag wider.

Mrs. Murphy peered back, eyes large in the darkened space. She burrowed deeper into the mail. "*Hee hee.*" Only it sounded to human ears like "kickle, kickle."

"Murphy, cut it out. You're going to scratch the mail. Federal property. Just think. You could be the first cat convicted of tampering with the mail. Federal offense. Jail. I can see the headlines now: Catastrophe."

"*Corny,*" the cat meowed.

"I can't get Pewter out either." Miranda bent down a bit more stiffly than Harry, but she'd been gardening on her knees for the last few days, too.

"*I can do it.*" Tee Tucker bounded over and bit, gently, first the large lump in one bag and then the larger lump in the other.

Two cats shot out of the bags as though shot out of cannons. They whirled on Tucker. After all, no human had jaws like that.

"*Charge!*" Mrs. Murphy ordered.

She leapt onto Tucker's back. Tucker rolled over to dispense with that but when she did, Pewter jumped on her belly. The dog loved it, of course, but this was accompanied by furious growling. A few tufts of fur floated in the air.

As Pewter clung to Tucker's white belly, Mrs. Murphy grabbed the corgi's head, literally crawling on top of her, biting her ears.

"*Uncle!*" the dog cried out.

"*You don't have an uncle.*" Mrs. Murphy laughed so hard she fell over, so now Tucker could put the cat's head in her mouth.

Pewter yelled, "*That's cheating!*"

"*No, it's not. Two against one is cheating.*" But of course the minute Tucker said this she released her grip on Mrs. Murphy, who escaped.

"*The jaws of death,*" the cat panted.

They'd all three exhausted themselves, so they fell in a heap between the mailbags.

"Crazy!" Miranda shook her head.

The front door swung open and Big Mim, wearing a flowered sundress and a straw hat, strolled in. "Don't worry." She held up her hands. "I know you haven't sorted the mail yet. Miranda, I've hired Dan Wheeler to play at your reunion. Okay?"

Miranda walked over to the divider. "He'll add so much to the event but we can't afford him. We've got the tiniest treasury."

Mim waved her hand. "I'll pay for it."

"Mim, that's very generous, especially since you graduated from Madeira."

"I might as well do something with the money. It appears I am never to have grandchildren."

Mim's daughter, divorced, was childless and not at all happy about either state. Her son, living in New York, was married to an elegant African-American model but they, too, had not produced an heir.

"They'll get around to it."

"I hope before I'm dead!" came the tart response.

"We've plenty of years left. Now you just come on back here and have a piece of my fresh pumpernickel."

"Love pumpernickel." Mim whizzed through the divider.

As Miranda cut through the warm bread the glorious scent intensified. Tucker opened an eye but couldn't bring herself to move. Harry brewed a fresh pot of coffee.

"Why hasn't Tracy Raz come to see me?"

"He's just gotten here." Miranda handed Mim a napkin.

"He's been here almost a week. You tell him I'm miffed. I expect a call. Maybe we didn't go to the same school but we were all friends. After all, I was home every holiday and every summer."

"Yes, dear." Miranda had learned how to handle Mim decades ago and was amazed that the woman's daughter had never figured out the trick: agree with her even when you don't. Over time, bit by bit, present opposing points of view. Nine times out of ten, Mim would hear it. But oppose her immediately or rain on her parade and her back would go up. You'd never get anywhere. Mim's mother was the same way, as was her ancient Aunt Tally, alive and exceedingly well.

"Harry, how's your reunion coming along?"

"BoomBoom has done a good job organizing. I have to give her credit. She has some original ideas."

"That's gracious of you." Mim beamed. "Now girls, I have a bone to pick with Market Shiflett and I want your support."

Both Harry and Miranda looked at one another and then back to Big Mim. "What?" they said in unison.

"He's moved that blue dumpster parallel with the alley. Looks dreadful. I should think it upsets you, Miranda."

"Well . . ." She measured her words. "He has created more parking and this was the only way he could do it."

"He could go back to garbage cans." Mim pronounced judgment.

"He even tried chaining the garbage cans. That didn't work. He painted them orange and people still ran over them," Harry offered.

"I know all that," Mim replied imperiously. "Then he can set the dumpster sideways under the privet hedge and he can build a palisade around it."

"But the dumpster is picked up once a week on a huge flatbed and a clean one put down in its place. I don't see how he can build a palisade around it." However, Miranda liked the idea.

"Oh yes, he can. Put big hinges on the long end, the end facing the parking lot, such as it is"—her voice dropped—"and put rollers on the bottom. In essence it's a big gate. When the pickup truck comes all Market has to do is roll that gate back or swing it out, whichever makes the most sense. He'll have to figure that out but I know it will work. I'm going over there to speak to him right now. Could one of you come with me?"

"Uh . . ." Harry stalled.

"Harry, go on. I'll sort the mail. You're better suited than I am."

"I don't know if that's true." Harry wiped her hands on the napkin.

"Harry," was all Mim said.

"Okay," she replied weakly, "but before we go in there, let's look closely at the site and the dumpster. Maybe we can figure out ways to improve it even more, you know, some plantings or something."

"Excellent!"

Miranda dropped her eyes lest she laugh by connecting with Harry. If there's one thing Mim couldn't resist it was a gardening idea. Harry was shrewd enough to maneuver her into yet another beautification plan.

As it was, Mim struggled valiantly with the garden club to

accept her plans for filling downtown Crozet with profusions of flowers for the spring, summer, and fall bolstered by masses of holly, pyracantha, and Scotch pine for the winter. Her master plan for the town was stunning and everyone admitted that Crozet needed help. But money could never be found in the town budget and Mim, generous though she was, felt strongly that if the plan didn't generate community support she wasn't going to cough up the funds. She'd enlisted Miranda's aid and if she could interest Harry and Harry's generation, she thought she just might pull it off.

Harry and Mim walked out the back door as Tracy walked in the front door. He'd finished his errands and returned to see Miranda.

Mrs. Murphy got up, stretched, and followed Harry out.

Tucker, exhaling loudly, did the same. Pewter, sound asleep, didn't even open an eye when Miranda picked her up, gently placing her in an empty mail cart.

The two humans and two animals stood before the blue dumpster. It was unsightly but at least it had a lid on it. Having it open would have been a lot worse.

Mim used her right hand. "Swing the dumpster around like so. He can still use it with ease but it will free up more space. The palisade on the alley side could swing out or roll back for transfer."

"If it swings out it will block traffic."

"How much traffic is on this alleyway," Mim snipped, then thought a minute. "You're right. If it rolls straight along, it will block his parking lot for a minute but the alley will be free. 'Course, the truck will be in it anyway. However, I take your point and think rollers toward us is a better idea. Did you think perhaps planter tubs on the parking lot side?"

"No. I thought since that palisade part is stable why not build three tiers and fill them with geraniums, petunias, and even ivy that could spill over."

"Now that is a good idea." Mim's eyes brightened. "It will add to the expense."

"He's got a daughter in college." Harry need say no more.

"H-m-m, I'll think of something."

"Something's not right." Tucker lifted her nose and sniffed deeply.

Mrs. Murphy, nose not as sensitive, also smelled blood. *"Let me jump up."*

"Lid's closed." Tucker barked loudly.

"Maybe we can get them to open it." Murphy soared onto the slanted lid, sliding a bit but quickly jumping over to the flat side. *"I smell blood, too. Maybe there's a beef carcass. I'll get some of it for you,"* Murphy promised her grounded friend.

"No, this isn't beef, sheep, or chicken. This is human," Tucker adamantly barked.

Mrs. Murphy thought a minute, then said, *"Together."*

The cat and dog howled in unison. The humans looked at them as Pewter hurried out the animal door to the post office. *"What's going on?"*

"Come up here."

She leapt up next to Mrs. Murphy, sliding down harder than the slender cat. Harry caught her.

"Yell," Mrs. Murphy directed.

Pewter bellowed. She surprised Harry so much that she dropped her. The cat shook herself, then leapt up again. This time she managed to get over to the flat side. *"Uh-oh."* She smelled it, too.

All three of them hollered for all they were worth.

"What's gotten into them?" Mim put her hand on her hip, then reached over and lifted up the slanted lid. She dropped the lid with a thud reverberating throughout the alley and sending the two cats off the dumpster. She took a faltering step back. Harry reached out to catch her.

Mim's face, bone-white, frightened Harry, who at first thought the older woman might have suffered a heart attack or stroke. Mim moved her lips but nothing came out. She pointed to the dumpster lid.

"Are you all right?"

Mim nodded her head. "Yes." Then she took a deep breath and opened the lid again.

"Oh, my God!" Harry exclaimed.

23

Sitting on top of the squad car, Mrs. Murphy laconically commented, *"Could have been worse."*

The assemblage by the dumpster would have disagreed with her if they had understood what she was saying. Mim called her husband, Jim, the mayor. He rushed over. Tracy put his arm around Miranda's waist. She was upset but holding together.

As luck would have it, Marcy Wiggins and Chris Sharpton had stopped by to pick up their mail. Fair Haristeen had also come to the P.O. Marcy fainted and Chris, with Fair's help, carried her into Market's air-conditioned store. Market, rushing around the store, revived her with a spot of brandy. As soon as she was somewhat recovered he hurried back outside again.

"In my dumpster!" He wrung his hands.

Tucker, as close to the dumpster as she could get without being in the way, asked Pewter, *"What did the body look like when you first could see in?"*

Pewter peered down from the limb of the pin oak where she was reposing. She wanted a different view than Mrs. Murphy. *"Leo's mouth was open and so were his eyes. He'd stiffened up but it wasn't too bad yet. They'll have a hell of a time getting him out of there now."*

"What I meant was, can you see how he was killed?" the dog persisted.

"*Right between the eyes. Like Charlie Ashcraft,*" Pewter informed her with some relish.

"*Flies are what made the humans sick.*" Murphy watched intently. "*They're in the dumpster so they crawled all over him but really, it could have been worse. He's not been dead half a day.*" She was matter-of-fact about these matters, but then, cats are.

Rick and Cynthia, having finished their work, had to turn to Jim Sanburne, the crowd growing by the minute behind the yellow tape. "Jim, I prefer they leave but I doubt they will so keep them back. If they break through the tape they may compromise evidence. Can you call in anyone to help you?"

Tracy stepped forward. "Sheriff, Tracy Raz, I can help."

Tracy was off in the service when Rick was young so he didn't remember him, but he knew the Raz name. "Thank you."

"I'll help, too." Fair towered over the other two men.

Tracy, accustomed to command, faced the murmuring crowd, some with handkerchiefs to their mouths. "Folks, I know this is extremely upsetting to you all but please leave. The more of us that crowd around, the more possibility that valuable evidence will be destroyed. Sheriff Shaw is doing all he can right now and he needs your help."

"Come on, gang." Fair gently shepherded his friends and neighbors back down the alleyway.

As people walked slowly they turned to see what else was happening. The last thing they saw was a big blue truck, Batten Services, come down the lane with Joe Batten emerging, his assistant and cousin, Harvey Batten, along with him. He ran the trash-removal company and he was going to take off the door to the dumpster so they could remove the body.

"You girls go back into the post office," Tracy soothingly directed, "because that's where people will gather and they'll need you to keep your heads."

"Quite right." Miranda nodded. Violent death shocked her. But she'd seen enough death in her life to accept it as inevitable, although she never could accept violence.

The cats and dog stayed at the scene of the crime. No one paid attention to them because they were careful to stay out of the way, even though Mrs. Murphy brazenly sat on top of Rick's squad car.

Joe glanced at the body, pulled a heavy wrench from his leather tool belt around his waist, and started turning a nut. "Harvey, you crippled?"

Harvey swallowed hard, walked over, and crouched down to work on the bottom bolt. He was eye-level with the loafers on the corpse but he did not look inside.

As the men worked, Diana Robb and the rescue squad crept down the alleyway, clogged with cars. The people moved away but they'd left their cars.

Diana hopped out, marched up to the opened dumpster, and peered inside. "Like Charlie. Powder burns."

"Uh-huh," Rick noncommittally grunted.

"You ready for us?" She noticed the crushed green and orange 7 Up cartons under the body.

"Yeah, you can take him." Rick leaned against the squad car to light a cigarette.

"*Those things will kill you*," Mrs. Murphy scolded.

He looked up at the cat looking down at him. "You don't miss a thing, do you?"

"*Nope.*"

"Need a hand?" Tracy offered.

"We've got it, thanks." Diana smiled.

Tracy asked Rick, "If you don't need me anymore I'll be going."

"Where to?"

"The post office."

"I mean, where do you come from?" Rick inhaled.

Tracy briefly filled the sheriff in on his background. "Retired now. Came back to help with our high-school reunion."

Rick reached out to shake his hand. "Rick Shaw, sheriff."

"Deputy Cynthia Cooper." She shook Tracy's hand also, as did Fair.

"I'm renting rooms at Harry's farm. If you need me I'll be there." He opened the back door to the post office, slipping inside.

Fair, face white with upset, hands in jeans pockets, said, "Quite an ending for someone as fastidious as Leo Burkey. To be dumped with garbage."

"Harry made a similar comment," Rick noted.

Market bustled back again. "Sheriff, I hope you don't think I did this. I couldn't stand Leo, but I wouldn't kill him. Besides, he lived far enough away he didn't work on my mood." Market's voice was tremulous, his hands were shaking.

"Market." Rick paused. "Why didn't you like him?"

"Smart-ass. In high school—well, always."

"Yes, he was," Fair confirmed.

"As bad as Charlie Ashcraft?" Cynthia watched as Joe and Harvey lifted the blue metal door off its hinges, leaning it up against the side of the dumpster.

"What's worse, reaching in the garbage or picking up the body?" Pewter giggled.

Tucker whirled around, hearing before the rest of them. *"What's worse is here comes Channel 29."*

Diana, now seeing the van with the dish on top, as she was looking down the alleyway, urged, "Come on, let's get him out of here and in a body bag before they jump out with the damned cameras."

Too late. Even before the van pulled over the cameraman was running toward them.

"Stand back!" Rick barked, holding up his hand.

A brief argument followed but the cameraman and on-air reporter did stay twenty yards back as Diana, with three assistants, lifted out the body. Since rigor was taking over, getting him into a body bag required effort.

"Why don't they break his arms and legs?" Pewter sensibly suggested.

"They'd pass out. Humans are touchy about their dead." Mrs. Murphy

noticed the outline of his wallet in his back pocket. It would appear robbery wasn't the motive.

Market returned to the question Cynthia had posed before they were interrupted by the television crew. "No, Leo wasn't as bad as Charlie Ashcraft. Charlie was in a class by himself. Leo wanted us to think he was a ladies' man but he was more bark than bite. He had a smart mouth, that's all. Hurt a lot of feelings. Or I should say he hurt mine. And he was handsome, I couldn't compete with him for the girls. Not too many of us could." He looked up at Fair. "Like you, the class ahead. You always got the girls."

"Hope I didn't have a smart mouth." Fair still watched fixedly as they struggled with the body.

"You were a good guy. Still are," Market said. He leaned against the car with Rick, as he couldn't stop shaking. "I don't know what's wrong with me. I feel dizzy."

"The shock of it." Rick patted Market on the back. "No one expects to come to work in the morning and find a dead body in the garbage."

"If I'd kept those old garbage cans it wouldn't have happened," Market moaned. "That will teach me to leave well enough alone."

"Until they scattered all over the alleyway again," Fair reminded him. "You did the right thing. Someone took advantage of it, that's all."

"*Someone who doesn't much care about how they dispose of bodies. Two men, same age, same high-school class, shot between the eyes and left for the world to see. There's a message here.*" Mrs. Murphy walked over the back window, careful not to smear paw prints on it. "*Like those stupid mailings. I think the message will get more clear in time.*"

"*Both senior superlatives, too.*" Pewter backed down the tree to join her friend. "*That's odd.*"

"*Mom's a senior superlative.*" Tucker barked so loud she distracted one of the rescue-squad men and he tripped, then righted himself.

"*We* know," the cats said. Then Murphy continued, "But *so far the murdered are handsome men, well-off. Don't panic yet.*"

"*I'm not panicking,*" the dog grumbled, "*only observing.*"

"*They say that when someone dies their features relax.*" Pewter walked toward the post office, her friends walking with her. "*But Leo Burkey looked surprised, like a bear had jumped out at him, like something totally out of the blue had shocked him.*"

"*We* didn't *see Charlie but it's a sure bet he was surprised, too.*" Tucker pushed through the animal door into the post office.

Mrs. Murphy sat in front of the door, irritating Tucker who stuck her head back through to see where the cats were. "*There's human intelligence to this. That's the trick, you see. Killers often start from an irrational premise and then are completely rational and logical when they act.*"

24

Glad to be home after an extremely upsetting day, Harry wearily pushed open the screened porch door. It didn't squeak. She noted the hinges had been oiled. She heard pounding behind the barn.

Mrs. Hogendobber had given her freshly baked corn bread in a square pan which the older woman had thoughtfully covered with tinfoil. Harry placed the pan inside the refrigerator.

"Look!" Pewter trilled.

Mrs. Murphy, whiskers swept forward, bounded up to Pewter in front of the refrigerator. Tucker ran over, too, her claws hitting the heart pine floorboards with clicks.

"Wow, this is a first," Tucker exclaimed.

Harry grinned. "Hasn't been this full since Mom was alive."

Milk, half-and-half, bottled water, and Dortmunder beer filled the beverage shelf. Chicken and steak, wrapped in cellophane, rested on another shelf. Fresh lettuce, collard greens, pattypan squash, and perfectly round cherry tomatoes spilled over the vegetable compartment. On the bottom shelf, neatly placed side by side, gleamed red cans of real Coca-Cola.

Stacked next to the refrigerator were a variety of cat and dog canned foods with a few small gourmet packs on top.

"A cornucopia of delight." Pewter flopped on her side, rolling over then rolling back in the other direction.

"He must be rich to buy so much food at once." Tucker admired the canned food, too.

"It is amazing." Murphy purred, too, excited by the sight of all those goodies.

Harry closed the door, turned to wash her hands in the sink, and noticed her yearbook and a 1950 yearbook resting on the table side by side. She opened the 1950 yearbook and saw Tracy's name in youthful script in the upper right-hand page. Strips of paper marked her yearbook. She flipped open to each one. Tracy had marked all the photographs in which Charlie Ashcraft and Leo Burkey appeared.

She closed the book and walked outside toward the sound of the pounding.

Tracy, shirt off, replaced worn fence boards with good, pressure-treated oak boards, piled neatly in one paddock.

"Tracy, you must be a good fairy or whatever the male version is." She smiled.

He pushed back his cowboy hat. "Oak lasts longer."

"Please give me the bill for the wood and the groceries. Otherwise, I'll feel like I'm taking advantage of you."

"I love for women to take advantage of me." He laughed. "Besides, you don't know how good it feels to be doing something. Bet the post office was wild today, wasn't it?"

She knew he'd changed the subject because he didn't want to hear anything more about repayment. "Yes."

"Damn fool thing. I read through your yearbook. I hope you don't mind."

"No."

"Dead bodies don't bother me. Got used to that in Korea. But wanton killing, that bothers me."

"Me, too. Can't make rhyme or reason of this."

"Patience." He lifted another board, she grabbed the far end to help.

"What's that expression, 'Grant me patience, Lord, but hurry.' I recall Mom saying that a lot." She stepped to the side, nearly stepping on Tucker, who jumped sideways. "Sorry, Tucker."

"Cutest dog."

"*Thank you.*" Tucker cocked her head at Tracy.

"Being all over the map, I couldn't keep a dog. Li had one. Well, I guess it was mine, too, but since I was on the road so much it was really hers. Beautiful German shepherd. Smart, too. I knew as long as Bruno was with her, she was safe. You know, two weeks after Li died, Bruno closed his eyes and died, too. Granted he was old by then but I believe his heart was broken." Tracy's eyes clouded over.

"*I couldn't live without Mom.*" Tucker put her head on her paws.

The cats listened to this with some interest but neither one would admit to such excessive devotion. The truth was, if anything ever happened to Harry, Mrs. Murphy would be devastated and Pewter . . . well, Pewter would be discomfited.

Harry stooped down to pat Tucker's head, since she was whining. "When I was little Mom and Dad had a German shepherd named King. Wonderful dog. He lived to be twenty-one. Back then we had cattle, polled Herefords and some horned Herefords, too, and Dad used King to bring in the cattle. Mom always had a corgi—those dogs herd as efficiently as shepherds. Someday I'd like to get another shepherd but only when I'm certain a puppy won't upset Tucker and the kitties. They might be jealous."

"*A puppy! I'll scratch its eyes out,*" Pewter hissed.

"*No, you won't. You'll hop up on the table or chairs. You like babies as much as I do.*" Murphy laughed at the gray blowhard.

"*No, I don't and I don't recall you liking puppies or kittens that much. I recall you telling those two kittens of Blair Bainbridge's ghost stories that scared the wits out of them.*"

Murphy giggled. "*They grew up into big healthy girls. Of course, we hardly see them since they spend half their life at the grooming parlor.*"

Harry lifted another board. She and Tracy were getting into a rhythm. "Corgis are amazing dogs. Very brave and intelligent. Tee Tucker's a Pembroke—no tail. The Cardigans have tails and to my eye look a little longer than the Pembrokes. Pound for pound, a corgi is a lot of dog." She bragged a touch on the breed, a common trait among corgi owners.

"I noticed when I came out back this morning—back of Market's, I mean—that Pewter was in a tree. She could see everything. Mrs. Murphy sat on the squad car. She, too, could see everything, as well as hear the squad radio calls. And Tucker sat just off to the side of the dumpster door. Her nose was straight in the air so she smelled everything. Miranda said it was the animals that called attention to the dumpster."

"I did." Tucker puffed out her white chest.

"*True, you have the best nose. I'd bet you against a bloodhound.*" Mrs. Murphy praised the dog.

"*Don't get carried away,*" Pewter dryly said to the tiger.

"Chatty, aren't they?" Tracy pounded in nails.

"You sure notice everything."

"That's my training. I noticed something else, too. When they pulled the body out of the dumpster there was a stain across the seat of his pants, noticeable, like a crease. The killer sat him on the edge of the dumpster before pushing him back into it. As Leo was a big man and as the crease was pronounced, he sat there for a minute or two at the least before the killer could maneuver the body into the dumpster and close the lid. That's what I surmise. Can't prove a thing, of course. And I asked Miranda if she heard a car back there but her bedroom is away from the alley side of the house. She said she heard nothing. I would assume, also, that the killer was smart enough to turn off his headlights and that Leo Burkey's car will turn up somewhere."

Harry stepped aside as he nailed in the last of the boards. He'd also brought out the fence stain so he could stain them right away. She counted twenty-seven boards that he'd replaced.

"I'll get another brush." She walked to the toolshed where she kept brushes of every shape and size, all of them cleaned and hung, brush side down, on nails. Harry never threw out a paint-brush in her life. By the time she returned he'd already painted one panel.

"It's not going to look right with some freshly painted and the others faded so I'm going to do the whole thing. Now you don't have to work with me. After all, this was my idea, not yours."

"I'd like to work with you. I'm so accustomed to doing the chores alone."

"When was the last time you stained these fences?"

"Eight years ago."

He studied the faded boards and posts. "That's good, Harry. Usually this stuff fades out after two or three years. I pulled five gallons out of the big drum you've got there. I'm impressed with your practicality. Had the drum on its side on two wrought-iron supports, drove a faucet in the front just like a cask of wine. You know your stuff, kid. What is this, by the way?"

"Fence coat black. You can only buy it in one place in the U.S., Lexington Paint and Supply in Lexington, Kentucky. They ship it out in fifty-five-gallon drums. I've tried everything. This is the only stuff that lasts."

"Smart girl." He whistled as he painted, carefully, as he did everything. He was a tidy and organized man. "Is there a con-necting link between the two victims?"

"Huh?"

"Leo and Charlie."

"Well, they graduated in 1980 from Crozet High School. They were both handsome. That's about it. They weren't friends. I don't think they saw one another after high school."

"Nothing else? Did they play football together or golf or did they ever date sisters or the same woman? Were they involved in financial dealings together?"

Harry was beginning to appreciate Tracy's ability to construct patterns, to look for the foundation under the building. "No. Charlie wasn't much of an athlete. He thought he was but he wasn't. Leo was much better. He played football and basketball in high school and then he played football in college, too."

"Where'd he go?"

"Uh, Wake Forest."

"What about Charlie?"

"He went up north. Charlie was always smart in a business way. He went to the University of Pennsylvania. Charlie had a lot of clients. He was an independent stockbroker. I don't know if Leo was one or not, though I doubt he was."

"Anything else?"

"They were both senior superlatives. I can't see that as much of a connection, though. Not for murder, anyway."

"I saw you had two superlatives."

"I know you were Most Athletic."

"Yep. We have that in common." He smiled at her. "Keep a notebook handy. Has to be little so you can stick it in a pocket. When ideas occur, write them down. No matter how silly. You'd be surprised at what you know that you don't know."

"Interesting." Murphy got up and headed for the barn.

"Where are you going?" Pewter enjoyed eavesdropping.

"Tackroom. I am determined to destroy those mice." She flicked her tail when she said that.

Tucker laughed. Murphy stopped, fixing the corgi with a stare, a special look employed by Southern women known as "the freeze." Then she walked off.

"We'll find the killer or killers before she gets one thieving mouse." Tucker laughed loudly.

That quick, Murphy turned, leapt over a startled Pewter, bounded in four great strides to the corgi. She flung herself upon the unsuspecting dog, rolling her over. Tucker bumped into the big paint bucket. A bit slopped out, splattering her white stomach.

"Murphy!" Harry yelled at her.

Murphy growled, spit, swatted the dog as she righted herself, then tore toward the barn, an outraged Tucker right after her. Just as Tucker closed the gap, Murphy, the picture of grace, leapt up, and the dog ran right under her. The cat twisted in midair, landed on the earth for one bound, was airborne again as she jumped onto the bumper of the red dually, then hurtled over the side into the bed. She rubbed salt into the wound by hanging over the side of the truck bed as the dog panted underneath.

"*Cat got your tongue?*"

"Murphy," Tucker said between pants, "*I'll get you for that.*"

"*Ha ha.*" Murphy jumped onto the dome of the cab.

The truck, parked in front of the barn entrance, gleamed in the rich late-afternoon light.

Harry laid her paintbrush on the side of the can. "Don't you dare put paw prints on my new truck." She advanced on the tiger, who glared insolently at her, then chased her tail on the cab hood to leave as many paw prints as possible.

Just as Harry reached the door to open it so she could step inside and gain some height to grab the little stinker, Murphy gathered herself together, hunched down, and then jumped way, way up. She just made it into the open hayloft, digging up the side with her back claws as she hung on with her front paws. Her jet stream rocked the light fixture, which looked like a big Chinaman's hat poised over the hayloft opening.

She looked down at her audience. "*I am the Number One Animal. Don't you forget it.*" Then she sauntered into the hayloft.

Tracy laughed so hard he doubled over. "That's quite a cat you've got there, Harry."

"*Heatstroke,*" Tucker grumbled furiously.

"*More like the big head,*" Pewter replied.

"*I still say she won't catch one lousy mouse.*"

"*Tucker, if I were you, I wouldn't say it any too loudly. Who knows what she'll do next?*" Pewter advised.

25

"—everybody."

"That's very edifying." Rick leaned toward BoomBoom sitting opposite him in her living room. "But I'd like to hear the names from your lips."

"Well, Leo Burkey of course, Bonnie Baltier, Denny Rablan, Chris Sharpton, Bitsy Valenzuela, Harry, Marcy Wiggins, who mostly stood around, and Susan."

"Then what?"

She shifted in her seat, irritated at his pickiness. "Have you interviewed everyone else?"

He counted names on his notepad. "No."

"Are you going to tell me who's left?"

"No. Now, BoomBoom, get on with it. What did you do, and so forth."

"We were reshooting the senior superlative which was Wittiest with Bonnie Baltier and Leo Burkey for the reunion. After we finished, everyone went to the Outback to eat. Marcy called her husband, Bill, who met her after work. They're making a point of spending time together. And Bitsy called her husband, E.R., to invite him. He took a pass, said he was tired. Funny, he was such a quiet guy in high school. To think he'd go out and start a cellular phone company. He has no class spirit, unfortunately. Neither does Bill."

"No tension at dinner?"

"No, because Harry went home. She doesn't like me," BoomBoom flatly stated. "And I have tried very hard to make amends. It's silly to carry around emotions, negative emotions."

"I wouldn't know." He reached in his pocket for the red Dunhill pack and offered her a cigarette. "Mind?"

"No. Those are expensive."

"And good. I tried to wean myself off smoking by buying generic brands. Awful stuff."

"I have some herbal remedies if you decide to stop again."

"I'll let you know."

"Anyway, nothing much happened. We all ate, told tales, bored Marcy and Chris and Bitsy, but they were gracious about it. Denny flirted with Chris. She didn't seem to mind. Then we went home."

"Did Leo linger with anyone in the parking lot? Talk to a waitress?"

She put her finger to her chin. "He cornered Bitsy for a minute as we left but well, you'd have to ask her. I think they were discussing mutual friends and whether E.R. could give Leo a deal on a cell phone."

"Uh-huh."

"Do you have any leads? I mean surely you've noticed the two victims were killed right after their senior superlative reshoot. That's what bothers me. That and those offensive, cheap mailings!"

"Yes, we have leads." He exhaled, then continued his questioning. "Did anyone wear L.L. Bean duck boots that night?"

"What?"

"You know, the boots that made L.L. Bean famous. We call them duck boots but I guess today that means the short rubber shoe. Short, tall, did anyone wear them?"

"No. That's an odd question."

"Did anyone wear heels? Not spike heels, but say about two inches."

"Do you think I spend my time cruising people's feet?" She laughed.

"I know you are a woman of fashion. I expect you take in everything, BoomBoom."

"Let's see." She studied a spot at the left-hand corner of the ceiling. "Baltier wore white espadrilles. Susan wore navy blue flats, Pappagallo. Susan loves Pappagallo. Bitsy wore a low heel, Marcy wore sandals, Chris wore a slingback with a bit of heel. Harry wore sneakers, as you would suspect, since it's summer."

"Why?"

"Harry wears sneakers in the summer, Bean boots in the rain, or riding boots. Oh yes, and her favorite pair of cowboy boots. That's the repertoire."

"Did she wear her Bean boots?"

"No, I just said, she wore sneakers."

He dropped his eyes to his notes. "So you did."

"How big are the footprints?" BoomBoom asked.

He crossed his arms over his chest, uncrossed them, picked up his cigarette out of the ashtray, taking another drag. "BoomBoom, you don't ask me questions. I ask you."

"I hate to think of Leo like that." Her eyes brimmed suddenly with tears, but then it was well known BoomBoom could cry at a telephone commercial. "He was such fun. He—" She shrugged, unable to continue.

Rick waited a moment. "He was an old friend."

"Yes," came the quiet reply.

"Did you know he was divorcing his wife?"

"Yes." She opened her hands, palms upward. "He told us at the Outback. I think he was upset, although Leo always made a joke about everything."

"Will you go to the funeral?"

"Of course I'll go."

"It's in Richmond, isn't it?"

"Yes. St. Thomas. The most fashionable church in Richmond."

"Leo from a good family?" He dropped the verb.

"Yes, but he married higher on the social ladder. His wife is a Smith. The Smiths."

"And I don't suppose they've named any of their daughters Pocahontas."

"Uh . . ." The corners of her mouth turned upward. "No."

"I expected you to be more upset." He ground his cigarette into the ashtray until tiny brown strands of tobacco popped out of the butt. "You're the emotional type."

"I guess I'm in denial. First Charlie. Now Leo. It's not real yet."

"Did they ever date the same girl?"

"In high school?"

"Any time that you can recall."

"No. Not even from grade school."

"Can you think of anyone who hated Leo?"

"No. His wit could rip like a blade sometimes. But a true enemy? No. And I don't think his wife hated him either. After all, divorce is such a pedestrian tragedy."

"That's poetic."

"Is it?" She batted her long eyelashes at Rick, not a conventionally handsome man but a very masculine one.

He smiled back. "If you think of anything, give me a call." He stood up to leave and she rose with him.

"Sheriff, do you think Charlie and Leo were killed by the same person or persons?"

"I don't know, and I'm not paid by your tax dollars to jump to conclusions."

She showed him the door and bid him good day.

Later that same day he compared notes with Cynthia Cooper. Between the two of them they had buttonholed everyone who'd been at the shoot that day. Better to catch people as soon after an incident as possible. Rick was a strong believer in that.

They'd found Leo's car still in the parking lot at the Outback. None of the restaurant staff remembered seeing him get into another car, but they had been inside working. The small gathering of friends didn't remember him getting into another car either.

They sat in his office drawing up a flow chart for Leo. Each person's story confirmed what every other person said. There were no glaring omissions, no obvious contradictions.

"Boss, he could have picked someone up after the dinner and gone to wherever they went in their car. Charlottesville is a college town. There's a semblance of night life." Not for her. She fell between the college students and the married, which put her in the minority.

"Could have."

"You think he knew the killer just as Charlie probably did, don't you?"

"If he didn't know the killer I'm convinced the killer is innocuous in some fashion. A nonthreatening person or functionary, you know, like a teacher." He stopped. "Someone you wouldn't look at twice in terms of physical fear. Leo could have been killed by a woman for that matter."

"She'd have to be fairly strong to hoist him into the dumpster," Cynthia said.

"Yes, but it could be done. The man Hunter Hughes saw go into the locker room at Farmington was thin. Average height, but as it was from a distance the man could have been shorter. Doesn't mean it's our killer, and it doesn't mean the same person killed both men. But it's odd."

"That it is."

"Have you talked to Charlie's ex-wives?"

Cynthia cracked her knuckles. "Yes. Finally reached Tiffany, wife number four—don't you love it—'Tiffany,' in Hawaii. Said she'd heard he was shot and she was sorry she hadn't done it herself.

When I asked for suspects she said apart from herself, the person who hated him most when she was married to him was Larry Johnson."

"Larry Johnson? That doesn't make any sense." Rick ran his hand over his balding head. "Or maybe it does."

"Abortions. Does Larry perform abortions?"

"He's a general practitioner, so no, he doesn't. But he knows where the bodies are buried, as they say." He noted the clock on the wall, five-thirty in the afternoon. "The best time to talk to Larry is in the morning. Maybe we should both make this visit. Oh, did you talk to Mim yet?"

"Yes, she's fine as long as she knows things before anyone else does."

"I asked BoomBoom about shoes. She remembered everybody's shoes. Another thing: for BoomBoom she was remarkably self-possessed. No vapors. No lace hankies to the eyes and thence to the bosom. Another oddity."

"What do you think of Tracy Raz?" Cynthia asked.

"A trained observer and a damned sharp one at that."

"Ran a check on him. Legit. Korea. A solid Army career, Major when he mustered out and into the CIA."

"If he hadn't pointed out those prints in front of the dumpster before more people walked around I might have missed them. He said nothing. He motioned with his eyes and then turned to push the gawkers back. He's a pro." He slapped his hand on his thigh. "You know what I'm going to do?" She shook her head and he continued. "Take the wife to the movies."

"Good for you." She wished she had someone in her life. She'd go out with a guy but eventually her schedule and work would turn him off. "I'll see you at Larry's office. Seven."

"Yep."

He stopped at the door. "Two footprints next to each other at the dumpster isn't much to go on. The Bean footprint is a man's, size eight and a half or nine. The heel footprint, well, we couldn't tell, since the toe would have been on a rock."

"Could have been a man and woman, side by side, heaving in Leo," Coop said. "He was a short, but stocky man. But then, some of the trash in there was heavier than cartons."

"Some memories are heavier than others, too." He opened the door. "I don't think it's coincidence that Charlie's death came now. And now Leo." He shrugged. "Gotta go."

26

Fair measured Poptart around the girth. He'd dropped by to see how Harry was doing after the shock. He glanced at last week's figures on the chart hanging outside each horse's stall.

Poptart quietly stood in the center aisle. The horse, a big girl, half-closed her eyes.

Mrs. Murphy, sitting on the tack trunk, asked, *"Don't you ever get hungry for meat?"*

"No."

"Not even an eensy piece?"

"Do you get hungry for timothy or for grain?" Poptart's large brown eyes focused on the tiger, now standing on her hind legs to touch noses with the large creature.

"No. You're right. I can't expect you to like what I like and vice versa."

"We like lots of the same things. Just not foods."

"You'll be surprised at how much less grain you'll need to feed her."

"I like my grain," Poptart protested.

"She's an easy keeper." Harry patted the gray neck. "I give her half a scoop, a couple of flakes of hay, plus she's got all that grass to eat."

Fair also patted Poptart on the neck, then led her out to the pasture behind the barn, where she kicked up her heels and joined Gin Fizz and Tomahawk, who had been measured before she had.

"How come you didn't tell me about Tracy Raz?"

"Fair, he just started renting here."

"Seems a good man."

"Miranda likes him. I've noticed she doesn't quote the Scriptures around him as much as she does around us."

Fair laughed as he leaned over the fence. Poptart bucked, twisted, and bucked some more.

They walked back to the house. The evening had begun to cool down. Tracy was calling on Big Mim. They sat in the kitchen together along with Murphy, Pewter, and Tucker.

"Sure you're okay?" He reached for her hand.

"Yes." She squeezed his offered hand. "It shocked the hell out of me. Both Mim and I about fell over."

"I would have about passed out myself."

"A dead body is bad enough but the"—she paused—"incongruity of it . . . that's what shocked me."

"It looks like this reunion might be, uh . . . eventful."

"Well, that's just it." She grew suddenly animated. "I don't remember anything from high school. I mean I don't remember some awful thing that would provoke revenge. Especially senior year, the big one."

"Yeah. I can't remember anything either. But maybe something did happen in your senior year. You know how sometimes things are vague or you're on the edges of it? Obviously, I was a freshman in college. All I remember from that year is missing you."

"I wrote you a letter a day. I can't believe I was that disciplined." She laughed.

"Maybe you loved me," he softly suggested.

"I did. Oh, Fair, those were wonderful and awful times. You feel everything for the first time. You have no perspective."

"You had some perspective by the time we married. I mean, you dated other men."

She patted his hand, removed hers, then noticed the animals, motionless, had been watching them. "Voyeurs."

"*Interested parties.*" Murphy smiled.

"*If this is going to get mushy I'm leaving,*" Pewter warned.

"*Bull. You're as nosy as we are.*" Tucker giggled.

"I feel like we're the entertainment tonight." Fair spoke to the animals.

"*You are,*" Pewter responded.

"They're my family," Harry said.

"So am I. Like it or not." Fair leaned forward in his chair. "Can you remember how you felt back then? The wild rush of emotion? The sense of being your own person?"

"I remember. People grow in lots of different ways. Sometimes they stop. I think Charlie stopped. Never got beyond high school. Leo got beyond it but his defenses stayed the same: shoot from the hip. Susan has matured." He thought for a moment. "I think I have, too."

"Have I?"

"Yes, but you won't trust anyone again."

"I trust Mrs. H. I trust Susan."

"I should have said men. You won't trust men."

"I trust Market."

"Harry, you know what I mean. You won't trust men as romantic partners. You won't let a man into your life."

"I guess." Her voice sounded resigned.

"You know, I dropped by tonight to see how you were— check the horses, too. I don't know if it's your reunion or because I'm getting close to forty . . . the murders or that this late summer has been uncommonly beautiful, but whatever it is—I love you. I have always loved you, even when I was acting a fool. And I think you love me. Love me the old way. Down deep."

She stared into his clear light eyes. Memories. Their first kiss.

Dancing on the football field to the car radio. Driving to colonial Williamsburg in Fair's old 1961 Chevy truck. Laughing. And finally, loving.

"Maybe I do."

"Equivocal?"

"I do."

He leaned across the table and kissed her.

"*It would be more romantic if they'd wash one another's heads,*" Pewter advised.

"*They're not cats,*" Mrs. Murphy said.

"*Nobody's perfect.*" Tucker burst out laughing.

27

At seven in the morning a haze softened the outline of trees, buildings, bridges. Rick Shaw and Cynthia Cooper, in separate vehicles, pulled into the paved driveway to the doctors' offices. Johnson & McIntire, a brass plaque, was discreetly placed next to the dark blue door.

The white clapboard building looked like the house it once was. Back in the early fifties, Larry Johnson bought it and the house next door, where he continued to live.

Larry, slightly stooped now, his hair a rich silver, opened the door himself when the officers of the law knocked.

"Come in, come in." He smiled genially. "If you all are up as early as I am, it must be important. The murders, I suppose."

"Yes." Rick closed the door behind him as they followed Larry into his office covered with a lifetime of service awards and his medical diploma.

"Can I get you all some coffee?"

"No, no, thank you. We're already tanked." Deputy Cooper fished her notebook from her back pocket.

"Larry." Rick called the doctor by his first name as did most people. "You knew Charlie Ashcraft and Leo Burkey."

"I delivered them. In those days you did everything. G.P. meant just that."

"You saw them grow up?" Rick stated as much as he asked.

"I did."

"And you would therefore have an assessment of their characters?"

"I think so, yes." Larry leaned back in his chair. "Are you asking for same?"

"Yes. I took the long way around." Rick laughed at himself.

"Charlie was a brilliant boy. Truly brilliant. He covered it up as any good Southern gentleman would do, of course. His success in the stock market didn't surprise me as it did others. He was upright in his business dealings. Even as a child he was interested in business, and honest. As you know, his downfall was women. He was like most men who were spoiled and coddled by a mother. They go through the rest of their life expecting this treatment and what amazes me is there is always a large pool of women willing to be used. But if you separated Charlie from the woman thing, he was a decent man."

"What about Leo?" Coop asked.

"Strong. Even as a child, quite physically strong. A pleasing boy. You had to like him. Another good-looking kid, not as dramatically handsome as Charlie but good-looking. I saw little of him after he left for college and then moved to Richmond."

"Did these two have anything in common that you could see?"

"No."

"What about medically? Was there anything they both suffered from? Depression or something?"

"No. Not as far as I know. After all, I stopped being Leo's doctor after high school. Both boys had the usual round of strep throat, flu, chicken pox. But nothing out of the ordinary."

"Could either man have infected sex partners with venereal diseases?" Rick was zeroing in on the area he sensed would be most fruitful.

Larry put his hands behind his head, leaning back. He glanced at the ceiling, then back at the two before him. "As you know, the relationship with a patient is confidential."

"We know, but both patients are dead and I hope and pray these murders are at an end. But Larry, what if? I've got to find out everything I can. Everything."

Larry's voice dropped as he brought his hands back on his desk. "Rick, the two men don't have anything in common medically. Again, I haven't seen Leo Burkey as a patient since he graduated from college, which had to be, well, 1984 or 1985, I guess."

Cynthia checked her notes. "Right. 1984."

"So there are no illegitimate children from high-school days? No follies?"

"Not for Leo. Again, not under my care. Charlie, as you would imagine, was quite a different matter."

"Yes," Rick said. "Tiffany said you'd know everything."

"She did, did she?" Larry shook his head. "Life is too short to be so unforgiving. Of all Charlie's ex-wives and ex-flames she's the one who hates the most. It will destroy her in the end."

"Could you be more specific?" Cynthia tried to hide her impatience.

"He fathered a child after graduating from high school. The child was put up for adoption. The rumor always was that he fathered the child in high school but it was during his college days. That was the beginning of a career of sexual irresponsibility that rivals that of any rock star. He refused to use any form of birth control. He believed if a woman went to bed with him that was her responsibility. He used to say, 'If she's dumb enough to want the baby, she should have it.' That sort of thing. He slept with so many people he contracted genital herpes, which he happily passed along. I treated him for gonorrhea eight times in his lifetime. Curiously, he never contracted syphilis."

"What about AIDS?"

Larry leveled his gaze. "Yes. At the time of his death he was

HIV-positive but showing no signs. He had resources and could afford every new drug that came down the pike, plus, apart from the sexual risks he took, he kept himself in good shape."

"He could have infected others?" Cynthia was scribbling as fast as she could.

"Could and did."

"Will you give us their names?" Rick knew he wouldn't.

"I can't do that."

"Any of them married?"

"Yes."

"Brother." Rick sighed.

"The husband doesn't know and I suppose he won't know until he discovers he's infected or his wife shows symptoms. People can be HIV-positive for years and not know it. This virus mutates, it alters its protein shell. In a strange fashion it's an intelligent virus. Every day we learn more but it's not enough."

"Charlie slept with woman A. Did she become positive immediately?"

"I don't honestly know. Yes, I can't give you a hard and fast answer. We do know of cases where an uninfected person has repeated contact with an infected person, sexually, and does not contract the disease. There's a famous case of two female cousins, African-American, who are prostitutes. They have been repeatedly exposed to AIDS, yet remain immune. The other oddity is that different people show clinical signs of infection at different times. A fifteen-year-old boy may show signs quite soon after becoming positive whereas a thirty-five-year-old man might not show any for years. It's puzzling, infuriating, and ultimately—terrifying."

Rick and Cynthia sat silent.

Cynthia finally spoke. "Does the woman know she's HIV-positive?"

"Yes. One is in denial. I see that quite often when a person learns they have a disease for which there is no cure. Flat denial." He folded his arms across his chest, glanced at the ceiling. "The other woman died last year. There were two. There may be more but I've only treated two. I'm not the only doctor in town."

"I see." Rick clasped and unclasped his hands.

"People are capable of great evil—even nice people. Life has taught me that. Korea opened my eyes and then general practice did the rest." He paused. "Having said that, I think I'm a good judge of character. The woman still alive would not kill Charlie Ashcraft. I really believe that. I don't think Leo Burkey is even in the picture on this one."

"Would Charlie Ashcraft ever sleep with men?" Cynthia surprised both men by asking what to her was obvious: Charlie and Leo could have been lovers.

A considered moment followed. Larry cleared his throat. "Under the right circumstances, yes. Charlie was driven—and I mean *driven*—by sex. He was irrational and irrationality is always dangerous. We tend to laugh off sexual dysfunction in men, especially if it's of the aggressive variety, satyriasis."

"Beg pardon?"

"The male version of nymphomania," Larry answered Cynthia.

"Oh."

"We laugh and tell jokes about what a stud he is but in fact he's sick. In Charlie's case he was sick in body as well as in mind."

"Did Tiffany know about the AIDS?" Rick inquired.

"He was not infected when they were divorced, which was three years ago. Charlie became HIV-positive shortly thereafter and displayed no signs of the disease. In other words, he was HIV-positive but he had not yet developed full-blown AIDS. I don't know if Tiffany knew about it. She would, of course, know about the genital herpes and she no doubt suspected there were unclaimed children along the way."

"More than the one?" Cynthia was surprised, although on second thought she wondered why.

"Yes—but only one lives here. The others were out of town."

"My God, did he provide for them or anything?" Like most

women, Cooper had a strong maternal streak and couldn't understand how some men could be so callous concerning their offspring.

"As far as I know he didn't do squat." Larry rose from his chair and sat on the edge of his desk before them. "We're professionals. You and I see things most people do not see and don't want to see. We aren't supposed to be emotional. Well, I fail because there were times when I could have killed Charlie myself—and yet, I liked the guy." He held up his hands.

"Larry, the mother might have strong motivation to kill Charlie."

"Not now. The child is in the late teens and in no danger from infection. Charlie became HIV-positive seventeen years after the child's birth. As for the other women, why kill him now? Furthermore, Rick, the murders of Charlie and Leo appear to be by the same person. Yes?"

"Yes."

"The connection is the answer and I don't have it." He cleared his throat. "When do you get the autopsy report on Leo?"

"Not until next week. Everyone is on vacation. The coroner's office is shorthanded."

"Would you like me to call in and ask for special blood work?"

"Yes, thank you. If they both were HIV-positive that would be a beginning."

"I'll call them right now. We can talk to them together." He glanced at the clock on his desk. "Someone will be there by now."

The rest of the day Cynthia Cooper thought about the young person in Crozet. She hoped the person would have Charlie's looks and his brilliance but not his grotesque irresponsibility. Then she thought how she looked at people every day but didn't really see them. They were all accustomed to one another. If there was a resemblance to Charlie, she'd missed it.

28

The slight drone of a bumblebee, growing stronger by the moment, irritated Mrs. Murphy to the point where she opened one glittering green eye. The marvel of insect engineering zoomed closer. She batted at it with a paw but the large black and yellow creature zigged out of the way.

"*Losing your touch,*" Tucker laconically commented.

"*Bull. I'm lying on my side. If I'd been sitting up that bomber wouldn't have had a chance. 'Course, if I'd been sitting up she wouldn't have come near me.*"

"*Yeah, yeah,*" Tucker, also on her side under a hydrangea bush, said.

Mrs. Murphy sat up. "*Where's Pewter?*"

"*In the post office. Leave the air-conditioning? Ha!*"

The sweltering heat intensified. Mrs. Murphy and Tucker had left the post office to scrounge around Miranda's garden in the late morning. It didn't seem so hot then but they couldn't find anything of interest despite a soft, lingering chipmunk scent, so they fell asleep.

BoomBoom's elegant BMW rumbled down the alleyway. She parked behind the post office, getting out of the driver's side as Marcy Wiggins and Chris Sharpton emerged from the passenger and rear doors.

Chris glanced over at the dumpster and shuddered.

"Guess I shouldn't have parked here." BoomBoom's hand flew to her mouth. "I didn't think of it. I haven't processed all this emotionally. I mean, I still have such unresolved—"

"Let's go inside." Chris cut her off before BoomBoom's lament could gather steam.

Marcy kept staring at the dumpster. "I heard he was covered in maggots."

"No." Chris shook her head. "Stop this."

Marcy began shaking.

Tucker and Mrs. Murphy crept to the edge of Miranda's yard to listen more closely.

"Marcy, are you going to be sick?" BoomBoom moved toward her to help.

"No, no, but I can't take this. People talking behind our backs. Talking about Bill killing Charlie. Talking about me and Charlie. This is a vicious little town!" She burst into tears. "I wish we'd never moved here. Why did I let Bill talk me into this? He wanted to come home. He said he'd be head of oncology faster in Charlottesville than in some huge city."

BoomBoom put her arm around the frail woman. "Things will get better."

Chris put her arm around her from the opposite side. "People gossip in big cities, too."

"But you can get away from them. Here, you're"—she gulped for air—"trapped. And I'm not working on your high-school reunion anymore! I'm sorry but it's too dangerous."

"Marcy, that's okay," BoomBoom soothingly said. "But this awful stuff doesn't have anything to do with our reunion. It's some bizarre coincidence. Come on, let's get you in the air-conditioning. Harry will let you sit in the back while you, uh, regain your composure."

Marcy allowed herself to be led into the post office.

"*Gossip.*" Tucker shook her head. "*People would be much improved if their tongues were cut out of their heads.*"

"Maybe." Mrs. Murphy yawned.

"If I say red, you say black. If I say apples you say oranges. You're contrary."

Mrs. Murphy smiled. "Sometimes I am, I guess. It's the feline in me."

"Bum excuse."

"Gossip is ugly stuff said about people behind their backs. But people, being a herd animal, need to be in touch. They need to talk about one another. There's good talk and bad talk but think about it, Tucker, the worst thing that can happen to a human being is not to be talked about," Murphy expounded.

"Never thought of that," Tucker replied.

"Follow me."

The dog padded after the cat, the small pieces of gravel hot in the sun. They stopped in front of the dumpster. The yellow cordoning tape had been removed.

"Nothing left."

"I'm not so sure. Let's look where they put the plaster casts. See, there's little bits of plaster left in the indentations."

"I see that," the dog crabbily said as she stared at the chain-link heel mark from the Bean boot and the high-heel mark not far from it. "Left foot and right."

"Could be anybody's and these marks may have nothing to do with Leo's demise but if Rick Shaw took plaster casts we ought to pay some attention to them. They're close together."

"Like two people, you mean. One holding him on the left side and one on the right. That's why the heel mark is deep on this right side."

"It's a possibility."

"So that means there are two people in on this."

"That, too, is a possibility." She lifted her head, sniffing the air. "Rain coming."

Tucker sniffed. "Tonight."

"The bullet into Leo's forehead was fired at close range. And the humans are saying that means he knew who killed him. But who else, I mean, what manner of stranger, would a man allow close to him?"

"A child."

"Or a woman."

"*Ah, the two marks. A woman. She kills him and her male partner helps dispose of the body.*"

"*I don't know, but I'm leaning that way.*"

"*It could have been Marcy and Bill Wiggins.*"

"*Could have been Laurel and Hardy, too.*"

"*There you go again. Smartmouth.*" The dog headed toward the animal door of the post office.

The cat came alongside, brushing against her friend. "*You're right. I'm awful.*" She walked a few steps, then stopped. "*What bothers me is that we're missing something and I won't feel reassured until we know it. I don't like that Mom knew these two as well as she did.*"

"*She wasn't romantically involved with either of them.*"

"*For which we should be grateful.*"

"*And no women have been killed.*"

"*Grateful for that, too.*"

Tucker blinked, then sneezed. "*Lily pollen.*"

"*It's on your coat, too.*"

"*Don't want Miranda to know I was in her lilies.*"

"*Roll in the dirt.*"

"*Then I'll get yelled at.*"

"*Better to be yelled at for that than for creeping through the lily beds.*"

"*You're right.*" Tucker rolled over.

When they slipped through the animal door no one noticed them, since everyone was ministering to Marcy Wiggins.

Tucker crawled under a mail cart. Mrs. Murphy hopped into it, landing on a recumbent Pewter, who jumped up, spitting and hissing.

"*Pewts, Pewts, I'm sorry,*" Murphy laughed.

Pewter, not yet in a forgiving frame of mind, lashed out, cuffing Mrs. Murphy on the cheek.

Mrs. Murphy returned the favor and soon the mail cart was rolling, thanks to their violence. Tucker's rear end stuck out behind the cart.

"Hey, you two!" Harry clapped her hands over the mail cart,

which diverted the cats' attention. Then her eye fell on a dirty corgi behind. "What have you done?"

"*Nothing,*" came the meek reply.

"Fleas," Mrs. Hogendobber declared. "Rolling in the dirt because of fleas."

"Guess it means a bath and flea powder when we get home." Harry sighed.

"*Thanks, Murphy,*" Tucker growled.

"*How was I to know?*" she said, then whispered to Pewter what had happened. Pewter giggled.

"It's like having children," Chris laughed.

"Marcy, feeling better?" Mrs. Hogendobber offered her more iced tea.

"Yes, thank you." She nodded, then turned to Harry. "I told BoomBoom and Chris I'm not working on your reunion anymore. Who knows what will happen next?"

"I understand." Harry didn't believe in trying to convince people to do what they didn't want to do.

"And I'll thank you all to stop talking about me."

"We aren't talking about you." Harry wrinkled her brow, puzzled.

"Everyone is. You think I don't know." She stood up and whirled on BoomBoom. "And don't tell me I need to drink chamomile tea or some other dipshit herbal remedy! You all think I'm having marital problems. You think I slept with Charlie Ashcraft and—"

"Marcy, you need to go home." Chris grabbed her friend under the elbow, pushing her out the back door as Marcy continued to babble.

"Paranoid," BoomBoom flatly said.

"That's a pretty harsh judgment," Harry countered.

"Call it what you like then."

"Well, BoomBoom, try to see it from her point of view. She doesn't have the advantage of being one of us," Harry said.

"*Right now I'd say that was not such an advantage,*" Pewter called out from the mail cart.

"Boom, you seem out of sorts today." Miranda hoped to calm the waters.

"I am." She glared at Harry. "Cynthia Cooper called on me this morning before I left for golf and do you know what she asked me? If I had had any illegitimate children with Charlie Ashcraft or if I had any sexually transmitted diseases!"

"How come you're yelling at me?"

"Because you baited her into it."

"Boom, I don't know anything about such . . . matters."

"Well, you obviously think my life is one big promiscuous party!"

"Girls." Miranda held up her hands. "I do wish you two would make some kind of peace."

"Peace? She nips at me like a Jack Russell. Sex. Always sex. Right, Harry?"

"Wrong." Harry's face darkened as the animals watched, fascinated. "I haven't said a word to Cynthia, and why would I even think about venereal disease? God, BoomBoom."

"Then who did?"

Miranda looked heavenward. "Please, dear Lord, don't send anyone into the P.O. for a while." She returned to the battling pair. "Time out. Now you two sit down, be civil, and discuss this or I am throwing you both out. Do you hear me?"

"Yes, ma'am," they both said, startled at Miranda's vehemence.

"Sit down." She pointed to the table. They sat. "Now, questions such as BoomBoom is asking do not come out of the blue. Instead of accusing Harry, why don't you both think back. Think back as far as you have to go."

They sat mute.

Harry fingered the grain on the old table. "Remember in our junior year, people whispered that Charlie got someone pregnant."

BoomBoom thought about it. "Yes, but no one left school."

"If the baby was due at the end of the summer she might not have had to leave," Miranda said. "Some women show less than others."

"There's always gym class. If someone was packing on the pounds, we'd know," Harry said.

"Did anyone get an excuse from gym class?"

"Lord, I don't know. That was twenty years ago."

"Perhaps it wasn't someone at your high school. There's St. Elizabeth's, or it may have been someone already out of school," Miranda offered.

"That's true. Cynthia must be getting desperate, running down ancient rumors." BoomBoom folded her arms across her ample chest.

"Charlie's death could have old roots."

"Twenty years is a long time to get even," BoomBoom said.

"Depends on how angry you are," Mrs. Murphy said. *"Someone hurt badly enough might live their entire life waiting for revenge."*

"What do you want in there?" Harry called out to the cats in the mail cart.

"Nothing. We're trying to help," Murphy replied.

"There were rumors about Charlie right up to the present." BoomBoom softened somewhat. "I'd heard that he'd gotten AIDS. Heard that at the club. He'd slept with some society queen in Washington, no surprise, but I heard she died a year ago. The papers hushed it up. Said she had heart failure."

"Did you tell Coop?"

"Yes. And I also told her that anyone infected with the AIDS virus by him could be mad enough to kill."

"A mother wishing to protect a child might also have plenty of motivation," Miranda added. "But it's a dreadful thing to do. I would think the child would find out who her father was, sooner or later."

"Her?" Harry looked quizzically at Miranda.

"Him."

"Do you know something we don't?" BoomBoom's voice grew stronger.

"No, I don't. But remember your Bible. Numbers. Chapter thirty-two, Verse twenty-three. 'Be sure your sin will find you out.'"

Chris popped her head back in the door. "BoomBoom, if you need more time, I'll run Marcy home. She's having a hard time."

BoomBoom rose. "I'll be right there." She paused before Miranda. "Do you think it's a sin to have a child out of wedlock?"

"No. I think it's inadvisable but not a sin. To me the sin is in not caring for the child."

BoomBoom silently opened the door and left.

"Miranda, you surprise me."

"You thought I'd say the woman should be stoned?" The older woman smiled ruefully. "Harry, I've lived long enough to know I can't sit in judgment of anyone. So many young women out there want to be loved and don't know the difference between sex and love."

"Then what sin were you referring to when you quoted Numbers?"

"Oh." She dropped her head for a moment. "The sin of cruelty. The sin of bruising another's heart, of abandoning someone to pain that you have caused. The sin of carelessness and callousness and self-centeredness. I don't know what Charlie's sins were, I mean, other than gossip. And I certainly don't know what Leo's sins were, but someone out there feels he or she has suffered enough."

29

"You're sure you want to do this?"

Mrs. Hogendobber tossed her head. "Absolutely. I used to be on the lacrosse team." She paused. "Granted that was some time ago but my athletic abilities haven't completely eroded."

Tracy placed two skateboards on the macadam surface. The parking lot at the back of the grade school was empty. Nobody driving by would see them, which was just how Miranda wanted it.

"H-m-m." He gingerly put one sneakered foot on the board to test the rollers.

Knee guards, elbow guards, and helmets made the two senior citizens look like creatures from outer space, or perhaps older space.

"Before I hop on, how do I stop?"

"Make a sharp turn in either direction and as you slow, tip the nose forward. At least, I think that's what you do."

"M-m-m." She breathed in. "Here goes." She put her right foot on the back of the board, her left foot on the front. Nothing happened.

Tracy, now aboard himself, coached, "Push off with your right foot."

She reached down and shoved off with more force than she had intended. "Whoa!"

Mrs. H. rolled along the level parking lot, her arms outstretched to balance her, laughing and hollering like a third-grader.

Tracy pulled alongside. "Not bad for our first time out!"

"Harry is going to die when I fly past her in the hallway."

"Cuddles, you won't be able to wait until the reunion. You'll surprise her before then." He started to wobble and hopped off.

"I thought you said turn sharply." Which she did.

"Didn't take my own advice." He bent over to pick up the skateboard. "I'll do it right this time." He hopped back on, pushed off, then practiced a stop. "I get it. Twist from the waist."

Miranda, watching him, tried it. She lurched to the side but didn't lose her balance. "Stopping is harder than moving on."

"Is in skiing, too."

"I don't know how young people go down banks, circle around in concrete pipes." She recalled footage she'd seen on television.

"We don't have to do that." He laughed as he rolled along even faster.

She picked up the skateboard, examined the brightly colored rollers, put it back on the macadam, and got on again. "You know, I don't do enough things like this. Oh!" She picked up speed.

"You're busy every minute. That's what Harry says." He executed another stop, better this time.

"Sedentary stuff. I need to get out more. Maybe then I'll lose a little weight. I don't know how you managed to keep your figure. I guess for men we don't say figure."

"Thank you, ma'am, but you look good to me."

"I don't believe you, but I love to hear it." She stopped. "I'm quite out of breath."

"Walk. You don't have to jog. Walking will do the trick. And if you really want to lose weight cut out the fats and sugars."

"Oh dear." She grimaced.

"It's either that or exercise for three hours a day. I work out for an hour in the gym, always have. Now that I'm doing farmwork, I'm getting double workouts."

She twisted her lower body and did a turnabout, didn't have enough speed and slipped off but caught herself, merely falling forward with three big steps. "Say, that's hard."

He tried it. "It is."

"How do you like Harry? They say you never really know someone until you live with them."

"I like her fine. She's paying off her ex-husband for the old truck, you know. Hardheaded, isn't she? He just redeposits the check in her account and then they fight about it."

"Has a fear of obligation. Whole family was like that. But she especially doesn't want to be beholden to him. He dropped by and told me he'd had a talk with Harry. He says he's going to aggressively win her back."

"Faint heart ne'er won fair lady." He crouched low to pick up speed. "This is fun, you know?"

"Yes, it is. Hate the helmet, though."

"They are weenie but your head is precious—Precious." He called her "Precious," then stood up, slowed down, and hopped off while the skateboard kept going. "Those babies are well balanced."

"And so are you."

They both laughed as Miranda cut sharply to the right and neatly stepped off.

A siren far away pierced the late-afternoon quiet.

"Heading east," Miranda observed.

Within a few moments another siren attracted their attention. A squad car roared down from Whitehall, past the grade school, into town. Then it, too, headed left.

"Good heavens, what could it be this time?" Miranda wondered.

30

Harry, tape measure around Tomahawk, heard the phone ring in the tackroom. She ignored it, then gave in.

"Hello."

"Marcy Wiggins has shot herself." Susan Tucker's voice had none of its customary lilt.

"What?"

"Shot herself in the temple with a .38. Bitsy Valenzuela found her when she stopped by to pick up a picnic hamper she'd lent Marcy."

"When?"

"About an hour ago. Maybe longer. Bill Wiggins called Ned asking for legal representation in case it isn't a suicide. Bill was the first person Rick questioned, too. That's all I know."

"Is she dead?"

"Yes."

"That poor woman." Harry put her hand to her temple. "She was definitely strange at the post office yesterday. Chris and BoomBoom took her home. She said everyone was talking about her and she couldn't stand it. Stuff like that. I should have paid more attention. Did she leave a note?"

"I don't know. Ned left the instant he hung up the phone. I believe this has something to do with Charlie."

"Yeah," Harry weakly replied. "What a September this has turned out to be."

31

Marcy's autopsy report revealed she had been HIV-positive. This, of course, was kept confidential. Leo Burkey's autopsy revealed him to be robustly healthy.

But the real shocker was when ballistics tests proved the gun that Marcy used to kill herself was the same one used to kill Charlie and Leo.

People assumed Marcy had been having an affair with Charlie. He tired of her. She snapped. Others said Bill killed Charlie but there was no evidence to link Bill to her demise. Rick and Cooper had been thorough on that count. She couldn't live with her guilt for betraying her husband. No one could figure out why she wanted to do in Leo but the scientific fact remained: it was her gun.

She did leave a suicide note which simply said, "I can't stand it anymore. Forgive me. Marcy."

The rest of September passed with no more murders. People breathed a sigh of relief.

The plans for the reunion remained in full swing. Dennis Rablan dated Chris Sharpton, which set tongues wagging. Some people thought she was wasting her time. Others thought he was dating her in hopes of getting her to wisely invest what little he had left. A few thought they made a cute couple. Dennis was happy again. Market asked her out once but she gracefully declined, saying she was focusing on Dennis. Blair Bainbridge dated Little Mim under the glare of a silently disapproving Big Mim. Everyone remarked how well they danced together but not in front of Big Mim, of course. The speculation on Blair and Little Mim was even hotter than the gossip concerning Dennis and Chris.

Harry went to the movies every Wednesday night with Fair, Tracy, and Miranda. However, she was in no hurry to get closer to her ex, but she did draw closer to Tracy—closer than she could have imagined. Theirs was a father-daughter sort of relationship. He, wisely, never asked about her romantic status with Fair, figuring sooner or later she would discuss it.

Once the sirocco of gossip died down, Crozet returned to normal. Mim bossed everyone about—but she was gaining more support for her gardening project. BoomBoom obsessed about the reunion. Harry was doing a great job on publicity. Susan had the caterers lined up. One for breakfast and lunch, a different one for dinner only because two of the participants ran catering businesses.

The horses gained weight on the alfalfa cubes. Harry had to cut back on the amount she was feeding them.

Pewter actually lost some weight during the September heat wave. Everyone commented on how good she looked.

Tucker endured a flea bath once a week.

Mrs. Murphy refused to accept that Marcy Wiggins had killed two men. No one paid any attention to her, so she finally shut up. Murphy kept repeating that she *wasn't the type.* It was Leo Burkey's murder that kept Murphy on alert.

She crouched in the tackroom just to the side of a mouse hole on this beautiful early-October day. Pewter walked in, as did Tucker.

"Hear anything?" Pewter inquired.

"They're singing again."

Tucker cocked her head. " 'The Old Gray Mare'—*where do they get these old songs?*"

"*Beats me.*" Mrs. Murphy, disgusted, shook her head. "I'll figure that out just about the time I figure out the murders."

"*Oh, Murph, don't start that again. It's over and done.*" Tucker put her head flat on the tackroom floor as she tried to peer into the mouse hole.

"*All right, but I'm telling you, something is coming out of left field. Just wait.*"

Pewter, opinionated, said, "*Why would a murderer jeopardize himself after getting off scot-free? I mean, if it wasn't Marcy, why would that person kill again?*"

"*Because the job isn't finished.*"

Tucker gave up on seeing the mice. "*Murphy, you always say that murders are committed over love or money. Marcy had the love angle.*"

"*No one was robbed. Nix the money,*" Pewter chipped in.

"*Remember the humans thought there might be an insurance payoff, but Leo left no insurance and Marcy's policy was quite small. No trust funds either,*" Tucker said.

" '. . . *she ain't what she used to be, ain't what she used to be . . .*' " The mice boomed out the chorus.

"*I hate them.*" Mrs. Murphy's striped tail lashed back and forth.

"*Let's go outside. Then we don't have to listen,*" Pewter sensibly suggested, and the three animals trotted to the roses at the back of the house.

"*Great year for roses.*" Pewter sniffed the huge blooms.

"*Silly refrain, 'ain't what she used to be many long years ago,*' " Murphy sang the chorus. Much as she scorned the song, she couldn't get it out of her head.

32

Crozet's citizens walked with a snap in their step. They were two days from a big weekend.

Crozet High would play Western Albemarle for Homecoming. The class of 1950 was having its fiftieth reunion and the class of 1980 was celebrating its twentieth.

The Apple Harvest Festival would follow that, filling up the following week.

Fall had arrived with its spectacular display of color and perfect sixty-degree days, followed by nights of light frost.

Everyone was in a good mood.

Harry sorted the mail. She liked the sound the paper made when she slipped envelopes into the metal post office boxes. She tossed her own mail over her shoulder. It scattered all over the floor.

Miranda glanced at the old railroad clock hanging on the wall. "Another fifteen minutes and Big Mim will be at the door." She pointed to Harry's mail on the floor. "Better get that up."

"Not yet!" Pewter meowed as she skidded onto the papers.

Mrs. Murphy followed.

"Copycat," Tucker smirked.

"*If this were a dead chicken you'd be rolling in it.*" Murphy bit into a brown manila envelope.

"*Of course.*" Tucker put her nose to the floor so her eyes would be even with Murphy, now on a maniacal destruction mission.

"*Dead chickens!*" Pewter pushed a white envelope with a cellophane window deeper into the small pile of increasingly tattered paper.

Harry knelt down. Two pairs of eyes, pupils huge, stared back at her. "Crazy cats."

"*Sorry human,*" Pewter replied.

"*You can't say that.*" Tucker defended Harry.

"*All humans are sorry. Doesn't mean I don't love her. Oh, this sounds divine.*" Pewter sank her fangs into the clear address panel and it crackled.

"*Tucker, you take life too seriously.*" Murphy had stretched to her full width over the mail.

"Enough." Harry started pulling papers from underneath the cats, who would smack down on the moving paper with their paws. "Let go."

"*No,*" Pewter sassed.

"She's a strong little booger." Harry finally pulled out a triple-folded piece of paper, stapled shut. Four claw rips shredded the top part. The staple popped off as she pulled on a small piece of paper attached to it.

Harry opened what was left. A small black ball, no message, was in the middle of the page. She checked the postmark: 22901, the main post office in Charlottesville. "Looks like another one."

"Oh, no." Miranda hurried over. "Well, I don't know."

"I'll check the other boxes."

Her classmates each had a letter, too.

Miranda was already dialing Rick Shaw.

Big Mim knocked at the front door. Harry unlocked it, letting her in at eight A.M. on the dot.

"Good morning, Harry."

Miranda hung up. "Morning, Mim."

"Look." Harry showed Big Mim the mailing.

"Not very original, is he?" Mim sniffed, as she held the torn paper in her gloved hands.

"No." Harry sighed. "But each murder occurred after each mailing."

"Call Rick?"

"Just did," Miranda said.

"Whoever this is seems determined to spoil your reunion." Mim tapped the countertop.

"He already has, in a way. We won't be talking about what we've learned in twenty years or remembering the dumb things we did in high school. We'll be talking about the murders." Harry was angry.

" 'Enter by the narrow gate; for the gate is wide and the way is easy, that leads to destruction, and those who enter it are many.' " Miranda quoted Matthew. Chapter seven, Verse thirteen. "I don't know why that just popped into my head."

33

Streamers dangled from clumps of shiny metallic balloons, hanging like bunches of grapes. Mrs. Murphy and Pewter raced around the gym, leaping upwards to bat the strings. Tucker sat under a ladder watching the reunion crew frantically hanging the blown-up photo posters of the senior superlatives.

A light frost covered the ground with a silvery glaze. The gym, large and unheated for decorating, proved chilly. Fortunately, it would be heated in the morning.

Harry and Chris had set up three long tables by the entrance. These they covered with white tablecloths. Sitting on the tablecloths were beautifully marked stand-up cards for each letter of the alphabet. In neat piles in front of the alphabet cards were the identification badges for each returning class member. Each badge, on the upper left-hand side, carried a small photograph of the individual from high-school days. This had proved costly, causing another row between Harry and BoomBoom, but even Boom admitted, once she saw the badges, that it was effective. Some people change so much that the high-school photograph would be the only way to recognize them.

Susan brought sandwiches. Always organized, she had arranged the food for the two-day celebration but she'd even thought of the hard work the night before. They only had Friday night in which to prepare, since Crozet High was in use throughout the week.

BoomBoom surprised everyone by having the photo frames built weeks before. Every balsa-wood frame was numbered, as were the low baskets in the shape of a running horse, the centerpieces on the table.

T-shirts were rolled and wrapped with blue and gold raffia. Disposable cameras, one for each participant, were also in the baskets, along with items from local merchants. Art Bushey threw in Ford key chains. Blue Ridge Graphics gave a deep discount on the T-shirts. The baseball caps, on the other hand, were on sale to raise money to pay for cost overruns. The T-shirts were meant to be money raisers but Bob Shoaf, who'd made a bundle in pro football, contributed the money for them so no one would be left out in case they hadn't enough money for mementos.

Harry's job was over. She'd stepped up publicity with each succeeding week. She'd done radio spots, appeared on Channel 29 Nightly News—along with BoomBoom, who never could resist a camera. She'd created clever newspaper ads using the mascot and pictures from 1980.

Local bed-and-breakfasts, as well as one hotel chain, offered discounts for returning members of the class of 1980 as well as the class of 1950.

Out of one hundred and thirty-two surviving classmates, seventy-four had sent in their deposits, as well as complaints about the strange mailings.

For Mrs. Hogendobber the return rate was one hundred percent. A fiftieth high-school reunion was too special to miss.

"Looks good." Harry admired the entrance tables. "It's simple. There's nothing to knock over. No centerpiece. They can pick up their badges and go."

"Now, where's the pile of badges for people you couldn't think of, I mean, you couldn't think of anything to say. You'll have to think fast," Chris said.

"They're here in this paper bag on my seat." Harry nervously pointed to the bag. "But I don't know if I'll be able to think of anything."

"Well, since I have no preconceived notions, I'll pop over from time to time and whisper in your ear—things like 'He looks like a warthog!'" She smiled. "Got your dress?"

"Yes. Miranda and Susan hauled me to town. Only have to wear it to the dance. I'm not wearing it the rest of the time."

A whoop from the hallway diverted their attention.

"Harry! You owe me ten dollars," Miranda's voice rang out.

Harry, along with the animals, hurried out into the long, polished hallway to behold Miranda on a skateboard, Tracy just behind her.

"I don't believe it!"

"Ten dollars." Miranda triumphantly held out her hand.

"Did I say ten dollars?" She grinned, then fished in her pocket. She'd forgotten the bet but vaguely remembered a crack about Miranda not being able to skateboard.

"She can do wheelies," Pewter remarked.

"Frightening, isn't it?" Tucker guffawed. *"That's a lot of lady to hit the ground."*

As though she understood the corgi, Miranda pushed off with her right foot and headed directly for the dog, who had the presence of mind to jump out of the way.

Mrs. Murphy said, *"She's lost a lot of weight, Tucker. There's not so much lady to hit the ground. But still . . ."*

"Sweetest ten dollars I ever made." Miranda held up the green bill after stopping.

Tracy stepped off his skateboard to put his arm around Miranda. "This girl practiced. She can even go down hills now."

"Mrs. H., you're something else." Harry laughed.

"Never underestimate the power of a woman." Miranda again waved the ten dollars in the air as Susan, BoomBoom, and Chris entered the hallway to see what was going on.

"*Hee hee.*" Mrs. Murphy, eyes gleaming, hopped on Miranda's skateboard, rolling a few yards down the hallway.

"Human. That cat is human," Chris marveled.

"*Don't flatter yourself.*" Mrs. Murphy got off, made a circle at a trot, then hopped on again, picking up a little speed.

Miranda finally took the skateboard from her, putting it behind the door of the cafeteria. Murphy would have pushed it out to play some more but Harry scooped her up to take her home. She was tired, even though the name-tag display hadn't been that trying. It was the anticipation that was exhausting her, that and a tiny ripple of dread.

34

Heart racing, Harry threw another log on the fire in the bedroom fireplace. She crawled into bed, finding the sheets cold. Then she crawled out, grabbed a sweatshirt, pulled it over her head, and slid back under the covers. Keeping an old house warm was a struggle, especially for Harry, who watched her pennies.

"*Will you settle down?*" Pewter grumbled from the other pillow.

The dry cherry log slowly caught fire, releasing a lovely scent throughout the room.

Harry tilted the nightstand light toward her, picked up her clipboard and reviewed tomorrow's agenda. Mrs. Murphy, cuddled on her left side, observed. Tucker was stretched out in front of the hearth, head on her paws.

"Okay. The tables are already set alongside the gym for breakfast. Susan's having the food delivered at seven-thirty. Bonnie Baltier said she'd be here in time to help me man the check-in table. She understands she has to write something, anything on the name cards with names only on them. The band will set up tonight when we go home to change. Amazing how many amps those electric guitars and stuff suck up. And I suppose we'll all hold BoomBoom's hand, who's really supposed to be in charge, but by now is Miss Basketcase Crozet High." She parked her pencil behind her right ear. "My second superlative photo didn't turn out so badly. I think it's better than BoomBoom's."

"*Me, too,*" Tucker called up to her.

"*Just don't draw a mustache on BoomBoom's, Mom—or at least wait until the end of the reunion.*"

"Mrs. Murphy, maybe I'll put a blue and gold bow on you for the festivities."

"*Won't she be fetching,*" Pewter meowed.

"*Don't be catty,*" Murphy rejoined.

"*Ha, ha,*" Tucker dryly commented.

"You guys are a regular gossip club tonight." Harry scanned her clipboard, then put it on the nightstand. She put her right hand over her heart. "My heart is thumping away. I don't know why I'm so nervous. I wasn't nervous at our fifteenth reunion." She stroked Murphy's silken head. "People know I'm divorced. Oh, I'm not really nervous about that. They can just hang if they don't like it. I'm hardly the only person in our class who's suffered romantic ups and downs. Don't know. Of course, how many divorced people are dating their exes? Guess it's seeing everybody at the same time. Overload."

"*Sure, Mom,*" Mrs. Murphy purred, closing her eyes.

She snatched her clipboard again. "Fair said he'd be there as a gofer. Everyone will be glad to see him. Half the girls in my class had a crush on him. I think he wants to be there—in case." She again spoke to Mrs. Murphy since Pewter had curled up in a ball, her back to Harry. "Say, can you believe Miranda on that skateboard? Or you, Murphy."

"*I can do anything.*"

"*Oh, please.*" Tucker rolled on her side. "*Why don't you two go to sleep. Tomorrow's going to be a long, long day.*"

As if in response, Harry replaced the clipboard and turned out the light.

35

Screams echoed up and down Crozet High School's green halls as classmates from 1980 and 1950 greeted one another. Southern women feel a greeting is not sufficiently friendly if not accompanied by screams, shouts, flurries of kisses, and one big hug. The men tone down the shouts but grasp hands firmly, pat one another on the back, punch one another on the arm, and if really overcome, whisper, "Sumbitch."

Harry, up at five-thirty, as was Tracy, finished her chores in record time, arriving at the school by seven. Tracy picked up Miranda so he arrived at seven-fifteen. Everything was actually organized so Harry sat next to Bonnie Baltier checking people in. Dennis Rablan, three cameras hanging around his neck, took photographs of everyone. Chris assisted him with long, smoldering looks as she handed him film.

Tucker sat under Harry's legs while Mrs. Murphy defiantly sat on the table. Pewter ditched all of them, heading toward the cafeteria for Miranda's reunion. The food would be better.

The class of 1950 arranged tables in a circle so everyone could chat and see one another. Pewter zoomed into the cafeteria, which was decorated with blue and gold stallions built like carousel horses and fixed to the support beams. Miranda had said that Tracy was working on something special but no one realized it would be this special. The beams themselves were wrapped with wide blue and gold metallic ribbons. The room was festooned with bunting. The cafeteria actually looked better than the gym with its huge photographs, then and now, and blue and gold streamers dangling from huge balloon clusters.

Best, to Pewter's way of thinking, was the breakfast room itself. Miranda had sewn blue and gold tablecloths. On each table was a low, pretty, fall floral bouquet.

Pewter noticed Miranda's and Tracy's skateboards resting behind the door. She also noticed that this reunion, forty-two strong, was quieter. There were more tears, more genuine affection. One member, a thin man with a neatly trimmed beard, sat in a wheelchair. A few others needed assistance due to the vicissitudes of injury or illness. Apart from that, Pewter thought that most of the class of 1950 looked impressive, younger than their years, with Miranda glowing. She'd lost twenty-five pounds since the beginning of September and Pewter had never realized how pretty Miranda really was. She wore a tartan wraparound skirt, a sparkling white blouse, and her usual sensible shoes. She also smiled every time she glanced at Tracy. He smiled at her a lot, too.

"Pewter Motor Scooter!" Miranda hailed her as the gray cat dashed into the room. "Welcome to the class of 1950."

"What a darling cat. A Confederate cat." A tiny lady in green clapped her hands together as the gray cat sauntered into the room.

"We work together," Miranda laughed, telling people about Pewter's mail-sorting abilities while feeding her sausage tidbits.

"I am so-o-o happy to be here," Pewter honestly said.

About ten minutes later Harry ducked her head into the room. "Hi, everybody. Aha, I thought I'd find you here."

"I like it here!"

"Folks, this is Doug Minor's girl—remember Doug and Grace Minor? Grace was a Hepworth, you know."

Martha Jones, quite tall, held out her hand. "I know your

mother very well. We were at Sweet Briar together. You greatly resemble Grace."

"Thank you, Miss Jones. People do tell me that."

"Your mother was the boldest rider. She took every fence at Sweet Briar, got bored, jumped out of the college grounds, and I believe she jumped every fence on every farm on the north side of Lynchburg."

People laughed.

Miranda said, "Mary Minor is a wonderful rider."

"Thanks, Mrs. H., but I'm not as good as Mom. She was in Mim's class."

"Where is Mimsy?" the thin man in the wheelchair bellowed.

"I'm here. You always were impatient, Carl Winters, and I can see that little has changed that." Mim swept in dressed in a buttery, burnt-sienna suede shirt and skirt. "You know, I wish I had graduated from Crozet High. Madeira wasn't half as much fun, but then, all-girls schools never are."

"You're really one of us, anyway." A plump lady kissed Mim on the cheek.

"I'll take my thief back to the gym," Harry said while the others talked.

"She can stay. She'll come back anyway. It's fine."

"*Please, Mom.*" Pewter's chartreuse eyes glistened with sincerity.

"Well . . . okay," Harry lowered her voice, leaning toward Miranda. "Your decorations are better." She raised her voice again. "Tracy, the carousel horses are spectacular!"

She left them smiling, talking, eating Miranda's famous orange sticky buns.

She ran into Bitsy Valenzuela and Chris Sharpton dragging an enormous coffee urn down the hall.

"Guys?"

"BoomBoom called me on the car phone and told me she was panicked. There wasn't enough coffee so we dashed over to Fred Tinsley's, which got Denny's nose out of joint since Chris was assisting him. I had to promise Fred six months free on his car phone to get this damn thing. E.R. will kill me," Bitsy moaned. "Is he here yet?"

"Yes, he brought miniature flashlights shaped like cell phones."

"That's my E.R. for you: ever the marketer."

"Would you like me to take a turn here? That looks heavy," Harry offered.

"Why don't you run in and get someone strong—like a man—to do this. That's what men are for." Bitsy gave up and slowly set down her side of the urn, as did Chris.

"Are we still allowed to say stuff like that?" Chris giggled.

"Yeah, among us girls we can say anything. We just can't say it publicly." Bitsy laughed, "Nor would I admit to E.R. that I need him. But I do need him."

Harry dashed into the gym, returning with Bob Shoaf, Most Athletic, who had played for seven years with the New York Giants as cornerback. Apart from having a great body, Bob wasn't hard to look at. He was, however, blissfully married, or so the newspapers always reported.

"Girls, you go on. I'll do this." He hoisted the urn up to his chest. "You two should look familiar to me but I'm afraid I can't place you."

"They helped us all summer and fall, Bob, but these two lovely damsels aren't from our class. Bitsy Valenzuela—Mrs. E. R. Valenzuela—and Chris Sharpton, a friend."

"Forgive me if I don't shake hands." He carried the urn into the gym, where BoomBoom greeted him as though he had brought back the Golden Fleece from Colchis.

Bitsy and Chris stopped inside the door. "It's odd."

"What?" Bitsy turned to Chris. "What's odd?"

"Seeing these people after staring at their yearbook pictures. It's like a photograph come to life."

"*Not always for the best.*" Mrs. Murphy lifted her long eyebrows. The class of 1980 had been on earth long enough for the telltale spider veins in the face to show for those who drank too much. The former druggies might look a bit healthier but brain cells had fried. A poignant vacancy in the eyes signaled them. A lot of the men were losing their hair. Others wore the inner tube of early middle age, not that any of them would admit that middle age had started. Nature thought otherwise. Bad dye jobs marred a few of the women but by and large the women looked better than the men, testimony to the cultural pressure for women to fuss over themselves.

Bonnie absentmindedly stroked Mrs. Murphy as she double-checked her list. Everyone had checked in except for Meredith McLaughlin, who wouldn't arrive until lunch. Harry rejoined her while Chris joined Dennis, wreathed in smiles now that she was back.

"Done." Bonnie put down her felt-tip pen.

"You're a fast thinker. I should have remembered that." Harry smiled. "When you came up with 'Secret Life, Televangelist' for Dennis Rablan, I could have died. That was perfect. Even he liked it!"

"Had to do something. What do you put down for the Best All-Round who has . . ." She shrugged.

"Zipped through a trust fund and unzipped too many times," Harry laughed.

"And then there's you. Most Likely to Succeed and Most Athletic, running the post office at Crozet," Bonnie said.

"I guess everyone thinks I'm a failure."

"*Not you, Mom, you're too special.*" Tucker reached up, putting her head in Harry's lap.

"No." Bonnie shook her head. "But if there were a category for underachiever, you'd have won. You were, and I guess still are, one of the smartest people in our class. What happened?"

Harry, dreading this conversation, which would be repeated in direct or subtle form over the next day and a half, breathed deeply. "I made a conscious choice to put my inner life ahead of my outer life. I don't know how else to say it."

"You can do both, you know," remarked Baltier, successful

herself in the material world. She ran an insurance company specializing in equine clients.

"Bonnie, I was an Art History major. What were my choices? I could work for a big auction house or a small gallery or I could teach at the college level, which meant I would have had to go on and get my Ph.D. I never wanted to do that and besides I married my first year out of college. I thought things were great and they were—for a while."

"I'm rude." Baltier pushed back a forelock. "I hate to see waste. Your brain seems wasted to me."

"If you measure it by material terms, it is."

"The problem with measuring it in any other way is that you can't."

"I think it's time we join the others. I'm hungry."

"You pissed at me?"

"No. If BoomBoom had asked me I'd be pissed." Harry then nodded in the direction of an attractive woman on the move up, one face-lift to her credit, holding court by the pyramid of Krispy Kreme doughnuts. "Or her."

Deborah Kingsmill, voted Most Intellectual, truly thought she was superior to others because she was book-smart and because she'd escaped her parents. And that's exactly where her intelligence ended. She'd never learned that people with "less" intelligence possessed other gifts.

Deborah and Zeke Lehr, the male Most Intellectual, were pictured together reading a big book in Alderman Library. Zeke owned a printing business in Roanoke. He'd done well, had three kids and kept himself in good shape. He was pouring himself a second cup of coffee while listening to BoomBoom discuss the sufferings of organizing the reunion.

"Hey, thanks for your work." Rex Harnett, already smelling like booze, kissed Harry on the cheek.

"You know, it turned out to be fun," Harry admitted to the broad, square-built fellow, who had been voted Most School Spirit and would easily have qualified for Most School Spirits.

"Fair coming?"

"He is but he's probably on call this morning. He'll get here as soon as he can. He's as much a part of our class as his."

"You two getting back together?"

"Not you, too!" Harry mocked despair.

"I have personal reasons. You see, if you aren't interested in the blond god then I'd like to ask you out."

"Rex?" Harry was surprised and mildly revolted.

Tucker, on the floor, was even more surprised. "*He's to the point. Gotta give him credit for that.*"

"I thought you were married."

"Divorced two years ago. Worst hell I've ever been through."

"Rex, I'm flattered by your attention"—she eased out of his request—"but we aren't the right mix."

He smiled. "Harry, you can say no nicer than any woman I know." He glanced across the room. "The redhead and the blonde look familiar but I can't place them."

"Bitsy Valenzuela, E.R.'s wife."

"The other woman?"

"Chris Sharpton. She moved here from Chicago and she and Bitsy helped us organize."

"Market looks the same. Less hair," Rex said. "Boom's the same."

"She's beautiful. She's surrounded by men," Harry flatly stated.

Bonnie Baltier, having grabbed a doughnut, joined them, as did Susan Tucker.

"Isn't this something?" Susan beamed.

"We've all got to go down the hall and congratulate the class of 1950," Harry suggested. "After breakfast. You can't believe how they've decorated the cafeteria."

"We can see ourselves thirty years from now." Rex smiled.

Bonnie was staring at the huge superlative photos. "You know who I miss? Aurora Hughes. What a good soul."

"I suppose with each reunion we'll miss a few more," Rex bluntly said.

"What a happy thought, you twit." Bonnie shook her head.

"Hell, Baltier, people die. For some, Charlie could have died even earlier."

Susan asked, "Remember the rumor that Charlie had an illegitimate child in our junior year?"

Rex shrugged. "Yeah."

Harry said, "Guys talk. You say things to each other you wouldn't say to us. Any ideas on who the mother was—or is, I should say?"

"No," Rex replied. "He dated a lot of girls. Raylene Ramsey was wild about him but she didn't leave school and she didn't gain weight. Wasn't her."

"Yeah, we thought the same thing," Susan said.

Bonnie dabbed the sugar crumbs from the corners of her mouth. "It doesn't matter. Let's concentrate on the good times."

"I'm for that. When's the bar open?" Rex held up his coffee cup.

"Six o'clock."

"I could be dead by then." He laughed as Bitsy, Chris, Bob, and Dennis joined their group. He slipped a flask from his pocket, taking a long swig.

"If you keep drinking the way you do, that's a possibility." Baltier let him have it.

"S-s-s-s." Rex made a burning sound, putting his finger on her skin.

36

By nine-thirty the whole group, including Fair, were called to attention by BoomBoom.

"Ladies and gentlemen, may I have your attention."

She didn't immediately get it.

Bob Shoaf cupped his hands to his lips. "Shut up, gang!"

The chatter frittered away, and all eyes turned toward BoomBoom, standing on a table. Modestly dressed by her standards, in a blue cashmere turtleneck, not too tight, a lovely deep-mustard skirt, and medium-height heels, she presented an imposing figure. She exuded an allure that baffled Harry, who saw BoomBoom as a silly goose. Harry wrote it off to the awesome physical asset that had given Olivia Ulrich her nickname. This was a mistake.

Women like Harry had a lot to learn from women like BoomBoom, who prey on male insecurities and unspoken dreams. Harry expected everyone, including men, to be rational, to know where lay their self-interest and to act on that self-interest. No wonder Mary Minor Haristeen was often surprised by people.

"Welcome, class of 1980." BoomBoom held out her hands as if in benediction. As the assemblage roared she turned her palms toward them for quiet. "All of us who worked on this reunion are thrilled that all of you have returned home. Mike Alvarez and Mignon, his wife, flew all the way from Los Angeles to be with us, winning Most Distance Traveled." Again the group roared approval.

As BoomBoom spoke the homilies reserved for such occasions, Harry, standing at the back with Mrs. Murphy and Tucker, surveyed her class. They were a spoiled generation.

Unlike Miranda's generation, who emerged from the tail end of World War II only to be dragged through Korea, Harry's generation knew the brief spasm of Desert Storm. Luckily they had missed Vietnam, which forever scarred its generation.

Everyone expected and owned one or two vehicles, one or more televisions, one or more computers, one or more telephones including mobile phones. They had dishwashers, washers and dryers, workout equipment, stereo systems, and most had enough money left over for personal pleasures: golf, riding horses, fly-fishing in Montana, a week or two's vacation in Florida or Hawaii during the worst of winter. They expected to send their children to college and they were beginning, vaguely, to wonder if there'd be any money left when their retirement occurred.

Most of them were white, about ten percent were black. She could discern no difference in expectations although there were the obvious differences in opportunities but even that had improved since Miranda's time. Walter Trevelyn, her Most Likely to Succeed partner, a café-au-lait-colored African-American, did just that. He was the youngest president of a bank in Richmond specializing in commercial loans, a bank poised to reap the rewards of the growth Richmond had experienced and expected to experience into the twenty-first century.

About half the class was working class, a gap in style as much as money, but those members also had one or more vehicles, televisions, and the like.

The sufferings her generation endured were self-inflicted, setting apart the specters of gender and race. She wondered what would happen if they ever really hit hard times: a great natural catastrophe, a war, a debilitating Depression.

Susan slid up next to her. "You can't be that interested in what BoomBoom is saying."

Harry whispered back, "Just wondering what our generation will do if the proverbial shit hits the proverbial fan."

"What every other generation of Americans has done: we'll get through it."

Harry smiled a halfway funny smile. "You know, Susan, you're absolutely right. I think too much."

"I can recall occasions where you didn't think at all," the tiger cat laconically added to the conversation.

Tucker, bored with the speeches, wandered to the food tables to eat up the crumbs on the floor.

"Harry!" BoomBoom called out.

Harry, like a kid caught napping in school, sheepishly blinked. "What?"

"The senior superlatives are asked to come forward."

"Oh, BoomBoom, everyone knows what I looked like then and now. You all go ahead."

Susan, her hand in the middle of Harry's back, propelled her toward the two big photographs as she peeled off to stand in front of her superlative, Best All-Round. Under the old photo the caption read Susan Diack. Under the new one, Susan Tucker. She glanced up at her high-school photograph. She and Dennis Rablan sat on a split-rail fence, wearing hunting attire, a fox curled up in her lap. Unlike Harry, she had changed physically. She was ten pounds heavier, although not plump. It was rather that solidness that comes to many in the middle thirties. Her hair was cut in the latest fashion. As a kid she had worn one long plait down her back. Dennis had grown another four inches.

Harry first stood at the Most Athletic, sharing a joke with Bob Shoaf, whom she liked despite his silly swagger. Then she dashed over to Most Likely to Succeed with Walter Trevelyn, who gave her a kiss on the cheek.

Everyone laughed as the superlatives laughed at their own young selves.

Then BoomBoom walked from her superlative, Best Looking, to Most Talented. "Folks, let's remember Aurora Hughes. Hank, what do you remember most about Aurora?" She turned to Hank Bittner, the Most Talented.

"Her kindness. She had a way of making you feel important." He smiled, remembering the girl dead almost twenty years.

Hank, talented though he was as a youth, had prudently chosen not to keep on with his rock band. Instead he moved to New York, began work in a music company, and had risen to become a powerful maker and breaker of rock groups.

Next BoomBoom walked to Most Popular. Meredith McLaughlin, late because of a prior commitment, had just skidded under her photographs. She glanced up at herself, young and old, and twice her former size to boot.

"Was that really me?" She hooted.

"Yes!" The group laughed with her.

"Meredith, what do you remember most about Ron Brindell?"

"The time he decided to wear a burnoose to class because we were studying the Middle East. Do you all remember that?" Many nodded in assent. "And old Mr. DiCrenscio pitched a fit and threw him out of class. Ron marched to Mr. Thomson, our principal, and said it was living history and he'd protest to the newspaper. Funniest thing I ever saw, Mr. Thomson trying to pacify both Ron and Mr. DiCrenscio."

"Thank you, Meredith."

She then walked over to Wittiest, where Bonnie Baltier muttered something under her breath, although by the time the tall woman reached her she was all smiles.

"What do you remember about Leo Burkey?" BoomBoom asked.

"His smart mouth. He got mad at Howie Maslow once and told him he could use his nose for a can opener."

People tittered. Howie Maslow, class president of 1978, had a nose like a hawk's beak. In fairness to Leo, the power had gone to Howie's head.

Then BoomBoom walked back to her own superlative and looked up at Charlie in 1980 and 2000. "He was always gorgeous. He was highly intelligent and fun. He had a terrific sense of fun. As to his weakness, well, who among us shall cast the first stone?"

A dead silence followed this until Hank Bittner called out, "I'll cast the first stone. He made my life miserable. Stole every girlfriend I ever had."

Everyone erupted at once. BoomBoom paled, waving her hands for people to quiet.

Finally, Fair, the tallest among them, bellowed, "Enough, guys, enough."

"Shut up, Fair, you're '79," Dennis Rablan hollered.

"Doesn't matter. Speak no ill of the dead." Market Shiflett defended his friend, Fair.

"Dead? Did they drive a stake through his heart? I'm sorry I missed the funeral," Bob Shoaf sputtered, and it was an amusing sight seeing a former cornerback and probably a man eventually to be inducted into the Hall of Fame, sputter.

"I'd like to find whoever shot him and give the guy a bottle of champagne," Hank called out.

The women silently observed the commotion among the men and without realizing it they gravitated together in the center of the room.

"This is going to ruin our reunion." BoomBoom wrung her hands.

"No, it won't. Let them get it out of their systems." Bitsy Valenzuela comforted Boom.

"People don't hold back here, do they?" Chris's eyes never left the arguing men.

Harry picked up Mrs. Murphy, who reached up at her to pat her face. "Boy, I haven't seen Market Shiflett this mad in years."

Market stood toe-to-toe with Bob Shoaf, shaking his fist in Bob's face. Rex Harnett stepped in, said something the ladies couldn't hear, and Market pasted him right in the nose. Dennis, like the paparazzo he longed to be, got the picture.

BoomBoom implored Harry, "Do something."

Harry, furious that BoomBoom expected her to solve the problem while she stood on the sidelines, stalked off, but as she did an idea occurred to her.

She walked to the corner of the room where Mike Alvarez had set up the dance tapes he'd made for the reunion. A huge tape deck, professional quality, loaded and ready to go, gave her the answer. She flipped the switch and Michael Jackson's "Off the Wall" blared out.

She coasted back to the women. "Okay, everyone grab a man and start dancing. If this doesn't work we'll go down the hall and visit the class of 1950. Maybe we'll learn something."

BoomBoom glided up to Bob Shoaf. Harry, with a shudder, took Rex Harnett. Chris paired off with Market Shiflett to his delight, Bitsy wavered then chose Mike Alvarez. Susan took Hank Bittner. Once all the men were accounted for, the place calmed down, except that Fair Haristeen strode up, tapping Rex on the shoulder.

"No," Rex replied.

"A tap on the shoulder means the same thing everywhere in the world, Rex."

"Lady's choice. I don't have to surrender this lovely woman even though you so foolishly did."

Fair, usually an even-tempered man but possibly overheated from the men's debacle, yanked Rex away from Harry.

Rex, fearing the bigger man, slunk to the sidelines, bitching and moaning with each step. Hank Bittner laughed at Rex as he passed him. In the great tradition of downward hostility, Rex hissed, "Faggot."

Shoaf, with his lightning-fast reflexes, tackled Rex as Fair grabbed Hank. The two combatants were hustled by their keepers outside the gym, Rex screaming at the top of his lungs. Tracy Raz, hearing the commotion, left his own reunion to assist Fair with Hank.

Although the music played the dancers stopped for a moment.

Chris was appalled. "Is that guy a Neanderthal or what?"

Harry said, "Neanderthal."

"What's he talking about?" Susan asked Dennis. "Calling Hank a faggot."

Dennis, lips white, replied, "I don't know."

37

Chris Sharpton headed for the door as Bitsy grabbed E.R. by the wrist, pulling him along to go outside.

BoomBoom hurried to them. "Don't let this bother you. It's just part of a reunion, confronting and resolving old issues."

"Hey, my reunion wasn't like this," Chris replied. "Then again, it's good theater. Bad manners but good theater."

E.R. stared. "BoomBoom, I don't believe old issues ever get resolved. It's all bullshit."

"Don't get started, E.R.," Bitsy said again, pulling her husband along. "I have to get my purse out of the car."

Chris watched them go down the hall, then followed.

Mrs. Murphy sauntered past BoomBoom. *"Ta ta."*

Harry, who hadn't heard E.R. tell Boom what he thought in plain English, followed her cat. Tucker had already zipped down the hall after Fair.

Harry walked down the hall to the far end, away from the parking lot, and pushed open the front doors. Fair and Hank stood under a flaming yellow and orange oak tree. Tucker sat at Fair's feet.

"Don't say it."

"I'm not saying anything." Harry tightly smiled as Hank shoved his hands in his pockets, his face red.

"Are you sufficiently calmed down?" She spoke to her old high-school friend.

"I suppose." He smiled. "It's funny. I live in New York City. I come back and it's like I never left."

Mrs. Murphy breathed in the October air for the day was deliciously warm, the temperature in the middle sixties. Tucker, far more interested than she was in these emotional moments, stayed glued to Fair. The tiger cat hitched her tail up with a twitch and a jerk.

"I'm going to walk around a little bit."

"I'm staying here," Tucker announced.

"Okay." Mrs. Murphy walked toward the back of the school. As she passed the parking lot she noticed Bitsy and E.R. heatedly talking at their car. Chris, carrying a large box of reunion T-shirts, pushed open the school doors with her back. They'd already sold out one box of T-shirts. Chris was resigned to being a gofer. She ignored Bitsy and E.R.

"You can stay, I am going!" Bitsy, hands on hips, faced her husband.

"Ah, honey, come on. It will get better."

Pewter circled the building from the other end. At the sight of the tiger cat, Pewter broke into a lope.

"You won't believe it." Her white whiskers swept forward in anticipation of her news. *"Rex Harnett is back there carrying on like sin. I mean, he needs to have his mouth inspected by the sanitation department."*

"Because of Hank?"

Pewter puffed out her chest. *"Hank, Charlie, Dennis, you name it. He's, uh, voluble."* She opened her right front paw, unleashed her claws, then folded them in again. *"Mostly it's babble about how he couldn't make the football team and was elected Most School Spirit as a sop. Get a life! He did say that he knows who Charlie got pregnant."*

"Well?"

"Nothing. He needed to sound important. I don't think he knows squat. Tracy Raz got disgusted and went back to his reunion. His parting words were 'Grow up.'"

"I'm not sure what really started the fight but I do know that Rex Harnett may be a drunk but that doesn't mean he's totally stupid. Maybe he does know something."

"Rex is hollering that he's no homosexual." Pewter loved the dirt. "Bob Shoaf told him to shut up. If Rex were homosexual, homosexuals would be grossed out. Pretty funny, really."

"I thought you were in the cafeteria with the golden oldies." Mrs. Murphy turned in a circle, then sat down.

"I ran out with Tracy. The hall amplifies noise." Pewter paused for effect, returning to the scene outside with Rex: "Then, and I tell you I about fell over, Rex started crying saying that no one ever liked him. He did not deny being a drunk, however. Are they all nuts or what? I thought reunions were supposed to be happy. Miranda's is. Anyway, Rex stormed off to the men's room. I think Bob walked around to the other side of the school to find Fair and Hank."

"The hormone level is a lot lower at Miranda's." The tiger smiled. "They're just animals, you know. That's what so sad. They spend their lifetime denying it but they're just animals. I can't see that we act any worse when our mating hormones are kicking in than they do."

"Paddy proves that," Pewter slyly said, making an oblique reference to Mrs. Murphy's great love, a black tom with white feet and a white chest, a most handsome cat but a cad.

"If you think you're going to provoke me, you aren't. I'm going back inside. Who knows, maybe someone else will blow up or reveal a secret from the past."

Pewter had hoped for a rise out of Murphy. "Me, too."

They bounced onto the steps of the side door. The old, two-story building had a front door with pilasters, a back door into the gym, and two side doors which were simple double doors.

One side door was propped open. They walked down the main hall toward the gym.

Susan Tucker, Deborah Kingsmill, and Bonnie Baltier barely noticed the cats as they walked by them.

"—ruin the whole reunion."

"They'll get over it," Susan replied.

"I wish everyone would stop speculating about who Charlie got pregnant. I fully expect everyone to sit down with their year-books and scrutinize every female in the book from all three classes. That's not why we're here and anyway, nothing anyone can do about it."

"Baltier, people love a mystery," Susan said.

"No one even knows if it's true," Deborah Kingsmill sensibly replied. "Because he was so handsome people make up stories. If it isn't true they want it to be true. It's like those tabloid stories you read about superstars drinking lizard blood."

The women laughed.

"What's so strange about drinking lizard blood?" Pewter asked.

"Pewter." Mrs. Murphy reached out and swatted Pewter's tail.

As the cats laughed and the three women headed back to the gym, Harry came into the hall from the front door.

Before the cats could run to her and Tucker, a shout from the men's locker room diverted their attention. Dennis Rablan threw open the door, stepped outside, leaned against the wall and slid down. He hit the floor with a thump. He scrambled up on his hands and knees, tried to clear his head and stood upright.

As Susan, Bonnie, and Deborah ran to him from one direction, Harry and Tucker ran from the other.

"Call an ambulance," Dennis croaked.

38

"Don't go in there." Dennis barred the way as Harry and Susan moved toward the men's locker-room door.

"They'll never notice us." Mrs. Murphy slipped in since the door was easy to push open. Pewter and Tucker followed.

They ran into the open square where the urinals were placed. Three toilet stalls were at a right angle to the urinals. A toilet stall door slowly swung open, not far.

"There." Pewter froze.

Rex Harnett's feet stuck out under the stall door.

"I'll check it out." Tucker dashed under the adjoining stall, then squeezed under the opening between the two stalls.

Mrs. Murphy, unable to contain her famous curiosity, slipped under from the other stall since Rex was in the middle one.

"He's dog meat," Mrs. Murphy blurted out, then glanced at Tucker. *"Sorry."*

"You'd better be."

"What is it? What is it?" Pewter meowed. Being a trifle squeamish, she remained outside.

Face distorted, turning purple, Rex's eyes bulged out of his head; the tight rope around his neck caused the unpleasant discoloration. His hands were tied behind his back, calf-roping style, quick, fast, and not expected to hold long. Between his eyes a neat hole bore evidence to a shot at close range with a small-caliber gun. No blood oozed from the entry point but blood did trickle out of his ears.

"Fast work." Murphy drew closer to the body. "*What does your nose tell you?*"

"*What is it!*" Pewter screeched.

"*Shot between the eyes. And trussed up, sort of, scaredy cat.*"

"*I'm not scared. I'm sensitive,*" Pewter responded to Murphy, a tough cat under any circumstances.

Although the odor of excrement and urine masked other smells as Rex's muscles had completely relaxed in death, Tucker sniffed the ankles, got on her hind legs and sniffed the inside of the wrists, since his arms were turned palm outward.

"*No fear smell. This is a fresh kill. Maybe he's been dead fifteen minutes. Maybe not even that, Murphy. So if he had been terrified, I'd know. That scent lingers, especially in human armpits.*" She reached higher. "*No. Either he never registered what hit him, or he didn't believe it. Like Charlie Ashcraft.*"

"*And Leo Burkey.*" The sleek cat emerged from under the stall to face a cross Pewter.

"*I am not a scaredy cat.*"

"*Shut up, Pewter.*" Murphy smacked her on the side of the face. "*Just shut up. You know what this means. It means the murders are about this reunion. And it means that Marcy Wiggins didn't kill Charlie. She may have been killed because she got too close. We can't discount her death as suicide.*"

"*What are we going to do?*" Tucker, upset and wanting to get Harry out of the school, whimpered.

"*I wish I knew.*" Murphy ran her paw over her whiskers, nervously.

"*We know one thing.*" Pewter moved toward the door. "*Whoever this is, is fast, cold-blooded, and wastes no opportunities.*"

"*We know something else.*" Tee Tucker softly padded up next to the gray cat. "The murderer wants the attention. Most murderers want to hide. This one wants everyone to know he's here."

"That's what scares me." Murphy solemnly pushed open the door as the humans from both reunions piled into the highly polished hallway.

39

Harry could hear the wheels of the gurney clicking over the polished hall as Diana Robb carted away Rex Harnett's body. Her stomach flopped over, a ripple of fear flushed her face. She took a deep breath.

"Damnedest thing I ever saw," Market Shiflett said under his breath.

Harry and Market walked into a classroom only to find Miranda, Tracy, and others there from the other reunion. The two cats and dog quietly filed in. Mrs. Murphy sat in the window ledge in the back, Pewter sat on Harry's desk, and Tucker watched from just inside the doorway.

Within moments, BoomBoom entered. "After all our hard work. Twenty years ruined."

"Really ruined for Rex," Harry said, but with no edge to her voice.

"Well . . . yes," BoomBoom said after a delay.

Susan ducked into the room. "Most people are filing back into the gym. Cynthia Cooper is herding us in there. I guess we'll be questioned en masse."

"Lot of good that will do." BoomBoom ran her forefinger through her long hair. "The murderer isn't going to confess. After all, any of the men could have killed Rex." Because she didn't protest that the murder had nothing to do with the reunion, meant she'd accepted the fact that it was connected.

"So every man is a suspect?" Harry's voice rose in disbelief.

"Girls, this won't get you anywhere." Miranda's lovely voice shut them up. "Whatever is going on presents a danger to everyone, but we can't let the killer erode the trust we've built over the years. The way to solve these heinous crimes is to draw closer together, not farther apart."

"You're right," Susan said.

"What if one of us were to see the killer? How long do you think we'd live?" BoomBoom trembled.

"Not long," Pewter answered.

"Let's not give way to fear," Market advised. "Hard not to, I know."

"Maybe the person who did it got away. That's why Cynthia and Rick want us in the gym, to count heads." BoomBoom allowed herself a moment of wishful thinking.

Tracy leaned toward her. "Whoever did this is in the gym."

"Come on then, let's get it over with." Harry marched out of the classroom.

"Come on." Mrs. Murphy tagged behind as Pewter and Tucker followed, too.

"If there's a killer in there, I'm not going." BoomBoom's voice rose.

"You're safer in there than you are out here." Miranda put her hand under BoomBoom's elbow, propelling her out of the classroom.

40

"Class of 1950 over here." Sheriff Shaw indicated the left side of the gym. "Class of 1980 to the right. Who has the rosters?"

"I do." Miranda stepped forward with her attendance list.

Rick took it from her hand. "Coop, go down the list with Miranda. Meet each person and check them off."

"Right, boss."

"Okay, what about 1980?"

"I've got it." Bonnie Baltier walked back to the table, picked up the Xeroxed sheets, and walked back, handing them to the sheriff.

"You stay with me. I want you to check off each name and show me who the person is. Use a colored pen. You've already got them checked off in black."

"Anyone got a colored pen?" Baltier called out.

"I do." Bitsy stepped forward, handing Bonnie a red pen. "E.R. is a member of this class and he was with me in the parking lot at the time of the murder," she told the sheriff.

E.R. called out, "Bitsy, don't bother the sheriff."

Chris Sharpton moved up alongside Rick. "It's not my reunion."

"Well, it is for now. Sit down." He pointed to the check-in

table. "I'll get to you last and then you can go home. I assume you want to go home."

"Yes," she nodded slowly.

"All right." Rick walked with Bonnie. "One-two-three."

As they worked their way down the line, Harry observed how differently people deal with authority. Some classmates answered directly. Others exhibited attitude, not at all helpful under the circumstances. The doctors in the room felt it necessary to behave like authority figures themselves. A few people were intimidated. Others were clearly frightened.

As they neared the end of the list, Hank Bittner asked to go to the bathroom.

"You'll have to wait until I'm through with this. Another five minutes. We're almost at the end."

Bob Shoaf called out, "Don't forget Fair Haristeen."

"I sent an officer out to find him." Rick's voice remained even. He felt as if he were a teacher with a room full of misbehaving children. In a way, he was.

"We're also missing Dennis Rablan." Bonnie scanned the familiar yet older faces. "Hey, anyone seen Dennis?"

"The last I saw, he'd come out of the bathroom," Harry spoke up, and a few others corroborated her statement.

"Did he walk down the hall? Go outside for a breath of fresh air?" Rick tapped his fingers against his thigh. He held on to his temper but he was greatly disturbed. Dennis might be the witness he needed—or the killer. However, there was a lot of commotion. People don't expect murder at their high-school reunion. And they don't think to keep track of one another.

"*Tucker, you stick with Mom. Pewter and I will scout around for Dennis,*" Mrs. Murphy ordered the corgi.

Pewter was out the door before Mrs. Murphy finished her sentence.

Since the class of 1950 consisted of forty-six people, Cynthia had finished the name check and was taking down whatever information the attendees might have. Nothing useful emerged since all of them, including Tracy Raz, were gathered in the cafeteria for the welcoming ceremonies.

"Boss"—Cynthia crossed over to Rick—"we can let them go.
At least, let them go back to the cafeteria."

"Yeah, okay."

Cynthia dismissed the class.

Martha Jones of the 1950 class said to a squatty fellow, bald
as a cue ball, "I'm not at all sure I want to go back to the cafeteria."

"There's safety in numbers," he replied. "This is their problem, not ours."

As the last member of the class of 1950 filed out, Cynthia
joined Rick.

"Let's divide them into groups of ten." He lowered his voice. "I
don't think I can hold them here all day. The best we can do is—"

Hank Bittner interrupted him. "Sheriff, the five minutes is
over."

"Go on." Rick waved him off. "Everyone else stay here."

Fair Haristeen passed Hank as he made for the men's room,
stopped in front of the one cordoned off, then turned heading in
the other direction, toward another bathroom.

As Rick questioned Fair, who sat next to Bitsy, E.R., and Chris,
Mrs. Murphy and Pewter prowled the hallway, sticking their
heads in every classroom.

*"Nothing here. If someone were dead and stuffed in a closet we could smell
him,"* Pewter remarked. *"Fresh blood carries."*

*"You know we have ten times the scent receptors in our nostrils than humans
do,"* Murphy casually said. *"And they say that hunting hounds have twenty
million receptors. More even than Tee Tucker."*

"I'd keep that to myself. You know how proud Tucker is of her scenting abilities." The tiger peeked into the cafeteria, where the class of 1950
was again getting settled, disquieted though they were. *"Pewter, let's
go upstairs."*

The cats turned around and walked to the stairway to the second floor. There was one stairwell at the end of the building but they walked up the main one, the wide one, which was in the middle of the hall. The risers bore thousands of scuff marks; the treads, beaten down also, bore testimony to the ceaseless pounding of teenaged feet. Although the school sanded and finished the stairs once a year the wood had become thin, concave in spots, the black rubber of sneakers leaving the most obvious marks on the worn surface.

The cats reached the second floor. A chair rail ran along the green walls; small bits had broken off and were painted over. The floor was as worn as the stair treads.

Mrs. Murphy turned into the first classroom, hopped on the windowsill, and looked down.

Pewter jumped up to join her. As she looked down she saw a bluejay dart from a majestic blue spruce. *"Hate those birds."*

"They don't like you either."

"What are we looking for?" Pewter sneezed. *"Dust,"* she said.

"Dennis Rablan. First order of business. Second order of business is to memorize the school. We can see a lot from here."

"Wonder if Dennis is dead?"

"I don't know." Mrs. Murphy put her paws on the wall, gently sliding down. *"He was an average-sized man. There aren't too many places a killer can stuff a fellow like that. Closets. Freezers. Let's check out each room, go down the back stairway, and then we can check out the cars. I don't remember what kind of car Denny drove, do you?"*

"No. Wasn't a car. It was one of those minivans."

They inspected each classroom, each bathroom, then trotted down the back stairs. They jumped on the hood of each car in the parking lot but no bodies were slumped over on the front seat.

"Don't jump on Mom's hood. She gets testy about paw prints." Pewter giggled.

A sheriff's department car pulled into the parking lot. Sitting in the front seat next to the officer was Dennis Rablan. The cats watched as the officer parked, got out, and Dennis, handcuffed, swung his feet out, touching the ground.

"Please take these off," Dennis pleaded. "I'm not a killer. Don't make me walk into the reunion like this."

"You left your reunion in a hurry, buddy, you can walk right back in wearing these bracelets. Eighty miles an hour in front of the Con-Agra Building. If you aren't guilty then you're running scared."

The cats followed behind the humans, who didn't notice them. As the officer, a young man of perhaps twenty-five, propelled Dennis into the gym, people turned. Their expressions ranged from disbelief to mild shock.

"I didn't do it!" Dennis shouted before anyone could say anything.

"Sheriff, I searched his van and found a hunting knife and a rope. No gun."

"Let me see the rope." Sheriff Shaw left for a moment as Dennis stood in the middle of the room.

He quickly returned, wearing thin rubber gloves, rope in hand. "Rablan, what's this?"

"I don't know. I didn't have a rope in my van this morning."

"Well, you sure have one in your van now."

"I didn't do it. I thought Rex Harnett was a worthless excuse for a man. I did. A useless parasite." He turned toward his classmates. "I can't remember him ever doing anything for anybody but himself."

"Maybe so but he didn't deserve to die for it." Hank Bittner, back from the bathroom, spoke calmly.

"*Tucker,*" Mrs. Murphy softly called, "*sniff the rope.*"

The beautiful corgi walked over to the sheriff, her claws clicking on the gym floor. She lifted her nose before Rick noticed. "*Talcum powder.*"

When the sheriff looked down at the dog looking up, he paused as if to say something but didn't. He stared at Harry instead, who whistled for Tucker. She instantly obeyed.

"I didn't do it." Dennis set his jaw.

BoomBoom folded her arms across her chest. "Sheriff, he's not the type."

"Then who is?" the sheriff snapped back. "I have seen little old ladies commit fraud, fifteen-year-old kids blow away their parents, and ministers debauch their flocks. You tell me, who is?"

"If none of you are going to stand up for me, I'll tell everything I know about our senior year," Dennis taunted the others.

"You bastard!" Bittner lunged forward, reaching Dennis before Cynthia could catch him. With one crunching uppercut he knocked Dennis off his feet.

Rick grabbed Hank's right arm as the young officer pinned the other one.

"He's a liar. He doesn't know anything about anybody," Hank snarled.

Bob Shoaf confirmed Hank's opinion. "Right, Rablan, make up stories to save your own ass."

Dennis, helped to his feet by Cynthia, sneered. "I'll tell what I want to when I want to and I'll extract maximum revenge. It was never my idea. I just happened to be there."

"Be where?" Rick asked.

"In the showers."

"Let me get this straight." Rick motioned for Jason, the young officer, to unlock the handcuffs. "You're talking about today? Or 1980?"

"*He's scared out of his wits,*" Pewter whispered.

Dennis looked around the room and his bravado seemed to fade. "I don't remember anything. But someone planted that rope in my van."

"Fool's blabbing about the rope before it's tested." Market Shiflett was disgusted with Dennis.

"Can I go home?" Chris sighed.

"No," Rick curtly answered.

Harry, next to Fair, said, "What did happen my senior year?"

Susan, on her other side, whispered, "Those that know are rapidly disappearing."

"Yeah, all part of the in-group clique." Harry felt dreadful, half-queasy over the deaths and the lingering presence of intended evil.

"All men," Susan again whispered.

"So far," Fair said. He was worried for all of them.

41

"Now what's the story." Rick folded his hands on the wooden desk with the slanted top, and leaned forward.

Cynthia remained in the gym checking everyone's hands for residue from firing the gun. She also checked their purses and pockets for surgical gloves. As lunchtime approached Rick decided the class of 1980 could enjoy their lunch as planned. Susan, in charge of the food, was rearranging tables with help. It would be a somber group that ate barbecue.

Rick meanwhile commandeered a classroom down the hall. Then he intended to interview the senior superlatives since they were the ones dying off, the men, anyway.

Market was number one on the list.

"I heard it second—no, thirdhand." Market coughed behind his hand. "I didn't think about it—even then—because Charlie was always bragging about himself. But . . ."

"Just tell me what you heard," Rick patiently asked.

"You know about senior superlatives?"

"Yes."

"I heard that on the day the class of 1980 elected theirs, which would have been mid-October, I think, there was the usual round of excitement and disappointment, depending on whether you were elected or not. But what I heard was that Charlie Ashcraft, Leo Burkey, Bob Shoaf, Dennis Rablan, and Rex Harnett pinned down Ron Brindell and raped him." Market grimaced. "They said if that faggot was going to be elected Most Popular they'd make sure he was popular. Or words to that effect. But Ron never reported them and he seemed on friendly terms with those guys. Just another one of those high-school rumors, like Charlie getting a girl pregnant."

Rick sighed. "Adolescent boys are terrified of sex and their own relation to it. Their answer to anything they don't understand is violence."

"I don't remember feeling all that violent," Market replied. "But I can't believe Ron would stay friendly with them after something like that."

"Depends on what he thought he had to do to survive. It's hard for many men to understand what it's like to be the victim of sexual violence," Rick said.

"I never thought of that." Market wondered what else he never thought of by virtue of being a man, a straight man.

"We worship violence in this country. Turn on your television. Go to the movies. I can tell you it makes my job a lot harder. Anyway, who told you this?" Rick returned to his questions.

"I wish I could remember. As I said, I dismissed the story and I never heard any more about it. I don't think the rumor made the rounds or it would have lasted longer. Damn, I wish I could remember who told me."

"Too bad."

"Maybe Ron wasn't a homosexual. Maybe he was just effeminate." Market thought a moment. "Must be hell to be a gay kid in high school."

"Anything else?"

"No. Well, Ron Brindell killed himself. His parents died shortly after that. From grief. He was their only son, you know. All that misery. I can't imagine killing myself."

"Self-hate." Rick offered Market a cigarette, which he refused. "All manner of things derail people: greed, lust, obsessions, sex, revenge, and self-hate. Then again I sometimes wonder if some people aren't born sorrowful." He inhaled. "Market, we've known each other for a long time. I don't mind telling you that we're sitting on a time bomb."

"Because everyone's gathered together?"

"Yes."

"But two murders took place before the reunion."

"That they did—with Marcy Wiggins' .38."

"Guess it was too good to be true." Market stopped. "I don't mean good that Marcy killed herself, but her gun . . . we all let our guard down."

Rick nodded in agreement. "Our first thought was a crime of passion. Bill had discovered the affair with Charlie, shot her, and made it look like suicide, taking the precaution to have her write a confession in her own hand. But Dr. Wiggins happened to be at the Fredericksburg Hospital that day. She could have been murdered by someone else but I don't think so. All indications were suicide."

"But her gun—"

Rick interrupted. "I know. I have a thousand theories and not one useful fact but I am willing to bet you a hundred dollars of my hard-earned pay that our murderer is sitting in the gymnasium right now. For whatever reason, this twentieth reunion has triggered him."

"Jeez, I just want to get out of here."

Rick frowned. "A normal response. I'm not sure I can let you all go. Not just yet, anyway."

As Market left the room, Rick thought about bringing in Dennis next. However, having Dennis in the gym would disquiet the others. Maybe he'd get more information from them if they stayed agitated. He decided to call Hank Bittner next.

Market walked back into the gym. Cynthia kept everyone on

a short leash. No one could rush up to Market. He sat down at the end of the table, his grim visage further upsetting the others. Market was usually so cheerful.

Walter Trevelyn asked Cynthia, "Are we trapped in the gym or what?"

"Once Rick finishes his interviews, he'll make a decision." She kept checking hands.

"I think we should forget the reunion," Linda Osterhoudt, who'd looked so forward to this reunion, suggested. "How can we go on? At least, I can't go on."

BoomBoom put down her barbecue sandwich. "If we cancel our reunion then the murderer wins. He's spoiled everything."

"I'd rather have him win than me be dead," came the sharp retort from Market.

Others spoke in agreement.

Mike Alvarez dissented. "I came all the way from Los Angeles. If we stick together what can he do?"

"I have something to say about that." Mike's attractive wife spoke up. "We came all the way from L.A. and it would be perfect if we could live to go all the way back—soon."

He declined to reply.

"We could market this," Bonnie quipped. "You know, like those mystery party games? We'll create one, Murder at the Reunion. If you get a lemon, make lemonade."

"Baltier, how insensitive," BoomBoom chided.

Hank Bittner returned, telling Bob Shoaf to go out. Bob glared at Dennis, who glared right back. Then Bob turned on his heel and left to join Rick Shaw.

Chris sat, avoiding eye contact with Dennis. Market moved and sat on the other side of Chris, as if to reassure her.

Rick returned with Bob Shoaf, who didn't seem as upset as Market had been on his return to the group. Rick still wasn't ready to pull Dennis out of the room.

BoomBoom started to cry. "All my hard work . . ."

"Oh for Christ's sake." Harry smashed her plastic fork down so hard it broke. "This isn't about you."

"I know that but I wanted it to be so great. It's your hard work, too, and Susan's and Mike's and Dennis's. I bet he didn't get any pictures either."

"Yes, I did. Up until the murder."

"How long will it take you to develop them?" Cynthia inquired.

"If I take the film to my studio I can be back in an hour."

"You're not going to let him go?" Hank Bittner was incredulous.

"There's not enough evidence to book him," Cynthia answered.

"He left the scene of the crime!" Hank exploded.

"I didn't do it."

The room erupted again as Rick shouted for quiet. "We've got your names and addresses. We've got the hotels where you're staying. We'll get in touch with you if we need to. I have no desire to make this more uncomfortable than it has to be."

"Are you going to book Dennis?" Hank insisted.

"No, I'm not, but I'm going back with him to his studio," Rick stated.

Dennis bit his lip until it bled, realized what he had done and wiped his mouth with a napkin.

As Rick and Dennis left, Cynthia remained. BoomBoom stood up, then sat down abruptly as Susan pulled her down. They whispered for a moment.

Mrs. Murphy followed Dennis and Rick out to the squad car.

"You don't believe me, do you?" Dennis demanded.

"Look, Dennis"—Rick put his hand on the man's shoulder—"I know you're scared. I don't know why you're scared and I wish you'd tell me. Think a moment. You have to live in this county. Whatever it is that frightens you can't be as bad as ending up dead."

"I didn't do it." Dennis stubbornly stopped, planting his feet wide. "I did not rape Ron Brindell."

Rick paused a minute as this was an unexpected response. "I believe you. Why are you so frightened? That was twenty years ago. I believe it happened. I believe you. Why did you run away today? The only thing I can figure is you ran away from the others who were in on it. Or you think you're next."

He mumbled, "I don't know. It's crazy. People don't come back from the dead."

"No, they don't, but there's someone in that gym who loved Ron Brindell. A girlfriend who wants retribution for his suffering. Another man perhaps. He could have had a lover. None of you knew. The man's come back for his revenge after all these years. He could be married and have children. How would you know? We called Ron's cousin in Lawrence, Kansas, to see if she had any ideas. She said they were never close. She lost contact with him after high school. Right now, Dennis, you're my only hope."

Dennis hung his head as Mrs. Murphy scampered back to tell Pewter and Tucker. "I don't know anything."

The cat could hear the shouting from the gym and she wasn't halfway down the hall. She loped to the open double doors to behold all the humans on their feet, everyone shouting and screaming. BoomBoom was the only person seated and she was in tears.

Tucker ran over to greet Mrs. Murphy. Pewter, wide-eyed, remained on the table. The commotion mesmerized her. She wasn't even stealing ham and barbecue off plates.

The only people not fighting were Harry, Susan, Fair, Bitsy, and Chris. Even E.R. was yelling at people.

"I thought we were a good class." Susan mournfully observed the outbreak of bad manners and pent-up emotion.

"Maybe we should go down to Miranda's reunion," Harry said.

"And ruin it?" Fair bent over and brushed the front of his

twill pants. "I say we all go home. No one in their right mind would stay for the dance tonight."

"Jesus, guys, what am I going to do with all the food that's been ordered? It's too late to cancel it. Someone's got to eat it."

"I never thought of that." Harry briskly walked back to the center of the melee. "Shut up!" No response. She stood on the table and yelled at the top of her lungs. "Shut up!"

One by one her classmates quieted, turning their faces to a woman they'd never had reason to doubt.

BoomBoom continued sobbing.

"Boom." Susan reached her, patting her on the back. "Wipe your eyes. Come on. We've got to make the best of it."

With all eyes on her, Harry took a deep breath, for she wasn't fond of public speaking. "We'll solve nothing by turning on one another. If anything, this is a time when we need one another's best efforts. As you know, the sheriff has released us. Before we scatter to the four corners of the globe, what are we to do with all the food Susan has ordered and you've paid for? Remember, we have the supper in the cafeteria tonight before the dance. We can't cancel it. We've paid for it. What do you want to do?"

"Let the class of 1950 have it," Hank said.

"They've organized their own dinner," Susan informed him.

"Can't we send it to the Salvation Army?" Deborah Kingsmill asked.

"I'll call them to find out." Susan left for her car. She'd left the cell phone inside it.

"We could eat our supper and go. It seems obscene to have a dance under these circumstances," Linda Osterhoudt said. "And it seems obscene to waste all that food if the Salvation Army won't take it."

Others murmured agreement.

"Shall we vote on it?" Harry asked.

"Wait until Susan comes back," Bonnie Baltier suggested.

"Even if we vote on it, it doesn't mean the majority rules." Market shook his head. "You can't make people come and eat."

"Well, we can count heads. And we can divide up what's left among those who choose to come back for supper." Harry turned as Susan reentered the room. "What'd they say?"

"Thanks for our generosity but they've only got six men in the shelter right now."

"Okay then, how many are willing to come back for supper in the cafeteria? No dance."

Feet shuffled, then a few hands were timidly raised. A few more moments and more hands shot up.

Fair and Harry counted.

"BoomBoom, surely you're coming." Susan handed her another tissue.

"I am," she weakly replied.

"You're coming, Cynthia?" Harry smiled as the deputy raised her hand.

"Wouldn't miss it for the world."

"Thirty."

"Thirty-one." Fair finished his count.

"How'd I miss one?" Harry wondered.

"You didn't. You just forgot to count yourself," he said.

"Okay then. We'll see you all tonight for supper, six o'clock in the cafeteria. Bring coolers and stuff so you can carry food back home." She put her hand on the edge of the table, swinging down, her feet touching the floor lightly.

"*Graceful—for a human,*" Mrs. Murphy noted.

"Where's Chris?" Susan didn't see her.

"The minute Rick said we were free to go she shot out of here. Just about the time everyone started yelling at everyone else," Harry said.

"Can't blame her. She'll probably never talk to us again." Susan sighed.

"It wasn't your fault." Fair smiled at Susan.

"In a way it was. I roped Chris into this because of a bet we made on a golf game this summer. Of course, she was really hoping to meet a man and she found Dennis. Right now, I doubt she's too happy about that, too."

"*I didn't say one thing about all that extra food.*" Pewter waited for praise to follow.

"*Miracle. I've lived to see a miracle.*" Mrs. Murphy gaily sped out of the gym.

Cynthia sat in her squad car in the parking lot. The school, even with the heat on, was a bit chilly. The car heater warmed her. She'd found no residue on anyone's hands or clothing. The killer probably wore plastic gloves. She'd had every garbage can at school checked. While she held everyone in the gym, Jason went through the dumpster. Nothing—but disposing of a thin pair of gloves would have been easy.

42

As Harry drove away from Crozet High School she glanced in her rearview mirror at the brick building. The four white pillars on the front lent what really was a simple structure a distinguished air. Stained glass over the double-door main entrance bore the initials CHS in blue against a yellow background.

Situated on a slight rise, the school overlooked a sweeping valley to the east, a view now partially obscured by the brand-new, expensive grade school on the opposite side of the state road. The mountains, to the west, provided a backdrop.

Like most high-school students, when she attended Crozet High she took it for granted. She never thought about architecture, the lovely setting, the nearness to the village of Crozet. She thought about her friends, the football games, her grades.

A memory floated into her mind, a soft breeze from an earlier time. She had been wearing a beautiful fuchsia sweater and Fair wore a deep turquoise one. They hadn't intended to color coordinate but the effect, when they stood together, was startling.

She remembered that junior year, hurrying from her classroom during break, hoping to catch sight of Fair as he moved on to his next class. When she'd see him her heart would skip a beat like in some corny song lyric. She didn't know exactly what she was feeling or why she was feeling it, only that the sensation was disquieting yet simultaneously pleasurable. She thought she was the only person in the world to feel like this. People didn't much talk about emotions at Crozet High or if they did, she'd missed it. Then, too, an extravagant display of emotion was for people who lived elsewhere—not Virginia. Young though they all were, they had learned that vital lesson. And today most of them had forgotten it, good manners worn out by fear, police questioning, and suspicion of one another.

Harry burst into tears.

"*Mom, what's the matter?*" Mrs. Murphy put her paws on Harry's shoulder to lick the right side of her face.

"*Don't worry, we'll protect you.*" Tucker's soft brown eyes seemed even kinder than usual.

"*Yeah, scratch that murderer's eyes out!*" Pewter puffed up.

"Damn, I never have Kleenex in the truck." She sniffled. "I don't know what's the matter with me. Nostalgia." She petted Murphy, then reached over her to pat the other two as she turned right toward home. "Why is it that when I look back, it seems better? I was so innocent, which is another word for stupid." She sniffed again but the tears continued to roll. "I fell in love with my high-school boyfriend and married him. I actually thought we'd live happily ever after. I never thought about—well—the things that happen. I never even thought about paying the bills. I supposed I would live on air." She pulled over to the side of the road, put on her flashers, and reached under the seat, pulling out a rag she used to clean the windshield. She wiped her eyes and blew her nose. "Smells like oil. I must have used this to check my oil. That's dumb—putting it back in the cab." She closed her eyes. A headache fast approached from the direction of lost youth.

"*We love you,*" Tucker said for all of them.

"I love you guys," she replied, then bawled anew, feeling, like so many people, that the only true love comes from one's pets. "I love Fair, but is it real? Or is it just the memories from before? This is one hell of a reunion."

Mrs. Murphy tried the sensible approach. "Time will tell. If you two can be together, you'll know it if you just go slow. About your reunion, how could anyone not feel terrible?"

"Some nutcase," Pewter said. "Someone who is now feeling very powerful."

Tucker nuzzled up to Harry. "Mom, it's the reunion. It's stirred up feelings, good and evil."

She blew her nose again, popped the truck in gear, and headed toward home. "I guess when I was in high school I thought trouble happened to other people, not to me. I had a wrong number." She ruefully laughed. "But you know, kids, that love is so pure when you're young. It never comes again. Maybe you fall in love again and maybe it's a wiser and better love but it's never that pure, uncomplicated love."

"Humans worry too much about time," Pewter observed. "Suppose they can't help it. There's clocks and watches and deadlines like April fifteenth. It'd make me a raving lunatic."

"Hasn't helped them any." Tucker nudged close to Harry and stared out the window as the familiar small houses and larger farms ticked by.

Mrs. Murphy sat on the back of the seat. She had an even higher view.

"I look around at everyone at the reunion and wonder what's happened to them. How'd we get here so fast? With a murderer in our midst. Our class? I read somewhere and I can't remember where, 'Time conquers time'—maybe it's true. Maybe I'll reach a time when I let it all go. Or when I'm renewed with a spiritual or even physical second wind."

"Mom, you've missed the turn!" Tucker acted like a backseat driver.

"She's clearing her head. Whenever she needs an inner vacation she cruises around. Cruising around in the dually is a statement." Mrs. Murphy didn't mind; she appreciated the plush upholstery covered with sheepskin. "She had to show up at her reunion in this new truck. Funny, isn't it? The desire to shine."

The warm autumn light turned the red of cow barns even deeper, the fire of the maples even brighter.

Harry loved the seasons but had never applied them, an obvious but potent metaphor, to her own life. "Know what's really funny? No one ever believes they'll get old. There must be a point where you accept it, like Mrs. Hogendobber." She thought a moment. "But then Mim hasn't truly accepted it. And she's the same age as Miranda." Her conversation picked up. The ride was invigorating her. "Here's what I don't get. First, someone is killing off men in the class of '80. Someone is actually carrying out a plan of revenge. I've been mad enough to kill people but I didn't. What trips someone over the edge? And then I think about death. Death is something out there, some shadow being, a feared acquaintance. He snatches you in a car wreck or through cancer. By design or by chance. But he's oddly impersonal. That's what gets me about this stuff. It's brutally personal."

43

Harry had no sooner walked through the kitchen door than the phone rang.

"Hello," Fair said. "I'm at the clinic but I can be there in fifteen minutes."

"I'm fine. I'll meet you at school for supper. Don't worry." She hung up the phone and it rang again.

"Hey," Susan said. "I dropped off two English boxwoods for Chris. I feel guilty. She's not coming to the dinner tonight, obviously. She was funny, though. She said if we survived our reunion she'd love to play golf next weekend. Oh, she's through with Dennis, too. Said she's shocked at the way he behaved. That's what really upset her."

"Well—good for her. Did you think of anything for Bitsy? It's really E.R.'s responsibility to thank her for her work but, well, I liked working with her."

"The full treatment at Vendome." Susan mentioned the most exclusive beauty parlor in town, where one could have a haircut, massage, waxing, manicure, pedicure, and complete makeover, emerging rejuvenated.

"That's a good idea. We'll get BoomBoom to cough up the money. Those two worked as hard on our reunion as we did."

"I paid for the boxwoods. It was my bet. If Boom won't pay for Vendome, I'll do it. It's only right."

"I'll split it with you."

"No, you won't. You put away that money you're getting on rent."

"I guess Tracy will leave after his reunion. He hasn't said anything. I'll tell you, though, his rent money has made my life easier."

"You're the truck queen of Crozet." Susan laughed, since she knew the rent money went to pay for the truck.

"Susan, are you scared?"

"About the dinner?" They'd known one another since infancy so elaborate explanations weren't needed, nor were transitions between subjects.

"Yeah."

"No. I'll have Ned with me. Also, I don't think we're involved except as bystanders."

"There won't be that many people there. I wonder if the killer will attend? And I wonder if we're doing the right thing. We haven't even had time to process Rex's murder. I feel like we're being whittled away."

"Are you scared?" Susan asked.

"Yes. I'm not afraid I'll get bumped off. I'm afraid of what I'll feel."

"Blindsided." Susan referred to the manner in which emotions flatten a person.

"You, too?"

A long pause followed. "Yes. I joked about who was that young person in the Best All-Round photograph but I meant it. And then I look at Danny and Brooks." She referred to her son and daughter. "And I realize they're feeling all the same emotions and confusions we did but in a different time. I'm beginning to believe that the human story is the same story over and over again, only the sets change."

"A in History," Harry laughed.

Susan thought back on her A's in History and just about everything else. "The difference is that I understand it now— before, I just knew it."

"Can you understand the murders?"

"No. I don't even know what to call the way I feel. Intense . . . disturbed? No, I don't understand it and I don't remember anything that horrible from high school. I mean, nothing out of the ordinary like two people hating one another so much it lasts for twenty years. But we're in the dark. Even Market seems to know something we don't, and Dennis—good Lord."

"Think Denny Rablan will show his face?"

"He doesn't dare."

44

Denny sat there as big as life and twice as smug. No one wanted to sit next to him. Finally Harry did, only because Susan had put out the exact number of chairs based on the head count. The sheer quantity of food overwhelmed the tables: spicy chicken wings, corn bread, perfectly roasted beef with a thin pepper crust, moist Virginia ham cooked to perfection, biscuits, shrimp remoulade, a mustard-based sauce for the beef, sweet potatoes candied and shining orange. Three different kinds of salad satisfied those who didn't wish such heavy foods. The women sat down, claiming they'd stick to the salads. That lasted five minutes.

The desserts, reposing on a distant table, beckoned after the main course. Carrot cake, tiny, high-impact brownies, fruit compote, luxurious cheeses from Denmark, England, and France rested among heaps of pale green grapes. If that wasn't enough, a thin, dense fruitcake with hard sauce filled out the menu.

The bar was open, which somewhat raised the conversation level.

The thirty-one people who came to the dinner ate themselves into a stupor. Mike Alvarez did not return. His wife had put her foot down but he left the tapes for everyone to enjoy, if "enjoy" was the right word. During dinner BoomBoom played the slow tapes. "Digestion tapes," she called them.

Mrs. Murphy, Pewter, and Tucker ate from paper plates on the floor under the table. Since there was so much food, Harry didn't think anyone would begrudge her animals.

Fair sat on the other side of Harry, her left side. Hank Bittner refused to sit next to Dennis even though he came in late and seats were taken. Bonnie Baltier switched seats with Hank so she sat on the other side of Dennis.

"Anything turn up in the lab?" Bonnie asked Dennis as her fork cut into the steaming sweet potato.

"No. Rick Shaw took the pictures and left. He said he had suspects but they always say that. I just said, 'Yeah, the whole class.'"

"Is there a digital time frame on the photographs?"

Dennis answered Harry. "No. I'm using a Nikon that's thirty years old. Never found a camera I liked better."

"Oh." Harry returned to her dinner.

Miranda and Tracy ducked their heads in the open doors. Susan waved them in. Harry hadn't seen them.

"Miranda, you look stunning." Fair stood up to compliment her.

"Sit down, sit down. I'll spoil your dinner." She blushed.

"She's the belle of the ball." Tracy beamed. "Doesn't that emerald green dress set off her hair and her eyes?"

"Yes," they agreed.

"Mrs. Hogendobber, come down to the studio in that outfit. I'll take a picture—for free. I should have my camera with me but I forgot it."

"You've," Miranda paused, "been discombobulated."

"Mrs. Hogendobber, you should be a diplomat," Hank Bittner laughed. "And you do look lovely. If the women look as good as you do when we have our fiftieth reunion, I'll be a happy man."

"You men will turn my head." She blushed some more as Tracy winked at the men.

"Come on, beautiful. I don't trust these guys." Tracy gently put his hand in the small of her back, guiding her out of the room.

Susan, on her way for second helpings, swooped past Harry. "Are they getting serious or what? She really does look fabulous. That treadmill has worked wonders."

"Tracy has worked wonders." Fair smiled. "It's a magic that never fails." He turned to Harry and whispered, "You'll always be magic to me, Sweetheart."

Harry blushed and mumbled, "Thanks."

BoomBoom raised her glass. "Here's to the class of 1980!"

The group hesitated, then raised their glasses. "Hear. Hear."

"What's left of us." Dennis held up his glass for a second toast.

"Rablan, shut up." Bittner stood and held up his glass. "To the organizers for their hard work and their heart when things didn't turn out quite as they—or any of us—expected."

Everyone cheered.

"I don't remember Hank being so eloquent," Fair remarked.

"He learned somewhere along the way." Bonnie leaned over Dennis. "Brightwood Records wouldn't promote an unpolished stone. I'd kill to have his stock options."

"You'd have to," Dennis laughed.

"You haven't exactly made a fortune. In fact, you lost one," Bonnie replied.

"You're right." He shut up.

The cats and Tucker decided to walk under the tables. This was a stroll, not a search for crumbs. They'd eaten too much.

"*Hee hee.*" Pewter nudged Mrs. Murphy as she watched a lady, heels off, run her foot over a man's calf. He wore charcoal pants.

Mrs. Murphy popped her head from under the tablecloth. "*BoomBoom.*"

Pewter ducked out on the other side. "*Bob Shoaf.*"

"*Figures,*" Murphy said as she walked back under the tablecloth.

"*He's married, isn't he?*" Tucker could have told them it was

BoomBoom since Tucker paid a lot of attention to shoes and smells.

"*Yes. He left the Mrs. at home, though,*" Pewter said.

Bored with their stroll, the animals emerged by the food tables.

"*I could probably eat one more piece of beef.*" Tucker gazed upward.

"*Don't. You've stuffed yourself. If you eat too much you'll get sick on the way home,*" Mrs. Murphy counseled.

Their conversation didn't finish because an explosion from Bonnie Baltier sent them back to that table.

"What are you talking about?" She slammed her hand on the table, making the plates jump.

"I thought you knew." Dennis blinked.

Hank leaned over Bonnie. "None of the women knew, you asshole!"

Bonnie stood up, walked around Dennis to Harry. "Did you know about a gang rape on the day senior superlatives were voted?"

"No." Harry gasped as did Susan.

"Is it true?" Bonnie, very upset, turned on Dennis. "It must be true. Why would anyone make something like that up!"

Bob Shoaf stopped playing footsies with BoomBoom. His eyes narrowed, he pushed back his seat as he strode over to Dennis, towering above him. "Rablan, there's something wrong with you. I'd call you a worm but that would insult worms." He bent over, menacing, as Fair rose from his seat just in case. "I don't know why you're making up this story about Ron Brindell getting raped in the showers but I do know that you were the person who found Rex Harnett dead and no one else was in the men's room. Do you think we're that stupid!"

Dennis, shaking with rage, stood up, facing off with Bob. "I'm not making it up. I wish I'd done something at the time. I felt guilty then and I feel guilty now."

Bob reached for Dennis's neck but Fair grabbed Bob's arms. Bob Shoaf had been a great pro football player but Fair Haristeen was a six-foot-four working equine vet. He was strong and he had one advantage: his knees still worked.

"You aren't going to listen to him! He's guilty and the sheriff is waiting for him to make a mistake," Bob exploded.

"Why would I kill Charlie Ashcraft and Leo Burkey?" Dennis became oddly calm.

"You tell me," Shoaf taunted. "It's like your story about knowing who Charlie Ashcraft knocked up. You don't know anything. You say these things to make yourself important. You don't know shit."

"I do. You know I do."

By now Hank Bittner was on his feet. Everyone else was watching.

"Then who's the mother?" Bob stepped back, already dismissing Dennis.

"Olivia Ulrich," Dennis loudly said.

"I am not!" BoomBoom flew out of her chair. "You liar. I am not."

"Come on, Boom. You loved his ass," Dennis mocked.

Susan, now at Harry's side, said, "I don't recall Dennis being this snide."

"Me neither. Something's sure brought it out of him."

"Fear," Mrs. Murphy said.

"If he was afraid he should have stayed home." Pewter moved farther away from the humans in case another fight broke out.

"Maybe he's safer here than at home," Tucker sagely noted. "He has no family. All alone. The killer might not want to slit his throat but there are a few people here who wouldn't mind. If I were Dennis, I'd rent a motel room for a couple of nights."

"Or maybe he has to be here," Murphy shrewdly said.

BoomBoom, shaking, pointed her finger in Dennis's face. "Because I'd never go to bed with you—this is your revenge. You waited twenty years for this. My God, you're pathetic."

"But you did have an illegitimate child."

"I did not and you can't prove it."

"You know, I take class pictures for the schools in town. And I recall a beautiful girl who graduated three years ago who had your coloring but Charlie's looks. Western Albemarle. You gave that girl up for adoption."

"Never! I would never do that." BoomBoom was so furious she couldn't move. She had never before felt a paralyzing rage.

"Boom, don't try to pull the wool over our eyes. You don't care about the consequences. You never did. You steal people's husbands." Dennis looked at Harry when he said that. "You dump inconvenient children. Why, if Kelly Craycroft had known about the girl he'd have never married you. You wanted his money."

"I married Kelly Craycroft after I graduated from college. Do you think I was thinking about marrying money in high school? You're out of your mind."

"*Think it's true?*" Pewter asked Murphy.

"*I don't know.*"

"And furthermore, I didn't steal anybody's husband. They aren't wallets. You can't just pick them up, you know." She put her hands on her hips. "As for the rest of you, I know what you think. The hell with you. I do as I please. Ladies, virtue is greatly over-rated!"

Harry whistled. "At long last, the real BoomBoom!"

BoomBoom stalked out of the room with Bob Shoaf following after her, reaching to slow her down.

Hank Bittner sat back down, calling over his shoulder, "Dennis, Rex may be physically dead, but buddy, you're dead socially."

Everyone started talking at once.

Mrs. Murphy watched Dennis sit down next to Hank. She hurried over to hear the conversation since there was so much noise.

"You're an even bigger coward than I am, Bittner. I just figured it out. Sheriff Shaw said something to me today. He said if these murders are revenge for Ron Brindell's rape then someone who loved Ron has to be committing them. He said what if Ron had a lover, another high-school boy that no one knew about. The boy stood back and didn't stop the rape. He didn't want anyone to know he was gay. He never lifted a finger to help Ron. And no one ever suspected. That was you."

Hank deliberately put down his fork, turned to Dennis, and said softly, "Dennis, if I were gay I would like to think I would have the courage to be what I am. I would like to think I would have fought for Ron. But I'm not gay. It wasn't me and I don't know what's wrong with you—unless that coward is you."

45

Sheriff Shaw had taken the precaution of having Dennis Rablan tailed to the reunion dinner. He also had a plainclothes officer watching Dennis's house in Bentivar, a subdivision up Route 29.

He'd pinned another flow chart to the long bulletin board in the hallway. The interior of the school was neatly drawn. Exits and entrances were outlined in red, as was each window.

Cynthia Cooper was to have attended the dinner but Rick changed his mind: he thought her presence might inhibit people. Little could have inhibited that group, though, and Coop hoped Harry and Susan would save the leftovers. She beseeched them to bring a lot of Ziploc bags and containers.

"You think the killer will crack?"

"It's his or her big night, isn't it? Whoever it is has waited twenty years."

"Are you expecting someone to be blown up in the parking lot?"

He shot her a sharp glance. "I wouldn't put it past our perp."

"I think he's enjoying the chaos—and the fear in the eyes of whoever is left on his list. I think he's sitting in that gym loving every second of it."

"Wish we knew more about Brindell. His parents have passed

away. His cousin was no help and snotty, to boot. There's got to be somebody who can tell us who his boyfriend was—or girlfriend. One of the girls could have loved him even if he was gay. People don't have much control over love. Mim Sanburne is proof of that." He smiled because the Queen of Crozet had married beneath her, although everyone conceded that Jim Sanburne, in his youth, was one sexy man.

"This is what bothers me." Cynthia, suddenly intense, stubbed out her lit cigarette. "The killer knows we know this is the big weekend. He knows we're expecting another incident at the dinner or right after since they canceled the dance. He knows," she repeated for emphasis. "Is he going to risk it? He knocked off two this summer. He's killed this morning. He might just wait, enjoy the panic, then strike when it suits him. Whoever he or she is—this lover or best friend—he's fooled us."

"You don't buy that it's Dennis Rablan. He had access to everyone. Not much in the way of alibis but then we've both seen ironclad alibis suddenly get produced in the courtroom, along with the expensive lawyer." The sheriff rubbed his chin, opened his drawer, pulling out a cordless electric razor.

"Boss, do that in the car. Let's go over there."

"Jason's in the parking lot."

"Like a neon sign."

"What are we, then?"

"I don't know but I think we ought to—" The phone rang, interrupting her.

"Sheriff Shaw," Rick answered as the operator put the call through. "Well, stay with him." He hung the phone up. "Jason says Dennis Rablan ran out of the high school, fired up his van, and is pulling out of the parking lot."

"Jason can stay with Dennis. Let's go to Crozet High."

"I hope so."

46

"Jesus, what a mess." Harry watched as the reunion dinner fell apart. "We might as well clean up and go home."

"Yeah." Susan, also dejected, picked up the plates, depositing them in huge trash bags. "One good thing, they ate more than I thought they would. We'll have a lot to take home but at least people enjoyed the food."

Fair stayed behind, as did Hank Bittner, Bonnie Baltier, Market Shiflett, and Linda Osterhoudt. Within an hour and a half the place looked as though they'd never been in it. The huge senior superlative photographs easily came down. Market rolled them up, placing them in large tubes.

"You might as well throw those out," Fair told him.

"Maybe our thirtieth reunion will be better. Anyway, there's plenty of space in the attic of the store. Who knows, huh?"

Mrs. Murphy, Pewter, and Tucker, tired from the rich food and the human fuss, sat down under the raised basketball backboard.

"Guess that's it." Harry put her hands on her hips, surveying the polished gym floor. "Too bad we couldn't have had the dance. Alvarez made serious tapes. He was always good at that kind of stuff."

"His wife sure tells him what to do," Hank Bittner laughed. "I thought he might sneak back to the dinner."

"She probably dragged him to Monticello. That's what all the out-of-towners want to see." Susan pressed her hand to the small of her back. All the bending over and lifting had made her ache a little. "I hate to see our reunion end this way."

"Yeah," the others agreed.

Harry asked Hank, "Do you believe the story about Bob, Rex, Charlie, and Leo attacking Ron?"

"Yes," Hank replied.

"Was Dennis there?" Harry continued her inquiry.

"I think he was. I think he stood by the door to watch out for Coach. I can't prove any of it but I believe it."

"How did you hear about it?" Fair asked.

"Ron told me," Hank said, looking truly sorrowful.

"Why didn't you go to the principal or Coach or somebody?" Harry blurted out. She didn't want to sound accusatory but she did.

"Because Ron said he would deny what happened. He didn't want anyone to know. He especially didn't want Deborah Kingsmill to know. He was taking her to the Christmas dance. He thought she'd break the date if she knew." Hank paused. "And if he'd told, who knows what they would have done to him. There was a kind of wisdom to his silence."

"If she really cared about him, she'd go anyway," Susan said.

"Not Deborah." Hank half-smiled. "She didn't care about anybody—which made the guys want her. And remember, she was a cheerleader and all that crap. Even then, her ambition made her cold. Ron felt like he was, I don't know, moving up, I guess, having a date with her."

"Did you know he was gay?" Harry wondered.

"Kinda." Hank shrugged. "What do you know at that age? I'm not sure even Ron knew. I do know that Leo, Charlie, Bob, and Rex spent the rest of the year teasing him but they weren't violent again."

"Maybe Dennis was his boyfriend?" Fair stooped over to pick up a carton loaded with food. He was going to start carrying food and drinks out to his truck, Harry's truck, and Susan's car.

"He's got two kids and one ex-wife," Susan said.

"That doesn't mean he's not gay." Hank also bent over to pick up a carton. "Hell, I've been married and divorced three times— to the same woman. That doesn't mean I'm nuts."

"Hank, I've been meaning to ask you about that." Fair smiled as the men walked out of the gym.

"I'm going home. Thanks for the food, Susan." Bonnie kissed Susan on the cheek.

"Drive safely." Susan kissed her back. "That ninety miles can get truly boring."

"Back to Washington." Linda Osterhoudt did her round of kisses. "Call me when you come up. The opera this year is worth the trip."

"We will," Susan and Harry said. "Hey, why don't you let the guys carry that out for you?"

"I'm not taking that much home." She lifted her small carton and left.

Market came back in for more tubes. Subdued, he waved and left.

Harry and Susan sighed simultaneously.

"It's a bitch," Harry exhaled.

"Yeah. I understand revenge. But why wreck the reunion for everyone else?"

"Guess your mind warps after a while. Hey, Boom let us all have it, didn't she? And you know, she's right. It's her body. A hus- band isn't a purse. You can't snatch him unless he wants to be snatched. I give her credit for fighting back."

"You're mellow."

Harry clapped her hands together for the animals. "Sick of it. Not mellow. I'm sick of being angry at her, angry at him, angry at me. Done is done. Took me a long enough time to get there, though. In a strange way this reunion has helped me."

"I'd like to know how?" Susan asked, genuinely interested.

"I've had ample proof of what carrying around anger, hate, and the desire for revenge can do to somebody—whoever that somebody is. So he's winning. Winning what? His life is reduced to this one issue, a very great pain, a terrible wound and it would seem an equally terrible act of cowardice. But life moves on. Our killer didn't. In my own little way, I don't want to be like that." She smiled as the three animals trotted toward her. "I've seen enough embittered women not to want to become one."

Susan hugged Harry fiercely. "I love you."

"I love you, too. I couldn't ask for a better friend."

The two women stood there with tears in their eyes.

"Maybe it wasn't such a bad reunion after all." Susan wiped away her tears and Harry's, too. "Shall we?"

They bent over to pick up two cartons and walked out the door. Harry paused for a moment to look back, then cut the lights. "Good-bye, class of 1980."

Mrs. Murphy and Pewter dashed ahead of the humans, turned a few very pretty kitty circles, and waited at the door. Tucker barked at the door; she'd barreled on ahead of them.

Harry put her carton down for a second. The faint sounds of fifties music wafted down the hall from the cafeteria. She wanted to stick her head in and watch but thought the better of it. Hank came back in for another carton.

"Should we dance?" He nodded toward the music.

"No. It's their night."

"Well, I'm not flying back to New York until Monday. If you change your mind about dancing, call me." He winked, picked up Harry's carton, and headed for the door. Harry turned to follow but thought she heard a sound on the stairwell.

The lights were out in the stairwell. She walked up a step and went over to turn them on to double-check.

A black-gloved hand came down over hers.

A man's tenor, a familiar voice, snarled, "Don't, you idiot!"

Before she could respond he drew back the side of his hand

and hit her hard in the windpipe. She staggered back, choking, falling off the one step. She saw briefly the back of a man, dressed in black, a black ski mask over his face as he jumped over her. Nimbly, he ran down the hall.

Tears of pain rolled down her face; she couldn't get up. She was fighting hard to breathe.

Mrs. Murphy noticed first. *"Something's wrong!"*

The three animals tore back down the hallway, their paws barely touching the ground. They were all going so fast that when they reached Harry they spun out of control.

Harry, on her hands and knees, gasped for air. Tucker licked her face.

"I'll catch him!" Pewter took off down the hall. Once the humans saw Harry, Murphy ran after Pewter.

"Harry? Harry!" Susan came running toward Harry, the sound of footsteps receding, fading into the fifties music.

Murphy left Harry, hit Mach One, sped past Pewter, sped past the running man, ducked into the cafeteria, pushed out a skateboard from behind the door, and pushed it so it would cross the man's path.

He never saw the skateboard. He hit it running flat out, fell down, and skidded on the polished floor. He struggled up and kept running, although his arm was crooked.

"Dennis Rablan! It's Dennis Rablan!" Murphy yelled, but only Pewter understood as she came alongside Murphy.

The two cats followed Dennis, running hard, his right arm hanging uselessly by his side. He turned, hit the doors with his left side, and escaped.

The double doors swung shut, keeping the cats inside.

"Damn!" Mrs. Murphy spit, the hair on her tail puffed, her eyes huge.

As Susan reached Harry, Tucker, hearing a second set of footsteps, bounded up the stairwell. Tucker, now on the second floor, heard footsteps thump down the far stairway. The corgi ran down the hall, reaching the top of the back stairwell as the human hit the bottom, turned right and, narrowly missing the cats, opened the doors and escaped. The cats escaped with him. He was in black sweats with a ski mask covering his face.

Within seconds Tucker was at the bottom of the stairs. With her greater bulk, she pushed a door open and followed the cats.

About a hundred yards ahead of them they heard footsteps drop over the bank; they followed as the figure ran toward the houses behind the school. He disappeared, they heard a car door slam and a car took off, heading west, no lights.

"*Damnit!*" Tucker cursed.

"*It was Dennis Rablan,*" Murphy panted.

"*But who was the guy upstairs?*" Tucker kept sniffing the ground.

"*Let's follow the tracks,*" Pewter wisely suggested. They followed two sets of tracks to the end of the schoolyard.

Looking down at the houses below, Murphy said, "*I would never have thought Dennis capable of these murders. I can't believe it but I smelled him. It was him.*"

"*Let's go back inside,*" Tucker said.

"*We can't open the doors.*" Pewter sat in the cool grass.

"*I can. Come on.*"

Once inside, they checked down the hall. Everyone was around Harry.

"*Let's go upstairs and work backwards. There may be a scent up there that will help us.*" Pewter started up the back stairs.

The other two followed.

Tucker, nose to the ground, moved along the hall. Pewter, pupils wide in the dark, checked each room, as did Mrs. Murphy.

"*English Leather.*" Tucker identified the cologne. "*Enough to mask the scent of an entire regiment. Odd. So heavy a scent even humans can smell it. Why advertise your presence like that?*"

"*What's this?*" Pewter stopped in the hall, patting at a thin, twisted piece of rope with a wooden dowel on each end.

"*A garotte!*" Mrs. Murphy exclaimed. "*He was going to strangle some-one.*"

"*Think we can get Susan or another human up here?*" Tucker said.

"*No, they're worried about Mom and we should be, too,*" Pewter replied.

"*We can't just leave it here.*" Murphy thought a moment. "*Tucker, pick it up. Drop it at their feet. When things quiet down one of the humans will notice.*"

Without another word, Tucker picked up the garotte, and hurried down the stairs to Harry.

Rick Shaw and Cynthia attended to her. They had just arrived at the school. Hank, Fair, and Susan knelt down with Harry.

"It's not crushed, thank God." Cynthia gently felt Harry's windpipe.

Harry still couldn't speak but she was breathing better.

Mrs. Murphy, Pewter, and Tucker quietly walked down the stairs.

Tucker dropped the garotte at Rick Shaw's feet. He pulled a handkerchief from his pocket, bent over, and picked it up. He whistled low.

Tucker eagerly looked up at him, then turned, walking toward the stairwell.

Harry whispered—her throat felt on fire—"They chased him."

"*There were two of them!*" Pewter, in frustration, yowled.

Rick followed Tucker up the stairs. The dog stopped where Pewter found the twisted rope. Although it was cool on the second floor—the heat was turned down for the weekend—Rick was sweating. He knew what a close call Harry had suffered. And he also knew because Jason called in on the squad car radio that he had lost Dennis Rablan at the intersection of Route 240 and Route 250. A big semi crossed the intersection and when Jason could finally turn, Dennis was out of sight. The officer drove down Beaver Dam Road, turned back on 250 to check that out, turned west on 250, and finally doubled back on 240. No trace.

Slowly he walked down the hallway, down the back stairwell, to the doors. He pushed open the doors, accompanied by Tucker, and walked to the edge of the hills.

He knelt down; the grass was flattened. He stood up and

quickly walked back to the school. He and Cynthia had locked the doors at the top of each stairwell. He walked up the stairs. The door was open, a stopper under it so it wouldn't swing back and forth. The lock had been neatly picked. He walked the length of the hall to find the other door, also propped open. It had been opened from the inside. Then he came downstairs and checked on Harry again.

Harry, sitting with her back against the wall, was pushing away a glass of water Susan wanted her to drink. She was breathing evenly now.

Rick knelt down with her. "Can you talk?"

"A little," she whispered. She told him about hearing a sound, going up a step to turn on the lights, and hearing a man's voice say, "Don't, you idiot." Then he hit hard and she fell back.

"Did the voice sound familiar?" Rick put his hand on her knee.

"Yes, but . . . it was just a whisper. I didn't recognize it and yet, there was something familiar. Eerie."

"Height?"

"Maybe five nine, ten, average, I guess."

"Build?"

"Average."

"And you couldn't see the face?"

"Ski mask." She reached for the water now. Susan handed it to her.

Rick stood back up, asked everyone where they were. In the parking lot, they all confirmed one another's presence, except for Susan, who waited at the doors for Harry.

"Listen to me," Rick commanded. "Say nothing of this. Harry, if you can't speak normally for the next few days, put out that you have laryngitis. Let's see if we can disturb our guy. He's going to want to know what you've seen."

"Okay."

"Next thing. Keep someone with you at all times."

"*I wish they could listen. Dennis Rablan!*" Murphy meowed, knowing it was hopeless.

"It's all right, Mrs. Murphy." Harry reached for the cat. Pewter came over, too.

"You're covered at work. Miranda is there," Rick said.

"I'll stay," Fair gladly volunteered.

"Z'at all right with you?" Cynthia, sensitive to the situation, asked Harry.

"Yes." Harry nodded.

"Do you think he was waiting in the stairwell for Harry?" Susan shuddered.

"I don't know," Rick grimly replied. "If he was up there throughout the dinner, he'd have seen who was leaving and who was staying. If he'd gone to the dinner and then come back, well, maybe he hoped his intended victim was still there." He turned to Harry and then Fair: "This is a highly intelligent and bold individual. Take nothing for granted." Rick was seething inside that he hadn't posted a man upstairs. He assumed locking the doors would do the job.

The three animals looked at one another. They knew they'd be on round-the-clock duty, too.

47

Like most stubborn people, Harry failed to realize how shock would affect her. She thought she was fine. She was happy to go home but surprised that when she walked through the kitchen door a wave of exhaustion washed over her, adding to the throb caused by the headache. She wanted to talk to Fair but couldn't keep her eyes open.

"Honey, you need to go to bed." He lifted her out of the chair into which she'd slumped.

"I'm sorry. I don't know why I'm so tired. Maybe I should take more painkiller."

"No. You've had enough."

Too wiped out to protest, she meekly let him walk her into the bedroom and fell into bed.

"*I'll sleep by the kitchen door,*" Tucker declared.

"*I'll take the front door.*" Mrs. Murphy chose her spot.

"*Well, I'll sleep in the bedroom then. What if someone climbs through the window?*" Pewter dashed to the bedroom before the others could protest.

Tracy came home at midnight, whistling as he opened the kitchen door. Fair, stretched out on the sofa, swung his long legs to the floor.

"Fair?"

"Had a good night?"

"Wonderful. I feel like a kid again. I even kissed Miranda on her doorstep." He smiled broadly, then considered Fair on the sofa. "Am I interrupting anything?"

"No." Fair walked into the kitchen, reached under the cupboard by the door, pulled out a bottle of Talisker scotch, and poured them each a nightcap. They moved to the cheerful, if threadbare, living room, where Fair told Tracy everything he could remember from the evening.

A long, long silence followed as Tracy stared into the pale gold liquid in his glass. "We were fiddling while Rome burned, I guess. That son of a bitch was over our heads the whole time."

"Harry could have been killed." Fair put his glass down on the coffee table, first sliding a coaster under it. "And whoever it is may fear she recognized him through his voice or way of going."

"Way of going?"

"Ah," Fair explained, "a horse has a special movement and I or any good horseman, really, can identify her by her gait. A way of going. For instance, you have an athlete's walk. I might be able to identify you even if you were in costume—or BoomBoom Craycroft, that sashay."

"The sheriff's command to act as though she has laryngitis is a good one for flushing him out but not so good for Harry. She knows she's bait?"

"Of course. Rick will have plainclothes men around the post office. He's got the house covered now. There's only one drive in and out."

"Somehow that's not very reassuring."

"No." Fair picked up his glass again, holding it between both hands.

"Do you have any ideas about who, what, why?"

"No, well, not exactly. I told you Rick Shaw's idea, that this is someone who was in love with Ron Brindell. Or at least is avenging him."

Tracy emptied his glass, then leaned toward Fair. "You know what, Buddy? I'm sixty-eight years old and I don't know a damn thing. Do people snap? Can anyone snap in a given situation? Are some weak and some strong? Are there really saints and sinners? Don't know but I do know once a person loses their fear of their own death, once they no longer care about belonging to other people, they'll do anything. Anything. My God, look at Rwanda. Sarajevo. Belfast. Kill children. Kill anything."

"Presumably those killings are politically motivated."

"Yeah, that's another load, too. Some people just want to kill. Give them a reason so they can cover up their murderous selves. The church can give them a reason, the state. I've seen enough to know there are no good reasons."

"I'm with you there."

"Whoever this is no longer cares. He's given up on people. He has nothing to lose. I also think he intended to finish off his list at the reunion and he's been thwarted. He's angry. And maybe, just maybe, he'll make a mistake."

Fair nodded in agreement. "The more I think about this reunion murderer, the more the finger points to Dennis Rablan."

"There are three left." Tracy held up three fingers.

"Two. Dennis Rablan and Bob Shoaf."

"Three. Hank Bittner."

"He said he wasn't in the locker room."

"He knows too much. Three. And there's a strong possibility one of the three is the killer."

"I'd hate to be one of those guys." Fair's deep voice dropped even lower.

Truer words were never spoken.

48

"Getting the flu?" Chris asked Harry sympathetically when she heard her voice on the phone that Sunday morning.

"Laryngitis," Harry replied.

"You do sound scratchy. I called to apologize. I chickened out. I could have at least said good-bye."

"You don't have to apologize to me. If I'd been in your shoes, I'd have melted my sneakers running—flat-out flying—out of there."

"You're not mad?"

"No."

"Anybody know anything? I mean, any clues?"

"Not that I know of but then Sheriff Shaw wouldn't tell me no matter what."

"Yes, I guess. He has to be careful. Well, I hope you feel better. I'll see you in the P.O. tomorrow."

"You bet." Harry hung up the tackroom phone.

She and Fair finished the barn chores and had decided to strip all the stalls to fill in the low spots and places where the horses had dug out.

"You need rubber mats or Equistall." Fair rolled in a wheelbarrow of black sand mixed with loam.

"Equistall costs me four hundred and fifty dollars a stall."

"It is expensive. Our alfalfa cube experiment was a big success."

"So far. I've been able to cut back on my feed bill but everyone's getting good nutrition. Maybe a little too much," she laughed, as she indicated Tomahawk in the paddock.

"If he were a man that'd be a beer belly." Fair shoveled the sand into the stall. "Tracy was up early this morning. At least their reunion is a smashing success. They're meeting for breakfast in the cafeteria."

"Chris sure wanted to know everything. Maybe I'm being suspicious. I guess it's natural since she and Denny have been pretty close. Right now I—" A car motor diverted her attention.

"Who goes!" Tucker barked, running out of the barn.

Pewter and Mrs. Murphy, sitting in the hayloft, saw BoomBoom's Beemer roll down the dusty drive.

"Wonder what she wants?" Mrs. Murphy said.

"Fair," Pewter sarcastically replied.

"We'll soon find out." The tiger cat tiptoed to the edge of the hayloft. She stayed still as she peered down into the center aisle.

Once BoomBoom parked her car and got out, Pewter joined her.

"Harry!" BoomBoom called out.

"In here," came the reply.

BoomBoom walked into the barn, saw Harry in the aisle, and then noticed Fair as he stepped out of the stall. Her expression changed slightly. "Oh, hello."

"Hi," he said.

"Has Bob Shoaf come by?"

"No. Why would he?" Harry said.

"I thought he might stop off to say good-bye before flying back up north. He always liked you."

"BoomBoom, I don't believe a word of this. What's wrong?" Harry leaned her rake against the stall door.

Her voice shot up half an octave. "I wanted to say good-bye myself, really."

"Why don't I go inside or why don't you two go inside? Maybe you can have this discussion without me." Fair tossed a shovelful of the sand mix into a stall.

"Uh . . . yes." BoomBoom backed out of the barn.

Mrs. Murphy and Pewter climbed down backwards from the ladder to the hayloft. They followed the two women, who stopped at the BMW.

BoomBoom, voice lowered, said, "He left without saying anything. I thought if he was still around I'd find out what was the matter."

"He's a jock, Boom. He's used to being fawned over and getting what he wants. As long as he didn't leave money on your dresser, I wouldn't worry." Harry immediately guessed what really happened.

BoomBoom's face flushed. "Harry, you have the most off-putting way of speaking sometimes." She reached in her skirt pocket. "He left this, though." A heavy, expensive Rolex gold watch gleamed in her hand.

"That costs as much as my new truck."

"Yes, I think it does. I really ought to return the watch but I can't send it to his house, now, can I?"

"Ah. . . . ?" Harry had forgotten about Bob's perfect wife and two perfect children. She took the watch from BoomBoom's palm. Nine-fifteen. She checked the old Hamilton she wore, her father's watch. Nine-fifteen.

"One other thing, I ought to check the school. I know you and Susan cleaned up last night but I am the Chair, and I should double-check everything."

"Well, go on."

"I'm afraid."

"Great. Why come to me?"

"Because Susan is at church with Ned and the kids and because—you're not afraid of much."

Within ten minutes Harry, Mrs. Murphy, Pewter, Tucker, BoomBoom, and Fair reached Crozet High.

The front main entrance was open because of the class of 1950's breakfast, the last scheduled event. The first place they checked was the gym, which was locked. BoomBoom had a set of keys. She unlocked the door. They looked around quickly. Everything was fine.

"*I'm going back upstairs,*" Tucker said. "*Maybe I missed something in the dark.*"

"*I can see in the dark. I didn't see anything,*" Pewter said.

"*There was a lot going on.*" Tucker headed up the stairs.

Pewter followed. Mrs. Murphy stayed with Harry as the humans checked the hallways and garbage cans.

"You all cleaned up everything. I don't have anything to do," BoomBoom said gratefully.

"*Murphy!*" Pewter howled from the top of the stairs.

Murphy hurried up the stairs, met Pewter and raced with her as she flew over the polished floor to the classroom next to the back stairwell.

Tucker sat in the classroom. The window was open. The blinds, pulled all the way to the top, had the white cord, beige with age, hanging out the window. That wasn't all that was hanging out the window.

Mrs. Murphy jumped to the windowsill. Bob Shoaf, tongue almost touching his breastbone, hung at the end of the venetian blind cord.

"*Should I get Mom?*" Pewter asked.

"*Not yet.*" Mrs. Murphy coolly surveyed the situation. "*The humans will track up everything. Let's investigate first.*" She asked the dog, "*Anything?*"

"*English Leather fading—and Dennis's scent.*"

Pewter jumped up next to Mrs. Murphy. "*His face is—I can't describe the color.*"

"*Don't worry about him.*" Murphy noted that the end classroom jutted out by the stairwell. The windows in a row could be seen from the road out front but the back window, set at a right angle to the others, was hidden from view. Bob probably wouldn't have been found until sometime Monday if they hadn't come upstairs. The frost preserved the body but even without a frost the humans wouldn't have smelled him for twenty-four to forty-eight hours, depending on the warmth of the day. She also noticed that rigor had set in. Nothing lay on the ground below.

The three animals prowled around the classroom. They walked the windowsills, checked under desks, sniffed and poked. Then they split up. Mrs. Murphy walked to the far stairwell. Tucker and Pewter checked the stairwell closest to the classroom.

They met in the downstairs hallway. No one had found anything unusual.

"Do you think the killer would have done this to Mom?" Tucker asked.

"No. But I think he would have killed her if she'd gotten too close. I know he would. But he wasn't hanging when she was attacked. Whoever did this in the wee hours of the morning hauled him back here. That's a lot of work." Mrs. Murphy spied the humans coming out of the cafeteria, each one eating a muffin from the class of 1950's breakfast.

"They'll wish they hadn't eaten," Pewter sighed.

"Well, let's get them upstairs." Tucker thought she'd pull on Fair's pants leg.

"BoomBoom is going to have a terrible time explaining that watch." Murphy headed toward the group.

49

All hell broke loose. The media from all over Virginia, Washington, and even Baltimore played up the murders. The attention was fueled by the fact that Rex and Bob had been killed on a weekend when news was especially slow and Bob had been a big sports celebrity.

Crozet, overrun by vans adorned with satellite dishes, pulled tight the shutters on the windows. Few chose to talk but among themselves the agreement was that the media was correct in dubbing these events the Reunion Murders.

The reporters waited outside the various churches, trying to nab the faithful as they emerged from late-morning services.

Public buildings were closed. The reporters were out of luck there but they hit up the convenience stores, including Market Shiflett's. The reporter from Channel 29, having done her homework, knew that Market was a member of the class under siege. Being quite pretty, she managed to extract a comment from him, which was played on the news relentlessly.

"The big cities have lots of nutcases. Guess it was Crozet's turn," Market said, looking into the camera from behind the cash register of the store.

Since few other quotes were available, Market made the airwaves up and down the Mid-Atlantic.

Mim Sanburne called a meeting at her house. Invited were those she considered the movers and shakers of the town. Harry and Miranda, part of the inner circle by virtue of birth and their jobs, sat with Herb Jones, Jim Sanburne, Larry Johnson, and Mim, discussing how to divert the bad publicity.

"That problem would be solved if we could apprehend the criminal," Harry, out of sorts, whispered, her voice still rough.

The older people quieted, each realizing that not being members of the class of 1980, they felt safe.

"You're quite right." Mim smoothed her hair.

50

Dennis Rablan was nowhere to be found. Rick Shaw scoured the photo shop and Rablan's house, called his parents and his friends. No one had seen or heard from him—at least, that's what they told Rick and Cynthia. He had stationed patrol cars at Dennis's home, his parents' home, and his ex-wife's home.

Standing next to the coroner, Rick hoped Dennis would open the doors to his business on Monday morning. He was sure Dennis knew something that he wasn't telling—assuming he was alive.

"This man died from a bullet to the brain. Apart from broken fingers, smashed knees, and both sides of his collarbone broken—the results of twelve years of pro football—this was a man in good health." The coroner shook his head. "I'd like to take every high-school football hero and show them what happens to people who continue to play this game throughout college and the pros. They get money and maybe fame but that's all they get."

"How long was he dead before he was found this morning?"

"I'd say the time of death occurred about four in the morning. You examined the site, of course."

"No sign of struggle." Rick hoped the embalmer at the funeral home would be able to get the dark color from Bob's face and he asked the coroner if that was possible.

"Usually. Once the blood drains out it will drain from the face, too, but I'm a coroner, not a funeral director." He smiled, perfectly at home with dead bodies. "If that doesn't work, I'd suggest a closed casket. There's the problem of the deep crease in the neck but if he staples the collar to the skin at the back of the neck it should stay up and not distress the family. I remember Bob's glory days at Crozet High." He peered over his half-moon glasses. "And beyond."

"Me, too." Cynthia finally spoke. Autopsies put her considerable composure to the test.

"Those days are over now," Rick simply stated. "Funny how an entire life reduces to that final moment. Bob probably thought he could get out of it, whatever or whoever. Self-confidence was never his problem."

"Same M.O.?" The coroner pulled the sheet up over Bob's discolored face.

"Yes. More than likely he wasn't shot at the school. His body was carried to the high school and up the steps. He's no feather either."

"One hundred and eighty-eight pounds, a good weight for a cornerback. Your killer will have sore legs unless he's a weight lifter."

When Rick and Cynthia drove away, Cynthia said, "Harry, Boom, and Fair certainly had a shock. They didn't know he'd been shot between the eyes until we hauled up the body. There's that moment when you see the corpse, the physical damage—it never leaves you."

"I was surprised that BoomBoom didn't swoon. She rarely misses an opportunity to give vent to her innermost feelings," Rick wryly commented.

"Remarkably restrained." Cynthia sighed. "Considering she'd slept with the man not six or seven hours before that."

"We've got her statement. She didn't waffle. I give her

credit." Rick headed back toward the department, then turned toward Crozet.

"School?"

"No. BoomBoom's."

They pulled into the driveway of the beautiful white brick home. BoomBoom's deceased husband had made a lot of money in the gravel and concrete business, a business she still owned although she did not attend to day-to-day operations. Flakey as Boom could be, she could read an accounting report with the best of them, and she made a point of dropping in at the quarry once or twice a week. She intended to profit handsomely from the building boom in Albemarle County.

A Toyota Camry was parked next to her BMW.

If anything, BoomBoom seemed relieved to see them again. Her eyes, red from crying, were anxious.

Chris Sharpton and Bitsy Valenzuela rose when Rick and Cynthia walked into the lavish living room.

"Should we leave?"

"Not yet," Rick said.

Boom offered refreshments, which they declined.

"Ladies, what are you doing here?" the sheriff asked.

"I called them," Boom said.

"That's fine but I didn't ask you." Rick smiled, as he'd known Olivia Ulrich Craycroft since she was tiny, and no offense was taken on her part.

"Like she said, she called me, she was crying and I drove over," Chris said. "I'm afraid I haven't been much comfort. I told her to take a vacation. In fact, everyone from her class should take a vacation."

"She called me, too." Bitsy confirmed BoomBoom's statement. "I asked E.R. if I could come over. He's worried about all this but he relented since Chris and I were driving over together."

"The victims are men." Cynthia leaned forward as Rick settled into his chair. "BoomBoom doesn't appear to be in danger."

"I'd hate to be the exception that proves the rule," BoomBoom said.

Rick waited, resting his head on his hand.

First she sat still, then she fidgeted. Finally she spoke. "I know you think I know something, sheriff, but I don't." Suddenly she got up and walked upstairs to her bedroom, returning with Bob's gold Rolex watch. She dropped it into Rick's upturned hand. "I didn't steal it. He left it here last night. Can you return it to his widow? I mean, you don't have to tell. Why should she know?"

"Fine." Rick slipped the heavy watch in his pocket.

"Were you two together in high school?" Cynthia asked.

"No. We just looked at one another at the supper and there it was. People told me these things happen at reunions but it wasn't a case of some old wish being fulfilled."

"Who did you date in high school? Any of the deceased?"

"Coop, I told you all this. No. My senior year I dated college guys mostly. The dances, let's see, I went with Bittner if my boyfriend at the time couldn't come."

"And where is this boyfriend?" Cynthia scribbled.

"A vice president at Coca-Cola in Atlanta. I think he'll be president someday. As you know, I married a hometown boy, although he was eight years older than I."

"Chris, sometimes outsiders can see more than insiders. What do you think?" Cynthia asked the blonde woman, who had been listening intently.

"That I'm glad I'm not part of this." She nervously glanced at BoomBoom. "Even if you are a woman and therefore probably safe, I'd be frightened."

"Did you notice anything unusual when you worked on the reunion?" Coop turned to Bitsy.

"Uh . . . well, they picked on one another. No one held much back." She smiled nervously. "But there wasn't enough hostility for murder."

"Did anyone ever discuss Charlie's illegitimate child from high school?"

Bitsy replied, "Not until Dennis lost his composure."

Chris looked Cynthia straight in the eye. "No. I didn't hear about that until later."

"You know that Dennis Rablan accused me of having Charlie's baby, but I didn't. I swear I didn't." BoomBoom frowned.

"But you know who did?" Rick quietly cornered her.

Boom's face turned red, then the color washed right out. "Oh God, I swore never to tell."

"You couldn't have foreseen this, and the information might have a bearing on the case." Rick remained calm and quiet.

Agitated, BoomBoom jumped from her chair. "No! I won't tell. She wouldn't have killed Charlie. She wouldn't. As for Leo and the others: Why? What could the motive possibly be? It makes no sense. I don't care what happened back then, if anything did happen. The murders make no sense."

"That's our job. To find out." Coop was now perched on the edge of her seat. "What may seem like no connection to you . . . well, there could be all kinds of reasons."

"But I thought these murders sprang from the supposed rape of Ron Brindell." Boom paced back and forth. "Isn't that what everyone's saying?"

"That's just it. No one admits to being there. Market Shiflett heard about it at school. Bittner says he wasn't there and the same for Dennis Rablan."

"What do you think?" BoomBoom asked Cynthia.

"It's not my job to point the finger until I have sufficient evidence. Right now what I think is immaterial."

"It's not immaterial to me." BoomBoom pouted, pacing faster. "You're asking me to betray a lifelong trust and I know in my heart that this woman has nothing to do with these awful murders." She sat down abruptly. "I know what you all think of me. You think I'm a dilettante. I have, as Mrs. Hogendobber so politely puts it, 'enthusiasms.' I sleep with men when I feel like it. That makes me a tramp, to some. I guess to most. You all think I take a new lover every night. I don't, of course. You think I'm overemotional, oversexed, and underpowered." She tapped her skull. "Think what you will, I still have honor. I refuse to tell."

"This could get you in a lot of trouble," Rick softly replied.

"Trouble on the outside, not trouble on the inside." She pointed to her heart.

51

Rick had been on the phone for fifteen minutes. On a hunch he had Cynthia call the San Francisco Police Department.

He decided he wanted to talk to the officers on the scene that night. Luckily, Tony Minton, now a captain, remembered the case.

"—you're sure the note was his handwriting?"

Captain Minton replied, "Yes. We searched his apartment after the suicide and the handwriting was his. Our graphologist confirmed."

"Enough is enough." Rick quoted Ron's suicide note.

"That was it."

"There were three reliable witnesses."

"And others who didn't stop. They reported a young man climbing on the Golden Gate Bridge, waving good-bye and leaping. We never found the body."

"And the witnesses could describe the victim?"

"Medium height. Thin build. Young. Dark hair."

"Yes." Rick covered his eyes with his palm for a moment. "Did he have a police record?"

"No."

"Captain Minton, thank you for going over this again. If you think of anything at all, please call me."

"I will."

Rick hung up the phone. He stood up, clapped his hat on his head, crooked his finger at Cynthia, who was again studying lab reports. "Let's go," he said.

Silently, she followed him. Within twenty minutes they were at Dede Rablan's front door.

She answered the door and allowed them to come inside. She then sent the two children, aged eight and ten, to their rooms and asked them not to interrupt them.

"I'm sorry to disturb you again, Mrs. Rablan."

"Sheriff, I want an answer to this as well as you do. Dennis wouldn't kill anyone. I know him."

"I hope you're right." Rick reassured her, by his tone of voice, that he felt the same way. "Has he called today?"

"No. He usually calls in the evening to check on the kids. He has them next weekend."

"You met just out of college?" Cynthia referred to her notes from an earlier questioning.

"Yes. I was working for a travel magazine. Just started. A researcher."

"Dede." Cynthia leaned toward her. She knew her socially, as they took dance classes together. "Did you ever get the feeling Dennis had a secret—even once?"

"I had hunches he was unfaithful to me." She lowered her eyes.

"Something darker?"

"Cynthia, no. I wish I could help but he's not a violent man. He's an undirected one. A spoiled one. If he had a dark secret, he kept it from me for twelve years. You have to be a pretty good actor to pull that off."

Rick cleared his throat. "Did you ever think that your husband might be a homosexual?"

Dede blinked rapidly, then laughed. "You've got to be kidding."

52

Monday proved to be even more chaotic than Sunday. Print reporters snagged people at work, and television vans rolled along
Route 240 and the Whitehall Road as reporters looked for possible interviews.

Harry and Miranda refused to speak to any media person.
Their patience was sorely tested when the TV cameras came
inside anyway, the interviewer pouncing on people as they
opened their mailboxes.

"*Ask me,*" Pewter shouted. "*I discovered the garotte.*"

"*I discovered the body. I smelled it out!*" Tucker tooted her own
horn.

"*You two better shut up. This is federal property and I don't think animals are
supposed to work in post offices,*" Murphy grumbled. "*They don't listen. They
never listen. It's Dennis Rablan—dumbbells—Dennis and someone drenched in
English Leather cologne.*"

"*Bull! The government rents the building. As long as they don't own it we can
do what we want.*" Pewter had learned that fact from Miranda,
though she had neglected to confirm that the renter could do as
they pleased. But then the federal government did whatever they
wanted, pretending to have the welfare of citizens at heart. The
fact that Americans believed this astonished the gray cat, who felt

all governments were no better than self-serving thieves. Cats are by instinct and inclination anarchists.

"*Pewter, if we appear on television, all it takes is one officious jerk to make life difficult,*" Murphy, calmer now, advised her.

"*I'll fight! I'll fight all the way to the Supreme Court!*" Pewter crowed.

"*Animals don't have political rights or legal ones, either.*" Tucker sat under the table. "*Humans think only of themselves.*"

"*Be glad of it.*" Mrs. Murphy watched from the divider. "*If humans decided to create laws for animals, where would it end? Would chickens have rights? Would we be allowed to hunt? Would the humans we live with have to buy hunting licenses for us? If we killed a bird would we go to jail? Remember, we're dealing with a species that denies its animal nature and wants to deny ours.*"

"*Hadn't thought of that,*" Pewter mumbled, then threw back her head and sang out. "*To hell with the Supreme Court! To hell with all human laws. Let's go back to the fang and the claw!*"

"*Someone has.*" Murphy jumped down as the TV camera swung her way.

Bitsy Valenzuela opened the door, saw the commotion and closed it. A few others did the same until the television people left.

"Damn, that makes me mad!" Harry cursed, her voice actually huskier than the day before. Her throat hurt more, too.

"They hop around like grasshoppers." Mrs. Hogendobber walked to the front window to watch the van back out into traffic. The sky was overcast. " 'But if any man hates his neighbor, and lies in wait for him, and attacks him, and wounds him mortally so that he dies, and the man flees into one of these cities, then the elders of his city shall send and fetch him from there, and hand him over to the avenger of blood, so that he may die.' " She quoted Deuteronomy, Chapter nineteen, Verses eleven and twelve.

"What made you think of that?"

"I don't know exactly." Miranda flipped up the hinged part of the divider and walked into the mailroom. "There's a pall of violence over the land, a miasma over America. We must be the most violent nation among the civilized nations of the earth."

"I think that depends on how you define civilized. You mean industrialized, I think."

"I suppose I do." Mrs. Hogendobber put her arm around Harry. "You could have been killed, child. I don't know what I'd do without you."

Tears welled up in their eyes and they hugged.

"The strange thing was, Mrs. H., that I wasn't scared until I got home. I was glad to have Fair there and Tracy, too."

"Tracy is very fond of you. He's . . ." She didn't finish her sentence. Bitsy slipped back in now that the television crew had left.

"Hi."

"Hi, Bitsy." Miranda greeted her.

"Just came for my mail."

Chris pushed open the door, said hello to everyone, then exhaled sharply. "It's like a circus out there. Do you think there'd be this many reporters if someone in town had won the Nobel Prize?"

"No. Goodness isn't as interesting as evil, it would seem," Harry said.

"Still under the weather?" Chris came up to the counter, followed by Bitsy.

"Laryngitis. Can't shake it."

"There's a dark red mark on your neck," Chris observed. "Girl, you'd better go to the doctor. That doesn't look like laryngitis to me. Come on, I'll run you over."

"No, no," Harry politely refused.

"If there's color on your neck, Harry, this could be something quite serious. You're being awfully nonchalant."

"Chris, don't tell me the seven warning signs of cancer," Harry rasped, then laughed.

"It's not funny!" Chris was deadly serious.

Miranda stepped up to the counter. "I'll take her at lunch. You're quite right to be concerned. Harry is bullheaded—and I'm being restrained in my description."

The animals watched as Chris and Bitsy left, each getting into separate cars.

"*Do you think those present can keep from telling what really happened to Mom Saturday night?*" Tucker worried.

"*They'd better. Mom is in enough trouble as it is.*" Pewter sat by the animal door. She couldn't make up her mind whether to stay inside, where it was cozy, or whether to take a little walk. She was feeling antsy.

"*But that's the deal. The killer will come into this post office. He'll know that Mom doesn't have laryngitis. If she pretends that is her problem, it could rattle his cage. I flat-out don't like it and I don't care what the humans say—this person will strike like a cobra. They think because there's a human with her at all times, that she's safe. Remember, this killer gets close to his victims. They aren't threatened. Then—pow!*" Tucker was deeply worried. How could two cats and one dog save Harry?

Murphy, listening intently, hummed "The Old Gray Mare" under her breath.

53

Coop, alone in her squad car, rolled by the post office at five in the afternoon. She knocked, then came through the back door.

"More black clouds piling up by the mountains. The storm will blow the leaves off the trees by sundown." She bent down to scratch Tucker's ears. "I hate that. The color has been spectacular. One of the prettiest falls I remember."

"Storm's not here yet." Harry tossed debris into a dark green garbage bag with yellow drawstrings. She looked at the bag. "Silly, but I hate going out to that dumpster."

"Not so silly. Where's Miranda?"

"Next door. She ran over to get half-and-half for her coffee." Diet or no diet, Miranda would not give up her half-and-half.

"Weird."

"What?"

"It's so quiet. This is the last place I would expect it to be quiet."

"Wasn't this morning. Half the town dragged themselves in before ten o'clock but the media attention finally irritated them. What's so unusual is, there's no fear unless it's one of my classmates. Oh, people are upset, outraged, full of ideas, but not afraid."

"Are you?"

"Yes," Harry replied without hesitation. "I'd be a fool not to be. I scan each face that comes through that door and wonder, 'Is he the one?' I scan each face and wonder which one is scanning mine." She sighed. "At least we haven't gotten any more stupid mailings. That seems to be the signal."

"Any unusual conversations, I mean, did anyone call attention to your voice?"

"Every single person who came in. Chris Sharpton wanted to take me to Larry Johnson to have him examine my throat. She was the only one who wanted to get a medical opinion. Big Mim suggested a hot toddy after taking echinacea. Little Mim said pills, shots, nothing works. It has to run through my system. Most comments were of that nature. Although, I must say that I was impressed with BoomBoom. She hasn't spilled the beans—'course, I guess she has a lot on her mind."

"Indeed . . . but Boom has sense underneath all that fluff. She's not going to willingly jeopardize you."

"Fair calls every half hour. He's driven by four times. I'm sure his patients are thrilled."

Coop laughed. "Fortunately, they can't complain."

"No, but their owners can." Harry tied up the bag, setting it by the back door. "Any sign of Dennis Rablan?"

"Not a hair. We've checked plane departures, the train, the bus. His van hasn't turned up either."

"Coop, he could be dead."

"That thought has occurred to me." Cynthia sat down at the table, licked her forefinger, and picked up crumbs.

"You eat like a bird." Harry opened the small refrigerator, bringing out two buttermilk biscuits that were left. "Here. Miranda's concoction for today."

Just then Mrs. H. walked through the front door; the large brown bag in her arms testified to the fact that she had bought more than a container of half-and-half. "Cynthia, how are you?"

"Frustrated."

"And hungry. She's been picking the crumbs up off the table."

"I can take care of that." Miranda lifted a huge sandwich from the bag. "You girls can share. I got a salad for me, but if you prefer that, Cynthia, I can divide it." Cynthia said she'd like half of Harry's sandwich. Miranda cut the turkey, bacon, lettuce, and provolone on whole wheat in half.

"I'm glad you're here." Harry smiled at Cynthia. "You're saving me from making a pig of myself."

Chris Sharpton pulled up, stuck her head in the front door. "Did you go to the doctor?"

"Miranda took me," Harry lied.

"And?"

"Laryngitis. He said the red mark isn't anything to worry about. I bruised myself but I can't remember how."

"You take care." Chris waved to the others, shut the door, and drove off.

As Cynthia gratefully ate, Miranda put a steaming cup of coffee before her, half coffee, half cream, with a twist of tiny orange rind, a favorite drink.

"If you have any leftovers, I'd be glad to eat them." Tucker wagged her nonexistent tail.

"Pig," was all Mrs. Murphy said. Her worry soured her usually buoyant spirits.

Pewter had eaten two biscuits earlier. She was full as a tick. "Murphy, would it do us any good to walk up to the high school? Maybe we've missed something."

"The only thing we've missed is the boiler room and the janitor's been in there today. Besides, all the kids are back in school. No scent. I'm at a loss, Pewter. I have not one good plan of action. I don't even know where to start."

Tucker, hearing this dispiriting talk, said, "We can read Harry's yearbook tonight. Maybe that will guide us."

"I'll try anything." Murphy flopped down on her side, putting her head on her outstretched arm. She felt so bad it made her tired.

"Dennis?" was all Mrs. Hogendobber asked Cynthia.

"Vanished. I was telling Harry. His landlord opened the office and lab. We crawled all over it. We took a locksmith to his house. Nothing has been disturbed and he hasn't been back. Luckily, he doesn't have pets but his plants are wilting. His neighbors haven't seen him. The state police haven't seen him on the highway."

Cynthia sipped her coffee. "You think it was Dennis?"

"He's the only one left standing," Miranda replied.

"Hank Bittner," Harry reminded her. "Lucky him. He's back in New York."

"The killer had no opportunities to nail Hank," Cynthia said. "At least, I don't think he did."

Harry poured herself a cup of tea, putting a small orange rind in it, too. She couldn't drink coffee. Made her too jumpy. "Maybe he did and maybe he didn't. Rex Harnett was killed in the bathroom. He wasn't dragged there. I wasn't keeping track of when the men went to the loo but our killer was probably in there or saw Rex in there and followed him. He worked fast. How he got out without anyone seeing him makes me think he crawled through the window. After all, the bathroom is on the first floor. And he was prepared for any opportunity. It's frightening how clever and fearless he is."

"You're right about him crawling through the bathroom window." Cynthia confirmed Harry's thesis.

"*You could have told us.*" Mrs. Murphy was miffed.

As if in reply to the cat, Cynthia said, "We can't tell you everything. Well, Boss worries more than I do. I know neither of you did it. Anyway, yes, he dropped on the other side, maybe a six-foot drop. The grass wasn't torn up, no clear prints, obviously, but the ground was slightly indented. He dropped over, brushed himself off, hid the gun somewhere, and strolled back into the gym."

"Wish we knew if he came back in before or after Dennis found Rex."

"Harry, Dennis could have done it, walked around, gone into the bathroom, and discovered the body. It would throw people off." Miranda tapped the end of her knife on the table, a counter-point to her words.

"Why didn't you arrest him?" Harry asked Cynthia.

"Not enough proof. But Harry, go back to Hank Bittner. You said the killer didn't have an opportunity to kill Hank if he was an intended victim."

"Remember when Hank asked you if he could go to the bath-room?"

"Yes. I made him wait."

"And he did. If the killer hadn't been in the gym with us, if he'd been upstairs, or outside or in the basement, he might have known Hank was alone. Well, probably not in the basement. But from upstairs he could have listened to the sounds coming up from the hall." She held up her hand. "A long shot. Still, he might have known. If he was in the gym with us, he couldn't follow any-one anywhere. You had us all pinned down. You had secured the bathroom where Rex was killed. Your men were out in the park-ing lot. You'd checked out the building and the grounds while we were penned up, right? I mean, that's why you wouldn't let Hank go to the bathroom. Not until your guys were done."

"You know, Harry, you're smart. Sometimes, I forget that."

"The killer knew what was going on while we sat there. And he's smarter than we are. Now it's possible he could have run away after killing Rex and come back later. But I don't think so. You would have known. You had that school covered."

"Yes, we did."

"All right. Later we had our dinner. Dennis makes a perfect ass of himself and leaves. You knew that, too. And I'm thinking Dennis's behavior was part of a plan."

"You're right. We had a man on the roof of the grade school across the street and we had a man in the parking lot in Tracy Raz's car. We had another officer tail him, although he lost him."

"So he could have come back. He could have snuck up behind the school."

"It's possible," she agreed. "But your cats and dog ran out the back of the school. The dog barked and that alerted our man in Tracy's car. Unfortunately, he didn't put two and two together fast enough, but then he doesn't really know your animals as I do. By the time he roused himself, all he knew was that someone had run across the lawn."

"Dennis could have come back." Miranda stuck to her guns.

"It is possible but when we sent cars out to look for his van, it was nowhere to be found on any of the roads around here."

"He could have pulled off on a dirt road," Miranda said, "or he could have used someone else's car or a closed garage."

"Yes." Cynthia put down her cup.

"When I started up the stairwell, he was waiting. I think he was waiting for Hank. He knew Dennis had left—that is, if it wasn't Dennis. He wanted the reunion to be his killing field— he set us up with Charlie and Leo. They were the overture. The reunion was going to be the big show. I swear it! And I got in the way."

"But the class of 1950 was in the cafeteria, that's what galls me." Miranda smacked her hand on the table. "Right there. He was over our heads and we never heard him. Nor did we see him come in and we may be old but we aren't blind."

"He never left," Harry said. "He may have gotten in his car when everyone drove away but he just circled around and hid his car. He'd been up there for hours. I can't prove it but it makes sense. You had the building covered. And even if you'd walked the halls, there are plenty of places to hide: broom closets, bathrooms. He could have stood on the john. You wouldn't have seen him. I tell you, he was there all the time."

"And you believe that he was going to kill Hank Bittner." Cynthia started to rise but Miranda jumped up and refilled her cup, handing her the half-and-half.

"If the stories are true then there are two witnesses or . . . participants alive from that rape." Harry thought out loud. "If

Hank Bittner had been killed and Dennis lived, I guess we'd have our answer." She stopped abruptly. "Dennis has a car phone. Has he used it?"

"No. We checked that, too."

"And you've called Hank Bittner, of course," Miranda pressed.

"We did. He left on the six forty-five A.M. flight for New York and showed up for work. We called again this afternoon to see if anyone from the class had called him. Nobody had. He didn't seem frightened but that could be a bluff."

"What if you bring him back to flush the game?"

"No go. He's not coming back to Crozet until we find the killer."

"Doesn't mean the killer won't go to him." Harry folded her arms across her chest. "Another thing. The gun that killed Rex and Bob. A different gun than Marcy Wiggins'?"

"Yes."

"With a silencer?"

"Exactly."

"They're illegal," Miranda exclaimed.

"So is murder," Harry said, and then they burst out laughing, relieving some of the tension.

54

That evening, Tracy Raz and Fair took turns staying awake while Harry slept. Pewter again stayed in the bedroom with Harry while Tucker rested by the kitchen door and Mrs. Murphy curled up at the front door.

At one in the morning Mrs. Murphy opened one eye. She heard the crunch of tires about a half mile away. Had she been wide awake she would have heard it earlier. With lightning speed she skidded down the hallway, turned through the living room, and soared through the kitchen, leaping over Tucker's head. The corgi, eyes now opened wide, shot through the animal door after Mrs. Murphy. The two best friends ran under the three-board fence, down over the sloping meadow, jumped a ditch and culvert, zigzagged through the protective fringe of woods by the front entrance, and came out on the paved road in time to see the taillights of a late-model car recede in the darkness.

"Damn!" Tucker shook herself.

"Make that a double damn. Even a minute earlier, we might have identified the car. You can bet it wasn't someone lost and turning around. No, that was our killer all right. Coming down the driveway. Saw Tracy's car and Fair's truck."

They turned, trotting over the light silvery frost covering the ground. The storm clouds still gathered at the mountaintops. The weather in the mountains varies from minute to minute. Although it appeared in the afternoon that a storm would hit by early evening, it waited. When the winds changed, those inky masses would roll down into the valley. Deer, raccoons, fox, and rabbits scampered about, each hoping to fill their bellies before the storm pinned them down.

As the cat and dog broke into the open meadow, a low *swoosh* flattened them to the ground. Mrs. Murphy twisted her head to look upward. A pair of huge talons, wide open, reached for her.

"*Ha! Ha!*" Flatface called as she brushed the edge of Mrs. Murphy's fur. Then she rose again in the dark air.

"*She's got a sick sense of humor,*" Tucker, rattled, growled.

"*Flatface. Flatface. Come back,*" Mrs. Murphy called out to the enormous owl.

Huge shadowy wings dipped, the owl banked, then silently settled before them. Rarely were the ground animals this close to the owl, easily three times taller than they were, with a massive chest and fearsome golden eyes. When they spoke to her or were reprimanded by her, she was usually in her perch in the cupola in the barn.

Speechless for a moment, Tucker swallowed. "*You scared us.*"

"*Groundlings,*" came the imperious reply.

"*Did you see the car that drove partways down the drive?*" Mrs. Murphy refused to back up even though Flatface took a step toward her, turning her head upside down for effect.

"*Wasn't a car. It was a van. It flashed the lights on when it turned into the driveway, then cut them off. Drove down the road with no lights. Fool.*"

"*Did you see who was driving it?*" Murphy asked.

"*No.*"

"*We think whoever is driving that van, most likely Dennis Rablan, will try to kill Mom,*" Tucker, ears forward, said.

"*Humans don't concern me.*"

"*She's different.*" Murphy puffed out her fur a bit.

Flatface swiveled her head around; a field mouse moved under the dried hay leavings. Full, she let the tiny creature pass. "*If you were a kitten I'd eat you for supper.*" She let out a low chortle, then stretched her wings out wide, a sight that would have frozen the blood even of the forty-pound bobcat who prowled this territory. To further emphasize her power she stepped forward, towering over the cat and dog.

Mrs. Murphy laughed. "*Have to catch me first. Maybe I'd put pepper on my tail.*"

Flatface folded her wings next to her body. She admired the sleek tiger cat's nerve. "*As I said, I don't care about humans but I like the barn. New people might change the routine. One never knows. Then again, Harry seems less human than most of them. I shouldn't like to see her killed.*"

"*If you see anything or if that van returns, fly down and see who is driving it. We think it's Dennis Rablan.*" Tucker finally spoke up.

"*All right.*"

The wind shifted. Mrs. Murphy beheld the first inky octopus leg of the storm slide down the mountain. "*Have you had any luck catching any of the barn mice?*"

The owl blinked. "*No—and they sing the most awful songs.*"

"*Ah, it isn't just me then.*" Murphy smiled.

Flatface hooted, opened her wings, and lifted off over their heads, a rush of air from her large wings flowing over their faces as the wind from the west picked up.

By the time they reached the screened-in porch, the first tiny ratshot of sleet slashed out of the sky. It hit the tin roof of the barn like machine-gun fire. Within seconds the *rat-tat-tat* increased to a steady roar.

"*Will be a hard night of it.*" Murphy shook herself, as did Tucker.

"*Wonder where he hides that van?*" Tucker shook the sleet off her fur.

"*Right under our noses.*"

"*Do you believe Pewter slept through everything?*" Tucker was appalled.

"Tracy's wide awake." Murphy watched as the older man pored over Harry's high-school yearbook.

"If this is Dennis, he knows that Tracy is our lodger. He doesn't take him seriously. I think it was Fair's truck that backed him off."

"Maybe he was checking us out for later."

55

The sleet turned to ice bits which turned to snow by mid-morning. The first snow of the season arrived punctually, right on November first.

Harry felt prepared, having driven her four-wheel drive F350 dually to work.

It was also the day of Bob Shoaf's funeral in Buffalo, New York, and Rex Harnett's in Columbia, South Carolina, where his mother was living. No one had organized memorial services in Crozet. When shopping in Market Shiflett's store, Ted Smith, a fellow in his seventies, displayed a little gallows humor when he said, "Funeral. You guys need a bulldozer to dig mass graves." Market didn't find that funny.

Nor did he find it funny when he asked Chris Sharpton to the movies and she allowed as to how he was a good man but she wasn't going out with anyone from his high-school class ever again, and if she ever saw Dennis Rablan again she'd tell him a thing or two.

In a fit of loneliness he asked Bitsy Valenzuela, later that morning, if she had any unmarried girlfriends from her home-town. He'd travel for a weekend date. She very kindly said she couldn't think of anyone off the top of her head, but if she did she'd let him know.

Morose, he waved but didn't smile when Harry threw a snowball at his window. She entered the post office as Miranda hung up the phone.

"They found Dennis's van!"

"Where?"

"Yancy's Body Shop." Yancy's also specialized in painting automobiles.

"No one noticed?" Harry was incredulous.

"Yancy's on vacation, hunting in Canada. The shop's been locked since the weekend. Cynthia said they've cordoned off the place and are dusting for prints, searching for any other evidence."

"Locked, but is there anyone in town who doesn't know where the key is? Over the doorjamb. It's been there since we were kids." She unwound her scarf. "Hey, it's something, I guess."

Tracy came in, bringing them a pepper plant. "Needed something cheerful on the first snowy day."

"Tracy, I appreciate you keeping watch but really, I have the animals."

The three furry creatures smiled.

"Yes, but now you have me, too. And while it's on my mind—"

"Honey, they've found Dennis Rablan's van!" Miranda interrupted him, then told him everything she'd just heard.

Harry called Susan, who called Bonnie Baltier in Richmond. One by one the remaining senior superlatives heard the news, including Mike Alvarez in Los Angeles. BoomBoom called Hank Bittner in New York. More worried than he cared to admit, he thanked her for her thoughtfulness.

"*Dennis has to be hiding somewhere close by.*" Pewter felt drowsy. Low-pressure systems did that to her.

"*Underground.*" Tucker used the old term from the underground railroad days.

In a manner of speaking, he was.

56

The following day, clear in the morning, clouded up by noon. The bite in the air meant snow, big snow. Snowstorms usually did not hit central Virginia until after Christmas and then continued up to early April. Then spring would magically appear. One day it is a gray, beige, black, and white world and the next, pink, yellow, white, and purple cover the hills.

The earliest snowstorm within Harry's memory was an October snow, when the leaves were still on the branches, and the weight of the snow with the leaves brought down huge limbs throughout the region. She remembered doing her homework that night to the sound of branches being torn down, screaming since the sap was still in them.

Market dashed in to get his mail. "No more toilet paper. Miranda, I put a six-pack inside your back door. People are crazy. You'd think the storm of the century was approaching." He paused. "The barometer sure is dropping, though. Ought to be a couple of days' worth or one big punch."

"I've got my snow shovel at the ready." Miranda winked.

"And Tracy to shovel it." Harry tossed a pile of fourth-class mail into the canvas cart.

"He'll do yours, too. He is a charitable soul."

"Bet the supermarket is running low on canned goods. I should have ordered more last week. But you know, I watch the weather and you'd think it was one volcano eruption, tornado, or hurricane after another. It's not weather anymore—it's melodrama. So I don't much listen."

"I go by my shinbone." Miranda reached down on the other side of the mailboxes. "Hey, almost forgot, Market, here's a package from European Coffees." She handed it over the counter, worn smooth and pale from use.

"Thanks. Oops, looks like Bitsy at the store. Better head back."

As he left, Harry waved. They'd discussed the finding of the van yesterday. There wasn't much more to say. Market didn't like being in the store alone but he had to make a living. He said he didn't think he was in danger. He wasn't part of the Ashcraft-Burkey-Shoaf "in" group but things were so crazy, how could one be sure?

"I'm going to walk about before the snow gets here. Anyone want to come along?"

"Murphy, it's twenty-seven degrees Fahrenheit out there," Pewter protested.

"I'll go," Tucker volunteered.

"You two are always showing off about how tough you are." Pewter hopped in an empty mail cart, curling up with her tail draped over her nose.

"See ya!" Both animals pushed through the dog door in the back. It hit the wall with a magnetic thwap.

Harry looked up in time to see the gray door flop back. She figured they had to empty their bladders.

Mrs. Murphy lifted her head, inhaling the sharp cold air. She and Tucker moved along, since they stayed warmer that way. They headed toward Yancy's Body Shop, a block beyond the railroad track underpass. Both animals stayed well off the road, having seen enough squashed critters to know never to trust a human behind the wheel.

They reached the closed-up shop within ten minutes.

Rick Shaw had removed the yellow cordon tape but a few pieces of it had stuck to the big double doors of the garage. They circled the concrete structure. At the back a black plastic accordion-style drainpipe protruded from the corner. A cinder block was loose next to it, the mortar having crumbled away years ago.

"Can't you push it out? You're stronger than I am."

"I can try." Tucker leaned her shoulder against the cold block. Little by little it gave way.

"Good!" Murphy wriggled in and turned around. "Can you make it?"

"If I can push out the second block, I can." Tucker wedged the cinder block sideways just enough so she could flatten and claw her way under.

The light darkened with each minute as the clouds grew gunmetal gray outside. Mrs. Murphy squinted because the old odor of grease, oil, and gasoline hurt her eyes. Both animals walked over to where the van had been parked. It was easy to discern the spot since every other inch of space was crammed with vehicles in various states of distress or undress.

"I give them credit," Tucker, nose to the ground, said. "Usually they muck up the scent but it smells like only two people were here."

"Tucker, I can't smell a thing. The gasoline masks everything. Makes me nauseous."

"Funny, doesn't bother humans much." Tucker lifted her black moist nose then stuck it to the ground again. "Dennis was here all right. There's a hint of the darkroom plus his cologne. Cold scent. I think the only reason there's scent left is the closed van kept it safe and the moisture coming up through the concrete floor held some of it, too." She sighed. "I have good powers but if we had a bloodhound, well, we'd know a lot more. There's also that English Leather smell— the same smell I picked up in Crozet High, upstairs."

"Great," Mrs. Murphy sarcastically said, for she was hoping that scent wouldn't be found. Guarding against two humans is harder than guarding against one.

Tucker looked at Mrs. Murphy, her deep brown eyes full of concern. "Two. Two for sure."

Murphy wanted to sit down a moment but the greasy floor dissuaded her. "*Tucker, let's get back to the post office.*"

They ran back to the post office. Cynthia Cooper's squad car was parked in the front.

As they pushed through the animal door, Pewter bounded to greet them. "*Dennis Rablan called! He threatened Mother.*"

"*What?*" Tucker and Murphy shouted.

"*Yes, he called about five minutes after you left and he said, 'Butt out, Butthead.' Then he said, 'Ron Brindell lives!' Mom called the sheriff, and Cynthia, who was around the corner, got here in less than two minutes, I can tell you. No one knows where he called from but Mom said he sounded like he was right next door.*"

Miranda kept her eye on the door. If someone came in she would go directly to the counter and help if they needed her. Cynthia and Harry sat at the table.

"He's not far, Coop. And he wasn't on a cell phone. The reception was too clear." Harry, surprisingly calm, spoke. "But Ron being alive? I don't believe it."

"I called 360° Communications just in case, got E.R. Valenzuela. He's checking every call within the last ten minutes."

"Can they do that?"

"Yes. The technology is amazing and evolving by the minute. They'll work backwards, from your number. Harry, go over the conversation again. In case something occurs to you, an inflection of voice, a background sound, anything at all."

Harry folded her hands on the table. "The phone rang. I picked it up. I recognized Dennis's voice immediately. His voice was clear and firm, I guess is how I'd describe it. He didn't shout or anything. He just said, 'Butt out, Butthead' and 'Ron Brindell lives' and hung up." She furrowed her brow. "Wait, he breathed out hard and I heard a clink. A metal sound but I can't tell you what really. Just something like metal touching metal."

"He knows you saw him, obviously." Coop ran her fingers across her forehead, then squeezed the back of her neck. She felt a whopper of a tension headache coming on.

"But we know Dennis is alive."

"Yes, that makes it easier. Now we have to find him. Do you think his saying 'Ron Brindell lives' is meant as literal truth or is it part of the revenge scenario?"

"I don't know. People saw Ron jump from the bridge. How could he live?"

Miranda walked back to them. "There have been a few survivors since the Golden Gate Bridge was built, but Dennis doesn't want to hurt you, Harry. I truly believe he's warning you. What 'Ron Brindell lives' means, who knows?"

Murphy yowled. *"The Old Gray Mare! I get it. Ain't what she used to be."*

"Hush, sweetie." Harry picked her up to pet her.

"Don't let your guard down!" Murphy put her paws on the table.

"Guess Dennis was Ron Brindell's boyfriend. Bittner was right."

"Oh, that's another thing." Coop spoke to Harry, then glanced up at Miranda. "Dennis called Bittner, too. Told Bittner he was next."

The Reverend Herb Jones stomped his feet, bent over to pick something up, then opened the door. "Three beautiful ladies. I've come to the right place." He turned over the soggy white envelope that he'd found on the ground outside. "Addressed to Mrs. George Hogendobber. Now Miranda, this has to be someone younger than we are. They should know that you address a widow differently. It should be Mrs. Miranda Hogendobber. The old ways let you know the important things, right off. No wonder the young waste so much time. They're slipping and sliding trying to find out the essentials." He laughed. "Listen to me! I'm getting old!"

"Not you." Miranda took the envelope.

"Must have slipped out of the door. It's been stepped on." Herb leaned over the counter as Miranda opened the note.

She read, "His power to punish is real. He is God's servant and carries out God's punishment on those who do evil." She thought a moment. "Romans, Chapter thirteen, Verse four."

"You know the Bible better than I do!" Herb complimented her.

She read the note again. "Cynthia, I think you might want to look at this. It could be a crank or it could be Dennis trying to justify himself."

"Dennis?" Herb's eyebrows raised in puzzlement.

"He's alive." Harry then told him what had just happened.

As she was filling in the good Reverend, the phone rang.

Miranda picked it up. "Cynthia, E.R. Valenzuela for you."

Cynthia listened, then hung up the phone. "Wasn't a cell phone."

"He's here," Harry said with resolution.

"There are two and one of them you can't see, I mean, none of us can see. We take him for granted!" Murphy howled.

"Here it comes." Herb called attention to the big snowflakes falling from the glowering sky.

57

"Don't drive to New York. We'll be stranded in the storm." Dennis, right hand chained to the passenger door, pleaded. His left hand was chained to his belt. His wrists were raw from the handcuffs he'd been wearing since Saturday.

Ron Brindell started the car. "You might be right about that. I'm bored, though. Hey, I'll get Harry."

"She hasn't done a thing to you."

"She saw you," Ron said. "You know. I don't care. I just feel like killing someone else from the bad old days."

"I had a ski mask on," Dennis said wearily. "Look, just kill me and get it over with. You don't care if she saw me or not. I called her and Hank. Want me to call BoomBoom and Baltier, too?" he asked. "Just kill me. You're saving me for last, anyway." Dennis held no illusions that Ron had a scrap of sanity left but he tried to reason with him.

"Why, Dennis, what a courageous thing to say," Ron replied sarcastically.

"All right then, let's drive to New York."

"I will get Bittner. Maybe not tonight but I'll get him."

"He didn't *do* anything." Dennis, haggard from his ordeal, stared at the closed garage doors.

"Exactly. He opened the door, saw what was going on, and closed it. Did precisely nothing."

"In shock, probably."

"He could have gotten the coach."

"We were all kids. Kids make bad decisions. He was probably as scared in his way as I was in my way. He's a father now. Have you no pity?"

"No." Ron turned his cold eyes on Dennis. "Why should I? I was pinned down, raped—and they laughed. Called me a faggot. I was a faggot. Do you know where the word 'faggot' comes from, Dennis? From the Middle Ages, when people burned witches. The woman was tied to the stake and surrounding her were homosexual men who were set on fire first. Instead of bundles of kindling, we were the kindling. I have no pity."

Ron checked his watch. "Lie down. I don't want your head to show." As Dennis squinched down, Ron reached over and stuck a rag in the poor man's mouth. "You should have stood up for me, you know. You just stood there. Oh, you told them to stop. I believe you said it once. If it had been you I'd have fought. I'd have given my life for you. Now you can give yours for me. Lie down, damnit!"

Dennis didn't even look at him as he slid down as far as he could. Since Ron had threatened to kill Dennis's two children, Dennis would do anything Ron said. Meanwhile, his brain overheated, trying to find a way out. If there was no way out, then he was determined to take out Ron. But how?

Ron hit the electronic button to raise the garage door, then pulled out into the snowy darkness.

"Hi ho, hi ho, it's off to work I go," he sang as he headed through town. Everyone was snug inside, their lights shining through the falling snow.

58

Harry and Tracy buzzed around the kitchen making pea soup, a favorite winter treat. Fair called to say he'd be late. A horse at Mountain Stables had badly cut his hind leg and needed stitching up. He didn't think he'd be back for another hour and a half because he needed to swing by the office and fill his truck with supplies. He had a hunch he'd be on plenty of calls the next couple of days as people kept their horses in stalls, feeding them too much grain. Colic often followed heavy snows. Since Tracy was there he felt Harry was okay.

Tucker jerked up her head. *Someone's coming. On foot!*

"Tucker, chill." Harry heard nothing.

Both cats ran to the kitchen door. A towel was stretched across the bottom of it to keep out the draft.

A knock on the door surprised the humans.

"Chris, what on earth are you doing here in this weather?" Harry opened the door.

"I was coming back from Waynesboro. I did a big shop at Harris Teeter in preparation for the storm and my car died. Absolutely dead. No lights. No nothing. Do you think you could run me home in your truck? I could throw everything in the back."

"Sure."

"I'll do it." Tracy plucked his coat off the peg.

"Thank you so much." Chris smiled. "I'm sorry to bother you on such a cold night. I saw Fair's truck parked at Mountain Stables when I came down the mountain. He never gets a break, does he?"

"No." Harry smiled. "Comes with the territory."

Tracy, his hand on the doorknob, said, "Call Fair, will you?" What he really meant was, call Rick Shaw and tell him you're alone, but he didn't want to say that in front of Chris since the sheriff had told them to keep it quiet.

"I will." She waved as the two walked out the door.

Harry picked up the phone, dialing the sheriff's number. "Hi," she said, but before she could finish her sentence Chris was back in the kitchen, a gun in her hand, leveled at Harry.

"Hang up. Come outside."

Tucker grabbed Chris's ankle but she leaned over and clunked the faithful creature on her head. Tucker dropped where she was hit.

"Tucker!" Mrs. Murphy screamed.

Pewter, thinking fast, shot out the kitchen door and through the screened-in porch door, which was easy to open. Much as Mrs. Murphy wanted to lick her fallen friend's face, she knew she had to follow.

The two cats ran into the barn. Nearly six inches of snow were already on the ground and the snow was so thick you couldn't see your hand in front of your face.

Tracy Raz lay in the snow facedown, blood oozing from the back of his head.

Again the cats couldn't stop to help him. They raced into the barn, climbing up into the loft. Once there, Mrs. Murphy stood on her hind legs, pushing up the latch. They wedged their paws at the side and pushed the door open.

"If she'll come this way we can jump down on her. The height will give us force."

"And if she doesn't?" Pewter breathed hard.

"We follow and do what we can."

Simon waddled over and saw Tracy. "Uh oh."

"Simon, help us push a bale of hay over to the opening," Murphy commanded.

The three small animals tried but they couldn't do it. Pewter kept running back and forth from the hay bale to the loft door opening.

"Here they come!"

Chris walked behind Harry. At least she let Harry pull on a jacket. On seeing Tracy lying in front of the barn, Harry rushed over.

"Forget him!"

"But he's . . ."

"Forget him."

"I take it you're not really Chris Sharpton." Harry kept talking as she knelt down and felt Tracy's pulse, which, thanks-be-to-God, was strong.

"No. Come on."

"Where's Dennis?"

"You'll see soon enough."

Murphy wriggled her rear end, then launched herself from the loft opening. She soared through the snowflakes with Pewter right behind her.

"Ooph!" Chris fell backwards as Mrs. Murphy hit her on the chest. A split second later Pewter hit her square in the face. Chris slipped in the snow, falling on her back.

Harry jumped on her.

The gun discharged.

The cats clawed and bit but couldn't do much damage through the winter clothes. Also, the humans were rolling in the snow. Harry, strong, wasn't as strong as Chris. Harry bit Chris's gun hand but Chris wouldn't drop the gun. The cats leapt off when the humans rolled back on the ground. They'd get up, slip and fall, but Harry never let go of Chris's gun hand no matter how hard Chris hit or kicked her.

"*We've got to get the gun!*" Pewter hollered.

Harry hung on as Chris flung her around, her feet off the ground. Harry dragged Chris down again but they struggled up. The cats kept circling the humans while Simon watched in horror, not knowing what to do.

Finally, Chris pushed Harry away far enough to hit her hard on the jaw with a left hook. The blow stunned Harry enough that she relaxed her grip. Chris hit her again. Harry let go of the gun hand as she slid back into the snow, the blood running from her mouth. The cats again climbed up Chris's legs but she barely noticed them.

She aimed her gun at Harry, who neither begged for life nor flinched. Chris fired, missing her, because Flatface had suddenly flown low overhead and scared her for an instant.

Murphy climbed up Chris's leg, her back, and reached up to claw deep into her face. Chris struggled to rise and throw off the cat. Pewter climbed up and hung on to Chris's gun hand, sinking her fangs into the fleshy part of the palm. Chris tried again to throw off the cats, slipped in the snow, and fell down, cats shredding her face and hand.

Harry scrambled and grabbed the gun as Chris flailed, screaming, struggling to her knees. Harry had gotten up and smashed the butt of the gun into her skull. Chris dropped face first into the snow. Harry kicked her in the ribs, then kicked her again, rolling her over. Chris was out cold. Harry wanted to kill her. But some voice inside reminding her "Thou shalt not kill" prevented her from her own rage and act of revenge.

She looked into the falling snow, the flakes sticking to her eyelashes. Half-dazed herself, she sank to the ground.

Mrs. Murphy, on her hind paws, licked Harry's face. "*Come on, Mom. You've got to tie her up before she comes to—come on.*"

Pewter licked the other side of her face.

Harry blinked and shook her head, then stood up, swayed a little but walked into the barn, grabbed a rope lead shank, and made quick work of tying Chris's hands behind her back and tying her feet up behind her, the rope also around her neck. If Chris kicked her feet she'd choke herself.

She hurried over to Tracy, who was slowly awakening. She rubbed snow on his face. He opened his eyes.

"Tracy, can you get up?"

She put his arm around her shoulder and they both slipped and slid into the kitchen, where a groggy, sore corgi wobbled to her feet.

59

Harry, Miranda, Tracy, Fair, Susan, and Cynthia sat before Harry's roaring fire in the living-room fireplace. It was past midnight but the friends had gathered together as the snow piled up outside.

Fair treated Tucker's knot on the head by holding her in his lap, applying an ice pack periodically.

"You were saved by the grace of God," Miranda, still terribly upset, said. "He sent his furry angels of deliverance." She started to cry again.

Tracy sat next to her on the sofa, putting his arm around her. "There, there, Cuddles. You're right, our guardian angels worked overtime." A bandage was wrapped around his head and one eye was swollen shut.

"Mrs. Murphy and Pewter are heroes." Harry sat cross-legged before the fire, her cats in her lap. "You know, I would never have figured this out. So much for my deductive powers."

"If it makes you feel any better, I don't think I would have figured it out either," Cynthia consoled her. "We waited for a mistake and he finally made one. Had it not been for Mrs. Murphy and Pewter, you all would be dead and Ron would be heading for New York to get Hank Bittner."

"Has he confessed?" Fair, both hands on Tucker, asked.

"Yes. He didn't expect to live. His plan was to kill Dennis and then himself after killing Bittner. He felt no particular animosity toward Harry but toward the end, the power went to his head. He chained Dennis in his basement, forcing him to cooperate. He told Dennis if he didn't help him he'd kill Dennis's children as well as others from the class of 1980. If Dennis would help—with a gun in his ribs—he'd confine himself to the locker room boys. He broke his promise, of course."

"What about the two footprints at the dumpster?" Harry asked. "Remember, an L.L. Bean chain print and a high heel. You told us about that after we pestered you."

"He had his boots on. The heel was someone else. That was the thing. He could still pass as a man, an effeminate one, if he again dressed in men's clothes. He swears he nailed Leo Burkey in the Outback parking lot. Says he came back around and got Leo in the car. As to Charlie, Ron came down the back stairs, dressed as a man, walked into the locker room and shot him. He always identified himself first. He said Charlie laughed and Leo turned white as a sheet."

"What an elaborate ritual of revenge." Tracy's head throbbed. "To fake his own death. He knew whoever jumped off that bridge would be swept to sea. They hardly ever retrieve the bodies of the people who jump or fall from the Golden Gate Bridge."

"It was a despondent man he met in a bar," Cynthia said. "They made a suicide pact, the other fellow jumped and Ron didn't. Ron wrote the note 'Enough is enough.' People were so shocked at seeing a man standing on the edge of the bridge they didn't notice another man creeping away."

"But the yearbook!" Harry stood up, brushing off her rear end. She was sore from the struggle and her left jaw, turning dark red, would soon turn black-and-blue.

"He rummaged around used-bookstores. Found yearbooks, leafing through them. He said he looked through hundreds until he found a picture of a tall, lanky dark-haired girl that would work. People don't study yearbook pictures. He knew you wouldn't scrutinize. He said he decided to live life a blonde, which would make you laugh. He somewhat resembled Chris Sharpton. He understood people in a cunning fashion. He especially understood the code of politeness. He knew people around here wouldn't pry."

"Is Chris Sharpton alive?"

"Yes. She's married for the second time and lives in Fort Wayne, Indiana. She married her high-school boyfriend, divorced him, and in a fit sold off everything they'd had together, including her high-school yearbook. The book found its way to a San Francisco used-bookshop. Sometimes those dealers buy in lots from other dealers. At least he didn't kill Chris Sharpton," Cynthia said. "Rick had our guys calling and checking everything the minute he started talking."

"Did he fake Marcy Wiggins' suicide?" Susan felt terrible for the dead woman.

"No, she really was despondent and was on antidepression medication for months. She kept her gun in the glove compartment of her car. He'd steal it, then put it back. Brazen. If she'd caught him, he'd have made up a story."

"When did he become a woman?" Miranda wanted to know.

"After college. He worked for a large pharmaceutical company, learned as much as he could about the process, saved his money, moved to San Francisco, and underwent the sex-change process there, which is time-consuming and costly. It didn't make him any happier, though. All those years he was transforming, his one motivation was to return and punish his tormentors."

"Time stopped for him." Fair removed the cold pack from Tucker's head for a moment, to the relief of the dog.

"He'll get the chair," Susan bluntly stated.

"He wants to die. His only regret is that he couldn't kill Hank Bittner and Dennis."

"What will happen to Dennis?" Harry wondered out loud. "Was he in on it from the beginning?"

"No. Dennis drove to Chris's after losing our tail. He put his van in Chris's garage—at her suggestion. Or should I say, his? He was upset from the reunion supper and wanted to talk. She lured him into sex games. He went to bed with her and that's how Chris—or Ron—got the cuffs on him without a struggle. After that Ron was always near him with a gun on him. He was up in the stairwell when Dennis hit you, Harry. They were waiting for Hank."

Cynthia shrugged. "Dennis was a coward in not fighting Leo, Charlie, Rex, and Bob in the locker room but then four against one isn't good odds. Two against four if Ron had fought back isn't good odds either, but Dennis was afraid to be discovered. He was in a sexual relationship with Ron. At least up until the rape. But you know, Dennis wasn't a coward once Chris revealed who she really was. He said he was prepared to die in order to save his children. Ron confirms that, too."

"Is Dennis gay?" Fair asked.

"I don't know. Ron was crazy about him and Dennis said at that time in his life getting laid was the most important thing in the world."

"In a way, I'm surprised more gay people don't lose it, become violent." Fair had never really thought about it.

"Statistically, they are one of the most nonviolent groups we have in America," Cynthia replied. "Yet they are still utterly despised by a lot of people. It was worse in Ron's youth. That doesn't justify what he's done. And the press will make a big hoo-ha over it. Every gay leader in the country will have something to say and every reactionary will point to this as proof positive that gays are the Devil's spawn, ignoring the fact that most violent crimes are committed by heterosexual males between the ages of fifteen and twenty-five. The truth is irrelevant."

"It always has been," Susan agreed. "My husband can tell you that."

Ned Tucker, being a lawyer, had seen enough lying, cheating, and getting-away-with-it to fill three lifetimes.

"No wonder we couldn't figure out what was happening,"

Harry said thoughtfully. "A man consumed by revenge, turns into a woman. One life is deformed, if you can stand that word, and four men die for it twenty years later. I would have never figured out that Chris Sharpton was Ron Brindell. I'm just glad to be alive—even if I am a little dumb."

"None of us would have figured it out." Susan, too, knew she wouldn't have put the pieces together.

"Then what was all that business about the mother of Charlie Ashcraft's illegitimate child?" Fair asked. "A couple of the victims mentioned that—and, well, there was a lot of loose talk."

"That was a red herring," Cynthia replied. "But at that stage no one except the victims knew this was connected to Ron Brindell. They thought Charlie's murder might have something to do with his past lovers or his illegitimate child."

"Does anyone know who that woman is?" Harry asked Cynthia.

"It has no bearing on the case," Cynthia quickly said.

"I'd like to know." Harry shrugged. "Curiosity."

"Forget about it." Susan sighed. "It will come out in time. All of Crozet's secrets eventually see the light of day."

"I can't believe all the times I was in Chris's company and I never thought anything. Although I thought she had awfully big feet," Harry exclaimed.

Cynthia said, "He was brilliant in his way."

"Well, I owe thanks to one brave dog and two kitties who flew through the air with the greatest of ease." Harry kissed Mrs. Murphy and Pewter.

Tracy said, "And I thank them, too. Ron hit me hard on the back of the head. If he'd shot me the noise would have warned you. He would have finished me off after he killed you."

"Tracy, you came all the way back from Hawaii for your reunion. I'm sorry it was spoiled," Harry said.

"Brought me home. I'm thankful for that. I might stay awhile." He squeezed Miranda to him.

"*I don't think I would have figured out that Chris was Ron.*" Mrs. Murphy rubbed against Harry's side as she was again seated on the floor.

"*She was as nice as she could be and she didn't seem masculine or anything—except she had this little Adam's apple. I never thought a thing about it,*" Pewter said.

"*I should have known.*" Tucker sat up on Fair's lap. "*Too much perfume. She masked her scent or rather lack of it. You can change forms but you can't really change scent but so much. That's probably why he doused his black sweats and black shirt with English Leather. It smells manly.*"

"*Well, we'd better go check on Simon.*" Mrs. Murphy left the room followed by Pewter and Tucker, too.

"Are you guys going potsie?" Harry asked.

"*God, I wish she wouldn't say that. It sounds so stupid. I love her, I'm thrilled she's alive, but is there any way to get her to drop 'potsie' from her vocabulary?*" Tucker laid her ears back.

"*Just say yes, you are, and come on,*" Pewter advised.

Outside, the cold bracing air felt clean as they breathed. The snow was now nearly eight to ten inches deep. Tucker ran to the barn, snow flying up behind her. Pewter and Mrs. Murphy, hopping from spot to spot since the snow was almost over their heads, soon followed.

Simon peered over the loft edge. The horses offered thanks to all. They'd been in their stalls and couldn't do anything to help.

"*Thank you, Simon,*" Murphy meowed.

"*Flatface,*" Pewter called up.

"*Who's there?*" said the enormous bird, who knew exactly who was there as she looked down from her high nest.

"*Thank you,*" they said in unison. "*Thank you for helping to save Harry.*"

"*Inept groundlings!*" came the Olympian reply.

Claws and Effect

Dedicated to the people who work
in animal shelters. You're overworked
and underpaid but you have given your
life to a different kind of reward.
God bless you.

Cast of Characters

Mrs. Murphy   Beautiful, brainy, saucy, she is the perfect cat. Just ask her.

Pewter   A gray cat with strong opinions, she is often reluctantly pulled into Mrs. Murphy's schemes.

Tee Tucker   A courageous corgi who loves Harry. She loves Mrs. Murphy and Pewter as well but she thinks the cats can be awful snobs.

Mary Minor "Harry" Haristeen   Energetic, organized, very task-oriented, she provides her friends with laughter just by being herself. She's the postmistress of Crozet although a graduate of Smith College. Many people consider her an underachiever.

Mrs. Miranda Hogendobber   She's older and a good friend to the thirtyish Harry. Her husband was the former postmaster of Crozet. She's widowed and rather religious.

Big Mim Sanburne   The Queen of Crozet, a contemporary of Miranda's, is imperious and relentless in her efforts to "improve" Crozet and its inhabitants.

Little Mim Sanburne   The Princess of Crozet is often resentful of languishing in her mother's shadow but she's beginning to emerge. It's about time; she's in her thirties.

Jim Sanburne   The Mayor of Crozet is the affable husband of Big Mim. He married well above his station.

Aunt Tally Urquhart   The Dowager Queen, in her nineties, she passed on control of the town to her niece years ago. This does not mean she doesn't want to get her own way.

The Reverend Herbert C. Jones   He's the beloved pastor of the Lutheran Church. By his position and by his nature, he can often help others.

His two cats, Cazenovia and Elocution, appear to have religious impulses.

Dr. Bruce Buxton   Sought out by athletes because he is a celebrated knee specialist, he's also sought out by single women because he's single. Bruce has a big head.

Sam Mahanes   The administrator for Crozet Hospital juggles the budget as well as the doctors' egos. With a few exceptions, he gets along with people.

Tussie Logan   The head nurse in Pediatrics is dedicated to her job. She's attractive and available.

Hank Brevard   The plant manager at Crozet Hospital lives to complain. People just tune him out.

Susan Tucker   As Harry's best friend she has to be a good sport. She's a wife and mother, drawing comfort from her family. She bred Tee Tucker.

Ned Tucker   Susan's lawyer husband, who works hard and loves his family.

Danny Tucker and Brooks Tucker   Their teenaged son and daughter, respectively.

BoomBoom Craycroft   She's a dazzler who upsets other women by simply walking into the room. Too many people assume that because she's beautiful, she's dumb. Boy, have they got a wrong number.

Dr. Larry Johnson   He's an older, trusted general practitioner who tried to retire once with dismal results. He knows many secrets and keeps all of them.

Sheriff Rick Shaw   Overworked, understaffed, and underpaid, he nonetheless loves his job and plays strictly by the book—well, most times.

Deputy Cynthia Cooper   Bright, on the rise in her profession, she, too, loves law enforcement. She hangs out with Harry and the gang in her free time and she's beginning to wonder if there's a man out there ready for a wife who's a cop.

Fair Haristeen, DVM   Harry's ex-husband is a sought-after equine practitioner, who still loves Harry. He's a big enough man to have learned from his mistakes. He's open-minded and thoughtful.

1

*P*eople tell me things. Of course, I have a kind face and I'm a good listener, but the real reason they tell me things is they think I can't repeat their secrets. They couldn't be more wrong."

"People tell <u>me</u> secrets." The corgi looked up at Mrs. Murphy, the tiger cat, reposing on the windowsill at the post office.

"You're delusional. Dogs blab." She nonchalantly flipped the end of her tail.

"You just said people think you can't repeat their secrets but they're wrong. So you blab, too."

"No, I don't. I can tell if I want to, that's all I'm saying."

Tucker sat up, shook her head, and walked closer to the windowsill. "Well, got any secrets?"

"No, it's been a dull stretch." She sighed. "Even Pewter hasn't dug up any dirt."

"I resent that." A little voice piped up from the bottom of a canvas mail cart.

"Wait until Miranda finds out what you've done to her garden. She hasn't a tulip bulb left, Pewter, and all because you thought there was a mole in there last week."

"*Her tulips were diseased. I've saved her a great deal of trouble.*" She paused a moment. "*And I was careful enough to pull mulch over the hole. She won't find out for another month or two. Who knows when spring will come?*"

"*I don't know about spring but here comes Mim the Magnificent.*" Tucker, on her hind legs, peered out the front window.

Mim Sanburne, the town's leading and richest citizen, closed the door of her Bentley Turbo, stepping gingerly onto the cleared walkway to the post office because ice covered much of central Virginia.

Odd that Mim would own a Bentley for she was a true Virginian, born and bred, plus her family had been in the state since the early 1600s. Driving anything as flashy as a Bentley was beyond the pale. The only thing worse would be to drive a Rolls-Royce. And Mim didn't flaunt her wealth. Miranda, who had known Mim all of her life, figured this was a quiet rebellion on her friend's part. As they both cruised into their sixties, not that they were advertising, this was Mim's salvo to youth: Get Out Of My Way.

People did.

Mary Minor "Harry" Haristeen smiled when Mim pushed open the door. "Good morning."

"Good morning, Harry. Did you have trouble driving in today?"

"Once I rolled down the driveway I was fine. The roads are clear."

"You didn't ask me if I had trouble." Miranda walked up to the counter dividing the post office staff from the public. As she lived immediately behind the post office, with just an alleyway in between, she slipped and slid as she made her way to work on foot.

"You haven't broken anything so I know you're fine." Mim leaned on the counter. "Gray. Gray. Cold. Hateful."

"Four degrees Fahrenheit last night." Miranda, passionate gardener that she was, kept close watch on the weather. "It must have been colder at Dalmally." She mentioned the name of Mim's estate just outside of town. As some of Mim's ancestors fled to America from Scotland they named their farm Dalmally, a remembrance of heather and home.

"Below zero." Mim strolled over to her postbox, took out her key, the brass lock clicking as she turned the key.

Curious, Mrs. Murphy dropped off the windowsill, jumped onto the wooden counter, then nimbly stepped off the counter onto the ledge that ran behind the postboxes, dividing the upper boxes from the larger, lower boxes. She enjoyed peering in the boxes. If a day dragged on she might reach in, shuffle some mail, or even bite the corners.

Today she noticed that Susan Tucker's mailbox had Cracker Jacks stuck on the bottom of it.

Mim's gloved hand, a luscious, soft turquoise suede, reached into her box. Murphy couldn't help herself; she peered down, then took both paws and grabbed Mim's hand, no claws.

"Mrs. Murphy. Let me have my mail." Mim bent down to see two beautiful green eyes staring back at her.

"Give me your glove. I love the smell of the suede."

"Harry, your cat won't let me go."

Harry walked over, slipped her fingers into the mailbox, and disengaged Murphy's paws. "Murphy, not everyone in Crozet thinks you're adorable."

"Thank you!" Pewter's voice rose up from the canvas mail cart.

Harry gently placed her tiger on the counter again. A pretty woman, young and fit, she stroked the cat.

Miranda checked the bookshelves for cartons. "Mim, got a package here for you. Looks like your coffee."

Mim belonged to a coffee club, receiving special beans from various world-famous cafés once a month. "Good." She stood at the counter sorting her mail. She removed one exquisite glove and slit open envelopes with her thumbnail, a habit Harry envied, since her own nails were worn down from farm work. The older, elegant woman opened a white envelope, read a few sentences, then tossed the letter and envelope in the trash. "Another chain letter. I just hate them and I wish there'd be a law against them. They're all pyramid schemes. This one wants you to send five dollars to Crozet Hospital's Indigent Patients Fund and then send out twenty copies of the letter. I just want to know who put my name on the list."

Harry flipped up the divider, walked over to the wastebasket, and fished out the offending letter.

"Sister Sophonisba will bring you good fortune." She scanned the rest of it. "There is no list of names. All it says is to pass this on to twenty other people. 'If you wish.'" Harry's voice filled the room. "Send five dollars to Crozet Hospital's Indigent Patients Fund or your microwave will die."

"It doesn't really say that, does it?" Miranda thought Harry was teasing her but then again . . .

"Nah." Harry flashed her crooked grin.

"Very funny." Mim reached for her letter again, which Harry handed to her. "Usually there's a list of names and the top one gets money. You know, your name works its way to the top of the list." She reread the letter, then guffawed, "Here's the part that always kills me about these things." She read aloud. "Mark Lintel sent five dollars and the Good Lord rewarded him with a promotion at work. Jerry Tinsley threw this letter in the trash and had a car wreck three days later." Mim peered over the letter. "I seem to recall Jerry's wreck. And I seem to recall he was liberally pickled in vodka. If he dies he'll come back as a rancid potato."

Harry laughed. "I guess he has to get rid of that old Camry somehow so he decided to wreck it."

"Harry," Miranda reprimanded her.

"Well, I liked your death threat to microwaves." Mim handed the letter over the worn counter to Harry, who tossed it back into the wastebasket, applauding herself for the "basket."

"Two points." Harry smiled.

"Seems to be local. The references are local. None of this 'Harold P. Beecher of Davenport, Iowa, won the lottery,'" Mim said. "Well, girls, you know things are slow around here if we've wasted this much time on a chain letter."

"The February blahs." Harry stuck her tongue out.

"Ever notice that humans' tongues aren't as pink as ours?" Tucker, the corgi, cocked her head, sticking her own tongue out.

"They are what they are," came the sepulchral voice from the mail bin.

"Oh, that's profound, Pewts." Mrs. Murphy giggled.

"The sage of Crozet has spoken," Pewter again rumbled, making her kitty voice deeper.

"Well, I don't know a thing. What about you two?"

"Mim, we thought you knew everything. You're the—" Harry stopped for a second because "the Queen of Crozet" dangled on the tip of her tongue, which was what they called Mim behind her back. "—uh, leader of the pack."

"At least you didn't say Laundromat." Mim referred to a popular song from the sixties, before Harry's time.

"How's Jim?" Miranda inquired after Mim's husband.

"Busy."

"Marilyn?" Miranda now asked about Mim's daughter, Harry's age, late thirties.

"The same, which is to say she has no purpose in this life, no beau, and she exists simply to contradict me. As for my son, since you're moving through the family, he and his wife are still in New York. No grandchildren in sight. What's the matter with your generation, Harry? We were settled down by the time we were thirty."

Harry shrugged. "We have more choices."

"Now what's that supposed to mean?" Mim put her hands on her slender hips. "All it means is you're more self-indulgent. I don't mind women getting an education. I received a splendid education but I knew my duty lay in marrying and producing children and raising them to be good people."

Miranda deftly deflected the conversation. "Don't look now, but Dr. Bruce Buxton is flat on his back coasting down Main Street."

"Ha!" Mim ran to the window, as did Mrs. Murphy and Tucker. "I hope he's black and blue from head to toe!"

Bruce spun around, finally grabbing onto a No Parking sign. Breathing heavily, he pulled himself up, but his feet insisted in traveling in opposite directions. Finally steadied, he half slid, half skated in the direction of the post office.

"Here he comes." Mim laughed. "Pompous as ever although he is handsome. I'll give him that."

Dr. Bruce Buxton stamped his feet on the post office steps, then pushed the door open.

Before he could speak, Mim dryly remarked, "I give you a 9.4," as she breezed past him, waving good-bye to Harry and Miranda.

"Supercilious snot!" he said only after the door closed because it wouldn't do to cross Mim publicly. Even Bruce Buxton, a star knee specialist at Crozet Hospital, knew better than to offend "The Diva," as he called her.

"Well, Dr. Buxton, I gave you points for distance. Mim gave you points for artistic expression." Harry laughed out loud.

Bruce, in his late thirties and single, couldn't resist a pretty woman so he laughed at himself as well. "I did cover ground. If it gets worse, I'm wearing my golf spikes."

"Good idea." Harry smiled as he opened his mailbox.

"Bills. More bills." He opened a white envelope, then chucked it. "Junk."

"Wouldn't be a letter from Sister Sophonisba, would it?" Harry asked.

"Sister Somebody. Chain letter."

"Mim got one, too. I didn't." Harry laughed at herself. "I miss all the good stuff. Say, how is Isabelle Otey?"

Harry was interested in the gifted forward for the University of Virginia's basketball team. She had shredded her anterior cruciate ligament during a tough game against Old Dominion. UVA won the game but lost Isabelle for the season.

"Fine. Arthroscopic surgery is done on an outpatient basis now. Six weeks she'll be as good as new, providing she follows instructions for six weeks. The human knee is a fascinating structure . . ." As he warmed to his subject—he was one of the leading knee surgeons in the country—Harry listened attentively. Miranda did, too.

"*My knees are better.*" Mrs. Murphy turned her back on Bruce, whom she considered a conceited ass. "*Everything about me is better. If people walked on four feet instead of two most of their problems would vanish.*"

"*Won't improve their minds any,*" came the voice from the mail cart, which now echoed slightly.

"*There's no help for that.*" Tucker sighed, for she loved Harry; but even that love couldn't obviate the slowness of human cogitation.

"*Pewter, why don't you get your ass out of the mail cart? You've been in there since eight this morning and it's eleven-thirty. We could go outside and track mice.*"

"*You don't want to go out in the cold any more than I do. You just want to make me look bad.*" There was a grain of truth in Pewter's accusation.

Bruce left, treading the ice with slow respect.

In ten minutes Hank Brevard, plant manager of Crozet Hospital, and Tussie Logan, head nurse in Pediatrics, arrived together in Tussie's little silver Tracker.

"Good morning." Tussie smiled. "It's almost noon. How are things in the P.O.?"

"The P.U.," Hank complained.

He was always complaining about something.

"I beg your pardon." Mrs. Miranda Hogendobber huffed up.

"Cat litter." He sniffed.

"Hank, there's no litter box. They go outside."

"Yeah, maybe it's you," Tussie teased him.

He grunted, ignoring them, opening his mailbox. "Bills, bills. Junk."

Despite his crabbing over his mail, he did open the envelopes, carefully stacking them on the table. He was a meticulous man as well as a faultfinder.

Tussie, by contrast, shuffled her envelopes like cards, firing appeals, advertisements, and form letters into the wastebasket.

Miranda flipped up the dividing counter, walked out, picked up the wastebasket, and started to head back to the mailbag room, as she dubbed the working portion of the post office building.

"Wait." Tussie swiftly dumped two more letters into the trash. "If you don't open form letters you add three years onto your productive life."

"Is that a fact?" Miranda smiled.

"Solemn," Tussie teased her.

Miranda carried the metal wastebasket around the table to Hank. "Any more?"

"Uh, no." He thumbed through his neatly stacked pile.

"Can't you ever do anything on impulse?" Tussie pulled her mittens from her coat pocket.

"Haste makes waste. If you saw the damaged equipment that I see, all because some jerk can't take the time. Yesterday a gurney was brought down with two wheels jammed. Now that only happens if an orderly doesn't take the time to tap the little foot brake. He pushed, got no response, then pushed with all his might." Hank kept on, filled with the importance of his task. "And there I was in the middle of testing a circuit breaker that kept tripping in the canteen. Too many appliances on that circuit." He took a breath, ready to recount more problems.

Tussie interrupted him. "The hospital does need a few things."

He jumped in again. "Complete and total electrical overhaul. New furnace for the old section but hey, who listens to me? I just run the place. Let a doctor squeal for something and oh, the earth stops in its orbit."

"That's not true. Bruce Buxton has been yelling for a brand new MRI unit and—"

"What's that?" Harry inquired.

"Magnetic Resonance Imaging. Another way to look into the body without invading it," Tussie explained. "Technology is exploding in our field. The new MRI machines cut down the time by half. Well, don't let me go off on technology." She stopped for a moment. "We will all live to see a cure for cancer, for childhood diabetes, for so many of the ills that plague us."

"Don't know how you can work with sick children. I can't look them in the eye." Hank frowned.

"They need me."

"Hear, hear," Miranda said as Harry nodded in agreement.

"Guess we need a lot of things," Hank remarked. "Still, I think the folks in the scrubs will get what they want before I get what I want." He took a breath. "I hate doctors." Hank placed the envelopes in the large inside pocket of his heavy coveralls.

"That's why you spend your life in the basement." Tussie winked. "He's still looking for the Underground Railroad."

"Oh, balls." Hank shook his head. If they had been outside, he would have spat.

"I've heard that story since I was a kid." Miranda leaned over the counter divider. "'Bout how the old stone section of the hospital used to be on the Underground Railroad for getting slaves to freedom."

"Every house and bush in Crozet has historical significance. Pass a street corner and some sign declares, 'Jefferson blew his nose here.' Come on, Tussie. I've got to get back to work."

"What are you doing here with doom and gloom?" Harry winked at Tussie.

Hank suppressed a little smile. He liked being Mr. Negative. People paid attention. He thought so anyway.

"Chuckles' car is in the shop."

"Don't call me that," Hank corrected her. "What if my wife hears you? She'll call me that."

"Oh, here I thought you'd say 'people will talk.'" Tussie expressed much disappointment.

"They do that anyway. Ought to have their tongues cut out."

"Hank, you'd have fit right in during the ninth century A.D. Be in your element." Tussie followed him to the door.

"Yeah, Hank. Why stop with cutting people's tongues out? Go for the throat." Harry winked at Tussie, who joined her.

"Mom's getting bloodthirsty." Mrs. Murphy laughed.

"Let me get Chuckles back to his lair." Tussie waved good-bye.

"Don't call me Chuckles!" He fussed at her as they climbed into the Tracker.

"They're a pair." Miranda observed Hank gesticulating.

"Pair of what?" Harry laughed as she emptied the wastebasket into a large garbage bag.

The day wore on, crawled really. The only other noteworthy event was when Sam Mahanes, director of the hospital, picked up his mail. Miranda, by way of chitchat, mentioned that Bruce Buxton had slid on his back down Main Street.

Sam's face darkened and he replied, "Too bad he didn't break his neck."

2

*W*hee!" Harry slid along the iced-over farm road, arms flailing. The horses watched from the pasture, convinced more than ever that humans were a brick shy of a load. Mrs. Murphy prowled the hayloft. Tucker raced along with Harry, and Pewter, no fool, reposed in the kitchen, snuggled tail over nose in front of the fireplace.

Susan Tucker, Harry's best friend since the cradle, slid along with her, the two friends laughing, tears in their eyes from the stinging cold.

Slowed to a stop, they grabbed hands, spinning each other around until Harry let go and Susan "skated" thirty yards before falling down.

"Good one."

"Your turn." Susan scrambled to her feet. Instead of spinning Harry, she got behind her and pushed her off.

After a half hour of this both women, tired, scooted up to the barn. They filled up water buckets, put out the hay, and called the three horses, Poptart, Tomahawk, and Gin Fizz, to come into their stalls. Then, chores completed, they hurried into the kitchen.

"I'll throw on another log if you make hot chocolate. You do a better job than I do."

"Only because you haven't the patience to warm the milk, Harry. You just pour hot water on the cocoa. Milk always makes it taste better even if you use one of those confections with powdered milk in it."

"I *like chocolate.*" Pewter lifted her head.

"She heard the word 'milk.'" Harry stirred the fire, then placed a split dry log over the rekindled flames. Once that caught she laid another log parallel to that, then placed two on top in the opposite direction.

"*I'd like some milk.*" Mrs. Murphy placed herself squarely on the kitchen table.

"Murph, off." Harry advanced on the beautiful cat, who hopped down onto a chair, her head peering over the top of the table.

"Here." Susan poured milk into a large bowl for the two cats, then reached into the stoneware cookie jar to give Tucker Milk-Bones. As Susan had bred Tee Tucker, she loved the dog. She'd kept one from the litter and thought someday she'd breed again.

"Did I tell you what Sam Mahanes said today? It was about the only interesting thing that happened."

"I threw out junk mail along with the Cracker Jacks in my post-box. That was the big interest in my day," Susan replied.

"I didn't do it."

"Then why didn't you clean it out? You're supposed to run a tight ship at the post office."

"Because whoever put the Cracker Jacks in there wanted you to have them." Harry smiled.

"That reduces the culprits to my esteemed husband, Ned. Not the Cracker Jacks type. Danny, m-m-m, more like his father. Must have been Brooks." She cited her teenaged daughter.

"I'll never tell."

"You won't have to because when I get home she'll wait for me to say something. When I don't she'll say, 'Mom, any mail today?' The longer I keep quiet, the crazier it will make her." Susan laughed. She loved her children and they were maddening as only adolescents can be but they were good people.

"The hard part was keeping Mrs. Murphy and Pewter from playing with the Cracker Jacks."

"What was your solution?"

Mrs. Murphy lifted her head from the milk bowl. *"Catnip in the Reverend Jones' box."*

Both women laughed as the cat spoke.

"She's got opinions," Susan remarked.

"I put catnip in Herb's mailbox." Harry giggled. "When he gets home and puts his mail on the table his two cats will shred it."

"Remember the time Cazenovia ate the communion wafers?" Susan howled recalling the time when Herb's sauciest cat got into the church closet, which was unwisely left open. "And I hear his younger kitty, Elocution, is learning from Cazenovia. Imagine kneeling at the communion rail being handed a wafer with fang marks in it."

Harry giggled. "The best church service I ever attended. But I hand it to Herb, he tore up bread crusts and communion continued."

"What happened with Sam Mahanes?" Susan asked. "Didn't mean to get off the track. I do it all the time and I'm not even old. Can you imagine me at eighty?"

"I can. You'll be the kind of old dear who walks in other people's kitchens to make herself a cup of tea."

"Well—at least I won't be boring. Eccentricity is worth something. You were going to tell me about Sam Mahanes in the post office today."

"Oh, that. Miranda told him that Bruce Buxton took a header on the ice. He turned a nifty shade of beet red and said, 'Too bad he didn't break his neck,' and then he slammed out of the P.O."

"Huh." Susan cupped her chin in her hand as she stirred her hot chocolate. "I thought those two were as thick as thieves."

"Yeah, although I don't know how anyone can stand Bruce on a long-term basis."

Susan shrugged. "I guess in order to be a good surgeon you need a big ego."

"Need one to be postmistress, too."

"You know, in order to be good at anything I suppose everyone needs a touch of ego. The trick is hiding it. Bruce might be wonderful at what he does but he's stupid about people. That's one of the things I've always admired about Fair. He's great at what he does but he never brags." She sipped a moment. "And how is your ex-husband?"

"Fine. It's breeding season so I won't see much of him until mares are bred for next year and this year's mares deliver." Fair was an expert on equine reproduction, a veterinarian much in demand.

"Oh, Harry." Exasperated, Susan cracked Harry's knuckles with a spoon.

"You asked how he was, not how we're doing."

"Don't get technical."

"All right. All right. We were keeping to our Wednesday-night dates until now. We're having fun." She shrugged. "I don't know if lightning can strike twice."

"Me either."

"I get so sick of people trying to get us back together. We've been divorced for four years. The first year was hell—"

Susan interrupted. "I remember."

"I don't know if time heals all wounds or if you just get smarter about yourself. Get more realistic about your expectations of other people and yourself."

"God, Harry, that sounds like the beginnings of maturity." Susan faked a gasp.

"Scary, isn't it?" She stood up. "Want more of your hot chocolate?"

"Yeah, let's finish off the lot." Susan stood up.

"Sit down."

"No, let me bring the cup to you. Easier to pour over the sink."

"Yeah, I guess you're right." Harry picked up the pan and carefully poured hot chocolate into Susan's cup and then refilled her own. "The weatherman says it's going to warm up to fifty degrees tomorrow."

"You wouldn't know it now. I don't mind snow but ice plucks my last nerve. Especially with the kids out driving in it. I know they have good reflexes but I also know they haven't experienced as much as we have and I wonder what they'll do in that first spinout. What if another car is coming in the opposite lane?"

"Susan, they'll learn and you can't protect them anyway."

"Yeah. Still."

"Aren't you amazed that Miranda has kept to her diet in the dead of winter?"

"Still baking things for the store and her friends. I never realized she had such discipline."

"Shows what love will do."

Miranda had lost her husband over ten years ago. By all accounts it was a happy marriage and when George Hogendobber passed away, Miranda consoled herself with food. Ten years of consoling takes a long time to remove. The incentive was the return of her high-school boyfriend, now a widower, for their high-school reunion. Sparks flew, and as Miranda described it, they were "keeping company."

"The football team."

"What?" Harry, accustomed to abrupt shifts in subject from her old friend—indeed she was often guilty of them herself—couldn't follow this one.

"I bet that's why Sam Mahanes is mad at Bruce Buxton. Because Bruce operates on all the football players, and didn't he just get a big write-up in the paper for his work on the safety? You know that kid that everyone thinks will make All-American next year if his knee comes back. And Isabelle Otey, the girls' basketball star. He gets all the stars. Jealousy?"

"Buxton's always gotten good press. Deserved, I guess. Being in Sam's position as director of the hospital I'd think he'd want Bruce to be celebrated, wouldn't you?" Harry asked.

"You've got a point there. Funny, every town, city, has closed little worlds where ego, jealousy, illicit love collide. Even the Crozet Preservation Society can be a tempestuous hotbed. Good God, all those old ladies and not one will forgive the other for some dreaded misdeed from 1952 or whenever."

"*Sex, drugs and rock and roll.*" Mrs. Murphy climbed back up on the chair to join the kitchen discussion.

"What, pussycat?" Harry reached over, stroking the sleek head.

"*People get mad at other people over juicy stuff.*"

"*Money. You forgot money.*" Tucker tidied up the floor, picking up her Milk-Bone debris.

"*A little bit around here wouldn't hurt,*" Pewter, ever conscious of her need for luxury, suggested.

"*Well?*" Mrs. Murphy pulled forward one side of her whiskers.

"*Well what?*" The rotund gray kitty leapt onto the remaining free kitchen chair.

"*You want money. Get your fat butt out there and earn some.*"

"*Very funny.*"

"*You could do shakedowns. People do it. Ask a small fee for not tearing up gar-*

dens, not leaving partially digested mice on the front steps, and not raiding the refrigerator."

Before unflattering words could be spoken, Harry leaned over, face-to-face with the cats. "I can't hear myself think."

"They certainly have many opinions," Susan said. "Not unlike their mother."

"M-m-m." Harry glanced out the window. "Damn."

Susan turned to observe.

"*More snow,*" Tucker lamented. Being low to the ground, she had to plow through snow. It was the only time she admitted to admiring larger canines.

_S_pike!" Isabelle Otey shouted from the sidelines as Harry, on the opposing team, rose up in the air, fist punching into the volley-ball. Although Isabelle's main sport was basketball, she loved most team sports and she enjoyed knowing the "townies," as residents of the county were called by UVA students. Languishing on the side-lines, she supported her team vocally.

Isabelle's team, knowing of Harry's skill, crouched in prepara-tion but not only was Harry strong, she was smart. She spiked the ball where they weren't.

"Game," the ref called as the score reached 21 to 18.

"Rocket arm." Cynthia Cooper slapped Harry on the back.

Isabelle, her crutches leaning against the bleachers, called out to Harry, "Too good, Mary Minor. You're too good."

Throwing a towel around her neck, Harry joined the coach of the opposing team. Coop, a deputy on the county's police force, joined them.

"Isabelle, they need you. Basketball team, too." Cynthia sat next to her.

"Four more weeks. You know it isn't really painful, the swelling went down fast but I don't want to go through this again so I'm doing what Dr. Buxton told me. What scares me more than anything is going out to the car, walking across the ice with crutches."

"Calling for rain tomorrow." Harry wiped her face with the white towel. "The good thing is it will melt some of the snow. Bad thing, won't melt all of it and at night everything will be more ice."

"Keeps me busy." Cynthia grinned. "I have to earn my salary somehow. You know, most people are pretty reasonable about fender benders. A few lose it."

"You must see a lot of stuff." Isabelle couldn't imagine being a law-enforcement officer. She envisioned a career as a pro basketball player.

"Mostly car wrecks, drunks, a few thefts and"—she smiled devilishly—"the occasional murder."

"I wonder if I could kill anyone."

"Isabelle, you'd be amazed at what you could do if your life depended on it," Cynthia said, running her fingers through her blonde hair.

"Sure. Self-defense, but I read about these serial killers in the paper or people who just go to a convenience store with a shotgun and blow everyone to bits."

"I have a few uncharitable thoughts in the post office from time to time," Harry giggled.

"Oh, Harry, you couldn't kill anyone—unless it was self-defense, of course," Isabelle said.

"It's not a subject I've thought much about. What about you, Coop? You're the professional."

"Most murders have a motive. Jealousy, inheritance money. The usual stuff. But every now and then one will come along that makes you believe some people are born evil. From my point of view our whole system allows them to get away with it."

"Are we going to have the discussion about suspending civil rights?" Harry asked Coop.

"No, we are not because I'm going to hit the showers. I've got a date tonight."

Both Harry and Isabelle perked right up. "With who?"

"Whom," Harry corrected Isabelle.

"With Harry's ex."

"For real?" Isabelle leaned forward.

"Take him. He's yours." Harry nonchalantly waved her right hand.

"Oh, don't be such a hardass. He loves you and you know it." Coop laughed at Harry; then her voice became animated. "That's it. Confess. You could have killed BoomBoom Craycroft when they had their affair."

"Ah, yes," Harry dryly replied. "The affair that ended my marriage. Actually, that's probably not true. Marriages end in a variety of ways. That was the straw that broke the camel's back. Could I have killed BoomBoom? No. She was no better than she should be. I could have killed him."

"So—why didn't you?" Isabelle, having not yet fallen in love, wanted to know.

"I don't know."

"Because you aren't a killer," Coop answered for Harry. "Everyone in this world has had times when they were provoked enough to kill but ninety-nine percent of us don't. I swear there are people who are genetically inclined to violence and murder, and I don't give a damn how unpopular that opinion is."

"Why are we sitting here discussing my former marriage?"

"Because I'm going on rounds with Fair tonight."

Fair Haristeen had invited Cynthia Cooper to accompany him when she expressed an interest in his work.

"I didn't know you were interested in horses." Isabelle stood up as Harry handed her her crutches.

"I like them but what I'm really interested in is seeing some of the farms from the back side. Meeting the barn workers. There might be a time when I need their help. And I'm curious about the technology."

"A lot of the stuff that's eventually used on humans is used in veterinary care first."

"Like the operation on my knee." Isabelle swung her leg over the bottom bleacher, stepping onto the wooden floor. "I wonder how many dogs, cats, and horses tore their anterior cruciate ligaments before I did." She paused a moment. "Har, I'm sorry if I put you on the spot about when your marriage broke up."

"Here, let me carry your purse." Harry picked up the alarmingly large satchel, throwing it over her shoulder. "Everyone in Crozet knows everything about everybody—or thinks they do. He fooled around and I got sick of it. And being married to a vet is like being married to a doctor. You can't plan on anything, really. Emergencies interrupt everything and sometimes days would go by and we'd hardly see one another. And I married too young."

They both watched with lurid fascination as BoomBoom Craycroft pushed open the gym doors. "Speak of the devil."

"Hi, girls." The buxom, quite good-looking woman waved to them.

"What are you doing here?" Harry asked, since BoomBoom had skipped gym in high school. Her only physical outlet, apart from the obvious, was golf.

"I saw everyone's cars parked outside and thought I might be missing something."

"You did. We beat the pants off them and then discussed whether we were capable of murder," Harry deadpanned.

"Ah. Well, the other reason I stopped by was that I saw Sheriff Shaw at Market Shiflett's store. Coop, he knows you have plans but will you work tonight? Bobby Yount came down with the flu and he thinks it's going to be one of those nights. He asked for you to call him in his car."

"Damn. Oh well. Thanks, Boom." Cynthia turned to Harry and Isabelle. "There goes my date with Fair." She knew this would tweak BoomBoom's raging curiosity.

Eyes widening, BoomBoom edged closer to Coop, hoping to unobtrusively pull her away from the other two women, to get the scoop on what sounded like a romance or at least a real date.

Harry took care of that by saying, "Gee, Boom, maybe you ought to fill in."

"You can be hateful. Really hateful." BoomBoom turned on her heel, the heel of an expensive snow boot bought in Aspen, and stormed off.

Isabelle's jaw dropped at the adults' antics.

"Spike." Coop clapped Harry on the back.

4

*I*n one of those weather shifts so common in the mountains, the next few days witnessed temperatures in the middle fifties. The sounds of running water, dripping water, and sloshing water filled everyone's ears as rivulets ran across state roads; thin streams crossed the low spots of meadows spilling into creeks; streams and rivers rose halfway to their banks, and were still rising.

The north faces of ravines held snow in their crevasses, lakes of pristine snow trackless since animals avoided the deep drifts. Ice, turquoise blue, was frozen in cascades over rocks on the north face of outcroppings.

Fearing the onslaught of another sweep of Arctic air soon, farmers scrubbed and filled water troughs, suburban gardeners added another layer of mulch on spring bulbs, car dealers washed their inventory.

An early riser, Harry knocked out her farm chores, rode one horse and ponied the other two, climbed up on the ladder to sweep debris out of the barn gutters and the house gutters also.

Mrs. Murphy hunted mice in the hayloft, careful not to disturb Simon, the sleeping possum, the hibernating blacksnake, or the huge owl dozing in the cupola. Pickings were slim, since the owl snatched everything up, so Simon ate grain from the tack room. However, neither the owl nor Murphy could eradicate the mice living in the walls between the tack room and the stalls. The mice would sit in their cozy home and sing just to torment the cat.

Pewter, not one to get her paws wet, reposed in the house, flopped on her back on the sofa. Tucker followed Harry, whom she considered her human mother, which meant her stomach was filthy but she too felt a great sense of accomplishment. She picked up the small twigs and branches which had fallen, dragging them over to the toolshed. Small though the corgi was, she could pull four times her weight.

She'd grab the fat end of a branch, plant her hind legs, jerk the weight up a bit, then backpedal. Her yard work always made Harry laugh.

By eleven Harry was ready to go to town this Saturday. Foxhunting was canceled since the rigs and vans would get stuck in the mud. Parking was always a problem on rainy or muddy days.

"Tucker, let's clean you up in the wash stall. You're not getting in the truck like that."

"*I could sit in one spot. I won't move.*" Her ears drooped since she wasn't thrilled about a bath in any way, shape, or form. On the other hand she'd happily sit in a puddle, leap into the creek. But there was something about soap married to water that offended her canine sensibilities.

"Come on."

"*Why don't you wash off Mrs. Murphy's paws, too?*" A gleeful malicious note crept into Tucker's voice as she headed into the barn.

"*I heard that, you twit.*" Murphy peeped over the side of the hayloft.

"Any luck?" Harry called to her beloved cat.

"No," came the growl.

"*Slowing down, aren't you?*" Tucker wanted to get a rise out of her friend. She was successful.

"*I could smoke you any day, lardass. Tailless wonder. Dog breath.*"

"Ha. Ha." Tucker refused to glance upward, which further infuriated the sleek, slightly egotistical cat.

"All right. If you won't stand I'm going to put you in the crossties," Harry warned the little dog.

Turning on the warm water, she hosed off Tucker's stomach, which now returned to its lovely white color.

Mrs. Murphy, keen to enjoy her friend's discomfort, hopped down from the hayloft to sit on the tack trunk in the aisle. "*Cleanliness is next to godliness.*"

"*You think you're so smart.*"

"*Cats are smarter than dogs.*"

"*That's what you say but it's not true. Cats don't save shipwrecked humans. Newfoundlands do that. Cats don't rescue people in avalanches. St. Bernards do that. Cats don't even herd cows or pull their weight in the fields. Corgis do that. So there.*"

"*Right. I told you cats were smarter than dogs. Further proof: You'll never get eight cats to pull a sled in the snow.*" She hurriedly washed her paws since she didn't want Harry to think she could wash her down.

"You two are chatty." Harry finished with Tucker, cut the hose, then wiped her off with an old towel.

A frugal soul, Harry saved everything. She had a pile of old towels in a hanging basket in the aisle outside the washroom. She also kept old towels in the tack room and she even picked up worn-out towels from the country club, purchasing them for a few dollars. For one thing, she needed them, but for another, Harry couldn't abide waste. It seemed like a sin to her.

"*Beauty basket.*" Murphy smiled slyly at Tucker.

"Thank you. I thought you'd never notice. If she's cleaning me up it means we're going somewhere. Wonder where?"

"Well, Augusta Co-op for feed, always high on Mom's list. Wal-Mart. A and N for jeans if she needs any. Oh, don't forget AutoZone. She'll pick up a case of motor oil, windshield-wiper fluid, oil filters. Then again she might go to James River Equipment to get oil and oil filters for the tractor. You know her. It won't be the jewelry store. She's the only woman I know who would like a new set of wrenches for Valentine's Day as opposed to earrings or even flowers."

Tucker laughed. "She loves flowers, though."

"She'll send Fair flowers." Murphy laughed because in most ways Harry was quite predictable, but then cats always knew humans better than humans knew cats.

"Let me look at you." Harry walked over to Mrs. Murphy, who didn't bother to run away from her. After all, if she did and made Harry mad, she wouldn't get to ride in the truck, and Murphy adored riding in the truck, lording it over lowly cars.

"Clean as a whistle."

Harry inspected each dark paw, the color of Mrs. Murphy's tiger stripes. "Pretty good there, pussycat."

"Told you."

Harry picked up an animal under each arm, strode outside and put them inside the truck. No dirty paw marks on her seat covers. To haul her horse trailer, a year ago she'd bought a new dually, a one-ton truck with four wheels in the back for greater stability. She'd agonized for years over this decision, fretting over the financial drain, but it worked out okay because Fair helped a bit and she watched her pennies. But for everyday running about she used the tough old 1978 Ford, four-wheel drive, half ton. She'd bought cushy sheepskin covers for the bench seat as she'd worn out the original sheepskin covers.

When she closed the door, she thought about Pewter, then

decided to let the cat sleep. True, Pewter would be grouchy on their return but she wanted to get rolling. Once a job was completed, Harry wanted to move on to the next one.

Her grandmother once said that Harry was "impatient of leisure," an apt description.

Once on the road they headed toward Crozet instead of going toward Route 64, which would take them to Waynesboro where Harry shopped. She avoided Charlottesville for the most part since it was so expensive.

"Bag Augusta Co-op." Murphy observed the sodden landscape.

Both animals were surprised when Harry turned down the long, tree-lined drive to Dalmally Farm, passed the chaste yet still imposing main house, and continued on to a lovely cottage in the rear not far from the stables, so beautiful most people would be thrilled to live in them.

"Little Mim?" Tucker was incredulous.

Little Mim, Harry's age, was not an especially close friend of Harry's. Little Mim had attended an expensive private school whereas Harry, Susan Tucker, BoomBoom, Fair, and the gang all attended Crozet High School. Then, too, Little Mim had a chip on her shoulder, which Harry usually knocked off. One would not describe them as close friends under any circumstances. Over the years they had learned to tolerate one another, always civil in dis-course as befit Virginians.

"Now don't get off the sidewalk or she won't allow you in the house. You hear?" Harry ordered.

"We hear."

Neither animal wanted to miss why Harry was calling on young Marilyn Sanburne.

Little Mim opened the door, greeted them all, seating Harry by the fireside. Her Brittany spaniel kissed Tucker, who didn't mind but felt the display of enthusiasm ought to be tempered. Murphy sat by the fireside.

"I'll get right to the point." Little Mim pushed over a bowl of candies toward Harry. "I'm going to run for mayor and I need your help."

"I didn't know your father was stepping down," Harry said innocently, for Jim Sanburne had been mayor of Crozet for almost thirty years. Jim was good at getting people together. Everyone said Mim had married beneath her when she selected Jim from her many beaus. She did, if money and class were the issues. But Jim was a real man, not some fop who had inherited a bundle of money but no brains nor balls. He worked hard, played hard, and was good for the town. His Achilles' heel proved to be women; but then men like Jim tend to attract more than their share. Mim used to hate him but over time they had worked things out. And she had to admit she'd married him on the rebound after a torrid affair with Dr. Larry Johnson back in the fifties. She'd had a breast cancer scare a few years back and that more than anything settled down Jim Sanburne.

"He's not," came Little Mim's blithe reply as she leaned back on her sofa.

"Uh, Marilyn, what's going on?"

"Crozet needs a change."

"I thought your dad was doing a great job."

"He has." She crossed one leg over the other. "But Dad wants to bring in more business and I think that's going to damage the town. We're doing fine. We don't need Diamond Mails."

"What's Diamond Mails?"

"Dad's trying to lure this big mail-order book club here from Hanover, Pennsylvania. You know those book clubs. There's all kinds of them: history, gardening, investing, best-seller clubs. He wants to build a huge warehouse out there just beyond the high school, where the abandoned apple-packing shed is, on the White Hall Road? The groves are still behind it—on that nasty curve."

"Sure. Everyone knows where it is."

"Well, that's where he wants them to relocate. He says he'll take the curve out of the road. The state will do it. Fat chance, I say, but Dad has friends in Richmond. Think about it. This monstrous ugly warehouse. About fifty to sixty jobs, which means sixty houses somewhere and worse, think of the mail. I mean, aren't you already on overload?"

"But they'll have their own shipping and mailing."

"Of course they will but the workers will go through you. Private mail."

"Well—that's true." Harry had just shoveled piles of Valentine's Day cards. A future with more canvas bags bursting with mail loomed in her imagination.

"It's time for our generation to make our contribution. You know everybody. People like you. I'd like your support."

"That's flattering." Harry's mind was spinning. She didn't want to offend Little Mim and she certainly didn't want to offend Mim's father, whom she liked. "This is an awful lot to think over. I'll need a little time. And I'm not crawfishing. I do want to think about it. Does your father know you plan to oppose him in the fall election?"

"Yes. He laughed at me and said there's many a slip twixt the cup and the lip." Her face darkened. "And I said that's for sure and who knows what will happen between now and November."

"What's your mother say?"

"Oh." Marilyn's face brightened. "She said she was neutral. She wouldn't get in the middle of it. That was really good of her, and I didn't expect that."

"Yes." Harry thought Big Mim was taking the only sane course of action.

"The other thing is that Dad and Sam Mahanes plan to raise the money for a new wing on the hospital, which I don't oppose but I want to make sure nothing slips under the table, you know, no sneaky bond issue. If they want a new wing then they can raise the money privately. Larry Johnson agreed to head the drive. Dad talked him into it."

"You wouldn't by any chance know what's going down between Sam and Bruce Buxton, would you?"

"Budget." She clipped her words.

"You mean the hospital?"

"Bruce wants everything brand spanking new. Sam preaches fiscal responsibility. That's what Dad says."

"Well, I guess people will always fight over resources." Harry had seen enough of that.

"It's turned into a feud too because other doctors support Bruce but the nurses support Sam. They say they know how to work the older equipment, old IVAC units and stuff, and they don't want stuff that's so technologically advanced that they have to go back to school to use it."

"Larry Johnson will calm them down." Harry knew that Larry and Mim had had an affair but as it was long before she was born she paid little attention to it. He'd come back from the war to establish a practice. He was handsome, but Mim's mother had felt he wasn't rich enough or classy enough for her daughter. She broke up the relationship and Mim had never forgiven herself for her cowardice. She should have defied her mother. Marrying Jim certainly was an act of defiance although too late for Larry, who had subsequently married a girl of his own class. As it turned out, Jim Sanburne had a gift for making money in construction, which over time had somewhat mollified Mrs. Urquhart, Mim's mother. And over time, Jim and Larry had become friends.

"He certainly will," Little Mim agreed.

"Thanks for asking me over. I've got to run some errands. The feed truck couldn't get into the farm last week and Thursday's delivery day. So I'd better get odds and ends just in case we get clobbered again. February is such a bitch."

"Doing anything for Valentine's Day?"

"No. You?"

"Blair's in Argentina on a photo shoot. So no." She paused. "Do you know if Bruce Buxton is dating anyone?"

Harry, wisely, did not comment on what Marilyn perceived of as a romance and what Blair Bainbridge thought of as a growing friendship. At least, that's what Harry thought was her peripatetic neighbor's position regarding Little Mim. "I don't know much about Bruce other than that he comes in for his mail. He's a little bit moody—but I never see him with a woman. Too busy, I guess."

Little Marilyn stood up, as did Harry. "You can talk to anyone you like about my candidacy. It's not a secret and I'll make a formal announcement March first."

"Okay." Harry reached the door, Mrs. Murphy and Tucker behind her, and then she turned and stopped. "Hey, did you get a chain letter last week?"

"I probably did but I throw them in the trash after reading the first line. Why?"

"Your mother got one and it upset her."

"Why?"

"Just junk mail, but you know how those things predict dire consequences if you don't send out the money and pass them along."

"A tidal wave will engulf your home in Tempe, Arizona." A gleam of humor illuminated Little Mim's attractive face.

"Right, that sort of thing. Oh well. I'll see you." Harry opened the door as her cat and dog scampered for the truck.

A tidal wave wasn't about to engulf Tempe, Arizona, but the creeks were rising fast in Crozet.

As Harry headed toward Route 64, she noticed Deputy Cynthia Cooper on Route 250 heading in the opposite direction, siren blaring, lights flashing. Harry pulled off the two-lane road.

"Another wreck, I'll bet," Harry said to her passengers.

"*Pretty bad.*" Mrs. Murphy, sharp-eyed, had noticed how grim Coop looked.

It occurred to Harry, the way things usually occurred to Harry—meaning it just popped into her head—that she didn't know what an IVAC unit was.

5

The straight corridors of lead pipes running overhead testified to the 1930s updating of the oldest section of the hospital. Like a metallic spiderweb, they led to the boiler room, a square cut deep down at the center of the old building. Smack in the middle of this deep square sat the enormous cast-iron boiler, as good as the day it was built in 1911.

Hunkered down, fingers touching the stone floor for balance, Rick Shaw, sheriff of Albemarle County, glanced up when his trusted deputy walked into the room.

She stopped a moment, surveyed the blood splattered on the wall ten feet away, then bent down on one knee next to her boss. "Jesus Christ."

Lying in front of her was the still-warm body of Hank Brevard. His throat had been cut straight across with such force that he was nearly decapitated. She could see his neckbone.

"Left to right." Rick pointed to the direction of the cut.

"Right-handed perp."

"Yep."

The blood had shot across the room when the victim was killed, his heart pumping furiously.

"Tracks?"

"No." Rick stood up. "Whoever did this must have come up behind him. He might not have much blood on him at all and then again even if he did, this is a hospital. Easy to dump your scrubs."

"I'll look around."

Coop hurried down the main corridor. She heard a door slam behind her, hearing the voices of the fingerprint and lab teams.

She pushed open grimy pea-green doors, each one guarding supplies, empty cartons, odds and ends. The old incinerating room was intact. Finally she found the laundry room for the old part of the hospital. Nothing there caught her eye.

Rejoining Rick she shrugged. "Nada." She paused a moment. "You know, I had a thought. I'll be back. But one quick thing. There may be laundry rooms for the newer sections of the hospital. We'll need to check them fast."

"Where are you going?"

"Incinerator."

She ran back down the corridor, opened the door, and walked in. In the old days the incinerating room burned body parts. These days such things were considered biohazards so they were hauled out of the hospital and burned somewhere else. It seemed odd, trucks of gallbladders and cirrhotic livers rolling down Main Street to their final destination, but the laws made such incongruity normal.

She searched each corner of the room, then picked up the iron hook and gingerly opened the incinerator. A sheet of flame swept near her face. Instinctively she slammed the door shut. If there had been any evidence tossed in there, it was gone now.

"Damn!" She wiped her face, put the hook back on its hanger, and left the room.

Rick had returned to the corpse. Wearing thin plastic gloves like the ones worn in the hospital he went through Hank's pockets. A set of keys hung from the dead man's belt. In his left pocket he had $57.29. His right pocket contained his car keys and a folded sheet of notepaper, a grocery list. Rick put everything back in Hank's pockets.

"All right, guys. Do what you can." He stood up again and propelled Coop away from the others. "Let's get to Hank's office before we notify the hospital staff."

"Boss, who called you? And why isn't anyone else here?"

"Bobby Minifee called me from his cell phone. I told him not to speak to anyone, to stay with the body. He's outside in the unmarked car with Petey."

Bobby Minifee was Hank's assistant.

Petey D'Angelo, a young officer on the force, showed a flair for his job. Both Rick and Coop, young herself at thirty-four, liked him.

"So you're hoping no one knows about this except for Bobby Minifee and whoever killed Hank?"

"Yeah. That's why I want to get to Hank's office. Bobby said it was at the northeast corner of the building. This is the center so we take that corridor." As they walked along in the dim underground light, Rick cursed. "Shit, this is like a maze from hell."

"You'd have to know your way around or you'd run into the Minotaur."

"I'll remember that." He vaguely remembered the Greek myth about the half-bull, half-man.

They arrived at an open door, the name Hank Brevard on a black sliding nameplate prominently displayed. The spacious office was jammed with file cabinets. Hank's desk, reasonably neat, had an old wooden teacher's swivel chair behind it and a newer, nicer chair in front for visitors.

Coop began flipping through drawers while Rick pulled out the file drawers.

"Records go back ten years. If this is only ten years I'd hate to see all of the records."

"I've got a pile of oil bills from Tiger Fuel. A picture of the wife and kids." She stopped. Who would get that awful job, telling them? She opened the long middle drawer. "Pencils, pens, a tiny light, paper clips. Ah . . ." She pulled the drawer out even farther. A few envelopes, lying flat, were at the rear. "Winter basketball league schedule. Repair bill for his car. A new alternator. Three hundred forty-nine dollars with labor. That hurts. And . . ." She turned. "You getting anything?"

"It will take half the force to go through these file cabinets and we'll do it, too, but no, nothing is jumping right out at me except the mouse droppings."

"Need Mrs. Murphy."

"You're getting as bad about that cat as Harry."

Coop opened the last letter; the end of the envelope had been slit. She took out the letter. "Sister Sophonisba will bring you good fortune." She laughed a low laugh. "Guess not." She glanced up at the date. "Guess he didn't make the twenty copies in time."

"What in the hell are you talking about?"

"A chain letter. Mail out twenty copies in three days. Well, it's past the three days."

Rick came over, snatched the chain letter, and read it. "'Ignore this letter at your peril.' Under the circumstances it's like a sick joke." He handed the letter back to Coop, who replaced it inside the envelope. "All right, let's find Sam Mahanes."

"Saturday night."

"H-m-m. I'll find Sam. You find out who's the head honcho Saturday night."

"Boss, when are we going to notify people?"

"Not until I talk to Sam and you talk to whoever. I think we're already too late. The killer's flown the coop."

"Or he's over our head." She looked up at the ceiling.

"There is that. I'll send Petey over to Lisa Brevard. He's going to have to learn to deliver the bad news. Might as well start now. I'll keep Bobby Minifee with me—for now."

"Rick, think Bobby could have done it?"

"I don't know. Right now I don't know much except that our killer is strong, very strong, and he knows where to cut."

6

*F*ace as white as the snow that remained in the crevices and cracks of the county, Bobby Minifee clung to the Jesus strap above the window on the passenger side of the squad car.

Rick lit up a Camel, unfiltered, opening the window a crack. "Mind?"

"You're the sheriff," Bobby said.

"You need me to pull over?"

"No. Why?"

"You look like you're going to be sick."

A jagged intake of breath and Bobby shook his head no. At twenty-one, Minifee was good-looking. He worked nights at the hospital to make ends meet. During the day he studied at Piedmont Community College. A poor boy, he had hopes of going on to Virginia Tech at Blacksburg. He was bright and he wanted a degree in mechanical engineering. The more he studied the more he realized he liked fluid dynamics, waves, water, anything that flowed. He wasn't sure where this would lead him but right now he was considering a different kind of flow.

"Sheriff, you must see stuff like that all the time. Blood and all."

"Enough. Car wrecks mostly. Well, and the occasional murder."

"I had no idea blood could shoot like that. It was all over the wall."

"When the jugular is cut, the heart, which is close to the throat, remember, pumps it out like a straight jet. It's amazing—the human body. Amazing. Was he still bleeding like that when you found him?" Rick slowly worked his way into more questions. When he arrived on the crime scene he had gone easy on Bobby because the kid was shaking like a leaf.

"No, oozing."

"Do you think he was still alive when you found him?"

"No. I felt for his pulse."

"How warm was his wrist or his hand when you touched him?"

"Warm. Not clammy or anything. Like he just died."

"The blood was bright red?" Bobby nodded yes, so Rick continued. "Sure? Not caked around the edges, or clumping up on his neck?"

"No, Sheriff. The reddest red I've ever seen, and I could smell it." He shook his head as if to clear his brain.

"It's the smell that gets you." Rick slowed down for a stoplight. "I'd say you were a lucky man."

"Me?"

"You, Minifee, could be lying there with Hank. I'd guess you were within five minutes of seeing the killer. Did you hear a footfall?"

"No. The boiler is pretty noisy."

"Freight train. Those old cast-iron babies go forever, though. Our ancestors expected what they built to last. Now we tear stuff down and build structures and systems that decay in seven years' time." He stubbed out his cigarette in the ashtray. "Didn't mean to lecture."

"Takes my mind off—"

"When I drive you home I'll give you a few names of people you can talk to, people who specialize in this kind of shock. It is a shock, Bobby, and don't do the stupid testosterone thing and go it alone."

"Okay." His voice faded.

"Did you like Hank Brevard?"

"He was a hardass. You know what I mean? One of those guys who likes to make you feel stupid. He always knew more than I did or anybody did. A real negative kind of guy."

"So you didn't like him?"

Bobby turned to directly stare at Rick. "Funny, but I did. I figured here's a real loser. In his fifties, mad about young guys coming up. Used to shit on me all the time about my studies. 'An ounce of experience is worth a pound of book learning,'" Bobby imitated Hank. "I kind of felt sorry for him because he really knew his stuff. He kept on top of everything and he could fix just about anything. Even computers and he's not a computer guy. He had a gift."

"Being plant manager of a hospital isn't a small job."

"No, but he couldn't rise any higher." Bobby sighed.

"Maybe he didn't want to."

"He did. You should have heard him gripe about baseball player salaries or basketball. He felt plenty trapped."

"Insightful for a young man."

"What's age got to do with it?" Bobby turned back to gaze out the window. The night seemed blacker than when they had driven away from the hospital.

"Oh, probably nothing. I'm just used to young people being self-absorbed. But then think of what I see every day."

"Yeah, I guess."

"The other men who worked under Hank, feel the same way you did?"

"I'm night shift. I don't know those guys."

"Can you think of anyone who might want to kill Hank?"

"He could really piss people off." Bobby paused. "But enough to kill him—" He shrugged. "No. I'd feel better if I could."

"Listen to me. When you return to work, stuff will fly through your head, when you first go back to that boiler room. Sometimes there's a telling detail. Call me. The other thing is, you might be scared for yourself. I know I would be. From my experience this doesn't look like a sicko killer. Sickos have signatures. Part of their game. Hank either crossed the wrong man or he surprised somebody."

"What could be down in the boiler room worth killing for?"

"That's my job." Rick coasted to a stop at Sam Mahanes' large, impressive home in Ednam Forest, a well-to-do subdivision off Route 250. "Bobby, come on in with me."

The two men walked to the red door, a graceful brass knocker in the middle. Rick knocked, then heard kids yelling, laughing in the background.

"I'll get it," a young voice declared, running feet heading toward the door.

"My turn," another voice, feet also running, called out.

The door swung open and two boys, aged six and eight, looked up in awe at the sheriff.

"Mommy!" The youngest scurried away.

"Hi. I'm Sheriff Shaw and we're here to see Daddy. Is he home?"

"Yes, sir." The eight-year-old opened the door wider.

Sally Mahanes, a well-groomed, very attractive woman in her middle thirties, appeared. "Kyle, honey, close the door. Hello, Sheriff. Hi, Bobby. What can I do for you?"

Kyle stood alongside his mother as his younger brother, Dennis, flattened himself along the door into the library.

"I'd like to see Sam."

"He's down in his shop. The Taj Mahal, I call it. Sam owns every gadget known to man. He's now building me a purple martin house and—" She smiled. "You don't need to know all that, do you?" She crossed over to the center stairwell, walked behind it, opened a door, and called, "Sam." Music blared up the stairs. "Kyle, go on down and get Daddy, will you?" She turned to Rick and Bobby. "Come on in the living room. Can I get you a drink or a bite to eat?"

"No, thanks." Rick liked Sally. Everyone did.

"No, thank you." Bobby sat on the edge of a mint-colored wing chair.

Sam, twenty years older than his wife, but in good shape and good-looking, entered the living room, his oldest son walking a step behind him. "Sheriff. Bobby?" He tilted his head a moment. "Bobby, is everything all right?"

"Uh—no."

"Boys, come upstairs." The boys reluctantly followed their mother's lead, Dennis looking over his shoulder. "Dennis. Come on."

Once Rick thought the children were out of earshot he quietly said, "Hank Brevard has been murdered in the boiler room of the hospital. Bobby found him."

Thunderstruck, Sam shouted, "What?"

"Right after sunset, I'd guess."

"How do you know he was murdered?" Sam was having difficulty taking this all in.

"His throat was cut clean from ear to ear," Rick calmly informed him.

Sam glanced to Bobby. "Bobby?"

Bobby turned his palms up, cleared his voice. "I came down the service elevator from the fourth floor. I checked the hot line for messages. None. So I thought I'd check the pressure of the boiler. Supposed to be cold tonight. I walked in and Hank was flat on his back, eyes staring up, and it's kind of strange but at first I didn't notice his wound. I noticed the blood on the wall. I thought maybe he threw a can of paint. You know, he had a temper. And then I guess I realized how bad it was and I knelt down. Then I saw his throat. I took his pulse. Nothing. I called the sheriff—"

Rick interrupted. "Sam, I ordered him not to call anyone else, not even you. I was there in five minutes. Coop took seven. He would have called you."

"I quite understand. Bobby, I'm very sorry this has happened to you. We'll get you some counseling."

"Thank you."

"Sam, running a hospital is a high-pressure job. I know you have many things on your mind, lots of staff, future building plans, but you did know Hank pretty well, didn't you?"

"Oh sure. He was there when I took over from Quincy Lowther. He was a good plant manager. Set in his ways but good."

"Did you like him?"

"Yes." Sam's face softened. "Once you got to know Hank, he was okay." A furrow crossed his brow, he leaned forward. "Have you told Lisa?"

"I have an officer over there right now."

"Unless you need to question her, Sally and I will go over."

"Pete will ask the basics if she's capable. I'll see her tomorrow. I'm sure she would be grateful for your comfort." Rick never grew accustomed to the grief of those left behind. "Do you have any idea who would kill Hank or why? Did he have a gambling problem? Was he having an affair? I know it's human nature to protect friends and staff but anything you know might lead me to his killer. If you hold back, Sam, the trail gets cold."

Sam folded his hands together. "Rick, I can't think of a thing. Bobby told you he had a hot temper but it flared up and then was over. We all shrugged it off. Unless he had a secret life, I really can't think of anyone or anything."

Rick reached in his shirt pocket. "Here. If you think of anything, tell me. Coop, too. If I'm not around, she'll handle it."

"I will." Sam shifted his gaze to Bobby. "Why don't you take off a few days—with pay. And"—he rose—"let me get those counselors' names for you."

"Sam, you get on over to Lisa. I'll give him some names." Rick stood up, as did Bobby.

"Right." Sam showed them to the door.

Rick drove Bobby home and as he pulled into the driveway of his rented apartment he asked, "Who's in charge of night maintenance?"

"Me."

"Upstairs?"

"You mean, who stands in for Sam?"

"Yeah."

"Usually the assistant director, Jordan Ivanic."

Rick clicked on the overhead light, scribbled the name on his notepad, tore off the sheet. "Can't hurt."

"Thanks." Bobby opened the squad car door, stepped out, then bent down. "Do you ever get used to this?"

"No, not really."

On the way back to the hospital, Rick called Coop. She'd questioned Jordan Ivanic. Not much there except she said he had nearly passed out. The body had been removed thirty minutes ago and was on its way to the morgue. The coroner was driving in to get to work immediately. She had ordered Ivanic to sit tight until Rick got there and she hadn't called the city desk at the newspaper, although she would as soon as Rick gave her the okay. If she helped the media, they would help her. It was an odd relationship, often tense, but she knew she'd better do a good job with the media tonight.

"Good work." Rick sighed over his car phone. "Coop, it's going to be a long night."

"This one's out of the blue."

"Yep."

7

t ten o'clock Saturday evening, Harry, already snuggled in bed, Mrs. Murphy on her pillow, Pewter next to her, and Tucker on the end of the bed, was reading *Remembrance of Things Past*. This was one of those books she'd promised herself to read back in college and she was finally making herself do it. Amazed at Proust's capacity for detail and even more amazed that readers of the day had endured it, she plowed through. Mostly she liked it, but she was only halfway through Volume I.

The phone rang.

"*Has to be Susan or Fair,*" Pewter grumbled.

"Hello." Harry picked up the receiver; the phone was on the nightstand by the bed.

"Har." Susan's voice was breathless. "Hank Brevard was found murdered at the hospital."

"Huh?" Harry sat up.

"Bobby Minifee found him in the boiler room, right after sunset. Throat slit. O-o-o." Susan shuddered.

Susan, one of Crozet's leading younger citizens, was on the hospital board. Sam Mahanes, responsible and quick, had called every member of the board, which also included Mim Sanburne and Larry Johnson.

"Oh, I wish I hadn't picked on him." Harry felt remorse. "Even if he was a crab."

"You know, Harry, a little expression of grief might be in order here."

"Oh, balls, Susan. I did express grief—a little, your qualifier! Besides, I'm talking to you."

A light giggle floated over the line. "He was a downer. Still—to have your throat slit."

"A swift death, I assume."

The animals pricked their ears.

Susan paused a second. "Do you think people die as they lived?"

"Uh, I don't know. No. No. I mean how can you die as you lived if someone sneaks up behind you and s-s-s-t."

"You don't have to produce sound effects."

"And how can you die as you lived if you're propped up in a hospital bed, tubes running everywhere. That's a slow slide down. I'd hate it. Well, I guess most people in that position hate it."

"Yeah, but I wonder sometimes. What I'm getting at is even if you're on that deathbed, let's say, you would approach death as you approached life. Some will face it head-on, others will deny it, others will put on a jolly face."

"Oh that. Yeah, then I suppose you do—I mean, you do die as you lived. Makes Hank's death even stranger. Someone grabs him and that's the end of it. Swift, brutal, effective. Three qualities I wouldn't assign to Hank."

"No, but we'd assign them to his killer."

Harry thought a long time. "I guess so. What's so weird is why anyone would want to kill Hank Brevard other than to stop hearing him talk about how our country is a cesspool of political corruption, Sam Mahanes works him too hard, and let's not forget Hank's theories on the Kennedy assassination."

"Fidel Castro," Susan filled in.

"I count that as part of the Kennedy assassination." Harry changed the subject slightly. "When do you have a board meeting? I'm assuming you'll have an emergency one."

"Which Mim will take over as soon as Sam opens it."

"He'd damn well better smile when she does it, too. She's one of the hospital's largest contributors. Anyway, imperious as Mim can be, she has good ideas. Which reminds me. I was going to call you tomorrow and tell you that Little Mim wants to run for mayor of Crozet."

"Tomorrow. You should have called me the minute you walked in the door," Susan chided her.

"Well, I kinda intended to but then I mopped the kitchen floor because it was a mud slide and then I trimmed Tucker's nails which she hates, the big baby."

"I do," Tucker replied.

"Has Marilyn lost her senses?"

"I don't know. She pressured me a little bit but not in a bad way. She said her father had done a pretty good job but she and he were falling on opposite sides of the fence over the development of Crozet, especially where industry is concerned, and you know, she did make a good point. She said it's time our generation got involved."

"We have been slugs," Susan agreed. "So what are you going to do? Between a rock and a hard place."

"I said I'd think about it. She'll ask you, too. We're all going to have to make choices and publicly, too."

"M-m-m, well, let me call Rev. Jones so he can get the Lutheran

Church ladies in gear. Miranda will organize the Church of the Holy Light group. We'd better all get over to Lisa Brevard's tomorrow morning."

"Right. What time are you going?"

"Nine."

"Okay. I'll be there at nine, too. See you." Harry hung up the phone, informed her three animal friends of the bizarre event, then thought about the morning's task.

Sitting next to grief disturbed her. But when her mother and father had died within a year of each other, she had cherished those people who came to share that grief, brought covered dishes, helped. How selfish to deny yourself to another person in need because their sorrow makes you uncomfortable. People feel uncomfortable for different reasons. Men feel terrible because they can't fix it and men are raised to fix things. Women empathize and try to soothe the sufferer. Perhaps the categories don't break down that neatly along gender lines but Harry thought they did.

She reached over and set her alarm a half hour early, to five A.M.

Then she clicked off the light. "Who in the world would want to kill Hank Brevard?"

"*Somebody very sure of himself,*" Mrs. Murphy sagely noted.

"*Why do you say that?*" Pewter asked.

"*Because he or she knew his way around the basement, probably he. He left the body. Humans who want to cover their tracks bury the body. At least, that's what I think. There's an element of arrogance in just leaving Hank crumpled there. And the killer either knew the schedule, the work routine, or he took the chance no one else would be in the basement.*"

"*You're right,*" Tucker said.

"Will you guys pipe down? I need my beauty sleep."

"*Try coma,*" Pewter smarted off.

The other two snickered but did quiet down.

8

*T*he scale needle dipped. Tom Yancy, the coroner, lifted off the brain. His assistant wrote down 2 *lb.* 9 *oz.*

Both Rick and Coop had attended enough autopsies not to be but so squeamish but Rick hated the part when the coroner sawed off the skullcap. The sound of those tiny blades cutting into fresh bone and the odor of the bone made him queasy. The rest of it didn't bother him. Most people got woozy when the body was opened from stem to stern but he could handle that just fine.

Each organ was lifted out of Hank Brevard.

"Liver's close to shot," Tom noted. "Booze."

"Funny. I never saw him drunk," Rick remarked.

"Well, it is possible to have liver disease without alcohol but this is cirrhosis. He drank."

"Maybe that's why he was so bitchy. He was hungover most of the time," Coop said.

"He wasn't exactly beauty and light, was he?" Tom poked around the heart. "Look. The heart is disproportionate. The left side should be about one half the right. His is smaller. Chances are he would have dropped sooner rather than later since this pump was working too hard. Every body has its secrets."

After the autopsy, Tom washed up.

"The obvious?" Rick asked.

"Oh yeah. No doubt about it. Left to right as you noted. Back to the bone. The C-3 vertebra was even nicked with the blade where I showed you. Damn near took his head off. A razor-sharp blade, too. Nothing sloppy or jagged about it. Very neat work."

"A surgeon's precision." Coop crossed her arms over her chest. She was getting tired and hungry.

"I'd say so, although there are plenty of people who could make that cut if the instrument was sharp enough. People have been slitting one another's throats since B.C. It's something we're good at." Tom smiled wryly.

"But the assailant had to be powerful." Rick hated the chemical smells of the lab.

"Yes. There's no way the killer could be female unless she bench-presses two hundred and fifty pounds and some do, some do. But from the nature of the wound it was someone a bit taller than Hank. Otherwise the wound would have been a bit downward, unless he drove Hank to his knees, but you said there was no sign of struggle at the site."

"None."

"Then my guess, which I'm sure is yours, too, is the killer came up behind him, was Hank's height or taller, grabbed his mouth and cut so fast Hank barely knew what hit him. I suppose there's comfort in that."

"How long did it take him to die?"

"Two minutes, more or less."

"There'd be no shortage of suitable knives in the hospital," Coop said.

"Or people who know how to use them." Tom opened the door to the corridor.

Flames darted behind the glass front of the red enamel wood-burning stove. Tussie Logan hung up the phone in the kitchen.

When she returned to the living room, Randy Sands, her house-mate and best friend, noticed her ashen face. "What's wrong?"

"Hank Brevard is dead."

"Heart attack?" Randy rose, walked over to Tussie, and put his arm around her shoulders.

"No. He was murdered."

"What?" Randy dropped his arm, turning to face her.

"Someone slit his throat."

"Good Lord." He sucked in his breath. "How primitive." He walked back to the sofa. "Come on, sit down beside me. Talking helps."

"I don't know what to say." She dropped next to him, which made his cushion rise up a little bit.

"Who just called to tell you?"

"Oh, Debbie, Jordan Ivanic's secretary. I guess we're all being called one by one. She said Sheriff Shaw or Deputy Cooper would be questioning us and—" She bit her lip.

"Not the most hospitable man but still." He put his arm around her again. "I'm sorry."

"You know, I was just in the post office with him and he was bitching and moaning about working a late shift because someone was sick or whatever. Half the time I tuned him out." She breathed in sharply. "Now I feel guilty as hell about it."

Randy patted her shoulder. "Everybody did that. He was boring."

A log popped in the stove.

Tussie flinched. "You never know. How trite." She rocked herself. "How utterly trite but it's true. Here I work in a hospital with these desperately sick children. I mean, Randy, we know most of them haven't a prayer but this shakes me."

"Working with terminally ill children is your profession. Having an associate or whatever you call Hank is quite another matter . . . having him murdered, I mean. Sometimes I open my mouth and I can't keep my tongue on track," he apologized.

"Start one sentence and bop into the second before you've finished the first." She smiled sadly. "Randy, I have to go back and work in that hospital and there's a killer loose." She shuddered.

"Now you don't know that. It could have been a random thing."

"A homicidal maniac goes to the hospital and selects Hank."

"Well," his voice lightened. "You know what I mean. It's got nothing to do with you."

"God, I hope not." She shuddered again and he kept patting her shoulder, keeping his arm around her.

"You'll be fine."

"Randy, I'm scared."

*O*nce a human being reaches a certain age, death, while not a friend, is an acquaintance. Sudden death, though, always catches people off guard.

Lisa Brevard, in her early fifties, was stunned by her husband's murder. To lose him was bad enough, but to have him murdered was doubly upsetting. She knew his faults but loved him anyway. Perhaps the same could have been said of him for her.

After Harry left the Brevards' she, Susan, Miranda Hogendobber, and Coop had lunch at Miranda's, she being the best cook in Crozet.

"When does Tracy get back?" Coop asked Miranda about her high-school boyfriend, who had struck up a courtship with her at their reunion last year.

"As soon as he sells the house." She placed the last dish on the table—mashed potatoes—sat down, and held Harry's and Coop's hands. Coop held Susan's hand so the circle was complete. "Heavenly Father, we thank Thee for Thy bounty to us both in food and in friendship. We ask that Thou sustain and comfort Lisa and the family in their time of sorrow. In Jesus' name we pray. Amen."

"Amen," the others echoed, as did the animals, who quickly pounced upon their dishes on the floor.

"You look wonderful, Miranda." Susan was proud of Miranda, who had lost forty pounds.

"Men fall in love with their eyes, women with their ears." Miranda smiled.

Coop glanced up, fork poised in midair. "I never thought of that."

"The Good Lord made us differently. There's no point complaining about it. We have to accept it, besides"—Miranda handed the bowl to her left—"I wouldn't have it any other way."

"Wh-o-o-o." Harry raised her eyebrows.

"Don't start, Harry." Miranda shot her a glance, mock fierce.

"I hope Tracy sells that house in Hawaii fast." Harry heaped salad into her bowl.

"I do, too. I feel like a girl again." Miranda beamed.

They talked about Tracy and others in the town but the conversation kept slipping back to Hank Brevard.

"Cooper, are you holding back?" Harry asked.

"No. It takes us time to piece together someone's life and that's what we have to do with Hank. Whatever he was, whatever he did, someone wanted him dead. Big time."

"He couldn't have, say, surprised someone doing—" Susan didn't finish her sentence as Harry jumped in.

"In the boiler room of the hospital?"

"Harry, someone could have been throwing evidence into the boiler," Susan defended herself.

"Most likely the incinerator." Cooper then described the bowels of the hospital building to them. "So you see, given the corridors, whoever did this knew their way around."

"Someone who works there," Miranda said.

"Or someone who services equipment there. We have to run down every single contractor, repairman, delivery boy who goes in and out of that place."

"What a lot of work," Miranda exclaimed. "Like that old TV show, *Dragnet*. You do throw a net over everything, don't you?"

Cooper nodded. "And sooner or later, Miranda, something turns up."

And so it did, but not at all where they thought it would.

10

*O*h boy." Harry closed the post office door behind her just as Rob Collier pulled up to the front door. She hurried through and opened the front door. "Monday, Monday."

"I've got stuff for you," he sang out as he hauled canvas bags stuffed with mail.

"Valentine's Day. I forgot." She grimaced as he tossed two extra bags onto the mailroom floor.

"Just think of all the love in those bags," he joked.

"You're in a good mood."

"I already got my Valentine's Day present this morning."

"No sex talk, Rob, I'm too delicate."

He grinned at her, hopped back in the big mail truck, and took off in the direction of White Hall, where a small post office awaited him.

"Think Mom got any love letters?" Tucker tugged at one of the bags.

"I don't think she cares. She has to sort her mail the same as everybody else's," Murphy replied.

"*Saint Valentine. There ought to be a Saint Catnip or how about a Saint Tuna?*" Pewter, having eaten a large breakfast, was already thinking about lunch at seven-thirty in the morning. "*I bet there wasn't even a real person called Valentine.*"

"*Yes, there was. He was a third-century martyr killed in Rome on the Flaminian Way under the reign of Claudius. There are conflicting stories but I stick to this one,*" Mrs. Murphy informed her gray friend.

"*How do you know all that?*" Pewter irritatedly asked.

"*Whatever Harry reads I read over her shoulder.*"

"*Reading bores me,*" Pewter honestly answered. "*Does it bore you, Tucker?*"

"*No.*"

"*Tucker, you can hardly read.*"

"*Oh yes I can.*" The corgi glared at Murphy. "*I'm not an Afghan hound, you know, obsessed with my appearance. I've learned a few things in this life. But I don't get what a murdered priest has to do with lovers. Isn't Valentine's Day about lovers?*"

With a superior air, Murphy lifted the tip of her tail, delicately grooming it, and replied, "*The old belief was that birds pair off on February fourteenth and I guess since that was the day Valentine was murdered somehow that pairing became associated with him.*"

"I'm sorry I'm late." Miranda bustled through the back door. "I overslept."

Harry, up to her elbows in mail, smiled. "You hardly ever do that."

They had spoken Sunday about the murder of Hank Brevard and, with that shorthand peculiar to people who have known one another a long time or lived through intense experiences together, they hopped right in.

"Accident?" Miranda placed packages on the shelves, each of which had numbers and letters on them so large parcels could be easily retrieved.

"Impossible."

"I guess I'm trying to find something—" A rap on the back door broke her train of thought.

"Who is it?" Harry called out.

"Miss Wonderful."

"Susan." Harry laughed as her best friend opened the door. "Help us out and make tea, will you? Rob showed up early and I haven't started a pot. What are you doing here this early, anyway?"

Susan washed out the teapot at the small sink in the rear. "Brooks' Volvo is in the shop so I dropped her at school. Danny's off on a field trip so I had to do it." Dan, her son, would be leaving for college this fall. "I swear that Volvo Ned bought her must be the prototype. What a tank but it's safe."

"What's the matter with it?" Miranda asked.

"I think the alternator died." She put tea bags in three cups, then came over to help sort mail until the water boiled. "You'd think most people would have mailed out their Valentine's cards before today."

"They did, but today"—Harry surveyed the volume of mail—"is just wild. There aren't even that many bills in here. The bills roll in here next week."

The teakettle whistled. "Okay, girls, how do you want your tea?"

"The usual," both called out, which meant Harry wanted hers black and Miranda wanted a teaspoon of honey and a drop of cream.

Susan brought them their cups and she drank one, too.

"*Murphy, what are you looking at?*"

"*This Jiffy bag smells funny.*" She pushed it.

Pewter and Tucker joined her.

"*Yeah.*" Pewter inhaled deeply. "*Addressed to Dr. Bruce Buxton.*"

Puzzled, Tucker cocked her head to the right and then to the left. *"Dried blood. Faint but it smells like dried blood."*

The cats looked at one another and then back to Tucker, whose nose was unimpeachable.

"All right, you guys. No messing with government property." Harry snatched the bag, read the recipient's name, then placed it on the bookshelves, because it was too large for his brass mailbox. "Ned tell you anything?" she asked Susan.

"No. Client relationship."

Susan's husband, a trusted and good lawyer, carried many a secret. Tempted though he was at times, he never betrayed a client's thoughts or deeds to his wife.

"Is Bobby Minifee under suspicion?" Miranda put her teacup on the divider between the public space and the work space.

"No. Not really," Susan replied.

"Anyone seen Coop?" Harry shot a load of mail into her ex-husband's mailbox.

"No. Working overtime with all this." Susan looked on the back of a white envelope. "Why would anyone send a letter without a return address, the mail being what it is. No offense to you, Harry, or you, Miranda."

"None taken." Harry folded one sack, now emptied. "Maybe they get busy and forget."

At eight on the dot, Marilyn Sanburne stood at the front door just as Miranda unlocked it.

"Good morning. Oh, Miranda, where did you get that sweater? The cranberry color compliments your complexion."

"Knitted it myself." The older woman smiled. "We've got so much mail—well, there's some mail in your box but you'd better check back this afternoon, too."

"Fine." Little Mim pulled out her brass mailbox key, opened the box, pulling out lots of mail. She quickly flipped through it, then loudly exclaimed, "A letter from Blair."

"Great." Harry spoke quickly because Little Mim feared Harry had designs on the handsome model herself, which she did not.

"I also wanted you ladies to be the first to know that I've rented the old brick pharmacy building and it's going to be my campaign headquarters."

"That's a lot of space," Harry blurted out.

"Yes." Little Mim smiled and bid them good-bye.

They watched as she got into her car and opened Blair's letter. She was so intent upon reading it that she didn't notice her mother pull up next to her.

Mim parked, emerged well-dressed as always, and walked over to the driver's side of her daughter's car. Little Mim didn't see her mother, so Big Mim rapped on the window with her forefinger.

Startled, Little Mim rolled down the window. "Mother."

"Daughter."

A silence followed. Little Mim had no desire to share her letter, and she wasn't thrilled that her mother saw how engrossed she was in it.

Shrewdly, she jumped onto a subject. "Mother, I've rented the pharmacy."

"I know."

"How do you know?"

"Zeb Berryhill called your father and wondered if he would be upset and your father said he would not. In fact, he was rather looking forward to a challenge. So that was that."

"Oh." Little Mim, vaguely disappointed, slipped the letter inside her coat. She was hoping to be the talk of the town.

"It must be good."

"Mother, I have to have some secrets."

"Why? Nobody else in this town does," said the woman who had secrets going back decades.

"Oh, everyone has secrets. Like the person who killed Hank Brevard."

"M-m-m, there is that. Well, I'm off to a Piedmont Environmental Council meeting. Happy Valentine's Day."

"You, too, Mumsy." Little Mim smiled entirely too much.

As she drove off, Big Mim entered the post office just as Dr. Buxton pulled into the parking space vacated by her daughter. At that moment her irritation with her daughter took over the more pressing gossip of the day.

"Girls," Mim addressed them, "I suppose you've heard of Marilyn's crackbrained plan to oppose her father."

"Yes," came the reply.

"*Not so crackbrained*," Pewter sassed.

Bruce walked in behind her, nodded hello to everyone, opened his box, and almost made it out the door before Miranda remembered his package. "Dr. Buxton, wait a minute. I've got a Jiffy bag for you."

"Thanks." He joined Mim at the divider.

She placed her elbows on the divider. "Bruce, what's going on at the hospital? The whole episode is shocking."

"I don't know. He wasn't the most pleasant guy in the world but I don't think that leads to murder. If it did a lot more of us would be dead." He looked Big Mim right in the eye.

"Was that your attempt at being subtle?" She bridled when people didn't properly defer to her.

"No. I'm not subtle. I'm from Missouri, remember?"

"*Two points.*" Murphy jumped onto the divider, Pewter followed.

"*Let me out,*" Tucker asked Harry, because she wanted to be right out there with Bruce and Mim.

"Crybaby." Harry opened the swinging door and the corgi padded out to the public section.

"You and Truman." Mim rapped the countertop with her long fingernails.

"Here we go." Miranda slid the bag across the counter.

"Ah." He squeezed the bag, examined the return address, which was his office at the hospital. "Huh," he said to himself but out loud. He flicked up the flat red tab with his fingernail, pulling it to open the top. He shook the bag and a large bloody scalpel fell out. "What the hell!"

11

*C*oop placed the scalpel in a plastic bag. Rick turned his attention to Dr. Bruce Buxton, not in a good mood.

"Any ideas?"

"No." Bruce's lower jaw jutted out as he answered the sheriff.

"Oh, come on now, Doc. You've got enemies. We've all got enemies. Someone's pointing the finger at you and saying, 'He's the killer and here's the evidence.'"

Bruce, a good four inches taller than Rick, squared his shoulders. "I told you, I don't know anyone who would do something like this and no, I didn't kill Hank Brevard."

"Wonder how many patients he's lost on the table?" Pewter, ever the cynic, said.

"He probably lost more due to bedside manner than incompetence," Mrs. Murphy shrewdly noted.

"He's not scared. I can smell fear and he's not giving off the scent." Tucker sniffed at Bruce's pants leg.

"You don't have to stop. You can still sort the mail. But first tell me where you saw the bag," the sheriff asked Harry, Miranda, and Susan, now stuck because she had dropped in to help. He had interviewed Mim first so that she could leave.

"*I saw it first,*" Tucker announced.

"*You did not. I did,*" Pewter contradicted the bright-eyed dog.

"*They don't care. If you gave these humans a week they wouldn't understand that we first noticed something peculiar.*" Murphy flopped on her side on the shelf between the upper and lower brass mailboxes.

"I saw the bag." Harry, feeling a chill, rolled up her turtleneck, which she had folded down originally. "Actually, Mrs. Murphy sniffed it out. Because she noticed it, I noticed it."

"*What a surprise.*" Mrs. Murphy's long silken eyebrows twitched upward.

"Look, Sheriff, I've got to be at the hospital scrubbed up in an hour." Bruce impatiently shifted his weight from foot to foot.

"When will you be finished?" Rick ignored Bruce's air of superiority.

"Barring complications, about four."

"I'll see you at your office at four then."

"There's no need to make this public, is there?" Bruce's voice, oddly light for such a tall man, rose.

"No."

"No need to tell Sam Mahanes unless it turns out to be the murder weapon and it won't."

Coop, sensitive to inflections and nuance, heard the suppressed anger when Bruce mentioned Sam Mahanes.

"Why are you so sure that isn't the murder weapon?" she asked.

"Because I didn't kill him."

"The scalpel could still be the murder weapon," she persisted.

"I heard that Hank was almost decapitated. You'd need a broad, long, sharp blade for that work. Which reminds me, the story was on all the news channels and in the paper. The hospital will be overrun with reporters. Are you sure you want to see me in my office?"

Rick replied, "Yes."

What Rick didn't say was that he wanted hospital staff to know he was calling upon Dr. Buxton. While there he would question other workers.

He couldn't be certain that the killer worked in the hospital. What he could be certain of was that the killer knew the layout of the basement.

Still, he hoped his presence might rattle some facts loose or even rattle the killer.

"Well, I'll see you at four." Bruce left without saying good-bye.

"Harry, what are you looking at?" Rick pointed at her.

"You."

"And?"

"You're good at reading people," she complimented him.

Surprised, he said, "Thanks"—took a deep breath— "and don't start poking your nose in this."

"I'm not poking my nose into it. I work here. The scalpel came through the mail." She threw up her hands.

"Harry, I know you." He nudged a mailbag with his toe. "All right then, you get back to work. Susan?"

"I dropped in for tea and to help. It's Valentine's Day."

"Oh, shit." He slapped his hand to his head.

"Shall I call in roses for your wife?" Miranda volunteered.

Rick gratefully smiled at her. "Miranda, you're a lifesaver. I'm not going to have a minute to call myself. The early days of a case are critical."

"I'd be glad to do that." Miranda moved toward the phone as Rick flipped up the divider and walked out the front. "Coop," he called over his shoulder. "Start on the basement of the hospital today. In case we missed something."

"Roger," she agreed as she reached in her pocket for the squad car keys.

They had arrived at the post office in separate cars.

"Any leads?" Harry asked the big question now that Rick was out of the post office.

"No," Cynthia Cooper truthfully answered. "It appears to be a straightforward case of murder. Brutal."

"Doesn't that usually mean revenge?" Susan, having read too many psychology books, commented.

"Yes and no." She folded her arms across her chest. "Many times when the killer harbors an intense hatred for the victim they'll disfigure the body. Fetish killings usually involve some type of ritual or weirdness, say, cutting off the nose. Just weird. This really is straightforward. The choice of a knife means the killer had to get physically close. It's more intimate than a gun but it's hard to get rid of a gun. Even if the killer had thrown it in the incinerator, something might be left. A knife is easy to hide, easy to dispose of, and not so easy to figure out. What I mean by that is, in lieu of the actual weapon, there are a variety of knife types that could do the job. It's not like pulling a .45 slug out of a body. Also, a knife is quiet."

"*Especially in the hands of someone who uses knives for a living.*" Murphy pounced on the third mailbag.

Cynthia, taller than the other women, reached her arms over her head and stretched. She was tired even though it was morning, and her body ached. She hadn't gotten much sleep since the murder.

Miranda hung up the phone, having ordered flowers for Rick's wife. "Did I miss anything? You girls talking without me?"

"No. No suspects," Harry told her.

"'Be sure your sin will find you out.' Numbers, thirty-second chapter." She reached into the third mailbag to discover that Murphy had wriggled inside. "Oh!" She opened the drawstring wider. "You little stinker."

"*Ha. Ha.*" Murphy backed farther into the mass of paper.

"Harry, if I get a day off anytime soon I'm coming out to your place." Coop smiled.

"Sure. If it's not too cold we can go for a ride. Oh, hey, before you go—and I know you must—have you heard that Little Mim is going to run against her father for the mayor's office?"

"No." Cynthia's shoulders cracked, she lowered her arms. "They'll be playing happy families at Dalmally." She laughed.

"Well." Harry shrugged, since the Sanburnes were a law unto themselves.

"Might shake things up a bit." Cynthia sighed, then headed for the door.

"I expect they've been shaken up enough already," Miranda wisely noted.

Harry made a quick swing to the hospital to find Larry Johnson. Although semi-retired, he seemed to work just as hard as he had before taking on Dr. Hayden McIntire as a partner.

She spied him turning into a room on the second-floor corridor.

She tiptoed to the room. No one was there except for Larry.

He looked up. "My article for the newsletter." He snapped his fingers. "It's in a brown manila envelope in the passenger seat of my car. Unlocked."

Harry looked at the TV bolted into the ceiling, at the hospital bed which could be raised and lowered. Then her attention was drawn to the IVAC unit, an infusion pump, a plastic bag on a pole. A needle was inserted usually into the patient's arm and the machine could be programmed to measure out the appropriate dose of medicine or solution.

"Larry, if I'm ever taken ill you'll be sure to fill my drip with Coca-Cola."

"Well, that's better than vodka—and I've seen alcohol sneaked into rooms in the most ingenious ways." He rolled the unit out of the way.

"Got any ideas?" She didn't need to say about the murder.

"No." He frowned.

"Nosy."

"I know." He smiled at her. "I apologize for not running my newsletter article to the post office. I'm a little behind today."

"No problem."

She left, found his red car easily, grasped the manila envelope, and drove home. Cindy Green, editor of the newsletter, would pick it up at the post office tomorrow.

If nothing else, the great thing about working at the post office was you were central to everybody.

12

*I*ntruder! Intruder!" Tucker barked at the sound of a truck rolling down the driveway.

Murphy, her fabulously sensitive ears forward, laconically said, "*It's Fair, you silly twit.*"

Murphy, like most cats, could identify tire sounds from a quarter of a mile away. Humans always wondered how cats knew when their mate or children had turned for home; they could hear the different crunching sounds. Humans could tell the difference between a big truck and a car but cats could identify the tire sounds of all vehicles.

Within a minute, Fair pulled up at the back door. Murphy jumped on the kitchen windowsill to watch him get out of the truck, then reach back in for a box wrapped in red paper with a white bow.

He glanced up at the sky, then walked to the porch, opened the door, stopped at the back kitchen door, and knocked. He opened the door before Harry could yell, "Come in."

"It's me."

"I know it's you." She walked out of the living room. "Your voice is deeper than Susan's."

"Happy Valentine's Day." He handed her the red box.

She kissed him on the cheek. "May I open it now?"

"That's the general idea." He removed his coat, hanging it on a peg by the back door.

"Wormer! Thanks." She kissed him again.

He'd given her a three-month supply of wormer for her horses. That might not be romantic to some women but Harry thought it was a perfect present. "I have one for you, too."

She skipped into the living room, returning with a book wrapped in brown butcher paper yet sporting a gleaming red ribbon and bow. "Happy Valentine's Day back at you."

He carefully opened the present, smoothing the paper and rolling up the ribbon. A leather-bound book, deep rich old tan with a red square between two raised welts on the spine, gave off a distinctive aroma. He opened to the title page. The publication date was in Roman numerals.

"Wow. 1792." He flipped through the pages. "Ever notice how in old books, the ink on the page is jet black because the letter was cut into the page?"

"Yeah. The best." She stood next to him admiring the book, an old veterinary text printed in London.

"This is a beautiful present." He wrapped his arms around her, kissing her with more than affection. "You're something else."

"*Just what, I'd like to know.*" Pewter, ready for extra crunchies, was in no mood for romance.

"I've got corn bread from Miranda, if you're hungry."

"*I am!*"

"Pewter, control yourself." Harry spoke to the now very vocal

Pewter, who decided to sing a few choruses from *Aïda* at high register.

Harry poured out crunchies.

"*Yahoo.*" The cat dove in.

"Anything to shut her up." Harry laughed.

"She's got you trained." He pulled two plates out of the cupboard as Harry removed the tinfoil from the corn bread.

As they sat and ate she told him what had happened at the post office with Bruce Buxton.

After hearing the story, Fair shook his head. "Sounds like a cheap trick."

"Bruce doesn't win friends and influence people," Harry truthfully remarked.

"Arrogant. A lot of doctors are like that, or at least I think they are. Then again, a lot of vets are that way. I don't know what there is about medical knowledge that makes a man feel like God but Bruce sure does."

"You've got a big ego but you keep it in check. Maybe that's why you're such a good equine vet. Not good, really, the best." She smiled at him.

"Hey, keep talking." He beamed.

"Come to think of it, I don't know anyone that really does like Bruce. Too bad they couldn't have seen his face when he opened the Jiffy bag. Whoever sent it would have been thrilled with their success. 'Course if they could see him in the hunt field, they'd have a giggle, too."

Bruce liked the excitement of the chase, the danger of it, but in truth he was a barely adequate rider, as was Sam Mahanes. It was one more place where they could get in each other's way.

"Don't you wonder what Hank Brevard did to get himself killed? I mean, there's another guy not exactly on the top of anyone's 'A' list." Fair cut a bigger piece of corn bread. "Still, you didn't want to kill him. Now I could see someone doing in Bruce. Being around him is like someone rubbing salt in your wound. Murder is—dislocating."

"For the victim." Harry laughed at him.

"You know what I'm trying to say. It calls everything you know into question. What would push you to kill another human being?"

"Yeah, we were talking about that at volleyball." She pressed her lips together and raised her eyebrows, her face a question. "Who knows?"

"Did you think Hank Brevard was smart?" Fair asked Harry. He trusted her reactions to people.

"M-m-m, he knew how to cover his ass. I'm not sure I would call him smart. I guess he was smart about mechanical things or he wouldn't have been plant manager. And I suppose he'd be pretty efficient, good at scheduling maintenance checks, that sort of thing."

"Yeah," Fair agreed.

"No sense of culture, the arts, enjoying people."

"Cut and dried. I think the only people really upset at his death are his wife and family." Fair stood up and walked to the window. "Damn, this weather is a bitch. This afternoon the mercury climbed to fifty-two degrees and here comes the snow."

"What's my thermometer read?" She had an outdoor ther-mometer on the kitchen window, the digital readout on the inside of the window.

"Twenty-nine degrees Fahrenheit."

"Let's hope it stays snow. I'm over it with the ice."

"Me, too. Those farm roads don't always get plowed and horses get colic more in the winter. Of course, if people would cut back their feed and give them plenty of warm water to drink I'd have fewer cases and they wouldn't have large vet bills. I can't understand people sometimes."

"Fair, it takes years and years to make a horseman. For most people a horse is like a living Toyota. God help the poor horse."

He looked back at her, a twinkle in his eyes. "Some horses know how to get even."

"Some people do, too."

13

The next day proved Fair's theory. The snow, light, deterred no one from foxhunting that morning. Foxhunting—or fox chasing, since the fox wasn't killed—was to Virginia what Indiana U. basketball was to the state of Indiana. Miranda happily took over the post office, since the mail lightened up after Valentine's Day. She felt Harry needed an outlet, since all she did was work at the post office and then work at the farm. As foxhunting was her young friend's great love, she liked seeing Harry get out. She also knew that Fair often hunted during the week and she still nurtured the hope that the two would get back together.

Cold though the day was when Harry first mounted up, the sun grew hotter and by eleven o'clock the temperature hit 47 degrees Fahrenheit. As the group rode along they looked at the tops of the mountains, each tree outlined in ice. As the sun reached the top of the mountains the crests exploded into millions of rainbows, glittering and brilliant.

At that exact moment, a medium-sized red fox decided to give everyone a merry chase.

Harry rode Tomahawk. Fair rode a 17.3 Hanoverian, the right size for Fair's height at six four and then some in his boots. Big Mim had so many fabulous horses Harry wondered how she chose her mount for the day. Little Mim, always impeccably turned out like her mother, sat astride a flaming chestnut. Sam Mahanes, taking the morning off, grasped his gelding, Ranulf, with a death grip, tight legs and tight hands. The gelding, a sensible fellow, put up with this all morning because they were only trotting. Once the fox burst into the open and the field took off flying, though, Sam gripped harder.

Coming into the first fence, a slip fence, everything was fine, but three strides beyond that was a stiff coop and the gelding had had quite enough. He cantered to the base of the jump, screeched on the brakes. Sam took the jump. His horse didn't. Harry, riding behind Sam, witnessed the sorry spectacle.

Sam lay flat on his back on the other side of the coop.

Harry hated to miss the run but she tried to be helpful so she pulled up Tomahawk, turning back to Sam, who resembled a turtle.

Dismounting, she bent down over him. "You're still breathing."

"Just. Wind knocked out of me," Sam gasped, a sharp rattle deep in his throat. "Where's Ranulf?"

"Standing over there by the walnut tree."

As Sam clambered up, brushed off his rear end, and adjusted his cap, Harry walked over to the horse, who nickered to Tomahawk. "Come on, buddy, I'm on your side." She flipped the reins over his head, bringing him back to Sam. "Sam, check your girth."

"Oh, yeah." He ran his fingers under the girth. "It's okay."

"There's a tree stump over there. Make it easy on yourself."

"Yeah." He finally got back in the saddle. "We'll have a lot of ground to make up."

"Don't worry. I'll get us there. Can you trot?"

"Sure."

As they trotted along, Harry was listening for hounds. She asked, "Ever been to Trey Young's?"

"No."

"He's a good trainer."

Still miffed because of his fall, which he blamed completely on his horse, Sam snapped, "You telling me I can't ride?"

Harry, uncharacteristically direct with someone to whom she wasn't close, fired back, "I'm telling you you can't ride that horse as well as you might. I take lessons, Sam. Ranulf is a nice horse but if you don't give with your hands and you squeeze with your legs, what do you expect? He's got nowhere to go but up or he'll just say, 'I've had enough.' And that's what he said."

"Yeah—well."

"This isn't squash." She mentioned his other sport. "There's another living creature involved. It's teamwork far more than mastery."

Sam rode along quietly. Ranulf loved this, of course. Finally, he said, "Maybe you're right."

"This is supposed to be fun. If it isn't fun you'll leave. Wouldn't want that." She smiled her flirtatious smile.

He unstiffened a little. "I've been under a lot of pressure lately."

"With Hank Brevard's murder, I guess."

"Oh, before that. That just added to it. Hospital budgets are about as complicated as the national budget. Everybody has a pet toy they want, but if everyone got what they wanted when they wanted it, we'd be out of business and a hospital is a business, like it or not."

"Must be difficult—juggling the egos, too."

"Bunch of goddamned prima donnas. Oh, you probably haven't heard yet. The blood on the blade sent to Bruce was chicken blood." He laughed a rat-a-tat laugh. "Can you believe that?"

Rick Shaw had contacted Sam when the blade arrived in the mail. When the lab report came back Rick called Bruce Buxton first and Sam second.

"Fast lab report."

"I guess chicken blood is easy to figure." Sam laughed again. "But who would do a fool thing like that? Sending something like that to Buxton?"

"One of his many fans," Harry dryly replied.

"He's not on the top of my love list but if you needed knee surgery, he'd be on top of yours. He's that good. When they fly him to operate on Jets linebackers, you know he's good."

She held up her hand. They stopped and listened. In the distance she heard the Huntsman's horn, so she knew exactly where to go.

"Sam, we're going to have to boogie."

"Okay."

They cantered over a meadow, the powdery snow swirling up. A stone wall, maybe two and a half feet, marked off one meadow from another.

Harry called to Sam, "Give with your hand. Grab mane. Never be afraid to grab mane." Taking her own advice she wrapped her fingers around a hunk of Tomahawk's mane and sailed over the low obstacle. She looked back at Sam and he reached forward with his hands, a small victory.

Ranulf popped over.

"Easy." Harry smiled.

The two of them threaded their way through a pine forest, emerging on a snowy farm road. Harry followed the hoofprints until they crossed a stream, ice clinging to the sides of the bank in rectangular crystals.

"Up over the hill." Sam pointed to the continuing tracks.

"Hounds are turning, Sam. We're smack in the way. Damn." She looked around for a place to get out of the way and hopefully not turn back the fox into the hounds, a cardinal sin in foxhunting.

Sam, not an experienced hunter, really thought they should charge up the hill but he deferred to Harry. After all, she'd been doing this since she was tiny.

She pushed Tomahawk into the woods, off the old farm road. They climbed over a rocky outgrowth and stopped about forty yards beyond that. No sooner had they reached their resting point than the red fox sauntered into view, loping onto the farm road. He crossed, hopped onto a log, trotted across that, scampered along, and then, for reasons only he knew, he flipped on the afterburners and was out of there before you could count to ten.

Within two minutes the first of the hounds, nose to the ground, reached the farm road.

Sam started to open his mouth.

"No," Harry whispered.

He gulped back his "Tally Ho," which would have only disturbed the hounds. "Tally Ho" was sometimes called out when a fox was seen but only if the witness was sure it was the hunted fox, and not a playful vagrant. Also, if hounds were close, the human voice could disturb them, making their task even more difficult. Yet it was human nature to want to declare seeing the fox.

In about five minutes, the Huntsman, the person actually controlling the hounds, who had been battling his way through a nasty briar patch, emerged onto the road.

"Okay, Sam, turn your horse in the direction in which you saw the fox, take off your cap, arm's length, and now you can say 'Tally Ho.' Hounds are far enough away."

Excited, Sam bellowed, "Tally Ho!"

The Huntsman glanced up, winked at Harry, and off he rode, following his hounds, who were on the line.

In another two minutes the field rode up, Harry and Sam joining them in the rear. Sam, being an inexperienced hunter, needed to
stay in the back out of other people's way.

They ran a merry chase until the red fox decided to disappear
and in that maddening way of foxes, he vanished.

Ending on a good note, the Huntsman, after conferring with the
Master, the person in charge of the hunt, called it a day.

Riding back, Sam thanked Harry.

Little Mim came alongside Harry as Sam rode up to Larry Johnson to chat. "Think he'll ever learn?"

"Yeah. At least he's not a know-it-all. He doesn't like advice but
eventually it sinks in."

"Men are like that," Little Mim remarked.

"Jeez, Marilyn, think of the women we know like that, too."

"You mean my mother?"

Harry held up her hand. "I didn't say your mother."

"Well, I mean my mother." Little Mim glanced over her shoulder to make certain Mother wasn't within earshot.

She wasn't. Big Mim at that very moment was pressing Susan
Tucker to join the Garden Club, which was supposed to be a great
honor, one Susan devoutly wished to sidestep.

Back at the trailers, people shared flasks, hot tea, and coffee.
Susan brought Mrs. Hogendobber's orange-glazed cinnamon buns.
The mood, already high, soared.

"Gee, I hate to go back to work." Harry laughed.

"Isn't it a shame we couldn't have been born rich?" Susan said
in a low voice, since a few around them had been, like Big Mim and
Little Mim.

"Breaks my heart."

"What'd Fair give you for Valentine's?"

"Wormer. Ivermectin."

"Hey, that's romantic." Susan, a hint of light sarcasm in her voice, laughed.

"I gave him a vet book from 1792."

"Hey, that is romantic." Susan handed Harry a mug of hot tea. "You know, this new thermos I bought is fabulous. We've been out for two and a half hours. I put the tea in the thermos a good hour before that and it's piping hot."

"Yeah. I'll have to get one."

Sam walked over. "Harry, thank you again."

"Sure." She offered him a sip of tea. He held up his flask.

"A wee nip before returning to drudgery." He bowed, said "Ladies," then walked back to his trailer.

Susan looked at Harry. Neither one said anything. They neither liked nor disliked Sam. He was just kind of there.

Larry Johnson, carrying a tin of chocolate-covered wafers, came over. "Ladies. Don't worry about the calories. I'm a doctor and I assure you any food eaten standing up loses half its caloric value."

They laughed, reaching in for the thin delicious wafers.

"How's the mood at the hospital?" Susan asked.

"Good. Hank's death may not be hospital related." He paused. "But as you know I'm semi-retired so I'm not there on a daily basis."

"Semi-retired." Harry laughed. "You work as hard as you did when I was a kid."

Larry had an office in his home. Years ago he had taken on a partner, Hayden McIntire, vowing he would retire, but he hadn't.

"That was good of you to nurse Sam along," Larry complimented Harry. "Soon you'll be in Tussie Logan's class. She's wonderful with children." He laughed low. "I kind of regard Sam in that light."

"You didn't see me stop to help him." Susan ate another chocolate-covered wafer. "The run was too good."

Larry, in his early seventies, was in great shape thanks to hunting and walking. "A straight-running fox, joy, pure joy. But you know, I think he doubled back. He was so close, then—" He snapped his fingers.

"Fox magic." Susan smiled, checked her watch, and sighed, "I'd better get home."

"Well, back to work for me." Harry finished off her tea.

om!" the animals cried when Harry bounced through the back door of the post office.

"Hi," she called out.

"Oh, Harry, I'm so glad you're here. Look." Miranda handed her an envelope, opened. "Susan left this for you. She forgot to give it to you at the breakfast."

Harry checked the addressee, Mrs. Tucker. "H-m-m." She slid out the letter and read it aloud:

"Dear Susan,

As you know, I will be running for the office of mayor of our great town of Crozet.

I need your support and the help of all our friends. I hope that you and Harry will throw your weight behind my campaign.

My top two priorities are keeping Crozet's rural character intact and working closely with the Albemarle Sheriff's Department to decrease crime.

Please call me at your earliest convenience.

Yours truly, Marilyn Sanburne."

Harry rattled the paper a bit. "Call her? She can nab any of us in the street. Waste of postage."

"It is rather formal but I don't think staying neutral is as easy as you do. And if we waffle too long we will gain her enmity," Miranda sensibly said.

"The thing is, did Little Mim get the support of the party?" Harry was surprised that Little Mim would write Susan. It seemed so distant.

"No. Not yet. Called Rev. Jones. He's on the party's local steering committee. He said that yes, they voted to support Marilyn at their monthly meeting, which was Saturday. They wouldn't make the vote public until the state steering committee gave them the okay. Herb said they would probably hear from them in Richmond today. He didn't anticipate any problems. After all, Jim Sanburne, as a Republican, has run unopposed for nearly twenty years. The Democrats ought to be thrilled with their candidate. Not only is someone challenging Jim, it's his own daughter."

Mrs. Murphy rubbed against her mother's leg. *"We checked in your mailbox, Mom. You only have bills."*

She reached down, scooping up the beautiful tiger cat. "Mrs. Murphy, you are the prettiest girl."

"Ha," came a croak from Pewter, reposing on her side on the small kitchen table in the rear. She wasn't supposed to be on the table but that never stopped her.

"Jealous." Harry walked over to rub Pewter's ears.

"I'm not jealous."

"Are, too," Murphy taunted her friend.

"Am not." Pewter stuck out her amazingly pink tongue, hot pink. Murphy wiggled out of Harry's arms, pouncing on Pewter. They

rolled over and over until they fell off the table with a thud, shook themselves, and walked in opposite directions as though this was the most natural event in the world.

"*Cats.*" Tucker cocked her head, then looked up at Harry. "*Mom, I don't like these chain letters. Something's not right.*"

Harry knelt down. "You are the best dog in the universe. Not even the solar system but the universe." She kissed her silky head.

"*Gag me.*" Pewter grimaced, then turned and walked over to sit beside Mrs. Murphy, their kitty spat forgotten as quickly as it flared up. "*Obsequious.*"

"*Dogs always are.*" Murphy knowingly nodded, but Tucker could have cared less.

Within the hour Coop drove up and ducked into the front door of the post office just as rain began to fall. "Is this weather crazy or what?" she said as she closed the door behind her.

"Find anything out?" Miranda flipped up the divider to allow her in the back.

"Yes." Cynthia stepped through, removed her jacket, and hung it on the Shaker peg by the back door. "Crozet Hospital is in turmoil. Jesus, what a petty place it is. Backstabbers."

"Well, I'm sorry to hear that. I guess a lot of businesses are like that." Mrs. Hogendobber was disappointed. "No suspects?"

"Not yet," Coop tensely replied.

"Oh great. There's a killer on the loose."

"*Harry.*" Mrs. Murphy spoke out loud. "*You humans rub shoulders with killers more than you imagine. I'm convinced the human animal is the only animal to derive pleasure from murder.*"

As though picking up on her cat's thoughts, Harry said aloud, "I wonder if Hank's killer enjoyed killing him."

"Yes," Cooper said without hesitation.

"Power?" Harry asked.

"Yes. No one likes to talk about that aspect of murder. The Lord giveth and the Lord taketh away. No one has the right to take another human life."

"Miranda, people may read their Bible but they don't follow the precepts," Cooper told her.

"You know, the post office is in the middle of everything. Action Central, sort of." Harry's eyes brightened. "We could help."

"No, you don't." Cooper's chin jutted out.

"*Yeah.*" Mrs. Murphy fluffed her tail. "*A little skulking about is good for a cat.*"

"*Which cat?*" Pewter grumbled.

Cynthia Cooper waggled her finger at Harry and Miranda. "No. No. And no."

15

A meeting that evening brought together the faithful of St. Luke's Lutheran Church, presided over by the Reverend Herbert C. Jones. While Harry considered herself a lapsed Lutheran she adored the Rev, as she called him. She liked that the Lutheran church—as well as the other churches in the area—hummed, a hive of activity, a honeycomb of human relationships. If someone was sickly, the word got out and people called upon him or her. If someone struggled with alcoholism, a church member who was also in Alcoholics Anonymous invariably paid a call.

The other major denominations, all represented, cooperated throughout major crises such as when someone's house burnt down. It wasn't necessary that the assisted person be a member of any church. All that mattered was that they lived in Crozet or its environs.

Reverend Jones, warm and wise, even pulled together the Baptist and Pentecostal churches, who had often felt slighted in the past by the "high" churches.

Mrs. Hogendobber, a devout member of the Church of the Holy Light, proved instrumental in this new area of cooperation.

Tonight the meeting concerned food deliveries and medical services for those people unable to shop for themselves and who had no families to help them. Often the recipients were quite elderly. They had literally outlived anyone who might be related to them. In other cases, the recipient was a mean old drunk who had driven away family and friends. The other group involved AIDS patients, most of whom had lost their families, self-righteous families who shrank into disapproval, leaving their own flesh and blood to die alone and lonely.

Harry especially felt a kinship with this group since many were young. She had expected to meet many gay men but was shocked to discover how many women were dying of the insidious disease, women who had fooled around with drugs, shared needles, or just had the bad luck to sleep with the wrong man. A few had been prostitutes in Washington, D.C., and when they could no longer survive in the city they slipped into the countryside.

Harry, well educated, was not an unsophisticated person. True, she chose country life over the flash and dash of the city, but she hardly qualified as a country bumpkin. Then again few people really did. The bumpkin was one of those stereotypes that seemed to satisfy some hunger in city people to feel superior to those not in the city. Still, she realized through this service how much she didn't know about her own country. There was an entire separate world devoted to drugs. It had its rules, its cultures, and, ultimately, its death sentence.

Sitting across from her in the chaste rectory was Bruce Buxton. Insufferable as he could be, he gave of his time and knowledge, visiting those that needed medical attention. How Herb had ever convinced him to participate puzzled her.

"—three teeth. But the jaw isn't broken." BoomBoom Craycroft read from her list of clients, as the group called their people.

Herb rubbed his chin, leaned back in his seat. "Can we get her down to the dentist? I mean can she get away from him and will she go if you take her?"

BoomBoom, becoming something of an expert on domestic violence, said, "I can try. He's perverse enough to knock out the new teeth if she gets them."

Bruce spoke up. He'd been quiet up to now. "What about a restraining order?"

"Too scared. Of him and of the system." BoomBoom had learned to understand the fear and mistrust the very poor had of the institutions of government and law enforcement. She'd also learned to understand that their mistrust was not unfounded. "I'll see if I can get her out of there or at least get her to the dentist. If I can't, I can't."

"You're very persuasive." Herb put his hand on his knee as he leaned forward in the chair a bit. His back was hurting. "Miranda."

"The girls and I"—she meant the choir at the Church of the Holy Light—"are going to replace the roof on Mrs. Weyman's house."

"Do the work yourself?" Little Mim asked. Though an Episcopalian and not a Lutheran, she attended for two reasons: one, she liked Herb, and two, it irritated her mother, who felt anything worth doing had to be done through the Episcopalian Church.

"Uh—no. We thought we'd give a series of concerts to raise money for the roof and then perhaps we could find some men to donate their labor. We're pretty sure we can come up with the money for materials."

"Here I had visions of you on the roof, Miranda." Herb laughed at her, then turned to Bruce, moving to the next topic on the agenda. "Any luck?"

Before Bruce could give his report they heard the door to the rectory open and close. Larry Johnson, removing his coat as he walked from the hall to the pleasant meeting room, nodded at them.

"Late and I apologize."

"Sit down, Larry, glad you could make it. Bruce was just about to give his report about the hospital cooperating with us concerning our people who can't pay for medical services."

Larry took a seat next to Miranda. He folded his hands, gazing at Bruce.

Bruce's pleasant speaking voice filled the room. "As you can imagine, the administration sees only problems. Both Sam and Jordan insist we could be liable to lawsuits. What if we treated an indigent patient who sued, that sort of thing. Their second area of concern is space. Both say Crozet Hospital lacks the space to take care of paying patients. The hospital has no room for the non-paying."

Little Mim raised her hand. Bruce acknowledged her.

"While I am not defending the hospital, this is true. One of my goals as a board member and your next mayor"—she paused to smile reflectively—"will be to raise the money privately for a new wing to be built."

"Thank you." Herb's gravelly voice was warm. He was amused at her campaigning.

"It is true," Bruce agreed, "but if we could bring people in on the off hours, before eight A.M. or after three P.M., we might at least be able to use equipment for tests. I know there is no way we will get hospital beds. Which brings me to the third area of concern voiced by the administration, the use of hospital equipment. The increased wear and tear on equipment, whether it's IVAC units, X-ray machines, whatever, will raise hospital operating costs. The budget can't absorb the increases." He breathed in. "That's where we are today. Obviously, Sam and Jordan don't want to give us a flat no. They are too politically astute for that. But there is no question in my mind that they evidence a profound lack of enthusiasm for our purpose."

The room fell silent, a silence punctuated when the door to the rectory was again opened and closed. The sound of a coat being removed, placed on the coatrack was heard.

Tussie Logan, face drawn, stepped into the room. "Sorry."

"Come on in. We know your time isn't always your own." Herb genially beckoned to her. "Bruce has just given us his progress report."

"Or lack thereof," Bruce forthrightly said. "Tussie, you look tired."

Bruce slid his chair over so she could wedge in between himself and BoomBoom.

"One of my kids, Dodie Santana, the little girl from Guatemala, had a bad day."

"We're sorry." Herb spoke for the group.

"We'll do a prayer vigil for her," Miranda volunteered.

"Thank you." Tussie smiled sadly. "I'm sorry. I didn't mean to interrupt."

"I'm glad you did." Larry lightened the mood. "It means I'm not the last one to the meeting."

"Back to business then." Herb turned to Bruce. "Can we get access to the hospital's insurance policy?"

"Yes. I don't think Sam would refuse that," Bruce replied.

"But who would understand it?" Larry said, half in jest. "I can't even understand the one Hayden and I have for the practice."

"I believe Ned Tucker will help us there." Herb watched as both Cazenovia and Elocution paraded into the room. "Harry?"

"I'll call him." She volunteered to ring up Susan's husband, a man well liked by all except those who crossed him in court.

"Bruce and I have spoken about this," Tussie joined in, "and—there's no way to delicately put this. Jordan Ivanic fears poor patients will steal—not just drugs, mind you, which would be most people's first thought, oh no, he thinks they'll steal toilet paper, pencils, you name it."

"He said that?" Harry was upset.

Cazzie jumped in her lap, which made her feel better. Elocution headed straight for Herb.

"Yes. Flat out said it." Tussie tapped her foot on the floor.

"My experience is the biggest thieves are the rich." Bruce rubbed his chin, perceived the frown on Little Mim's face, and hastened to add, "Think of Mike Milken, all those Wall Street traders."

"Well, I think I'd better call upon Sam and Jordan." Herb petted his youngest cat, who purred loudly.

"*Meow.*" Elocution closed her eyes.

Bruce said, "I've been able to secure the cooperation of at least one physician in each department. Our problem now is convincing Sam Mahanes to use a portion of the hospital, even a room, to initially screen these people.

"He did voice one other small concern." Bruce's voice was filled with sarcasm. "And that is the paying patients. He didn't feel they should be around the charity cases. It would engender hard feelings. You know, they're paying and these people aren't. So he said if we could find space and if we could solve the liability problem, where are we going to put people so they wouldn't be visible?"

"Ah." Herb exhaled.

Miranda shifted in her seat, looked down at the floor, took a deep breath, then looked at the group. "Bruce, you weren't born and raised here so I don't expect you to know this but sequestering or separating the poor gets us awfully close to segregation. In the old days the waiting rooms in the back were always for colored people. That was the proper and polite term then, and I tell you no white person ever went through the back door and vice versa. It brings back an uneasy feeling for me and I expect it does for those of us in this room old enough to remember. The other problem is that a goodly number of our people are African-American or Scotch-Irish. Those seem to be the two primary ethnic groups that we serve and I couldn't tell you why. Anyway, I think Sam needs to be—" She looked at Herb and shrugged.

"I know." Herb read her perfectly. After all, Sam was a Virginian and should know better, but one of the problems with Virginians was that many of them longed for a return to the time of Thomas Jefferson. Of course, none of them ever imagined themselves as slaves or poor white indentured servants. They always thought of themselves as the masters on the hill.

The group continued their progress reports and then adjourned for tea, coffee, and Miranda's baked goods.

BoomBoom walked over to Harry. "I'm glad we're working together."

"It's a good cause." Harry knew BoomBoom wanted to heal the wounds and she admitted to herself that BoomBoom was right, although every now and then Harry's mean streak would kick up and she wanted to make Boom squirm.

"Are you going to work on Little Mim's campaign?"

"Uh—I don't know but I know I can't sit in the middle. I mean, I think Jim's a good mayor." She grabbed another biscuit. "What about you?"

"I'm going to do it. Work for Little Mim. She's right when she says our generation needs to get involved and since Big Mim will sit this out we won't offend her."

"But what about offending Jim?" Harry asked as Cazenovia rubbed her leg.

"Some ham biscuit please."

Harry dropped ham for the cat.

"He won't be offended. I think he's going to enjoy the fight. Really, he's run unopposed for decades." BoomBoom laughed.

Bruce, his eye on BoomBoom—indeed, most men's eyes were on BoomBoom—joined them. "Ladies."

"Our little group has never had anyone as dynamic as you. We are so grateful to you." BoomBoom fluttered her long eyelashes.

"Oh—thank you. Being a doctor isn't always about money, you know."

"We are grateful." Harry echoed BoomBoom's praise minus the fluttering eyelashes. "Oh, I heard about the chicken blood on the blade. I'm sorry. Whoever did that ought to be horsewhipped."

"Damn straight," he growled.

"What?" BoomBoom's eyes widened.

This gave Harry the opportunity to slip away. Bruce could tell BoomBoom about his experience and she could flirt some more.

"Harry." Herb handed her a brownie.

When his back was turned from the table, both cats jumped onto it. People just picked up the two sneaks and put them back on the floor.

"M-m-m, this thing could send me into sugar shock." She laughed.

He lowered his voice as he stood beside her. "I'm very disturbed by Sam's attitude. I think some of the problem may be that it was Bruce who asked. Sam can't stand him, as you know."

"He'll talk to you."

"I think so." He picked up another brownie for himself. "There goes the diet. How are things with you? I haven't had any time to catch up with you."

"Pretty good."

"Good." His gravelly voice deepened.

"Rev, do me a favor. I know Sam will talk to you—even more than he'll talk to Rick Shaw or Coop. Ask him flat out who he thinks killed Hank Brevard. Something doesn't add up. I don't know. Just—"

"Preys on your mind." He dusted off his fingers. "I will."

"I asked Bruce before the meeting started what he thought

about Brevard," Harry continued. "He said he thought he was a royal pain in the ass—and maybe now the hospital can hire a really good plant manager. Pretty blunt."

"That's Bruce." Herb put his arm around her reassuringly, then smiled. "You and your curiosity."

Tussie, her back to Herb, reached for a plate, took a step back, and bumped into him. "Oh, I'm sorry."

"Take more than a little slip of a girl like you to knock me down."

"He's right. Tussie, you're getting too skinny. You're working too hard," Harry said.

"Runs in the family. The older we get, the thinner we get."

"Sure doesn't run in my family," Miranda called out from the other side of the table, worked her way around the three-bean salad, and joined them.

"Do you think poor patients will steal?" Harry asked Tussie.

"No," she said with conviction.

"Aren't hospitals full of drugs?" Miranda paused, then laughed at herself. "Well, that's obvious but I mean the drugs I read about in the paper—cocaine, morphine."

"Yes and those drugs are kept under lock and key. Any physician or head nurse signs in, writes down the amount used and for what patient, the attending physician then locks the cabinet back up. That's that."

"But someone like Hank Brevard would know how to get into the drug cabinets, storage." Harry's eyebrows raised.

"Well—I suppose, but if something was missing, we'd know." Tussie's lower lip jutted out ever so slightly.

"Maybe. But if he was smart, he could replace cocaine with something that looks like it, powdered something, powdered milk of magnesia even."

Slightly irritated, Tussie gulped down a bite of creamy carrot salad. "We'd know when the patient for whom the drug was prescribed didn't respond."

"Oh hell, Tussie, if they're sick enough to prescribe cocaine or morphine, they're probably on their way out. I bet for a smart person who knows the routine, who is apprised of patients' chances, it would be like stealing candy from a baby." Harry didn't mean to be argumentative; the wheels were turning in her mind, that was all.

"You watch too much TV." Tussie's anger flashed for a second. "If you'll excuse me I need to talk to BoomBoom."

Harry, Miranda, and Herb looked at one another and shrugged.

"She's a little testy," Miranda observed.

"Pressure," Herb flatly stated.

"I guess. Guess I wouldn't want to be working where someone was murdered. See, Miranda, imagine a murder at the post office— The body stuffed in the mailbag." Harry's voice took on the cadence of a radio announcer's: "The front and back door locked, a fortune in stock certificates jammed into one of the larger, bottom postboxes."

"Harry, you're too much." Miranda winked at her.

"And remember what I said about your curiosity, young lady. I've known you all your life and you can't stand not knowing something." Herb put his arm around her.

16

*I*t was that curiosity that got Harry in trouble. After the meeting she cruised by the hospital when she should have driven home. The puddles from the melted ice glistened like mica on the asphalt parking lot.

Impulsively, she turned into the parking lot, drove around behind the hospital to the back delivery door, which wasn't far from the railroad tracks. She paused a moment before continuing around the corner to the back door into the basement.

She parked, got out, and carefully put her hand on the cold doorknob. Slowly she turned it so the latch wouldn't click. She opened the door. Low lights ran along the top of the hallway. The dimness was creepy. Surely, the hospital didn't have to save money by using such low-wattage bulbs. She wondered if Sam Mahanes really was a good hospital director or if they were all cheap where the public couldn't observe.

She tiptoed down the main corridor which ran to the center of the building, the oldest part of the complex, built long before the

War Between the States. She counted halls off this main one but wished like Hansel and Gretel she had dropped bread crumbs, because if she ducked into some of these offshoot halls she wouldn't find her way out quickly. Bearing that in mind, she kept to the center hall corridor.

If she'd thought about it, she would have waited for this nighttime exploration until she could bring Mrs. Murphy, Pewter, and Tucker. Their eyes and ears were far better than her own, plus Tucker's sense of smell was a godsend. However, she'd taken them home after work, whipped off her barn chores, and hopped over to the rectory for the meeting.

She thought she heard voices somewhere to her right. Instinctively she flattened against the wall. She wanted to find the boiler room. The voices faded away, men's voices. A closed door was to her right.

Stealthily she crept forward. A flickering light to her right told her a room lay ahead. The voices sounded farther away, and then—silence.

The door behind her opened. She hurried away, slipping into the boiler room. She'd found her goal. Again, she flattened against the wall listening for the footfall but the boiler gurgling drowned out subtle sounds.

She quickly noted that another exit from the boiler room lay immediately in front of her on the other side of the room.

Glancing around she took a deep breath, walked to the boiler. The chalk outline of Hank's body had nearly worn away. She knelt down, then looked at the wall. Though it was scrubbed, a light bloodstain remained visible. Shuddering at the picture of blood spurting from Hank's throat, jetting across the room, she started to rise.

Harry never made it to her feet. A clunk was the last thing she heard.

17

*S*heriff Rick Shaw and Deputy Cynthia Cooper hit the swinging doors of the emergency room so hard they nearly popped off their hinges.

"Where is she?" Rick asked a startled ER nurse.

The young woman wordlessly pointed to yet another set of doors and Rick and Cynthia blasted through them.

A woozy Harry, covered with a blanket, lay on a recovery-room bed. A quiet night at the hospital, no other patients were in the room.

Jordan Ivanic, a sickly smile on his face, greeted the officers. "Why does everything happen on my watch?"

"Just lucky, I guess," Dr. Bruce Buxton growled at him. Bruce considered Jordan a worm. He had little love for any administrative type but Jordan's whining and worrying curdled his stomach.

"Well?" Rick demanded, staring at Bruce.

He pointed to the right side of Harry's head. "Blow. Blunt instrument. We've washed the blood off and cleaned and shaved the wound. I've taken X rays. She's fine. She's stitched up. A mild concussion at the worst."

"Harry, can you hear me?" Cynthia leaned down, speaking low.
"Yes."

"Did you see who hit you?"

"No, the son of a bitch."

Her reply made Cooper laugh. "You'll be just fine."

"Who found her?" Rick asked Jordan.

"Booty Weyman. New on the job and I guess he just happened to be checking the boiler room. We don't know how long she was there. We don't know exactly what happened either."

"I can tell you what happened," Rick snapped. "What happened was someone hit her on the head."

"Perhaps she fell and struck her head." Jordan tried to find another solution.

"In the boiler room? The only thing she could have hit her head on is the boiler and then we'd see burns. Don't pull this shit, Ivanic." Rick rarely swore, considering it unprofessional, but he was deeply disturbed and surges of white-hot anger shot through him. "There's something wrong in this hospital. If you know what it is you'd better come clean because I am going to turn this place upside down!"

Jordan held up his hands placatingly. "Now Sheriff, I'm as upset about this as you are."

"The hell you are."

This made Bruce laugh.

"Dr. Buxton." Cynthia leaned toward the tall man. "When did you get here?"

"I came a little bit after the meeting at the rectory, the God's Love group, you know. Herb's group."

"Yes." She nodded.

"Stopped at the convenience store. So I guess I got here about eight forty-five."

"Did you go to the boiler room yourself?" Rick asked the doctor.

"No. She was brought to me. When Booty Weyman found her, he had the sense to call for two orderlies. Scared to death." Bruce remembered Booty's face, which had been bone white.

"Well, if you won't be needing me I'll go back to my office." Jordan moved toward the door.

"Not so fast." Rick stopped him in his tracks. "I want the blueprints to the hospital. I want every single person's work schedule. I don't care who it is, doctors, receptionists, maintenance workers. I want the records for every delivery and trash removal for the last year and I want all this within twenty-four hours."

"Uh." Jordan's mind spun. "I'll do my best."

"Twenty-four hours!" Rick raised his voice.

"Is that all?" Jordan felt like he was strangling on his voice, which got thinner and higher the more nervous he became.

"No. Have you had any patients die under mysterious or unexplained circumstances?"

"Certainly not!" Jordan held his hands together.

"You would say that." Rick got right in his face.

"Because it's true. And I remind you, Sheriff," Jordan found a bit of courage to snap back, "whatever has occurred here has occurred in the basement. There are no patients in the basement."

"Get out." Rick dismissed him with a parting shot. "Twenty-four hours, on my desk."

"I'm glad he left before he peed his pants," Bruce snorted.

"I did not pee my pants," Harry thickly said.

"Not you, Harry. Just relax." Cooper reached for her hand.

Rick whispered to Bruce, "Do you think Harry is in danger?"

"No. Her pulse is strong. She's strong. She's going to have a tender spot on her head." He pointed to the three tiny, tight stitches. "These will drive her crazy."

"The blow was that hard?" Cynthia carefully studied the wound.

"No. If it was that hard, Deputy, we'd have seen a fracture in the skull. Whoever hit her knew just how hard to hit her, which is interesting in and of itself. But the skin on the skull is thin and tears quite easily. Also, as you know, the head bleeds profusely. If I hadn't stitched up what was a relatively small tear, the wound would have seeped for days. She might scratch it, infecting it or tearing it further. Something like this doesn't throb as much as it stings and itches." He smiled warmly. He had a nice smile, and it was a pity he didn't smile more often.

"Do you have any idea what she was doing here? Did she mention coming to the hospital at the meeting?" Cynthia asked.

"No."

Rick sighed, a long, frustrated sigh. "Mary Minor Haristeen can be damned nosy."

"Drugs." Harry tried to raise her voice but couldn't.

"What?" Cooper bent low.

"Drugs. I bet you someone is stealing drugs."

Bruce sighed. "It's as good an explanation as any other." He rubbed his hands together.

"I'd like to keep her here overnight for observation."

"I'll bring her home and stay with her," Cynthia declared.

"You said she was in no danger." Rick, understanding Cynthia's concern, stared at Bruce.

Bruce cupped his chin in his hand. "From a medical point of view, I don't think she is. She might suffer a bit of dizziness or nausea. Occasionally vision will be impaired. Again, I don't think the blow was that hard."

"She has a hard head." Rick smiled ruefully.

"You got that right, Sheriff." Bruce smiled back at him.

18

*O*w." Harry touched her stitches as Cynthia Cooper drove her home in her own truck.

As they walked through the kitchen door the two cats and dog ran up to their human, all talking at once. She knelt down, petting each one, assuring them that she was fine.

"*We can skip breakfast, Mom, if you feel punk,*" Tucker volunteered.

"*No, we can't.*" Pewter meowed so loudly that Cynthia laughed, walked over to the kitchen counter, and opened a can of food. "I'll do that."

"Harry, sit down. I can feed the cats and dog."

"Thanks."

Mrs. Murphy, now on Harry's lap, licked her face. "*We were scared. We didn't know where you were.*"

"*Yes, don't leave us. You need a brave dog to guard you.*" Tucker's lovely brown eyes shone with concern.

Harry rose to make a pot of coffee. Mrs. Murphy walked beside her.

"Sit down. I'll do it." Cynthia laughed to herself. Harry had a hard time accepting help. "Besides, I need to know what happened and your full concentration is necessary."

"I can concentrate while I make the coffee."

"All right." Coop put out the food as Pewter danced on her hind legs.

She then put down Tucker's food.

"*Thank you.*" Tucker dove in.

"Okay. I went to the God's Love meeting. Regular cast of characters. On the way home I thought, why not cruise the hospital." Harry noticed Mrs. Murphy sticking to her like glue. "Murphy, I'm fine. Go eat." The tiger cat joined Pewter at the food bowl.

"I'm with you so far." Coop smiled, wondering how Harry would explain nosing around the basement.

"Well, I zipped into the parking lot and I don't know, the idea occurred to me that I might go around the back. I did that and then, uh, no one was around so I thought, 'Why not just take a peek?' I wasn't being ghoulish. I just wanted to see the room where Hank was killed."

"What time was this?"

"Um, eight-thirty or nine."

"Go on." Cynthia began frying eggs.

"Okay. I parked the truck. I got out. The door was unlocked. I opened it. Boy, the lights are dim down there. Cheapskates. Well, I walked down the hall. I passed a closed door on my right and up ahead, a wash of light spilled out onto the hallway and I heard voices. Low. Sounded like men's voices. I froze. I couldn't hear too much because I was outside the boiler room. Anyway, I kind of slid down, peeked into the room and no one was there. They left but I don't know how. I mean I noticed doors in there but I didn't hear any open or close. I tiptoed over to the chalk marks for Hank's body.

Not much of them left. I knelt down and I looked over to the wall. At least I think that was the wall where the blood splashed. The light is pretty good in the boiler room. There's discoloration on that wall. I started to get up and—that's all I remember."

"Whoever hit you, hit you hard enough to knock you out but not hard enough to do damage, real damage. That tells me something."

"Oh?"

"Yes." Coop slid the eggs onto a plate Harry handed to her. "Either your assailant is a medical person who knows his stuff, or your assailant knew you and didn't want you dead. Or both. Everyone who knows you knows you can't resist a mystery, Harry. But the fact remains that the assailant was merciful, if you can stand the term, given your stitches."

"Ah." Harry hadn't thought of that, but then she hadn't had time to think of anything.

"*Merciful, hell,*" Tucker growled. "*Wait until I sink my fangs into his leg.*"

"*I'll scratch his eyes out,*" Mrs. Murphy hissed.

"*I'll regurgitate on him,*" Pewter offered.

"*Gross!*" Mrs. Murphy stepped back from the food bowl as Pewter pretended to gag.

"*Ha ha,*" Pewter giggled.

"Lot of talk around here," Harry teased her animals.

Coop, now sitting at the table, leaned across it slightly. "Harry, just what in the hell did you think you would find?"

Harry put down her fork, her eyes brightened. "I asked myself— what goes on in a hospital? Life or death. Every single day. Right?"

"Right." Coop shook pepper on her eggs.

"What if there is an incompetent doctor or technician? One false move on the anesthesiologist's part and—" She snapped her fingers to signify the patient dying instantly. "One misapplied medication to a critically ill patient or one angel of death." Noticing

Coop's noncomprehension she hastened to explain. "A nurse who wants to ease patient suffering or who decides old people can just die and get out of the way. There are hundreds of secrets at a hospital and I would imagine hundreds of potential lawsuits. We all know doctors cover for one another."

"Yes." Cynthia thoughtfully chewed for a moment. "But given that they have to work together and cooperate closely, I suppose that's natural. Cops cover for one another, too."

"But you see where I was heading. I mean what if there's a problem person, an inadequate physician?"

"I understand. I'm still trying to link this to Hank Brevard."

"Yeah, me, too. The head of maintenance wouldn't exactly be in the know if the problems were medical." She paused. "Unless he had to hide evidence or bury it or he was stealing drugs."

"Be pretty damn hard to cart a body or bodies out of the hospital. Or down into the basement. Now, drugs, that's another matter."

"Then, too, people do just fall into things. Pop up at the wrong place at the wrong time." Harry jabbed at her eggs.

"True."

"Or maybe Hank had a problem. Gambling. Just an example. They nailed him at work. It might not have anything to do with the hospital but I think it does. If he owed money I'd think a killer would shoot him somewhere else. There are easier ways to get rid of somebody than the way he was killed."

Coop reached for the toast. "That's what I think, too. Rick isn't saying much. But we're all traveling down the same path."

"I even thought it might have something to do with harvesting body parts. A patient dies. Okay, now how would the family know if the liver or kidneys have been removed?"

"The undertaker would certainly know if there'd been an autopsy but—he wouldn't necessarily know if any body parts or organs had been removed."

"If the family requests an autopsy, and most do, it would be so easy. And in some hospitals aren't autopsies a matter of course?"

"I don't know. They aren't in Crozet." Coop tapped her fork on the side of the plate, an absentminded gesture.

"Let's go with my thesis. Organs. A healthy kidney is worth five thousand dollars. In any given week a hospital the size of Crozet, a small but good place, will have, I would think, at least three people die with healthy organs. I mean that's not far-fetched. A black market for body parts."

"No, I guess it isn't far-fetched. We can clone ourselves now. So much for reproduction." Her light eyes twinkled.

"Don't worry. Old ways are the best ways."

The two women laughed.

"Where to hide the organs before shipping them out?" Cynthia knew how Harry thought.

"I've seen those containers. They're not big. They're packed with dry ice. They'd be pretty easy to stash away in the basement. A nurse or doctor might find that kidney upstairs but who goes into the basement? Hank was in on it. The key is in the basement. Maybe it really was part of the Underground Railroad once. There'd be lots of places to hide stuff in then."

"Well, it's a theory. However, I don't think organs last very long. And donor types need to match. Still, it's something to investigate."

"And I can help."

"There she goes again." Tucker shook her head.

"What I want from you is: keep your mouth shut. Don't you dare go back into that hospital without me. Whoever hit you knows you, I think. You show up again and the blow might be—" Coop's voice trailed off.

"Is Rick mad at me?"

"Of course. He'll get over it."

"Who found me?"

"Booty Weyman, new on the job. Poor kid. Scared him half to death."

"Who stitched me up?"

"Bruce Buxton—and for free."

Surprised, she said, "That was nice of him." Glancing at the old railroad clock on the wall, Harry said, "I've got to feed horses, turn out, and get to work."

"You feel good enough to go to work?"

"Yeah. It hurts but it's okay. I'll stuff myself with Motrin."

"How about if I help you feed? One other little thing, don't tell people where you were or what you were doing. You've got until you walk into the post office to come up with a good story. The last thing we need on this case is to draw everyone's attention to the basement. It's much better if the killer or killers get a little breathing room. Whatever they are doing, if indeed it does involve the hospital, let them get back to it. Rick is even delaying talking to Sam about this for twenty-four hours. The trick is to get everyone to let down, relax."

"You need someone on the inside."

"I know."

"Larry Johnson still goes to the hospital. He's true blue."

"Larry is in his seventies. I need a younger man," Coop replied.

"Old Doc might be in his seventies but he's tough as nails and twice as smart. I'd put my money on him any day of the week."

"Well—I'll talk to Rick."

"The other thing is, Larry's a deep well. Whatever goes in doesn't come out."

"That's true. Well, come on, girl. If you're going to work we'd better get cracking in the barn."

"Hey, Coop, thanks. Thanks for everything."

"You'd do the same for me."

As the humans pulled on their coats, Mrs. Murphy said to her friends, "She's right about one thing. A hospital is life and death."

19

"What happened to you?" Miranda practically shouted when Harry walked through the back door at work.

Harry trusted Miranda, a well-founded trust, so she told her everything as they sorted the mail, fortunately light that morning.

"Oh, honey, I hope you haven't stirred up a hornet's nest." The older woman was quick to grasp the implications of what Harry had done.

In fact, Miranda's mind clicked along at a speedy pace. Most people upon meeting her beheld a pleasant-looking woman somewhere in her early sixties, late fifties on a good day. She used to be plump but she'd slimmed down quite a bit upon reigniting the flame with her high-school beau. She wore deep or bright colors, had a real flair for presenting herself without calling undue attention to herself, the Virginia ideal. But most people who didn't really know Mrs. George Hogendobber had slight insight into how bright she was. She always knew where the power in the room resided, a vital political and social survival tool. She was able to separate the wheat from the chaff. She also understood to the marrow of her bones that actions have consequences, a law of nature as yet unlearned by a large portion of the American population. She'd happily chat about her garden, cooking, the womanly skills at which she excelled. It was easy for people to overlook her. Over the years of working together, Harry had come to appreciate Miranda's intelligence, compassion, and concern. Without being fully conscious of it she relied on Miranda. And for Miranda's part, she had become a surrogate mother to Harry, who needed one.

Naturally, the cats and dog understood Miranda perfectly upon first introduction. In the beginning Miranda did not esteem cats but Mrs. Murphy set her right. The two became fast friends, and even Pewter, a far more self-indulgent soul, liked Miranda and vice versa.

Pewter couldn't understand why humans didn't talk more about tuna. They mostly talked about one another so she often tuned out. Or as she put it to herself, tuna-ed out.

Nobody was tuning out this morning though. The animals were worried and simultaneously furious that Harry had taken such a dumb chance. Furthermore, she had left them home. Had they been with her, the crack on the head would have never happened.

As the morning wore on, everyone who opened a postbox commented on the square shaved spot on Harry's head and the stitches. Her story was that she clunked herself in the barn. Big Mim, no slouch herself in the brain department, closely examined the wound and wondered just what could do that.

Harry fibbed, saying she'd hung a scythe over the beam closest to the hayloft ladder and when she slid down the ladder—she never climbed down, she'd put a foot on either side of the ladder and slide down—she forgot about the scythe. The story was stupid enough to be believable.

After Mim left, Miranda wryly said, "Harry, couldn't you have just said you bumped your head?"

"Yeah, but I had to bump it on something hard enough to break skin." She touched the spot. "It hurts."

"I'm sure it does and it's going to keep hurting, too. You promise me you won't pull a stunt like that again?"

"I didn't think it was such a stunt."

"You wouldn't." Miranda put her hands on her hips. "Now look here, girlie. I know you. I have known you since you came out of the womb. You don't go around that hospital by yourself. A man's been murdered there."

"You're right. I shouldn't have gone alone."

Right before lunch Bruce Buxton walked in. "How's my patient?"

"Okay."

He inspected his handiwork. "A nice tight stitch if I do say so myself."

As luck would have it, Sam Mahanes dropped in. As no one had thought to tell Bruce to keep his mouth shut, he told Sam what happened to Harry.

"You stitched her up, discharged her, and didn't inform me?" Sam was aghast, and then wondered why Rick Shaw hadn't told him immediately.

"I'm telling you now," Bruce coolly responded, secretly delighted at Sam's distress.

"Buxton, you should have been on the phone the minute this happened. And whoever was down there"—he waited for a name to be forthcoming but Bruce was not about to finger Booty Weyman so Sam continued—"should have reported to me, too."

"First off, I gave the order to the orderlies that carried her up, to the nurse, to shut up. I said that I'd talk to you. I'm talking to you right now. I was going to call you this morning." He checked his watch. "In twenty minutes to be exact. Don't blow this out of proportion."

"I don't see how it could be any worse." Sam's jaw clapped shut.

"Oh, trust me, Sam Mahanes. It could be a lot worse."

This comment so enraged the hospital director that he turned on his heel, didn't even say good-bye to the ladies, and strode out of the post office, slamming the door hard behind him.

20

Sam, still angry, cut off Tussie Logan as she was trying to back into a space in the parking lot reserved for staff.

He lurched into his space, slammed the door, and locked his car as she finally backed in, avoiding his eyes.

Tussie knew the director's rages only too well. She didn't want to cross him and she didn't want her new Volkswagen Passat station wagon scratched.

Larry Johnson, who had been driving behind Sam at a distance, observed the incident.

Sam strode toward the hospital without a hello or wave of acknowledgment.

After parking, Larry stepped out of his car as Tussie reached into hers, retrieving her worn leather satchel.

"Good morning, Dr. Johnson." She put her arm through the leather strap while closing her car door.

"Morning, Tussie. He damn near knocked you out of the box."

"One of his funks."

"I don't remember Sam being such a moody man." The older doctor fell into step next to Tussie.

"The last month, I don't know, maybe it's been longer. He's tense, critical, nothing we do is right. Maybe he's having problems at home."

"Perhaps, but Sally seems happy enough. I've always prided myself on being able to read people but Sam eludes me."

"I know what you mean." She turned up the collar of her coat, an expensive Jaeger three-quarter-length that flowed when she walked. "I guess you've seen everything and everybody in this burg."

"Oh—some," he modestly replied. "But you still get surprised. Hank Brevard. I wouldn't think he could have aroused enough passion in another person to kill him."

"Maybe he got the better of someone in a car deal." She said this with little conviction.

Hank had put his mechanical skills to work in fixing up old cars and trucks. His hobby became an obsession and occasionally a source of income, as he'd repair and sell a DeSoto or Morgan.

"God knows, he had his own car lot. This last year he must have gone on a buying spree. I don't remember him having so many cars. I'd love to buy the 1938 Plymouth. No such luck." Larry laughed.

"I bet once the dust settles, Lisa will sell his collection."

"Ah, Tussie, even if she did, I couldn't afford the Plymouth."

"Maybe you could. You've got to treat yourself every now and then. And what we do is draining. There are days when I love it as much as my first day out of nursing school and there are other days when I'm tired of being on my feet."

"Tussie, you're a wonderful nurse."

"Why, thank you, Doctor."

He smiled. "Here we are." He opened the front door. "Into the fray." He paused a moment, then said, "If you see anything off track, please tell me. In confidence. If there is something wrong here we've got to get to the bottom of it. This is too good of a hospital to be smeared with mud."

Surprised, she shrank back a moment, caught herself, and relaxed. "I agree. I'm a little touchy right now. A little watchful."

"We all are, Tussie. We all are."

21

Four medium-sized smooth river stones anchored the corners of the large blueprint that covered Sheriff Shaw's desk. He leaned over with a magnifying glass, puffing away like a furnace on his cigarette. The smoke stung his eyes as he took the cigarette out, peered closely, then stuck the weed back in his mouth.

Cynthia, also smoking, stood next to him. She told herself she was smoking in self-defense but she was smoking because that little hit of nicotine coated her frayed nerve endings.

He pointed a stubby finger at the boiler room, put down the magnifying glass, and placed his left forefinger on the incinerator room. This meant his cigarette dangled from his mouth, a pillar of smoke rising into his eyes.

Coop took the cigarette out of his mouth, putting it in an ashtray.

"Thanks." He breathed deeply. "The two easiest spots to destroy evidence."

"Right but I don't think that's our problem."

"Oh?" His eyebrows arched upward. "I wouldn't mind finding the damned knife."

She shook her head. "That's not what I mean. We aren't going to find the knife. It's burned to a crisp or he could have taken it right back up to where those things are steamed or boiled or whatever they do. Fruitless."

"I like that word, fruitless." He reached for his cigarette again with his right hand but kept his left forefinger square on the incinerator room. "What's cooking in your brain?"

"You know, Harry had some good ideas last night."

"Oh." He snorted. "This I've got to hear."

"She thought maybe someone is pirating body parts, organs."

He paused a long time, lifted up his left finger. "Uh-huh."

"Or stealing drugs."

He stubbed out his cigarette, which he'd smoked to a nub. "The other angle is that his killer was an enemy and knew this would be the best place to find him. The killer knew his habits but then most killers do know the habits of their victims. Until Harry got clunked on the head I was not convinced the crime was tied to the hospital. Now I am."

"Me, too," Cooper agreed. "Now the trick is to find out what is at the hospital. What doesn't add up for me about Hank is—if he were in on a crooked deal, wouldn't he have lived higher on the hog? He didn't appear to live beyond his means."

Rick rubbed his chin. "Maybe not. Maybe not. Wait for retirement and then whoosh." He put his hands together and fluttered his fingers like a flyaway bird.

"He was in a position to take kickbacks from the fuel company, the electrical supply company, from everybody. For instance, those low-wattage lightbulbs. I noticed that when we answered Bobby Minifee's call. How do we know he didn't charge for a hundred watts but put in sixty? Now I went over those records and know that he didn't but I mean, for example. He was in the perfect position to skim."

"Wouldn't have been killed for that, I wouldn't reckon. But if he was corrupt it would have been damned hard to pin down. Those records, he could have falsified them, tossed the originals in the incinerator." He rubbed his palms together. "Right now, Coop, we're grasping at straws. We've got a hundred theories and not one hard piece of evidence."

"Let's go back to the basement. Don't tell Sam Mahanes when we're there. Call and tell him our people will be there next Tuesday. Then you and I go in Monday night. Someone might be tempted to move something out. But even if that isn't the case we'd be down there without Sam or anyone knowing except for the maintenance man on duty and we can take care of him."

"That's not a bad idea."

"A light hammer might help. To tap walls."

Rick smiled. She was good. She was good.

22

The sunset over the Blue Ridge Mountains arced out like a pin-wheel of fire, oriflamme radiating from the mountaintops, an edge of pink gold on each spoke.

Harry paused at the creek dividing her property from the property of her neighbor, Blair Bainbridge. The sky overhead deepened from robin's-egg blue to a blue-gray shot through with orange. She never tired of nature's palette.

As she watched the display, so did Rick Shaw and Cynthia Cooper. They had parked an unmarked car along the railroad tracks near the hospital just below the old switching station, a smallish stone house, finally abandoned by the C & O Railroad in the 1930s.

"Something," Rick murmured.

"Yeah." Coop watched the sky darken to velvety Prussian blue, one of her favorite colors.

One by one lights switched on, dots of life. Drivers turned on their headlights and Crozet's residents hurried home for supper.

"When's the last time you went to a movie?" Rick asked.

"Uh—I don't know."

"Me, too. I think I'll surprise the wife tomorrow night and take her to a movie. Dinner."

"She'll like that."

He smiled. "I will, too. I don't know how I had the sense to pick her and I don't know why she married me. Really."

"You're a—well, you know, you're a butch kind of guy. Women like that."

He smiled even bigger. "You think?"

"I think."

He pulled out a Camel, offered her one, then lit up for both of them. "Coop, when you going to find what you're looking for? You still thinking about Blair Bainbridge?"

She avoided the question. "I meant to ask you the other day, when did you switch to Camels? You used to smoke Chesterfields."

"Oh," he exhaled. "I thought if I tried different brands"—he inhaled—"I might learn to hate the taste."

"Marlboro."

"Merit." He grimaced.

"Kool."

"I hate menthol."

"Dunhill. Red pack."

"Do you know any cop can afford Dunhills?"

"No. Shepheard's Hotel. Another good but real expensive weed."

"You must be hanging out with rich folk."

"Nah—every now and then someone will offer me a cigarette. That's how I smoked a Shepheard's Hotel."

"M-m-m, what's the name of that brand, all natural, kind of thirties look to the pack, an Indian logo. Where did I see those?" he pondered.

She shrugged. "I don't know." A beat. "Viceroy."

"Pall Mall. You're too young to remember."

"No, I'm not. Winstons."

He waited, took a deep drag. "I go to the convenience store. I ask for cigarettes, I see all those brands stacked up and now I can't think of any more."

"Foreign ones. Gauloises. French. Those Turkish cigarettes. They'll knock your socks off."

He grunted, then brightened. "Virginia Slims."

"Lucky Strike."

"Good one. And I note you haven't answered my question about Blair Bainbridge."

Blair Bainbridge worked as a model, flying all over the world for photo shoots. Little Mim Sanburne more or less claimed him but he was maddeningly noncommittal. Many people thought he was the right man for Harry, being tall and handsome, but Blair and Harry, while recognizing one another's attractiveness, had evolved into friends.

"Well, he is drop-dead gorgeous," she sighed.

"Have I ever spoken to you about your personal life?" He turned toward her, his eyebrows quizzically raised.

"No." She laughed. "Because I don't have a personal life."

"Yeah, well, anyway, you and I have been on this force a good long time. You're in your thirties now. You're a good-looking woman."

"Thanks, boss." She blushed.

He held up his hand, palm facing her. "Don't waste your time on a pretty man. They're always trouble. Find a guy who works hard and who loves you for you. Okay, maybe he won't be the best-looking guy in the world or the most exciting but you know, for the long run you want a doer, not a looker."

She gazed out the window, touched that he had thought about her life away from work. "You're right."

"That's all I have to say on the subject except for one more little thing. He has to meet my approval."

They both laughed as the darkness gathered around them. They got out of the car and walked up the railroad tracks to the hospital, slipping down over the embankment at the track.

They opened the back door. Each carried a flashlight and a small hammer. Both had memorized the blueprints.

Wordlessly, they walked down the main corridor to the boiler room. The boiler room sat smack in the middle of the basement. The thick back wall of the room was almost two and a half feet of solid rock, an effective barrier should the boiler ever blow up. The other three walls each had corridors coming into the boiler room.

The only other hallway not connecting into the boiler room was one along the east side of the building at the elevator pool. But in the middle of that east hallway, intersecting it perpendicularly, the east corridor ran into the boiler room.

Offices and storage rooms were off of each of these corridors. The incinerator room was not far from the boiler room.

Coop tapped the solid wall behind the boiler. No empty sound hinted at a hidden storage vault. The two prowled each corridor, noted the doors that were locked, and checked every open room.

The silence downstairs was eerie. Every now and then they could hear the elevator doors open and close, the bell ringing as the doors shut. They heard a footfall and then nothing.

The opened rooms contained maintenance items for the most part. Each corridor had mops, pails, and waxers strategically placed so they could be easily carried to the elevators. A few rooms, dark green walls adding to the gloom, contained banks of ancient file cabinets.

As they quietly walked along, the linoleum under their feet

squeaked. Back at the oldest part of the building, the floors were cut stone.

"Three locked doors. Let's find Bobby Minifee." Rick checked his watch. They'd been in there for two and a half hours.

Bobby hadn't taken over Hank Brevard's old office until that morning. The Sheriff's Department had crawled over every inch, every record. Satisfied that nothing had escaped the department's attention, the office was released for use.

"Bobby." Rick knocked on the open door.

Startled, he looked up and blinked. "Sheriff."

"We need your help."

"Sure." He put down the scheduling sheet he was working on.

"Bring all your keys."

"Yes, sir." Minifee lifted a huge ring full of keys.

The three walked to the first locked door, which was between Hank's office and a storage room full of paper towels and toilet paper.

After fumbling with keys, Bobby found the right one. The door swung open and he switched on the light. Shelves were jammed with every kind of lightbulb imaginable.

"Hank made us keep this locked because he said people would lift the bulbs. They're expensive, you know, especially the ones used in the operating room."

"People would steal them."

Bobby nodded yes. "Hank used to say they'd steal a hot stove and come back for the smoke. I never saw much of it myself." He politely waited while Rick and Cooper double-checked the long room, tapping on walls.

"Okay. Next one," Rick commanded.

The second locked room contained stationery and office supplies.

"Other hot items?" Coop asked.

"Yep. It's funny but people think taking a notebook isn't stealing."

"Everyone's got that problem, I think." The sheriff flipped up a dozen bound legal pads. "If I had a dollar for every pen that's walked off my desk I'd have my car paid for."

The third room, much larger than the others and quite well lit, contained a few pieces of equipment—one blood-infusion pump, one oscillator, two EEG units.

"Expensive stuff." Rick whistled.

"Yes. Usually it's shipped out within forty-eight hours to the manufacturer or the repair company. For a hospital this size, though, we have few repairs. We're lucky that way." Bobby walked through the room with Rick and Cynthia. "Hank took care of that. He was very conscientious about the big stuff. He'd call the manufacturer, he'd describe the problem, he'd arrange for the shipping. He'd be at the door for the receiving. You couldn't fault him that way."

"Huh," was all Rick said.

"Where do you keep the organ transplants?"

Bobby's eyes widened. "Not here."

"You don't receive them at the shipping door?" Coop asked.

"Oh, no. The organ transplants are hand-walked right into the front door, the deliverer checks in at the front desk, and then they are delivered immediately to the physician. They know almost to the minute when something like that is coming in. Most of the time the patient is ready for the transplant. They'd *never* let us handle something like that."

"I see." Rick ran his forefinger over the darkened screen of an oscilloscope.

"Let's say someone has a leg amputated. What happens to the leg?" Coop asked.

Bobby grimaced slightly. "Hank said in the old days the body parts were burned in the middle of the night in the incinerator.

Now stuff like that is wrapped up, sealed off, and picked up daily by a company that handles hazardous biological material. They burn it somewhere else."

"In the middle of nowhere, I'd guess, because of the smell," Coop said.

"No." Rick shook his head. "They use high heat like a crematorium. It's fast." He smiled smugly, having done his homework.

"I'm glad. I wouldn't throw arms and legs into the incinerator." Bobby shuddered.

"People were tougher in the old days." Rick wanted another cigarette. "Well, thank you, Bobby. Keep it to yourself that we were here."

"Yes, sir."

Rick clapped him on the back. "You doing okay?"

"Yeah." He shrugged.

"Notice any change in the routine here?" Coop clicked off her flashlight as Bobby walked them to the back door by the railroad tracks.

"No. Not down here. I'm duplicating Hank's routine. He'll be hard to replace. We're not as efficient right now. At least, that's what I think."

"Anyone coming down here who usually doesn't come down?"

"Sam and Jordan made separate appearances. But now that things have settled a little it's business as usual—no one cares much about our work. If something isn't done we hear about it but we don't receive compliments for doing a good job. We're kind of invisible." A slight smirk played on Bobby's lips.

"Has anyone ever offered you drugs? Uppers. Downers. Cocaine?"

"No. I haven't even been offered a beer." The corners of his mouth turned up. Dimples showed when he smiled.

Rick opened the back door. "Well, if anything pops into your head, no matter how small it seems, you call me or Coop."

"I will."

The temperature had dropped below freezing. They climbed up the bank to the tracks.

"Ideas?"

"No, boss. Wish I had even one."

"Yeah, me, too."

It had never occurred to them to tap the floors in the basement.

That same Monday evening, Big Mim and Larry Johnson dined at Dalmally. Jim Sanburne was at a county commissioners' meeting in Old Lane High School, now the county offices, in Charlottesville. Little Mim was ensconced in her cottage.

The two dear friends chatted over fresh lobster, rice, vegetables, a crisp arugula salad, and a very expensive white Chilean wine.

"—his face." Larry laughed.

"I haven't thought of that in years." Mim laughed, remembering a gentleman enamored of her Aunt Tally.

He had tried to impress the independent lady by his skill at golf. They were playing in a foursome during a club tournament. He was in the rough just off the green, which was surrounded by spectators. The day being sultry, ladies wore halter tops or camp shirts and shorts. The men wore shorts and short-sleeved shirts, straw hats with bright ribbon bands.

The poor fellow hit a high shot off the rough which landed right in the ample bosom of Florence Taliaferro. She screamed, fell down, but the golf ball was not dislodged from its creamy resting place.

No one knew of a rule to cover such an eventuality. He couldn't play the ball but he was loath to drop a ball and take a penalty shot.

His contentious attitude so soured the caustic Tally that the moment they turned in their cards, she never spoke to him again.

Larry cracked a lobster claw. "I'm amazed at what flutters through my mind. An event from 1950 seems as real as what's happening this moment."

"Y-e-s." She drew out the word as the candlelight reflected off her beautiful pearls.

Larry knew Mim always dined by candlelight; the loveliness of the setting proved that Mim needed luxury, beauty, perfect proportion.

Gretchen glided in to remove one course and bring out another. She and Big Mim had been together since girlhood. Gretchen's family had worked for Mim's parents.

"What do you think about my daughter opposing my husband?"

"Ah-ha! I knew you had an agenda."

"She shouldn't do it," Gretchen piped up.

"Did I ask you?"

"No, Miss Mim, that's why I'm telling you. I have to get a word in edgewise."

"You poor benighted creature," Big Mim mocked.

"Don't you forget it." Gretchen disappeared.

Larry smiled. "You two would make a great sitcom. Hollywood needs you."

"You're too kind," Mim replied, a hint of acid in her tone.

"What do I think? I think it's good for Marilyn but it creates stress for the residents of Crozet. No one ever wants to offend a Sanburne."

"There is that," Mim thoughtfully considered. "Although Jim has been quite clear that he doesn't mind."

"It still makes people nervous. No one wants to be on the losing side."

"Yes." Mim put down her fork. "Should I tell her to stop?"

"No."

"I can't very well suggest to Jim that he step down. He's been a good mayor."

"Indeed."

"This is a pickle."

"For all of us." He chewed a bit of lobster, sweet and delicious. "But people will pay attention to the election; issues might get discussed. We've gotten accustomed to apathy—only because Jim takes care of things."

"I suppose. Crozet abounds with groups. People do pitch in but yes, you're right, there is a kind of political apathy. Not just here. Everywhere."

"People vote with their feet. They're bored, with a capital B."

"Larry," she leaned closer. "What's going on at Crozet Hospital? I know you know more than you're telling me and I know Harry didn't cut her head on a scythe."

"What's Harry got to do with it?"

"There's no way she could stay away from the murder site. She's been fascinated with solving things since she was tiny. Now really, character is everything, is it not?" He nodded assent so she continued. "I'd bet my earrings that Harry snuck over to the hospital and got hurt."

"She could have gotten hurt sticking her nose somewhere else. What if she snuck around Hank Brevard's house?"

"I know Mary Minor Haristeen."

A ripple of silence followed. Then Larry sighed. "Dear Mim, you are one of the most intelligent women I have ever known."

She smiled broadly. "Thank you."

"Whether your thesis is correct or not I really don't know. Harry hasn't said anything to me when I grace the post office with my presence." He was telling the truth.

"But you have been associated with the hospital for, well, almost fifty years. You must know something."

"Until the incident I can't say that I noticed anything, how shall I say, untoward. The usual personality clashes, nurses grumbling about doctors, doctors jostling one another for status or perks or pretty nurses." He held up his hand. "Oh yes, plenty of that."

"Really." Mim's left eyebrow arched upward.

"But Mim, that's every hospital. It's a closed world with its own rules. People work in a highly charged atmosphere. They're going to fall for one another."

"Yes."

"But there has been an increase of tension and it predates the dispatch of Hank Brevard. Sam Mahanes has lacked discretion, shall we say?"

"Oh."

"People don't want to see that sort of thing—especially in their boss or leader."

"Who?"

"Tussie Logan."

"Ah."

"They avoid one another in a theatrical manner. But Sam isn't always working during those late nights." He held up his left palm, a gesture of questioning and appeasement. "Judge not lest ye be judged."

"Is that meant for me?"

"No, dear. We've gracefully accommodated one another's faults."

"It was me, not you."

"I should have fought harder. I've told you that. I should have banged on this front door and had it out with your father. But I didn't. And somehow, sweetheart, it has all worked out. You married and had two good children."

"A son who rarely comes home," she sniffed.

"Whose fault is that?" he gently chided her.

"I've made amends."

"And he and his wife will finally move down from New York some fine day. Dixie claims all her children. But whatever the gods have in store for us—it's right. It's right that you married Jim, I married Annabella, God rest her soul. It's right that we've become friends over the years. Who is to say that our bond may not be even stronger *because* of our past. Being husband and wife might have weakened our connection."

"Do you really think so?" She had never considered this.

"I do."

"I shall have to think about it. You know, I cherish our little talks. I have always been able to say anything to you."

"I cherish them as well."

A car drove up, parked, the door slammed, the back door opened.

Jim slapped Gretchen on the fanny. "Put out a plate for me, doll."

"Sexual harassment."

"You wish," he teased her.

"Ha. You'll never know."

He strode into the dining room. "Finished early. A first in the history of Albemarle County."

"Hooray." Mim smiled.

Jim clapped Larry on the back, then sat down. "Looks fabulous."

"Wait until you taste the rice. Gretchen has put tiny bits of orange rind in it." Mim glanced up as Gretchen came into the room.

"Isn't that just perfect."

"Of course. I prepared it." Gretchen served Jim rice, vegetables, then tossed salad for him.

The small gathering chattered away, much to Larry's relief. Had he continued to be alone with Mim she would have returned to her questions about the hospital.

Mim had to know everything. It was her nature, just as solving puzzles was Harry's.

And Larry did know more than he was telling. He could never lie to Mim. He was glad he didn't have to try.

23

*E*ach day of the week grew warmer until by Saturday the noon temperature rose into the low sixties. March was just around the corner bringing with it the traditional stiff winds, the first crocus and robin, as well as hopes of spring to come. Everybody knew that nature could and often did throw a curveball, dumping a snowstorm onto the mountains and valley in early April, but still, the days were longer, the quality of light changed from diffuse to brighter, and folks began to think about losing weight, gardening, and frolicking.

Hunt season ended in mid-March, bringing conflicting emotions for Harry and her friends. They loved hunting yet they were thrilled to say good-bye to winter.

This particular Saturday the hunt left from Harry's farm. Given the weather, over forty people turned out, quite unusual for a February hunt.

As they rode off, Mrs. Murphy, Pewter, and an enraged Tucker watched from the barn.

"I don't see why I can't go. I can run as fast as any old foxhound." Tucker pouted.

"You aren't trained as a foxhound." Mrs. Murphy calmly stated the obvious, which she was forced to do once a year when the hunt met at Harry's farm.

"Ha!" The little dog barked. "Walk around, nose to the ground. Pick up a little scent and wave your tail. Then you move a bit faster and finally you open your big yap and say, 'Got a line.' How hard is that?"

"Tail," Pewter laconically replied.

"How's zat?" The dog barked even louder as the hounds moved farther away, ignoring her complaints.

"You haven't got a tail, Tucker. So you can't signal the start of something mildly interesting." The tiger was enjoying Tucker's state almost as much as Pewter, who did have the tiniest malicious streak.

"You don't believe that, do you?" She was incredulous, her large dog eyes imploring.

"Sure we do." The two cats grinned in unison.

"I could run after them. I could catch up and show my stuff."

"And have a whipper-in on your butt." Pewter laughed, mentioning the bold outriders responsible for seeing that hounds behaved.

"Wouldn't be on my butt. Would be on a hound's," Tucker smugly replied. "I think Mom should whip-in. She'd be good at it. She's got hound sense, you know, but only because I taught her everything she knows—about canines."

"Pin a rose on you," Pewter sarcastically replied.

Tucker swept her ears back for a second, then swept them forward. "You don't know a thing about hunting unless it's mice and you aren't doing so hot on that front. And then there's the bluejay who dive-bombs you, gets right in front of you, Pewter, and you can't grab him."

"Oh, I'd like to see you tangle with that bluejay. He'd peck your eyes out, mutt." Pewter's temper flared.

"Hey, they hit a line right at the creek bed." Mrs. Murphy, a keen hunter

of all game, trotted out of the barn, past Poptart and Gin Fizz, angry at not hunting themselves. She leapt onto the fence, positioning herself on a corner post.

Tucker scrambled, slid around the corner of the paddock, then sat down. Pewter, with far less enthusiasm, climbed up on a fence post near Mrs. Murphy.

"*Tally Ho!*" Tucker bounded up and down on all fours.

"*That's the Tutweiler fox. He'll lead them straight across the meadows and dump them about two miles away. He always runs through the culvert there at the entrance to the Tutweiler farm, then jumps on the zigzag fence. I don't know why they can't get his scent off the fence but they don't.*" Mrs. Murphy enjoyed watching the unfolding panorama.

"*How do you know so much?*" Tucker kept bouncing.

"*Because he told me.*"

"*When?*"

"*When you were asleep, you dumb dog. I hunt at night sometimes. By myself since both of you are the laziest slugs the Great Cat in the Sky ever put on earth.*"

"*Hey, look at Harry. She took that coop in style.*" Pewter admired her mother's form over fences.

"*She would have taken it better with me,*" a very sour Gin Fizz grumbled. "*Why she bothers with Tomahawk, I'll never know. He's too rough at the trot and he gets too close to the fence.*"

As Gin was now quite elderly, in his middle twenties, but in great shape, the other animals knew not to disagree with him.

Poptart, the young horse Harry was bringing along, respectfully kept quiet. A big mare with an easy stride, she couldn't wait for the day when she'd be Harry's go-to hunter. She listened to Gin because he knew the game.

As the animals watched, Miranda drove up with church ladies in tow. She cooked a hunt breakfast for Harry once a year and Harry made a nice donation to her Church of the Holy Light. Each lady emerged from the church van carrying plates of food, bowls of soup, baskets of fresh-baked breads and rolls. Although called a breakfast, hunters usually don't get to eat until twelve or one in the afternoon, so the selection of food ranged from eggs to roasts to biscuits, breads, and all manner of casseroles.

The enticing aroma of honey-cured Virginia ham reached Tucker's delicate nostrils. She forgot to be upset about the hounds. Her determination to trail the hounds wavered. Her left shoulder began to lean toward the house.

"*I bet Miranda needs help,*" Tucker said in her most solicitous tone.

"*Sure.*" Murphy laughed at her while observing Sam Mahanes lurch over a coop. "*That man rides like a sack of potatoes.*"

Sam was followed by Dr. Larry Johnson, who rode as his generation was taught to ride: forward and at pace. Larry soared over the coop, top hat not even wobbling, big grin on his clean, open face.

"*Amazing.*" Pewter licked a paw, rubbing it behind her ears.

"*Larry?*" Murphy wondered.

"*Yes. You know humans would be better off if they didn't know arithmetic. They count their birthdays and it weakens their mind. You are what you are. Like us, for instance.*" Pewter out of the corner of her eye saw Tucker paddle to the back door. "*Do you believe her?*"

"*She can't help it. Dogs.*" Murphy shrugged. "*You were saying?*"

"*Counting.*" Pewter's voice boomed a bit louder than she had anticipated, scaring Poptart for a minute. "*Sorry, Pop. Okay, look at you and me, Mrs. Murphy. Do we worry about our birthdays?*"

"*No. Oh boy, there goes Little Mim. She just blew by Mother. That'll set them off. Ha.*" Murphy relished that discussion, since Harry hated to be passed in the hunt field.

"*Tomahawk's too slow.*" Gin Fizz, disgruntled though he may have been, was telling the truth. "*She needs a Thoroughbred. Of course, Little Mim* can buy as many hunters as she wants and the price is irrelevant. Mom has to make her own horses. She does a good job, I think." Gin loved Harry.

"But I'm only half a Thoroughbred," Poptart wailed. "Does that mean we'll be stuck in the rear?"

Gin Fizz consoled the youngster. "No. You can jump the moon. As the others fall by the wayside, you'll be going strong as long as you take your conditioning seriously. But on the flat, well, yes, you might get passed. Don't worry. You'll be fine."

"I don't want to be passed," the young horse said fiercely.

"Nobody does." Gin Fizz laughed.

"Am I going to get to finish my thought or what?" Pewter snarled. She liked horses but herbivores bored her. Grass eaters. How could they eat grass? She only ate grass when she needed to throw up.

"Sorry." Gin smiled.

"As I was saying," Pewter declaimed. "Humans count. Numbers. They count money. They count their years. It's a bizarre obsession with them. So a human turns thirty and begins to fret. A little fret. Turns forty. Bigger. Is it not the dumbest thing? How you feel is what matters. If you feel bad, it doesn't matter if you're fifteen. If you feel fabulous like Larry, what's seventy-five? Stupid numbers. I really think they should dump the whole idea of birthdays. They wouldn't know any better then. They'd be happier."

"They'd find a way to screw it up." Murphy looked over at her gray friend. "They fear happiness like we fear lightning. I don't understand it. I accept it, though."

"They're so worried about something bad happening that they make it happen. I truly believe that." Pewter, for all her concentration on food and luxury, was an intelligent animal.

"Yeah, I think they do that all the time and don't know it. They've got to give up the idea that they can control life. They've got to be more catlike."

"Or horselike." Gin smiled wryly.

"They've got to eat some meat, Gin. I mean they're omnivores," Pewter replied.

"I'm not talking about food, I'm talking about attitude. Look at us. We have good *food, a beautiful place to live, and someone to love and we love her. It's a perfect life. Even if we didn't have a barn to live in, it's a perfect life. I don't think horses were born with barns anyway. Harry needs to think more like a horse. Just go with the flow."* Gin used an old term from his youth.

"Uh—*yeah,*" Pewter agreed.

Harry may not have gone with the flow but she certainly followed her fox. Just as Mrs. Murphy predicted, the Tutweiler fox bolted straightaway. Two miles later he scurried under a culvert, hopped onto a zigzag fence to disappear, ready to run another day.

The hounds picked up a fading scent but that fox didn't run as well as the Tutweiler fox. He dove into his den. After three hours of glorious fun, the field turned for home.

Harry quickly cleaned up Tomahawk, turning him out with Poptart and Gin Fizz, who wanted to know how the other horses behaved on the hunt.

Her house overflowed with people, reminding her of her childhood, because her mother and father had loved to entertain. She figured most people came because of Mrs. Hogendobber's cooking. The driveway, lined with cars all the way down to the paved road, bore testimony to that. Many of the celebrants didn't hunt, but the tradition of hunt breakfast was, whoever was invited could come and eat whether they rode or not.

Bobby Minifee and Booty Weyman attended, knowing they would be welcome. The Minifees were night hunters so Bobby would pick a good hillock upon which to observe hounds. Night hunters did just that, hunted at night on foot. Usually they chased raccoons but most hunters enjoyed hunting, period, and Bobby and Booty loved to hear the hounds.

Sam Mahanes had parted company with his horse at a creek bed and didn't much like Bruce Buxton reminding him of that fact.

Big Mim Sanburne declared the fences were much higher when

she was in her twenties and Little Mim, out of Mother's earshot, remarked, "Must have been 1890."

Everyone praised Miranda Hogendobber, who filled the table with ham biscuits, corn bread, smoked turkey, venison in currant sauce, scrambled eggs, deviled eggs, pickled eggs, pumpernickel quite fresh, raw oysters, salad with arugula, blood oranges, mounds of almond cake, a roast loin of pork, cheese grits and regular grits, potato cakes with applesauce, cherry pie, apple pie, devil's food cake, and, as always, Mrs. Hogendobber's famous cinnamon buns with an orange glaze.

Cynthia Cooper, off this Saturday, ate herself into a stupor, as did Pewter, who couldn't move from the arm of the sofa.

Tussie Logan and Randy Sands milled about. Because they lived together people assumed they were lovers but they weren't. They didn't bother to deny the rumors. If they did it would only confirm what everyone thought. Out of the corner of her eye, Tussie observed Sam.

Tucker snagged every crumb that hit the floor. Mrs. Murphy, after four delicious oysters, reposed, satiated, in the kitchen window. Eyes half closed, she dozed off and on but missed little.

"Where's Fair today?" Bruce Buxton asked Harry.

"Conference in Leesburg at the Marion Dupont Scott Equine Medical Center. He hates to miss any cooking of Mrs. Hogendobber's and the Church of the Holy Light but duty called."

"I think I would have been less dutiful." Bruce laughed.

"Mrs. H.," Susan Tucker called out. "You said you and the girls had practiced 'John Peel.'"

"And so we have." A flushed, happy Miranda held up her hands, the choir ladies gathered round, and she blew a note on the pitch pipe. They burst into song about a famous nineteenth-century English foxhunter, a song most kids learn in second grade. But the choir gave it a special resonance and soon the assemblage joined in on the chorus.

Mrs. H., while singing, pointed to Larry Johnson, who came and stood beside her. The choir silenced as he sang a verse in his clear, lovely tenor and then everyone boomed in on the chorus again.

After the choir finished, groups sporadically sang whatever came into their heads, including a medley of Billy Ray Cyrus songs, Cole Porter, and various nursery rhymes, while Ned Tucker, Susan's husband, accompanied them on the piano.

Many of the guests, liberally fueling themselves from the bar, upped the volume.

Tucker, ears sensitive, walked into Harry's bedroom and wiggled under the bed.

Pewter finally moved off the sofa arm but not to the bedroom, which would have been the sensible solution. No, she returned to the table to squeeze in one more sliver of honey-cured ham.

"*You're going to barf all over the place.*" Mrs. Murphy opened one eye.

"*No, I'm not. I'll walk it off.*"

"*Ha.*"

Coop grabbed another ham biscuit as people crowded around the long table. Larry Johnson, uplifted from the hunt and three desert-dry martinis, slapped the deputy on the back.

"You need to hunt with us."

"Harry gets after me. I will. Of course, I'd better learn to jump first."

"Why? Sam Mahanes never bothered." He couldn't help himself and his laughter sputtered out like machine-gun fire.

It didn't help that Sam, talking to Bruce, heard this aspersion cast his way. He ignored it.

"Harry would let you take lessons on Gin Fizz. He's a wonderful old guy." Susan volunteered her best friend's horse, then bellowed over the din. "Harry, I'm lending Gin Fizz to Coop."

"What a princess you are, Susan," Harry yelled back.

"See, that's all there is to it." Larry beamed. "And by the way, I'll catch up with you tomorrow."

Before Coop could whisper some prudence in his ear—after all, why would he need to see her—he tacked in the direction of Little Mim, who smiled when she saw him. People generally smiled in Larry's company.

Mrs. Murphy had both eyes open now, fixed on Coop, whose jaw dropped slightly ajar.

Miranda walked up next to the tall blonde. "I don't know when I've seen Larry Johnson this happy. There must be something to this hunting."

"*Depends on what you're hunting.*" Mrs. Murphy looked back out the window at the horses tied to the vans and trailers. Each horse wore a cooler, often in its stable colors. They were a very pretty sight.

24

*M*iranda stayed behind to help Harry clean up, as did Susan Tucker. The last guest tottered along at six in the evening, ushered out by soft twilight.

"I think that was the most successful breakfast we've had all year. Thanks to you." Harry scrubbed down the kitchen counters.

"Right," Susan concurred.

"Thank you." Miranda smiled. She enjoyed making people happy. "When your parents were alive this house was full of people. I remember one apple blossom party, oh my, the Korean War had just ended and the apple trees bloomed like we'd never seen them. Your father decided we had to celebrate the end of the war and the blossoms, the whole valley was filled with apple fragrance. So he begged, borrowed, and stole just about every table in Crozet, put them out front under the trees. Your mother made centerpieces using apple blossoms and iris, now that was beautiful. Uncle Olin, my uncle, he died before you were born, brought down his band from up Winchester way. Your dad built, built from scratch, a dance floor that he put together in sections. I think all of Crozet came to that party and we danced all night. Uncle Olin played until sunup, liberally fueled by Nelson County country waters." She laughed, using the old Virginia term for moonshine. "George and I danced to sunrise. Those were the days." She instinctively put her hand to her heart. "It's good to see this house full of people again."

"*They step on my tail,*" Pewter grumbled, rejoining them from the screened-in porch and, hard to believe, hungry again.

"*Because it's fat like the rest of you.*" Mrs. Murphy giggled.

"*Cats don't have fat tails,*" Pewter haughtily responded.

"*You do,*" Murphy cackled, then jumped on the sofa, rolled over, four legs in the air, and turned her head upside down so she could watch her gray friend, who decided to stalk her.

Pewter crouched, edged forward, and when she reached the sofa she wiggled her hind end, then catapulted up in the air right onto the waiting Murphy.

"*Banzai. Death to the Emperor!*" Pewter, who had watched too many old movies, shouted.

The cats rolled over, finally thumping onto the floor.

"What's gotten into you two?" Harry laughed at them from the kitchen.

"You know, I've heard people say that animals take on the personality of their owner," Miranda, eyes twinkling, said.

"Is that a fact?" Harry stepped into the living room as the cats continued their wrestling match with lots of fake hissing and puffing.

"Must be true, Harry. You lie on the sofa and wait for someone to pounce on you." Susan laughed.

"Humor. Small, pathetic, but an attempt at humor nonetheless." Harry loved it when her friends teased her.

"Is that true?" Miranda appeared scandalized. "You're a sex bomb?" The words "sex bomb" coming out of Miranda's mouth

seemed so incongruous that Harry and Susan burst out laughing and were at pains to explain exactly why.

Tucker, dead asleep in the hallway to the bedroom, slowly raised her head when the cats broke away from one another, ran to her, and jumped over her in both directions. Then Pewter bit Tucker's ear.

"*Pewts, that was mean.*" Mrs. Murphy laughed. "*Do the other one.*"

"*Ouch.*" Tucker shook her head.

"*Come on, lazybones. Let's play and guess what, there are leftovers,*" an excited, slightly frenzied Pewter reported before she tore back into the living room, jumped on the sofa, launched herself from the sofa to the bookcases, and miraculously made it.

Mrs. Murphy followed her. Once she and Pewter were on the same shelf, they had a serious decision to make: which books to throw on the floor.

Harry, sensing their plan, rushed over. "No, you don't."

"*Yes, we do.*" Mrs. Murphy pulled out *The Eighth Day* by Thornton Wilder.

Crash.

"I will smack you silly." Harry reached for the striped devil but she easily eluded her human.

Pewter prudently jumped off but not before knocking off a silver cup Harry had won years before at a hunter pace. As the clanging rang in her ears, the cat spun out, slid around the wing chair, bolted into the kitchen where Miranda was putting Saran Wrap over the remains of the honey-cured ham, stole a hunk of ham, and crouched under the kitchen table to gnaw it.

"I've seen everything." Miranda shook her head.

"Wild." Susan knelt down as Tucker walked into the kitchen. "Aren't you glad you're not a crazy kitty?"

"*Got her a piece of ham,*" Tucker solemnly stated.

Harry surveyed the house. "We did a good job."

Mrs. Murphy joined Pewter under the table.

"*I'm not giving you any. I stole this myself with no help from you.*"

"*I'm not hungry.*"

"*Liar,*" Pewter said.

Harry peered under the table. "Radical."

"*That's us.*" Murphy purred back.

Harry examined the ham before Miranda put it in the refrigerator. "She tore a hunk right off of there, didn't she?"

"Before my very eyes. Little savage."

"Might as well cut the piece smooth." Harry lifted up the corner of the Saran Wrap and sliced off the raggedy piece. She divided it into three pieces, one for each animal. "Hey, anyone want coffee, tea, or something stronger? The coffee's made. Will only take me a second to brew tea."

"I'd like a cuppa." Miranda wrapped the last of the food, then she reached into the cupboard, bringing down the loose Irish tea that Harry saved for special occasions. "How about this?"

"My fave." She turned to Susan. "What will you have?"

"Uh, I'll finish off the coffee and sit up all night. Drives Ned nuts when I do it but I just feel like a cup of coffee. Hey, before I forget, is that possum still in the hayloft?"

"Yeah, why?"

"I saved the broken chocolate bits for him."

"He'll like that. He has a sweet tooth."

"*I don't know how Simon*"—Mrs. Murphy called the possum by his proper name—"*can eat chocolate. The taste is awful.*"

"*I don't think it's so bad.*" Tucker polished off her ham. "*Although dogs aren't supposed to eat it. But it tastes okay.*"

"*You're a dog.*" Murphy shook her head in case any tiny food bits lingered on her whiskers. She'd follow this up with a sweep of her whiskers with her forearm.

"So?"

"You'll eat anything whether it's good for you or not."

Tucker eyed Mrs. Murphy, then turned her sweet brown eyes onto Pewter. "She eats anything."

"I don't eat celery," Pewter protested vigorously.

As the animals chatted so did the humans. The hunt was bracing, the breakfast a huge success, the house was cleaned up, the barn chores done. They sat and rehashed everything that had happened in the hunt field for Miranda's benefit as well as their own. Then all shared what they'd seen and heard at the party, laughing over who became tipsy, who insulted whom, who flirted with whom (everybody flirted with everybody), who believed it, who didn't, who tried to sell a horse (again, everybody), who tried to buy a horse (half the room), who tried to weasel recipes out of Miranda, various theories about Hank Brevard, and who looked good as well as who didn't.

"I heard only twenty people attended Hank's funeral." Miranda felt badly that a man wasn't well liked enough to pack the church. It is one's last social engagement, after all.

"As you sow so ye shall reap." Harry quoted the Bible not quite accurately to Miranda, which made the older woman smile.

"Some people never learn to get along with others. Maybe they're born that way." Susan lost all self-restraint and took the last cinnamon bun with the orange glaze.

"Susan Tucker," Harry said in a singsong voice.

"Oh, I know," came the weak reply.

"You girls have good figures. Stop worrying." Miranda reached down to scratch Tucker's head. "I wonder about that. I mean how it is that some people draw others to them and other people just manage to say the wrong thing or just put out a funny feeling. I'm not able to say what I mean but do you know what I mean?"

"Bad vibes," Harry simply said, and they laughed together.

"These aren't bad vibes but Little Mim was working the party. She's really serious about being mayor." Susan was amazed because Little Mim had never had much purpose in life.

"Maybe it would be good," Harry said thoughtfully. "Maybe we need some fresh ideas.

"But we can't go against her father. He's a good mayor and he knows everybody. People listen to Jim." Harry wondered how it would all turn out. "I don't see why he can't take her on as vice-mayor."

"Harry, there is no vice-mayor," Miranda corrected her.

"Yeah," she answered back. "But why can't we create the position? If we ask for it now either as a fait accompli or charge the city council to create a referendum, it's a lot easier than waiting until November."

"Oh, ladies, all you have to do is tell Jim your idea and he'll appoint her. You know the city council will back him up. Besides, no one wants to see a knock-down-drag-out between father and daughter—not that Jim would fight, he won't. But we all know that Little Mim hasn't much chance. Your solution is a good one, Harry. Good for everybody. The day will come when Jim can't be mayor and this way we'd have a smooth transition. You go talk to Jim Sanburne," Miranda encouraged her.

"Maybe I should talk to Mim first." Harry drained her teacup.

"There is that," Susan said, "but then Jim hears it first from his wife. Better to go to him first since he is the elected official and on the same day call on her. She can't be but so mad."

"You're right." Harry looked determined, scribbling the idea on her napkin.

The phone rang. They sat for a moment.

"I'll get it." Mrs. Murphy jumped onto the counter, knocking the wall phone receiver off the hook.

"Her latest trick." Harry smiled, got up, and picked up the phone. "Hello." She paused. "Coop, I can't believe it." She paused again. "All right. Thanks." She turned to her friends, her face drained white. "Larry Johnson has been shot."

"Oh my God." Miranda's hands flew to her face. "Is he—?" She couldn't say the word.

25

*T*he revolving blue light from Rick's squad car cast a sad glow over the scene. Cynthia stood with him behind the three barns at Twisted Creek Stables. The parking lot for trailers and vans was placed behind the barns, out of sight. Those renting stalls could use the space for their rigs.

Larry Johnson, who lived in town, boarded his horse here. He'd always boarded horses, declaring he wasn't a farm boy and he wasn't going to start now. He'd boarded his horses ever since he started his practice after the war.

Facedown in the grass, one bullet in his back, another having taken off part of the back of his skull, he'd been dead for hours. How long was hard to say, since the mercury was plummeting. He was frozen stiff.

He would have lain there all night if Krystal Norton, a barn worker, hadn't come to the back barn to bring up extra feed. She thought she heard a motor running behind the barn, walked outside, and sure enough, Larry's truck was parked, engine still humming. She didn't notice him until she was halfway to the truck to cut the motor.

"Krystal," Cynthia sympathetically questioned, "what's the routine? What would Larry have done after the hunt breakfast?"

"He would drive to the first barn, unload his horse, put him in his stall, and then drive back here, unhitch his trailer, and drive home in his truck."

"And he'd unloaded his horse?"

"Yes." Krystal wiped her runny nose; she'd been sobbing both from shock and because she loved Dr. Johnson. Everybody did.

"Nobody noticed that he hadn't pulled out?" Cynthia led Krystal a few steps away from the body.

"No. We're all pretty busy. There's people coming and going out of this hack barn all the time." She used the term "hack barn," which meant a boarders' barn.

"You didn't hear a pop?"

"No."

"Sometimes gunfire sounds like a pop. It's not quite like the movies." Coop noticed a pair of headlights swerving into the long driveway and hoped it was the whiz kids, as she called the fingerprint man, the photographer, and the coroner.

"We crank up the radio." Krystal hung her head, then looked at the deputy. "How can something like this happen?"

"I don't know but it's my job to find out. How long have you worked here?"

"Two years."

"Krystal, go on back to the barn. We'll tell you when you can go home but there's no need to stand out here in the cold. This has been awful and I'm sorry."

"Is there some—some deranged weirdo on the loose?"

"No," Cynthia replied with authority. "What there is is a cold-blooded killer who's protecting something, but I don't know what. This isn't a crime of passion. It's not a sex crime or theft. I don't believe you are in danger. If you get worried though, you call me."

"Okay." Krystal wiped her nose again as she walked back into the barn.

The headlights belonged to Mim Sanburne's big-ass Bentley. She slammed the door and sprinted over to Larry Johnson. She knelt down to take him up in her arms.

The sheriff, gently but firmly, grabbed her by the shoulders. "Don't touch him, Mrs. Sanburne. You might destroy evidence."

"Oh God." Mim sank to her knees, putting her head in her hands. She knelt next to the body, saw the piece of skull missing, the hole in his back.

Rick motioned Coop to come on over fast.

Cynthia's long legs covered the distance between the barn and the parking lot quickly. She knelt down next to Mim. "Miz San-burne, let me take you back to your car."

"No. No. I want to stay with him until they take him away."

Another pair of headlights snaked down the driveway. Miranda Hogendobber stepped out of her Ford Falcon, which still ran like a top. Behind her in Susan's Audi station wagon came Susan, Harry, and the two cats and dog.

Rick squinted into the light. "Damn."

Coop, voice low, whispered, "They can help." She tilted her head toward Mim.

"Help with what?" Mim cried. "He's gone! The best man God ever put on this earth is gone."

Miranda hurried over, acknowledged Rick, and then knelt down next to Mim. She shuddered when she saw Larry's frozen body. "Mim, I'm going to take you to my place."

"I can't leave him. I left him once, you know."

Miranda did know. Friends since birth, they shared the secrets of their generation, secrets hardly suspected by their children or younger friends who always thought the world began with their arrival.

Taking a deep breath, Miranda put her cheek next to Mim's. "You did what you had to do, Mimsy. And your mother would have killed you."

"I was a coward!" Mim screamed so loud she scared everyone.

Susan and Harry hung back. They wouldn't come forward until Miranda got Mim out of there.

"*Make a wide circle so the humans don't notice,*" Mrs. Murphy told Pewter and Tucker. "*We need to inspect the body before other humans muck it up.*"

"*I'm not big on dead bodies.*" Pewter turned up her nose.

"*It's not like he's been moldering out here for days,*" Murphy snapped. "*Follow me.*"

The three animals walked in a semicircle, reaching the back of the two-horse trailer. They scrunched under the trailer, wriggling out by the body but careful not to move too quickly.

"Come on, Mim, you can't stay here. This can't get in the papers. I'll take care of you." Miranda struggled to lift up Mim, who was dead weight even though she was elegant and thin. Coop gently held Mim's right arm, pulling her up along with Miranda's efforts.

"I don't care. I don't care who knows."

"You can make that decision later," Miranda wisely counseled.

Mim glanced over her shoulder at the fallen man. "I loved him. I don't care who knows it. I loved him. He was the only man I ever truly loved, and I threw him aside. For what?"

"Those were different times. We did what we were told." Miranda tugged.

Mim turned to Cynthia. "I don't know if you know what love is but I did. If you do fall in love, don't lose it. Don't lose it because someone tells you he isn't a suitable husband."

"I won't, Mrs. Sanburne." Coop asked Miranda, "What car?"

"Hers. I'll drive. Ask Harry to bring my car home later."

"Yes." Coop helped fold Mim into the passenger seat. Her eyes were glassy. She looked ahead without seeing.

Miranda turned on the ignition, found the seat controls, moved the seat back, then reached over to grasp Mim's left hand. "It's going to be a long, long night, honey. I don't know how to use that thing." She indicated the built-in telephone. "But if you call Jim or Marilyn, I'll tell them we're having a slumber party. Just leave it to me."

Wordlessly, Mim dialed her home number, handing the phone to Miranda.

As they drove back down the drive, they passed the coroner driving in.

Tucker, nose to the ground, sniffed around the body. Rick noticed and shooed her away. The cats climbed into the two-horse trailer tack room.

Although the night was dark they could see well enough. No spent shells glittered on the floor of the trailer. A plastic bucket, red, with a rag and a brush in it sat on the floor of the small tack room. The dirty bridle still hung on the tack hook, a bar of glycerin soap on the floor.

"*Guess he was going to clean his bridle and saddle before going home,*" Pewter speculated.

"*I don't smell anything but the horse and Larry. No other human was in here.*" Mrs. Murphy spoke low. "*Although Tucker is better at this than we are.*"

Tucker, chased off again by Rick, hopped into the tack room. "*Nothing.*"

"*Check in here,*" Pewter requested.

With diligence and speed, the corgi moved through the trailer. "*Nothing.*"

"*That's what we thought, too.*" Mrs. Murphy jumped out of the open tack room door, breaking into a run away from the parking lot and the barns.

"Where's she going?" Tucker's ears stood straight up.

Pewter hesitated for a second. *"We'd better find out."*

Harry didn't notice her pets streaking across the paddock. She and Susan walked over to Larry's body.

"I'll kill whoever did this!" Harry started crying.

"I didn't hear that." Rick sighed, for he, too, admired the older man.

"He brought me into this world." Susan cried, too. "Of all people, why Larry?"

"He got too close." Coop, not one to usually express an opinion unsolicited, buttoned up her coat.

"This is my fault." A wave of sickening guilt washed over the sheriff. "I asked him to keep his eyes and ears open at the hospital and he did. He sure did."

"If only we knew. Boss, he kind of said something at Harry's breakfast today. He'd had a little bit to drink, a little loud. He said—" She thought a moment to try and accurately quote him. "'Yes,' he said, 'I'll catch up with you tomorrow.'"

"Who heard him?" Rick was glad when Tom Yancy pulled up. He trusted the coroner absolutely.

"Everyone," Harry answered for her. "It wasn't like he had a big secret. He didn't say it that way. He was happy, just—happy and flushed."

"Harry, I want a list of everyone who was at your breakfast this morning," Rick ordered.

"Yes, sir."

"Go sit in the car to get warm and write it out. Susan, help her. A sharp pencil is better than a long memory." He pointed toward Susan's station wagon.

The two women walked back to Susan's vehicle as Tom Yancy bent down over the body. He, too, was upset but he was professional. His old friend Dr. Larry Johnson would have expected nothing less of him.

Mrs. Murphy stopped on a medium-sized hill about a quarter of a mile from the barn.

"*What?*" Tucker, whose eyes weren't as good in the dark, asked.

"*Two places the killer could stand. On top of the barn. On top of this hill—or he could have been flat on his stomach.*"

"*How do you figure that?*" Pewter asked.

"*Powder burns. No powder burns or Tucker would have mentioned it. He had to have been killed with a high-powered rifle. With a scope—easy.*"

"*Shooting from here would be easier than climbing on the roof of one of the barns,*" Pewter suggested. "*And the killer could hide his car.*"

The three animals stared behind them where an old farm road meandered into the woods.

"*It would have been simple. Hide the car, walk to here. Wait for your chance. Someone who knew his routine.*" Tucker appreciated Mrs. Murphy's logic.

"*Yeah. And it's hunting season. People carry rifles, handguns. There's nothing unusual about that.*" Pewter ruffled her fur. She wasn't a kitty who enjoyed the cold.

"*We'd better go back before Harry starts worrying.*" Mrs. Murphy lifted her head to the sky. The stars shone icy bright as they only do in the winter. "*Whoever this guy is, he's able to move quickly. He was at the breakfast. He heard Larry. I guarantee that.*"

"*Do you think it's the same person who hit Mother over the head?*" Pewter asked.

"*Could be.*" Mrs. Murphy loped down the hill.

"*That doesn't give me a warm and fuzzy feeling.*" Tucker felt a sinking pit in her stomach.

26

The fire crackled in Miranda's fireplace, the Napoleon clock on the mantel ticked in counter rhythm to the flames. Mim reclined on the sofa, an afghan Miranda had knitted decades ago wrapped over her legs. A cup of hot cocoa steamed on the coffee table. Miranda sat in an overstuffed chair across from Mim.

"I hope he didn't suffer."

"I don't think he did." Miranda sipped from her big cup of cocoa. She enjoyed cocoa at night or warm milk and hoped the substance might soothe her friend a little bit.

"Miranda, I've been a fool." Mim's lovely features contracted in pain.

Mim could pass for a woman in her middle forties and often did. Rich, she could afford every possible procedure to ensure that beauty. She'd grown distant and haughty with the years. She was always imperious, even as a child. Giving orders was the breath of life to Mim. She had to be in the center of everything and those who knew and loved her accepted it. Others loathed it. The people jockeying for power in their groups, the developer ready to rip through the countryside, the errant politician, promising one thing and delivering another or nothing, Mim was anathema to them.

Her relationship with her daughter alternated between adversarial and cordial, depending on the day, for Mim was not an effusive mother. Her relationship with her son, married and living in New York City, had transformed from adulation to fury to coldness to gradual acceptance of him. The fury erupted because he married an African-American model and that just wasn't done by people of Mim's generation. But Stafford displayed that independence of spirit exhibited and prized by his mother. Over time and with the help of Mary Minor Haristeen, a friend to Stafford, Mim confronted her own racism and laid it to rest.

Her aunt, Tally Urquhart, flying along in her nineties, said to Mim constantly, "Change is life." Sometimes Mim understood and sometimes she didn't. Usually she thought change involved other people, not herself.

"You haven't been a fool. You've done a lot of good in this life," Miranda truthfully told her.

Mim looked at her directly, light eyes bright. "But have I been good to myself? I want for nothing. I suppose in that way I've been good to myself but in other ways, I've treated myself harshly. I've suppressed things, I've put off others, I've throttled my deepest emotions." She patted a tear away with an embroidered linen handkerchief. "And now he's gone. I can never make it up to him."

The years allowed Miranda to be brutally direct. "Would you? He was in his seventies. Would you?"

Mim cried anew. "Oh, I wish I could say yes. I wish I had done a lot of things. Why didn't you tell me?"

"Tell you? Mim, no one can tell you anything. You tell us."

"But you know me, Miranda. You know how I am."

"It's been a long road, hasn't it? Long and full of surprises." She breathed in deeply. "If it was meant to be, it was meant to be. You and Larry." She gazed into the fire for a moment. "What a long time ago that was. You were beautiful. I envied you, your beauty. Never the money. Just the beauty. And he was handsome in his naval uniform."

"Somewhere along the way we grew old." Mim dropped a bejeweled hand on her breast. "I'm not quite sure how." She sat up. "Miranda, I will find who killed Larry. I will pursue him to the ends of the earth like the harpies pursued Orestes. With God as my witness, I swear it."

"The Lord will extract His vengeance. You go about your business, Mimsy. Whoever did this wouldn't stop at killing you either. They hit Harry on the head."

"Yes, her story sounded fishy."

Miranda shut her eyes. It had popped out of her mouth, and after she'd promised Harry not to tell. "Oh, me. Well, the cat's out of the bag. Harry snooped in the basement of the hospital and someone cracked her on the noggin. It's supposed to be a secret and I, well, you can keep a secret—obviously."

"Funny, isn't it? We live cheek by jowl, everyone knows everyone in Crozet, and yet each of us carries secrets—sometimes to the grave."

"People say we should be honest, we should tell the truth, but they aren't ready to hear it," Miranda sagely noted.

"Mother certainly wasn't," Mim simply said.

"Well, dear, Jim Sanburne was quite a payback."

A slight smile played over Mim's lips. "Damn near killed her. Aunt Tally understood but then Aunt Tally understands more than the rest of us. She keeps reminding me, too."

"Why *did* you marry Jim?"

"He was big, handsome, a take-charge guy. An up-and-comer as Dad would say. Of course, he came from the lower orders. That killed Mother but by then I'd learned."

"What?"

"I'd learned to just go ahead. The hell with everybody. I knew she wasn't going to cut me out of the will."

"But did you love him?"

A long, long silence transpired; then Mim leaned back. "I wanted to be in love. I wanted, well, I wanted the things you want when you're young. I never loved Jim the way I loved Larry. He's a different sort of man. You know, those early years I'd see Larry driving to work at the hospital, driving back to his private practice, at the country club with Bella. At first the sight of him hurt me because I was wrong. I knew I was wrong. But he always said he forgave me. I was young. I wasn't quite twenty, you know, when I fell in love with Larry. He was so kind. I think a little part of me died when he got married but I understood. And—" She opened her hands as though they might have contained treasure. "What could I do?"

"Love never dies. The people die but love is eternal. I believe that with all my heart and soul. And I believe God gives us chances to love again."

"If you envy me my looks, I envy you your faith."

"You can't reason your way to faith, Mim. You just open your heart."

"As we both know, I haven't been too good at that. I sometimes wonder if I would have been a more loving woman had I rebelled earlier against my family and married Larry. I think I would have. I closed off. I became guarded. I lost myself along the way. Now I've lost him. You see, even though we weren't lovers anymore, even though we lived separate lives, I knew he was there. I knew he was there." She cried harder now. "Oh, Miranda, I loved him so."

Miranda rose from her chair to sit on the edge of the sofa. She took Mim's hand in both of hers. "Mimsy, he knew you loved him."

"In time, Jim knew, too. I think that's why he redefined the word 'unfaithful'—well, that and the fact that he wearied of me bossing him around. It's rather difficult for a man when the wife has all the money. I think it's difficult in reverse, too, but the culture supports it, plus we've been raised to be simpletons. Really." Mim's modulated voice wavered. "That, too, was one of the things I loved about Larry. He respected my mind."

"It's like that Amish saying, 'We grow too soon old and too late smart.'" Miranda smiled. "But Jim grew out of it or he grew old. I don't know which."

"Breast cancer. Scared both of us. I believe that's when Jim came back to me, realized he loved me and maybe we'd both been foolish. Well, that's all behind me. My cancer hasn't recurred in five years' time nor has Jim's unfaithfulness." She smiled slightly. She sighed. "What did Jim say when you spoke to him? I don't remember. I know you told me but I don't even remember you driving me here."

"He said to call him if you needed him. He was going straight to Twisted Creek Stables." She let go of Mim's hand, reached over to the coffee table, and brought up Mim's cup. "This really will make you feel a little better."

Mim drank, handed the cup back to Miranda. "Thank you."

"I wouldn't want to be in Sheriff Shaw's shoes right now."

"I mistakenly assumed this had nothing to do with us." She made a dismissive gesture with her hand. "When Hank Brevard was found with a slit throat I thought it was brutal, but Hank lacked the fine art of endearing himself to others. That someone would finally kill him didn't seem too far-fetched. One had only to find the reason. But now—everything's different now."

"Yes." Miranda nodded.

"I think of death as an affront. I know you don't. You think you'll join up with Jesus. I hope you're right."

"'For I have no pleasure in the death of anyone, says the Lord God; so turn and live.' Ezekiel, chapter eighteen, verse thirty-two. Turn and live," Miranda emphasized.

"You've changed, too, Miranda."

"I know. After George's death the church was my comfort. Perhaps I tried too strenuously to comfort others." A smile played on her lips. "It all takes time."

"And Tracy." Mim mentioned Miranda's high-school boyfriend, who had returned to her life but was currently in Hawaii selling his home.

"I feel alive again. And you will, too. We need to think of something to do to honor Larry, something he would have loved."

"I thought I'd establish a scholarship at the University of Virginia Medical School in his name—for family practice."

"Jim?"

"He'll like the idea. Jim's not mean-spirited."

"I know that." Miranda smiled. "Do you think you could ever talk to him about those years?"

Mim shook her head no. "Why? You know, Miranda, I believe there are some things best left unsaid in a marriage. And I think every woman knows that."

"Mim, I think every man knows that, too."

"I always think they know less than we do, most of them anyway."

"Don't fool yourself." Miranda got up and threw another log on the fire. "More cocoa?"

"No."

"Do you think you can sleep? The spare bedroom is toasty."

"I think I can." Mim threw off the afghan and stood up. "I take you for granted, Miranda. I think I've taken many people for granted. You're a good friend to me. Better than I am to you."

"I don't think like that, Mim. There's only love. You do for the people you love."

"Well." This was hard for Mim. "I love you."

"I love you, too."

The old friends embraced. Miranda led Mim to the spare bedroom.

"Miranda, whoever killed Larry had no conscience. That's the real danger."

27

While most of the residents of Crozet spent the night in shock and tears, Sheriff Shaw worked like a demon, as did Cynthia Cooper.

Once Larry's body was loaded on the ambulance, Shaw and Cooper sped on their way to Sam Mahanes.

They knocked on the door.

Sally opened it. "Sheriff Shaw, Coop, come on in."

They could hear the boys upstairs in the bathroom, splashing and shouting.

"Sorry to disturb you, Sally, but it's important."

"I know that." She smiled genuinely, revealing broad, even teeth. "He's in his shop."

"We'll just go on down." Rick had his hand on the doorknob.

"Fine." She turned back, heading up the stairs, since the water noise was taking on a tidal wave quality.

"Sam," Rick called to him.

The tall director, bent over a workbench, his hands gripping a tiny soldering iron, finished the small seam, then turned off the implement. "Rick, had to finish this or it'd be ruined."

Rick and Cynthia admired the thin wooden box with inlaid gold and silver.

"Beautiful." Coop admired his work.

"Thank you. Keeps me sane."

Rick scoped the shop. Sam had the best woodworking equipment, soldering equipment, even a small, very expensive lapidary saw. "Back door?"

"Sometimes I slip in to escape the boys. I love 'em but I need to get away. Dennis is at the age where he wants to pick up everything. I lock the doors. I think when they're a little older I'll let them work with me."

"Good idea." Rick smiled. As there was no place to sit down, he suggested going upstairs.

Once settled in the library Rick got to the point. "Sam, Larry Johnson was shot twice and killed at Twisted Creek Stables."

"What?"

"As soon as we finished examining the body and the scene of the murder I drove to you. I wanted to talk to you before the reporters get to you."

"Thank you," Sam said.

"And I wanted to reach you before your phone started ringing off the hook." Rick noticed how pale Sam's face was, so pale from the shock that his cheeks looked like chalk. "Level with me, Sam. Do you know what's going on at your hospital? Any idea?"

"I don't. Nothing makes sense to me and—this may not be related to Crozet Hospital."

"No, but I have to take into consideration that Larry's murder might be connected to events there."

Cynthia discreetly flipped open her notepad.

"Yes—of course." Sam swallowed hard.

"We've considered black-market traffic in organs."

"Good God, Rick, you can't be serious."

"I have to think of anything worth killing for and money surely seems to be number one on the list."

"There's no selling of kidneys and livers. I'd know about it."

"Sam, maybe not. Hypothetical situation. You've got a young intern on the take. A person dies—someone in fairly good condition—the intern harvests the kidney, packs it up, and sends it off."

"But we have records of pickups and deliveries. Besides, families often request autopsies. If a kidney were missing we'd know. The family would know. There'd be hell to pay and lawsuits until kingdom come."

"What if the person responsible for the autopsies is in on it, too?"

Sam's brow furrowed, he ran his forefinger across the top of his lip, a nervous gesture. "The more people involved, the more opportunity for mistakes or loose talk."

"If there is a ring, Hank Brevard would have been in a good position to reap the benefits. He could ship organs out of there without anyone knowing."

"The pickup would know."

"The pickup gets a cut. You don't know how many trucks go down to the back door or to loading and unloading. But the back door is my guess there because it's simply a service entrance for the workers. All someone has to do is walk in, go to Hank's office or wherever the organs are stored, and walk out. They could be in a carton, surrounded by a plastic bag filled with dry ice—any number of unobtrusive carriers."

"For one thing, Sheriff, we know who uses operating rooms. I don't think it's possible. Just not possible."

"The patients are dead, Sam. They could cut them and sew them in a broom closet, in a bathtub. All they'd need is water to wash the blood, then zip the body back up in a body bag and off to the morgue—or they could cut them up at the morgue."

"Procedures in the morgue are as strict as in the operating room. Sheriff, I understand you need to consider every angle but this one is just not possible."

"What about fraud? Double-billing—?"

Sam shrugged. "Over time that, too, would show up. And we have few complaints in that department—other than shock at medical costs, but no, that's out."

"Has anyone been acting peculiar? Anyone attracting your attention?"

"No." Sam held out his hands as if in supplication. "Apart from Hank Brevard's death, everything is routine. The trains run on time. I can't think of anyone behaving in an untoward manner. Bruce is hostile towards me but he's always hostile towards me." Sam smirked slightly.

Rick persisted. "Are there other ways to create illicit profit, if you can stand that phrase? Something specific to hospitals of which Coop and I might be unaware?"

"Drugs. That's obvious. We keep them under lock and key but a clever head nurse or doctor can find ways to pilfer."

"Enough to make a lot of money?"

"We'd notice fairly soon but enough to make one quick, big hit. It's possible to do that and get away with it."

"Do you think any of your staff is on drugs?" Rick kept his face impassive.

"Yes. It's part of the hospital business. It takes some time to find them out but there's usually a nurse, a doctor, an orderly taking uppers or downers. The doctor creates false dosages for a patient. Again, we'll sniff it out but it takes some time—and I hasten to add it's part of our culture."

"How often has this happened at the hospital?"

Sam hesitated. "I think I ought to have the hospital lawyer here for this conversation."

"For Christ's sake, Sam, Larry Johnson is dead and you're worried about hospital liability! I'm not going to the press with this but I've got to know and if you don't tell me I'll dig it out and in the process uproot other things as well. It will get everyone in an uproar. How often has this happened?"

"Last year we found two people stealing Darvocet, codeine-based pills, Quaaludes. We fired them. End of story." He took a deep breath. "As I said, drug abuse is as American as apple pie."

"Once fired from a hospital that person will never work in a hospital again unless he or she goes to Honduras—am I right?"

"And they might not even get work in Central America. They'd have to go where people were so desperate they didn't care about their records from anywhere else. It definitely would be a career killer."

"All those years of medical school, all those bills—for nothing." Rick folded his hands together, leaning forward. "Other ways to steal or make money?"

"Oh, patient jewelry, wallets, and credit cards."

"Equipment?"

Sam exhaled. "No. Who would they sell it to? Also, we'd notice it immediately."

"Was Hank Brevard a good plant manager?"

"Yes. We discussed that before. He was conscientious. Apart from his obvious personality flaw that he was resistant to new technology. He wanted to do everything the way it always had been done."

"Remind me, had he ever been disciplined during his career at Crozet Hospital?" Rick glanced over at Coop.

"No. Well." Sam opened his hands, palms upward. "I'd routinely meet with him and request he, uh, lighten up. But no, Hank was no trouble."

"Ever hear about affairs?"

"Hank?" Sam's eyebrows shot upward. "No."

"Gambling?"

"No. Sheriff, we've been over this."

"You're right. Was Larry Johnson off the rails at any time?"

"I beg your pardon?"

"Did people feel he was too old to practice? Was he carried for old times' sake?"

"No. Quite the contrary. He was a G.P., of course." Sam abbreviated General Practitioner. "So he wasn't a glamour boy but he was a good, solid doctor and always open to new procedures, medical advances. He is, I mean was, a remarkable human being."

"Could he have been stealing drugs?"

"Absolutely not." Sam's voice raised. "Never."

"Sam, I have to ask these questions."

"There is no blemish on that man's record."

"Then I must respectfully suggest he got too close to whoever is blemished."

"The murder of Larry Johnson may not be related to Crozet Hospital. You're jumping to conclusions."

"Perhaps but you see, Sam, he was my man on the inside." The color drained from Sam's face as Rick continued, "I believe the murders are related and I will prove it."

"You should have told me."

"What if you're in on it?" Rick said bluntly.

"Thank you for the vote of confidence." Sam's face now turned red, and he fought back his anger.

"Or Jordan Ivanic. He's in a position to pull strings—excuse the worn phrase."

"Jordan." Sam's lips pursed together. "No. He's a man devoid of all imagination. He does everything by the book."

"You don't like him?"

"Oh, he's one of those men who can't think on his own. He has to find a precedent, a procedure, but he's honest. We aren't the best team personality-wise but Jordan isn't a criminal."

"He has three speeding tickets in two years' time. Had to take a driver's course mandated by the state."

"That doesn't make him a criminal." Sam's patience was wearing thin.

"Did you know about the tickets?"

"No. Sheriff, why would I know? You're grasping at straws. You assume my hospital, and I do think of it as my hospital, is a hotbed of crime. You connect two murders which while heinous may not be connected. As for Larry Johnson being your spy, that still doesn't prove his murder's connected to the hospital. He may have had a secret life." Sam's eyes blazed.

"I see." Rick stared at his shoes for a moment, then looked up at Sam. "What about the hospital killing people through negligence?"

"I resent that!"

"It happens." Rick raised his voice. "It happens every day all over America. It has to have happened at your hospital, too."

"I won't discuss this without a lawyer." Sam's jaw hardened.

"Well, you just do that, Sam. You'd better hire a public-relations firm, too, because I won't rest until I find out everything, Sam, everything and that means just who the hell was killed at your hospital because some bozo forgot to read their chart, gave the wrong medicine, or the anesthesiologist screwed up. Shit happens even in Crozet Hospital!" Rick stood up, his face darkening. Coop stood up, too. "And I'll have your ass for interfering with a law-enforcement officer in the prosecution of his duties!"

Rick stormed out, leaving an angry Sam sitting in the library with his mouth hanging wide open.

Coop, wisely, slipped behind the wheel of the squad car before Rick could do it. She had no desire to peel out of the Mahanes' driveway, then careen down the road at eighty miles an hour. Rick drove fast anyway; angry, he flew.

He slammed the passenger door.

"Where to?"

"Goddamned Jordan Ivanic, that's where. Maybe that smart bastard will tell us something."

She headed toward the hospital, saying nothing because she knew the boss. The misery over Larry's death swamped him and this was his way of showing it. Then again, he had a good reason to be livid. Someone was killing people and making him look like a jerk.

"Boss, this is a tough case. Go easy on yourself."

"Shut up."

"Right."

"I'll nail Sam Mahanes. I will fry him. I will slice and dice him. You know patients have died from stupidity. It happens!"

"Yes, but Sam's job is to protect the reputation of the hospital. Covering up one or two mistakes is one thing, covering up a rash of them is something else—and Larry would have known, boss. Doctors may be able to keep secrets from patients and patient families but not from one another, not for long, anyway."

"Larry would have known." Rick lit a cigarette. "Coop, I'm stuck. Everywhere I turn there's a wall." He slammed his fist into the dash. "I know this is about the hospital. I know it!"

"Any one of our ideas could provoke someone to kill."

"You know what really worries me?" He turned his face to her. "What if it's something else? What if it's something we can't imagine?"

No sooner had Rick Shaw and Cynthia Cooper pulled out of the driveway than Sam Mahanes made a beeline to his shop, grabbed his cell phone, and dialed Tussie Logan.

"Hello."

"Tussie."

"Oh, hello." Her voice softened.

"I'm glad you're home. Have you heard the terrible news about Larry Johnson?"

"No."

"He was found shot at Twisted Creek Stables."

"Larry Johnson." She couldn't believe it.

"Listen, Tussie, Sheriff Shaw and that tall deputy of his are going to be all over the hospital. We're going to have to cool it for a while."

A long pause followed. "I understand."

28

*T*he streets, alleys, and byways leading to the Lutheran Church were parked solid. The funeral service slated to start at eleven A.M. brought out all of Crozet, much of Albemarle County, plus the friends and family flying in from places Virginians often forgot, like Oklahoma.

At quarter to eleven some people were frantically trying to find places to park. Sheriff Shaw figured this would happen. He instructed the two officer escorts for the funeral cortege to ignore double-parking and parking in a No Parking zone. He did not waive the rules on parking by a fire hydrant.

Businesses opened their parking lots to everyone. The crush of people was so great that over two hundred had to file into the offices and hallways of the church, the church itself being full. At eleven there were still over seventy-five people standing outside, and the day turned crisp, clear, and cold.

The Reverend Herbert C. Jones, anticipating this, hung up speakers outside as well as in the hallways. Yesterday had been Ash Wednesday, so he wore his Lenten vestments.

Herb had known Larry all his life. He pondered over his eulogy, pondered over the life of a good man being snuffed out so violently. As a man of God he accepted the will of God but as a friend, a human of great feeling, he couldn't help but question.

The upper-management staff of Crozet Hospital filled the left-hand, front side of the church. Behind Sam Mahanes, Jordan Ivanic, Dr. Bruce Buxton, and others were those support people who worked with Larry over the years, Tussie Logan, other nurses, secretaries, people who had learned to love him because he valued them. Larry hadn't had an ounce of snobbery in his soul.

On the right-hand side of the church, at the front, sat distant relatives, nephews and nieces and their children. Larry's brother, a lawyer who had moved to Norman, Oklahoma, after World War II, was there. Handsome people, the Johnsons shared many of Larry's qualities: down-to-earth, respectful, hardworking. One great-nephew in particular looked much like Larry himself at twenty-five.

When Mim Sanburne saw this young man she burst into tears. Both Jim and Little Mim put their arms around her, but this reminder in the flesh, this genetic recall, tore at her heart. Larry was irretrievably gone and with him, Mim's youth and passion.

Harry, Susan, and Miranda sat together near the front on the right-hand side of the church. All three women wore hats, as was proper. In Harry's case the hat also served to cover the stitches.

The walnut casket, closed, sat at the nave, down below the altar. The scent of the massed floral arrangements overpowered those in the front. For those in the rear the sweet odors brought hopes of the not-too-distant spring, an exquisite season in the Blue Ridge Mountains.

The murmur of voices hushed when Herb opened the door behind the lectern. Two acolytes were already seated, one by the lectern, the other by the pulpit. When Herb entered, the congrega-

tion stood. He walked to the center, held his hands up, and the congregation was seated.

As the service for the dead progressed, those who knew the
good reverend felt the force of his deep voice, felt the genuine emotion. By the time he read his sermon, liberally sprinkled with paw-
prints from his cats, people knew this was the greatest sermon Herb
had ever given.

He eschewed the usual easy words about the deceased being
with the angels. He spoke of a life well lived, of a life spent in service to others, of a life devoted to easing pain, to healing, to friendship. He spoke of foxhunting and fly-fishing, Larry's favorite
pastimes. He recalled his record in the Navy, his youthful practice,
his rapport with people. He argued with God, Herb did.

"Lord, why did you take Thy faithful servant when we have such
need of him here on earth?" He read Psalm 102. "'Hear my prayer,
O Lord; let my cry come to Thee! Do not hide thy face from me in
the day of my distress! Incline thy ear to me; answer me speedily in
the day when I call! For my days pass away like smoke and my bones
burn like a furnace. My heart is smitten like grass, and withered; I
forget to eat my bread.'"

As Herb continued with the psalm, Mrs. Hogendobber quietly
recited it with him, her memory of the Good Book being a source
of comfort to her and astonishment to others.

At the end of the service, Herb asked that people join hands
and repeat the prayers with him. "Larry spent his life bringing people together. Whoever is on your right, whoever is on your left,
remember that Dr. Larry Johnson has brought you together even in
death."

After the service the church doors opened. People slowly left
the church, almost unwilling to go because the emotions holding
them there were so powerful.

Mim, in control now, walked to the car. From here the group would wind its way to the cemetery just southwest of town.

Harry reached her truck, stepped on the running board to get in, and noticed a dead chicken, its neck broken, in the bed of the truck.

She reached over, picking it up. There was nothing special about it except that it was tossed deliberately in the back of her truck.

She had an old canvas tarp which she pulled over the bird. It wouldn't do to drive to the entombment with feathers flying.

She knew in her bones this was a cheap warning.

29

Mrs. Murphy's tail stuck out from under the canvas in the back of the truck.

"*Throw it down to me,*" Tucker's bright eyes implored her kitty friend.

"*No way, José.*" The tiger cat sank her fangs in one red leg, backing out, pulling the heavy chicken with her.

Pewter, also sitting in the bed of the truck, called out, "*We aren't stupid, Tucker.*"

"*I just want to sniff it. I can tell you how long it's been dead.*"

"*Liar.*" Murphy inspected the corpse. "*Been dead since this morning.*"

"*It's cold. Maybe it's freezing up,*" Tucker called from the ground.

"*Maybe.*" Murphy hopped over the side of the truck, softly landing on the ground.

Pewter chose the less athletic route. She carefully eased herself over the closed tailgate, her hind paws touching the bumper. Then she dropped down on her front paws and jumped off to the ground.

The animals heard the story of the funeral and the dead chicken when Harry and Miranda returned to work. The post office front door was always unlocked but the back door and the counter divider could be locked. There was a pulldown door, like a garage door, which pulled to the counter divider, locking from the back side. Because stamps were valuable, Miranda and Harry had wrapped up everything tight before leaving for the funeral. It wasn't that anyone had ever stolen anything from the post office other than rubber bands and pencils but the murders inspired them to caution. Then, too, they had put the cats and dog in the locked portion along with a big bowl of water and crunchies on the small table out of Tucker's reach. As there was an animal door in the back of the post office, Harry had locked that, too.

Usually when humans returned, the animals bolted outside, but they wanted to hear the events. Once Harry told about the chicken they bolted and now they sat, fur ruffled against the cold with the northwest wind kicking up. Harry planned on taking the chicken home to feed the fox living on her land.

"I say we go to the hospital." Tucker was resolute. "It's a fifteen-minute jog." Tucker cut time off the trip to make it more attractive.

"We'll last five minutes. You know how fussy humans are at hospitals. Insulting, really. We're cleaner than they are. All those humans with diseases." Pewter shuddered in distaste.

"We won't go in the front door." Tucker knew Pewter was trying to get out of the walk in the cold to the hospital.

"Oh." The gray cat ducked underneath the truck to escape the wind. It was a good idea but the wind whipped underneath the truck as well as swirling around it.

"We go to the back door."

"Tucker, the back door is closed." Pewter didn't like this idea one bit.

"The loading dock isn't," Murphy thought out loud. "We could slip in there and work our way to the basement."

"What if we get locked in? We could starve in there."

"*Pewter.*" Mrs. Murphy maliciously smiled. "*You could eat cast-off body parts. How about a fresh liver?*"

"*I hate you,*" Pewter spit.

"*Well, fine, you big weenie. You stay here and we'll go.*" Tucker wanted to get over there.

"*Oh sure, and hear from you two for the next eleven years about what a fat chicken I am.*" She thought about the chicken a moment, then continued, "*Besides, you don't know everything. I see things you miss.*"

"*Then shut up and come on. Time's a-wasting. Harry will be out of here at five and it's already one-thirty.*" Mrs. Murphy looked down both sides of the road, then scampered across heading north toward the hospital, the wind in her face.

The three animals stayed off the road, dashing through lawns, hopping creeks, and eluding the occasional house dog upset because three animals crossed his or her lawn.

They reached the hospital by two-ten. To test their luck they hurried to the back door first. The doorknob was reachable but the cats couldn't turn it.

By now they were cold so they ran around the side of the building to the loading dock, one level up from the back door. It was child's play to elude the humans working the dock. There was only one truck and one unloader. Neither noticed the animals. Once inside the building, grateful for the warmth, the three headed away from the dock.

Murphy led them to an elevator pool.

"*We can't take that,*" Tucker said.

"*I know but stairwells are usually near elevator pools so start looking, genius.*" Her voice was sarcastic.

Sure enough, the stairwell was tucked in the corner, the door unlocked. Tucker, a strong dog for her size, pushed it open and the animals sped downstairs, opening the unlocked door with a red BASEMENT neatly painted across it.

They had landed on the east side of the building, site of the elevator bank.

"*Come on, let's get out of here before someone steps off that thing.*" Murphy turned left, not out of any sense of where she was going but just to escape possible detection. They raced past storage rooms, finally arriving at the boiler room, the hub of all corridors.

"*Oh.*" Pewter saw the blood on the wall; most of it had been washed off, but enough had stained into the old stone wall that she could see it.

The three sat down for a moment, considering where Hank Brevard's body had been crumpled.

"*This is where Mom got hit on the head. In this room.*" Tucker put her nose to the ground but all she could smell was oil from the furnace.

"*She should never have come in here by herself,*" Pewter complained. "*She has no fear and that isn't always a good thing.*"

"*Boy, you'd think the hospital could afford better lights.*" The dog noted the low wattage.

"*That's why we're here.*" Mrs. Murphy systematically checked out each corner of the room. "*Let's go outside.*"

"*Which door?*" Tucker asked.

"*The one in the opposite direction. We came in from the east. Let's go west.*"

"*I hope you remember because it all looks the same to me.*" The basement gave Pewter the creeps.

"*Wimp.*"

"*I'm not a wimp.*" Pewter smacked Murphy, who smacked her back.

"*Girls,*" Tucker growled.

The cats stopped following the dog as she pushed open the door, which wasn't latched. A hallway led to the end of the building. The light from the small square in the door was brighter than the lights overhead.

"*Is that the door we first tried?*" Pewter asked.

"*Yes. It's the only door downstairs on the west side.*"

They slowly walked down the hall, the storage rooms appearing as innocuous to them as they had to the humans. Satisfying themselves that nothing was amiss in that hall, they returned to the boiler room and went down the southerly corridor, the one which contained the incinerator.

Tucker sniffed when they entered the room. "*This incinerator could destroy a multitude of sins.*"

"*And does, I'm sure,*" Pewter said.

"*Nothing in here.*" Tucker had thoroughly sniffed everything.

They returned to the corridor, poking their heads in rooms. Hearing voices, they ducked into a room that had empty cartons neatly stacked against the wall.

Bobby Minifee and Booty Weyman walked by. Bobby had been promoted to Hank's job and Booty had moved up to day schedule. Engrossed in conversation, they didn't even glance into the storage room.

Tucker put her nose to the ground once the men passed. The cats heard them turn toward the boiler room.

"*Someone's been here recently.*" Tucker moved along the cartons.

"*That doesn't mean anything. People have probably been in each of these rooms for one thing or another.*" Pewter was getting peckish.

Tucker paid no attention to her. Murphy knew her canine friend well enough to put her own nose to the ground. She could smell shoes, one with leather soles, one with rubber.

"*Hands.*" Tucker stopped over a spot on the old slate floor. "*I can smell the oil on their hands. They've been here today.*"

"Hands on the floor?" Pewter's gray eyebrows shot upward, for the dog was sniffing where the wall met the floor.

"*Yes.*" Tucker kept sniffing. "*Here, just above the floor.*"

"*Pewter, look for a handle or something,*" Murphy ordered her.

"*In the wall?*"

"*Yes, you dimwit!*"

"*I'm not a dimwit.*" Pewter declined to further the argument because she, too, was intrigued.

The animals sniffed the walls. Murphy, claws out, tapped and patted each stone, part of the original foundation.

"*Hey.*" Pewter stopped. "*Do that again.*"

The two cats strained to hear. Murphy rapped her claws harder this time. A faint hollow sound rewarded her efforts.

"*Flat down,*" Tucker whispered as Bobby and Booty returned, but once again the two men didn't look toward the room full of boxes.

When they passed, the dog came over to the cats. She sniffed the wall as high up as she reached. "*Yes, here. Human hands.*"

"*Let's push it,*" Murphy said and the three leaned against the square stone.

A smooth, soft sliding sound rewarded their efforts, then a soft clink surprised them. The floor opened up. One big slate stone slid under another one, revealing a ladder. It was dark as pitch down there.

"*Tucker, you stay here. Pewter, you with me?*" Murphy climbed down the ladder.

Wordlessly, Pewter followed. Once down there their eyes adjusted.

"*It's a bunch of machines.*" Pewter was puzzled.

"*Yeah, those drip things. They don't look broken up.*"

"*Get out of there. Someone's coming!*" Tucker yelled.

The two cats shot up the ladder, the three animals leaned against the stone in the wall, and the slate rolled back into place.

Breathlessly they listened as the steps came closer.

"*Behind this carton.*" They crouched behind a tumbled-down carton as Jordan Ivanic walked into the room and threw a switch. He plucked a carton off the top of the neat pile, turned, hit the switch off, and left.

"*Let's get out of here before we're trapped,*" Pewter whispered.

"*You know, I think you're right,*" Mrs. Murphy agreed.

They hurried down the corridor, pushed open the stairwell door, ran back up one flight of stairs, and dashed out onto the loading dock. They jumped off and ran the whole way back to the post office, bursting through the animals' door.

"Where have you been?" Harry noted the time at four-thirty.

"*You'll never guess what we found,*" Pewter breathlessly told her.

"*She won't get it.*" Tucker sat down.

"*It's just as well. The last thing we want is Harry back in that hospital.*" Murphy wondered what to do next.

*W*hat is this?" Mim pushed a letter across the counter.

Mrs. Murphy, with quick reflexes, smacked her paw down on the 8" x 11" white sheet of paper before it skidded off onto the floor. "Got it."

Pewter, also on the counter, peered down at the typewritten page. She read aloud,

"Meet me. I will be the next victim. I need your help to escape. Why you?
You are the only person rich enough not to be corrupted. Put a notice for a
lost dog named Bristol on the post office bulletin board if you will help me.
I will get back to you with when and where."

Harry slid the paper from underneath the tiger's paw.

"Well?" Miranda walked over to read over her shoulder.

"Well, this is a crackpot of the first water." Miranda pushed her glasses back up on her head. "I'm calling the sheriff." She flipped up the divider.

"Wait. Let's talk about this for a minute," Harry said.

"This could be the killer playing some kind of weird game." Mim headed for the phone.

"Sit down, Mim. You've had a shock." Miranda propelled her to the table.

"Shock? Seismic." The thin, beautifully dressed woman sank into the wooden kitchen chair at the back table.

"This letter is from someone who knows our community, knows it well." Miranda searched her mind for some explanation but could come up with nothing.

Harry noticed the time, eight-thirty in the morning. She had a habit of checking clocks when she'd walk or drive by, then she'd check her wristwatch, her father's old watch. Ran like a top. Mim usually preceded everyone else into the post office in the morning. Like Harry and Miranda she was an early riser and early risers find each other just as night owls do. She tiptoed around Mim, knowing how hard Larry's death had hit her.

"Trap." Tucker found the letter irritating.

"Possibly." Mrs. Murphy twitched the fur along her spine.

"Flea?" Pewter innocently asked.

"In February?" Mrs. Murphy shot her a dirty look.

"We spend much of our time indoors. They could be laying eggs in the carpet, the eggs hatch, and you know the rest of the story."

"You're getting some kind of thrill out of this. Besides, if I had fleas you'd have them, too." The tiger swatted at the gray cat.

"Not me." Pewter smiled, revealing her white fangs. "I'm allergic to fleas."

"Doesn't mean you don't get them, Pewter, it means once you do get them you also get scabs all over." Tucker giggled. "Then Mother has to wash and powder you and it's a big mess."

"She hides the powder until she's grabbed you." Mrs. Murphy relished Pewter's discomfort at bath time. "First the sink, a little warm water, baby shampoo, lots of lather. My what a pretty cat you are in soapsuds. Then a rinsing. A second soaping. More rinsing. A dip with medicated junk. Drying with a towel. You look like a rock star with your spiky do. Pewter, the Queen of Hip-Hop."

"I don't listen to hip-hop." The rotund gray kitty sniffed.

"You hip-hop. You shake one hind leg, then the other. Real disco." Murphy howled with laughter.

"You know." Tucker, on the floor, paced as the humans discussed the letter. "What if this plea is like Mom with the flea powder? What's hidden?"

Murphy leapt down to sit next to her friend. "But we know what's hidden."

Pewter put her front paws on the wood, then slowly slid down. "Not exactly, Murphy. We know those machines, those IVAC units are under the basement floor but maybe that was the only place to store them. So we don't really know what's hidden and we don't know what this letter is hiding."

"Why Mim? Why not Sheriff Shaw?" Tucker frowned, confused.

"Because the writer is tainted somehow. The sheriff would pose a danger. Mim's powerful but not the law." Mrs. Murphy leaned into Tucker. She often sat tight with the dog or slept with her, her head curled up next to Tucker's head.

"Put up the notice. Put one up in the supermarket, too." Harry put her hands together, making a steeple with her forefingers. "Everyone will see it. That we know. Then do like the letter requests: wait for directions."

"Without calling Sheriff Shaw!" Mim was incredulous.

"Well—don't you think he'll want to keep you under watch? It would be clumsy. The letter writer would notice."

"Are you suggesting I be bait?" Mim slapped her hand on the table.

"No."

"What are you suggesting, Harry?" Miranda folded her arms across her chest.

"That we wait for directions."

"We? You don't know when and where I might receive these directions. I could be hustled into a car and no one would know."

"She's right," Miranda agreed.

"Yeah." Harry sighed. "Instant meeting. Just add danger."

"My point exactly. Harry, let the professionals deal with this." Mim got up and dialed Sheriff Shaw.

"I still think we should try the missing-dog notice by ourselves," Harry said to Miranda, who shook her head no as Mim read the letter over the phone to Rick Shaw.

"*Now that Larry Johnson's been killed, Mother won't rest. She wants to find the killer probably worse than Rick Shaw and Coop.*" Murphy worried. "*I don't know if we can keep her away from the hospital.*"

"*Well, I know one thing,*" Tucker solemnly declared. "*We'd better stick with her.*"

"*And I think what's under the floor is dangerous. Pewter, those IVAC units aren't down there for lack of space. I predict if someone stumbles onto that room there will be another dead human.*" Mrs. Murphy put her paw on the postage scale.

31

For Sheriff Rick Shaw and Deputy Cynthia Cooper it was the week from hell. The ballistics report ascertained that Larry Johnson was killed by a shell from a twenty-gauge shotgun.

While Rick spent the week questioning everyone who had been at the hunt meet, the barns, on Larry's patient list, Coop dipped into the state computer file on twenty-gauge shotguns.

There were twenty-six registered firearms of that description in Albemarle County, ranging from a handmade Italian model costing $252,000, owned by Sir H. Vane-Tempest, a very wealthy Englishman who had moved to Crozet five years ago, to the more common $2,789 version, a good working shotgun made by Sturm & Ruger.

Coop patiently called on each shotgun owner. No one reported a firearm stolen. She asked each owner if they would allow the shotgun to be checked to see if it had been fired recently. Everyone agreed. Everyone wrote down the last time they had used their shotgun. Even Vane-Tempest, a pompous man whom she intensely disliked, cooperated.

Of the twenty-six firearms, four had been used recently and each owner readily volunteered when and where they had used their shotgun. All four belonged to the Kettle and Drum Gun Club. None of the four had any connection that Coop could discover to anyone at the hospital.

Being in law enforcement, she expected people to lie to her. She knew in time she might find a connection but she also knew the chances were slim.

The weapon that killed Larry was most likely unregistered. It could have been bought years ago, before registration became the norm in America. It could have been stolen from another state. Could have, should have, would have—it was driving Coop crazy.

Rick and Coop studied patient logs, pored over maintenance records kept by Hank Brevard. They even walked through the delivery of a human kidney right up to the operating room.

The hospital routine was becoming familiar to them. The various doctors, nurses, orderlies, and receptionists were fixed in their minds. The one unit that upset both of them was Tussie Logan's. The sight of those terminally ill children brought them close to tears.

When Rick came back into the office he found Coop bent over the blueprints of the hospital.

"So?" He grunted as he removed his heavy jacket, quick to pluck the cigarette pack from the pocket. He offered her one, which she gratefully took. He lit hers, then he lit his. They both inhaled deeply, then relaxed imperceptibly.

Nicotine's faults were publicized and criticized but the drug's power to soothe temporarily never abated.

She pointed to the center of the blueprint with the glowing tip of the cigarette. "There."

He put his elbows on the table to look closely. "There what? You're back at the boiler room."

"This old part of the building. Eighteen thirty-one, this old square right here. The boiler room and the one hallway off of the boiler room. The rest was added in 1929. And it's been renovated three times since then. Right?"

"Right." He put his weight on his elbows as the pressure eased off his lower back, which felt stiff in the cold.

"The old part was originally built as a granary. Heavy stone flooring, heavy stone walls, whole tree-trunk beams. The original structure will last centuries. I was thinking about that. Now what I've been able to piece together about the history here"—she paused, took another drag—"thanks to Herb Jones's help, he's quite the history buff, well, anyway, he says the rumors always were that the granary was a way station on the Underground Railroad. No one was ever able to prove it but the owners, the Craycrofts, opposed slavery. Peaceably, but opposed, nonetheless. But as Herb says, no one ever proved a thing and the Craycrofts, despite their opposition to slavery, fought for the Confederacy."

"Yeah, well, you tend to do that when people invade your back-yard." Rick straightened up.

"The Craycrofts lost everything, like everyone else around here. They sold the granary in 1877 to the Yancys. Herb also said that the granary was used as a makeshift hospital during the war, but then so was every other building in the county."

"Yeah, they shipped in the wounded by rail from Manassas, Richmond, Fredericksburg. God, it must have been awful. Did you know that the War Between the States was the first where the rail-road was used?"

"Yes, I did." She pointed again to the boiler room. "If this was a way station on the Underground Railroad then there are probably hidden rooms. I doubt there'd be anything like that in the new part."

"When did the granary cease being a granary?" Rick sat down, realizing he was more tired than he thought.

"Nineteen hundred and eleven. The Krakenbills bought it. Kept it in good repair and used it for hay storage. They were the ones who sold it to Crozet United, Incorporated, the parent company for the hospital. There are Krakenbills in Louisa County. I contacted Roger, the eldest. He said he remembered his great-uncle mentioning the granary. He doesn't remember much else but he, too, had heard stories about the Underground Railroad."

"What you're getting at is that maybe the location of Hank's murder is more important than we thought."

"I don't know. Boss, maybe I'm grasping at straws, but it looked like a hurry-up job."

"Yeah." He exhaled heavily, a spiral of gray-blue smoke swirling upward.

"I keep coming back to how Hank was killed and where he was killed. If this were a revenge killing, the murderer, unless he is stone-stupid, would pick a better place. The risks of killing Hank at work are pretty high—for an outsider. For an insider, knowing the routine and the physical layout of the hospital, killing Hank could be a matter of opportunity as well as planning. The risk diminishes. The way he was killed strongly suggests knowledge of the human body, height, and physical power. Whoever killed him had to hold him long enough to slit his throat from left to right. Hank wasn't a weak man."

"I'll agree with you except on the point about knowledge of the human body. Most of us could slit a throat if we had to. It doesn't take a surgeon."

"But it was so neat, a clean, one-sweep wound."

"I could do that."

"I don't know if I could."

"If your victim were weaker than you or you had him helpless in some way, sure, you could make a neat cut. The trick to slitting a throat is speed and force. If you hesitate or stick the knife straight in instead of starting from the side, you botch it. I've seen the botched jobs."

She tightened her lips. "Yeah, me, too. But boss, the weapon was perfect, sharp."

"A layman could grind a knife to perfection, but I grant you this looks like an inside job, someone picked up a big scalpel or whatever and s-s-s-t. You know, it would be easy to throw away the instrument or return it to where surgical instruments are cleaned. We've been through that."

"Okay. We're on the same wave here." She held out her hands as if on a surfboard, which made him laugh, then cough because he'd inhaled too much. She slapped him on the back, then continued. "Big foxhunt at Harry's farm. Everyone's in a great mood. They view the fox. The fox gets away per usual. People are lined up for the breakfast like a movie premiere. Everyone and her brother is there. You can hardly move it's so packed. The food is great. Larry drinks a little, gets a little loud, and says he'll meet up with me. There couldn't be too many reasons for Larry to meet with me. I'm not a patient. It's not a big stretch to think he had something professional to tell me, my profession, that is. But it's not like it's a big deal. He didn't make it a big deal. Over fifteen or twenty people near the table had to have heard him. But again, it didn't seem like a big deal. He didn't use a dark tone of voice, no hints at evil deeds. However, he knew procedures cold. He knew the people. He probably knew more than even he knew he knew. What I'm saying is that he's known his stuff for so long he forgot how much he did know. An observation from him was worth a hell of a lot more than an observation, say, from Bruce Buxton. See?"

"Kind of."

"I don't think Larry knew what was wrong at Crozet Hospital. Not yet anyway but our killer feared him, feared he'd put two and two together quickly once he sobered up. Whatever Larry did observe, our killer made certain I wouldn't know."

Rick's eyes opened wider. "Our perp was in the room, or if he or she has an accomplice they could have called to warn about Larry spilling the beans." He inhaled. "We know from ballistics and the entry point of the bullet that the killer was flat on the hill about a quarter of a mile from the barn. Larry never knew what hit him. The killer crawls back off the hill in case anyone hears the shots. He was damned lucky those kids keep the radio on full blast but maybe he knew that. Maybe he rides. Or he's a hunt follower. He knew where Larry stabled his horse."

Coop added her thoughts. "He crawls back down the hill, gets in his car or truck, whatever, and pulls away as the sun sets. I checked for tracks. Too many of them. Nothing definitive. I had casts taken just in case."

"Good work." He crossed his arms over his chest, bit his lower lip for a moment.

"There's one last thing."

"What?"

"The attack on Harry."

His face fell. He took a last drag, then stubbed out the cigarette, the odor of smoke and tar wafting up from the ashtray. "Damn."

"In the boiler room."

He looked back at the blueprints. "Damn!"

32

*B*ox of rocks." Fair touched his forehead with his right forefinger.

"Don't start with me," Harry warned as she walked down the
steps to the lower parking lot.

On the tarmac the jet warmed its engine, the whine piercing the
still February air. Fair had just returned from his conference.

"You didn't even call to tell me."

"Accident." Harry felt like picking a fight.

"I'm so glad I have a girlfriend with a bald spot." He indicated
the small patch on her head with the stitches.

"Yeah, be glad you have a girlfriend. Of course, BoomBoom
could always fill in if I'm gone."

"You know, Harry, you find the belt and then hit below it."

"Hey, isn't that where you guys live?"

"Thanks a lot, pardner." He reached her truck, swung his bag
over the side.

It dropped into the bed with a thud. He put his kit bag on the
floor of the passenger side.

They said nothing until Harry paid the parking fee, turned right, and drove down to the Y in the road. "I think I'll go the back way. Through Earlysville."

"I should have known when you didn't call me that you'd gotten in trouble. But 'No,' I told myself, 'she knows how intense these conferences are and she's busy, too.'"

"You could have called me." Harry pouted slightly.

"I wish I had. Not that you would have told me."

"Who did?"

"I've known you since grade school, Sheezits." He called her by her childhood nickname. "You don't have farm accidents."

"I broke my collarbone in seventh grade."

"Roller skating."

"Yeah." She scanned her past for a salvaging incident.

"You stuck your nose where it doesn't belong."

"Did not."

"Miranda told me."

"I knew it!" Harry's face reddened. "I'll never tell her anything again."

Naturally, she would.

A few miles west, the panorama of the Blue Ridge opened before them, deep blue against a grainy, gray sky, a true February sky.

Fair broke the silence. "You could have been killed."

"But I wasn't." She bit her lower lip. "You know, I drove by the hospital and I kind of thought, 'Well, I'll go see where Hank met his maker.' And I walked in the back door. I mean I just didn't think I'd be a threat or whatever I was."

"And now Larry. Oh boy, that's hard to believe. It hasn't really sunk in yet. I think it will when I go by his house or to the next hunt and he's not there."

"Mim's taking it pretty hard. Quietly, obviously."

He stared out at the rolling hills punctuated with barns and houses. "Funny how love persists no matter what."

"Yes."

He looked at her. "Promise me you won't do anything like that again."

"Be specific," she hedged.

"You won't go back into the hospital. You won't snoop around."

"Oh—all right." This was said with no conviction whatsoever.

"Harry."

"Okay, okay, I won't go alone. How's that for a compromise?"

"Not a very good one. You are the most curious thing."

"Runs in the family."

"And that reminds me, if you don't think about reproducing soon the line stops with you." He spoke like a vet whose specialty was breeding. "You've got that good Hepworth and Minor blood, Harry. Time."

"I see. Who's the stud?"

"I'd thought that would be obvious."

33

"You and I will never see eye to eye." Bruce Buxton slammed the door to Sam Mahanes's office.

Sam, on his feet, hurried to the door, yanking it open. "Because you don't see the whole picture. You only see your part, dammit."

Bruce kept walking but Sam's secretary buried her head in her work.

"Ruth, how do you stand that asshole?" Bruce said as he walked by, ignored the elevator, and opened the door to the stairwell. He needed the steps to cool down.

Sam stopped at Ruth's desk. "He thinks I should open all the books, everything, to Sheriff Shaw. Says forget the lawyers. All they do is make everything worse. This was interspersed with complaints about everything but the weather."

"Perhaps he doesn't hold you responsible for that," Ruth dryly replied.

"Huh? Oh." Sam half smiled, then darkened. "Ruth, you're on the pipeline. What are people saying?"

"About what?"

"For starters, about Hank Brevard. Then Larry."

"Well." She put down her pencil, neatly, parallel to her computer keyboard. "At first no one knew what to make of Hank's murder. He wasn't popular and, well—" She paused, collecting her thoughts. "Larry's killing set them off. Now people think the two are connected."

"Are they criticizing me?"

"Uh—some do, most don't."

"I don't know what more I can do." His voice dropped low. "I'm not hiding anything but I can't just open our books to Rick Shaw. I will allow him to study anything and everything with our lawyers *present*."

"The Board of Directors will find some comfort in that decision, Sam." Her tone of voice betrayed neither agreement nor disagreement. As they were close, Ruth used his first name when it was only the two of them around. Otherwise she called him Mr. Mahanes.

"Bruce also wants me to issue a press statement emphasizing all the good things about Crozet Hospital and also emphasizing that—" He stopped. "What the hell good is a press statement? Larry wasn't killed on hospital grounds. Until it's proven that his murder is connected to Hank's murder, I'd be a damn fool to issue a press statement. All that would do is link the two murders in people's minds—those who haven't made that linkage. You ride out bad publicity. A press statement is just asking for trouble at this time. Now I'm not saying I won't do one—" he paused—"when the time is right."

"How long can we fend off the reporters? We can't stop the television crew from shooting in front of the hospital. We can stop them from coming inside but they've made the connection despite us."

"Six o'clock news." He sat on the edge of her desk. "Well, all Dee"—he used the reporter's name—"said was that a member of the staff was killed. She couldn't say Larry's death was related to Hank's."

"No, but she said Hank was killed two weeks ago. Was it two weeks ago?" Ruth sighed. "It seems like a year."

"Yes, it does." He ran his fingers through his hair, thick wavy hair of which he was quite proud.

"Sam, issue the press statement. A good offense is better than a good defense."

He crossed his arms over his chest. "I hate for that jerk to think he's one ahead of me or that I listened to him."

"Oh, Bruce is Bruce. Ignore him. I do. If he's really obnoxious just imagine what he'd be like as an ob-gyn."

"Huh?"

"He'd think every baby he delivered was his." She tittered.

Sam laughed. "You're right." He slid off her desk, stretching his arms over his head. "Rick or Coop pestering you?"

"Not as much as I thought they would. Mostly they wanted to know hospital routine, my duties, anything unusual. They were to the point. That Coop is an attractive woman. I think I'll tell my nephew about her."

"Ruth, you must have been Cupid in another life."

"I thought I was Cupid in this one." She picked up her pencil, sliding it behind her ear, and turned back to her computer.

"All right. I'll write the damned press release." He trudged back to his office.

34

*C*oop pulled white cartons of Chinese food out of a brown paper bag, setting them in the middle of Harry's kitchen table. Harry put out the plates, silverware, and napkins.

"Milk, Coke, tea, coffee, beer?"

"Beer." Coop wearily sat down, narrowly avoiding Tucker, who had positioned herself by the chair leg. She appeared glued to it. "I'll have coffee with dessert."

"You got dessert?"

"Yes, but I'm not telling you what it is until we eat this first. Sit down."

"Okay." Harry sat down, reaching for the pork lo mein as Coop dished out cashew chicken.

"I don't do Chinese." Mrs. Murphy sat in the kitchen window.

"Worth a try. You can fish out the pork bits." Pewter extended one talon.

"I had enough to eat," said the tiger cat, who kept her figure.

"I thought you'd be spending the night with Fair after picking him up at the airport."

"Oh, I wasn't in the mood for manly bullshit tonight," Harry airily replied.

"Like what?"

"Like him telling me what to do and how to do it."

"Mother, that's not exactly the way Fair does things. He suggests and you get pissed off." Murphy laughed.

"And what did he tell you to do? Something for your own good." Cynthia mixed soy sauce in her white rice, then dug in with her chopsticks. "Right?"

"Well—well, I know it's for my own good but I don't like hearing it. He told me not to go back to the hospital and not to snoop around anywhere by myself, and then he said I looked like a punk rocker who couldn't quite make it." She pointed to her stitches. "I suppose I could spend the next six weeks wearing a beret."

"Not you, Harry."

"Okay, a baseball cap. Orioles or maybe the Braves. Nah, don't like the logo."

"I was thinking more along the lines of a black cowboy hat— with black chaps and black fringe."

"Coop, is there something about you I should know?" Harry's eyes twinkled.

"Uh—no." She bent her blonde head over the food. "Just a thought. Fair would like it."

"Maybe you ought to play dress-up." Harry giggled.

"For one thing I don't own a pair of chaps and I won't buy the ready-made ones. If you're going to have chaps you've got two choices and only two choices: Chuck Pinnell or Journeyman Saddlery."

"How do you know that?"

"You told me."

"Early Alzheimer's." Harry smacked her head with the butt of her palm.

"Maybe it's not so early."

"Up yours, Coop. I'm a long way from forty."

"Oh—I suppose you were never a whiz at arithmetic. I count three years."

"Thirty-seven is a long way—" Harry smirked slightly. "And you aren't far behind, girlfriend."

"Scary, isn't it? What would I do with those chaps? No one to play dress-up with and I'm not going to wear them in the squad car."

"Oh, why not? It would be such a nice touch. Everyone thinks lady cops are butch anyway."

"You really know how to please a girl." Coop sighed because she knew it was true.

"Yeah, but I didn't say you were butch. You're not, you know. You're really very feminine. Lots more than I am."

"No, I'm not."

"You're tall and willowy. People think that's feminine until they see the badge and the pressed pleats in your pants. The shoes are winners, too. High heels. You could kick some poor bastard into next week but you'd never get your heel out of his butt. Police brutality."

"Harry." Cynthia laughed.

"See what Fair does to me. Just turns me into an evil wench. I think unclean thoughts."

"You don't need Fair for that. It's just that usually you keep them to yourself."

"Can you imagine me talking like this to Miranda? Smelling salts. And when she came to she'd have to pray for me at the Church of the Holy Light. I love her but there are things you don't say to Mrs. H."

Chopsticks poised in the air, Coop put them down for a moment. "I bet she knows more than she says. That generation didn't talk about stuff."

"Do you really think so?"

"Yeah. I think they did everything we do but they were quiet about it. Not out of shame or anything but because they were raised

with guidelines about proper conversation. I bet they didn't even discuss some of this stuff with their doctors."

"The chaps. I wouldn't discuss that either." Harry laughed. "Better chaps than some of those silk things at Victoria's Secret. They look good on the models but if I put something like that on I'd get laughed out of the bedroom."

"I wish they'd stop talking about sex and drop some food," Tucker whined.

"Get on your hind legs. Coop's a sucker for that," Pewter advised. *"I'll rub Mother's legs. It ought to be good for one little piece of cashew chicken."*

The two performed their routine. It worked.

"You guys." Murphy giggled, then glanced back out the window. *"Simon's on a food search."* She saw the possum leave the barn.

"All he has to do is go to the feed room or get under the feed bucket in Tomahawk's stall. That horse throws grain around like there's no tomorrow. He wouldn't be so wasteful if he had to pay the feed bill." Pewter hated food being wasted.

"He's a pig. Wouldn't matter if he paid the bill or not." Murphy liked Tomahawk but was conversant with his faults.

"Any word on Tracy selling his house in Hawaii?"

Harry leaned over to grab another egg roll. "No takers yet but he'll sell it soon. He writes her every day. Isn't that romantic? It's much better than a phone call or e-mail. There's something so personal about a person's handwriting."

"I can't imagine a man sitting down to write me a letter a day."

"Me neither. I suppose Fair would write me a prescription a day—for the horses." She laughed.

"He's a good guy." Coop paused. "You love him?"

"I love him. I always loved him. I don't know about the in-love part, though. Sometimes I look at him and think it's still there. Other times, I don't know. You see, he's all I know. I dated him in high school and married him out of college. I dated a few men after our divorce but nothing clicked. Know what I mean?"

"Does the sun rise in the east?"

"I don't even know if I'm searching for anything or anyone. But he is a good man. And I'm over it."

"What?"

"Over the mess we made."

"At least you have a mess, a past."

"Coop?"

"All I meet are deadbeat dads, drunks, drug addicts, and the occasional armed burglar. The armed-robbery guys are actually pretty bright. You might even say sexy." The pretty officer smiled.

"Really?" Harry pushed out the last of the lo mein with her chopsticks. "If you want more of this you'd better holler."

"I'll finish off the chicken."

"Deal. So the armed robbers are sexy?"

"Yes. They're usually very masculine, intelligent, risk takers. Unfortunately they don't believe in any form of restraint, hence their profession."

"What about murderers?"

"Funny you ask that. Murderers are usually quite ordinary. Well, set aside the occasional whacked-out serial killer. But the guy who blasts his girlfriend's new lover into kingdom come, ordinary."

"No electricity?"

"No."

"Maybe murder is closer to us than we think. We're all capable of it, but we aren't all capable of armed robbery. Does that make sense?"

"Yes. Given the right set of circumstances or the wrong set, I believe most of us are capable of just about anything."

"Probably true."

"*Drop one last little piece of chicken,*" Pewter meowed.

"Pewter, I don't have anything else unless you want fried noodles."

"*I'll try them.*"

Harry laughed and put down a handful of the noodles, which

the cat devoured in an instant because Tucker was moving in her direction.

"*Your claws click. That always gives you away.*" Pewter laughed.

"*There are more important things in this life than retractable claws.*"

"*Name one,*" Pewter challenged the dog, although she sounded garbled since her mouth was full.

"*The ability to scent a dead body three feet underground.*"

"*Gross!*" Pewter grimaced.

"*She's trying to get a rise out of you.*" Mrs. Murphy watched as Simon re-entered the barn. "*Simon's heading for the tack room. I guess he walked around the barn and decided no bears were near. He's a funny fellow.*"

"*I'd like to know what good possums contribute to the world.*" Pewter licked her lips with her shockingly pink tongue.

"*Think what possums say about cats,*" Tucker needled the gray cat.

"*I catch mice. I dispatch vermin.*"

"*Not lately,*" came the dry canine reply, which so enraged the fat cat she bopped the corgi right on her sensitive nose.

"Pewter. Hateful." Harry noticed.

"*I'm leaving.*" Pewter turned, sashaying into the living room with the hauteur of a disgruntled cat.

"I think cats and dogs are more expressive than we are." Cynthia laughed as Pewter exaggerated her walk for effect. "They can use their ears, turn them back and forth and out, they can wiggle their whiskers and their tail, they can make the hackles rise on their neck and back. They have lots of facial expressions."

"*Pewter's major expression is boredom.*" Tucker giggled.

"*Don't start with me.*"

"*Start? She hasn't stopped,*" Murphy called from the window.

"Lots of talk. Lots of talk." Harry pointed her finger at each animal in succession, then returned to Coop. "I agree. They are more expressive."

"I'm beat."

"Go in the living room. I'll bring you a cup of coffee and dessert. What is it, by the way?"

"Phish Food. I put it in the freezer."

"Ben and Jerry's. Coop, the best." Harry raced for the freezer, retrieved the pint of ice cream, pulled two bowls out of the cupboard. "The ice cream can soften while I make coffee. I've got Colombian, hazelnut, chicory, and regular. Oh, I've got decaf, too."

"Colombian." Cynthia sat on the sofa, bent over, and removed her shoes. "Oh, that feels too good. Foot massage. We need someone in Crozet who can give a good foot massage."

"Body massage. It's been years since I had a massage. Oh, they feel so good. I get such knots in my back." She waited for the coffee to run through the coffeemaker, filling the kitchen with rich aroma.

Cynthia got up to retrieve her briefcase, which she had put down by the kitchen door. She reached the sofa and lay down. She couldn't resist. When Harry brought in the coffee and a bowl of ice cream she sat up.

"Work?"

"Yeah. I need just enough energy to go over these bills from the hospital."

"I'll help you."

"It's supposed to be confidential."

"I won't tell anyone. Cross my heart and hope to—"

"*Don't finish that,*" Mrs. Murphy hollered as she jumped off the kitchen counter. "*Enough has happened around here.*"

"Murphy?" Harry wondered if something was wrong with her cat, who hurried over, leaping into her lap.

"Okay, here are the procedure billings, you know, cost of a tonsillectomy. I'll go over the equipment bills."

"What am I looking for?"

"I don't know. Anything that seems off."

Harry's eyes fell onto a bill for a gallbladder operation. "Jeez, two thousand dollars for the surgeon, a thousand for the anesthesiologist, two hundred a day for a semi-private room. Wow, look at these medication prices. This is outrageous!"

"And this is a nation that doesn't want comprehensive health care. It will kill you—getting sick."

"Sure will at Crozet Hospital." Harry smiled weakly. "Sorry."

Coop flipped her fingers, a dismissive gesture. "You develop gallows humor after a while. Otherwise you lose it."

"Here's a bill for breast removal. When you break down these bills it's like an avalanche. I mean every single physician bills separately. The rent on your room is separate. I can imagine you'd think you'd seen the last bill and here comes another one."

They worked in silence for about an hour, occasionally commenting on the cost of this or the fact that they didn't know so-and-so's sister had a pin put in her leg.

"Hank Brevard kept meticulous records," Harry noted.

"He wrote them out by hand and then I think someone else entered them on the computer. Hank wasn't that computer literate." Coop paused. "Boy, am I dumb. I'd better find out who did that for him."

Harry frowned. "I guess so. After a while everything and everyone seems suspicious. It's weird."

"Salvage Masters."

"Oh, that's a good one. The Dumpster people?"

"No, a company that rehabilitates infusion pumps. You know, the units next to a patient's bed that drip saline solution or morphine or whatever." She studied the bill. "Middleburg postmark. I think I'll drive up there Saturday if Rick says okay."

"He will."

"Want to go with me?"

"Yeah. I'd love to go."

35

"*M*ug *shot.*" Mrs. Murphy scrutinized the lost-dog photo taped on the wall by the postboxes.

"*Ever notice you hardly ever see photographs of lost cats? We don't get lost.*" Pewter ran her tongue over her lips.

"*Ha. It means people don't care as much about their cats,*" Tucker said, malice intended.

"*Bull!*" Pewter snarled and was about to attack the sturdy canine when the first human of the day entered the post office.

Reverend Herb Jones picked up the church's mail, then strode over to the sign. "Now that's a new one."

"What?" Harry called out from behind the divider.

She was dumping out a mail sack, letters cascading over the table, onto the floor.

"Bristol. I thought I knew every dog in this district. Who owns Bristol?" Herb frowned.

"You know, I don't know. The notice was slipped under the front door. I put it up. I don't recognize the pooch either except that he's awfully cute."

"Yeah. Hope he's found," Herb agreed.

"Where's Miranda?"

"Home. She said she'd be a little late this morning."

"Well, I'd better get a move on. The vestry committee meets this morning and I have to deliver the blow that we must replumb the rectory."

"That will cost a pretty penny."

"Yes, it will." He leaned over the counter for a second. "If money is your objective, Harry, become a plumber."

"I'll remember that."

He waved as he left.

A few minutes later BoomBoom Craycroft, tanned, came in. "I'm back!"

"So I see."

"She really is beautiful," Tucker had to admit.

"A week in Florida in the winter restores my spirits." She stopped. "Except I've come home to such—such sadness."

"No one quite believes it." Harry continued to sort through catalogues.

BoomBoom glanced at the lost-dog notice, said nothing, cleaned out her mailbox, then went over to the counter. "More."

Harry walked over, taking the yellow slip indicating there was more mail than the mailbox could hold. She put the overflow in a white plastic box with handles. She retrieved it, heaving it over the counter.

"Here you go."

"Thanks." BoomBoom picked up the box.

Harry flipped up the divider, trotting to the front door, which she opened. "It's slippery."

"Sometimes I think winter will never end. Thanks."

Harry closed the front door as Miranda entered through the back.

"Yoo-hoo."

"Hi." The animals greeted the older woman.

"Hello, you little furry angels."

"*Oh, yes.*" Tucker flopped over on her back.

"*That's more stomach than I care to see,*" Pewter snipped.

"*Look who's talking,*" Tucker responded.

Tussie hurried through the front door. "Hi, late." She slipped her key in the brass mailbox, scooped out the contents, shut the door with a clang, glancing at the lost-dog notice. "Poor puppy." She dashed out the front door.

Jordan Ivanic followed, read the notice, said nothing.

Later that day Susan dropped by. "We ought to put up posters of marriageable daughters."

"Right next to lost dogs," Harry remarked.

"Or goats."

By the end of the day neither Harry nor Miranda had observed anything unusual regarding the poster. Harry called in to Coop.

"You know, even though Rick must have someone watching Mim, I'd rather she hadn't done that," Miranda worried out loud as Harry spoke to Coop.

"*If it's the killer versus Mim, catnip's on Mim,*" Mrs. Murphy declared.

"It's been a while since I've been up there. I enjoy walking around the shops—after my duty is done, of course." Coop referred to their planned trip to Middleburg.

"You could get measured for chaps."

"Harry."

"Hee hee."

36

*M*other, do you really think you can stay neutral?"

A languid, melancholy Mim replied, "I have no choice."

"You don't think I should run against Dad, do you?"

"No."

A slight red blotch appeared on Little Mim's forehead, a hint of suppressed anger. "Why? He's been mayor long enough."

"I believe in letting sleeping dogs lie." The older woman patted the arm of her overstuffed chair; a fire crackling in the fireplace added to the warm atmosphere of the drawing room.

"Change never happens that way."

"Oh, Marilyn, change happens even when you sleep. I just don't see the point in stirring things up. Your father is a wonderful mayor and this town has flourished under his guidance."

"And your money."

"That, too." Mim glanced out the window. Low gray clouds moved in fast from the west.

"You never support me."

A flicker of irritation crossed Mim's regular, lovely features. "Oh? You live in a handsome house, provided by me. You have a car, clothing, horses, jewelry. You are denied nothing. You had the best education money can buy and when you married, I believe the only wedding more sumptuous was that between Grace Kelly and Prince Rainier. And when you divorced we dealt with that, too. Just exactly what is the problem?"

Pouting, not an attractive trait in a woman in her mid-thirties, Little Mim rose from her chair opposite her mother's and walked to the window. "I want to do something on my own. Is that so hard to understand?"

"No. Get a job."

"Doing what?"

"How should I know, Marilyn? It's your life. You have talents. I think you do a wonderful job with the hunt club newsletter. Really, I do."

"Thanks. Storm's coming in."

"Yes. February never fails to depress."

"Mother." She bit her lower lip, then continued. "I have no purpose in life."

"I'm sorry. No one can provide that for you."

Turning to face her mother, arms crossed over her chest, Little Mim said, "I want to do something."

"Charity work has meaning."

"No. That was for your generation. You married and that was that."

"Marriage might improve your humor." A slight smile played over Mim's lips, mocha lipstick perfectly applied.

"And what's that supposed to mean?"

"Just that we are meant to go in twos. Remember the animals on Noah's Ark?"

The younger woman, lithe and as well dressed as her mother, returned, gracefully lowering herself into the chair. "I'd like to marry again but Blair isn't going to ask me. He's not in love with me."

"I'm glad you realize that. Anyway, he travels too much for his work. Men who travel are never faithful."

"Neither are men who stay at home." Marilyn was fully aware of her father's peccadilloes.

"Touché."

"I'm sorry. That was a low blow."

Mim smoothed her skirt. "The truth isn't tidy, is it?"

"I'm out of sorts. Every time I think of Blair my heart leaps but when I'm with him I don't feel—I don't feel *there*. Does that make sense?"

"Any man that gorgeous will get your blood up. That's the animal in you. When you're with him you don't feel anything because there's nothing coming off his body. When a man likes you, wants you, you feel it. It's electric."

The daughter looked at her mother, a flash of recognition illuminating her features. "Right. Did you feel that for Dad?"

"Eventually. I learned to love your father."

"You were always in love with Larry, weren't you, Mother?"

As they had never discussed this, a surprising silence fell over them for a few moments.

"Yes."

"I'm sorry, Mother." Marilyn meant it.

"Life is strange. Hardly a profound thought but I never know what will happen from one minute to the next even though I live a well-ordered life. The mistake I made, and I share this with you only in the hopes that you won't repeat my mistakes, is that I valued form over substance, appearances over emotion. I was a perfect fool."

"Mother." Little Mim was shocked.

"The money gets in the way, darling. And social expectations are deadening. I ought to know, I've spent a lifetime meeting and enforcing them." She leaned over to turn on the lamp by her chair as the sky darkened. "Going to be a good one."

"First snowflake."

They both stopped to watch the skies open.

Finally, Mim said, "If you're determined to run against your father, go ahead, but consider what you really want to do as mayor. If you win, stick to it. If you lose, support your father."

"I suppose."

"Maybe there's another path. I don't know. I haven't been thinking too clearly these last days."

"It's awful that Larry's dead." Marilyn had loved him as though he were a kindly uncle.

"Quite. Snatched from life. He had so much to give. He'd given so much and someone took aim. I don't think Rick Shaw has one clue."

"They have the ballistics report." Marilyn wanted to sound hopeful.

"Little good it does without the finger that pulled the trigger." Mim's eyes clouded over. "As you age you learn there is such a thing as a good death. His was a good death in that it was swift, and apart from the shock of getting hit with a bullet, I should think the pain didn't last. He died as he lived, no trouble to anyone."

"I don't have any ideas; do you?"

"No, unfortunately. So often you have a premonition, an inkling, a sense of what's wrong or who's wrong. I don't have that. I'd give my eyeteeth to find Larry's murderer. I don't know where to look. The hospital? A lunatic patient? I just have no feel for this."

"I don't think anyone does, but now that you mention the hospital, what do you think of Bruce Buxton?"

"Arrogant."

"That's all?"

"Arrogant and handsome. Does that make you feel better?"

"He's brilliant. Everyone says that."

"I suppose he is."

"But you don't like him, do you?"

"Ah, well, I can't explain it, Marilyn. And it's not important anyway. Are you interested in Bruce? At least he rides reasonably well. You can't possibly be interested in a man who can't ride, you know. Another reason Blair's not for you."

Little Mim laughed because it was true. Horse people shouldn't marry non-horse people. It rarely worked. "That's something."

"Bruce rides like most men. Squeeze, jerk. Squeeze, jerk, but a bit of teaching could improve that. He doesn't intend to be abusive and he's not as abusive as most. Women are better with horses. Always will be." This was stated with ironclad conviction. "Women make up eighty percent of the hunt field but only twenty percent of the accidents."

"Harry's been riding well, hasn't she?"

"You two ought to ride in the hunt pairs when we have our hunter trials."

"Harry and I aren't close."

"You don't have to be close. Your horses are matched."

This was followed by an exhaustive discussion of the merits of relative mounts, carried out with the enthusiasm and total concentration peculiar to horse people. To anyone else the conversation would have been a bloody bore.

"Mother," Little Mim said, changing the subject. "Would you give one of your famous teas and invite Bruce?"

"I can't see the stables." Mim noted the thickness of the falling snow. "A tea?"

"You give the best teas. Things always happen at your parties. I wish I had your gift."

"You could have it if you wanted it, Marilyn. One learns to give parties just as one learns to dress. Oh, what was that I heard Harry and Susan say a few days ago? The 'fashion police.' Yes, the fashion police. They were laughing about Jordan Ivanic's tie and said he needed to be arrested by the fashion police."

"Harry in her white T-shirt, jeans, and paddock boots?"

"Ah, but Marilyn, it works for her. It really does and she has a wonderful body. I wish she and Fair would get back together again but once trust is broken it's hard to mend that fence. Well, a tea? You can learn."

"I can do the physical stuff. I will. I'll help with all that, but you have a gift for putting people together. Like I said, Mother, something always happens at your parties."

"The time Ulrich jumped the fence, cantered across the lawn, and jumped the picnic table was unforgettable." She smiled, remembering a naughty horse.

"What about the time Fair and Blair got into a fistfight and Herb Jones had to break it up? That was pretty exciting."

Mim brightened. "Or the time Aunt Tally cracked her cane over Ned Tucker's head and we had to take Ned to the emergency room."

"Why did Aunt Tally do that?"

"You were eleven at the time, I think. Your brother, Stafford, was thirteen. I'll tell you why. Ned became head of the Republican Party in the county and Aunt Tally took umbrage. She told him Tucker was an old Virginia name and he had no business registering Republican. He could vote Republican but he couldn't register that way. It just wasn't done. And Ned, who is usually an intelligent man, was dumb enough to argue with her. He said Lyndon Johnson handed the South to the Republican Party in 1968 when he signed the Voter Rights Act. That did it. Pow!" Mim clapped her hands. "I suppose Aunt Tally will enliven this tea as well. Let's sic her on Sam Mahanes, who is getting entirely too serious."

"With good reason."

"He's not the only person with troubles. All right. Your tea. How about two weeks from today? March sixth."

"Mother, you're lovely."

"I wouldn't go that far."

37

*B*ruce dropped by Pediatrics to check on a ten-year-old boy on whom he had operated.

Tussie Logan stood by the sleeping boy, hair dirty blond. She adjusted the drip of the infusion pump, took his pulse, and whispered on his progress to Bruce, who didn't wish to wake him.

They walked back into the hall.

"That pump's old, an IVAC 560 model. I keep pushing Sam for new equipment but I might as well be talking to a wall."

"Forget new pumps. These work perfectly well and the nurses know how to use them." Tussie had no desire to get in the middle of a Bruce versus Sam disagreement. The nurse always loses.

"They can learn."

"Dr. Buxton, they are overworked now. Keep it simple. The old pumps are really simple."

"You sound like Sam."

Her face tightened. "I hope not."

"Cheap."

"We do have budget restraints."

"We're falling way behind the technology curve, Nurse Logan. He's got to spend money to catch up. Go in debt, if necessary. He's too cheap, I tell you."

"Dr. Buxton, I can't really criticize the director of this hospital. It's not a wise policy." A flicker of fear danced in her hazel eyes. "And if you're going to fight for new equipment, fight for another MRI unit or something. Leave the nurses out of it."

"Afraid to lose your job?" He snorted. "Cover your ass. Ah, yes, the great American answer to the future, cover your ass."

"If you'll excuse me." She turned, walking down the hall to disappear into another patient's room.

"Chickenshit. Everyone around here is just chickenshit." Disgusted, he headed back toward his office in the newest wing of the hospital.

38

*C*hain store after chain store lined Route 29; fast-food restaurants, large signs blazing, further added to the dolorous destruction of what had once been beautiful and usable farmland. The strip, as it was known, could have been anywhere in the United States: same stores, same merchandise, same food. Whatever comfort value there was in consistency was lost aesthetically.

Back in the late sixties the Barracks Road shopping center at the intersection of Garth Road and Emmet Street, Route 29, broadcast the first hint of things to come. It seemed so far out then, three miles north of the University of Virginia.

By the year 2000 the shopping centers had marched north almost to the Greene County line. Even Greene County had a shopping center, at the intersection of Routes 29 and 33.

The city of Warrenton wisely submitted to a beltway around its old town. Charlottesville eschewed this solution to traffic congestion, with the result that anyone wishing to travel through that fair city could expect to lose a half hour to forty-five minutes, depending on the time of day.

As Harry and Coop headed north on Route 29 they wondered how long before gridlock would become a fact of life.

They chatted through Culpeper, the Blue Ridge standing sentinel to their left, the west. At Warrenton they latched onto Route 17 North which ran them straight up to Route 50 where they turned right and within six miles, they were at the door of Salvage Masters, a new four-story building nestled in the wealthy hills of Upperville, ten miles west of Middleburg proper.

Harry's chaps, needing repair, were tossed in the back of the Jeep, Coop's personal vehicle. She didn't want to draw attention to herself by driving a squad car, although she could have flown up Route 29 without fear of reprisal from another policeman lurking in the hollows, radar at the ready. The small towns relied on that income although they were loath to admit it, ever declaring public safety as their primary concern for ticketing speeders.

"Think my chaps will be okay?" Harry asked automatically, then grinned.

"There must be millions of people here just waiting to steal a pair of chaps needing repair—because you wore them." The blonde woman laughed as she picked up a leather envelope containing papers.

When they knocked on the door, a pleasant assistant ushered them in.

Joe Cramer, a tall muscular man at six four walked out of his office. "Hello. Come on in. Would either of you like coffee, or a Coke?"

"No thanks. I'm Deputy Cynthia Cooper and this is Mary Minor Haristeen, Harry, who has been involved in the case." Cynthia shook his hand, as did Harry.

"Come on." He guided them into his office, a comfortable space.

"This is quite an operation." Coop looked around at the employees seated at benches, working on IVAC units.

"Infusion pumps are sent to us from all over the world. These machines are built to last and for the most part, they do."

"You aren't from Virginia, are you, Mr. Cramer?" The lean deputy smiled. "Do you mind giving me a little background about how you developed this business?"

"No. I'm originally from Long Island. Went to college in the Northeast and started working in the medical industry. I was fascinated by the technology of medicine. I worked for years for a huge corporation in New Jersey, Medtronic. That's when I came up with the idea of rehabilitating infusion pumps and other equipment. The smaller hospitals can afford to repair their equipment and they can often afford to buy used equipment, but they often can't afford to buy new equipment. As I said, most of these machines are well built and will last for decades if properly maintained."

"Do you visit your accounts?"

"Yes. I haven't visited our accounts in India," he answered in his warm light baritone. "But I've visited many of the accounts here."

"What about Crozet Hospital?"

"Oh, I think I was there four years ago. I haven't had much business from them in the last few years."

"You haven't?" Cynthia's voice rose.

"No. And the machines need to be serviced every six months."

"Let me show you something." She pulled invoices out of the leather envelope, placing them before him.

Joe studied the invoices, then hit a button on his telephone. "Honey, can you come over to the shop for a minute?"

A voice answered. "Sure. Be a minute."

"My wife," he said. "We put everything on the computer but I trust her memory more than the computer." He punched another button. "Michael, pull up the Crozet Hospital file, will you?"

"Okay."

A tall, elegant woman swept into Joe's office. "Hello."

"Honey, this is Deputy Cynthia Cooper from the Albemarle Sheriff's Department and Mary Haristeen. Uh, Harry."

"Laura Cramer." She shook their hands.

"Do you remember the last time we got an order from Crozet Hospital?"

"Oh—at least four years."

Just then Michael walked into the office. "Here."

Joe reached up for the papers as Michael left. He and Laura read over the figures. "Here, Deputy, look at this."

She reached for the papers. The bills stopped four years ago. "They've given us no notice of moving their business," Laura said.

"Well, Mr. and Mrs. Cramer, the last billing date on the last invoice I have is December second of last year."

"It's our letterhead," Joe said, as Coop handed him an invoice.

"It's our paper, too." Laura studied the invoices, tapping them with her forefinger. "But Joe, these aren't our numbers." She looked up at Coop and Harry. "We have our own numbering system. These fake invoices copied the numbers from four years ago, running them up sequentially. But each year I alter the numbers. It's our internal code for keeping track of business, repair cycles, and it's all in those numbers."

"It'd be a pretty easy matter to print up invoices with your logo," Harry volunteered. "Someone with a good laser printer could do it and it would be cheaper than going to a printer. Also, no records of the printing job."

"Some of those laser systems are very sophisticated," Laura said, obviously upset.

"Has there been a problem with the equipment? Is that why you're here?" Joe asked because the reputation of his business was vitally important to him.

"No. Not that we know of." Coop walked around and sat back down, as did Harry.

"Can you tell me just what it is that you check on the infusion pumps, if check is the correct term?"

"We check for electrical safety, something like good current leakage. Or a power cord might be damaged. Sometimes orderlies will drop a unit. Stuff happens. We take the unit apart and check the circuits. Here, let me show you." He stood up and ushered them into the spanking-clean shop area.

"Here." Laura pointed to the digital screen on the face of the unit, above a keyboard of numbers like telephone push buttons. "The nurse punches in the flow, the time frame, the amount of fluid, and the rate, which is displayed here." She pointed to the screen. "The nurse on duty or doctor has only to look on the screen to know how much is left in the unit, whether to increase flow or whatever."

Harry remembered Larry punching in information on a unit.

"And you can put any fluid in the bag?" Coop pointed to boxes filled with sterile bags.

Joe nodded. "Sure. Blood. Morphine. Saline solution. Anesthesia. OBs use IVAC units to drop Pitocin, which stimulates the uterus to go into labor. The infusion pump is very versatile."

"And simple," Laura added.

"Here." Joe picked up a unit from the table. "You can even medicate yourself." He placed a round button attached to a black cord into Coop's hand. "You hit the button and you get more drip."

"Are these units well made?" Harry was curious.

"Oh sure. They're built to last and it's like everything else, newer models are more expensive, more bells and whistles, but I service units that are twenty years old—they usually come in from Third World countries."

"May I ask you something?" Laura smiled.

"Of course."

"Is someone stealing IVACs and selling them to poor countries?"

"What we have are two murders which we believe are connected, and I think we just found the connection. We don't know if the units are sold on the black market or not. What we have to go on right now are these false bills."

"Murders?" Laura's eyes widened.

"Yes, the plant manager of the hospital was killed three weeks ago and a doctor was killed just a week ago." She paused. "Both of those men must have stumbled onto something relating to these billings."

"Have you added up the amount of the billings? You've got three years' worth." Laura checked the figures and the dates.

"Yes, we have. It comes to seven hundred fifty thousand dollars for that time period."

"Someone's rolling in dough," Laura flatly stated.

"We've looked for that, too, Mr. and Mrs. Cramer. We didn't know this was the problem but we knew something had to be going on. We had no reports of suspicious patient deaths. We thought there might be a black market in human organs."

"There is." Joe leaned forward. "A huge black market."

"We found that out, too, but we also discovered that wasn't our problem. You two have shown me what's at stake here, a lot of money and more to come, I should guess."

"Joe, I think we'd better contact our lawyers. Officer, do you mind if I make copies of these?"

"No, but I ask you both to keep quiet about this. You can't sue anyone until we catch them and we won't catch them if they have warning."

"I understand," Laura agreed.

"This just knocks me out." Joe shook his head.

"The only reason the sheriff and I noticed these particular invoices, and it took time, I might add, was we crawled over the hospital, over billings, maintenance bills, you name it, but what finally caught our eye was that these bills were so neat."

"What do you mean?" Laura was curious.

"Well, they have a receipt date, as you can see." Coop pointed to the round red circle in the middle of each bill. "They have a pay date." She pointed to another circle, this one in blue with a date running across it diagonally. "But the invoices are so white and crisp."

"What do you mean?" Laura picked up an invoice.

"The other bills and invoices had gone through a couple of hands, a couple of shufflings. Fingerprints were on the paper, corners were a little dog-eared. These are pristine. It was a long shot but it was just peculiar enough for me to come up here."

"I'm glad you did." Joe, upset, looked into the young officer's eyes.

"Is there anyone who stands out in your mind at Crozet Hospital?" Coop had been making notes in her notebook.

"No. Well, I met the director and the assistant director, that sort of thing. I talked to a few of the nurses. The nurses are the ones who use the infusion pumps. That's why the simpler the model, the better it is. You can make these devices too complicated. Nurses have to use them, they're overburdened, tired—keep it simple." His voice boomed.

"How serious would a malfunctioning unit be?" Coop asked.

"Life and death." Laura folded her long fingers together as if in prayer. "An improper dosage could kill a patient."

After they left Salvage Masters they drove east on Route 50, ten miles into Middleburg. Harry took her chaps to Journeyman Saddlery to have them repaired, since Chuck Pinnell in Charlottesville was off to another Olympics. As he was one of the best leatherworkers in the nation, with a deep understanding of riders' needs, he had been invited to the Olympics to repair tack for all the competitors, not just Americans.

"Coop, look at these neat colors and the trims you can get, too."

Cynthia felt the samples, played with putting colors together. "It really is beautiful."

"They can put your initials on the back or on the side. They can make leather rosebuds on the belt or whatever. It's just incredible."

"I can see that."

"Mine's a plain pair of pigskin chaps with cream trim and my initials on the back, see?" Harry showed her the back of the chaps belt.

"Uh-huh." Cynthia was gravitating toward black calfskin.

"You know, if you had a pair of chaps made to your body, you might even learn to jump. I'd let you ride Gin Fizz. He's a sweetie. Then, too, chaps have other uses." She had a devilish glitter in her eye.

Coop weakened, allowing herself to be measured. She chose black calfskin, smooth side out, no fringe, and a thin green contrasting strip down the leg and on the belt, also calfskin. She had her initials centered on the back of the belt in a small diamond configuration. The waiting period would be three months.

All the way back to Crozet the two women discussed uses for the chaps as well as the pressing matter at hand: how to trap the killer or killers into making a mistake.

It only takes one mistake.

39

The two cats and the dog had heard about the trip to Upperville and Middleburg. They huddled in the back of the post office by the animal door. Outside a hard frost was melting as the temperature at ten in the morning was forty-five degrees and rising quickly. February could run you crazy with the wild weather fluctuations.

"*That's what those machines are we found. The pumps that should have gone to Salvage Masters.*" Pewter held her tail in her paw. She'd meant to clean it but in the excitement of the news she'd forgotten.

Mrs. Murphy, already one step ahead of her, replied, "*Yes, of course, but that's not the real problem. You see—*" As the two animals drew closer to her she lowered her voice. "*Those machines have to be rehabbed. That's why they're down there. Whoever is stashing them can't put them back into use without cleaning them, right?*"

"*Why not?*" Tucker asked.

"*Either they won't work or they'll work improperly. Which means complaints to Salvage Masters and the game is up. Whoever is doing this has to crawl down in that space and clean the pumps. I should think that part wouldn't be too hard. Well, the* person has to get in and out undetected. *What's difficult is if a machine needs more work than just cleaning. See?"* Mrs. Murphy swept her pointed, refined ears forward.

"No, I don't see," Pewter confessed.

"I do." Tucker licked the gray cat's face. "*Someone has to understand these machines."*

"Oh." Pewter's face brightened. "*I get it."*

"*Think it through,"* Murphy counseled patiently. "*The infusion pumps are small. One person, a small person, a child even, can pick them up, roll them, move them around. The hospital routine isn't ruffled. For years these pumps have been removed for cleaning. Right?"* The dog and other cat nodded in agreement. "*Whoever picks them up is in on it."*

"*Not necessarily,"* Tucker contradicted her. "*An orderly or janitor could pick them up and take them to the basement for shipping out. Then they could be removed to where we found them."*

"True." The pretty tiger was getting excited because she felt she was getting close to figuring this out. "*That's a good point, Tucker. The fewer people who know, the better. And someone has to run off the fake invoices. H-m-m."*

"*Okay, let's review."* Tucker caught Murphy's excitement. "*We have a person or persons good at using a computer. It sounds easy, copying a bill, but it isn't and the paper matches, too. So they're pretty good. We have a person or persons with mechanical skill. Right?"*

"Right," the two kitties echoed.

"*And there has to be someone higher up. Someone who can cover for them. Someone very, very smart because the chances are, that's the mastermind behind this. That person recruited the others. How often does an employee woo the boss into crime?"* Tucker stood up, panting from her mental efforts.

"*Well done, Tucker."* Mrs. Murphy rubbed along the dog's body.

"*How can we get a human to the hidden room?"* Pewter cocked her head, her long whiskers twitching.

"*We can't,"* Mrs. Murphy flatly replied. "*First off, anyone we might lure* there in the hospital could be in on it. We'd wait downstairs and who is downstairs but the plant crew, as Sam Mahanes calls them. You know one of them has to be in on it. Has to be. We'd be toast."

"Hank Brevard." Pewter's green eyes grew large. "He was the one. And he had his throat slit."

"Maybe he got greedy. If he'd kept at his task why kill him? Think about it. Whoever is on top of this sordid little pyramid is creaming the bulk of the profits. Hank figured out somewhere along the line that he was an important person in the profit chain and he wanted more. He asks for more or threatens. Sayonara." Murphy glanced at Miranda and Harry sorting out the parcels, tossing them in various bins or putting them on the shelves, numbers like the postboxes.

"Which means if the money is to keep rolling in, our Number One Guy will soon need to recruit someone else." Tucker was getting an uneasy feeling.

"He might be able to do the work himself," Pewter said.

"That's possible but if he's high up on the totem pole he isn't going to have the time, number one, and number two, he isn't going to be seen heading to the basement a lot. Eventually that would be a tip-off, especially after Hank's death." Mrs. Murphy's mind raced along.

"When Mom got clunked on the head—it must have been him." Tucker hoped Harry wouldn't go back to the hospital but she knew her mother's burning curiosity, which was why she'd been feeling uneasy.

"Everyone knows that Harry is both smart and curious. Smart for a human. I hope as long as she stays away from the hospital, she's okay, but she's friends with Coop. If I were the killer that would be worrisome. Look how fast he struck when Larry was finding discrepancies, and they probably weren't critical yet because if they were Larry would have gone straight to Sheriff Shaw. He wouldn't have waited." The tiger began to pace.

"If it were just one person . . ." Pewter's voice trailed off; then she spoke louder. "We've got at least two. Mom might be able to handle one but two—well, I don't know."

"*And no bites yet on Bristol, the missing dog? We've got to find out who that is,*" Mrs. Murphy fretted.

"*Mim would tell Rick if anything had happened,*" Tucker said.

"*Well, nothing's happened on that front yet.*" Murphy sighed. They were wrong about that.

40

Fair stood at the divider counter sorting out his mail. "You know Dr. Flynn's got two gorgeous stallions standing at Barracks Stud."

"Yeah. I thought I'd breed Poptart in a few years. She's still pretty young and I need her. If she's bred . . ." Harry's voice trailed off as there was no need to say she'd be out of work for at least the last three months of her pregnancy and then out of work until the foal was weaned.

"I like Fred Astaire, too." Fair mentioned a beautifully bred Thoroughbred stallion at Albemarle Stud.

"Doesn't everyone?" Harry smiled as she threw metered mail in one pile, since it needed a second hand-cancellation for the date.

"Now's what's the difference between one stallion and another?" Mrs. Hogendobber, not a horse person, asked.

"Kind of the difference between one man and another." Fair laughed.

"Don't get racy. I'll blush." Miranda's cheeks did turn rosier.

"It depends on what you're looking for, Miranda. Let's say you have a good Thoroughbred mare, she's well bred and she has good conformation. She didn't win a lot of races but she's pretty good. You'll search around—and you can do this on the Net, by the way—for a stallion whose bloodlines are compatible and who also has good conformation. You might want more speed or more bone or more staying power. That's in the blood. Breeding is as much an art as a science."

"Don't forget luck." Harry pressed the heavy rubber stamp in the maroon postal ink.

"There sure is that," the tall blond man agreed. "Miranda, if breeding were just a matter of study, we'd all be winning the Triple Crown. So much can happen. If you get a live foal—"

"What do you mean, a live foal?" The older woman assumed they'd all be live.

"A mare can slip or not catch in the first place." Noticing the puzzled look he explained, "A mare can not get pregnant even though you've done everything by the book. Or she can get pregnant yet abort early in the pregnancy. Strange as it may sound, it isn't that easy to get mares pregnant. A conception rate of sixty percent by a vet specializing in breeding is respectable. There's a vet in Pennsylvania who averages in the ninety percent range, but he's extraordinary. Let's say your mare gives birth. A mare can have a breech delivery the same as a woman but it's much worse for a mare. If those long legs with hooves get twisted up or tear her womb you can imagine the crisis. Foals can strangle on the umbilical cord or be starved for oxygen and never be quite right. They can be born dead."

"It sounds awful."

"Most times it isn't but sometimes it really is and your heart sinks to your toes. You know how much the owner has put into the breeding both financially and emotionally. Around here people are attached to their mares. We don't have huge breeding establishments so just about everything I see is a homebred. Lots of emotion."

"Yes, I can see that. Why, if Mrs. Murphy had kittens I think I'd be so concerned for her."

"*Thank you.*" Murphy, half asleep in the mail cart, yawned.

Pewter, curled up next to her, giggled. "*Some mother you'd be.*"

"*Look who's talking. You selfish thing, you'd starve your own children if there weren't enough food. I can see the headlines now. 'Cat starves kittens. Is fat as a tick.'*"

"*Shut up.*"

"*You started it.*"

"*Did not,*" Pewter hissed.

"*Did too.*"

"*Not.*"

"*Too.*" Murphy swatted Pewter right on the head.

"*Bully!*" Pewter rolled over to grapple with the thinner cat.

A great hissing, growling, and flailing was heard from the mail cart. Harry and Miranda tiptoed over to view the excitement. Fair watched from the other side of the counter.

Tucker, on her side, lifted her head, then dropped it. "*Cats.*"

"*Fatty, fatty, two by four,*" Murphy sang out.

"*Mean. Hateful and mean!*" Pewter was holding her own.

The mail cart rolled a bit. Harry, devilish, gave it a shove.

"*Hey!*" Murphy clambered over the side, dropped to the ground, put her ears back, and stomped right by her mother.

"*Whee!*" Pewter crouched down for the ride.

Harry trotted over, grabbed the end of the mail cart. "Okey dokey, smoky. Here we go." She pushed the mail cart all around the back of the post office as Pewter rose up to put her paws on the front. The cat loved it. Murphy sulked, finally going over to Tucker to sit next to the dog, who wanted no part of a cat fight.

"It's a three-ring circus around here." Miranda laughed.

"You look good in hunter green. I meant to tell you that when I walked in." Fair complimented her dress.

"Why, thank you, Fair. Now where were we before Mrs. Murphy and Pewter interrupted us?"

"Mares. Actually once you deliver a healthy foal life begins to shine a little. There are always worries. The mare's milk could be lacking in proper nutrition. The foal's legs could be crooked although usually they straighten out and if not then I go to work. Nothing intrusive. I believe less is more and let nature do her work. But short of a foal running through a board fence in a thunderstorm, once you've got a healthy baby on the ground, you're doing great."

"What about diseases?"

"Usually protection comes in the mother's milk. In that sense it's like kittens or puppies. They receive immunity from the mother. In time that immunity wears off and then you need to be vigilant. But nature truly is amazing and a foal arrives much more prepared to negotiate the world than a human baby. With both babies, the more they're handled the better they become. I think, anyway."

"You're the doctor." Mrs. H. smiled.

"Here, why don't you take these back?" He shoved bills across the counter.

"Happy to." She playfully grabbed them.

"Want mine, too?" Harry usually got to her own mail last.

"We could burn them," Fair suggested.

"They'd just come back," Harry ruefully observed.

"Somewhere in this vast nation exists a person with an incredible mind, a person who can crack computer codes. I pray that person will wipe out everyone's IRS files and save our country. I dream about it at night. I believe in a national sales tax. Then everyone knows what they're paying. No hidden taxes. If the government can't run itself on those monies then the government can cut back. If I have to cut back as a private citizen I can expect my government to do the same. That's exactly what I think."

"Bravo." Harry finished canceling the metered mail. "Run for office."

"Little Mim has beat me to it." He shuffled his mail, organizing it into a pile according to letter size.

"That rebellion has taken second place to the mess around here. Maybe that's a good thing. Little Mim doesn't seem to know what she's searching for but young people worry more these days than we did."

"I don't know," said Harry. "Maybe after a long time you forget. You know, you forget the pain but hold on to the good part of the memory."

"Could be. Could be." Miranda smiled at Fair, who smiled back, as both were hoping Harry had done this with memories of her marriage.

"Tucker, why don't we sneak out tonight and go to the hospital? I bet those pumps get brought in as well as cleaned at night."

Pewter called out from the mail cart. *"That's a seven-mile hike and it's cold at night, real cold."* Her voice lowered.

"I don't mean from the farm, dimwit. I mean just before Harry leaves work we run off."

"Oh, I don't know. She'll catch us." Pewter wanted to go home after work. Supper beckoned.

"Not if we run under Mrs. Hogendobber's porch."

"Murphy, we could head straight to the hospital. All we have to do is go through yards. One road crossing but we can handle that." Tucker was thinking out loud.

"If we do that, she'll follow us. If we get close enough to the hospital I know she'll go in. She'll forget her promises and just go right in. Can't have that." Mrs. Murphy knew her human to the bone.

"It will be cold," came the mournful whine from the mail cart.

"That's why you have fur," Murphy tartly replied.

"Fine."

Murphy and Tucker looked at one another and shrugged.

At closing the tiger and corgi blasted out the back animal door. Pewter stuck close to Harry as she chased her bad pets. Although curious, the gray cat wanted to snuggle up on the sofa in front of the fire after her tuna supper. She wasn't that curious.

Harry and Miranda tried to cut off the cat and dog but the animals easily eluded them.

"Every now and then." Harry shook her head.

"I'll keep my eyes open for them."

"Thanks, Miranda. I'll leave the animal door unlocked, too. I don't know what it is. They get a notion." She glanced up at the sky. "At least it looks like it will be a clear night. No storms rolling in."

Defeated, Harry bundled Pewter into the cab of the old truck to head home.

"*They're very naughty.*" Pewter sat right next to Harry.

"You're a good kitty." Harry rubbed her head.

"*I'd like fresh tuna, please,*" Pewter purred, half closing her eyes, which gave her a sweet countenance.

Murphy and Tucker reached the hospital just as the loading dock was shutting down. They scooted in, hearing the big rolling doors lock behind them.

"*Going to be a long night,*" Murphy observed.

"*Yeah but someone might open the back door later. We'll get out.*"

"*No matter what, we know we can escape in the morning. I bet if we scrounge around we'll find something to eat.*"

They could hear the elevator doors open and close. The shift was changing. Day workers were going home and the night crew, much smaller in number, was coming to work. Then silence. Not even a footfall.

Just to make sure they remembered the layout they walked down the halls, checked the boiler room in the center, poked their heads into those closet doors that were open.

Finally they walked into the carton room.

"*Clever, leaving this door open, filling it with cartons. As though there is nothing to hide,*" Murphy noted.

"*You can hide better than I can.*" Tucker searched the room. "*What if I lie flat over here in the darkest corner and you push a carton over me. I think that will work. After all, no one is expecting a corgi here.*"

"*Right.*"

As Murphy covered up Tucker they both heard a footfall, a light footfall.

Wordlessly, the cat climbed to the top of the cartons, wedging herself between two of them. She could see everything. Tucker's face, ears covered, poked out from the carton in the dark corner. Both held their breath.

Tussie Logan softly walked inside carrying a pump. She pressed the stone in the wall. The floor door slid aside. She climbed down the ladder, pressed a button down there, and the floor quietly closed up.

Neither animal moved. Three hours later the floor yawned open. Tussie climbed up the ladder, then pressed the stone. She watched the flagstone roll back, tested it with her foot, brushed off her hands, put her nurse's cap back on, and left, yawning as she walked.

They could hear her move down the hall but she didn't go to the elevator bank. Instead she opened the back door and left.

Tucker grunted as she shook off the carton. "*That floor is cold.*"

"*Let's see if we can get out of here.*"

The two hurried to the lone door at the end of the hall.

Tucker stood on her hind legs. "*You maybe can do this.*"

Murphy reached up but it was a little high. "*Nope.*"

"*Get on my back.*"

The cat hopped onto the corgi's strong back. She easily reached

the doorknob and her clever paws did the rest. They opened the door and scooted out without bothering to close it.

Within twenty minutes they were scratching at Miranda's back door.

She opened it. "Nine-thirty at night and cold. Now just what were you two bad critters doing out there?"

"*If only we could tell you,*" Mrs. Murphy sighed.

"Come on. Bet you're hungry," said the kindly woman, who would feed the world if she could figure out how.

When the phone rang at ten that same cold night Mim, early to bed, grudgingly picked it up.

A muffled voice said, "Your barn, tomorrow morning at nine." Then hung up.

Mim had caller ID and quickly called Sheriff Shaw at home.

"823–9497." He repeated the number as she read it to him.

"She must have had fabric or something over the mouthpiece but it was a woman," Mim stated, "and she sounded familiar."

"Thanks. You've done good work. I'll have someone in the hayloft tomorrow and another officer flat in the backseat of your car. Park your car at the barn."

"I will."

When Rick checked the phone number it turned out to be the pay phone in the supermarket parking lot.

Harry chastised Mrs. Murphy and Tucker, neither of whom appeared remorseful, which only infuriated her more. She thanked Miranda for keeping them overnight. That was at seven in the morning.

By seven-thirty Rob Collier had dropped off two canvas sacks of mail, a light day. As Harry sorted mail and Miranda tackled the packages and manila envelopes, the two bold creatures told Pewter everything.

"Nurse Logan. Tussie Logan?" Pewter couldn't believe it. "It's hard to imagine her as a killer."

"We didn't say she was the killer. Only that she went down into the room and came back out three hours later. We assume she's cleaning the infusion pumps." Mrs. Murphy allowed herself a lordly tone.

"Remember the first three letters of assume." Pewter smarted off.

41

A spiral of blue smoke lazed upward for a few feet, then flattened out. Whenever smoke descended hunters felt that scent would be good. Rick, not being a foxhunter, would have gladly picked up a good scent, figuratively speaking. He felt he was on the cusp of knowledge yet it eluded him like a receding wave.

The temperature hovered in the low forties but the air carried the hint of snow. He looked west at the gunmetal-blue clouds peeping over the tops of the Blue Ridge Mountains. Turning up the collar of his jacket, he stood on a knoll a half mile from Mim's barn. Coop, next to him, held a cell phone in her hand. They waited for the call from the barn.

"You know I've always felt that killers, like painters, eventually leave a body of work behind so distinctive that you can identify them—by looking at the canvas. Some people kill out of self-defense. Understandable. Admirable even, and hard to fault." A plume of air escaped his lips.

"As long as those killers are men. If a wife kills in self-defense against an abusive husband people find reasons why she shouldn't have done so. In fact, boss, killing seems to still be male turf."

"Yep, for the most part it is. We jealously guard our propensity for violence. That's the real reason the services have trouble with women in combat. Scares the men." He half laughed. "If she's got an Uzi, she's as powerful as I am."

She hunched up. The wind picked up. She checked her watch. Nine-fifteen. No call.

They waited until ten-thirty, then walked back to the barn. Mim and the two officers at the barn were bitterly disappointed.

Mim returned to her house accompanied by one of the officers.

"Stay in the barn office until noon unless you hear from me," Rick ordered the other man. Then he and Cooper trudged through the woods to their squad car parked in the hay shed on a farm road. The ground was frozen. They'd drive out without getting stuck.

Once inside the car they sat for a moment while the heater warmed the vehicle and Rick squashed his cigarette in the ashtray.

"Boss." Coop unzipped her coat. "Harry had an idea."

"Sweet Jesus." He whistled.

"The Cramers foxhunt with Middleburg Hunt and Orange, too."

"What's that supposed to mean?" He turned toward her, his heavy beard shadow giving his jaw a bluish tinge.

"According to Harry it means they hunt with fast packs, they're good riders."

"So what?"

"So, she said invite them down to hunt. It might rattle our killer."

"Harry thought of that, did she?" He leaned back, putting both hands behind his head. "Remind me to take that girl to lunch."

"The sight of them might provoke our guy to do something stupid."

"We still have to keep somebody with them. No chances. Can you ride good enough to stay with them?"

"No, but Graham Pitsenberger can and so can Lieutenant-Colonel Dennis Foster. They're both tough guys. They'll be armed, .38s tucked away in arm holsters or the small of the back. We can trust them."

"You've asked them?"

"Yes. Graham will come over from Staunton. Dennis will drive down from Leesburg. Harry said she'll mount them."

"That sounds exciting," he wryly noted.

"I'll go with the Hilltoppers."

"God, Cooper, I can't keep track of all this horse lingo."

"Hilltoppers don't jump. It will take me a while before I can negotiate those jumps. I will though." A determined set to her jaw made her look the way she must have looked as a child when told no by her mother.

"I'll stick to fishing. Not that I have the time. I've been promising Herb we'd go over to Highland County to fish for the last four years." He sighed, cracking his knuckles behind his head.

"You haven't spit on dogs or cussed Christians so I guess it's all right?"

"Where do you get these expressions?" He smiled at her. "I'm a Virginia boy and I haven't heard some of them."

"I get around." She winked.

"When are the Cramers coming?"

"This Saturday."

"I'll try to get there for part of it, anyway."

"Roger."

"Let's cruise." He put the car in gear. "Maybe if we're lucky we'll catch this perp before there's more harm done."

What neither of them knew was that they were already too late.

42

*R*an down over everything, part of my ceiling fell in." Randy
Sands, bone white, coughed, composed himself, and continued, "so
I banged on the door and shouted and then I opened the door. I
guess that's when I knew something was—was not right." He
coughed again.

Rick sympathetically put his arm around Randy's thin shoulders.
"Quite a shock, Randy."

"Well, I yelled for her but she didn't answer so I went straight to
the bathroom." His lower lip trembled. "The rest you know."

In the background the rescue squad removed the body of Tussie
Logan. The fingerprint team had come and gone.

Coop figured from the body that Tussie had been in the tub perhaps four or five hours. Whoever shot her had come up behind her
and shot down through the heart, one shot.

"Randy, how long have you owned this house?" Rick asked as
Coop joined him.

"Since Momma died." Randy thought this information was sufficient.

"When was that?"

"Nineteen ninety-two." He fidgeted when the body was rolled out on the gurney even though it was in a body bag. "She was a good-looking woman. I hated to see her like that."

"Yes." Rick guided him to the sofa. "Sit down, Randy. Your first impressions are valuable to us and I know you're shaken but I have to ask questions."

Shaken though he was, it wasn't often that Randy Sands was the center of attention. He sat on the wicker sofa, brightly colored cushions behind him. Rick sat in a chair opposite the sofa. Coop quietly examined each room in the airy upstairs apartment.

"Did Tussie lock her doors?"

The clapboard house with the wraparound porch built in 1904 was halfway between Charlottesville and Crozet, situated back off Garth Road. The location was convenient to the hospital yet afforded privacy and a touch of the country. Randy couldn't always keep up with the forty-two acres. Tussie enjoyed mowing the lawn on the riding mower, edging the flower beds, and hanging plants on the porch.

"Where were you today?"

"At work. I came home around five-thirty. Finished a little early today. That's when I found Tussie."

"Where do you work, Randy?"

"Chromatech. Off the downtown mall. My bosses Lucia and Chuck Morse can verify my hours." A slightly belligerent tone infected his voice.

"I'm sure they can. Now do you have any idea who would kill Tussie?"

"No." He shook his head.

"Drugs?"

"No. Never."

"Drinking?"

"No. Well, socially but I never saw her drunk. I can't imagine who would do this."

"Is anything obvious missing? Jewelry? Money? Paintings?"

"I didn't check her jewelry box. I stayed right here in the living room. I—" He didn't want to say he was afraid to walk from room to room.

"Boss." Cynthia Cooper called from the glassed-in back porch, which had been a sleeping loft in the old days.

"Excuse me, Randy. You wait here." Rick walked down the hall-way to the back.

The porch overlooked the meadows, the mountains beyond. Filled with light, it was a wonderful place to work. A bookshelf rested against the back wall. Her desk, a door over two file cabinets, was in the middle of the narrow room, coldish except for a space heater on the floor.

"Here." Coop pointed to a very expensive computer and laser printer.

"Huh. Must have cost close to six thousand dollars."

"This computer and printer can do anything. The quality is very high."

"Invoices?" Rick wanted another cigarette but stopped himself from reaching for the pack in his inside coat pocket. "Maybe."

"Is everything all right?" Randy's querulous voice wafted back to them.

"Yes, fine," Rick called back. "Coop, can you get into the computer?"

"Yes, I think so."

"I'll keep Randy busy. Maybe I'll walk him outside. He can show me if there's a back way in." Rick winked and returned to the slender man in the corduroy pants.

Coop sat down, flicked on the computer. Tussie had lots of

e-mail. She had been plugged into a nurses' chat room. She'd taped a list of passwords on the side of her computer, a defense against forgetfulness perhaps. Coop went through the passwords finally hitting pay dirt with "Nightingale." Coop perused the messages. She then pulled up the graphics package, which was extensive.

"I could sit here all day and play with this," Coop said to herself, wishing she could afford the same system.

Tussie had a code. Coop couldn't crack it.

After checking out what she could, she shut off the computer and walked to the bedroom. With gloved hands she lifted the lid on the leather jewelry box. Earrings, bracelets, and necklaces were thrown in together. She opened the top drawer of the dresser. Silk underwear was jumbled. A green savings bankbook rested under the eggplant-colored underwear.

She pulled it out, flipped the white pages to the last balance. "Wow." She whistled.

Tussie's savings account balance as of February 25 was $139,990.36.

"I'm beginning to get the picture," Coop said to herself.

Once she and Rick were together in the squad car she informed him of her finds. They wondered where and how Hank Brevard had hidden his profits. To date they'd found nothing in that department.

Rick picked up the phone, calling in to headquarters. He ordered the department computer whiz to see if he could crack Tussie's code.

"Screwy, isn't it?" Coop wiggled down in her seat, hunching her shoulders. "What's the plan, boss?"

"First we'll go to Sam Mahanes, which means he'll call for his lawyers."

"Right. Then he'll express grief."

"Then we'll go to Bruce Buxton."

"More shock and dismay but in a different way."

"We'll go to her Pediatric unit. And then you and I are going to walk through this hospital one more time. As many times as it takes over the next few days, weeks, or whatever. We know there are false billings. We know those infusion pumps have to be cleaned and rehabbed. They have to be in that hospital somewhere. Damn, it's right under our noses!"

Coop, having heard that before, sat up straight and said nothing. She was wondering why a woman like Tussie Logan got involved in the scam in the first place. Tussie seemed like a nice enough person. She knew right from wrong. She knew what she was doing was wrong—even before the murders. Maybe Tussie was one of the murderers. How does a woman like that get into something like this? She knew what Tussie Logan had done was wrong and she knew Tussie knew it was wrong.

Coop expected more of women than men. It surprised her. She'd never thought of herself as a sexist but her response to Tussie's criminal behavior gave her a gleam of insight into her own self. She wasn't sure she liked it.

43

The Church of the Holy Light, in order to raise money for Herb's God's Love group, was holding a bake sale at the small old train station. Given that the ladies of the church had earned fame for their skills, the place was mobbed.

Miranda Hogendobber baked orange-glazed cinnamon buns as well as luscious breads.

Harry held down the fort at the post office. She and Miranda spelled one another. Sometimes it was nice to scoot out of work early or take a long lunch.

Everyone noticed when the Rescue Squad ambulance pulled out of the brick garage and they also noticed when it drove by, heading out of town.

Big Mim, as Crozet's leading citizen, felt she should be informed of every single event the moment it occurred. She flipped out her tiny cell phone, dialing the sheriff's office.

"Mother." Little Mim thought her mother could have at least walked outside to call, but then again it was cold.

"Don't tell me what to do." She tapped her foot, clad in exquisite crocodile loafers. "Ah, hello. Is the sheriff in? Well, have him call me then, Natalie." She dropped her voice as she worked over the daytime dispatcher. "You don't know who just rolled by in the ambulance, do you? Well, have him call me on my cell phone. Thanks. Bye." She pressed the Off button, folded her phone, slipping it in her purse.

"People do have heart attacks without consulting you." The daughter smiled sweetly as she drove home a light barb.

"They shouldn't. They shouldn't do anything without consulting me." Mim smiled sweetly right back. "I suppose I ought to buy some brownies."

"The orange cinnamons are all gone."

"Really, Miranda should open her own bakery. She's got a gift." Mim noticed the squad car with Rick and Coop stopping at the post office. "Here." She handed her daughter fifty dollars. "I'm going across the street."

"Without me?"

"Oh, Marilyn. Just buy the stuff and join me." Mim was out the door before she finished her sentence.

Rick and Cooper set foot in the post office but before they could open their mouths, Mim charged in. "Did Natalie call you?"

"About one minute ago." He exhaled from his nostrils. "I was going to call you as soon as I finished here."

Big Mim's eyebrows raised up. What could be so important that Harry had to be consulted first?

"*Bad news.*" Pewter trotted over from the small table in the rear.

"Why don't you all come back here?" Harry flipped up the divider as Mrs. Murphy stretched herself on the narrow shelf behind the postboxes. Tucker, awake, watched.

Rick realized he was going to have to tell Mim something, so he thought he'd get that over with first. "Randy Sands found Tussie Logan in her bathtub shot to death."

"What?" Mim clapped her hands together, a gesture of surprise.

"How did he know?" Harry asked the pointed question.

"The water was running and it came through his ceiling below. He came home from work, noticed it, and ran upstairs. He's in a bad way. I called Reverend Jones to go on out there."

"Shot." Mim sat down hard in one of the wooden chairs at the table.

"*Well, that's no surprise to us,*" Mrs. Murphy said.

"*Being in on it and being dead are two different things,*" Tucker sagely noted.

"Ugh." Pewter hated the thought of dead big bodies. She didn't mind mice, mole, or bird bodies but anything larger than that turned her stomach.

"Good Lord. I wonder if it was Tussie who called me?" Mim was incredulous.

"*Her death ought to tell you that.*" Murphy paced on the narrow ledge.

"*If they knew what we knew, it would.*" Tucker had more patience with human frailty than the cat.

"How long had she been dead?" Harry was figuring in her mind whether the killer crept up by night or by day.

Rick added, "It's hard to tell. Tom Yancy will know."

"Struggle?" Harry was still reeling from the news of the murder and that Tussie was the chain-letter writer.

"No," Coop simply stated.

"Whoever it was may have been known to her but having any-one walk into your bath ought to provoke some sort of response from a lady." Mim saw her daughter, laden with food, leave the train station to put the booty in her car.

"I don't know but it wouldn't be terribly difficult to walk into a bathroom and pull the trigger. She wouldn't have time to struggle.

This was fast and effective." Rick slipped a cigarette out of the pack. "Ladies?"

"No. I thought you quit." Mim didn't care if anyone smoked or not.

"I quit frequently." He lit up.

"*Why do humans do that?*" Pewter hated the smell.

"*To soothe their nerves,*" Murphy said.

"*It ruins their lungs.*" Tucker also hated the smell.

"*You don't see cats smoking,*" Pewter smugly said, secure that this proved yet again the superiority of cats.

Murphy kept pacing. "*Rick's not just here to deliver the news. Mom wouldn't be first for that.*"

"*Yeah, that's true,*" Tucker agreed.

"Harry, I think we'd better cancel having the Cramers hunt tomorrow. It's too dangerous. And I'm going to have Coop stay with you at night until—" He noticed Little Mim walking toward the post office.

"The Cramers?" Mim's voice rose. "Do I know the Cramers?"

"No." Harry quickly spoke for she, too, saw Little Mim. "They hunt with Orange and Middleburg."

"Must be good." Mim wanted to know what was going on.

"Mrs. Sanburne." Rick leaned over. "We're close to our killer here. I know you like to be in on everything but right now I would expose you to danger, serious danger. The reason I'm here with Harry is that she was struck over the head at the hospital."

Mim raised an eyebrow, saying nothing, since Miranda had sworn her to secrecy when she told her, but Mim had figured it out anyway. Rick continued. "I can't take a chance. The killer or killers may think she knows more than she does."

"And I don't know anything." Harry shrugged. "Wish I did."

"What do the Cramers have to do with Harry?"

"Well, uh, we were going to hunt together tomorrow. They're in the hospital business and—"

"Mrs. Sanburne, I promise you I'll fill you in as soon as we're—" He paused, searching for the right words. "Over the hump. Now could I ask you to intercept your daughter before she gets in here? Just give me two minutes with Harry."

Mollified slightly, Mim stood up, walked over, flipping up the divider, and caught Marilyn just as her hand was on the doorknob. She ushered her back toward the car across the street.

"Rick. Let the Cramers hunt. It will be the straw that breaks the camel's back. We've got Graham, we've got Dennis. They're military men. They're horsemen. They know what they're doing. They can protect the Cramers. Dennis is riding down with them in their rig and he'll ride back. I really believe we can shake our gorilla out of the tree tomorrow."

"It's a hell of a chance." Rick ran his fingers through his thinning hair. He knew Harry had a point but he hated to risk civilians, as he thought of them.

"Coop, I know we can do this. I wouldn't use the Cramers as bait if I didn't think it would flush him out," Harry pleaded.

"Yeah, Harry, I know, but I just saw Tussie Logan."

Rick and Coop stared at one another.

Rick puffed, then put down his cigarette. "Okay."

44

The Hunt Club hounds met at Tally Urquhart's farm at ten in the morning. Rose Hill, one of the oldest and most beautiful farms in Albemarle County, was a plum fixture, fixture being what meeting places are called.

The home itself, built of bricks baked on-site in the mid-eighteenth century, glowed with the patina of age. Tally herself glowed with the patina of age at ninety-two. She said ninety-two. Mim, her niece, swore that Tally was a hair older but at least everyone agreed she was triumphantly in her nineties.

Tally would stride into a room, still walking mostly upright, shake her silver-headed cane, a hound's head, at the congregation and declare, "I am two years older than God so do what I say and get out of my way."

And people did. Even Mim.

Years ago, back in the 1960s, Tally had been Master of the Jefferson Hunt. Her imperiousness wore thin but her ample contributions to the treasury ensured a long mastership. She finally retired on her eightieth birthday, amid much fanfare.

Everyone thought Mim would vie to be Master but she declined, saying she had enough to do, which was true. But truthfully, Mim wanted to keep her hunting pure fun and if she were Master it would be pure politics. She practiced that in other arenas.

Jane Arnold found herself elected Master and had remained at her post ever since.

A chill from the mountains settled into the meadows. Harry's hands were so cold she stiffly fastened Poptart's girth. She had introduced Laura and Joe Cramer to Jane per custom. There was no need to introduce Graham Pitsenberger, Joint-Master of Glenmore Hunt, nor Lt. Col. Dennis Foster, the Director of the Master of Foxhounds of America Association.

Master and staff didn't know the true reason for their company. Jane graciously invited these guests to ride up front with her.

Harry breathed a sigh of relief. If Joe and Laura were up front, nothing much could happen that she could foresee. If they fell behind, well, anything was possible.

Aunt Tally waved everyone off, then hurried back to the house before the chill could get her. Also, she was hosting the breakfast and it had to be perfect.

Dennis and Graham had conferred by phone before the hunt. Each man wore a .38 under his coat, low near the belt so the gun could be easily retrieved if needed.

Susan, Little Mim, and Harry rode behind Big Mim, who rode immediately behind the Cramers and the two men. It would never do to pass Big Mim in the hunt field, but since her Thoroughbreds were fast and she was a consummate rider, there was little chance that would happen.

The hounds hit right behind the cattle barns and within minutes everyone was flying up the hill behind the barns, down into the narrow ravine, across the creek, and then they boomed over open meadows which would soon be sown with oats.

Sam Mahanes rode in the middle of the pack, as did the bulk of the field. A few stragglers, struggling at the creek, brought up the rear.

Dr. Bruce Buxton rode back with the Hilltoppers since he was trying a new horse. Being a cautious rider, he wasn't ready to ride a new horse in the first flight.

They flew along for fifteen minutes, then stopped. The hounds, noses to the ground, tried to figure out just where Reynard lost them. A lovely tricolored female ran up a large tree, blown over in a windstorm, its top branches caught in the branches of another large tree. The angle of the fallen tree must have been thirty degrees. The top of the tree hung over a large, swift-moving creek.

Finally a brave hound plunged into the creek and started working on the other side.

"*He's on this side,*" the hound called out to his companions.

"I knew it!" the tricolor female, still on the tree, shouted. "*He ran up this tree and dropped into the creek. Swam to the other side. Oh, he's a smart one, he is.*"

Within a minute the whole pack had crossed the creek. The humans and horses, however, slipped and slid, trying to find a negotiable crossing. Jane, leading the humans, rode about one hundred yards downstream to find a better place. She motioned for the others to follow her quickly for the hounds were streaking across the meadow.

Laura Cramer, sitting her horse beautifully, jumped down the bank, trotted across the creek, and then jumped out. Her husband followed. Mim, of course, rode this as though she were at Madison Square Garden. Everybody made it except for a little girl on a pony. The water swirled up over the saddle. She let out a yell. Her mom retrieved her, and both walked back home, the kid crying her eyes out, not because she was cold and wet but because her mother made her stop hunting. She didn't care if she caught a cold. It would mean she might miss some school. Mothers could be mean.

Harry and Poptart observed a movement out of the corner of their eyes. The fox had turned, heading back toward the creek.

Harry stopped, turned her half-bred in the direction of the fox, took off her hunt cap, counted to twenty to give the fox a sporting chance, and then said, "Tally Ho."

Jane raised her whip hand, stopping the field. Everyone got a splendid view of a medium-sized red fox rolling along at a trot. He reached the creek, jumped in, but didn't emerge on the other side. He swam downstream, finally jumping out, and he then walked across a log, stopped, checked where the hounds were. Then he decided to put some distance between himself and these canine cousins.

Graham stood up in his stirrups and laughed. He was a man who enjoyed being outsmarted by this varmint. Dennis noticed the First Whipper-In flying along the top of the ridge ahead of the hounds but to the right of the fox. No hunting person, staff or field, ever wants to turn the fox.

The Huntsman watched proudly as his hounds curved back, soared off the bank into the creek, coming out on the other side. Now they had to find the scent, which was along the bank but a good football field or more downstream. The Huntsman jumped straight down the bank.

Laura whispered to Joe, "Think we'll have to do that?"

"You go first." He laughed.

Jane wheeled back, deciding that discretion was the better part of valor. She'd recross at their original crossing site and then gallop along the stream to try and catch up, for she knew the Huntsman would push his hounds up to the line of scent as fast as he could.

Within minutes the hounds sang out. Harry's blood raced. Susan giggled. She always giggled when the pedal pushed to the metal.

They slopped across the creek, jumped up the bank, and thundered alongside it, jumping fallen logs, dodging debris. The path opened up; an abandoned meadow beckoned ahead, a few scraggly opportunistic cedars marring it.

They shot across that meadow, hounds now flying. They crossed a narrow creek, much easier, and headed up the side of a steep hill, the tree line silhouetted against a gray, threatening sky.

Once they reached the crest of the hill, the hounds turned toward the mountains. The field began to stretch out. Some whose horses were not in condition pooped out. Others bought some real estate, mud stains advertising the fact. About half the field was still riding hard when the crest of the ridge thinned out, finally dipping into a wide ravine with yet another swift-running creek in it.

They reached the bottom to watch all the hounds furiously digging at an old tree trunk. The fox had ducked into his den. There was no way the hounds, much too big for the den, could flush him out, plus he had lots of hidden exits if things grew too hot. But the Huntsman dismounted to blow, "Gone to ground." The hounds leapt up, dug, bayed, full of themselves.

The fox moved farther back into the den, utterly disgusted with the noise. Why a member of the canine family would want to live with humans baffled the fox. Humans smelled bad, plus they were so dumb. No amount of regular food could overcome those flaws.

After a fulsome celebration, the Huntsman mounted back up.

"Shall I hunt them back, Master?"

"Oh, why not?" She smiled.

On the way back they picked up a bit of scent but by the time Tally's farm came into view, fingers and toes craved warmth.

Everyone untacked their horses, threw sweat sheets and then blankets over them, tied them to the trailers, and hurried into Tally's beautiful house.

Harry thought to herself, "So far, so good."

45

hy, the fences were four feet then. We rode Thoroughbreds of course and flew like the wind." Tally leaned on her cane. It wasn't her back that had given out on her but her left knee and she refused to have arthroscopic surgery. She said she was too damned old to have some doctor punching holes in her knee.

Dennis listened, a twinkle in his eyes. The fences were always bigger when recalled at a distance of decades but in truth, they were.

A crowd filled the house: Miranda, Ned Tucker, Jordan Ivanic, Herb Jones, plus stablehands, more lawyers and doctors, and the neighbors for miles around. When Miss Tally threw a hunt breakfast, best to be there.

"Sam," Joe Cramer greeted him warmly. "I didn't have time to talk to you during the hunt. Say, it was a good one, wasn't it?"

"Those creek crossings—" Sam noticed Bruce out of the corner of his eye. "Well, I haven't seen you for some time, Joe. I'm glad you could come on down and hunt with us."

"Yes, Harry invited us," Joe almost said but caught himself.

Cynthia Cooper brushed by, a plate loaded with food, including biscuits drenched in redeye gravy, her favorite.

Bruce joined Joe and Sam. He spoke to Joe. "Forgive me. I know I've met you but I can't recall where."

"Salvage Masters. Joe Cramer." Joe held out his hand. "We rehab infusion pumps, every brand."

"Why, yes, of course." Bruce warily shook his hand. "What brings you to Crozet?"

"Harry Haristeen invited my wife and I to hunt today. You know, February is usually a good month."

Laura glided up next to her husband. "The dog foxes are courting."

"My wife, Laura. Laura, this is Dr. Bruce Buxton and Sam Mahanes, director of Crozet Hospital."

"Glad to meet you." She shook their hands.

"You ride quite well," Sam said admiringly.

"Good horse," she said.

"Good hands." Graham Pitsenberger, smiling, squeezed into the group, the fireplace immediately behind them providing much needed warmth. "Time to thaw out."

"My butt's cold, too." Bruce smiled.

"Sam." Joe held his hands behind his back to the fire. "You know, your infusion pumps are way overdue on a cleaning." Joe just blurted this out in the excitement of it all. He was supposed to say nothing.

Sam paused a moment. "They are?"

"Years."

"I'll look into that. I can't imagine it because our plant manager, Hank Brevard, was meticulous in his duties. I'll check the records."

Troubled, Bruce cleared his throat. "We've had a shake-up at the hospital, Mr. and Mrs. Cramer. You may have heard."

Joe and Laura played dumb, as did Graham.

Sam, jovially, touched Joe's elbow as he spoke to Bruce. "No need to go over that, Bruce. Foxhunting shouldn't be plagued with work troubles. Joe, I'll get out the files Monday and give you a call."

"Here's my card." Joe slipped his hand into his inside hacking jacket, producing a business card printed on expensive paper, really printed, not thermographed.

He'd changed from his hunting coat to a hacking jacket for the breakfast, which was proper. Not that Tally would have pitched a fit. She didn't care if anyone came into her house in a muddy or torn frock or melton so long as they regaled her with stories. She did draw the line at lots of makeup in the hunt field though. Tally felt that hunting favored the naturally beautiful woman while exposing the artificial one.

Sam took the card, excusing himself. As he headed for the bar, Bruce tagged after him.

"Sam, what's going on? The equipment is overdue for cleaning." He gulped down his drink. "Why the hell won't you listen to me about this—our reputation is taking a beating."

"Let's have this discussion at another time."

"It's a damned sorry mess if we're using pumps that need work. It's beyond sorry."

"Bruce." Sam's voice was firm but low. "As far as I know those infusion pumps are working beautifully. The nurses would report it to the head nurse in a heartbeat. You know that. But I will definitely check the records. Hank would never let anything get out of hand or worn down. He just wouldn't and I don't think Bobby Minifee will either, once he feels comfortable in his position."

Rick Shaw and Big Mim whispered to one another in the corner for a moment.

"When will Tussie's death be written up in the paper?"

"Tomorrow." Rick sighed. "I used every chit I had to hold the story. The only people who know are you, Marilyn, Harry, and Randy."

"Rescue Squad."

"They understand perfectly well. Diana Robb can shut up the two people who came out with her for another twenty-four hours."

"I hope so." Mim's eyes darted around the room.

"Randy called the hospital and told her boss that Tussie had a family emergency. She wouldn't be in to work until Sunday."

"If this ruse works, Rick, our fox should bolt the den."

Rick smiled. "You hunters crack me up."

She smiled and they parted to mix with the others.

Little Mim cleverly maneuvered toward Bruce Buxton who, face flushed, was now talking with Harry, Susan, and Miranda.

"You all will be receiving invitations to one of Mother's teas," Little Mim said, her luxurious chestnut hair falling straight to her shoulders.

"More mail to sort." Harry winked.

Miranda's stomach growled. She put her hand on it, saying, "News from the interior."

"Time to eat," Susan added. "Harry, you've only eaten once. You must be ready for another plate."

"Cold makes me hungry."

The three women made a beeline for the table, leaving Marilyn to flirt with Bruce, who didn't seem to mind.

Fair strode through the door.

Tally called out to him. "Why didn't you hunt today?"

"Breeding season, Miss Urquhart. But I had to drop by to see you."

"Liar. You dropped by for the food!" He kissed her cheek.

"I came to see you." He kissed the other cheek. "Prettiest girl in the county."

"You go." She blushed a little. "Go on, your girlfriend's back at the table. She can eat, Fair, my, how she can eat. In my day a lady hid her appetite. Of course, she never puts on a pound. Me neither."

"Your figure is the envy of women half your age."

"Fifty!" Tally triumphantly said.

"Actually, I was thinking more like thirty-five."

"Mercy. You get out of here before I forget myself." She pushed him toward the dining room.

Fair cut into the line to be with Harry.

"Cheater," Susan humorously complained.

"Tally called me a liar. You're calling me a cheater. Anyone else want to unburden themselves?" He stared down at his ex-wife's pretty head. "I retract that offer."

Harry reached for and squeezed his hand. Laura Cramer was on the other side of the table.

"This is a lively group." Laura laughed.

"Wait until the drinks hit." Susan giggled.

Harry introduced Fair to Laura as they moved around the table.

He gallantly carried her plate, put both plates down on the long coffee table, and headed to the bar for Cokes for each of them. Fair never drank during the day, although he did drink socially.

Cooper walked over. "Some party."

"Have you had anything to eat?"

"Yes. Too much. I'm going back for dessert."

"Come sit with us." Harry indicated they'd sit on the floor.

The Cramers also sat on the floor, using the coffee table as their table. Graham, Dennis, Cooper, Susan, and Miranda squeezed in. Fair and Joe talked medical talk, since veterinary medicine used many of the same procedures and machines as human medical science. In fact, some procedures successful on humans were pioneered by veterinarians.

Graham regaled Cynthia Cooper with tales of training green racehorses to use the starting gate. Dennis Foster and Laura compared packs of hounds in northern Virginia, always a subject of passionate interest to foxhunters. Susan listened intently and Laura invited her, the whole table, to join them at Middleburg Hunt for a ripsnorter.

At one point Joe leaned over, whispering to Harry what he'd said to Sam and Bruce. Just then Jordan Ivanic bent over to say his hellos and Joe repeated what he'd told Sam and Bruce to Jordan, who blanched.

"I'll look into it. We've had some unfortunate occurrences." Jordan smiled tightly.

"I think murder qualifies as an unfortunate occurrence." Graham picked up a piece of corn bread.

"Now, Mr. Pitsenberger, we only know that Hank Brevard was killed in the basement of the hospital. We have no information that would connect other irregularities to that incident," Jordan smoothly replied.

"That's not what the newspaper says," Graham needled him.

"Newspapers sell issues for the benefit of advertisers. Now if you all will excuse me. It's nice to see you again." Jordan nodded to the Cramers.

"That's a cool cucumber," Graham remarked as Jordan was out of earshot.

"He wasn't so cool when Hank was murdered," Susan filled him in. "At least that's what I heard."

The visiting hunters had been well briefed about Hank's demise and Larry Johnson's murder. They knew nothing about Tussie Logan.

"For a small community you don't lack for excitement," Laura dryly said.

A shout at the front door attracted everyone's attention.

"George Moore, what are you doing here?" Tally laughed as a tall man breezed through her front door.

"I'm here to sweep you off your feet." He picked her up.

"Brute!" She threw up her hands in mock despair.

He carefully placed her down. "Have you eaten any of your own food?"

"No. I've been the hostess with the mostest."

"Well, come on. I'll be your breakfast date." He slipped her arm through his, walking her to the table.

Everyone knew George so there was lots of catcalling and waving.

Little Mim teased Bruce Buxton. "With a name like George, you have a lot to live up to in Virginia."

The breakfast rolled on for hours. Tally had hired a pianist, which augmented the already high spirits. After everyone had eaten they crowded around the piano to sing, a habit common to Tally's generation and all but lost by the time Harry's generation was raised.

As the guests finally left one by one, Dennis accompanied the Cramers.

Rick quietly watched everyone from the front windows of the house. Coop used the excuse of helping Harry load her horses to go back to the trailers.

"I'll ride home with you." Cynthia's voice indicated this was an order not a request.

"Great."

"Rick's going to push Sam and Jordan about the records and he wants me to stick with you."

"I'd say there's someone at this breakfast today who is sweating bullets."

"You know, here's where the human ego baffles me. Why not take the money and run? If you're the kingpin of this scam, you know the noose is being tightened—just run," Coop said.

"Maybe the money is not easily retrieved."

"All the more reason to run." Coop shrugged.

"I think it's ego. He thinks he can outsmart all of us."

"Could be. He's done a good job so far." Coop waved as the Cramers and Dennis pulled out.

By the time Harry and Coop reached the farm, unloaded the horses, fed them, cleaned up, they were tired.

As they discussed the events of the day, the animals listened.

"I hate to admit this but I'm hungry again." Harry laughed.

"I can always eat."

They raided the refrigerator.

"You know, Mom has that chirpy quality," Tucker noticed.

"That means she's going to do something really dumb." Murphy said what Tucker and Pewter were thinking.

46

Rick walked into his office just as the dispatcher told him to pick up line one.

"Sheriff Shaw."

"Hi, Sam Mahanes. I dropped back by the hospital after Tally's breakfast and we do have records for cleaning out the infusion pumps. Joe Cramer must have been confused."

"Where are you now?"

"Home."

"Can anyone working a computer terminal at the hospital pull up a maintenance file?"

"No. If people could do that they could also get into medical records, which are strictly confidential. The only people accessing the maintenance file would be myself. Well, Ruth, of course, Hank Brevard, and now Bobby Minifee."

"What about the men working with Bobby? Someone like Booty Weyman. Wouldn't Bobby teach him to use the computer? Anybody responsible for equipment, for shipping, would have to access the records."

"I'll double-check with Bobby on Monday. I'm not sure. I always assumed Hank gave marching orders and that was that."

"Maybe he did but it would have made his life a lot easier if someone could work the computer, otherwise he'd have been bugged on his days off, on vacation." Rick paused. "And Jordan Ivanic. As your second-in-command he would have the maintenance records or know how to get them."

Sam airily dismissed Jordan. "He could, I suppose, if he felt it germane but Jordan shows little interest in those matters. He likes to focus on 'above the line' as he calls it. He feels that maintenance, orderlies, janitorial, and even nurses are 'below the line.'"

"Speaking of nurses, are you on good terms with Tussie Logan?"

"Yes. She's one of our best." A questioning note filtered through Sam's even voice.

"H-m-m, why don't you meet me in your office in about an hour? Jordan will be on duty this weekend. We can all go over this together."

"Sheriff, an oversight about infusion pumps seems small beer compared to the murders."

"On the contrary, Sam, this may be the key." He paused. "Anything not quite on the tracks at Crozet Hospital interests me right now. And one other little thing. Joe and Laura Cramer have examined the invoices. The billing numbers aren't their billing numbers. These invoices are bogus, Sam." Rick could hear a sharp intake of breath.

"In an hour. Eight-fifteen."

47

"Coop, are you going to spend the night?" Harry innocently asked.

"Yes." Cynthia checked her watch. It had been losing time.

"Seven." Harry answered without being asked.

"I'd much rather the damn thing gained time than lost it. Well, it only cost me forty dollars so I suppose I could afford another one. There's no sense wearing good watches on my job." She reset her watch, to synchronize with Harry's: seven o'clock.

"Those Navy Seals watches are pretty neat. They glow in the dark."

"So do people who live near nuclear reactors," Coop joked.

"Ha ha." Harry stuck out her tongue. "Wouldn't it be helpful if you could read the dial in the dark? What if you're creeping up on a suspect or you have to coordinate times, synchronize in the dark?"

"Your fervid imagination just runs riot."

"*You should live here.*" Pewter yawned.

"Coop, there's two of us. I've got a .38 pistol. You've got your service revolver."

"Harry, where is this leading?"

"To Crozet Hospital."

"What?!"

"Now hear me out. Three people are dead. My stitches still itch. Joe baited Sam, Bruce, and Jordan. Right?"

"Right."

"What we're looking for has to be in that basement. Has to be."

"Rick Shaw and I crawled over that basement with a fine-tooth comb. We studied the blueprints. We tapped the walls to see if any are hollow. I don't see how we could have missed anything."

"*The floor,*" Murphy practically screeched in frustration.

"Pussycat, do you have a tummy ache?" Harry swung her legs off the sofa but Murphy jumped on her lap to save her the trip to the chair.

"*I am fine. I am better than fine. What you want is underneath your feet.*"

"*Yeah!*" Pewter joined the chorus.

"*It's so obvious once you know,*" Tucker barked.

"Pipe down." Harry covered her ears and they shut up.

"Something provoked them."

"*Human stupidity,*" Murphy growled.

"Maybe you need a tiny shot of Pepto-Bismol."

"*Never.*" Mrs. Murphy shot off Harry's lap so fast she left tiny claw marks in Harry's thigh.

"Ouch. Murphy, behave yourself."

"*You ought to listen to us.*" Tucker stared at her mother, her liquid brown eyes soulful.

"Here's my idea. We take our guns. We take a good flashlight and we go back down there together. I even think we should take Mrs. Murphy, Pewter, and Tucker. They can sense and smell things we can't. Coop, you know Rick won't let me or the kids down there and what we need is there. Has to be."

"You're repeating yourself."

"This is our only chance. It's nighttime. There won't be as many people around. The loading dock will be closed. We'll have to contend with whoever is on night duty, assuming we can find him. Come on. You're a trained officer of the law. You can handle any situation."

It was the appeal to Cooper's vanity that wore down her defenses. "It's one thing if I gamble with my life, it's another if I gamble with yours."

"What about mine?" an insulted Pewter yowled.

"God, Pewter, you can't be hungry again." Harry returned her attention to Cynthia Cooper. "You gamble every day you put your foot out of bed. Life is a gamble. I really want to get whoever killed Larry Johnson. I can't say I'm motivated by Hank's death or Tussie's, not that I wished them dead, but Larry was my doctor, my friend, and a good man. I'm doing this for him."

Cooper thought a long time. "If I take you, will you shut up? As in never mention this to Rick?"

"Scout's honor."

Another long pause. "All right."

"Oh brother." Tucker hid her eyes behind her paws.

48

*H*arry drove her old blue truck around to the back of the hospital. Everyone in town knew that truck but it was less obvious than Coop's squad car. She parked next to the back door. Had Harry parked out in the open parking lot even though she was at the rear of the hospital, the truck would have been more noticeable.

Cynthia checked her watch. It was seven-fifteen.

Harry double-checked hers. "Seven-fifteen."

The young officer checked her .357, which she wore in a shoulder holster. It was a heavy, long-barreled revolver. She favored long barrels since she felt they gave her more accuracy, not that she looked forward to shooting anyone.

Harry shoved her .38 into the top of her jeans.

"*Mom, you ought to get a holster,*" Tucker advised.

"*She ought to get a new brain. She has no business being here.*" Pewter, a grumbler by nature, was nonetheless correct.

"*We'd better be on red alert. We can't turn her back.*" Murphy's tail puffed up, then relaxed. She had a bad feeling about this.

Coop opened the back door as the animals scampered in. Harry noiselessly stepped through and Coop shut the door without clicking the latch. They walked down toward the boiler room, stopped, and listened. Far away they could hear the rattle of the elevator cables; the doors would open and close but they heard no one step out. Then the cables rattled more.

The animals listened intently. They, too, heard no one.

The two women stepped inside the boiler room, the large boiler gurgling and spewing for the night was cold. Coop checked the pressure gauge. She had respect for these old units. The trick was keeping the pressure in the middle of the gauge, which looked like a fat thermometer.

"This place was supposed to be on the Underground Railroad. The first thing we checked when Hank was killed was whether the wall was hollow behind what had been the old fireplace. Nothing," Cynthia whispered.

"You checked all the walls?"

"In every single room."

"*Follow me,*" Mrs. Murphy commanded.

"*Yeah, come on,*" Tucker seconded her best friend.

As the animals pushed and prodded the two humans, Sam Mahanes pulled into his reserved parking space right next to Jordan Ivanic's car. It was seven twenty-five. If the two of them were to meet with Rick Shaw at eight-fifteen then he'd better prepare Jordan, who, he felt, was a ninny. While Rick asked them about the invoices, Ivanic was capable of babbling about an anesthesiologist who nearly lost a patient. Those things happened in hospitals and Sam was determined that everyone stay on track.

Down in the basement, after a combination of nips, yowls, and pleading, Harry and Coop at last followed Mrs. Murphy and Tucker. Pewter walked along, too, but in a foul mood. Mrs. Murphy and

Tucker were showing off too much for her and the only reason she accompanied everyone tonight was that her curiosity got the best of her.

In the distance the animals and humans heard a siren. Someone was being rushed to the emergency room. In the country that usually meant a heart attack, a car accident, or a farm accident.

"*In here!*" The tiger's tail stood straight up.

Harry reached for the light but Coop put her hand over Harry's. "No." She clicked on the flashlight, half closing the door behind her.

The cartons, neatly stacked, offered no clue to the treasure below.

Tucker ran to the wall, stood on her hind legs, and pressed the stone. Although low to the ground and short, the corgi was powerfully built with heavy bones. The flagstone opened with a sliding sound and thump.

"I'll be damned," Cooper swore under her breath as she flashed the light into the entrance.

In the distance the elevator chains rattled, the doors opened and closed.

The humans didn't hear but the animals did.

"*Human. Human off the elevator.*" Pewter's fur stood straight up.

"*Quick. Down the hatch!*" Mrs. Murphy hopped onto the ladder, her paws making a soft sound on the wood as she hurried down into the hiding room.

"Murphy!" Harry whispered loudly.

Pewter, no fool, followed suit. Tucker, never one for ladders, turned around and backed down with encouragement from the cats.

By now the humans could hear a distant footfall heading their way.

"Come on." Harry grabbed the top of the ladder, swung herself around, and slid down, her feet on the outside.

Cooper reached down, giving Harry the flashlight, but as she turned around to climb down she knocked over a carton. It tumbled down. She grabbed it, putting it back up, then dropped down the ladder.

"How do we close this damn thing?" Harry realized she might have trapped everyone.

Mrs. Murphy pressed a round red button on the side of the ladder. The top slowly closed.

"Murphy," Harry whispered.

"Hide. Get in the back here and hide behind the machines," the tiger advised.

As the animals ran to the back, the humans heard the heavy footsteps overhead. Whoever was up there was bigger than they were. They moved to the back, crouching down behind pumps stacked on a table.

Cynthia put her finger to her lips, pulled out her gun. Harry did the same. Then Coop cut the flashlight.

The flagstone slid open.

"Can you smell him?" Mrs. Murphy asked Tucker.

"Too far away. All I can smell is this dank cellar."

The light was turned on. The humans crouched lower. One foot touched the top rung of the ladder, then stopped.

"Hey." Bobby Minifee's voice sounded loud and clear. "What are you doing?"

They heard a crack and a thud and then Bobby was tossed down the ladder. He landed heavily, blood pouring from his head. The flagstone closed overhead.

Pewter and Murphy ran to Bobby. Coop crept forward. Overhead they heard something heavy being pulled over the sliding trapdoor.

Harry, too, quietly moved forward. The two women bent over the crumpled young man. Harry took his pulse. Coop opened his eye.

"His pulse is strong," Harry whispered.

Coop looked around for towels, an old shirt, anything. "We've got to wrap his head up. See if you can find anything."

"Here." She handed Coop a smock, unaware that it had been Tussie Logan's.

Coop tore it into strips, wrapping Bobby's head as best she could. "Let's get him off this cold floor."

Harry cleared off a table and with effort they put him on top of it.

As the humans tended to Bobby, Mrs. Murphy considered their options. *"Coop and Mom are armed. That's cold comfort."*

"I'd rather have them armed than unarmed," Pewter sensibly replied.

"We'd better find a way out of here. For all we know, he's sitting up there trying to figure out how to kill us all."

"There's something over the trapdoor but since it's a sliding door, we could try." Pewter didn't like the cold, damp hole.

"Try what? To open the door?" Tucker asked.

"Yeah, press the button and see what happens." Pewter reached out with her paw.

"Pewter, no," Murphy ordered. *"You don't know what's sitting on the trapdoor. You don't know what will fall down. Hospitals have all kinds of stuff like sulfuric acid. Whatever he put up there he figured would either hold us or hurt us. He's a quick thinker. Remember Larry Johnson."*

"And he's merciless. Remember Hank Brevard and Tussie Logan," Tucker thoughtfully added.

"My hunch is, he'll come back. He doesn't know who's down here but he suspects something. And he has to come back to kill Bobby. He heard the carton drop. I know he did. He was moving up faster than the humans could hear." Mrs. Murphy's tail twitched back and forth. She was agitated.

"I don't fancy being a duck in a shooting gallery," Pewter wailed.

"Get a grip," Tucker growled.

"I'm as tough as you are. I'm expressing my feelings, that's all."

"Express them once we're out of this mess." Mrs. Murphy prowled along the walls. "Pewter, take that wall. Tucker, the back. Listen for anything. If this was part of the Underground Railroad then there has to be a tunnel off this room. They had to get the slaves out of here somehow."

"Why couldn't they take them out in the middle of the night? Out the back door?" Pewter did, however, go to the wall to listen.

"If everyone is still telling stories about the Underground Railroad, this place was closely watched. Since no one was ever caught, I believe they had tunnels or at least one tunnel." Murphy strained to hear anything in the walls.

"Hey." Pewter's green eyes glittered. "Rats."

Mrs. Murphy and Tucker trotted over, putting their ears to the wall. They could hear the claws click as the rats moved about; occasionally they'd catch a snippet of conversation.

"Now, how do we get in?" Tucker sniffed the floor, moving along the wall. "Nothing but mildew."

"Pewter, you check the ceiling, I'll study the wall." Mrs. Murphy slowly walked along the wall.

"Why am I checking the ceiling?" Pewter rankled at taking orders and she'd been taking too many, in her mind.

"Maybe the way they got out was to crawl between the ceiling and the floorboards upstairs."

"Murphy," Tucker said, "the rats sound lower than that."

"We've got to try everything." Murphy walked the length of the wall, then returned, stopping at a large stone at the base. "Tucker, Pewter, let's push. This might be it."

They grunted and groaned, feeling the stone budge.

"Harry!" Tucker barked.

Harry turned from Bobby to see her three friends pushing the stone. She walked over, knelt down, putting her own shoulder to the large stone. Sure enough it rolled in. "Coop!"

Cooper turned her flashlight into the small dark cavern and a narrow tunnel appeared, rats scurrying in all directions. One would have to walk hunched over but it could be done. "It *was* part of the Underground Railroad!"

"*He's back!*" Tucker barked as she heard the heavy burden being slowly slid off the trapdoor.

"*He knows we're here now,*" Murphy warned after Tucker barked.

Harry heard it, too. She ran back and cut the lights. "Let's go." She ducked down and squeezed into the tunnel, crawling on all fours. Cooper followed as the animals ran past them. The two women rolled the stone back in place, then stood up, bending over to keep from bumping their heads.

"Bobby, we left Bobby." Harry's face bled white.

"Harry, we'll have to leave him to God. Let's hope whoever this is comes after us first. He had to have heard Tucker."

"*Sorry,*" Tucker whimpered.

"*No time for that,*" Mrs. Murphy crisply meowed. "*We've got to go wherever this leads and hope we make it.*" She shot ahead followed by Pewter, who was feeling claustrophobic.

The humans ran along as fast as they could, flashlight bobbling. Harry noticed scratchings along the wall. She reached for Cooper's hand, halting her for a moment. She took the flashlight, turning it on the wall. It read: *Bappy Crewes, age 26m 1853.* They ran along knowing that Bappy, buried in the wall, never found freedom. Right now they hoped that they would.

"*He's rolling the stone.*" Tucker could hear behind them.

"*Nip at their heels, Tucker. Make them go faster. We don't know what's at the end of this and it might take us a little time to figure it out.*"

"*Oh, great,*" Pewter moaned when Murphy said that.

"*Your eyes are the best. Run ahead. Maybe you can figure it out,*" Tucker told the cats.

The two cats sped away as the light dimmed. The tunnel turned hard right. The rats cursed them. They skidded, turned right, then finally reached the end of the tunnel. They waited a moment while their eyes adjusted. They could see the flashlight shining on the wall where the tunnel turned right.

"We have to go up. There's no other way," Pewter observed.

"Oh, thank the Great Cat in the Sky." Murphy breathed a prayer. A ladder made from six-inch tree trunks lay on its side. *"Maybe we can make it."*

Harry and Cooper now turned right; they were running harder now because whoever was behind them was firing into the dark.

Harry saw the ladder since Murphy was helpfully sitting on it. The two women hoisted it up. Cooper turned to train her gun on the turn in the tunnel.

"Get up and push with all your might!" the deputy said between gritted teeth.

Harry's foot went through one rotted rung but the rest were okay. She pushed and the top opened with surprising ease. She reached down, picking up Murphy, whom she tossed up. Then she did the same for Pewter and finally she carried Tucker, much heavier, under her arm.

She turned back for Coop, who extinguished the flashlight so as not to give their pursuer, who was approaching the right-hand turn, a target. Cooper, in great shape, leapt up, grabbing the top rung. She was out of the tunnel in moments.

"Where are we?" Pewter asked.

Harry quickly flopped down the heavy lid. "Let's get out of here."

"We're in the old switching station." Cooper was amazed. "My God, they literally put them on the trains."

"Smart people, our ancestors." Harry opened the door to the old switching station and they plunged into the darkness, running for all they were worth.

"Down here." Cynthia scrambled down a ditch by the side of the railroad tracks, the typical drainage ditch. "Lie flat. If he comes out I might be able to drop him."

They waited for fifteen minutes in the bitter cold but the door to the switching station never opened.

The railroad, begun by Claudius Crozet in 1849, had been in continuous use since then, with upgrades. The small switching station had been replaced by computers housed in large stations in the major cities. A nerve network fanned out from there, so the individual stations had fallen into disuse.

"Let's go back." Coop, shivering, stood up, brushing herself off.

"Mrs. Murphy, Pewter, and Tucker, I think we owe you big time."

"*We're not out of the woods yet.*" Murphy's senses stayed razor sharp as Tucker's hackles rose.

"*I vote for warmth.*" Pewter moved ahead toward the hospital parking lot.

Cynthia checked her wristwatch. "Eight-ten." As they drew closer to the front door she noticed Rick's squad car. "Well, we might get our asses chewed out but let's find him."

They walked into the main reception area just as Sam Mahanes, disheveled, was greeting Rick. Cooper's hands were torn up and the sleeves of Harry's jacket were shredded where her arms had slid against the stone wall when her foot went through the rotted rung of the ladder to the switching house.

"You look like the dogs got at you under the porch." Rick frowned. "And just what are you doing here?"

It took a second but both Harry and Coop looked down at Sam's shoes, scuffed with dirt on the soles.

"Harry, you've got to take those animals out of here. This is a hospital," Sam reprimanded her as he moved toward the front door.

"He smells like the tunnel!" Tucker hit him from behind. If they'd been playing football the corgi would have been penalized for clipping.

Harry may have been a human but she trusted her dog. "Coop, it's him!"

Sam lurched to his feet, kicked at the dog, and ran for all he was worth.

"Stop!" Cooper dropped to one knee.

He didn't stop, reaching the revolving door. Coop fired one shot and blew out his kneecap. He dropped like a stone.

The few people in the hospital at that hour screamed. The receptionist ducked behind the desk. Rick ran up and handcuffed Sam's hands behind him.

"Call a doctor," he shouted at the receptionist.

"Call two," Cooper also shouted. "There's a man badly injured in the basement. I'll take the doctor to him."

Sam was cussing and spitting, blood flowing from his shattered kneecap.

"How'd you know?" Rick admiringly asked his deputy.

"It's a long story." She smiled.

49

*T*hat's so awful about Tussie Logan." Miranda wrung her hands.
The group of dear friends gathered at Miranda's house that Sun-
day morning. The article about Tussie's murder was front-page news.
Harry and Cooper filled them in on all that happened.

"He made enough money. He didn't have to steal any." Big Mim
was horrified by the whole episode.

"'And he said to them, Take heed, and beware of all covetousness;
for a man's life does not consist in the abundance of his possessions.'
Luke, chapter twelve, verse fifteen." Miranda recalled the Scriptures.

"Well, that's what's wrong with this country. It's money. All anyone ever thinks about is money." Mim tapped her foot on the rug.

"Mimsy, that's easy for you to say. You inherited a boatload of it."
Miranda was the only one in the room who could say that to Mim.

Fair sat so close to his ex-wife he was glued to her. "I'll never
forgive myself for not keeping a closer watch over you."

"Fair, honey, it's breeding season. You can't. You have to earn a
living. We all do. Well, most of us do."

"All right. I was born with a silver spoon in my mouth but that doesn't mean I don't understand this nation's malaise. I do. I can't help being born who and what I am any more than the rest of you," Mim said.

"Of course, dear, but I simply wanted to point out that it's rather easy to declare money the root of all evil when one is secure." Miranda's voice was soothing.

Susan, rather disappointed to have missed the action, asked, "I thought Sam Mahanes had an alibi for Hank Brevard's death?"

"He was in his work space, as he calls it." Cooper nodded. "Rick questioned Sally Mahanes in a relaxed way. The night of Hank's murder she didn't see him come in. He used the private entrance to his shop. It was easy for him to slip in. He left the radio on. Easy. Hank got greedy, threatened him, and Sam took him out. Quick. Efficient."

"And Larry?" Mim's lower lip trembled a moment.

"We'll never know what Larry knew." Cooper shook her head. "But he was such an intelligent man. Sam took no prisoners. Poor Tussie, after Hank's murder she must have lived in terror."

"Caught in a web and couldn't get out." Miranda felt the nurse's life had been squandered.

"And how much money are we talking about?" Mim got down to brass tacks.

"Close to a million over the years. Just out of Crozet Hospital. He confessed that they billed for more than infusion pumps. They worked this scam on anything they could fix, including air conditioners. But the IVAC units—easy to fix, Tussie knew them inside and out—were the cash cow."

"Well, I thank you for apprehending Larry's killer. I feel I owe you a reward, Cynthia, Harry." Mim's voice was low but steady as she fought with her own emotions.

"I was doing my duty, Mrs. Sanburne. You don't owe me a thing."

"And I don't deserve anything either. The real detectives were Mrs. Murphy, Pewter, and Tucker. How they figured out where the hiding room was, I'll never know, and then they discovered the tunnel. They're the ones."

Mim eyed the three animals eagerly looking at her. "Then I shall make a large contribution to the local SPCA."

"*No! Food!*" Pewter wailed.

"*Good God.*" Murphy grimaced. "*At least, ask for catnip.*"

"Perhaps my largesse is unappreciated." Mim laughed.

"No." Harry smiled. "They want treats."

"And they shall have them!" Mim smiled. "Liver and kidneys and chicken. I'll cook them myself."

"*This is wonderful.*" Tucker turned a circle. She was that excited.

A knock on the door drew their attention.

"Come in," Miranda called out.

Little Mim, face flushed, let herself in, hurriedly taking off her gorgeous sheepskin coat dyed hunter green; even the baby lamb's wool was dyed hunter green. "I'm sorry I'm late but Daddy and I just had a meeting. I'm going to run for vice-mayor and he's going to create the position. So now, Mother, will you support me?"

"With enthusiasm." Big Mim smiled.

"*Why does it take people so long to find the obvious solution?*" Pewter tilted her head as she spoke to Murphy.

"*Too much time on their hands.*" Tucker turned another circle just thinking about kidneys.

"*She's probably right. When they had to fight lions and tigers and bears, when they had to till the soil and run from thunderbolts, they didn't have time to think about themselves so much,*" Pewter thoughtfully added.

"*Who was it said, 'The unexamined life is not worth living'? That contradicts your point,*" Tucker said.

"*Yeah, who said that?*" Pewter asked.

"*Not a cat so who cares?*" Mrs. Murphy burst into uproarious laughter.